THE CHAOS BALANCE

L.E. Modesitt, Jr.

TOR
fantasy ®

A TOM DOHERTY ASSOCIATES BOOK
NEW YORK

NOTE: If you purchased this book without a cover you should be aware that this book is stolen property. It was reported as "unsold and destroyed" to the publisher, and neither the author nor the publisher has received any payment for this "stripped book."

This is a work of fiction. All the characters and events portrayed in this book are either products of the author's imagination or are used fictitiously.

THE CHAOS BALANCE

Copyright © 1997 by L. E. Modesitt, Jr.

All rights reserved, including the right to reproduce this book, or portions thereof, in any form.

Edited by David G. Hartwell

A Tor Book
Published by Tom Doherty Associates, Inc.
175 Fifth Avenue
New York, NY 10010

Tor Books on the World Wide Web:
http://www.tor.com

Tor® is a registered trademark of Tom Doherty Associates, Inc.

ISBN: 0-812-57130-4
Library of Congress Card Catalog Number: 97-16431

First edition: September 1997
First mass market edition: June 1998

Printed in the United States of America

0 9 8 7 6 5 4 3 2 1

To Lara,
and her mother

NORTHERN

CANDAR

Gulf of Murr

Gulf of Candar

RECLUCE

EASTERN OCEAN

The WORLD

"Fascinating! A big, exciting novel of the battle between good and evil, and the path betwee̶̶̶̶. . . ."
                    —Gordon R̶̶̶̶̶̶ ̶̶̶̶ on *The Magic of Recluce*

"This is a very special fanta̶̶̶̶. . . in its slow and thoughtful use of familiar fantast̶̶̶̶̶ its skillful development of character."
                    —*Asimov's SF Magazine* on ̶̶̶̶̶̶̶ *Recluce*

"I could not put it down. This is an outstanding f̶antasy tale."
                    —Andre Norton on *The Towers of Sunset*

"This is a writer who cares about his characters and his world. This is disciplined fantasy, not fluff. L. E. Modesitt, Jr., is uncompromising when it comes to the effects of magic, both on the natural world and on the human heart. There are no cheap solutions to the problems of Reluce. Because of that, it is a world worth returning to."
                    —Megan Lindholm on *The Magic Engineer*

"A thinking person's fantasy novel, with world-building of the first order. A complex, compelling, exciting, and rewarding tale from first page to last."
                    —Robert J. Sawyer on *The Order War*

TOR BOOKS BY L. E. MODESITT, JR.

THE SAGA OF RECLUCE
The Magic of Recluce
The Towers of the Sunset
The Magic Engineer
The Order War
Fall of Angels
The Chaos Balance
The White Order
Colors of Chaos*

THE ECOLITAN MATTER
The Ecologic Envoy
The Ecolitan Operation
The Ecologic Secession
The Ecolitan Enigma

THE FOREVER HERO
Dawn for a Distant Earth
The Silent Warrior
In Endless Twilight

THE SPELLSONG CHRONICLES
The Soprano Sorceress
The Spellsong War*

Of Tangible Ghosts
The Ghost of the Revelator*

The Timegod
Timediver's Dawn

The Green Progression
The Parafaith War
The Hammer of Darkness
Adiamante

*forthcoming

OCEAN

AUSTRA

Gulf of Austra

Brysta

Valmurl

NORDLA

WESTERN OCEAN

Swartheld

Luba

Cigoerne

AFRIT

Atla

South River

MEROWEY

HAMOR

I

THE ANGELS OF darkness made the Roof of the World their home, and after deceiving the followers of light who had eagerly welcomed them, they wielded the ancient and dreadful weapons of Heaven and vanquished those who rejoiced in the light.

In those first dark years, there were none at first among the dark ones who could descend to the lower lands and bear the heat, and the lords of mankind, their true daughters, and their consorts rejoiced that this was so.

For the angels of temptation bore blades that slashed through armor and loosed arrowheads that treated iron bucklers as if they were rotten wood, and they raised a mighty stronghold called Westwind, anchored on Tower Black, that rivaled Freyja in power. And the followers of light, who had ages earlier forsaken the powers of the heavens, relinquished the barren heights to the dark angels and their evil powers.

The dark angels were women who made a mockery out of hearth and home, who reviled men and laughed as they destroyed all the armies of the Westhorns sent against them, as they forced the great lords to heap dust and ashes upon their own heads and to bend their knees and pay tribute, and to stand helplessly as their daughters were tempted from their hearths and consorts.

Yet an even more deadly evil was to flow from the Roof of the World, and none knew it, from the mighty Nylan, smith of the angels, he who built the Tower Black, he who forged the blades of night and the arrows of the storms. . . .

Colors of White
(Manual of the Guild at Fairhaven)
Preface

II

THE WIRY AND silver-haired man paused at the end of the causeway from Tower Black, his breath white in the sunlit chill. His eyes lifted from the cleared stones that led from Tower Black—the tower whose stones he had wrested from the mountains, the tower he had raised to shelter the angel crew of the *Winterlance*.

Another dozen steps before him, the causeway melded into the metaled road. Beyond the road was the expanse of softening snow that stretched in every direction—eastward to the kay-plus-deep drop-off that overhung the high forest, and to the mountains that bordered Westwind on the south and west. Softening or not, the snow was still well over Nylan's head just about everywhere and twice that in spots. That depth explained the ski traces and trails that paralleled the road, though many were just there as remnants of training exercises for the newer guards.

From the mountains to the south rose Freyja, that impossibly ice-needled peak that dominated the Roof of the World, glittering through the cold green-blue skies.

Nylan, wearing only a light jacket over his smithing clothes, walked slowly out to the road, nodding at the barely raised patterns in the snow to his right that marked the walls outlining the outdoor weapons practice yard.

Beyond the practice yard the stones of the road rose slowly to the west, past the smithy he had built, to the canyon that held the stables carved out of the stone of the mountainside itself. A thin plume of white smoke rose from the forge chimney. To his left, the road ran eastward for a hundred paces or so, then curved northward over the stone bridge that marked the channel for the tower drains and outfalls. Beyond the bridge, the metaled road began to climb the slope to the top of the ridge, and the watchtower.

Nylan shivered as his eyes traversed the snow-covered

slope to the north, east of the road. Beneath the melting snow lay the ashes that were all that remained of the armies of Gallos and Lornth—and of a third of the guards of Westwind. Once the snow melted, in the eight-days ahead, he hoped that the spring grasses would cover that desolate grayness quickly.

From the east his eyes turned south, toward the hummocks where dark stones had begun to protrude from beneath the snow. Three large cairns—and twenty-two individual cairns—bore witness to the harshness of two years of struggle against the lords of Candar and the Roof of the World itself.

Yet Tower Black held more than the nine survivors of the thirty-one from the *Winterlance* who had made planetfall. More than two score filled the six levels of the black stone tower—most of them women and refugees who had sought a new life on the Roof of the World. Of the seven ship's officers, there remained four—Ryba, Nylan, Saryn, and Ayrlyn. Of the twenty-four elite marines, five remained—Huldran, Llyselle, Istril, Siret, and Weindre.

Outside of Daryn, the blond young standard-bearer from Gallos who had been wounded on the north side of the ridge and protected by Hryessa—no one wanted to cross the spitfire from Lornth—Nylan was the only adult male remaining in Westwind, scarcely surprising given Ryba's distrust of most men.

He began to walk uphill between the heaps of snow and ice that flanked the road toward the smithy. Until an eight-day earlier, the road itself had been covered with that ice and snow, packed into a thick crust, but with midday temperatures slightly above freezing, Saryn had had the guards clear the sections near the tower, extending the cleared areas daily— as much to begin physically conditioning the upper bodies of refugees as for the need to return the road to the condition necessary for the timber carts that would begin to roll once the way to the high forests below Westwind was clear.

The smith frowned as he turned off the road and crossed the packed snow to the door of the smithy. This winter there had been enough wood for the furnaces, and for hot water in the bathhouse, unlike the first winter on the Roof of the World. They'd still had to slaughter some of the sheep for lack of fodder, but only a few.

Nylan eased open the smithy door, closing it behind him, before he spoke to Huldran. "You were up here early."

"It was noisy this morning. Dephnay was howling, and neither Siret nor Istril could quiet her. So," the stocky blond guard beside the forge shrugged, "all three were awake. Yours, thank darkness, don't howl. They just babble. But I don't sleep that well with babbling."

"I'm sorry, Huldran."

"It isn't your fault. Istril keeps telling me that, as if every guard doesn't know it."

"She didn't have—"

"Ser . . . you're not perfect and neither is the Marshal, but between the two of you, you've saved us, and a lot of women on this forsaken planet. No one else could have designed and built Tower Black."

Nylan reached for the leather apron.

"Not much left in the way of charcoal." The stocky Huldran fed another set of short logs to the forge fire. "We're back to starting with wood coals."

"Saryn said the wood crews could do a charcoal burn early this spring. She's got enough bodies."

"Warm bodies we've got," Huldran snorted. "Trained guards we don't, and two of the best are Siret and Istril." She broke off.

"I know. I know." And Nylan did. Both the silver-haired guards had children less than a year old, and both children were his—through Ryba's manipulation of the last residue of angel high-technology. He tightened his lips. While he loved both Kyalynn and Weryl—and Dyliess, his daughter by Ryba—having been an involuntary and ignorant stud still grated on his nerves.

Yet what could he do? He had to admit Ryba had been right about the cultures that surrounded them, and angels weren't exactly welcomed anywhere. Nor did he feel right even thinking about leaving his children, whether he'd been an involuntary stud or not.

Yet Ryba was getting harder and harder to take, and each day felt like a balancing act. Ryba, former captain of the *U.F.F. Winterlance,* was now Marshal of Westwind, and undisputed ruler of that chunk of the Westhorns known as the Roof of the World—a land so high and cold that very few of the locals could survive more than short stretches outside in full winter. Then, Ryba and all of the surviving ship's marines—now the guards of Westwind—were full-blooded Sybran, born to an even colder heritage than the Roof of the World, unlike Nylan and Ayrlyn.

Nylan shook his head and removed his jacket, hanging it on one of the wooden pegs beside the front double doors. Reminiscing and mentally complaining wouldn't forge blades—and Ryba wanted more of the deadly weapons he had developed. For her all-too-accurate visions indicated that, in the seasons and years ahead, scores of women would seek out the refuge that Westwind had become. Was that his destiny—armorer of the angels, forger of weapons of death and destruction? And involuntary stud? So far he'd avoided repeating that—since the great battle—but he could feel the pressure building.

The smith took the flat and crude shovel formed from lander alloys and eased the scarce charcoal from the basket across the forge coals. He nodded to Huldran, and the blond guard pumped the great bellows while Nylan took out his hammers and a strip of lander alloy—not that there was much left, but he would use it while he could. Then he'd have to figure out another way to make high-quality blades—if he could.

On the forge shelf rested a local blade—broken and melted around the edges from the devastation Nylan had created by merging one dying weapons laser with the "order fields" of this unknown world, so like and yet so unlike the powernets he had ridden as the engineer of the *Winterlance.* More than a thousand such local blades were stacked, like cords of wood, behind the smithy. Some were whole, some partly melted, and some broken.

A wry smile crossed the smith's lips. And a year ago he'd worried about metal stocks?

"Ready, ser?" asked Huldran.

"Ready as ever." He laid the alloy on the coals. From bitter experience he'd learned that, in the initial stages of forging blades, the softer local iron had to be forge-welded into the alloy, not the other way around.

By the time the midday chimes rang from the tower, they had managed to flatten the iron of the local blade into the strip of alloy, flatten the mixed metals, fold them and flatten them once, twice, and three times, then yet again. A dozen or more such fold-weld-flattenings, and Nylan would have metal ready to forge into a blade itself. He knew that even more of the pattern-welding would have been better, but time was short, and Ryba less than perfectly patient. In any case, the later forge steps would go more quickly.

All winter long he and Huldran had forged blades, spurred on by Ryba's insistence that every guard—every recruit— should have at least two of the shortswords that were equally deadly as blades or missiles. All of the blades were essentially modified copies of the pair that Ryba had brought down from the *Winterlance*—the Sybran nomad blades the Marshal and former captain of the angel ship had carried and practiced with throughout her service career.

"I'll bank the coals, ser, not that we've much to bank."

"You up to starting one of your own this afternoon?"

"Why not?"

"Then dump some logs on the fire."

Huldran grinned. "You going to practice after you eat? That's dangerous."

"I'll be careful." Either Saryn or Istril or Siret would single him out. He and Ryba avoided practicing skills against each other—there was too much resentment there for it to be safe for either of them.

Nylan racked the hammers and checked the metal blank that would soon be another deadly shortsword, then eased on his jacket before heading out of the smithy and down toward the tower.

A handful of newer guards, led by Murkassa, one of the first locals to seek out Westwind, walked swiftly down from the canyon that held livestock and mounts, but they were several hundred paces up the road from the smithy. The round-faced and brown-haired guard lifted a hand in greeting, and Nylan returned it before turning onto the road.

Nylan had barely cooled off before he stepped through the main door to Tower Black. He squinted in the far dimmer light of the tower, but took a deep breath of the fresh-baked dark bread that Blynnal did so well and the aroma of something else—the mint-spiced stew, he thought, probably created around the remnants of the deer that Ayrlyn had brought in two days earlier, after the light dusting of snow from a spring storm.

"Nylan?" Istril, carrying her son Weryl in her arms, motioned from the de facto nursery on the left side of the tower entry area.

He turned and crossed the stones of the entry hall.

Her face was slightly flushed, as though she had been outside in the cold. Weryl's face was also red.

"You were outside?" Nylan asked.

"We walked up to the stables with Siret and Kyalynn. Ydrall went with us, but she was cold the whole way. Kyalynn and Weryl just babbled the whole time." Istril grinned down at her son. "The cold like this doesn't bother him at all."

"With what you wrapped him in, I imagine not."

"I am glad you got another snow cat. Once I have it tanned, it will make a good parka."

"For a year or two." Nylan laughed.

"Da!" offered Weryl, thrusting a chubby hand toward his father.

"Da to you, too," returned Nylan, taking his son, and still half wondering at the circumstances that had resulted in three of the four infants in Westwind being his—when he'd only slept with Ryba at that time.

"We'll have five more lambs," the silver-haired Istril announced quietly.

"Practicing your healing, again?"

Weryl tugged at Nylan's index finger, his grip firm. Nylan smiled at his son.

"The more healers the better. You and Ayrlyn can't do it all, and what happens if you're hurt, like in the big battle with the Lornians and the Gallosians?" asked Istril.

"I was glad you'd practiced."

"So was the Marshal. Her arm was a mess."

"You wouldn't know it now."

"She used to get tired faster when she practiced blades, but she's almost over that now," noted Istril.

"Slow, she's faster than anyone else."

"Except you and Saryn. You're as fast as she is, but you don't like to go for the kill. Saryn's even more of a killer than the Marshal." Istril held out her arms for Weryl. "You need to eat. He's eaten."

"What about you?" asked Nylan as he handed his son back to Istril, disengaging Weryl's fingers from his own index finger.

"Antyl will watch him while I eat." Istril smiled warmly and carried their silver-haired son back to the nursery.

Nylan turned, then stopped to avoid running into one of the cooks.

"Greetings, ser." Blynnal bowed her head, about all she dared bow, as pregnant as she was and carrying the large baskets of fresh-baked bread up from the kitchen on the lower level of the tower.

Nylan had no doubts about the father. Blynnal had worshiped Relyn before the one-armed man had slipped out of Westwind one step ahead of a vengeful Ryba. And Relyn had worried a lot about the cook—pretty, but timid, and one of the few women in Westwind with no desire to lift a blade against the majority of men in Candar.

After following Blynnal past the lower tables, Nylan slipped around her and into the space at the end of the bench at the first table, the position that had always been his. The hearth to his right was dark—but between the warmth that drifted up from the kitchen on the level below and the residual heat from the wood-fired furnace, the high-ceilinged room was warm enough.

Saryn sat across from Nylan, while Huldran eased onto the bench on Nylan's left. Ayrlyn, her flame-red hair seemingly glinting with its own light, slipped onto the bench across from the smith-engineer.

Even before Nylan poured the steaming tea in his mug, Ryba sat down at the end of the table in the only chair in the great hall.

"How is the forging coming?" she asked politely.

"We're working on two more blades," he answered. "From what I figure, that will bring us to nearly a hundred of them—about a score more than two per guard. We've had to go back to starting the forge with wood, and we'll be out of charcoal in another eight-day."

"I'd appreciate it if you'd just work on blades until the charcoal goes."

"More visions?" he asked quietly.

"Such as they are." Ryba broke off a chunk of bread.

Nylan took a chunk of the dark bread after her and passed the basket to Huldran, then looked across the table, noting the pallor in Ayrlyn's face. "Dephnay again?" he asked.

"She's getting better, but Tryssa got burned with hot grease. Cold water helped—except for her eyelids."

Nylan winced at the thought of grease across the eyes, and the effort it must have cost the flame-haired healer. Healing through the order fields was exhausting, as he knew from experience. He'd collapsed more than once. "How is she?"

"She'll be fine."

"How about you?"

"I'll need a nap after I eat. A long one." Ayrlyn took a long swallow of the hot tea.

Nylan nodded sympathetically, then took a sip of his own tea while waiting for the huge crockpot filled with stew to reach him.

"You need to eat more," Hryessa badgered Daryn from the foot of the table.

"You need to be strong to return to Gallos," suggested Murkassa, a glint in her eye.

"I cannot return," said Daryn quietly, a flush stealing over his fair-complected face. "You know that. One of the standard-bearers of Gallos? A single survivor? I would be suspected of treachery . . . or worse."

"We've been through this before," said Ayrlyn, interrupting the teasing, straight-faced. "You certainly weren't the only survivor, just the only one daring enough to entice a guard. Some of the wounded in the lower camp made their way back to Lornth and Gallos."

Daryn flushed again, then replied. "Most died. You know that, healer. Those that did return reached their homes before the winter snows. After a winter on the Roof of the World . . ." Daryn shrugged.

"You could not have traveled. You almost died," said Hryessa.

"No." Daryn laughed, not quite bitterly. "It is difficult for a one-footed man to travel the Westhorns."

"Almost as difficult as for a single woman to travel Candar unmolested," added Ryba dryly.

A murmur of assent ran across the tables.

Nylan wanted to shake his head. Candar was a powerflux ready to explode, and just by founding Westwind Ryba had started the energy cascade.

"Daryn?" asked the Marshal.

"Yes, Marshal," answered the youth warily.

"What do you know about a place called Cyador?"

"Only what the traders tell, ser. It is the ancient home of those who follow the white way, and filled with silver and malachite, and great buildings walled with mirrors that catch and hold the sun. Even the smallest of dwellings are like palaces."

"Exactly where is this paradise?"

"Somewhere beyond the Westhorns—that is all I know."

"What brought that up?" Nylan asked Ryba.

"I've been studying some of those scrolls Ayrlyn picked up, and there are some disturbing references to Cyador, especially to how the ancient ones channeled the rivers and built the grass hills to turn back travelers. Oh, and about how some daughters of Cyador fled to the barbarians." Ryba's voice turned dry. "I wonder about paradise if those daughters fled."

A murmur of laughter went around the table.

"It must be beyond Lornth, then," said Ayrlyn. "Relyn never mentioned it. Nor did Nerliat."

"Relyn's probably spreading tales about the great new ancient one," suggested Hryessa.

"That will only cause more trouble," said Ryba quietly. Her eyes turned on Nylan momentarily, before she took a mouthful of the mint stew.

Not about to get into a discussion about Relyn and his efforts to create a new religion based on what he had learned from Nylan, the smith ate quietly, occasionally glancing at Ayrlyn, pleased to see some of the pallor leaving her face as the healer ate.

"Eating helps, doesn't it?" he said, knowing it was an inane comment, but wanting to reach out.

"Somewhat. With some rest, I'll feel better," answered Ayrlyn.

"If someone needs something that way," he offered, "send them to me. Or Istril. She's practicing her skills."

"I told her to. I'm glad she is."

"We will need more healers," Ryba said coolly, and the certainty of her words chilled Nylan. What else was she seeing?

Ayrlyn and Nylan exchanged glances, then continued to eat without speaking.

After the midday meal, Nylan walked up the five flights of the stone steps to the top level, turning right into his quarters, across from Ryba's. He looked around the bare room—one window, glazed in wavery local glass; a lander couch that made a hard bed, but better than anything of local manufacture; a crude table and stool; and a rocking chair for when he sang Dyliess to sleep.

"Nylan?"

He turned.

The dark-haired Marshal of Westwind stood in the door, carrying a squirming silver-haired child, more than an infant, but not quite a toddler. "Could you take her? I'd like to practice. Or you could practice first—"

"Go ahead. I'll practice after you." The smith-engineer extended his hands for his daughter, and she extended hers.

"Gaaaa . . ."

"Gaaa to you, too." Nylan lifted Dyliess to his shoulder and hugged her.

"I'll be down below," Ryba repeated. "Then . . . I don't know."

"Fine." Nylan eased himself into the crude rocking chair he'd crafted just so that he could have one in his own quarters to rock Dyliess.

As he rocked, her fingers grasped the edge of the carvings on the back of the chair, and then his silver hair—and his ear.

"Easy there, young lady. Your father's ears are tender." He lowered her and sat her in his lap, beginning to sing to her.

"On top of old Freyja, all covered in ice . . ."

His voice was getting hoarse when there was a rap on the door.

"Yes?"

"Ser . . ." A thin-faced woman with mahogany hair stood at his door. "The Marshal sent me up—"

"You're going to take care of Dyliess while I practice, Antyl?"

"If you'd wish it, ser."

"That's fine." Trust Ryba to send someone else to Nylan for Dyliess. Despite the close quarters of the tower, Ryba avoided Nylan as much as possible, asking as little as possible, as though he were the unreasonable one. He'd been tricked into being a stud, manipulated into incinerating thousands, and deceived in who knew how many little ways, but he was unreasonable—even though he'd essentially built and armed Westwind. And Ryba wondered why he didn't want anything to do with her? If it weren't for Dyliess and the other children . . .

But they were his and linked to Westwind, and there was no changing that, none at all.

He stood up from the rocking chair and eased Dyliess to his shoulder for a moment, patting her back. Then he half-lowered her and kissed her cheek before easing her into Antyl's arms.

"How's Jakon?"

"He be fine, ser, a strong baby. He sleeps now." With a broad smile, the brunette turned and headed down the stone steps of the tower.

Nylan stripped off his jacket and headed down the steps to the dimness of the fifth level, where practicing was a contest not only against his partner, but against the gloom and uncertain lighting. Ryba claimed that blades were as much feel as vision, and perhaps she was right. Nylan wasn't certain he'd even seen half the men he'd killed with a blade over the past two years. He'd certainly felt their deaths, suffused with white agony, but had he really seen them with his eyes?

That was the problem with Ryba. She was almost always right, but he hated her insistence that power—or cold iron—was the only true solution to surviving in Candar.

"Here's the engineer," called Istril, holding Weryl and watching the sparring floor.

"Catch!" called Saryn.

Nylan's hand reached out almost automatically and caught the hardwood wand, flipping it again and catching the hilt end. As he did, he absently wondered how he had gotten so proficient in handling antique weapons of destruction—except he wasn't. He could defend himself against most, and he had killed more than a few raiders and attackers—one at a time, since, after the first or second killing, the white-infused waves of pain that flowed through him left him virtually incapacitated.

He wasn't unique. All those who showed the innate ability to manipulate the order fields to heal—all the silver-haired ones and Ayrlyn—had the same problem. Ryba couldn't heal, but she could certainly kill.

Interestingly, Nylan reflected as he flexed the wand, try-

ing to warm up briefly, all of those who showed those healing traits had survived, even despite the battles they had been
forced to fight.

"Watch this," Saryn told the handful of recruits lining the
chalked-off practice floor.

Nylan knew only about half the faces by name, and he
wished they wouldn't watch. He glanced to the corner where
Daryn sat on a stool. The smith probably needed to craft some
sort of prosthetic device for the youth's foot, as he had for
Relyn's lost hand.

"Ready, Nylan?"

"Not really." The smith lifted the hardwood wand, trying
to let the feeling of unseen darkness and order flow around
him and through him.

Saryn lifted her wand, a shimmering laserlike force that
probed and slashed through the gloom of the fifth-level practice area.

As usual, Nylan felt awkward, barely parrying Saryn's initial attacks, giving ground and retreating, trying to capture the
sense of order that was his only salvation from bruises or, in
actual combat, death.

As he melded with the hardwood wand that mirrored a
blade, he finally surrendered to the flow of order and let the
wand take its own course.

"...engineer's so good...bet not even the Marshal could
touch him..."

"...notice, though...he never strikes...all defense..."

But how long could he only defend? How long?

III

THUS CONTINUED THE conflict between order and chaos, between
those who would force order and those who would not, and between those who followed the blade and those who followed the
spirit.

On the Roof of the World, those first angels raised crops amid the eternal ice, and builded walls, and made bricks, and all manner of devisings of the most miraculous, from the black blades that never dulled to the water that flowed amidst the ice of winter and the tower that remained yet warm from a single fire.

Of the great ones in those times were, first, Ryba of the twin blades, Nylan of the forge of order, Gerlich the hunter, Saryn the mighty, and Ayrlyn, of the songs that forged the guards of Westwind.

For as the skilled and terrible smith Nylan forged the terrible black blades of Westwind, and wrenched the very stones from the mountains for the tower called Black, so did Ryba guide the guards of Westwind, letting no man triumph upon the Roof of the World.

For as each lord of the demons said, 'I will not suffer those angel women to survive,' and as each angel fell, Ryba created yet another from those who fled the demons, until there were none that could stand against Tower Black.

So too, as did each of the forges of Heaven fail, did the mighty smith Nylan bend the fires of the world to his will and forge yet anew the black blades of Westwind.

Yet, despite Nylan's efforts in smiting the legions of the demons into dust, Ryba the mighty was not satisfied, and she asked for more black blades than the snowflakes that fell upon Tower Black, and for arrows that no armor could stop. And Nylan bent the forges to his will, and it was so, and still was Ryba displeased. . . .

. . . and so it came to pass that Ryba was the last of the angels to rule the heavens and the angel who set forth the Legend for all to heed. . . .

Book of Ayrlyn
Section I
(Restricted Text)

IV

Most Illustrious Lord, Protector of the Steps to Paradise, and—"

"Enough, Themphi. Enough," answered the silver-robed figure who sat easily in the sculpted malachite and silver chair on the dais. "What is the problem? This time?"

The man in white bowed. "My lord Lephi . . . the snows were mighty, and the Great East River rises."

"And all the rice fields in Geliendra will be washed away?"

"Yes, Sire. And those in Jakaafra." The white wizard bowed again, more deeply.

"What of the northern dams, and the diversions?"

"The . . . storms . . ." stammered Themphi. "You were—"

"They destroyed those as well as the locks of Kuliat? Why was I not informed of that?"

"Your Mightiness received the scrolls in the field . . ." Themphi offered a stained scroll. ". . . as you did this one at Guarstyad—"

"I am supposed to remember details of waterworks when I am trying to rebuild the fireships? Or commanding an army? Or remember that I received a scroll in the midst of dark confusions?" Lephi's eyes flickered toward the two sets of ornate open grillwork that flanked the dais and concealed the Archers of the Rational Stars. Then he leaned forward in the malachite and silver chair, his silver linens rustling. "Themphi, my wizard of the Throne of Reason, Emperor and heir to the Rational Stars I may be, but even emperors do not recall everything—especially in these times." He paused. "Why do the eastern barbarian kingdoms no longer respect Cyador?"

"Sire?"

"You are thinking of rice fields, Themphi. We will address those in a moment. Why is mighty Cyad no longer respected?"

"Cyador remains mighty."

"Yet barbarian traders attempted to establish a fortified enclave at Guarstyad, miserable corner of the word that it is. Why?"

"It is on the borders of Cyador, and there are no Mirror Lancers or Shining Foot there."

"In my grandsire's days, they would not have dared. Why do they dare now?"

The wizard frowned ever so slightly. "You routed them, Sire. They will not try again."

"Had we the great fire cannons or were the fireship completed, they would not have dared." Lephi leaned back in the shimmering throne. "The barbarians have short memories and respect little save force. We must restore our abilities to supply that force."

"Yes, Sire."

"You humor me, Themphi. You think I am erratic and obsessed. Perhaps I am. An emperor must be obsessed. How else can he guide his people?"

The wizard nodded.

"Answer me! How else?"

"Any ruler must guide his people."

"You talk, and you say nothing. Would that I did not need you and your kind. Would that . . . but wishes are but fluttering breezes dashed against stone." Lephi sighed. "Now . . . you may proceed with the rice fields."

"I should have seen that you were informed once you returned, Your Mightiness," offered Themphi.

"Someone should have. Someone should have." Lephi eased back in his throne. "Can we send the White Engineers?"

"The Second is at hand . . ." offered the wizard.

"No . . . the fireship project comes first. I will not let those thieves from Ruzor or Lydiar or Spidlar . . ." Lephi let his words break off.

"The Third Company could go. You sent the first to Fyrad—"

"To rebuild the trading piers and the levees. I recall. With the Second engaged here . . . Yes, send the Third." Lephi paused. "And send one of the Mirror Legions. Whichever one Queras can spare most."

"Yes, Your Mightiness." Themphi bowed as if to depart.

"Have we heard from the northern barbarians?"

"About the reopening of the copper mines?"

"Exactly."

"No, Sire. The messenger could not have reached Lornth yet, even upon the fastest of Your Mightiness's steeds."

Perspiration beaded on the white wizard's forehead as Lephi's eyes narrowed.

"Are you suggesting, white wizard, that I am impatient?" asked the Lord of Cyador.

"No, Sire. Only that Lornth is far beyond the Walls of the North."

"Those walls will move northward again. We will need the copper for the fireships to come." Lephi smiled. "Inform me when we receive word from Lornth. In the meantime, best you study the old tomes on the diversions, Themphi. And on containing chaos within ship boilers."

"Yes, Mightiness." The white mage's voice was even.

V

NYLAN STEPPED FROM the smithy, even before Blynnal rang the chimes for the midday meal, squinting as the snow-reflected glare cascaded around him.

"Frigging bright," mumbled Huldran as she stumbled out into the light after the smith.

"Sun and snow." The smith nodded and began to walk downhill. Despite the comparative warmth and the disappearance of the snow and ice cover from the south side of the rocky cairns and some sections around the canyon mouths, he hadn't seen any signs of snow lilies. Did that mean they'd have more spring snows? Or had the guards done something in their cultivation to kill off the lilies?

Nylan didn't know. There was so much that they had yet to learn about this world. The similarities to Heaven-type worlds helped, but there were certainly differences, like the semideciduous trees that looked H-norm, but had green leaves that turned gray and curled up around the branchlets that held them. Only about half the leaves fell every year.

And the reference to Cyador had surprised Nylan. Ryba had intimated that the place was almost a throwback to the white demons of Rationalism, but again, in almost two years no traders or locals had mentioned Cyador. He'd never even heard the name before, and that kind of surprise bothered him. Had Ryba gotten another vision? He had begun to wish long before that her visions were not so devastatingly accurate.

"Did you ever hear the name Cyador?" he asked Huldran.

"Before the Marshal mentioned it the other day? No. Maybe the healer had, but no one else had, either, except for Ydrall, but she came from coins."

"What did Ydrall know?"

"Not much more than Daryn, except that they don't let traders in and that they keep their women locked up. They have trading stations at the borders—or they used to. Lornth had problems with Cyador years ago, and there hasn't been much trading since. Ydrall didn't know what kind of problems, though."

A culture even harder on women than Lornth and those of the lands bordering Westwind? He shook his head, then rubbed his chin. He really needed a shave. He didn't care for the local bearded look at all, but shaving with a blade, a real dagger-edge blade, had taken some learning, and not a few cuts along the way. Of course, some of the local recruits had wondered if he was actually a man, since he didn't have a beard—as if hair made the man. He snorted.

As they reached the outer end of the causeway to the tower, Blynnal appeared and used the wooden mallet to hammer out a rough melody on the chimes that had replaced the old triangle. She wore a burlaplike apron over her gray trousers and tunic, and a jacket thrown over everything. The brunette smiled shyly at Nylan. "I do not have the touch of the healer, not with the songs, but I try."

"You have the touch with the food," the smith-engineer responded. "And we're all very thankful for that."

"It is good to have so many people who like what I cook. Dyemeni—he never liked anything." Her eyes went to Nylan. "Would that all men were like you." Then she smiled again. "Today, we have the noodles with the hot sauce, and the flat bread."

"Good." Nylan inadvertently licked his lips. When Blynnal said food was hot—it was spiced hot and then some.

"The tea is cold—for you." Blynnal laughed, then struck the chimes again.

Huldran grinned and glanced at the smith.

"You'll need that tea, too," Nylan predicted.

"Probably, but it's a lot better than the slop poor Kadran fixed."

As Nylan walked into the entryway, Siret stood by the nursery with Kyalynn, waiting. Smiling at the tall silver-haired guard and mother of his other daughter, the smith wondered if the two silver-haired guards had an informal arrangement as to which child he would see before the noon meal. Still, he had to admit he looked forward to seeing the children, more than a little.

"How is she?" he asked.

"Sleepy. She was restless last night. Teeth, I think. Ayrlyn touched her, but there is no chaos, just a trace of white around her teeth. I felt it, but I wasn't sure."

Nylan cradled Kyalynn in his left arm, and she looked up with a yawn, the dark green eyes mirrors of her mother's, her hands slowly reaching toward Nylan's face. "Waaaa . . . dah!"

"Somehow, I don't think she's asking for water," Nylan observed. "I'll probably wake her up, and she'll be cranky all night."

"That won't be any change from last night."

"So you were a grumpy girl, and you kept your mother up all night, all the time. That wasn't a nice thing to do . . ."

"Waaaa-daa-da . . . ooo . . ."

"No, it wasn't. It really wasn't."

Kyalynn yawned again, as Nylan rocked her, then once more, and shut her eyes. Shortly, a snort and a soft snore followed.

"You can always get her to sleep," said Siret.

"That's true," the smith said. "When I talk, I can put anyone to sleep, especially if I talk about building something." But the building was done, mostly, and now he was a weapons smith, forging more destruction. Did it always take force and more force?

He walked slowly toward the nursery and the corner bed that was Kyalynn's. There he eased her down, and patted her back gently for a moment, murmuring softly, until he was certain she would sleep.

Nylan glanced at the bed beside Kyalynn's, and patted a sleeping Dyliess on the back for a moment. Half the time in the nursery he still felt amazed.

Antyl smiled from the inside corner where she nursed her own son Jakon, rocking slightly in the plain wooden rocker that all the guards had helped craft early in the long winter.

Istril was burping Weryl, but she studiously avoided looking at Siret or Nylan, confirming the smith's suspicions about the oh-so-casual prearrangements.

Nylan and Siret eased out of the nursery and toward the great room.

"She still looks like you," the engineer said quietly.

"She takes things in like you do. She sees them, and she doesn't make a fuss, but she *knows*—I swore she could feel you healers when you worked on Llyselle's hand. Her eyes got wide, and she just watched."

"Could be," mused Nylan, stopping at the end of the lowest table. The aromas of mint and spice and bread filled the room. "We both have the talent. You'll have to be careful when she gets older."

"She might be too sensitive? I've thought of that." Siret nodded, then gestured. "I can see the Marshal's waiting for you." Her voice cooled.

Nylan smiled wryly, then wiped the smile away before turning and continuing toward the hearth and head table.

"How are the blades coming?" asked Ryba.

"I'm starting another. The one we finished yesterday is ready to sharpen." Nylan stepped around Ryba's chair and slid into his place on the bench next to Huldran.

"Another one?" groaned Saryn from across the table.

"Another one." Nylan offered a bright smile. "And Huldran will have another finished late today or tomorrow."

"Two?" Saryn shrugged, then wiped her steaming forehead. "You two keep this up, and we'll have enough of those killer blades for a complete U.F.F. legion."

"Isn't that the idea?" asked the engineer, ladling out Blynnal's noodles.

"I haven't figured out any other way to stop the locals. Have you?" asked Ryba mildly.

Nylan shrugged. That was the problem with Ryba. While her answers to questions were usually right, they all too often involved the maximum application of force necessary before someone else did the same. And the few times when the angels hadn't been able to apply such force had been near-disastrous. Had he avoided leadership because he didn't like the preemptive use of force? Or because he knew it was necessary on the violent world where the angels had landed? Or both?

Ayrlyn slipped into her seat across from Nylan. Her eyebrows lifted momentarily, but she said nothing, instead pouring some tea and drinking half a mugful almost immediately.

By the second bite of the noodles, despite the leavening effect of the flat bread, Nylan's forehead was sweating more than if he were standing before his forge. The cool tea helped, if not enough.

"The food here—it is always good." That comment came from Daryn.

Nylan looked at the young armsman, wanting to shake his head. Did all the locals like things spiced? Was it a survival ploy to cover the taste of meat or flour that wasn't quite right?

"We try to make everything good," offered Ryba.

"And you do, honored Marshal. Westwind is truly amazing."

The youth had been trained well in Gallos, at least in manners, Nylan reflected, and he was adaptable, more so than Gerlich had been. The former weapons officer had never accepted that Ryba was his better in everything from commanding to armed and unarmed combat. Of course, Gerlich had died in his attempt to storm Westwind. He'd also gotten a lot of guards killed unnecessarily, as well as one of the white wizards of Lornth. *That* hadn't bothered Nylan. Those white wizards were innately nasty, although why they were was yet another unanswered mystery.

"We try, Daryn. We try." Ryba's tone was light, but carried the edge that never left her voice anymore.

Nylan blotted his forehead.

"Do you think you should start training someone else in smithing?" asked Ryba.

"Cessya was working, but . . ." Nylan shrugged and glanced toward Huldran.

"Gerlich's wizard got her," Huldran finished. "Ydrall's shown some interest in the past. She liked your fancy pikes."

"If she is interested, I think it might be a good idea," Ryba suggested, lifting her mug to her lips. "Otherwise, find someone else."

"What's the urgency?" asked the smith.

"You said you wanted to work on building your mill," Ryba pointed out. "If you do, you can't smith, not all the time, and we're going to need a lot of smithwork. So I'd like you and Huldran to start training whoever it is in the next few eight-days, before the snows clear and you're back building the sawmill."

Nylan concealed a frown. All of what Ryba said was correct, but the words felt somehow wrong, and that bothered him. His eyes crossed those of Ayrlyn, and he got the faintest of nods in confirmation.

"There's been more snow this winter, and that means more mud," the engineer said. "That means it will be longer until we can reach the brickworks and the millpond down there—"

"Good," answered the black-haired Marshal. "You'll have more time to do blades and train another smith."

Her answer felt even more wrong to Nylan, but the quickest of frowns from Ayrlyn warned him not to push Ryba.

"Did you find out any more in those scrolls about Cyador?" he asked easily.

"There wasn't much," Ryba admitted. "I get the feeling that it's some sort of Rationalist leftover, with a heavy dose of chauvinism." She shrugged. "Right now I don't have much to go on, but it bothers me."

The name *Cyador* chilled Nylan, too, but he had even less reason to be worried than Ryba. After all, he was just a smith and an engineer. Just a hardworking technical stiff and one-time involuntary stud who really didn't have a mission anymore, now that the tower and the attached facilities were complete and the armies of Lornth and Gallos annihilated. He took another helping of noodles and then blotted his forehead.

"You're a glutton for punishment, ser," said Huldran.

"That's definitely one way of putting it," the smith agreed as he broke off another chunk of the flat bread. "A true glutton for punishment."

He ignored the bluelike flash from Ayrlyn's eyes, even as the tightness in his guts told him he shouldn't. But he felt as though everyone else were directing him, guiding him, from Istril and Siret arranging which child he saw to Ryba's efforts to boost Westwind's armory—almost endlessly, it seemed.

And the worst part was that he had no answers, no direction, except to keep forging destruction.

He swallowed more tea. Maybe he'd feel better if he worked on that foot for Daryn—something besides destruction.

VI

THE THREE—a blond woman, a gray-and-black-haired man, and a younger black-haired man—sat around a small and ancient table in the tower room that had belonged to the Lady Ellindyja before her exile to the Groves in Carpa. All three bore a resemblance to each other.

The older man lifted the scroll. "I told you both about this . . ."

The blond woman with green eyes glanced toward the window and the dark spring clouds framed by the dark wood, clouds looming over Lornth, and, as lightning flashed, then to the door.

"He'll be all right, Zeldyan," said the younger man.

"I do not like to leave him, not after . . . everything," said Zeldyan.

"Get young Nesslek, then. He's certainly not old enough to repeat what we say." The older man laughed.

"I would feel better." Zeldyan nodded and rose.

After she stepped through the door, the younger man turned. "Do you think she dotes upon him too much? She trusts no one with him."

"In this time of uncertainty? Hardly, Fornal. Your sister knows that her doting is limited. It is those women who refuse to understand that—like Lady Ellindyja—who cause trouble. Darkness knows we have more than enough trouble, anyway." The older man's index finger touched the scroll. "We could use one of those white wizards that Sillek squandered on the Roof of the World."

"He did not have much choice."

"The greater price we pay for such folly." Gethen shook his head. "And Sillek knew it was folly. We talked of it, but, no, he was young, and the holders would not accept that he had wisdom beyond his years. Nor would his most esteemed mother."

"You hate the Lady Ellindyja," said Fornal. "Yet she was only trying to uphold Sillek's honor with the older holders."

"I have no problem with honor, Fornal. Honor and trust are a man's greatest allies, but the Lady Ellindyja used her idea of honor to destroy the holders' trust in Sillek. He could have been the greatest lord of Lornth, and he loved Zeldyan in a way that the poets claim is common—and seldom happens in life. Yet his own mother incited her friends, and the old holders, to push for the war against Westwind. Where lies honor in that?" Gethen shrugged. "Now . . . we have a regent's council, which is always suspect. We have Ildyrom free to nibble at the grasslands, and Karthanos protected by the demon angels and free to wreak his will on eastern Candar."

Fornal frowned before answering. "He will not cross the Westhorns against the dark angels."

"Not across their lands, but what will happen after he takes Spidlar? He will, sooner or later. Can he not move all his troops south into Analeria and swing through the southern passes into Cerlyn?"

Fornal stroked his black beard, rubbed his chin, then looked up as Zeldyan closed the door behind her. She carried the blond Nesslek, his eyes closed, cradled in her arms.

"You were speaking of Karthanos?" she asked, easing herself back into the wooden armchair. "Best we consider the scroll, first. How long has it been since word has come out of Cyador?"

"Almost a generation. Genglois found one scroll in the old library, and there are others, but I bid him cease searching," said Fornal. "It also referred to the copper mines. Genglois said that Berphi—he was the Lord of Cyador then—died thereafter, and the Cyadorans never pursued the issue."

Gethen lifted the scroll. "Do we ignore the demand? Do we ask for recompense? We cannot fight another land . . . not after last fall."

"Why do we not send a polite answer that says nothing?" asked Zeldyan. "As if we totally misunderstood? They think we are ignorant forest-dwellers anyway."

"It might buy time, and we can use much of that," mused Gethen. "But why does the Emperor of Cyador trouble us now?"

"According to Skiodra and the other traders that frequent the outlying stations—"

"Outlying stations?" asked Fornal.

"They do not permit outsiders' parties within Cyador—a few travelers perhaps, but certainly not traders, especially not after the Kyphrans tried to seize that isolated port town," Zeldyan explained.

"Guarstyad," confirmed Gethen. "It seems to have roused this Lephi against us all. What do we know of him?"

"Some of the Cyadorans have no great love of this Lephi. There was a struggle for the succession, and he ousted his beloved younger brother."

"I recall that," Fornal noted. "In the end, the older brother murdered the younger, but they called it a battle." The dark-haired man smiled crookedly. "Younger brothers have a way of being loved, I gather. Especially after they're dead."

"I don't think Relyn is dead," said Zeldyan. "And I don't appreciate the comment. I have always loved you both."

Fornal looked down at the table. "I am sorry, sister. That was uncalled for."

"What do you think about Zeldyan's idea?" asked Gethen, his weathered face carefully impassive.

The younger man nodded. "If we make the response flowery enough, we can manage several exchanges of messages. Especially if we express our concerns that it has been so long since last we heard from the great and mighty land of Cyador."

"We'll have to give in or express defiance sooner or later," the blond woman cautioned.

"It takes a fast messenger nearly two eight-days to reach Cyad," said Gethen, "and we cannot be expected to respond the day we receive such a message."

"Fine," said Zeldyan, opening her blouse and easing Nesslek to her breast. "We can buy a season, perhaps a year. Then what?"

"Give the copper mines to Ildyrom," suggested Fornal, "and let him cope with Cyador, except that wouldn't be honorable."

"Even if it were honorable, I would prefer another course," said Gethen. "But the longer before we must face any other land in battle the better."

The three nodded, not exactly in unison, but in agreement.

VII

IN THE DIM light cast by the fat candles—one on each of the six tables—Nylan pushed the platter away. He'd eaten too much, too quickly. Then he smiled at the irony. A year ago, they'd all been on the verge of starvation—that had certainly contributed to Ellysia's weakness and the chaos fever that had killed her and left Dephnay an orphan. Now, Westwind had enough in its larders that Nylan felt comfortably full.

Blynnal's cooking had also helped.

Ryba had pulled her chair to the side, and the glowing embers in the hearth added some light and a gentle warmth to the big room. The Marshal rocked Dyliess in her arms, gently.

"That was good," Huldran said.

Nylan nodded.

Holding a sleepy Dyliess to her shoulder, and patting her back, Ryba pushed back her chair and glanced at Ayrlyn. "Could we have a song?"

"I'll get my lutar." The healer/singer rose. Behind her, so did Istril.

"It's good Ayrlyn's teaching Istril and Llyselle the songs," the Marshal remarked quietly.

"I didn't know that Llyselle was learning them." Nylan took a long swallow of water from his goblet. He didn't like the bitterness of the tea in the evening, not unless his muscles were exceedingly sore from smithing, and, despite his wiry frame, that soreness didn't occur that often anymore. Then, after almost two years, he'd adjusted to a lot of heavy labor, from smithing to practicing with metal weapons designed to inflict maximum damage on other individuals—preferably while escaping the receipt of similar injuries.

"Like the songs . . ."

". . . some of them . . ."

". . . singer makes them sound so good . . ."

Ayrlyn did make them sound good—if she'd just refrain from ever performing the song she'd composed about the mighty smith Nylan. That one, reflected the silver-haired man, was truly awful. He shifted his weight on the bench and took another sip of the cold water, glad that he'd had a chance to take a warm shower—warm for Westwind, anyway—before the evening meal. His self-designed water system had not frozen once during the winter, and all the recruits who had helped with the repairs were even gladder than he had been. They hadn't been so glad the previous fall when he'd insisted on greater cover for the water lines and a few other laborious details.

Ayrlyn slipped back into the great room almost unnoticed until she stood at the hearth, her flame-red hair glinting with a light of its own. Istril eased up beside her.

The two strummed a few chords, looked at each other, then began to sing.

"On the Roof of the World, all covered with white,
I took up my blade there, and I brought back the night.
With a blade in each hand, there, and the stars at my boots,
With the Legend in song, then, I set down my roots.
The demons have claimed you, forever in light,
But the darkness of order will put them to flight,
Will break them in twain, soon, and return you your pride,
For the Legend is kept by the blades at your side.
The blades at your side, now, must always be bright,
And the Legend we hold to is that of the right.
For never will guards lose the heights of the sky,
And never can Westwind this Legend deny . . .
And never can Westwind this Legend deny."

"Good!" offered Ryba, amid the scattered applause. "Each time it gets better."

Nylan had to agree with that, although he knew that Ayrlyn had more than mixed feelings about creating songs to fuel a female militaristic culture. So did he, but given the reception they had gotten from the locals, there weren't many options, not on a planet where women had virtually no rights—at least anywhere the angels had heard of so far.

At the same time, Nylan reflected, he had, in some ways, even fewer options. His guts tightened, reminding him that he was deceiving himself. In Candar, any man had some options. He swallowed, wondering why his growing mastery of the local order fields was accompanied by an equal vulnerability to the pain of death and increasing discomfort with deception and untruth. And by increasing uneasiness with Ryba, he reminded himself, an uneasiness compounded by his feelings of responsibility toward his children.

Or is it a worry about the alternative? About having to face an unfamiliar outside world alone? He shook his head, again recognizing that there was something about the order fields that forced more self-examination, self-examination that was never exactly welcome.

The smith's eyes went through the darkness, no barrier to any of the silver-haired guards, to study Daryn. The blond young man fidgeted ever so slightly on the bench beside Hryessa. Hryessa, one of the first refugees to Westwind, had developed into a first-class guard, a demon with a blade according to Saryn. Her eyes were rapt and fixed on Ayrlyn.

"A ballad," called Llyselle. "The Sybran one."

The redheaded healer readjusted the lutar, touching the tuning pegs and strumming the strings before she began.

> *"When the snow drops on the stone*
> *When the wind song's all alone*
> *When the ice swords form in twain,*
> *Sing of the hearths where we've lain.*
>
> *"When the green tips break the snow,*
> *When the cold streams start to flow,*
> *When the snow hares turn to black*
> *Sing out to call our love back.*
>
> *"When the plains grass whispers gold*
> *When the red blooms flower bold,*
> *When the year's foals gallop long,*
> *Hold to the fall and our song. . . ."*

The stillness was almost absolute in the hall, punctuated by a scattered cough or two. The memory of Sybra was still too raw for the survivors, and the grief was too palpable even to the women from Candar.

"Something cheerier?" suggested Huldran.

Ayrlyn nodded, murmured to Istril, and began again.

> *"All day I dragged a boat of stone*
> *and came home when you weren't alone,*
> *so I took all those blasted rocks*
> *and buried all your boyish fancy locks . . .*
> *and took you for a ride in my boat of stone. . . ."*

Nylan wasn't certain how much cheerier the song was, but the locals especially loved it, perhaps because Ayrlyn had reversed the sexes in the verses.

In the end, the last song was predictably the same.

"The guard song . . . the guard song!" chanted the newer recruits.

Ayrlyn looked wryly at Nylan; Istril just looked at the floor. Ayrlyn stood before the hearth, lutar in hand, adjusting the tuning pegs and striking several strong chords before beginning.

> *"From the skies of long-lost Heaven*
> *to the heights of Westwind keep*
> *we will hold our blades in order*
> *and never let our honor sleep.*
>
> *"From the skies of light-iced towers*
> *to the demons' place on earth,*
> *we will hold fast lightning's powers*
> *and never count gold's worth.*
>
> *"As the guards of Westwind keep*
> *our souls hold winter's sweep;*
> *we will hold our blades in order,*
> *and never let our honor sleep. . . ."*

Nylan still wasn't sure about honor, since it seemed to him that people who talked a lot about it killed a lot of people and then paid a far higher price than anyone ever intended.

He managed to stifle a yawn as he rose from the bench and rubbed his stiff backside. The benches were wood, and hard, after sitting for a long time, songs or no songs.

He glanced around, but Ayrlyn was gone, and so were Istril, Siret, Huldran, and Ryba.

He shrugged and headed for the jakes before bed. Tomorrow, there would be more smithing—more blades—and he still wasn't quite sure they were a good idea, but he had none better.

The rough form for Daryn's foot was taking longer, far longer, than he had thought, since he had to squeeze it in—just as Relyn's handhook had taken longer and had had to be worked in between the endless weapons creation.

He stifled another yawn as he turned toward the lower-level jakes, stifled a yawn and tried not to think about children and Ryba and the darkness that was Candar.

VIII

THE STOCKY GRAY-HAIRED man waited as Zeldyan knelt, patting Nesslek's back until the boy's breathing was regular. Then she eased him from his side to his back and covered him with the blanket.

After a last look at her son, she rose, crossed the room, and sat opposite Gethen across the low table, where she filled both goblets that rested there. She took a small sip from her own, followed by a nibble from the pastry she had started earlier.

"You were saying?" he asked quietly.

"Father," said Zeldyan slowly. "You remember Hissl, the wizard who tried to claim the Ironwoods by leading an expedition to defeat the dark angels?"

"I heard about it. I was in Rulyarth at the time, you recall." Gethen lifted the goblet and sipped the wine. "The angels destroyed them to the last man, despite Hissl's wizardry. The angels had a black mage. I suppose they still do."

"He was the one who used the fires of Heaven . . ." Zeldyan broke off the sentence, and looked down at the table. "Just like Sillek, he probably didn't have any choice. If he hadn't killed . . . he would have died."

"You don't hate him?" asked Gethen.

"Why? You know who I hate." Zeldyan toyed with her goblet, then set it down without drinking. "Hissl did not lead the first expedition, the one after Relyn's, I mean. The leader was a big man from the Roof of the World."

"That seems strange, if true. Why do you mention that?"

"For Nesslek's sake, I have to think. I cannot be bound by old hates or tradition." The blonde took another small sip of wine. "I doubt that there is a single land where everyone is happy. People come to Lornth from Jerans, or go from here to Westwind or Suthya."

"As far as I can see, only women go to Westwind." Gethen refilled his goblet.

"Once they came to Lornth from Cyador, those who weren't slaughtered . . . according to the old tales."

"You still raise the disturbing questions, daughter, after all these years."

"I cannot be who I am not. That, too, is a form of . . . honor. I learned that from Sillek."

Gethen waited.

"What do we know of Westwind, really know?" asked Zeldyan. "Except that they destroyed two armies?"

"Not much," agreed Gethen.

"I think we should be alert to learn what we can. Perhaps the dark angels might have something we can use."

"Against Cyador? You were certain that it would come to battle when we discussed this before." Gethen took another sip of the wine.

"Unless matters change," she said. "Fornal would fight. If he thinks he must fight, he will want to fight immediately."

"Sometimes that view is correct."

"Sometimes," said Zeldyan without agreeing. "I would rather avoid battles."

"One cannot always do that. Sillek hated battles, but he was right to take the fight to Ildyrom."

"So long as he had Koric and a wizard to leave in Clynya. Now what will we do—add to the armsmen there?" The blonde lifted a small handful of nuts from the dish on the table. "I suppose we must. Fornal has fortified Rulyarth, and the people there would not submit to Suthya now. Our tribute to Westwind keeps the east safe. If Cyador brings trouble, we will need forces in the south anyway."

"You just said you would avoid battle. What do you seek from the dark ones?" Gethen laughed.

"Do you disagree that battles are costly?" Zeldyan turned toward the window as the roll of thunder rumbled across Lornth, heralding more spring rain.

"Hardly. But what has this to do with the dark angels?" Gethen frowned.

"Perhaps nothing. I do think we should talk with any who leave, if any do, and set out word that they are to be treated kindly and escorted to Lornth."

"That will not set well with some," pointed out Gethen.

"Send those who wish to fight to Clynya."

"Including the Lady Ellindyja?"

"I wish I could send her to Westwind or feed her to Ildyrom's dogs."

"That would not be good for the dogs," said Gethen, "even if they do belong to Ildyrom."

IX

NYLAN LAY ON his couch in the darkness, listening to the wind as it rattled the shutters.

He'd scarcely seen Ayrlyn in the past two days, not since she'd sung the night before last. Was she avoiding him? Why?

The shutters rattled again.

What did he want? To live alone, to stay alone at the top of the tower he had built? To forge enough peerless blades to last generations—until Ryba needed his talents for some other form of mass destruction?

What did he want from his life, this life that had changed so much in the blink of a ship's powernet that had fluxed and crashed? Then, had he known what he had wanted before, or just let the service dictate things? Building the tower had been the first big thing he had wanted . . . and it was done, and building another wouldn't be the same, even if it were needed.

He shook his head.

The shutters rattled yet once more, and the smith turned on his couch until his eyes rested on the closed window and shutters. He and Ayrlyn had started to get close before winter closed in around them, but the confinement of the tower hadn't helped. Or had that been an excuse?

He and Ayrlyn had agreed not to sleep together regularly because . . . because why? Because he was treading on thin ice with Ryba? Because he didn't want to just drift into another relationship? Because he recognized that Ayrlyn needed a total commitment, and he didn't want to be forced?

With a deep breath, he turned back over, away from the rattling of the window and the low whistle of the wind.

Plick! A drop of water splattered on the planked floor, probably from the slowly melting ice making its way through the slates of the tower roof, in places where two winters had frozen and crumbled the mortar they had used instead of the roofing tar they did not have.

Plick!

The smith took another long breath, then paused at what sounded like a whisper outside his door—or bare feet on the cold stones of the tower steps. But Ryba's door had not opened. He would have heard if it had, and he had had nothing to do with Ryba since before the great battle of the previous autumn.

Plick!

His own door opened, and Nylan glanced through the darkness, not that it hampered his view. The strange underjump that had translated the *Winterlance* to whatever world they had found—like all worlds, the natives merely called it "the world" or "the earth"—the underjump that had turned his hair living silver had also given him night vision that was nearly as good as his day vision.

Plick!

The figure that slipped into his room did not have Ayrlyn's flame-red hair, but silver hair.

"Istril?" he whispered, half sitting up.

Her finger touched his lips and her lips whispered in his ear. "Just tonight. I talked with the healer, and we agreed." There was a pause. "Unlike some, Nylan, I wouldn't deceive you."

"But—"

"I want a daughter, and I want you to be her father. This is one of *my* visions."

Before he could protest again, the slight and wiry figure eased out of the robe she had worn and under the thin blanket, her skin smooth and warm against his—except for very cold feet.

"Your feet—"

"They're cold, but don't make fun of me. This is hard . . ." Istril shivered, and buried her head in his shoulder for a moment.

Nylan could feel the dampness of her cheeks on his bare skin. He eased his arms around her, even as he wondered. Ayrlyn? Istril would not have lied, not for anything.

Ayrlyn? Why would she have agreed?

He stroked Istril's silver hair for a long time before he kissed her, gently, before her lips trembled under his, before he chose not to resist what had been offered.

X

LEPHI GAZED OUT across the polished white tiles of the Great Hall of Cyad and stifled a yawn. Just below the oversized malachite and silver throne, to the Lord of Cyador's right, stood the white wizard Themphi. Farther below and to the left loomed Duhru, the Voice of His Mightiness.

"We might as well get this façade over with," muttered the Lord of Cyador. "Announce the receiving of petitions."

"His Mightiness Lephi the White, Lord of Cyador, ruler of all lands from the mountains of the skies to the oceans of the west, Protector of the Steps to Paradise, Son of the Rational Stars, stands ready to receive the petitions of his people. Those with worthy petitions, draw near with good conscience." Duhru's voice boomed across the great hall, and the three-story-high gilded doors in the rear of the hall slid open nearly silently, the hiss of steam merely a whisper lost in the vastness of the chamber.

Three figures slowly marched across the white tiles and stood on the shimmering and spotless tiles beneath the throne.

"Declare your petition," rumbled Duhru, "if you are without darkness and a follower of the way of whiteness."

· The first petitioner—a mid-aged man wearing the white surplice of a petitioner over heavy work trousers and tunic—bowed. "Most powerful Lord of Cyador, Protector of the Steps to Paradise, hear my petition."

"The Lord hears all," responded Duhru. "State your petition."

"The officers of the Eighth Mirror Lancers have dishonored

my youngest daughter, and I ask redress. Only you can restore her honor."

Lephi glanced toward Themphi.

"They say they used no force, and that they offered a dozen silvers toward her dowry," whispered the white wizard.

"Those officers have honored your daughter," declared Lephi. "I will also increase that honor by adding two golds to that dowry."

The stocky man bowed, his forehead slick with sweat. "I seek no dowry. I seek honor. I humbly ask that you dishonor those officers. No officer of the greatest lord should defile a young girl."

"The Lord of Cyador has heard your petition," boomed Duhru. "You may go and tell all of his generosity."

"NO!" The white-clad man charged the steps to the dais. "Your officers are pigs. They are sows, and you slop them."

A flaming arrow flashed from the balcony gratework, the mark of an Archer of the Rational Stars, catching the man in the chest. The other two petitioners watched, mouths partly open as the first petitioner crumpled.

After a nod from Lephi toward Themphi, a fireball arced toward the dying man, then exploded. Only a handful of scattered ashes sifted through the air.

"Question the lancer officers. If they dishonored the girl, do what is necessary. If not, have her join her father."

"So it is with unworthy petitions and petitioners, and those who reject the generosity of the lord," intoned Duhru. "Let the next petitioner offer his petition."

"Most puissant Lord of Cyador, Protector of the Steps to Paradise, the citizens of Wybar humbly beseech Your Mightiness for a token of his support for the blessing of the new river piers." The elderly man in the white surplice added in a wavering tone, "Only a token, Your Mightiness."

"They are fearful because Wybar is downstream from the Accursed Forest," Themphi explained.

Lephi nodded. "You shall have such a token. May your piers bring all prosperity and good trade."

"May the next petitioner approach," rumbled Duhru, "if he

is without darkness and a follower of the way of whiteness."

"Your Supreme Mightiness . . . the peasants in Geliendra have presented a petition, and the regional governor has endorsed it." The functionary in gold bowed twice. On the second bow, droplets of perspiration splattered on the polished white tiles of the floor.

"Lick those up, Husenar. I don't like the floors soiled, especially when my administrators are acting for others."

Husenar complied, then straightened, standing stiffly.

"What about this petition? Why need it be brought to me? Why did they not present it themselves?"

"The Accursed . . . Forest . . . rods and rods of the rice fields and the bean fields—those not already flooded—they are gone."

"Gone?"

"The forest has awakened—"

"The Forest of the Nameless? Have the wards failed? The wards have never failed."

Husenar bowed again. "The wards are no more, and the forest lives."

"I have taken their petition under advisement, and I will act accordingly."

After the petitioners and Duhru departed and the doors closed, Lephi turned to Themphi. "About that mess with the Eighth Mirror—"

"They could not so dishonor a peasant."

"Themphi . . . did you not hear what I said? When a man is so distraught he will die rather than accept two years' wages for a dowry, something is wrong. She is doubtless a spineless wench, but when peasants believe such girls are innocent they do not pay taxes, except under duress, and we do not need that now. I tell you again: you will find the guilty parties. If they are the officers, they can also choose duty to protect the people of Geliendra from the Accursed Forest—for the rest of their lives." Lephi smiled coldly. "I want every peasant to know that I heard and acted, and every officer to know that girls outside the households of officers or the pleasure class are to be left untouched. I do not care how many paid concubines they have, but they must be sure that the purchases of concubines are well witnessed. Well witnessed." He paused. "Of course, if it is the girl, and you had best be *very* sure, then she should be publicly violated by at least a company of Mirror armsmen. Whatever happens, I want both punishment choices made public, so that I receive no more petitions such as this."

Themphi swallowed.

"Send some of the engineers to check the forest, and the wards. How could they possibly have failed?"

"I do not know." Themphi shifted his weight from one foot to the other. "The wards are very old, and the ancient accounts record that the forest was cunning and patient before it was restrained."

"Then you will go and repair the damage, and restrain the forest once again. After you complete your work on this mess with the girl. Send no engineers from the Second. We need them to re-create the fireships, to reclaim the ocean from the eastern traders." Lephi stared at the wizard. "Had your predecessors not allowed the ancient fireships to deteriorate, we would have no such problems."

"Sire, they had no choice."

"There is always a choice."

"Not where chaos is concerned." Themphi ignored the dampness on his forehead.

"Do you question your Emperor, Themphi?"

"Emperors have choices, Sire, except where order and chaos meet. The same is true of wizards. I cannot change what was and is, even at your command."

"Bah . . . you sound just like Triendar. Do they cast spells over you when you are young so that you all sound alike?"

"Chaos and order do not change because we exist, Sire." Themphi shifted his weight again.

"Wizard, your powers must serve Cyad, not the other way around. See that they do, or your nephew's children or his children's children will bow under the yoke of the easterners.

Lands either become more powerful or less powerful and then perish. I intend to make sure Cyador becomes more powerful. You may go."

"Yes, Sire."

XI

EVEN BEFORE NYLAN sat at the table and balanced Dyliess on his right knee, his eyes kept ranging to the end of the great room toward the central pedestal and the staircase. He could feel the slight movement of warm air from the furnace ducts set in the central stone pedestal that held the stairs and around which the tower was built. Interspersed with the warmth were gusts of cold dry air from the opening of the main tower door as guards headed up to handle livestock details or wood-carrying.

Breakfast was the usual—some bread, some cheese, and for the stout-hearted, some thin porridge. Eating one-handed, Nylan suffered through the yellow-green bitter root-and-leaf tea, taking quick sips and keeping the mug out of reach of Dyliess's curious fingers. The bread was dark and cold, but hearty and chewy.

"Gaaaa . . . da . . . oooo . . . ." His daughter's hands grasped for his bread.

"Grabby, isn't she, ser?" said Hryessa from farther down the table.

"They all are at this age, from what I can tell," Nylan answered. "They want to grab the world and explore."

"Don't we all?" mumbled Huldran, finishing a wedge of cheese and some bread.

Nylan reached out and redirected Dyliess's wandering hand, in time to keep her from grasping the spout of the teapot. "Exploration gets dangerous."

"True enough even when you get older." Saryn frowned, then added after a moment of silence, "Ryba said you were working on more blades."

"We've been working on blades on and off all winter. Don't you have enough yet?"

"For now. She insists we'll have over fourscore guards by fall, maybe more, that we'll have to convert half the fifth level into a barracks room or something." Saryn turned her head as if Ryba were to appear, and the short, dark brown hair seemed almost black in the great room lit by only the four armaglass windows.

"Or start adding to the tower," Nylan said.

"You said it would hold over a hundred."

"It will," the smith answered, his eyes still seeking Ayrlyn. He hadn't seen Istril, either. "How many years will it take to build the addition if each stone has to be chipped out of the canyon with a sledge and chisel?" Somehow, Nylan wasn't thrilled about adding to Westwind, but he wasn't about to voice that lack of enthusiasm.

"Oh . . ."

"Exactly." Nylan fed Dyliess a morsel of bread, although she'd already eaten. Dyliess promptly gummed it and deposited starchy brown drool on Nylan's hand.

"I was wondering," ventured the dark-haired former ship's pilot. "Is there any way you could forge more bows? I mean, you started on the first blades with the laser, but you managed to forge the others."

"There's cormclit left," Nylan acknowledged, "but it's a directional heatshield composite. I had the demon's own time cutting it with a laser. It just fragments into strands when I've tried to cut it with a chisel, and bench shears just jam or chew it into shreds. Then there are the alloys. I can't even soften the lightweight, high-temp ones, and those were what I used for those bows." He shook his head. "I've tried, but . . ."

He frowned. Had that flash of flame-red been Ayrlyn headed down to the kitchen?

"I thought I'd ask. We've only got sixteen of those killer bows." Saryn coughed. All too many guards coughed through the winter, probably from too much mouth breathing outside in the chill of the Roof of the World. "We only lost one in the battle."

"You threatened to dismember any guard who lost one, even if she were dying," said Huldran. "I remember that."

"I was right," Saryn said. "They're twice as good as anything the locals have, and they're not replaceable."

"There's still too much up here that's not replaceable," Nylan offered. "We need a better low-tech base."

"Like your sawmill?" Saryn grinned. "What comes after that?"

"I thought about a flour mill, but we're too high to grow grain—"

"He never stops thinking, does he?" The number two of the Westwind guards finished her tea with a gulp.

There was too much to think about, reflected Nylan, from Ryba's coldness to children to Ayrlyn, not to mention smithing. He'd still only rough-formed the prosthetic foot for Daryn—something for a man would certainly be low on Ryba's priority list, he suspected, far below weapons.

"Got to run," added Saryn. "We're going to see what it's like down below near that grove of hardwoods off the lower meadow below the brickworks. You remember those ironwood trees? They're lousy for woodworking, but the healer says they'll make good charcoal. You did say you needed charcoal."

"I did. We can't do much at the smithy without it."

"Daaaa . . ." injected Dyliess, lurching toward Nylan's mug again.

By the time he had intercepted her grasping fingers and had his tea under control, Saryn was headed out of the great hall.

"She's a handful," said Huldran.

"Saryn? She's not bad."

"I meant your daughter." Huldran laughed. "Already, she has a mind of her own."

Like her mother, Nylan thought, but he only said, "She does." Then he finished the last of his own tea and a last morsel of cheese before standing and lurching off the bench and toward the stairs to the tower's lower level.

Still carrying Dyliess, Nylan made his way down the stone stairs into the warmth below. Turning away from the heat of the kitchen, where Blynnal and her crew labored, Nylan found

Ayrlyn in the corner of the lowest-level room in the tower—in the corner of the woodworking area, sitting on a stool and practicing chords on her lutar. She was not singing, and her eyes were puffy.

"I kept looking for you," he said, shifting Dyliess.

"Why?" she asked.

"Because I wanted to talk to you."

"Ouuuu," mimicked Dyliess.

"There's nothing to talk about."

"Yes, there is."

"What?" Ayrlyn's voice was flat.

"What about last night? Why? And why wouldn't you come to breakfast?"

"Because . . ." Ayrlyn took a deep breath. "I don't like sharing you, but I can't do what Ryba did. First, there's no technology left, and, second, I wouldn't trick you. It's not easy." The healer took a deep shuddering breath. "Her daughter will be all Istril really ever has, you know? How could I deny her that? You've saved her life twice, and she worships you, and it . . . it has to be more personal . . ." Tears oozed from the corners of the healer's deep brown eyes.

"What about Weryl?" Nylan shook his head. "I'm missing something. A lot of somethings." He reached out and took her hand with his left hand, the free one. "That can wait. I've been thinking . . ."

"About time . . ." Ayrlyn swallowed once, twice, then spoke again. "How long can Istril count on Weryl staying in Westwind with Ryba's distrust of men? Until he's fifteen or twenty and slips off?" Ayrlyn coughed, trying to clear her throat. "He is your son. Do you really think he'll buy all of Ryba's propaganda? Especially with all the legends about you?"

"You talk as if I won't be there."

"You won't. You and Ryba barely tolerate each other. Everyone sees it, but no one says anything. Ryba still needs more blades, and you feel responsible for Dyliess, and Weryl, and Kyalynn. How long can you hang in there for the children before . . ." The flame-haired healer shook her head. "Nylan . . . you're sweet, but you're dense about some things."

"I know. I know." Nylan glanced toward the end of the room where Murkassa entered, along with two other new guards—one called Jiess, Nylan thought. "Let's take a walk."

"Now?"

"Now," the smith insisted. "Or as soon as I can hand Dyliess over to Antyl for a little bit."

"Just a moment." Ayrlyn eased the lutar into the case and then set the case up on one of the empty shelves that had held planks and timber earlier in the winter. "I'll meet you at the end of the causeway. Don't be long, or I'll freeze solid."

"It's spring."

"I'll freeze half-solid."

"I'll hurry."

Nylan trudged back up to the nursery and looked around, finally seeing Antyl in the corner nearest the north door that led to the bathhouse and laundry.

"Be wondering how long afore you'd be here," said the mahogany-haired woman, extending her arms to Dyliess. "Jakon misses the silver-heads. He be telling when they're not here. So's Dephnay. It's like they reassure the others. Like you do, ser."

Part of their heritage? An earlier manifestation of sensitivity to the order fields—the black "magic" of Candar?

"Me?" asked Nylan involuntarily.

"You and the flame-healer. And the other silvertops. People settle down round you. Except the Marshal, but she's the Angel, and that's different. Don't know as to what some of us had done, weren't for Westwind. Now, don't ye be minding me. Your little ones be fine."

Nylan smiled and headed for the main door to the tower—the south door, pausing as Llyselle passed, carrying in an armload of stove wood for Blynnal.

"How's the hand?" he asked.

"Almost healed." The silver-haired guard shook her head. "So stupid. I just took my eyes off the saw an instant. You survive battles, and almost lose a hand to a saw, a frigging handsaw."

"It happens."

"It's still stupid, but I was lucky you and the healer were near." With a last smile, Llyselle headed toward the lower level. The engineer-smith closed the tower door behind himself and hurried out to the end of the causeway, his ship-jacket closed only halfway.

Despite the bright sun, the first green tendrils of the snow lilies rising through the melting whiteness, and the dampness at the ends of the snow piles flanking the road, Ayrlyn's jacket was fastened all the way up, her gloved hands in the pockets of the worn heavy-weather parka that was one of the handful that had come down in the landers from the *Winterlance*.

"Cold?" he asked.

"I'm always cold here, even in summer." Her brown eyes flashed in that way that conveyed a blueness, even though the smith intellectually knew that the blue flash he saw was more an order field manifestation than anything visual. Order field or not, it meant anger. "I've done pretty well for someone not raised in a freezer like the rest of you. I don't hide in the tower, and I don't crouch by the kitchen stove. Darkness knows, I feel like it. But I don't."

"I never said anything about that."

"You don't have to. You're not as bad as the others, but all of you are so damned condescending about it. I'd love to get you down in the lowlands in summer, and then smile at you while the sweat pours off your forehead and you feel like you're going to fall over from heatstroke."

Nylan pursed his lips. Was he really that bad? "Am I that bad?"

"No. Not usually, but I'm in a lousy mood. And you ought to know why. *That* is something you should know."

"You've been here for me . . ." he said slowly. "When no one else was . . . not anyone who understood."

"There were others? You told me—"

"There weren't any others. Except . . . for last night . . . there never have been . ... not since almost a season before the battle last fall. I told you that, and it was true. There weren't any others, because I don't get close to just bodies. I'm not a Gerlich. I never have been. And I can't talk about it."

"That's been clear, and I've tried to be understanding."
Ayrlyn shook her head, her eyes glistening.

"Then . . . why?" he asked helplessly.

Ayrlyn walked from the causeway out to the road and
turned toward the ridge, leaving Nylan standing by himself.

He turned to follow, repeating his question. "Why?"

"Don't you understand, Nylan? I won't beg. I won't ask."
The flame-haired healer began to walk more briskly out toward the bridge.

Nylan hurried after her, then settled into a quick walk beside her. For a time he walked silently, hoping she would say
more. She didn't.

"Did you ever think that I don't like begging, either?" he
finally asked.

"Begging? When all you have to do is lift a finger, and any
guard in the tower would crawl to your couch?" Ayrlyn
stopped in the middle of the small bridge and turned eastward,
looking out across the slow-melting snow, into the glare of
the mid-morning sun off the expanse of white. Beyond the
drop-off, in the distance rose the dark spires of the high forest, now that the evergreens had shed their cloak of winter
white.

"I didn't notice you crawling," he said slowly. "And I
haven't lifted my finger, as you put it, to beckon anyone else."

"I won't crawl. For you. For anyone. And you didn't turn
Istril away, not at all."

Nylan sighed. "It didn't seem right to have her in my bed,
and it didn't seem right to turn her away. Especially when she
said she'd talked to you. She doesn't lie."

"That's a great line. I bedded her because she doesn't lie."

Nylan winced, as though a Lornian arrow had slammed
through him. "That isn't what I meant. It wasn't an easy situation."

"You think it was easy for me? You ought to know by now
how I feel. Yet you stand there and look at me as if I had four
heads or spouted chaos and fireballs with every word."

Nylan looked down at the cold, cold stones of the bridge
underfoot. After a moment, he forced his eyes up and to meet

Ayrlyn's. "Would you believe"—he swallowed, trying to force the words out—"that you're so honest that it scares me worse than facing those wizards did?"

Her eyes did not flicker, just waited.

"I'm not that honest. And I'm not very brave. I never wanted to be captain. You know that. How could a man who deep inside fears *everything* . . . how could I ever lead people? How could I ask you . . . ?"

A faint smile crossed her lips, like the glimmer of sunshine after a storm. "The way you just did . . . by being honest with me . . . by not trying to be the solid engineer that no one touches. I don't want a hero image. I don't want a male version of Ryba. I have fears, Nylan. Everyone does. You do. I can deal with that. I just can't deal with a man who hides from himself."

Hides from himself . . . yes, you do. The engineer licked his lips, ignoring the chill ice that coated them, then sublimated away. "I have a lot . . . to learn."

"So do I. Will you learn it with me?"

"If you're gentle with me . . . that kind of honesty is hard," he admitted.

"All honesty is hard. So is love." Her eyes were brown, soft, and deep, and he felt lost in them, lost in wondering what he had not seen, what must have been so obvious. His hands reached for hers as they stood on the stones of the bridge he had built, in the cold spring of Westwind.

XII

THE WHITE-ROBED wizard stood near the front of the barge, on the raised section of deck right behind the three-cubit-wide bronze cleats, each shaped like a horned ox, around which the two ropes had been wound.

"Gee-ah . . ." The low sounds of the boat drovers whispered

across the canal surface in the gray before dawn as the four oxen pulled the gilded *White Lily* northward from Fyrad, their hoofs clicking faintly on the worn paving stones originally laid for the ancient steam tugs that long ago pulled the barges from the city of the Winter Palace, propelled by the same chaos engines that the Second Company of White Engineers was laboring to re-create for His Mightiness's fireship under construction at Cyad.

Themphi frowned. These days, oxen were more dependable, far more dependable. As for building a replica of an ancient fireship . . . he shook his head. Maintaining the steam device for the palace doors was tiring enough, yet Lephi wanted a fireship, with an ancient fire cannon, regardless of the cost and the impact on that precarious balance between order and chaos.

He glanced back at the low superstructure that held the privileged passengers, and the seven remaining guilty Mirror Lancer officers, then at the canvas awning under which the other passengers slept. One of the officers had attempted to assault the wizard. Themphi had turned the proceeds from the resale of that officer's household and concubines over to the wronged peasant girl along with a year's pay from each officer. In that, Lephi had been right. Erratic as the Emperor was, he was more often correct than not. The white wizard shook his head as he glanced westward in the general direction of Cyad.

"A peasant girl . . . and she will be the richest woman in . . . what is that wretched place . . . Nystrad." Themphi stretched and looked at the deckhouse where young Fissar still slept. The young always slept, unaware of the continual balancing acts required of their elders.

Far behind the deckhouse were the piers of Fyrad where the swift coaster had brought him from Cyad, far more swiftly than taking the North Highway.

Then his eyes dropped back to the glasslike surface of the canal.

Water bugs, almost as large as the wizard's clenched fist, skimmed across the shimmering surface, darting between the stalks of the reeds trimmed back to less than a cubit above the water, even with the smooth graystone blocks that formed the side of the west towpath of the waterway. The barge glided northward from Fyrad along the Great Canal, past trimmed reeds and ancient stone canal walls.

A kay or so to the east of the canal, the river wound a more sinuous course, and one more dangerous, with its population of stun lizards and sharp-toothed crocodators. The river was used by the peasants who had no coins to pay the tolls of the canal—and those who wished to avoid the keen-eyed Imperial inspectors.

"Gee . . . ah . . ."

Themphi fingered his smooth-shaven chin, looking straight down and catching sight of his own angel-shaded reflection in the silver-gray waters.

The white-trimmed blue barge continued to glide through the mirror-smooth waters of the Great Canal, another work that Themphi knew could not be replicated by the Empire he served. North toward the Accursed Forest, that expanse of . . . who knew what that had been bounded by white stone walls and wards since the founding of Cyador—and perhaps before.

He shivered as he thought of the teetering balance between order and chaos that awaited him.

XIII

THE MARE'S HOOFS squushed as she carried Nylan down the muddy road toward the brickworks—and the millpond. Beside him, Ayrlyn rode a chestnut mare. As usual, her jacket was fastened—all but the very top—and Nylan's was only loosely closed.

Less than a hundred cubits to their right—west—the rock rose in a sheer cliff nearly a kay up to the high meadow plateau that held Westwind. The two had started their ride after breakfast, and it was approaching mid-morning, although they had not pushed their mounts. Riding in the mud took longer, especially crossing the occasional snowdrifts, some of which remained nearly waist high, and the route was anything but direct. The direct route would have been over the cliff. Instead, they had to ride along the road from the tower up the ridge and down the ridge. From the fork below the ridge, they headed south and then west along the circular trail that eventually led downhill through the true upper forests of the Westhorns to border the cliff face. Nylan supposed the road eventually led somewhere in Lornth, but it wasn't the main road, and neither he nor Ayrlyn had taken it much beyond the brickworks. Neither had had much time for idle travel, and on Ayrlyn's trading runs the previous year, she'd followed the best roads, which were certainly slow enough.

Nylan's eyes flitted from the road to the trees, and his ears and order senses scanned the forest beyond the road, though he could sense nothing except rodents, tree rats, and some birds.

Piles of dirty snow lay under the spreading branches of the evergreens, where the trees had shed their winter coats that had not yet completely melted. For the first time since last fall, Nylan could hear bird calls, even the raucous comments of the loud-mouthed traitor bird.

Both the smith and the healer wore the twin black steel alloyed blades, and in the combined quiver/case behind Nylan's saddle was one of the composite bows he had created with the last energy from the laser, and more than a dozen shafts sporting the black iron arrowheads he had forged. The smith hoped that he wouldn't have to use the weapons.

"It's muddier this year," observed Ayrlyn as a glob of mud flicked by Nylan's mount struck her trousers just above her riding boots.

"We had more snow, and it melted later. The snow lilies are just poking through the crust now."

"I wondered about that."

"So did I. I suppose our plantings will be later, too."

"The big red deer have only started into the higher forests. Which winter is more typical?"

"This one." Nylan laughed. "It's a good thing the first winter was mild."

"I'd never call that mild. With ice coating all the inside walls of the tower? Mild?"

"We didn't have enough firewood. Or windows. The shutters just couldn't keep out the wind."

"Or blankets. Or food." Ayrlyn shifted her weight in the saddle. "Look! Tracks." She pointed to the sets of prints in the shaded expanse of snow under the firs to the right of the trail.

"A big snow cat, but they're melted out a bit. Yesterday or the day before, I'd guess. Istril keeps hoping that I'll be able to kill another one, or two so that Weryl can have a parka." The smith laughed. "The first one almost got me, and the second wasn't much better."

"Their coats are warm—and soft."

"They also have claws as long as a dagger and sharper."

"Like Ryba," offered Ayrlyn.

"I'd bet on her against the cat, bare-handed, even."

"And take odds," added the healer.

They both laughed, and the sound echoed briefly, then vanished into the tall firs and pines that lined the rough road.

After they eased the mares through yet another deeper and slushy snowdrift, a narrow canyon appeared to the left, like a gash in the cliff that supported the Roof of the World. The two eased their mounts up the narrow road, widened the year before to allow a cart passage, until they reached a natural clearing where the brook curved around the exposed clay bank. Behind that was a low building.

"There you are—the fabled brickworks." Ayrlyn leaned over from the saddle and studied the road and the interspersed patches of snow. "I don't see anything but animal tracks. Hares, deer, and an old snow cat print, I think."

"Be surprised if the locals were this high this early, but you never know." Nylan urged the mare over the rushing rivulet toward the small shuttered brick building and the two loaf-shaped outdoor ovens that comprised the brickworks. The clay pit to the right and downslope of the ovens was filled with water and chunks of ice.

The smith reined up by the pit and studied the slumping sides. Then he shook his head. "Now we need a pump. Every time I think I've gotten caught up, there's something else I need to make."

"That's true everywhere." Ayrlyn stopped her chestnut and turned her face into the sun. "Without the breeze, it feels almost warm."

"It is warm," Nylan protested, loosening his jacket, almost theatrically.

"For those of you raised in the Sybran freezer, maybe. For normal souls, it's still cold as mid-winter on decent worlds."

"Decent is a matter of opinion, my beloved healer."

"You never called me your beloved healer before, even joking."

"I should have. I thought it."

"I need to hear things like that. I may feel your pain, dear engineer, but my ability to sense order flows in bodies doesn't translate thoughts, no matter what people say."

"You never called me 'dear' before, either," Nylan said.

"Tit for tat." Ayrlyn grinned, then gestured. "This project looks all right."

"I worry more about the mill. We just had to leave it, you know."

"Your heroics on the battlefield didn't leave you in any shape to do much until well after the snows came, you might recall."

"They weren't heroics," Nylan said dryly. "And you weren't in much better shape, I believe." The engineer patted the mare's shoulder, then urged her uphill past the ovens toward the uncompleted sawmill—mostly a flat expanse that comprised the foundation for the mill, and the stone and brick wall next to the end of the snow-filled millrace. The troubles he'd had trying to create even the center of the mill wheel the fall before!

The smith flicked the reins and eased the mare uphill again through the knee-deep slush and toward the dark wall of the mill pond that extended from the canyon rock face on his right to the hillside slope a hundred cubits or more to his left.

He reined up short of the water that poured downhill like ice-blue crystal. Shards of ice still littered the frozen sand and rocky edges of the narrow creek. A gaping hole had been ripped in the millpond wall between the two drainage gates.

"Who did that?" asked Ayrlyn, halting her mount farther downstream.

"Ice, probably." The smith shook his head. "I'd guess it will be two eight-days before the ground's melted and firm enough to start repairs. Next year, we ought to drain it in the fall, leave both gates open."

The mare *whuffed,* and Nylan turned her downhill, letting her walk until she was out of the snow and on the narrow road by the brickworks. While he waited for Ayrlyn, he studied the area again. The mill was going to be as much of a pain as he'd remembered. Maybe that was why the oldtime millers were always wealthy. Somehow, he didn't feel so enthusiastic about building the mill.

"You know," said Ayrlyn as she stopped her mount beside his and fastened her jacket up as the breeze stiffened. "You talk as if there will be a next year."

"No one's going to challenge Westwind this year, are they? Karthanos spent a lot of golds, too much if he intended another battle. He's lost two armies in less than a year. And Lornth—who do they have left to send against us? This Cyador's farther south, and from what I can determine, they'd have to march over Lornth to get to us."

Ayrlyn brushed back the flame-red hair off her forehead, but the breeze whipped the fine short stands right back across her eyes. "I wasn't thinking about Westwind. I was thinking about you."

"Me?"

"What happened to Gerlich?"

"I'm not like him."

"I know that, but does Ryba? More to the point, does it matter?" Ayrlyn brushed back her hair again in exasperation. "Almost every guard in Westwind would throw herself in front of an arrow or a blade for you. How long will Ryba stand that? You've already told her you won't stand for stud on her terms. That makes you a social gelding."

Nylan winced. Ryba had slaughtered the geldings for food the first winter, and he could remember asking himself if that would be his eventual fate. Ayrlyn was suggesting his time might be coming sooner than he'd thought.

"I can see that the thought isn't totally unforeseen."

"I was thinking about geldings in Westwind," Nylan admitted.

"That . . . you're not. I mean, that's not what I meant." The healer and singer flushed almost as brightly as her hair.

"It isn't?"

Ayrlyn eased the chestnut closer to the mare. "You know, Nylan," she began with a grin, "sometimes you are such a noble and honorable pain in the ass, such an agonizingly long-suffering and noble pain. Nylan will take it on; Nylan will make it right." The grin grew wider. "And then you do."

"I'm not that bad," he protested. "I'm not."

"Ryba thinks so." The grin vanished. "I'm serious. Why does she have you working so hard, making weapons that the guards won't need for years? Why is she suggesting that you train more smiths?"

"I'd wondered about that, but she thinks so far in advance."

"It's about time we did."

"We?" Nylan forced a grin.

"We. Istril got the last favor. The *very* last favor of that nature."

"I was thinking that Siret . . ."

Ayrlyn put her free left hand on the hilt of the shortsword and drew it enough to show black steel. "You do, and I won't wait for Ryba for this gelding business."

"I get the point, woman."

"If you don't, you will." Ayrlyn resheathed her blade with a wicked grin. "And no more of this sleeping alone."

Nylan groaned, loudly. Then he grinned.

After a moment, so did Ayrlyn.

The wind whistled, more loudly, and they both looked up to see the leading edge of a cloud bank appearing over the cliff edge above.

Ayrlyn shivered. "I'm cold. Can we start back?"

Nylan nodded, and flicked the mare's reins. Ayrlyn eased the chestnut up beside him as they began the long and muddy ride back up to Westwind.

Geldings? Was that what he had to look forward to? Why didn't he want to face the fact that Ryba had killed or driven out every man who'd opposed her will?

Because you share a child? Because you fear an unknown world? Because your feeling of responsibility for children you didn't intend to sire is at war with your common sense?

He tried not to sigh, tried to focus on the healer—the woman by whom he had no children, and yet who cared more for him than Ryba ever had.

XIV

As NYLAN SET the iron-alloy mix back on the coals to reheat, the alarm triangle rang from the watchtower on the ridge—two doublets.

Nylan set the hammer on the rack, and used the tongs to ease the metal to the forge shelf. "Traders. I suppose I should go. Do you want to finish this one?"

"I'd rather work one myself, if you don't mind." Huldran nodded toward Ydrall, who straightened from the bellows. "That way I can show Ydrall what I'm doing. Besides, you do strange things to the metal. I can't get something you've started working to come out quite right." Unlike Nylan, who labored over a true anvil, Huldran used the smith's original makeshift anvil, created by bending lander alloy around a stone block and wedging the result between the fork of a green fir sunk into the ground.

"Traders . . ." mused the smith. "Early this year. I should see why."

"You're just tired of doing blades, ser."

"I admit it." The smith took a deep breath. "Let's get two dozen of the best of those local crowbars out from the covered stack in back. I'll have Ayrlyn send the cart for them. Use the good anvil, and have Ydrall try something simple—like spikes—from one of the broken blades."

Spikes weren't that simple—nothing was, but she'd have to start somewhere.

"A merchant's daughter, and I am learning to be a smith," said the dark-haired young woman. "Mother would be pleased."

"And your father?"

"He would be most offended. That is why I am here." Ydrall offered a musical laugh at odds with her muscular figure. "That is why there will be others."

Nylan didn't doubt that, not from what little he'd seen of Candarian treatment of women. And the mysterious Cyador was supposedly worse? "Let's get the blades."

It took only a few trips for the three to stack the Lornian and Gallosian blades that Nylan selected beside the front door of the smithy. Then Nylan headed down toward the tower and the bathhouse. He had time to wash up. In Candar, trading, while not snaillike in progress, was definitely a leisurely pursuit.

As he reentered the tower from washing and shaving, with only a single cut on his chin and dressed in dark gray leathers, Ryba was coming down the stairs, wearing the lighter gray leathers of the Marshal of Westwind. "You intended to go?"

"I thought I might be useful. We also could use another anvil and some hammers, if you'd like us to make better progress in training Ydrall."

"I'll have the mare waiting for you. Saryn's bringing down mounts from the stable," Ryba said. "You are getting your blades? Traders around here aren't always the most peaceful."

"They're laid out," the smith confirmed, biting back a retort. He'd been there the last time Skiodra had tried his treachery. So why had Ryba brought it up? Another attempt to put him in his place? Or what Ryba thought was his place?

He hurried up the steps to his quarters where he strapped on both blades, one at his waist and one in the shoulder harness. He descended more carefully, still cautious about tripping over the scabbard and going down the stone steps headfirst. Except for meeting traders and possible battles, he didn't carry a blade. They just got in the way.

Everyone was waiting by the causeway by the time he hurried across the stones.

Ayrlyn held the reins to the brown mare and extended them to him. "We just got here."

"Let's go," said Ryba.

A chill wind blew across the ridge, coming in from the northeast, as they followed the stone road up toward the watchtower. Farther behind creaked the cart pulled by a single horse. The cart horse was led by Effama, another new guard Nylan knew only by name.

"Which traders?" asked the Marshal.

"Skiodra's bunch, it looks like," answered Saryn.

"Good thing we've got a full squad."

"That's why we do," affirmed Saryn. "They've all got the engineer's bows." She stood in the stirrups as they reached the top of the ridge and looked downslope. "They're set up to trade all right."

Nylan and Ayrlyn rode side-by-side behind Ryba and Saryn down the damp clay track on the north side of the ridge, a track that should be turned into a metaled road, Nylan reflected. He smiled ironically as he recognized the way he'd thought of the need—not as something he had to do, but something that needed doing. Was he accepting emotionally, not just rationally, the truth of what Ayrlyn had been telling him?

"That's an odd smile," the redheaded healer said.

"I'll tell you later," he whispered back, hoping his words were lost in the hissing of the wind and the clop of hoofs . . .

and the more distant creaking of the cart carrying the swords that would be used as trading currency.

At that, recalling another trading incident, he extended his order senses to the trees that flanked the base of the ridge, but could detect no hidden armsmen or archers.

"Nothing in the trees," he reported.

"Good" was the only answer from Ryba. Saryn nodded, as if his report were expected.

The traders, dressed in half-open quilted jackets and cloaks, had halted to the north of the trading banner they had planted in the flat and damp ground at the foot of the ridge. Seven traders stood, hands very clear of their blades, behind the banner, with ten others farther west, tending the horses and the three carts.

As Ryba and Saryn reined up, then Nylan and Ayrlyn and the armed guard squad following, led by Llyselle, for a long moment, the sole sounds were those of the wind and the breathing of the angels' mounts.

Skiodra, still the biggest man among the traders and wearing in his shoulder harness the huge broadsword he had always carried, stepped forward and offered a lopsided smile. "I am Skiodra, and I have again returned." While the trader continued to speak in old Anglorat, the local language seemed almost second nature to Nylan now. Across the back of Skiodra's hand was a scab, and Nylan could almost sense the pus and pain beneath, the white chaos of infection.

He looked at Ayrlyn, and she nodded.

"Greetings, trader." Ryba's voice was polite, indifferent. She was no longer worried about having things to trade, not with the plunder of nearly two thousand armsmen stored in Westwind.

Skiodra bowed deeply. "Your fame has carried far, honored angel, and all of Candar bows to your might. We bring more supplies. I had hoped you might have blades to trade."

"We do have a few," said Ryba.

Skiodra looked at the mounted riders. Nylan got the picture, and, handing the mare's reins to Ayrlyn, dismounted and walked forward.

"You still do not let many others do the speaking, O mage?"

Mage? Even after his successes in mastering certain of the "magical" order fields of the world, Nylan certainly had no illusions about his being a mage. Or an armsman, he thought, despite all the hardware he carried.

"They are warriors, Skiodra." He shrugged.

"Aye," offered the big trader. "Warriors indeed. But now is the time to trade."

The first cart—as had always been the case—not only bore Skiodra's banner, but was filled with barrels.

"I have the lord of flours, not just from the fertile plains of Gallos, but from those heads grown on the flattest and darkest bottomland in Candar."

"You have grown more eloquent, Skiodra," Nylan said, ignoring Ryba for the moment. "I hope we do not pay for such eloquence."

"It is good flour. The very best." Skiodra offered Nylan a bow nearly as deep as the one accorded Ryba. "You as a mage should know good flour."

"We all appreciate good flour," agreed Nylan. "But the softer flour does not always store as well as that from harder grains." That was a point he'd picked up from listening to Blynnal.

"I forget, O honored mage, that you came from a long and distinguished line of usurers," responded Skiodra. "A line that must extend across the heavens back into the days of the most ancient. Still, I must insist that this is good flour, the best flour. You can store it longer, far, far longer. At a silver and a copper a barrel, I am offering you angels my very best price."

"Last year, your very best price was nine coppers a barrel, and the harvests in the lowlands were good."

"O mage, your memory extends as far as your ancestry. But it is harder and longer to travel the Westhorns in the spring, when mud clings to hoofs and heels and wheels." Skiodra bowed. "Take pity on an honest merchant."

Nylan wanted to laugh, for Skiodra was known for almost everything but honesty—unless he knew his customer was as willing to slaughter as to trade. At the same time, the smith tried not to sigh. After seasons, even, the trading sessions never seemed to change, and the haggling seemed almost routine, a ritual that was required.

"Can't we get on with this?" said Ryba quietly, shifting her weight on the big roan, her fingers touching the hilt of the Westwind blade.

"Pity is fine for charity," Nylan offered, "but bad for trading. Six coppers a barrel."

"Six coppers! That is not trading; it is robbery. No, it is murder, for we would all die of hunger ere we returned to our ruined homes." Skiodra touched the tip of his broad mustache. "You have mighty black blades, but can you eat that cold metal until your harvests come in? Or your guards, will they not grow thin on cold iron? A fair man am I, and for a silver a barrel I will prove that fairness."

"Aye," said Nylan. "A fair profit that would be. Fair and fine enough to bring you smoked fowl on gold and chains of silver round the necks of all the women around you." Nylan offered a broad and amused smile.

"I trade in good faith, mage. In true good faith." The big trader rolled his eyes.

"I scarcely question your faith," answered Nylan. "Only your price."

"You are a mage. Oh, I have said that, and said that, and the whole of Candar knows how mighty you are, but your father could not have been a mere usurer, but a usurer to usurers. You would have my horses grub chaff from the poorest miller's leavings."

"At eight coppers a barrel, because I would reward your efforts to climb here, you would still have golden bridles for your mounts."

"Not a single barrel at nine coppers. Not one," protested Skiodra. "The harvests were good, as you say. But the traders from Cyad had already cleaned the granaries in Ruzor."

"Someone is always trading," Nylan offered.

"There were floods in Cyador, they said. Nine coppers a barrel—that will break me with what I paid because flour was short. But I, the noble Skiodra, knew that you could use flour."

"How about ten barrels for a gold?" Nylan offered, sensing the growing chaos and tension in Skiodra.

"Done, even though you will ruin me, mage."

"If all were so successful at being ruined, noble Skiodra, all the world would be traders."

Skiodra frowned momentarily.

Ryba's face was cool as she watched Nylan haggle.

Ayrlyn's eyes took in both the traders and the Marshal, and her eyes went to Skiodra's hand again. Quietly, she dismounted and passed the two sets of reins to Saryn.

Skiodra frowned as the healer stepped up, and he paused in his description of the anvil in the cart.

"A token of good faith," Ayrlyn said, and her fingers brushed his wrist, settling there lightly.

Perspiration beaded on the trader's forehead.

Nylan wanted to laugh at the man's fear, but instead he only let his own senses follow Ayrlyn as she eased the forces of order around the infected hand and pressed out the chaos and infection.

"Now," she said. "It will heal properly."

Skiodra swallowed, and began to sweat even more as the healer remounted, sending a faint smile to the big trader. The faintest of frowns crossed Ryba's countenance, then vanished.

In the end, a half-dozen blades paid for not quite two dozen barrels of wheat flour, a barrel of maize flour, two barrels of kerneled corn for the chickens, the second true anvil that Nylan had wanted, two large wedges of cheese, and a keg of nails.

"Do you have to go through all those charades?" Ryba asked as the guards rode back up the ridge, the cart creaking behind them, while Skiodra and his entourage headed slowly westward along the road that wound toward Lornth.

"They seem to expect it," Saryn said, looking back over her shoulder at both the departing traders, and at the darkening clouds that foretold a possible late afternoon storm. "Ayrlyn's little effort knocked something off the prices, too, I'd bet."

Ayrlyn brushed her hair off her forehead, but said nothing.

"What do you think, Ayrlyn?" asked Ryba.

"Skiodra's heart wasn't in it. He's afraid of us."

"You certainly added to that," pointed out Ryba.

"If he died from that infection, and with the lack of medical knowledge here, he could have, then we'd have to break in another traveling trader."

"I'd rather not," said Nylan, recalling how long it had taken to convince Skiodra.

"So why is he here now?" asked Saryn. "Westwind isn't exactly the crossroads of Candar, and he's afraid of us."

"Business is bad elsewhere," hazarded Nylan.

"The war . . . it couldn't have bankrupted Gallos or Lornth—not over a few thousand armsmen."

"Something else, then," said Nylan. "The floods in Cyador."

"Are you sure he wasn't inventing that?" asked Ryba.

"I don't think so." Nylan shrugged. "I don't know. We'll have to keep our ears open."

"With all the travelers flocking through the Westhorns?" Ryba snorted.

Behind her, Nylan and Ayrlyn exchanged glances.

"This is the first time Skiodra hasn't tried something," Saryn pointed out.

"It's also the first time since we wiped out two armies," replied Ryba, unsheathing one of her blades and running through an exercise with it.

Behind them, Effama flicked the leads to the cart horse, and the cart creaked slowly through the damp ground uphill toward the top of the ridge and the stone road that would make the descent easier.

"I'd like to have gotten more flour," Nylan said to Ayrlyn. "But he didn't have any, and he knows we'll buy it. That's why I think he was telling the truth about the floods."

"Cyador again. Why haven't we heard about this place before?"

"They could be isolationists, like the Rats."

"In a low-tech culture?" asked Saryn from in front of them, turning in her saddle for a moment.

"It's easier in a low-tech culture," the engineer pointed out.

Ayrlyn shivered and fastened her jacket as they reached the top of the ridge where the wind was stronger.

Nylan rode the mare all the way back past the tower and up to the stables, unlike Ryba, who dismounted at the causeway and let one of the guards in Llyselle's squad guide her roan up past the smithy and into the canyon that held the stable.

Ayrlyn rode beside Nylan, a pensive look on her face.

After unsaddling and grooming their mounts, they walked back down toward the tower, alone on the stones of the road, since Nylan was among the slowest in grooming and handling mounts.

"What do you think?" Nylan asked.

"What do *you* think?" the healer replied. "Trust your own feelings. If I disagree, I'll tell you, but don't look to me to interpret what you feel."

Nylan flushed slightly, then coughed. "All right. When I'm uncertain, I try to feel out others before saying anything."

"I know. What do you feel?"

"Ryba's angry. She's looking for things to get angry at me for. We've always had to haggle with Skiodra. Didn't you have to haggle on all those trading runs you made last year?"

"Everyone in Candar likes to haggle, I think."

"She didn't even want me to come, and then she said something about remembering my blades—as if I hadn't dealt with Skiodra before or that ambush they set up with the herder. She's suddenly treating me like a child."

The healer nodded, hunched into her jacket against the late afternoon wind.

"I don't like it. It's like the way she treated Gerlich, except she hasn't drawn steel against me."

"She can't do that. You may be a pain in her Marshal's ass, dear, but all her guards love you, and they'd like to do it from closer than they do." Ayrlyn paused. "Don't let them."

"I've gotten that word." He grinned, but only momentarily. "That's going to be more of a problem."

"I know. What do you think you should do?"

The smith shook his head. "I don't like it. I've darkness near killed myself making a safe haven here, and it's not going to be pleasant any longer. It may not even be safe for me much longer. I'm not a Gerlich, and trying a coup would only destroy Westwind, even if I could do it. And that would only make things worse for the children . . . for everyone but us, probably."

"You're right there." Ayrlyn paused by the practice yard, well up the road from the end of the causeway. Her eyes drifted toward a last drooping snow lily that arched out of one of the few remaining patches of snow on the north side of the loose-stacked stones of the practice yard wall. "Can't you just avoid Ryba?"

"How? Westwind isn't that big. If I do what she says, she'll push for me to do more and more—or make me less and less useful—like with this smith training bit. She's good at maneuvering, and pretty soon I'll look either as obstinate as Gerlich or as useless as Nerliat was. At least, I think so. What do you think?"

"It doesn't matter what I think. I can just be a meek healer and stay in the background. You've got a lot of support from Siret, Istril, even Huldran and Llyselle, though," mused Ayrlyn.

"Right," Nylan snorted. "Saryn sides with Ryba, and she trains most of the new guards—or Ryba does. Maybe . . . what? Seven of forty guards think I'm good for something. Most of the new guards dislike or distrust men, and they accept me because I'm not like the men they knew—but I'm a man. Just how long will it be before there are a hundred guards, and half don't even know me?"

"That would take a while."

"Like being buried in a slow avalanche or being tied down and consumed by ants over the years." Nylan winced at his own image.

"You don't sound happy. What do you want to do?"

"It's not a question of wanting. It's a question of seeing the storm on the horizon and finding cover." He laughed, once, harshly. "Why is it so hard? I could see the need for a tower before anyone else, and I built it. I can see the need to leave, and I avoid facing it. What's the difference?"

"Three children?"

"That . . . and, I told you before, deep inside . . ." He swallowed. "It's not exactly . . . easy . . . to face an unknown world alone. I don't like it. I don't know where to go, and it feels like everything I've done is almost wasted."

"Is it?"

Nylan shook his head. "Dyliess, Kyalynn, Weryl—they'll be safe."

Ayrlyn frowned at the last name, but did not speak.

"They'll be safe," Nylan repeated. "It isn't easy to admit that. I don't know about us, though."

"I'm glad you said us . . . but . . . you never asked me."

"That's where you've been guiding me, dear. Don't think I didn't notice."

"You could have asked . . ." A glimmer of a smile flitted around the corners of her mouth.

"All right. I am planning to descend into the hot depths of the demon's hell to avoid jeopardizing everyone else and my children. Would you like to accompany me on this foolhardy expedition?"

"I thought you'd never get around to inviting me."

Nylan put his right arm around Ayrlyn as they walked. "You're cold."

"I'm always cold up here. Why do you think I agreed?"

"Not for my charm?"

"Not *just* for your charm."

A wry smile settled on Nylan's face for a moment, then vanished as his eyes took in the upper level of Tower Black, and the window to the Marshal's quarters.

XV

ZELDYAN HANDED THE scroll to Fornal with her free hand. The dark-haired regent slowly read through it, occasionally stopping and puzzling out an unfamiliar word. As he read, the blond woman rocked Nesslek on her knee, steering his fingers away from the goblet on the table before her.

The gray-haired Gethen looked toward the window, then rose and walked to it, sliding it wide open. The cool breeze carried the damp scent of recent spring rain into the tower room. For a moment, Gethen looked across Lornth to the orange ball of the sun that hung over the river to the west of the hold. Then he walked back to the table, where he refilled his goblet before reseating himself.

"This is one of your best," Zeldyan offered, taking a sip of the dark red wine, before setting her goblet down more toward the center of the table, out of Nesslek's reach.

"It is good. Even the Suthyans paid extra for it."

Fornal squinted, as though he wanted to shut out the conversation and concentrate on the scroll. His frown became more pronounced as his eyes traveled down the scribed lines.

"Lygon of Bleyans? I hope you made him pay triple."

"Only double," Gethen said. "Lady Ellindyja found him useful."

"I know."

"The lord of Cyador . . . how . . . to suggest that the copper mines of south Cerlyn have always belonged to Cyador . . . to ask for tribute and immediate return . . ." stuttered Fornal, letting the scroll roll up with a snap. "This is an insult!"

"Yes," agreed Zeldyan. "It is. Yet they gave up the mines, ages back."

"That was when they found the copper in Delapra. It was closer to the surface," said Gethen, "and closer to Cyad, much closer."

"They use the white bronze the way we do iron."

"They have to," pointed out the older man. "Iron and chaos do not mix."

"Mix or not, it remains an insult," snapped Fornal.

"Aaaahhhh . . ." added Nesslek, lunging for the goblet. Zeldyan restrained him just short of the crystal.

"To our way of thinking, it is an insult," commented Gethen, pausing to take a sip of his wine. "We must remember that Cyador is an old land. The legends say that it dates to the time of the true white demons, that they tamed the ancient forest and molded the paths of the rivers. Then, Lornth did not exist, and the copper mines may well have been part of Cyador."

"Not in generations," said Fornal. "I cannot claim Middlevale because Mother's grandsire lived there."

"No," admitted Gethen. "I was but noting how they think."

"It remains an insult." Fornal turned to his sister. "What would you do about it?"

"Since we're in no position to fight, I suggest we send back a message which notes that the scroll could have been interpreted as insulting by some, but that we trust our reading somehow did not find the courtesy for which the lord of Cyador is so justly known—"

"He's a butcher. We know that already." Fornal lifted his goblet and downed the half remaining in a single gulp. "Why would flattery help?"

"Fornal," said Gethen, drawing out his words, "if you insist on treating good wine like inn swill, I will bring you a pitcher of the Crab's finest, and save this for those who appreciate it." The gray-haired man smiled.

"I am sorry. It is good wine, but . . . I cannot believe . . ." Fornal turned to his sister. "You were about to say?"

"If we flatter him, Fornal, while we make ready, what harm can we do?" asked Gethen.

"None, I suppose, so long as we do make ready."

"Is it wise to fight?" asked Zeldyan.

"No," conceded the older man. "But it is more foolish not to. If we fight, and fight well, then the lord of Cyador will only take what he needs. If we surrender the mines, he will take them and ask for more, and then we will have to fight anyway."

Zeldyan nodded, shifting Nesslek from one knee to the other. "Most respect only force. Cold iron, if you will."

"Can you think of anything that deserves more respect?" asked Fornal, pouring more wine. "Cold iron is the shield of honor."

Zeldyan smoothed away a frown. "After I put Nesslek down, I will draft a response and then read it to you both."

"You always did have the better hand, sister. For writing." Fornal raised his goblet.

Gethen turned his head to the window and the setting sun.

XVI

IN THE DEEP twilight after the evening meal, Nylan sat in the chair by the north window in his room, rocking Dyliess, singing softly.

> *". . . hush little girl, and don't you sigh,*
> *Daddy's forging toys by and by,*
> *and if those toys should fail to please,*
> *Daddy's going to sing and put you at ease . . ."*

"Toys?" asked Ryba from the door to his quarters. "You have time to forge toys?"

"Not at the moment, but I can sing about them." He shifted Dyliess on his shoulder and kept rocking, patting her back. She lifted her head, seeking her mother.

As Dyliess looked at her mother, Ryba's voice softened, and she smiled. "Hello, there, silvertop." After a moment, she added, "She is beautiful."

"She is," Nylan admitted.

"I came to get her for bed, but I wanted to talk to you for

a moment. It's been half a year, and you really never did deal with the questions I had."

"That's possible," the smith said. "I try to avoid those kinds of questions." He kept rocking slowly, and Dyliess put her head down on his shoulder again.

"We've only got four children, a couple on the way, and we don't know how our genes mix with the locals—or if they will."

"They will," the smith affirmed. "I can feel how things mesh. This world is H-norm, or planoformed thoroughly to be that way. Things will work out."

"We don't have time just to let them work out."

"Oh . . . what did you have in mind?" Nylan wanted to take back the words even as they slipped out.

"Ydrall likes you," Ryba said. "And we do need to find out how the genes mix. Feeling it isn't enough."

"I'm not interested."

"You were interested enough in Istril that night an eight-day or so ago."

Nylan contained a wince. "That was a moment of weakness. I'm not the Gerlich type."

"When it comes to women who take their fancy, all men are Gerlich types. There just aren't as many who appeal to you. I thought Ydrall might be your type." Ryba shrugged. "Find someone else, but find them."

"What do I tell Ayrlyn?" Nylan asked. Why was she so diffident, so uncaring? Had she always been that way, or was it another push? Another shove to tell him to leave?

"Whatever you want. You're good with words when you choose to be. I really don't care. You're the only stud around here, except for Daryn, and that's a match between locals."

"You could certainly entice him." Nylan wanted to wince as the words burst out. *She's trying to provoke you. Don't drop to her level.*

"Be serious. Only Nylan the mighty smith can stand up to the Angel of Westwind." Ryba laughed harshly.

"That wasn't fair," he admitted. Dyliess shivered, and

Nylan patted her back again. Then she hiccupped and raised her head again.

"You actually considered whether it was fair. I'm amazed."

Dyliess hiccupped again.

"Take it easy." Nylan slipped to his feet and began to walk around the room, patting his daughter's back and humming. "I try," he answered Ryba.

"Sometimes." The Marshal's eyes turned to her daughter. "Is she hungry?"

"I don't think so," Nylan answered softly. "Just sleepy, and a little gassy." He kept walking, for a time, then slipped past Ryba and across to her quarters, where he slipped Dyliess into her small bed in the inside corner away from the drafts.

Ryba waited until he returned, then said, "We need more children—or we will."

"That takes men—or technology—or both, and I don't see much of either around here. You didn't have to chase Relyn off, you know?" Nylan walked toward the window, but stopped by the former lander couch that was his bed.

"I didn't. You warned him off, and he was local anyway."

The smith took a long, slow breath. He didn't want to get into a discussion of Relyn. It wouldn't do any good, not when Ryba would start pointing out that Relyn's religious view of the world's order fields would eventually hurt Westwind. What did she mean by eventually, anyway? Five hundred years later?

"What do you want?" he finally asked.

"I told you. Find a local to bed. Or another guard."

"I'll think about it."

"Don't think too long," Ryba said. "I've given you the chance to think all winter."

"I won't take that long," he promised.

With a curt nod, Ryba turned toward the door, then stopped. "Will you be here?"

"I have some notes to do—on the mill."

"Will you listen for Dyliess, then, until I get back?"

"Of course."

Another nod, and the Marshal was gone.

Nylan walked to the window and looked out, up toward the ridge and the watchtower. He couldn't see the ice-needle Freyja from his single window.

After he studied the mountains for a time, and his muscles began to relax, he went back to the work table, where he used the striker to light the single candle. Although his night vision was nearly as good as his day vision for most matters, the candle did help in writing and reading. As the flame lengthened, and cast light from the polished bronze reflector onto the table, he sat down on the stool and looked at the papers weighted down under the ornate hilt of a blade that had broken at the tang. He had found it in the plunder from the great battle, long since separated from the actual blade. The hilt was heavy, overdone, and had doubtless added a poor balance that had contributed to the blade's breaking, along with a tang that had been too narrow, but the hilt itself made a decorative paperweight.

In the dim candlelight, Nylan squinted at the crude paper on the table, then dipped the quill into the ink and began to draw—slowly and carefully. Each section of the mill had to be laid out so that there would be no mistakes. The purple outside the open window turned velvet black, and the chirp and whistle of unnamed insects rose and fell.

At the tap on the door, he looked up. Ayrlyn's face peered in.

He motioned, and the healer entered, easing the door shut behind her.

"Ryba and Saryn are still down in the great room, talking over something obscure, like whether caltrops are really that effective except in defending fixed emplacements and whether two-handed blades are useful in mounted attacks. Saryn was advocating lances and beefed-up stirrups . . ."

Nylan smiled wryly.

The healer shook her head and pointed at the stack of papers before Nylan. "What are you working on there?"

"The plans for the sawmill."

"You didn't do that for the tower, or the bathhouse, or the smithy," she pointed out, then leaned over him and kissed the back of his neck.

"I didn't have to. I was here."

"You are serious, aren't you?"

"Ryba practically ordered me to bed Ydrall. She wants to see the gene mix with locals."

"I take it you were reluctant."

"That wasn't the real point. She was giving me another shove. I told her I'd think about it. I have no intention of thinking about it." He rubbed his forehead.

"You got ink on your forehead," Ayrlyn said.

He tried to blot it away with the back of his hand. "Then, when I said I wasn't the Gerlich type, she said I was, except that fewer women appealed to me, and if Ydrall didn't appeal to find a local who did so that she could confirm that the genes mixed."

"Did she put it that way?"

"Pretty much."

Ayrlyn pursed her lips. "That makes you angry."

"That, and basically being told my prime value is as a stud."

"She's angry at you for choosing me."

"I'm glad I did," Nylan said. "I wish I'd seen who you were earlier."

"I wasn't who I am now back then, if that makes sense. I was a mousy comm officer."

"Neither was I. I was a withdrawn engineer. I still am."

Ayrlyn's eyes dropped to the papers. "Are you going to tell Ryba about all these plans?"

"Not until we're on our way out of here."

"She may not let us have mounts."

"That's why we need to make it quick," Nylan said. "Right now, there's sympathy for me, for you. If we let her drag it out, it will get so unpleasant that people will just want us gone. She's proved she's good at that."

"For someone who wasn't sure about leaving, you've reached a big decision quickly."

The engineer-smith-healer shook his head. "To see something I should have seen two years ago? Hardly. Hardly." He took a deep breath.

Ayrlyn bent over and blew out the candle, then kissed the back of his neck again. "You were almost finished for tonight, weren't you?"

"If you say so . . ." Nylan eased out of the chair.

XVII

THE WHITE WIZARD and the senior lancer officer rode side by side, the hoofs of their mounts clacking on the time-polished stones of the Lord's East Road.

They passed a kaystone with sculpted and fluted edges, mounted on a tan stone platform that bore the inscription "GELIENDRA—3 K." The lancer glanced at Themphi. "Ser wizard?"

"Yes, Jyncka?"

"One should not question His Mightiness, or white brethren, but could you hazard a thought as to why our punishment was so harsh?"

"Harsh?" Themphi raised his eyebrows.

"Harsh," repeated Jyncka. "We are allowed to buy any peasant girl for a concubine, if we offer double her dowry. We can slay any peasant who raises a hand against us, yet for taking liberties with a peasant girl—and we did not hurt her—we have been destroyed: either executed, allowed to suicide, or condemned to spend the rest of a short life battling the accursed forest. How did this happen? Is our world slowly unraveling, and I cannot see it? Or have I been blind all my years?"

Themphi frowned. "I can tell you what happened. The girl's father refused two golds and said that you were worse than sows. Then he ran toward His Mightiness. The peasant died. After that, our Lord turned to me and made his judgment. He said that when peasants defied his presence, matters needed attending to. And he sent me, his wizard of wizards, with the injunction that I should not return until the forest was contained." The wizard smiled coldly.

"So you are exiled as well?"

"In effect." Themphi shrugged. "Unless we can vanquish the forest."

"Is that likely?"

"I do not know. I do know that it took all the might and skill of the ancients to contain it."

"And you must combat it alone?" asked Jyncka.

"With your help and that of those living nearby—that is His Mightiness's command."

Jyncka raised his eyebrows. "I would not term that any great reward for service."

"Rulers do not reward for service, Majer, nor for realistic assessments. They reward for results."

"Times change," murmured Jyncka. "A great ship rises in the works at Cyad, a ship like the ancient fireships. They say the lancers ride north to bring the Grass Hills within the Walls of Cyad. Yet we are accorded less honor than before, and those who speak what they believe to be truth are dishonored."

"They do change," agreed Themphi dryly. "That is because His Mightiness works to restore what once was Cyad's, and he has little patience for those who caution against such efforts."

". . . for all that . . . unraveling from the great skein . . ." murmured a voice from the lancers somewhere behind. "Fewer steamwagons, fewer wizards . . ."

Themphi hoped the voice was not Fissar's, but he did not turn in the saddle. His eyes flicked northward toward the smudge of green on the horizon, and he shifted his weight in the hard saddle.

"Is the world of Cyador unraveling, ser wizard?" asked Jyncka. "Would you enlighten me?"

Themphi shrugged. "You have seen more than I, Majer. Do you think so?"

"I have not seen everything, but what I have seen disturbs me."

"It disturbs me as well," said Themphi. His eyes went back to the horizon, and he did not speak for a long time.

XVIII

Nylan studied the room again—lander couch, rocking chair, table, stool, bed—that was all. Stone walls . . . he'd laid almost every stone. Window casements—his design. The entire tower had been his dream, his way of making the Roof of the World safe for the angels, for the children he had known would come, if not as he had expected.

He glanced at the pair of blades on the couch, the single composite bow and quiver, and the two saddlebags—one filled with his few clothes and a spare pair of boots, the other with hard bread and cheese, and some dried venison.

His jacket was rolled inside the makeshift bedroll that lay on the saddlebags. In the bags were those few items he owned—after two lives, really. Two lives, and those few items were all. And—once again—he had no idea where he was going or what he was doing—not beyond escaping.

He took a deep breath and swallowed, hoping Ayrlyn was ready, knowing she'd been ready long before he had. Then, she'd never really been at home on the Roof of the World, and he'd been the one to build Tower Black. His eyes went to the open window, through which he could see puffy clouds marching out of the northeast across the green-blue sky.

The smith took another deep breath, squared his shoulders, crossed the landing, and stepped into the Marshal's quarters.

Ryba—the Marshal of Westwind—sat in the rocking chair, Dyliess in her lap. Her pale green eyes fixed on Nylan. "You've finally decided to leave, haven't you?"

Nylan nodded. "You knew all along. Your visions told you that I'd have to leave. You knew seasons ago, but you wouldn't share them. You never have shared those visions, and you never will. You wouldn't change anything because it might jeopardize Westwind. And you'd never jeopardize Westwind."

Ryba's arms tightened ever so slightly around her daughter, "I wouldn't do anything to threaten Dyliess."

The silver-haired girl wriggled as if Ryba were holding her too tightly. "Ah . . . wah! Wah!"

"I know." Nylan's voice was flat. "Nothing can be allowed to threaten her—or your dreams."

"What about your dreams? Your mighty tower? What about your plans for the sawmill?"

"I've written them out, with sketches, and I've discussed them all with Huldran—even the gearing. She can finish building the mill. She'll do what you want, just like all the others."

"The smith and the singer . . . off into the sunset, leaving the hard work for everyone else." Ryba's lips twisted. Her eyes seemed bright, brighter than usual, and she looked down at the plank floor, then out the window. Her left hand stroked Dyliess's hair.

"You have a strange definition of hard work, Ryba." Nylan snorted. "I did the building, and you and everyone else thought I was obsessed, crazy. But this past winter, no one complained when they were warm and cozy, when they had running warm and cold water.

"You schemed behind my back. You used me to get Siret and Istril pregnant. Who knows who else you tried with? And I didn't even see it. I should have, but I didn't. In my own clumsy way, I trusted you." He looked toward the empty trundle bed in the corner. The cradle he had made was down on the fourth level with the guards. He swallowed. Should he even try to say more? "You don't trust anyone."

"You've decided, haven't you?" she asked again. "The words don't matter. You've decided. You and Ayrlyn. Just go. Take what you need. I know you. You're so guilt-ridden you'll be more than fair. Just go. Let us get on with life."

"Leave me some time with Dyliess."

"Why? You're leaving."

"You owe me more than that. I'm only asking for a little

time with my daughter. She won't remember it—but I will."

"You don't have to leave." Ryba's voice was even, almost emotionless. "You've built Westwind. As you keep telling me."

"No. I don't have to leave. I can have every guard here pity me. I can live here for the rest of my life, wondering whether I can trust you. I can risk everything and then wonder if you care, or if it's just for another monument or legacy for the future. Because I've come to care for someone else, what would happen to her? Would you drive her out or dispose of her?" Nylan's voice remained level. "After all, nothing can be allowed to get in the way of your dream."

"It's not like that. I did what had to be done. Do you think that I liked killing Mran? Or seeing two-thirds of my crew wiped out? I relive that a lot. Do you think that I like seeing you leave, no matter what I've done? Do you think that I'll enjoy looking at all those cairns at the end of the meadow for the rest of my life? It's easy to criticize and to leave, Nylan. It's a lot harder to build something and live with the pain."

"*How* you build is important, too," the engineer answered. "I built you and the guards an honest tower. An honest bathhouse. An honest smithy. Honest stables. Even the beginning of an honest metaled road to the rest of the world. You built with deception. You deceived me. You deceived Istril, Ayrlyn, and Siret. And, in the end, however long Westwind lasts, that deception will bring down your work."

"You won't change, Nylan. You're just as deceptive as I am. The difference is that I recognize it, and you won't." Ryba stood, waiting for Nylan to take Dyliess. "What I build will last, and only your name will remain, a vague legend about a mighty mythical smith, and that will be because I had Ayrlyn write a song about you."

"You have an answer for everything, don't you?"

"So do you," she answered. "Take Dyliess. Sing to her, and I will tell her you did. Yes, I will. For her sake, not yours."

Nylan stepped forward.

"Ah . . . ooo . . ." Dyliess stretched her arms out to her father, looking up, a blanket wrapped around her waist and legs. Nylan picked her up, cradling her against his shoulder, and rocking back and forth, holding her tightly.

Ryba slipped to the door. "I'll be back in a while."

Still holding his silver-haired daughter, Nylan walked toward the trundle bed he had made and looked down. He stepped back across the smoothed plank floor to the rocking chair, where, cradling her against his shoulder, he sat down and began to rock . . . gently.

> *"Oh, my dear, my dear little child,*
> *What can we do in a place so wild,*
> *Where the sky is so green and so deep*
> *And who will rock you to sleep?*
> *Your daddy is leaving; he's going away*
> *There's only a cradle and nothing to say,*
> *but when the stars shine over the western sky,*
> *try to remember that he once said good-bye."*

The tears rolled down the smith's cheeks, and his vision, his superb day and night vision, showed him nothing. Nothing at all.

In time, he finally stood, laid the sleeping Dyliess in her cradle, and returned to his quarters to gather everything together.

With a last look at the sleeping child, he started down the steps, loaded with all his gear, moving slowly to avoid tripping over the blade at his waist. The one in the shoulder harness would be easier to use, far easier, once he was mounted. Some of the customs of Candar made sense—usually those having to do with arms.

As he trudged down to the fourth level, Siret glanced up after slipping on a work tunic. Her eyes took in all that Nylan carried, and, with a quick look to the bed where Kyalynn sat wrestling with a crude stuffed bear that Hryessa had made, Siret hurried across the wide planked floor to the stairs.

The engineer paused.

"Nylan? You're leaving, aren't you?" Her deep green eyes caught his.

He nodded.

"I could see it coming. Nothing you do pleases her."

He shrugged. "I'm not like Gerlich. I won't be back, not that way."

"You won't be back. This world needs you."

He blinked, not expecting such a comment.

"Ryba will fight the world. She will make the men who rule come to her and be defeated—but they won't. They'll let us rule the mountains, and let the truly unhappy women come to us." She smiled bitterly. "I've thought about it. People don't think I do, but I do . . . a lot. The Marshal . . . and especially you . . . gave me that."

"Me?" Nylan was feeling totally confused, wondering what else he had done that he hadn't seen.

"I watched you, Nylan. You don't talk much about why you do what you do. You do it. You push yourself, and . . . people take, and they take. I started asking why. So . . ." She shrugged, and her eyes were bright. "I had to tell you that I am grateful for all you've given . . . to let you know I wasn't like so many of the others." After a moment she swallowed. "Westwind is too small for you, and you're not full Sybran so you can leave here."

"I'm not looking forward to the heat," he said, trying not to choke up, and wondering if his decision to leave were such a good one after all.

"The healer's going with you, isn't she? Some guards will suffer. And the children." Her eyes darted to the bed where Kyalynn looked down at the bear that lay across her chubby legs.

"Istril, Llyselle, even you have some of the talent." He smiled wryly. "You'll be able to do as well as we can, if you can't already."

"We'll manage, but we'll never be as good. But I knew that it had to happen. Relyn said it would."

"Relyn? He's been gone since the battle." Not that Nylan hadn't wondered about the one-handed man, especially after Blynnal had turned up pregnant—but Nylan had been the one who advised Relyn to leave before Ryba found a way to eliminate the former Lornian noble because he'd found religion.

Nylan snorted to himself. The idea that he—a former angel ship's engineer—was the prophet of a new faith of order was almost ludicrous. Even more absurd was Ryba's contention that Relyn's preaching such a faith would undermine West-wind. Not so absurd had been her intent to remove Relyn in the chaos that followed the great battle—except Relyn, warned by Nylan, had slipped off into the night.

"Ryba said that he has already been preaching his new gospel of order." Siret looked around. "I heard her talking to Saryn. Tryssa—she was one of the last new recruits to reach us before the snows—she was talking about the one-handed prophet in black who forecast the fall of the old ways and the rise of order. He's also preaching about building a Temple of Order."

"Great." Nylan glanced up the steps.

"He said that, sooner or later, you would have to leave, and that the healer would go with you." Siret smiled sadly. "I listen, you know?"

"I know." He shook his head. "But everyone seems to know what I'm doing before I do." Then he added. "Thank you. I didn't stop to have you make me feel good."

"I know. You're a good man, a good person."

He dropped his eyes. Much as he appreciated the compliment, Nylan knew he wasn't that good. If he were, so many things would have turned out differently. "Where's Istril? I should say good-bye."

"She took Weryl out earlier. She was taking him on a ride. She had so many things I wondered if she were leaving, but she said she'd be back." Siret frowned. "She never lies. But she looked sad. I wonder if she knew you were leaving."

"I don't know." Istril knew a lot, a lot that the wiry guard didn't voice.

"You need to go. You need to say good-bye to Kyalynn." She darted across the room and scooped up their daughter, bringing her back to him.

As Nylan hugged his daughter, his tears bathed them both, and he wanted to rage—against fate, against Ryba, against himself. Why was it that everything had so high a price?

He finally eased his silver-haired daughter back to her mother. "Take care of her."

"I will. And I will make sure she knows who you are. A man and not a legend."

He half-walked, half-stumbled down the rest of the stairs and out the main door. Perhaps some guards watched, but Istril was not among them, nor Weryl, and he saw none of their faces as he forced himself up the road to the stable.

Most of the guards were out in the fields, or down below the ridge in the timber camps. He heard the sound of hammers as he passed the smithy, but he did not stop. He wasn't up for another emotional parting, and Huldran, of all people, would understand. Still . . . he put his feet forward, wondering where Istril and Weryl were.

Under the load he carried, despite the muscles developed from smithing, he was sweating and panting when he reached the stable.

Ayrlyn had both mounts saddled and waiting in the shade of the stable door. "You look like chaos. What happened?"

"I had to say good-bye to Dyliess and Kyalynn . . ." He coughed. "I couldn't find Weryl." He dropped the gear in a pile, then lifted the saddlebags and began to strap them in place.

At the *thump* of the dropped equipment, a chicken scurried away from the stable and uphill toward the shelter that had held the livestock through the long winter.

Ayrlyn lifted the bow. "Won't Ryba be a little angry about this?"

"She said I could take what I needed, that I was so guilt-ridden I'd be fair."

"She has that right," Ayrlyn said softly. "I'm glad you brought it. You've done so much for everyone else. I brought six extra blades—two of your blades, and four small crow-bars for trading. Ryba won't miss the crowbars, and you deserve some of your own. You wouldn't bring them, and you might not ever have the chance to forge replacements. They're all packed away. And all my trading silvers."

"Practical woman. I don't think I have more than a half-dozen silvers and a few coppers." The engineer eased the bedroll into place. "I did bring one spare blade, besides the pair."

"Good. I also brought some water bottles for you. You'll need them when we get down into Lornth."

"You still think that's the right way to go?"

Ayrlyn lifted her shoulders as she strapped a water bottle in place. "We go east and run into Karthanos and Gallos, and the easterners feel even nastier than the Lornians. Also, something about the west—"

"Feels better?"

The healer nodded. "I couldn't say why."

"I'll trust a good feeling over sterile reasoning any day, especially here."

"I don't know," mused Ayrlyn. "There's more to the order magic of this world. It's not just feeling. There's a system, somewhere."

"You're talking like an engineer, not a healer."

"Aren't they really the same?"

Nylan laughed, then began to readjust the shoulder harness that would hold his second blade. With one at his waist and the other in the shoulder harness, he should have access to one weapon in any situation. Even as he hoped he didn't have to find out, he knew he would. Candar was that sort of place.

After he tightened the harness and checked his ability to draw the blade easily, he looked at Ayrlyn. "Are you ready?"

Ayrlyn glanced out the open stable door and down the narrow canyon. "I can't believe Istril wouldn't bring Weryl."

"I didn't exactly broadcast our departure. Did you?"

"No . . . but she would have known."

Nylan led the mare out into the sun and climbed into the saddle. "Maybe we'll see her on the way out."

"Maybe." Ayrlyn sounded doubtful.

In the still-cool light of spring, they let the mounts carry them down the road and past the smithy.

Ydrall and Huldran stood by the door to the structure that Nylan had designed and built—and where he had forged scores of the deadly Westwind blades. At least, he had managed to finish one more nondestructive item—a foot for Daryn, along with all the blades.

"Take care, engineer . . . healer," offered the blonde.

"You, too," said Nylan. His voice was thick.

As they passed the causeway, a handful of guards in the bean field straightened. One pointed in their direction and waved. Nylan waved back.

His vision blurred as he looked beyond the indistinct faces, as he saw the cairns in the background, with the dark green stalks that would bear starflowers rising from the rocks.

When the mare's hoofs struck the stones of the bridge, his eyes went to the tower, but no one stood on the causeway or waved.

Nor was there any farewell from the watchtower as they crossed the top of the ridge and headed down, down to the road that would take them west.

As the two rode past the scattered trees on the lower ridge and eased the mare onto the road to the west, the same road used by the Lornians and Gerlich the year before to attack Westwind, Nylan could sense a figure moving through the trees.

"Someone's coming," said Ayrlyn.

Nylan glanced back toward the ridge, though he could not see the tower beyond, and his hand went to the blade at his waist. With both eyes and senses, he tried to track the approaching rider.

Beside him, Ayrlyn shifted in her saddle. "No chaos there."

Istril rode forward, out of the trees, Weryl strapped to her chest. She also wore twin blades. Her free hand patted Weryl on the back.

"Nylan?" Istril's eyes were red, as if she had been crying, and her voice was hoarse.

"Istril? I looked for you and Weryl, but Siret said you'd taken Weryl off riding." Nylan eased the mare to a stop, and Ayrlyn stopped the chestnut. "I didn't mean to go off without saying anything."

"I knew." Istril coughed as she reined up. "Knew you'd

have to leave." She turned to Ayrlyn. "I'm sorry for the trouble and the hurt I caused you, healer. But you'll understand, I hope."

"Istril . . ." began Ayrlyn.

"Hear me out, please, 'fore you say anything." The silver-haired guard turned to Nylan. "You have to take Weryl, ser. He's your son. He has to go with you. I know he does."

Nylan winced. "He's yours, too, Istril, far more than mine."

"What kind of life will he have here? He's got your blood. The Marshal'll drive him out before he's even grown. He can live in the lowlands. I can tell that. I can't. It'll be all right for the next one. The Marshal's not the only one who sees the future. I'll call her Shierl. She's a girl, and the Marshal looks fond on girls."

"Why?"

"You saved my life, ser, more than once, and Weryl's all I can give, and you'll raise him right. You do everything right. You will."

Beside him Ayrlyn offered the faintest of smiles.

"Da?" asked Weryl, stretching out his hands.

Istril fumbled with the straps of the carry-pouch. After a slow and lingering embrace, she slowly eased Weryl away from her and lifted the silver-haired boy toward Nylan.

Nylan stretched out his own hands, too, even though he knew that the single syllable meant little enough, and that giving him Weryl was the most painful action Istril could ever have taken.

As the smith struggled to settle Weryl in place in the pack on his own chest, readjusting the sword harness and the blade itself, Istril dismounted and began to unfasten the two bags behind her saddle. Her cheeks were again tear-stained. "One's food—the best I can do; the other's clothes. They're not much."

"I'll carry one," Ayrlyn offered.

"You'll be good to the engineer . . . and Weryl." Istril swallowed and coughed. ". . . hate this . . . hate it . . . but I'd have nothing . . . without you two."

"You would have done fine," Nylan protested.

"Without you two, every last one of us'd be dead or slaves or both." Istril cleared her throat. "This way . . . this way . . . I'll have Shierl and a life, and Weryl'll have the best . . . he can, too."

Nylan didn't know what to say, and he patted his son on the back and looked helplessly at Istril.

"Won't stand here weeping . . . like some fool." Istril threw herself into the saddle, took a long look at Weryl, then urged her mount into a trot back up the road to the ridge and the tower.

"Daaaa . . ." said Weryl, and Nylan wondered if the sound were as sad as he thought, or if the sadness were his.

How did he get into such messes? Was it life, fate, or his own inability to see all the patterns? He could see enough to know that Westwind had needed a tower, and all the buildings, and the smithy and the mill, yet—where people were concerned—he felt so blind, so inadequate.

He glanced at Ayrlyn, sitting stone-faced on the chestnut.

"You haven't said much." The engineer looked at Ayrlyn.

"I feel sorry for Istril, and I'm angry at Ryba. It didn't have to happen this way." The healer took a deep breath. "I need to think about all of this. If it were anyone but Istril . . . anyone—"

"You'd leave me?"

"Probably." Ayrlyn shook her head. "No. I wouldn't, but I'd be angrier, a whole lot angrier. Istril's not the self-pitying, self-sacrificing type. She *knows* what would happen to Weryl, and it's tearing her apart. And it would only be worse if you rode back to Westwind. So don't even think about it. Istril didn't mean it as a guilt-trip. But I'm angry. In effect, we have a child before we've really had a chance to sort anything out, and I can't really even be angry at you. Except I am. Part of me says that it wasn't your fault, and part of me wants to know why you're so frigging noble that you always end up picking up the pieces." She flicked the reins. "We'd better get moving. Sitting here on the trail doesn't solve anything."

No . . . it didn't.

Nylan cleared his throat, patted Weryl on the back, wondered how long before the boy would be hungry, and flicked the mare's reins, beginning a journey whose end he didn't know for reasons he could feel but not articulate, with a son he barely knew in some ways—and they were headed for a land where they were probably hated because he couldn't stay where he had built a safe haven.

Life was just so fair, so wonderfully equitable. His jaw tightened as he eased the mare after Ayrlyn.

XIX

THE BROWN-HAIRED man in the silver robes waited as the officer in the green uniform and white sash advanced into the small receiving hall—a marble-floored room merely large enough for two or three of the Cyadoran steam wagons whose numbers had dwindled from legion to a mere score or so.

"Majer Piataphi?"

"Yes, Your Mightiness?"

"Sit down."

The majer glanced at the two padded stools, each armless and backless, that faced the table desk behind which sat Lephi on a high-backed stool. Finally, Piataphi seated himself on the front edge of the left stool.

Lephi lifted the scroll. "This is the response we received from the Lornian barbarians. Do you know what it says?"

"No, Sire." A faint sheen coated Piataphi's forehead.

"It says nothing—except that we are discourteous. We of the land of Cyador, ancient and mighty, are discourteous. We of Cyador, who brought order out of disorder, cities out of wild forests, we are discourteous. We who brought metalworking and the first trade ships to cross the oceans, we are discourteous. There is no remembrance of the daughters they enticed away generations ago, nor of the dangers to life our ancestors eliminated, such as the stun lizards that were everywhere."

Piataphi waited.

"That in itself is no matter, Majer. No matter." Lephi stood and stepped from behind the white-lacquered table desk that dated through at least eight generations of Lords of Cyador. The Emperor walked toward the tinted glass windows, then paused before the oiled wooden frames as his eyes ranged over Cyad, down from the hillside site of the White Palace, toward the harbor, toward the piers that once housed the White Fleet of the ancients, before his grandsire had decided that the barbarians around the Western Ocean had nothing to offer. He smiled faintly as he took in the cranes and the timbers at the shipworks to the west of the white stone piers.

The white-paved streets glistened, glistened from the hiss of brooms as the sweepers continued their endless work to ensure that the White City remained shimmering white. Those who walked the streets were well clad, clean, and scented with oils and spices, as they should have been.

Without turning back to face Piataphi, Lephi continued. "You will teach the barbarians the meaning of discourtesy. They have forgotten that all that they possess came from the ancients of Cyador. Since they have no gratitude, we must use fear. They have existed on the sufferance of Cyador, and we will not suffer that misapprehension to continue."

"Yes, Sire." Piataphi remained nearly motionless on the edge of the stool.

"Would that we had the fire cannons. Or the lances of light, but those will be with us again before long."

"We cannot duplicate the fittings yet, Lord. Nor fill the reservoirs."

"We cannot duplicate them now," mused Lephi. "But that is changing. Already, we build a fireship. Then we will re-create the fire cannons. You will not need them now. Cyador is larger, more prosperous than in the time of my grandsire." He turned back toward Piataphi. "We must have the copper mines of the north; those in Delapra will not last. Take all the even-numbered Mirror Lancers and the Shield Foot—"

"All, Your Mightiness?"

"I am not aware of any other challenges to Cyador. Are you?"

"No, Sire."

"I wish the barbarians annihilated—those within fifty kays of the mines. The others you may handle as you see fit. If they will not respect us out of gratitude, they will respect the forces you command."

"There are doubtless many more—they breed like lizards, Sire—than in years previous."

"You may also take the Shining Foot."

"Thank you, Sire."

"Begin your preparations tomorrow. You may use half the steamwagons on the North Highway."

"As you command, Sire."

"As I command . . . yes, as I command, Majer. And I command you to leave a swath of destruction around any that oppose the might of Cyador. Or forget what we have bestowed upon them."

The majer nodded.

"You may go."

Piataphi stood and stiffened to attention. "All honor to Your Mightiness and to the glory of Cyador."

"Go . . ." Lephi gestured, as if to wave away a fly.

The majer saluted, turned, and marched from the small receiving room.

Lephi's brown eyes went to the ancient painting on the inside wall—the etched-metal depiction of a wheeled steamwagon with a fire cannon turning a section of trees and animals into ashes. Even a giant stun lizard was shown flaring into flame.

"Cyador will become yet more mighty," he whispered. "We will have more steamwagons and fire cannon. We will. As I will it to be. As it was in the beginning, and will be evermore."

XX

THE STREAM GURGLED and splashed, not quite overflowing its banks, if well below the clay track that was something more than a trail and less than a road.

The gray leaves on the willowlike trees had spread but not turned to the fuller green of summer, and the new leaves were but half-open. A few starflowers bloomed in patches on the far side of the water, nestled in sun-warmed patches of green between the piles of weathered rock that had peeled off the canyon walls over the years. A steel-blue bird chittered from the top of a scrawny pine as the two horses carried their riders downhill and generally westward.

Nylan patted Weryl gently, trying to encourage the boy to keep sleeping. For whatever reason, carrying his son seemed to make him saddlesore more quickly, yet a year-old child didn't weigh that much. Or was it the weight of two blades—or all of it together? He lifted his weight off the saddle a moment, and his knees protested.

"Do we have any ideas where we ought to be going—besides west?" Ayrlyn asked.

"No. I wish I did, but . . ." Nylan turned in the saddle and looked back over his shoulder toward the ice needle that was Freyja—now barely visible above the gray rock walls of the canyon that the road followed, downward and usually westward. He took a deep breath. "In a way, I feel lost. I always let someone else decide. The service needed engineers, and so I became one. Ryba and the marines needed a safe haven, and I built it. Now . . ." He shrugged as he looked toward Ayrlyn. "Now, I have to figure out where we're going and what I want from life, and I can't—or I haven't so far."

Ayrlyn nodded. "You're getting more honest with yourself, and that's a start."

"Great. I now know that everyone else has been determining my destiny. It doesn't make finding it any easier—on me or you."

"We share that, Nylan." She offered a soft smile. "We'll work it out."

"Even with Weryl?"

"In some ways, it's easier. He's so young."

The smith moistened his lips, then asked, "How long will it take to get out of the Westhorns? You've traveled these roads more than I have."

"Four or five trips don't make me an expert. We didn't exactly have a lot of time to learn about this place, and I was more worried about trading for the things we needed and avoiding the local armsmen."

"This isn't the most popular route." So far as Nylan could tell, the only tracks on the narrow winding road were those of Skiodra's traders, and those had been nearly weathered away. In places, the tracks of deer, and in one section, a bear, were superimposed over the traces of the traders' carts. Clearly, not too many locals traveled the Westhorns—not in spring, anyway.

"It will get more popular. Ryba has made sure most of the brigands are dead, or they've gone elsewhere."

"We hope. I'm not exactly convinced they're all gone." Nylan glanced ahead, at the narrow valley sloping away, and at the thick green canopy on the left side of the road, probably growing out of marshy ground beside the stream. The greenery was enough to hide anything, including bandits.

"Ryba will take care of any that are left," Ayrlyn offered.

"In the same way she takes care of everything else," Nylan added sardonically. "With a sharper blade applied more quickly." He squinted at the road ahead. The mention of brigands bothered him, though he couldn't say why.

"You're bothered."

The engineer nodded.

"We'll just have to be careful."

"I hope that will help." After a moment, he added, "It would help if Ryba improved some of the stream fords, put in bridges." Nylan wiped his forehead.

"Still the engineer, I see." Ayrlyn laughed.

"I probably always will be." He tried to loosen his jacket all the way, but stopped as Weryl, who had been sleeping, gave a lurch. Ayrlyn still wore her jacket mostly closed. He hoped the lowlands wouldn't be too hot—there was a difference between being able to survive and surviving in something other than total misery.

"Waaa . . ." Weryl squirmed in the carrypak, and Nylan could sense his son's discomfort—again! The odor confirmed Nylan's senses.

"We need to stop again." The smith wanted to laugh at the look on Ayrlyn's face. "You were the one who said he traveled well."

"I shouldn't have spoken so soon."

They had to travel almost a kay before they descended enough into the canyon valley and reached a spot where the approach to the stream was both gentle enough and open enough through the tangled willows—with a shelf of coarse sand—for easy access to the water.

Nylan extracted Weryl from the carrypak again, hanging it over a low willow branch, followed by Weryl's loose trousers. The pants were dry, thank darkness, but the cloth beneath was anything but.

Nylan took a deep breath and stepped toward the stream.

At the first touch of the cold water, Weryl began to howl.

"I'm sorry, little fellow," Nylan said, "but you don't like being a mess, and I don't like smelling it."

The cries were interspersed with sobs, which drifted into sobs alone by the time Nylan had his son back in dry clothes.

"Can you hold him while I wash out what he was wearing?" Nylan asked Ayrlyn.

"I would have helped, but you seemed to have everything under control. You will attack changing him like an engineering problem, though."

"I suppose so. It is a waste disposal problem."

"He's your son, not a waste disposal problem."

"He may be my son, but being my son isn't going to make him less smelly or more comfortable." Nylan handed Weryl to Ayrlyn, who lifted him to her shoulder and patted his back, rocking as she did so.

Nylan's hands were red from the cold water of the stream by the time he had the cloth squares clean. "I'll have to fasten them over the bags or something so that they'll dry."

"He's hungry, I think," suggested Ayrlyn.

"We'll try the biscuit things, with water." After draping the cloth squares over the saddlebags, the engineer opened Weryl's food pack.

There had been no such things as baby bottles on Westwind, not when all the milk was breast milk, but in the food pack was a crude wooden cup with a carved cover that had a small spout. Nylan had breathed one sigh of relief when he had seen that.

"Let me sense the water," Ayrlyn offered. After a moment, she added, "It's safe enough. They don't have river rodents here—not that we've seen. Sometimes, they foul the water."

Nylan filled the cup and capped it. He still worried about getting the boy to eat enough of whatever was necessary for a proper dietary balance, but Weryl happily gummed his way through a biscuit and half-sucked, half-drank some of the stream water.

After that, the engineer eased him into the carrypak again and remounted. "How long before we have to stop again?"

"We don't have a timetable, you know," Ayrlyn pointed out.

"I know. But I feel as though there's something we'll have to do and that time's running out."

"You always feel that way."

"Maybe." But Nylan didn't think so. His eyes took a last look at Freyja as the track carried them around a wide curve formed by the stream, and the ice needle vanished behind a wall of gray rock covered with scattered evergreens.

XXI

How FAR TO the wards?" asked Themphi.

The headman, who bounced in the saddle of a swaybacked roan that had the look of a cart horse, offered an expression that could be a shrug. "How far, honored wizard? That would be hard to say."

"Why?" asked the wizard, his tone resigned.

"Because . . . the wards, they are no more, and the wall has been covered with shoots and creepers."

The dark-haired wizard wanted to sigh, but did not. "What happened to them?"

"We do not know. The forest covered them. Since before my grandsire's grandsire's grandsire the forest has been there, and the walls have been there, and neither has changed. I can remember walking the walls all day and not even reaching the north corner. It is more than fifteen kays from Geliendra, ser wizard. When I was young, I kept a whole kay of the wall myself. I trimmed, and I pruned. Once I even climbed over the wall, but I climbed back—quickly. There was the largest forest cat I ever saw. Now . . . we cannot even see the white of the walls."

"And you did not send anyone to check the wards?"

"We did. My sister's son Byudur. He was the village wizard. He did not return. Nor did the wizard from Forestnorth." The headman peered toward Themphi. "So we sent our petition to His Mightiness. Surely, the Lord of Cyador would know. And you, the wizard of wizards, are here."

Behind them, from the mounted lancer officers, came a chuckle. Themphi ignored it. "I am here, and I am sorry to hear of your sister's son. Did anyone find any trace?"

"The Accursed Forest leaves no traces."

Themphi did sigh, but under his breath. Worse and worse,

and Lephi had no real idea of what went on in Cyador, not with his dreams of rebuilding past glories.

The wizard frowned as he caught sight of the wall of green that stretched across the horizon, above the fields through which the packed clay road passed. Ahead the road ended at a wooden gate in a low wooden fence. The gate to the field was ajar, and there were hoof prints in the damp soil.

"There! You see. Even since yesterday, the Accursed Forest has grown."

The white wizard eased his mount through the gate into the field and rode another hundred cubits or so before he reined up.

A line of green creepers had covered half the field, and he could almost see the green edging toward him. He blinked, and blinked again. Was the green closer?

"You see, honored wizard?" said the headman of Geliendra.

To the east, beyond the rebuilt dike that held the irrigated rice field, the scene was worse. There . . . trees had sprouted. Not all that high, perhaps knee-high, but knee-high in a season? Or less than a season?

As the headman had said, Themphi could not see the retaining walls. They could have been a few hundred cubits back behind the advancing greenery—or farther. He studied the forest again, mentally calculating. The taller trees, the older ones, began no more than two hundred cubits back from the creepers and the lower undergrowth. A chest-high line of green, barely visible, stretched from west to east—the wall, covered in vines.

The wizard dismounted and handed the gray's reins to Jyncka. Then he stepped forward, gathering whiteness around him.

Light flared, as if from the forest, and Themphi staggered on the soft ground that had been turned and sowed, where sprouts of green peered through the dark soil. Themphi forced himself erect, ignoring the dampness on his forehead.

After another glance toward the wall of green nearly a hundred rods north of the long green creepers, his brows furrowed, and a firebolt arced into the green. The vines and knife grass blazed for a moment, and a circle of ashes spread until it was nearly thirty cubits wide before the flames died.

The white wizard wiped his sweating forehead, and he turned.

"Jyncka. We will do this the hard way, the way our forefathers did. Make arrangements for torches and barrels of pitch."

Jyncka nodded. "Yes, honored wizard."

The headman smiled nervously.

Themphi studied the forest for a time. Then he turned and took the gray's reins from Jyncka and remounted. "It will be a large undertaking, but mainly tedious." Then he swung the gray back toward Geliendra.

Behind him followed the headman, Fissar, and the disgraced lancers.

XXII

FOR A TIME after they ate, Nylan just lay on the bedroll in the early twilight. His rear was too sore to sit on anything, and the muscles above his knees ached too much to stand. His hands were raw from cold water washing off everything from their few pots to Weryl's cloth undersquares, and his head ached faintly.

So, facing Weryl, he lay on his stomach, wearing his shirt and a tunic, but no jacket. Down the needle-strewn slope, the stream rushed and gurgled. The faint hum of insects rose as the light dimmed. A faint and chill breeze swept across their campsite from the higher and ice-covered peaks to the east.

Ayrlyn sat sideways on the blanket behind the silver-haired infant. She wore her jacket, but had not fastened it.

"You know, it took just moments when I brought the lander across what it's taken us three days to cover by horse."

". . . ooo . . ." Pudgy fingers grasping for the wood, Weryl crawled across the blanket toward the smooth stick Nylan had shaved clean and rounded with his dagger.

Ayrlyn pulled off her boots and massaged her calves. "I'd forgotten how many muscles riding affects. The skiing helped, though. It isn't as bad this year as it was last."

"Hmmm . . ." said Nylan as he held the stick.

"We're lucky it's early in the year. The mosquitoes aren't out yet. None of the big flies, either. That will change when we get lower."

"Wonderful."

"Gaaaa!" Weryl's fingers grasped the stick.

"He's strong."

Nylan nodded. "He'll be walking before summer's end—sooner, perhaps. If we travel too far, I'll have to make some sort of seat for him. He already gets heavy."

"I've noticed when I've carried him. He also squirms."

The engineer rolled on his side, containing a wince as various muscles protested. Weryl began to climb over his shoulder.

"Not so fast, young man." Nylan set the boy back in the middle of the blanket, and Weryl charged across it on hands and knees, again climbing across Nylan.

"Like his father, he doesn't give up."

"I'm tired, and he's just getting started."

"Well . . . he sleeps most of the day," the healer pointed out.

"The motion of riding and the carrypak must be soothing." Nylan let the silver-haired boy climb almost all the way over him before he picked his son up and set him back in the middle of the blanket again.

Weryl laughed.

"He thinks it's a game," Ayrlyn said with a chuckle.

"I'll really be worn out by the time he's tired."

"You, the untiring iron smith? The tower builder who never stopped? Tired by a child?" Ayrlyn's smile got broader. "You could just go to sleep."

"Just sleep? Not a chance." Nylan grinned back, ignoring the twinge in his shoulder as he set Weryl back on the center of the blanket once more.

Weryl charged toward Nylan's knees, instead of his chest.

"It sounds like a triumph of lust over common sense. Do you think I'm interested? You didn't ask."

"Are you interested?"

"I'll have to see. You only asked when I forced you to." The healer tossed her head, and the flame-red hair glinted with a light of its own in the gloom.

"I'll try to do better in the future." Nylan lifted Weryl overhead. "Your powerpaks are still fully charged, aren't they?"

"Oooo . . ." Suspended over Nylan, Weryl immediately drooled, and the liquid dropped on the smith's chin. Nylan set his son on the blanket and wiped his face.

"Serves you right," Ayrlyn said.

"Thanks. I'll remember that when we're . ... whatever." The smith absently reclaimed Weryl once more. "Doing what we can where we can. You know, in some ways, it was idiotic to just leave. No destination, no plans."

"It would have been better to wait until Ryba found a way to dispose of me or turn you into an armless stud, the way she threatened Gerlich? Sometimes, O rational smith, you have to go with your feelings. By the time you can rationally figure it out, it's too late."

"Maybe . . . I don't know as I'm a very good smith, though."

"The locals thought you were, and that's one test."

"Maybe," Nylan repeated.

"Don't you think you could be a smith somewhere?" Ayrlyn asked.

"I don't know. I'd guess it would have to be a small town, somewhere they don't have one. The locals have to be better than I am."

"I wonder about that. You can feel the metals, and most people here don't seem to have that ability. Both Nerliat and Relyn were clear on that. Lord Sillek managed to survive because he had three white wizards—three in an entire kingdom. That tells me that the talent for wizardry—or the ability to use it—isn't common."

Nylan scooped up Weryl and just held him for a moment,

hoping the involuntary stasis would break the try-to-escape pattern the boy had adopted.

"Waaaa-daa-daaaa!"

"All right." Nylan set Weryl back on the blanket, and the silverhead dropped on his knees and crawled toward Ayrlyn.

"It's my turn?" Ayrlyn scooped Weryl up and set him back on the blanket.

Weryl laughed.

"I think it's luck and chance. We've all ridden the angel powernets, and sensing the order flows, the chaos flows, whatever it is that passes for magic here, is a lot easier if you have." Nylan intercepted Weryl's attempt to crawl over his boots. "Look at Westwind. Only three of the original marines had any talent, but all of the officers who had to ride the fluxes showed up with it."

Ayrlyn shrugged. "Could be. My point stands. There can't be that many smiths who have your talents."

"That may be, but I don't have any tools either."

"You're too guilt-ridden to take any." ·

They both laughed, before Ayrlyn had to grab Weryl again.

XXIII

THE VAN OF the Mirror Lancers rode four abreast, heading east on the great North Highway, and yet there was room for a steamwagon beside them. The white stones of the roadbed, which shimmered at a distance, would have displayed slight pits and hairline cracks if examined too closely.

Behind the van came the full Second of the lancers, then the Fourth, and then the Sixth. Even four abreast, the column of horse stretched almost a full kay.

Then came the steamwagons, only half a score, for all their individual bulk and power, their iron-tired wheels rumbling, engines puffing, brass rods and pistons moving and glittering under the white-gold sun. Each wagon pulled two long trailers laden with supplies and covered with white tarpaulins.

Behind the wagons rode the Eighth Mirror Lancers, and then the Tenth, and behind them streamed the Shield Foot, followed, a half kay farther back, by the Shining Foot. All in all, the assemblage of horses, wagons, and foot extended more than three kays along the North Highway.

In the first third of the column, immediately before the steam wagons, rode Majer Piataphi, with two captains flanking him. All wore the white and green of the lancers, and their saddles were of hard-finished white leather.

"The Shining Foot cannot walk as fast as the lancers or the wagons," observed the balding captain to Piataphi's right. "We are slowed to their pace."

"I doubt the barbarians will note, Captain," responded the majer. "They are convinced it will be seasons before we act."

"It will take more than an eight-day to reach Syadtar, even with the steamwagons, and another eight-day through the Grass Hills to the mines," pointed out the other captain.

"From the screeing mirrors, we can tell that the barbarians have few armsmen left from their petty wars, and fewer coins. There are no horse moving, no foot being gathered, not even their ragtag levies. We will be at the mines before they can gather forces." Piataphi coughed as the wind swirled ashes and cinders from the steamwagons around him. "Taking the mines will be harder than holding them. These barbarians will sneak through the trees and the hills, and loose their jagged-edged arrows and be gone before you know they are there. Screeing glasses are not much good for small bodies of fighters."

"Is not that why the Lord Protector of Cyador told us to clear the area around the mines?" asked the balding captain.

"Yes, Miatorphi." Piataphi lowered his voice. "We still have to maintain that area. It is one thing to destroy or drive out everyone; it is another to hold it—as his great-grandsire found out. That is why we must strike quickly and annihilate everyone." He coughed again as the following wind swirled down more smoke. "Let us ride up with the van until the wind changes."

He guided his mount to the clear left side of the white stone high-way, then urged it to carry him ahead of the exhaust gases from the mighty wagons.

XXIV

THE MARE WAS breathing heavily as she carried Nylan out of the narrow space in the rocky defile where the road finally leveled and started back down once more.

Nylan glanced ahead, where the orange white sun had just dropped below the Westhorns, and where the shadows cast by the peaks to the west had cloaked the road and the wooded valley ahead in gloom. The smith shifted his weight in the saddle and, as his eyes adjusted to the dimmer light, rubbed his forehead in relief from the glare he had been facing for what had seemed so long.

"It's hard riding into the sunset," he said, half over his shoulder to Ayrlyn, whose chestnut followed.

"Gaaa-dah!" answered Weryl, windmilling his arms.

"By this time of day, any riding is hard," Ayrlyn snorted. "Even your son thinks so."

"He has sense. Tell me again why doing this is a good idea."

"Because all the other ideas are worse," suggested the flame-haired healer.

"That has some merit, but not the sort of thing you read about or see on trideo screens."

"We saw our last trideo screens a long time ago," she pointed out, "but you're right. Fictional characters always have one good choice. They just have to find it."

"And us?"

"The least of terrible choices, and sometimes all choices are bad."

The smith straightened his legs, easing himself up in the saddle, prompting another set of arm-windmills by Weryl. Ahead appeared two crude long walls, forming a half-roofed triangle that faced a stone-ringed firepit. To the left was an overgrown path—leading presumably through the trees to the stream. Nylan could smell the dampness from the marshy flats beyond the structure, borne on the cooling light wind out of the west.

"That looks like a rough sort of way station," Nylan said.

"It is," said Ayrlyn. "We used it once, I think. There are lots of mosquitoes on the path to the stream. I remember that."

"Should we go on?"

"There's not much else. The road gets rocky and narrow beyond the valley, and winds away from the stream."

"Great. I hate mosquitoes."

"It's quiet," said Ayrlyn, as they rode toward the triangular shelter.

Nylan strained his ears, in between Weryl's interruptions, but could hear nothing, not even the normal whirrs and insect chirps. His eyes went to the road, and he frowned, then pointed. "Hoof prints, there."

"They're more recent," Ayrlyn said, standing in her stirrups and scanning the area behind the shelter.

The smith's eyes flicked to the structure, but no one lurked in the back, and the flat area around the fire seemed untouched in the growing dimness. He studied the trees again, but the thick foliage revealed nothing.

Twirrrppp . . . twirrrppp . . .

Nylan didn't recognize the annoyingly cheerful bird call, and only saw a flash of yellow-banded black wings. "What's that bird?" He felt there was something about it he should remember.

"They're noisy." Ayrlyn frowned as though she were trying to recall something as well.

The yellow and black bird perched on a shrub on the other side of the rock-circled firesite, its head cocked in a perky attitude. *Twirrrppp . . . twirrrppp . . .*

Nylan started to extend his senses beyond what his eyes could see when he heard the faintest of clinks, and his hand reached for the blade in the shoulder harness, realizing all too late that he should have drawn the blade first. The bird was a traitor bird!

"Daaa-dah!" Both Weryl's chubby hands grasped at his arm.

"No." Nylan eased his hand free and grasped the blade. "No!"

Whhsstt! One arrow hissed past his shoulder, and he lurched forward, before he stopped, the reflex halted by Weryl's strangled yell and bulk in the carrypak.

A line of fire creased Nylan's left shoulder, and he spurred the mare in toward the shelter, hoping that he could use the log walls as a barrier to the archer, and knowing that he was too close to flee without becoming an even better target.

Hoofs thundered out of the woods toward the two angels. Awkwardly, Nylan struggled to get his blade free, hampered by Weryl's very presence and the boy's anger at being nearly squashed—and two very active and windmilling arms. He didn't look at Ayrlyn, having his hands full in trying to turn the mare and raise his own blade.

Five riders burst up the path, led by a tall and bearded man on a roan, who wore brown leathers and swung a hand-and-a-half blade like the crowbar it resembled toward Nylan's head with a yell. "Haaaiii!"

All too conscious of Weryl on his chest, Nylan somehow parried the first brigand's wild cut, half-ducking as the man rode past and toward Ayrlyn. He barely managed to get the blade back up before the second and third riders were on him.

The second rider, in gray, missed with a slash, and the third, in tattered brown leathers, lifted a rusty blade with a black-toothed smile.

Desperately, Nylan threw his first blade, as he had learned through much trial over the past two years. Then, trying to yank the mare away from the two with one hand, he struggled with Weryl, the mare, and his unsteady seat in an effort to clear the second shortsword from the waist scabbard. The mare skittered sideways.

"Get him, Skittor . . . get—"

"Watch the other."

A wave of whiteness swept over Nylan, leaving him momentarily blind, as his thrown blade slammed through the second brigand. He tried to duck, again hampered by Weryl and the carrypak . . . and by his son's whimpers and flailing arms.

A slash of fire and a dull ache slammed the smith's left shoulder—the off-center blade of the third bandit—and Nylan half-slumped in the saddle before somehow jerking the second blade clear of its sheath. He had to stop them—if not for himself, for Weryl.

Another dull impact slammed across the top of his left thigh as he brought the dark gray blade up in time to parry a third half-wild slash. Despite the pain-blinded and intermittent images relayed by chaos-stressed eyes, he managed to block another flurry of weak slashes before his eyes cleared enough and his blade, following Ryba's and Istril's training, brought down the third brigand.

Fighting white flashes like renewed knives in his eyes, he turned the mare back toward the road, where a single rider slashed at Ayrlyn.

The man barely had a chance to look up in surprise before the Westwind shortsword cut through him.

Then . . . Nylan clung to the saddle, effectively blind, with his eyes providing but scattered images that strobed against the increasing darkness of the twilight, while he struggled to keep his fingers around the heavy blade in his right hand.

"Daa . . . daaa . . . wah-dah?"

"Your daddy's hurt." Ayrlyn's voice came from a great distance, although the smith knew that she had reined up beside him.

"Wah-dah?"

Nylan forced another deep breath . . . and another, telling himself to concentrate on breathing, hoping that no more brigands showed up.

"I'm having some trouble seeing, but you don't look like you can see at all. I'm going to tie up my mount, and help you and Weryl down. Can you hold on for a moment?"

"Yes," he croaked.

Whufff . . . uffff. His mare tossed her head.

"Easy," he muttered, squinting against the white knives that jabbed from his eyes into his skull. "Shit . . . can't even defend . . . without friggin' blindness. . . ."

"Daa?"

"We'll be all right." He hoped so. At least, he could hear the chitter of insects, and the whine of something else. Mosquitoes seeking free blood?

"Waa-dah?"

"Have to wait." He forced his eyes open, ignoring the pain. Was it less? Scattered images flicked at him, then vanished, then returned in an annoying pastiche of vision and blackness.

Nylan looked slowly around the former camp/way station, trying to make sense of each image.

Two mounts snorted by the stream, riderless. The bandit in tattered brown leathers lay sprawled facedown beside the ashes of the fire, a dark splotch around his shoulder.

The one in the gray shirt lay faceup, his head at an angle, nearly at the feet of Nylan's mount.

Ayrlyn walked slowly past the fire site back toward the smith.

A third mount—a gelding, Nylan noted in a clear and somehow detached way—skittered sideways on the slope leading to the stream, his hoofs raising puffs of dust. The figure on the gelding's back twitched, then slid ponderously from the saddle into a heap in the dry dirt scraped by the hoofs.

He turned his head, slowly, feeling the light stabbing in his right shoulder, and the dull aching throbs in his left. His right thigh hurt, and he looked down. The leathers were unbroken. A bruise from the flat of a blade?

"Daaaa . . ." whimpered Weryl. "Daaaa . . ."

". . . all right . . . it's all right," mumbled the smith.

"Like flame . . . it is," snapped Ayrlyn as she took the reins and started to lead his mount toward the shelter. "You're bleeding . . . like a hounded . . . deer . . . look lower than . . . clam shit."

"Had trouble . . ." Nylan turned his head, trying to see if

any more brigands could be around. His neck twitched, and the muscular quiver sent more arrows of fire into his skull.

"We . . . got them all," Ayrlyn affirmed, still speaking between heavy breaths. "Don't . . . know . . . how . . ."

Beyond her, he saw another riderless mount, and a horse struggling—and failing—to rise.

"Friggin' . . . mess."

The engineer had to agree.

"Can you get down? Hand me your blade."

"Oh." He looked stupidly at the shortsword, lowered it, and let her take it. Then he managed to swing his uninjured leg over the saddle and started to climb out, but his fingers lost their grip on the saddle rim he had used to steady himself, and he half-dismounted, half-fell against Ayrlyn.

"Oofff. You're still heavy."

"Daaa . . ." protested Weryl.

"Sorry . . . son."

Still blinking against both the throbbing and aches from all over his body, and the white flashes that interrupted his vision, Nylan half-stood, half-leaned against the timbers of the shelter. Ayrlyn quickly unfastened and laid out his bedroll, then eased Weryl out of the carrypak.

"Sit down," the healer said, holding the silver-haired boy.

Nylan sat. His thigh and shoulder protested, and his vision wavered as he did.

"Stay put!" Ayrlyn snapped at Weryl as she stripped the carrypak off Nylan and studied the wound in the smith's shoulder. The boy blinked and stayed put on the foot of the bedroll.

"You really took a gash here," she mumbled. "I'm glad I brought some dressings."

He sat quietly as she lit a small candle and used its light to see as she began to clean and bind both shoulder wounds. Around them the darkness grew, and the whuffing of the bandits' mounts breathing diminished as the insect chorus swelled, backed by the sound of the stream.

"I can tell we're not going anywhere for a day or two."

"I'll ride tomorrow."

"No, you won't."

"Wah-dah?" asked Weryl.

"In a moment," Nylan said, his night vision taking in again the carnage that surrounded the crude way station. Even in leaving Westwind, they didn't seem to be able to get away from violence—from the fact that force determined destiny. He started to shake his head.

"Don't move. I still have to clean out the rest of this mess. Let me see that arm."

Nylan raised his right arm, and the redhead peeled back the sleeve slightly. Nylan could feel her reordering the fields around his wounds and using her skills and senses to push back the whitish chaos of infection.

"You've never gotten this beaten up before," she said.

"You try fighting with a carrypak," the smith offered wryly, "and with Weryl flailing around." He took a deep breath. "I need to figure out some other way to carry him before long."

"Always the engineer."

Nylan wished he could be just an engineer, or even a smith. Instead, he found himself using blades. He did shake his head. Who was he deceiving? Even the U.F.F. had only wanted his destructive skills as a combat power engineer. Would it ever be different?

"There." Ayrlyn rose. "Now I need to see about the horses and the purses of those brigands."

"Are you all right?" he asked. "I can't see very well."

"Bruised—some little gashes. Nothing like you." A ragged smile crossed her lips.

"I can help."

"No, you can't. You just watch Weryl. You've lost more blood than you think."

Weryl looked toward Nylan. "Wah-dah?"

Ayrlyn fumbled with the harness on Nylan's mare and handed him the bottle.

"Thank you," he said, unstoppering it and offering it to his son, trying not to wince as he bent forward.

Ayrlyn started toward one of the bandit horses, her steps heavy in the gloom.

XXV

I DO NOT think your stratagem was terribly effective," said Gethen, looking over at his daughter and his grandson. "This scroll—it promises to flay us for our discourtesy, with all the might of Cyador."

"No one else had a better one." Zeldyan laughed, a trace of bitterness creeping into her tone. Nesslek sat in a small chair and grabbed at pieces of biscuit as she offered them. "We would be flayed anyway, discourtesy or not. How come your efforts to gather levies and armsmen?"

"Those in Cerlyn and the south are willing. They will even offer more than the required levies." Gethen snorted. "Their memories are long. They recall the old days when any woman could be bought as a concubine and any father who protested executed."

"I think they remember the executions more than the dishonored daughters." Zeldyan sliced a small corner of a pearapple and offered it to her son. Nesslek rolled it around his mouth before finally swallowing.

"Sadly, daughter, I would have to agree, but we must take any way station possible in this storm."

"Have you heard from Fornal?"

"No. I fear he will have difficulty in obtaining any armsmen from Dosai."

"Could he not use the levies for the border patrol with Jerans?" Her eyes went to the window and the thunderstorm that had rolled out of the southeast.

"I suggested that to him, and that may free a few good armsmen, but we will have to leave some there for seasoning and expertise."

"You still do not trust Ildyrom?" She took a few sections of pastry herself and ate slowly, then sipped cold greenjuice from the goblet.

"Ahhhh . . ." Nesslek reached for the goblet.

"This is your mother's," Zeldyan said firmly, looking toward her own father. "I will feed you more later."

"Sillek did not, and I did not, and I see no reason to change my views." Gethen coughed. "Ildyrom will show the sharp side of his blade again when it suits his needs."

"As will most holders and lords," Zeldyan said, more to herself than her sire.

Gethen raised his eyebrows, but did not answer.

XXVI

NYLAN TURNED IN the mare's saddle and glanced back to the east at the tree-covered hills that concealed most of the rocky and ice-covered peaks of the Westhorns. He almost shook his head. Eight days, or was it nine? But three had been spent recovering from the bandit attack.

"Darkness . . ." he murmured, shifting Weryl in the carry-pak. His son seemed to grow heavier with each kay they rode, and he hadn't been really carrying Weryl much until the last day or so. With his bad shoulder, Ayrlyn had done most of that.

"Do you want me to take him? You shouldn't overdo it." Ayrlyn turned her eyes from the tether to the gray that followed with the extra packs on it. The other bandit horse that hadn't fled had been so lame that they had left the beast free.

"Overdo it? I haven't done much of anything—except ride."

"You did enough in the last two years for three people. Why are you so hard on yourself?"

"We've actually ridden six days," Nylan said, to change the subject. "Did it take you this long on your trading runs?"

"Five to this point, I think. But we also didn't run into bandits, and we didn't have to stop so often."

"I can't ride if he's uncomfortable," Nylan admitted. "Not hard-hearted enough, I guess."

"It's been hard for me, too," Ayrlyn admitted. "I sense when he doesn't feel good. Or when you don't."

"My sensitive healer." In medically primitive Candar, Nylan had again become very glad she had that talent. At times his shoulder didn't even hurt.

"Just remember that. You're also my sensitive engineer, mage, and smith."

"I still don't know about the mage part."

"You're a mage. Don't fight it." The healer studied the forest to the left, the south side of the road. "More broad-leafed trees there. You can tell we're lower."

After Nylan blotted his forehead in the still air, his eyes went to the clear blue-green sky. "It's hotter."

"It's getting comfortable."

"By the time you're comfortable, I'll be roasted or broiled . . . or something." He cleared his throat. "We still haven't seen anyone."

"There were sheep in the meadows between the woods up ahead, last fall. It might be early for that, yet. I don't know." The redhead stood in the stirrups for a moment.

"Stiff?" the engineer asked.

"A little."

"You weren't last night."

Ayrlyn flushed. "You are impossible. After a wound like that . . . I wouldn't have believed—"

"You're a good healer."

"Too good . . ."

Nylan's mare whuffed as the road curved to the north around a hill crowded with evergreens bearing grayish green needles. Nylan patted her shoulder, then Weryl's back. The boy squirmed, and jabbed a heel into Nylan's diaphragm.

"I felt that. Kick him again, Weryl. He deserves it."

Instead, Weryl looked up at his father and said, "Daaa-waa!"

"If that means something, I haven't decoded it yet." Nylan glanced at Ayrlyn. "Aren't there any people here?"

"Not many. Lornth isn't that heavily populated around here. There's a town, or a hamlet, or a village, whatever you want to call a collection of huts about a half-day on."

"That's something."

"Not much more than something," replied the healer. "It's pretty bleak."

"Isn't there some civilization . . . somewhere?"

"Well . . . Lornth must have some. They have good metal-work, wines, and traders."

"Lornth—isn't that the name of the country?"

"Nylan," said Ayrlyn slowly. "Lornth is a city-state. The capital is a city called Lornth. The locals say this road goes to the city of Lornth. The lord of Lornth holds these lands, except he has other lesser lords that—"

"Please . . . not an elementary civics lesson. I asked a dumb question. Next time, just tell me it was a stupid question."

"You don't like women who tell you that."

Feeling like he had been gut-punched in a different way, the smith took a deep breath, then glanced beyond Ayrlyn to his right. "The trees are different." Nylan wiped his forehead, although he wore no jacket, just a shirt and tunic.

"I hadn't noticed," Ayrlyn said.

"They are different," Nylan repeated.

"How?"

"Their tops barely move in the wind, and . . . look at the roots. They're gnarled and huge and above the ground."

"What wind?" Even Ayrlyn had blotted her forehead.

"Higher on the hills—see the tops of the broadleaves. They're bending. We must be down in a protected area."

Ayrlyn eased the chestnut closer to the side of the road, extended a hand, then drew it back quickly. "They've got thorns, like spikes. They're like the ironwoods we were going to make charcoal out of, except bigger and thornier."

"You get spiked?"

"No. Almost. That was a dumb idea." She took out her own water bottle and drank.

"Waaa-daaa," demanded Weryl.

"That's water, in Weryl's terms," noted Ayrlyn.

Nylan got out the water bottle, and ended up getting more water on the carrypak and his own trousers, but Weryl kept gulping for a time. Nylan tried to keep the bottle from bouncing into his son's face, and ended up getting his fingers half-gouged by the few teeth Weryl had. Finally, he put the bottle back in the holder.

Ahead the road ran straight for a time toward a dip between two hills. The one on the right was covered with the gray-green ironwoods; the one on the left with high grass. Nylan squinted. Was there a hut in the middle of the meadow?

"So . . . the trees are different. What does that mean?" asked Ayrlyn.

"Nothing, I suppose. Except ironwoods aren't something that you can cut. The branches don't bend."

"Ironwoods . . ." mused Ayrlyn. "That's it!"

"What's it?" Nylan sniffed, suspecting an all too familiar odor creeping upward from the carrypak.

"Da . . . wa-wa!" Weryl grinned.

"These are the ironwoods. You can't cut them. You can't ride through them without getting slashed to bits."

"So . . ." Nylan wrinkled his nose and looked down at his grinning son.

"Relyn . . . he attacked Westwind to get lands and a title. Lord of the Ironwoods, I think was what he told me." Ayrlyn laughed. "And the lands are almost worthless to this culture. They can't have the kind of tools you need to use the wood. How can you clear something that tears you to shreds?"

"You can't. You mean that Sillek, or someone, was offering mostly worthless lands to encourage attacks on Westwind?"

"That's what it feels like." Ayrlyn shook her head. "Darkness . . . the politicians never change. He sounds as bad as half the U.F.A."

"I don't think we're going to have to worry about the United Faith Alliance ever again. The descendants of some Rationalists, but not the U.F.A."

Ayrlyn eased the chestnut closer to Nylan. "Oh . . . I can smell him from here."

"The stream gets closer to the road ahead, there." Nylan's shoulder had begun to throb more strongly, again, and he probably needed to let Ayrlyn carry Weryl, much as it bothered him to ask her—even if he had been the one to insist on his turns once he had felt the shoulder would take the strain. He just hoped they wouldn't run into any more bandits—not any time soon.

"We can't get there too soon." Ayrlyn eased her mount slightly away from Nylan—and Weryl.

Nylan tried not to breathe deeply and looked ahead to the stream.

XXVII

NYLAN GLANCED FROM the white-orange sun that hung in the deepening green-blue sky, barely above the rolling hills to the west, to the group of houses—or hovels—that clustered on the uphill side of the road that stretched before them.

A dull rumble of thunder cascaded down from the hills, and the engineer-smith turned in his saddle. A line of white and gray clouds roiled above the Westhorns, headed westward and toward the travelers, clouds that swelled skyward and blackened as Nylan watched.

"We've been lucky," Ayrlyn observed. "Ten days in the open, and no rain. You couldn't have asked for better weather. We can find a shelter up there."

Nylan looked from the hamlet ahead back to the storm, trying to sense the energy patterns. He failed, as he usually did unless a storm was almost on top of him. "It seems like it's going to rain for a long time."

He looked down at Weryl. The rain wouldn't be good for him, or his still-healing wounds, and it wouldn't be good for his son.

"It's a big storm," Ayrlyn confirmed.

As their mounts plodded down the gentle grade, and the gray gelding plodded after them, the smith studied the hamlet ahead. The walls were of crudely chipped stones, not so much mortared in place as stacked and chinked. The roofs were rough-boarded wooden planks, the joints covered with thinner strips of wood.

Even from more than a hundred cubits east of the village, Nylan could see the gold and brown chickens clustering behind one hut. "Chickens . . . they have chickens."

"Everyone has chickens here. Even farther south on the flats, where it's hotter, they have chickens."

"It gets hotter and flatter and lower?"

"Of course."

Nylan groaned. "It's only spring."

Behind them, closer now, the thunder rolled again. Weryl shivered in the carrypak, as if he could sense while asleep the order and chaos conflict in the storm as it bore down on them.

"How were you received here?" asked Nylan.

"They didn't close all the shutters."

"Oh?" Nylan shifted Weryl again, ignoring the twinges in his shoulder.

"They don't have shutters—or much of anything else here, except food. Actually, they do have shutters. They don't have glass for their windows, though."

"Can we buy some food? Some grain would be good for the horses."

"I have before, but it depends on how their harvests were."

"We got some coins from the bandits."

"Five silvers and a dozen coppers—not exactly fair compensation for the wounds and bruises."

"And a gray packhorse and saddle." Nylan took another quick look over his shoulder, but the storm was not that much closer. Then, distances tended to be deceiving in the clear air of Candar. The two continued to ride as the thunder rolled again out of the Westhorns.

"A solid storm," affirmed Ayrlyn as they neared the hamlet. "Lots of chaos up there."

"You can feel that?"

"You can't?"

"No, not until it gets close," he admitted. "You're better with the winds, I think."

"Fancy that . . . and you admitted I was better."

"It's hard." He forced a grin.

He got a quick smile that faded as Ayrlyn turned her eyes back to the hovels ahead. There were no walks between the dwellings, just pathways worn in the soil by years of foot travel, and small structures to the side or rear of the main houses. Outhouses, Nylan realized, as a certain odor drifted in his direction on the stiffening breeze—outhouses not too carefully tended.

Cleared and turned plots behind the houses were clearly gardens, and their careful tending contrasted with the scattered debris piled beside the doors of several dwellings.

"It's the trader woman! No one has hair like that . . . there's a silver-haired one with her." The youth darted inside the second dwelling.

"They'll be disappointed to see I'm a man." Nylan shifted his weight in the saddle and Weryl yawned. Of course, the boy was waking up. They were about to stop.

"The men will be. I don't know about the women." Ayrlyn grinned. "You'd better not try to find out, either."

"With my friend here?"

"Are you saying you would if Weryl weren't here?"

"No . . ." stammered Nylan. "That's not what I meant."

"That is not what you said."

Nylan wanted to wipe his forehead. Why was he always saying dumb things? On the one hand, Ayrlyn wanted him to be more forthcoming. On the other, being forthcoming meant being less cautious, and less cautious meant . . . He sighed.

"Why the sigh?"

"Later," he temporized as an old woman stepped out from the first hovel.

Ayrlyn slowed, then stopped the chestnut, and Nylan reined up beside her, glancing around. Three houses farther along the road a man appeared at the door, bearing a staff, but the bearded figure did not move, just watched.

"Trader? Where is your cart?" asked the gray-haired woman.

With a start Nylan realized the woman was not that old, possibly not much older than he was. Behind her, in the doorway of the stone-walled structure, stood a child, perhaps waist high, with a twisted leg that dragged as the girl limped out onto the rock stoop.

The gray eyes beneath the gray hair turned to the smith.

"A silver-hair bearing a child."

"He is a man and a smith," Ayrlyn said.

"He has no beard. Are all the silver-haired men such as that? A man with no beard? A silver-haired man with a child. No man of Lornth would carry a child."

"A beard is too hot," Nylan said quietly as Weryl began to squirm. He winced as heels jabbed into his diaphragm, but he didn't want to get his son from the carrypak until he knew how friendly their reception was going to be.

"Waaa-daa."

He compromised by unfastening the water bottle and letting Weryl drink—and drool water over his left trouser leg. A gust of wind whistled through Nylan's hair, and a roll of thunder rumbled across the hamlet.

"A smith, you say . . . well . . . the angels are different." She laughed, almost a cackle. "And with those blades and the fires of Heaven, so I've heard tell, I'll not be one to question. Need you any chickens, lady trader?"

"No chickens. We are traveling, not trading." Ayrlyn paused. "Who might share a roof with us?"

"Hisek might have room, and he has a large shed that would shelter your mounts." The woman pointed. "At the other side, just beyond the burned hut. That was Jirt's place. Not much, and since Hisek's consort died, Jirt and his woman live with Hisek. Hisek's his sire. They have a large common, and even a separate room for the two. Imagine that. Hisek built it for Gistene. Said it was what they did in Lornth. Much good it did her." The eyes sharpened. "Why be you traveling so early in the year?"

"Because it would not have been healthy for me or my son to remain on the Roof of the World," Nylan temporized.

"That place be not healthy for many, so I've heard." The lame girl tugged at her mother's arm, and the gray-haired woman nodded. "The pot's boiling. Go see Hisek."

The brown-bearded man merely watched as they rode past his house, his eyes flicking from Nylan to Ayrlyn and then to Weryl. Nylan nodded politely, but the man did not respond. Then they rode past the burned home—little remained beyond the blackened stones and the charred remnants of roof timbers.

"That must have happened this winter," Ayrlyn remarked.

"Winter . . ." Of course—winter was when people had fires for heat, and when few were outside to see if a spark had caught something.

Ayrlyn and Nylan reined up outside the larger stone house—it even had a rudimentary covered porch, and there was a long shed to the side of the dwelling. A long, lowing sound indicated that at least one ox was in the shed.

"Greetings!" called Ayrlyn as she dismounted.

Nylan watched as a heavyset, white-haired man stepped out under the porch.

"You might be Hisek," Ayrlyn began gently. "I am Ayrlyn—"

"The angel trader. I have seen you before." A puzzled look crossed Hisek's face. "I have naught to trade."

"We seek a roof for the night. We were told you had a large common."

"Aye."

"A few coppers," suggested Ayrlyn.

"I do not know . . . a flame-hair and silver-hair . . . two angel women . . ." The squat Hisek pulled on a straggly white beard, and his eyes turned to Nylan, who was struggling with Weryl's efforts to reach the water bottle.

"Nylan is my consort. The angel men often do not wear beards."

Nylan looked at Hisek. "It would be good if Weryl had a roof over his head in a storm."

"A man carrying a child—"

"I'm also a smith," Nylan said. He could tell the business of explaining that he was a man would get old. Still, he was stubborn enough that he didn't intend to grow a beard. Even though he hadn't shaved every day, his whiskers were so silver-transparent that they weren't obvious from any distance.

"And a warrior, I would wager, with the ease you bear those blades. Cold iron weighs heavy."

"We only fight to defend ourselves," Ayrlyn said.

Another roll of thunder cascaded across the valley, and the wind whistled, gusting enough that Hisek looked to the east and squinted. "Quite a storm coming out of the east. Quite a storm." He pursed his lips. "Three coppers, say, and you share our stew." His eyes twinkled for a moment. "Course it'd taste better if a trader could add something—"

"Some dried meat, that's about it," Ayrlyn said with a smile in return.

"Let me show you the shed. Wouldn't want your mounts out in this, and old Nerm, he likes company. Never knew an ox that didn't."

Nylan dismounted, carefully, to avoid squeezing Weryl against the mare, and followed the others to the shed.

"See . . . like a stall if you tie them at this end."

The ox looked up placidly, then lowed again.

"Told you, Nerm, he likes company. Oxen better for tilling than horses. Smarter, too."

"You take Weryl," Ayrlyn said, turning to Nylan. "He needs exercise, or we won't sleep tonight. I'll get the mounts and the gray."

Nylan carried the bags off his mare and lugged them up to the house, and a squirming Weryl in the carrypak as well. His shoulder had begun to throb before they were halfway to the house.

"Must be a smith. You're a slender fellow, but don't know as I could haul two heavy blades, a rollicking child and a stone's worth of baggage." Hisek panted as he walked beside the smith.

"Iron is heavy, but working the hammers was the hard part," Nylan admitted. "There were times when I felt my arms would fall off."

"My sire—he always told me—yes, he did, never to mess with a smith. 'Hisek,' he said, 'any man who makes his living beating iron won't have much trouble beatin' you.' That's what he said."

Nylan didn't feel that ironlike, not at all, and he wondered again how long before the shoulder would heal completely.

More thunder, closer, rolled out of the east. Overhead, the sky was covered, except for the western horizon, with dark clouds.

"Best check the supper," puffed the white-beard as he stepped onto the narrow porch and then into the house through the open door. "Just set your stuff in the corner, there."

The common room had a hearth at the west end, with coals over which a large iron kettle was hung on an iron swivel mortared into the side wall. An oblong trestle table filled the center part of the room, with a bench tucked under each side. In the hearth corner at the back of the room was a narrow pallet bed. A kitchen-type work table stood wedged into the other hearth corner, with pitchers and boxes on it, and several kegs and small barrels underneath.

Nylan unloaded the gear in the corner away from the hearth. Then he eased Weryl out of the carrypak, carted him out to the front porch and set the boy on the stones. Weryl immediately crawled for the front edge of the porch. Nylan scooped him away and set him down by the door, but Weryl started for the edge again. The smith moved him.

"They be determined . . . young ones." Standing in the doorway was a heavy young woman, scarcely more than a girl, perhaps not much older than Niera, the orphaned girl at Westwind, whose mother had died in Gerlich's attack.

"They can be," he answered pleasantly.

"I be Kisen. Jirt is my consort. He has the flock in the low meadow." Kisen sat on one corner of the stone porch, letting her feet dangle.

Nylan set Weryl back down. This time, the boy looked at Kisen, his eyes wide.

"Boy?" she asked.

"My son." Nylan realized that the brown-eyed girl wasn't really heavy, but pregnant.

"He has hair like you, not like . . . the other angel. Do the angels all have silver or flame hair?" She shifted her weight, as if uncomfortable.

"No. Some have black hair, or brown hair, or blond hair. Even among the angels the silver and flame hair is not that common." Even as he spoke Nylan wondered. Only one of the angels with the flame-red hair or the silver hair had died in the first two years, one of six. Only four of the other twenty-seven had survived. Was that luck? Or did the traits tied to hair color . . . he shook his head. All those with the strange hair could sense the order/chaos/fields, and that had to help with survival.

"First, thought you were another woman angel. Hard like the others. How come you don't grow a beard?"

"Beards are uncomfortable. Hot."

Kisen nodded. "They say you folks like things colder. That true?"

"That's true, mostly." Nylan lurched to recover Weryl again.

Another gust of wind carried a few raindrops under the porch roof. Ayrlyn hurried around the corner and onto the porch, carrying the saddlebags, her bedroll, and Weryl's second bag.

"I put them in the back corner," Nylan said.

"Both of you carry two blades . . . ?" asked Kisen.

"That way you can throw one," Ayrlyn said dryly, as she stepped into the dwelling, banging the door with one of the shortswords as she did.

"You throw them, too?"

"Yes."

"Killed anyone?"

Nylan winced, then nodded.

"Lots?" pursued the girl.

"Too many," Nylan said.

Another gust of wind brought more rain, and Nylan scooped up Weryl. "Time to go inside, Weryl."

In the common room, Ayrlyn was breaking off a number of chunks of dried meat and easing them into the iron kettle that hung over the hearth. "They should cook for a time longer."

"Be a while 'fore Jirt gets back anyhow." Hisek looked at Kisen. "You make some biscuits, Kisen?"

"Can try, anyhow." Kisen headed toward the table in the corner.

Nylan sat on a three-legged stool by their gear and set Weryl on the floor—rough planks laid edge to edge and smoothed by feet and boots. Weryl grasped Nylan's trousers and pulled himself up, tottering on short legs for a moment before plopping down in a heap. After a moment, his fingers grasped the leather trousers again.

"He'll be walking sooner than you think," said Ayrlyn, taking the other stool and setting it beside Nylan.

"Looks that way."

After another attempt, and another, Weryl gurgled and smiled.

Nylan sniffed and reached for the boy. "Is there a well or stream?" he asked more loudly.

"Use the well by the shed. Bucket's there," said Hisek.

Nylan grabbed a clean cloth undersquare from Weryl's pack and carted the boy out through the light rain to the well. While the well water was warmer than the icy stream water of the Westhorns, his hands were still red and raw by the time Weryl and the soiled undersquare were clean and they were back at the house.

Another figure stood inside the door, and Nylan had to stop suddenly to avoid running into the shorter man.

"This be my son, Jirt," offered Hisek. "These are angel folk, travelers, 'cepting that the flame-hair's also a trader at times. Silver-hair's a smith."

"My sire's guests are welcome." Jirt frowned as he looked

at Nylan, obviously confused at the lack of whiskers until he saw the stubble.

"The flock?" asked Hisek.

"They're in the corral. No cats—so the lambs are all there. Cats be out later." Jirt was square like his sire, but brown-haired and brown-bearded.

"Good! We can eat now. You brought the meat, trader lady. You serve," said Hisek. "Sit." Hisek indicated that Ayrlyn and Nylan should take the end places on the benches.

As the others sat at the trestle table, Ayrlyn ladled out the stew. Another crash of thunder seemed to rock the house just as Ayrlyn served herself, and the rain splashed down in sheets.

"We're very thankful to be here," she told Hisek.

The stew wasn't bad, neither as awful as the messes that Kadran had made in learning to cook nor as good as Blynnal's cooking. It was plain and filling, and the dried venison helped a lot. Kisen's biscuits were heavy, but the one that Nylan offered Weryl seemed to keep the boy busy, half as food and half as a teething ring of sorts. At least, Nylan managed to eat a good dozen mouthfuls before he went back to alternating spoonfuls between Weryl and himself.

"You have a lot of trouble with the cats?" Nylan asked Jirt.

"Depends. Last year was bad. Lost half the lambs," answered the herder, his mouth full. "This year . . . not so bad. Yet. Cold winters make easier springs."

"Why is that?" asked Ayrlyn.

"The deer. Cold winter, the deer have it hard. They get weaker, and that makes it easier for the cats. Cats are smart. Rather go after a deer than a sheep and a herder that could kill 'em." Jirt reached for another heavy biscuit. "Solid biscuits, sweet. Like 'em that way."

Kisen smiled.

"True what they say about the angels," ventured Hisek, "that they—you folk—destroyed all Lord Sillek's armsmen and some eighty score of Lord Karthanos's folk?"

"That's about right. We didn't want to, but when you have two thousand armed men trying to kill you—" Ayrlyn shrugged.

"Idiots . . ." mumbled Hisek through his food. "Can't live there. Can't even pasture up there 'less you're a rich lord. All it's good for is bandits, and been a lot less of them since the angels showed. Got more from you, trader, than from the folk out of Lornth."

"Peace, now," said Nylan. "Both Karthanos and the regents of Lornth agreed to let Westwind be if Westwind keeps the roads safe of brigands."

"Some sense after all," noted Jirt.

"Only one who gets killed is the common man," said Hisek. "Golar was a levy. Lucky to come back alive. Brother didn't. That grassland lord of Jerans killed him. Him and his bitch consort."

After more small talk and after all the biscuits were gone, and after Nylan changed Weryl again—thankfully he was only wet—the three men dragged the table to one side of the room.

"There's the best we can do," offered Hisek.

"That's fine," said Ayrlyn.

"Much better than outside in this weather," Nylan agreed.

Jirt and Kisen retreated through the mishung door to the small bedroom, and Nylan rolled out his bedroll in the corner away from the fire, letting Ayrlyn have the closer space. After easing Weryl onto the side closest the fire, he stretched out, glad to get the weight off his feet and buttocks. For a time, he felt better. Then he began to notice that the plank floor was hard, as hard as if it were made of the rock that comprised the walls.

Plick! A raindrop splatted on the floor behind his head.

The engineer turned his head toward Ayrlyn. Her eyes met his, and she gave a half-shrug with the shoulder she wasn't lying on.

"Better than being outside," she said.

Plick! Plick! As if to emphasize her statement, the hissing of the rain became a heavier splashing, and another set of thunder rolls echoed outside.

Nylan turned slightly, careful not to roll onto or into Weryl, or to put his weight on the healing shoulder.

Plick!

Across the room, the older man began to snore, like a cross-cut saw that rasped across Nylan's nerves.

Plick! Plick!

He closed his eyes again.

Plick!

The engineer opened them and turned, whispering to Ayrlyn, "Tell me how it's better than being outside again."

In the darkness she smiled, and her hand reached out and squeezed his. "It is. You're dry."

He was dry. He was also tired, and his wounds and muscles ached.

Plick!

He took a deep breath, trying to relax.

Beside him, Weryl turned, but Ayrlyn squeezed his hand again.

XXVIII

NYLAN GLANCED ALONG the road, a road that now bore a few more cart tracks and hoofprints, then overhead at a patchwork of green-blue sky and white and gray clouds that moved rapidly westward.

In the fields to the left of the road stood a small hut, surrounded by gardens, where a woman in tattered trousers and a frayed gray shirt mechanically scraped away weeds with a warren. She did not even look toward the road.

"You still think we should go to Lornth? Why?" asked Nylan, shrugging his shoulders and enjoying the freedom of not carrying Weryl.

"Call it a feeling . . ." This morning, she wore the carrypak that held Weryl, and the silver-haired boy was awake and quiet—watching the long-horned cattle behind the split-rail fence on the south side of the road.

In turn, Nylan had the rope that led back to the gray. He glanced over his shoulder, but the gelding followed quietly.

The ironwoods again flanked the north side of the road, and Nylan wondered how many kays they stretched. There were none on the south side. Because the peasants got rid of them immediately? Nylan would have. They couldn't remove those on the north side because the lands belonged to the lord of Lornth, at least from what Nylan had figured out.

"You have any thoughts on why you feel Lornth is where we should go?" he pursued.

"Not really. Something tells me—it could be because one of the regents is a woman—that Lornth would be better."

"That's like saying Ryba would be more merciful." Nylan laughed harshly. "Women aren't necessarily more charitable because they're women. You're more charitable because you're you."

"That may be." Ayrlyn shrugged. "It doesn't change the way I feel about it."

"I hope you're right." Nylan grinned at Weryl.

The boy waved both arms, jabbing one back into Ayrlyn's ribs.

"Ooohhh . . . you've got sharp elbows, Weryl." The healer rubbed her ribs. "We need to think about designing some sort of seat, behind the saddle, perhaps."

"Behind?"

"It's safer, and it would leave your arms free for a blade or a bow if we ran into brigands. Or have you forgotten how you got all chopped up."

"No. You're right. I'll think about it . . . when we get someplace where I could make it." Ahead, around the gentle curve in the road that arced to the right, Nylan could see another hut, similar to the last, except that no one tended the garden.

"You said you had a dream? What sort of dream?" Ayrlyn asked, easing the chestnut closer to Nylan.

"Trees—old trees, and they were struggling against something. Order and chaos were twisted together. But what was funny was that it made sense, and I don't see how twisting order and chaos together could make any sense at all."

"Daaa!" called Weryl, thrusting a chubby fist into the moist air.

"Daaa to you, too," answered Nylan.

"Waaa-daaaa . . ."

"All right, all right," said Ayrlyn as she reached for the water bottle. "Try not to drool all over me."

"Good luck." Nylan laughed.

"I'm doing this because of my great good will . . .. and because I love you, you hardheaded smith, but don't push it. That shoulder is getting well enough."

"Thanks to you."

"The order-healing helps, especially against infection, but we really need antiseptics."

"We could distill alcohol out of wine."

"How? Isn't tubing and that sort of thing hard to forge?" She eased the bottle to the boy's lips. Surprisingly, little spilled.

"You're good at that."

"Of course." Ayrlyn grinned as she slipped the cork back in the bottle and stowed it in the holder.

"Hmmm . . . tubing would be hard, but maybe only a little has to be metal. Fire and glaze the rest. Also, we could increase the alcohol content by freezing the wine or whatever, and removing the ice. They used to make winter-wine that way."

"I thought you'd think up a way." Ayrlyn disengaged Weryl's hand from the hilt of her blade. "Was there anything else about your dream?"

"There must have been. It seemed to last a long time, but the order and the chaos and the trees were all mixed together."

"It means something," mused Ayrlyn.

A shadow passed across the road, extending far around the curve, as a cloud scudded across the sun.

"Probably." But what? That trees needed both order and chaos? Nylan frowned. True chaos would kill trees . . . wouldn't it? And what did the trees have to do with the future—another idea pushed forward by his subconscious that indicated how mixed up he was? He pushed the ideas to the back of his mind, then glanced upward. The sky remained the same mixture of sun and clouds, but the breeze seemed cooler without the sunlight.

"How far to Lornth?" he asked after a time.

"Another five days or so."

"Five days?" Nylan groaned.

"Or so."

Nylan glanced at the road, at the seemingly endless range of ironwoods to his right. Maybe there were other ironwood areas. He couldn't believe that a stretch of ironwoods that took five days to ride was worthless.

Then, a lot of Candar took some believing, starting with his own abilities and those of Ayrlyn. He shook his head, and shifted his weight in the saddle. Five more days?

Weryl gurgled happily and jabbed an elbow into Ayrlyn's ribs again. She took his arm firmly and moved it. "No."

Nylan could almost feel the mental force of that denial.

Weryl's face crumpled, and he began to cry.

Ayrlyn shook her head. "He can't be allowed to hurt people." Then she reached down and hugged him with one arm. "It's all right."

The boy sobbed for a few hundred cubits more, then stared at the cattle on the south side of the road once more. But he didn't jab Ayrlyn with his elbows again.

XXIX

NYLAN LOOKED UP from the way station's hearth fire as Ayrlyn slipped inside, bearing Weryl's damp clothes. She left the sagging door open, mainly for light, since there was but a single window with loose-fitting shutters. Her hands were red from the cold stream water.

The smith extended an arm to bar the silver-haired boy from nearing the few flames that rose from the shavings. "No."

Weryl looked puzzled, but stopped trying to climb over his father's limb.

"He understands," said Ayrlyn.

"He's too young to understand. I learned that years ago in child psychology."

"Child psychology? You were an engineer." Ayrlyn hung the undersquares and Weryl's trousers and shirt across a low roof brace. "He's going to need larger clothes before long. These are getting tight."

"I know. Maybe we can find a tailor or something in Lornth."

"Ha! People here make children's clothes."

"I forget about things like that." Nylan added more of the pencil wood to the fire, his eyes half on Weryl as he did, but the boy remained on hands and knees, just looking at the small tongues of flame from the shavings that licked at the wood.

"Child psychology?" prompted the healer. "You never answered."

"Distributional requirements. I wasn't from the Institute. I had to take courses at the university in something other than power physics. I thought I might have children some day; so child psychology seemed more useful than institutional behavior, sociology of the exotics, or alien metapsychology." Nylan added another chunk of slightly larger wood to the growing hearth fire, glancing at the two pots that waited.

"Child psychology or not, he understands 'no.' "

Nylan shrugged, wondering if Weryl were already sensitive to the order fields, if somehow he'd picked up on the emotional energy or disturbance or something associated with negatives. If so, they'd have to be careful, very careful. He wanted to groan again. It seemed like everywhere he turned, he had to be careful.

"Why the groan?"

"Because . . . if you're right, and Weryl understands no . . ." He went on to explain the sensitivity problems.

Ayrlyn bent down, picked up Weryl, and hugged him, then eased him into a more comfortable position. "You have to give him lots of affection. It can't be false, either, then, because he'll know the difference."

The engineer wanted to groan again. He didn't need a son who was an emotional lie detector. Then, his son hadn't exactly asked for the talent, and Nylan and Ayrlyn both had some abilities in that direction, as had Istril. Why was every talent a curse as well?

He slipped a larger chunk of wood onto the fire and swung the single bracket that bore both pots over the flames. The wrought iron creaked and wobbled, as if it might pull out of the crudely mortared stones—but it held.

"It will be a while before the stew, such as it is, is ready," he said absently. "I'm glad you found those wild onions. They'll help with the seasoning."

Nylan folded the wax away from the cheese and carefully sliced small slivers so that they dropped onto outer cloth that had covered the wax. When he had a small stack, he offered the first to Weryl, who half-chewed, half-gummed the sliver before swallowing and opening his mouth for more.

"He's hungry," affirmed Ayrlyn, after sitting on the hearth stones and holding Weryl so that Nylan could feed him.

"Aren't we all? That unplanned stop took more food." The smith offered more cheese and glanced at the fire. "It's going to be a while."

"That's all right. He's going to need his exercise anyway."

"At least we've been making good time—and only one storm since we left your first hamlet—the one without a name."

"It has a name. I just never learned it."

"I'm glad they have some of these way stations. It's good to have a roof, especially with Weryl, and I get an uneasy feeling when I think about staying in an inn or in some of the towns."

"The way stations are mostly for traders, I think. Lornth isn't nearly as well populated as the lands east of the Westhorns, and they need more trade, I'd guess."

"Wonder if that's because of the ironwoods. We've seen a lot of them."

Ayrlyn frowned.

"It takes time, good tools, and manpower to clear them. They're not much good for anything, and some of the bigger ones you couldn't budge with heavy industrial equipment. That means it's a slow tedious business—"

"That could be. I don't know."

Nylan crumbled more of the hard cheese into little pieces, and tried to coax more of it into Weryl's mouth. Without milk, trying to balance the nutrients for his son was hard, especially since fruits and vegetables weren't in season.

"Have you ever wondered why we're doing this?" Nylan mused. "Here we are, riding almost blindly into a country that was an enemy. If you look at it rationally, it verges on the insane."

"Yes and no. Was it sane to stay in Westwind?" asked the healer.

"Probably not, given Ryba's mindset."

"Would you rather have gone east, into Gallos?"

Nylan grinned wryly. "No."

"What other direction could we head? Or would you prefer to hide out in the mountains for the rest of what would be quite short lives?"

"When you put it that way, I feel a little better. A little." Considering that he still hadn't the faintest idea of what he really wanted to do, except . . . except what? Survival wasn't anything except survival, and life had to be more than that. Didn't it? He shook his head.

Weryl drooled out the last section of cheese, a whitish-yellow mess that oozed across Ayrlyn's wrist.

"I think he's had enough." Ayrlyn eased the child onto the packed clay floor and unstopped a water bottle to wash the small mess from her wrist onto the hearth stones. A sizzle followed when some of the water touched a coal.

Nylan used a stick he had whittled clean to stir the stew, but kept his eyes on Weryl. "It's still going to be a while. Maybe you could get out the lutar and sing something?"

"Later." Ayrlyn glanced at Weryl, who was crawling rapidly toward the waystation's door and the twilight outside. "Later."

Nylan handed the stirring stick to Ayrlyn and hurried after his son.

XXX

By MID-AFTERNOON of the next day, the two angels had ridden far enough north and west that hills had flattened more, and there were cots and even farms scattered here and there on both sides of the road.

Nylan absently wiggled his fingers in front of Weryl, and the boy grabbed his index finger. The smith tugged, just hard enough that Weryl could hang on for a time.

Nylan rubbed his chin, glad that he'd spent the time to shave away the stubble that had been approaching a beard and getting hot and sweaty in the afternoons. Ahead, the engineer could see a wagon drawn by a pair of horses headed in their direction.

"The road's getting busier," he said with a laugh, turning his head toward Ayrlyn, again wiggling his fingers for Weryl to wrestle with.

"It's about time."

As the wagon neared, Nylan and Ayrlyn eased their mounts, and the trailing gray, to the right side of the road, onto the shoulder where shorter stalks of green grass sprouted up underneath the dead grass of the previous year. The creaking of the battered wagon grew loud enough to silence the scattered calls of the ground birds in the meadow to the right of the road.

"Greetings," Nylan offered pleasantly as the wagon drew abreast of the two angels.

The gray-haired driver glanced at the two without speaking, then looked away quickly, his eyes on the road before him.

"Pleasant sort," Nylan said conversationally.

"You'll find more than a few like that. They think we're evil spirits or something." Ayrlyn gestured ahead. "We should be coming to a town before long. It could be right past that hill. I remember there was a hill where the road curved just before we got there. It's called Ginpa, or Hinpa, or something like that. After the town, the road follows the river almost straight north to Lornth. We didn't go nearly that far when we were trading last year, because the towns get a lot closer together now."

As they rode down the gentle grade toward the curve in the road, a gray stone no more than knee-high and partly obscured by grass appeared on the right side of the road. The kaystone read "HENSPA—3K."

"I knew it was something like that," said Ayrlyn.

"What's it like?"

"They're all alike. If they're really small, you have one muddy street, or dusty if it's been dry, and there are a few stores, usually a chandlery—that's where you can find travel goods, leather, candles, sometimes cheese—a cooper's, maybe a cabinetmaker. They'll have a smithy farther out, and some have a mill by the water. The bigger towns sometimes have a square with an inn, and a public room. The food's not too bad, but the rooms are pretty awful—bugs and worse. The smell gets worse in the bigger towns."

"You make it sound so attractive." Nylan looked down. Weryl had dozed off.

"They don't have your fetish for proper sanitation—or building."

"I wouldn't quite call it a fetish."

"Most of the guards would—except Huldran. She's as bad as you." Ayrlyn grinned. "I liked the semiwarm water, too."

"Thanks."

At the base of the hill were clustered several houses around a large barn and some outbuildings. One man guided a horse-drawn plow, turning back the dark soil in an even row. Two others seemed to be shearing black-faced sheep.

"I've never seen black-faced sheep before," Nylan said.

"The Rats have them—even sheep that are totally black."

"That seems odd, when they revere white and mirror reflections." The engineer glanced down again, but Weryl continued to sleep.

"People aren't nearly so logical as they'd like to believe." Ayrlyn's tone was dry. "Even the cold and logical Ryba can be illogical. Forcing you out of Westwind wasn't the most logical thing to do."

"That depends on what's important, I suppose."

A boy near the road, holding a scythe, looked at the two riders, dropped the scythe and ran down the lane toward the two who were shearing.

"I don't like that," said Nylan.

"Neither do I, but you'll find it happens. Some of the older children have been fed tales about everything from our eating babies to causing ewes to abort their lambs—or worse. It was probably easier for Gerlich because he didn't have flame hair or silver hair."

"That's not any more reassuring."

As the road straightened on the other side of the hill, Nylan studied the town that lay ahead. Just a brown clay road leading to what appeared to be a small square. The houses were not stone, but some form of stucco, whitewashed, probably over mud bricks or something akin. The roofs were made of a dull clay tile, and many of the tiles appeared cracked or askew.

A short-haired, golden-brown dog appeared on the edge of the road, its tail stiff, almost pointing at the riders, but as they passed, Nylan detected the faintest wag.

A young woman, with a toddler tied to a rope wound around her waist, struggled to fold laundry on a crude outdoor trestle table on the sunny south side of a small hut. Chickens pecked nearly around her bare feet. The woman scarcely looked up at the two.

A black dog chained to a small hut yapped, and kept yapping.

Farther toward the center of the town, a partly bald white-haired man openly stared as they passed.

"Greetings," offered Ayrlyn. She got no response, and no lessening of the stare.

"This place has a square, anyway." Nylan eased the mare to a slow walk as they approached the center of the town.

The square was barely that, with a pedestal and a battered statue in the middle of the road, surrounded by a knee-high brick wall.

On one side of the road was a cooper's. Nylan could tell that from the barrel hung over the open doorway. Beside the cooper's was another shop, or something, which had no sign. Across from the unnamed shop was a larger building, bearing a sign that showed two crudely drawn crossed yellow candles. Beside the candle-signed building was a stable and beyond that an inn—or the equivalent—with a sign showing a black bull on a weathered grayish background.

"The crossed candles mean a chandlery." Ayrlyn continued to survey the town, but the cooper kept pounding on the rim of a barrel outside his shop, while a heavyset gray-haired woman sat on a stool outside the adjoining building. She nodded at Ayrlyn, who smiled and returned the nod.

"We could use more cheese," Nylan said. "I worry about Weryl."

"He's fine, but we could use the cheese—and you might think about cloth—if it's not too expensive. Cloth's never cheap in low-tech cultures."

He turned the mare toward the chandlery. Although there was a stone hitching post with a brass ring outside, no mounts were tied there.

"Should we stay in the inn? Or have a hot meal? It's getting toward sunset," Nylan said almost absently as he dismounted and tied the mare to the bronze ring in the stone post outside the chandlery.

"See what sort of reception you get." Ayrlyn slipped off the chestnut and tied her beside Nylan's mount. Then she urged the gray forward and tethered him as well. "I'll carry Weryl."

"I can carry him."

"I just have this feeling . . ." insisted Ayrlyn. "How is your shoulder?"

"Fine—as long as no one puts a blade through it." Nylan grinned and eased Weryl from the carrypak and to Ayrlyn. The boy squirmed for a moment, flailing arms and elbows, then quieted.

The comparative silence of the late afternoon was broken by the sound of hoofs—cantering or galloping into the town.

"Told you so!" yelled a voice.

"Angels!" said another.

Nylan turned to his left, where two men vaulted from mounts across the street, tied them quickly outside the cooper's, and ran toward the chandlery. Two others remained mounted by the tied horses.

"Careful," murmured Ayrlyn.

The smith wasn't exactly certain how he could be careful with two armed men heading toward him, but this time he wasn't about to let anyone get in the first slash.

"You killed my brother!" A bearded blond man dragged the huge blade from the shoulder harness and lumbered toward Nylan. Lagging behind was a smaller black-bearded figure.

The smith stepped off the wooden plank walk, turning to face the local, wondering what to do, even as his tongue and mind triggered the combat step-up reflexes and his hands drew the blade from his waist scabbard.

The huge crowbarlike blade seemed both to fly at Nylan and to move in slow motion. He whipped the Westwind blade into a parry—one of those designed by Ryba to slide the big blades. Nylan did not strike, although the blond was totally exposed for a time, and instead stepped back, holding his blade ready.

"Murdering bitches!" The blond levered the crowbar around for another massive slash.

Behind the blond, the black-haired man waited, licking his lips.

Absently, Nylan wondered why having no beard made everyone assume he was a woman. Or was it his wiry build as well? He eased away another massive slash, almost effortlessly, and said, slowly, so slowly, it seemed, in old Anglorat, "We're just travelers. I only wanted to buy some cheese." As he spoke, he decided he sounded idiotic, but he slipped to one side and avoided another grunt-driven, wild slash.

The black-haired man suddenly raised his blade and darted forward.

Nylan threw the blade and ducked, half-rolling and coming up with the second blade, even as his mind automatically performed the ordered flux-smoothing that targeted the first blade.

The smaller man pitched backward, the black blade buried nearly to its hilt in his chest.

Nylan staggered, blinded with the white fire that slashed at him from the death of the smaller man. He backed up, knowing the mounts weren't that far behind him, and feeling the renewed throbbing from his left shoulder.

The blond man charged again, grunting and bringing the huge two-handed blade around like a crowbar.

Nylan's muscles followed the well-drilled patterns, and, as suddenly as it had begun, the blond lay on the street, dead from the slash that had nearly severed shoulder and arm from trunk.

"Stand still . . ." came Ayrlyn's voice out of the white fog that battered at him.

Nylan stood very still for a moment, almost blind, before, squinting through the flashes of white that intermittently blinded him, he bent and withdrew the black blade, cleaning it on the dead man's tunic. His guts churned, but he wondered if that feeling came from Ayrlyn, relayed through the order fields he had tapped, or came from the strain of reflex step-up. His shoulder had begun to burn and throb again as well.

"His purse," whispered Ayrlyn.

Mechanically, Nylan bent and used the shortsword's edge to cut loose the dead blond's wallet. Then he slowly walked toward the smaller man and repeated the process. He struggled to reclaim the thrown blade, his hands clumsy, but finally pulled it clear. Dumbly, he stood there with a blade in each hand, one clean, one still streaked with blood.

The two others started to ride across the clay of the street toward Nylan. He squinted, backed up, and fumbled the clean blade into the waist scabbard as the two riders slowly spread, as if to flank him.

Behind the smith, Ayrlyn set Weryl by her feet and drew the blade from her right scabbard, stepping into the street past the boy.

"Stop!" screamed the gray-haired woman who dashed into the street in front of the two Lornians. "You'll get killed, just like Gustor and Buil did. They're the black angels! Don't you see?"

Nylan waited, blinking through intermittent vision, trying to see better, breathing heavily, but not daring to drop out of reflex boost.

"The angel didn't attack him," insisted the gray-haired woman. "He pushed aside Gustor's blade, two or three times. He said he was a traveler. They got a child, and Gustor went for a blade."

The brown-haired man reined up, nearly on top of the woman. "Jenny-leu . . . you're Gustor's cousin, and you stick up for those . . . always knew you were a woman-lover."

"Wister, I be forgiving that this time. I never want to hear it again. Understand?"

Surprisingly, the rider lowered his head.

"I be no idiot, either. I know one thing. They never attack first. You attack, and they be killing you. You see, Wister, how fast he moved."

Nylan hoped that belief in angels never attacking first, but being deadly, spread far and wide. He still gripped the blade—ready to throw it, if necessary, although he doubted that he'd be able to function, let alone move, if he had to kill another Lornian.

Jennyleu and Wister stared at Nylan, but his eyes went to the second horseman. The other had reined up also.

"See," Jennyleu finally said. "A man and a woman and their child, and Gustor's dead. If someone went for you and your kid, wouldn't you stop 'em?"

Wister lowered the blade, smaller than Gustor's but still nearly twice the length of the shortswords Nylan had used, and looked toward the smith. "You done, angel?"

"I never wanted to fight. All I wanted was to buy some cheese for my son." He swallowed. "I could have held off the first man, without hurting him, for a while, but not two at once."

"Idiots!" snorted Jennyleu. "Hotheads! A man wants to buy cheese, and you four darkness-near go off getting yourselves killed."

Wister kept looking at his mount's mane, and the fourth rider eased his mount back toward the cooper's. The cooper stood by the barrel, eyes wide, wooden mallet in hand.

After glancing at Ayrlyn and Weryl, Nylan fumbled out the rag and cleaned the blade before sheathing it. Wister and the other rider sheathed theirs slowly. Ayrlyn did not, but no one said anything. Then Nylan bent and slowly lifted the blond man and carried the body across the street, draping it over the man's saddle. Then he did the same for the smaller man. His eyes burned, and so did his shoulder. He hadn't wanted to kill anyone.

"See that. He picked up Gustor like he was a baby," murmured Jennyleu to Wister. She turned to Nylan. "All you angels that strong?"

"He's a smith," answered Ayrlyn. Her eyes flicked to Nylan's left shoulder.

The smith shook his head.

"Glare!" snapped the woman. "Not only . . . never you mind. Wister, take 'em home to Furste, and tell him that I don't want to see any of his kin in town for a while. Not until he's done some thinking."

"Tomorrow's market day."

"We won't sell to any of you—not tomorrow."

After the four horses—two bearing riders and two bearing bodies—trudged east out of Henspa, Nylan crossed the street again, Ayrlyn at his side.

"I'm sorry," he said to Jennyleu. "I didn't mean to cause trouble. I'm glad you were here."

"I can't say as I be so glad you are here, angel, but fair is fair. I saw you trying not to fight, and I saw Gustor not listening, and then that sneak brother of his. Weren't they cousins I'd sent 'em to darkness long ago."

"Who are you?" asked Ayrlyn. "Why . . . ?"

"Me? Why'd they listen to an old lady? Oh . . . I figured out a way to card wool faster, long time back, me and Vernt did, but Vernt died, and I had to do it by myself—three young-uns, you know. One thing led to another. Own half the Black Bull now. My boy Essin owns the other half."

"We were looking for a good meal," Nylan said. "We have some coins."

"Bull's better 'n most, do say so myself. I'll go over with you."

"There won't be any trouble?" Ayrlyn glanced after the vanished riders.

"Furste's Vernt's little brother. He'll fume, and he'll call me names, but Essin'd take him apart if I couldn't. Don't you worry."

"Daaaa!" exclaimed Weryl, extending a chubby fist.

"Fine boy." Jennyleu nodded. "Be bigger than you, I'd wager."

"I think so." Nylan grinned sheepishly. "He already kicks hard."

"Tell you what. You eat at the Bull. You stay there tonight, and go to the chandler's tomorrow."

Ayrlyn gave the slightest of nods to Nylan, and he answered. "We'd be happy to. Sleeping on a bedroll gets tiring."

"No pests in the rooms, either," Jennyleu added. "Bring your mounts."

The two angels untied their mounts and the gray and followed the matriarch, first to the inn stable, and then, packs over their arms, to the Black Bull.

A tall mahogany-haired man with a matching beard met them at the recently painted white door. Nylan noted that the polished plank floors had been recently swept, perhaps even mopped.

"Essin, these are travelers, like any others. Treat 'em right," Jennyleu announced.

Nylan glanced up at Essin. The young giant would have overtopped Gerlich by a head. No wonder Jennyleu said Essin had no troubles with people.

"Pleased to meet you, angels." The innkeeper grinned.

"Saw the last of that fight." He shook his head at Nylan. "Any fool could tell you were trying not to hurt him. Then that little sneak Buil messed it all up. He ever did. I always said he'd get Gustor in big trouble." A rumbling cough followed. "You can have the big room for the regular."

"How much is regular?" asked Ayrlyn.

"Four coppers for the two."

The flame-haired angel extracted the coppers. "What about the stable?"

"Comes with the room, 'less you want grain instead of hay. A copper more for each mount—that's all the grain they can eat."

Ayrlyn handed over three more coppers. "They've carried us a long ways."

"Good to see folks who understand." Essin palmed the coins. "Stew comes with the room. Brew or jack's extra. Be serving pretty near after you get your gear stowed. You can carry your blades in the public room, but no bare steel, 'cepting an eating dagger." The big young man gestured, and a small girl scurried over. "Lessa, these are angels. They get the big front corner room."

"Sers—you are warriors?" asked the girl, who barely reached Nylan's chest.

"Yes," Ayrlyn answered.

"Good. I want to bear a blade when I'm bigger." She headed up the wooden stairs as if she expected them to follow.

Ayrlyn smiled and headed up the steps. After a moment, Nylan shifted his grip on Weryl, who grabbed for the brass lamp in a wall sconce, and followed.

After going down a short wide hall, Lessa opened a solid wooden door, oiled, rather than painted.

Nylan was impressed—the room had two windows and a wide bed with a coverlet, plus a table with a pitcher and wash basin, and a chamber pot in the corner. The windows were not glazed, but bore both solid outer shutters and louvered inner shutters. There was a small lamp on the wash table. "This is nice."

"My favorite," said Lessa. "You can bolt the door, but you don't need to. No one ever does anything bad here."

Nylan kept from grinning at the serious tone. "Thank you."

"Someday, I want to use a blade like yours." Lessa bowed slightly, then slipped out.

"We were lucky," Ayrlyn said quietly. "I was lucky here before, and I'm beginning to understand why."

"Because Jennyleu runs this town?"

"It looks that way, doesn't it?"

"I told you that not all women in Candar were oppressed," Nylan said.

"Not all—but too many. Places like this are rare."

Nylan set the saddlebags in the corner, along with the bag containing Weryl's clothes. "I'm hungry."

"So am I." Her face darkened. "Did you have to dive into the dust? Your shoulder isn't that well."

"I wasn't thinking about that. I just didn't want another blade touching me."

"Nylan—"

"What else was I supposed to do?"

"Let me check it."

Nylan set Weryl on the floor and slipped off the carrypak harness, waiting as Ayrlyn lifted his shirt. Her fingers were cool and precise on his skin.

"Everything you've done has spread the stitches . . . but there's no infection. That's probably because you can use the order fields now that you're stronger. You will have a darkness-huge scar there, to match the stitching in the shirt." She let his shirt fall. "Now, I'd like to get some of the dust off."

"After you, dear." The engineer took Weryl, and Ayrlyn poured water into the wash bowl. One-handed, he opened the two wallets. One had two silvers and a handful of coppers, the second a silver and four coppers.

"That's a lot for here," observed Ayrlyn.

Did that mean that he'd killed two of the wealthier young men in town? Nylan worried. Or that people carried more of their assets in a low-tech culture? He didn't know.

When they had both washed, and washed Weryl, they started out the door.

"Do you think things will be safe?" asked Nylan.

"Not everywhere . . . but here." Ayrlyn nodded toward the floor below.

At her expression, Nylan grinned. He couldn't imagine many travelers taking on Essin—in anything.

The smell of cooking, not grease, struck Nylan even before his boots touched the bottom step of the stairs. He followed his eyes and nose to his left and through open double doors into the public room.

There were no more than a half dozen tables, with four simple dowel-backed chairs around each square wooden table. Three tables were taken—one by a single man in dark brown leathers and a beard nearly as dark, one by three older men with only mugs before them, and one by two narrow-faced men.

Ayrlyn and Nylan took the remaining corner table, and were barely seated when a round-faced woman appeared.

"Sers . . . the stew comes with the room. A copper extra for chops, but forgo them tonight. Greenjuice is one, and brew or jack two." She raised her eyebrows.

"Stew, and juice," said Ayrlyn.

"The same," Nylan added, "but could I have a wedge of cheese, a small one for my son?"

"A small one . . . that be no problem. Gies would not charge for that, not with the juice. Two coppers, then."

Nylan fumbled out the coins.

"Be back with the juice." She scurried past the table with the three older men, and refilled all three mugs from the pitcher she bore, almost without stopping.

Before Nylan had finished looking around the room, the server was back with two large mugs.

"There." She was off again, after flashing a quick smile at Weryl, whose eyes followed her back toward the kitchen.

Nylan sipped the juice. "Good."

Two narrow-faced men sat at the other corner table. The

dark-haired one nodded toward the angels, and Nylan tried to catch the gist of the conversation.

". . . angel travelers, Jennyleu said . . . heard about Gustor . . ."

". . . good riddance . . . scattered Lyswer's flock last summer . . . for fun . . ."

". . . got a child . . . silverhair's a man . . . picked up Gustor's body like a dead dog . . . said he's a smith . . ."

". . . wonder . . . those blades . . ."

". . . not touch one myself . . ."

". . . regents made peace . . ."

". . . wouldn't you . . . old holders the problem . . . couldn't care . . ."

As the talk drifted toward other matters, Nylan took a sip of the cold greenjuice, happy for anything besides water and bitter tea.

"Here you be!" The round-faced serving girl deposited two large bowls, a loaf of bread, and a long thin wedge of cheese—and no utensils.

"Thank you."

The woman looked at Weryl. "Boy or girl?"

"Boy," the two answered together.

"Daaaa . . ." said Weryl, from Nylan's lap.

"Good-looking. Wager he be making hearts trip when he be grown."

"I hope he doesn't make a habit of it," said Ayrlyn.

Nylan laughed softly at her tone.

With a smile, the server was gone, and Nylan dug his spoon from his small belt pouch. Ayrlyn retrieved hers as well.

Nylan ate the big bowl of stew slowly, offering small spoonfuls to Weryl, interspersed with small bits of the biscuit and bits of the cheese the serving girl had brought.

"Good," Ayrlyn affirmed. "Almost as good as Blynnal's."

Nylan wondered how the pregnant cook happened to be getting along, even as he spooned more stew into Weryl's mouth. Then, he concentrated on feeding Weryl. He had to put aside the past and look to the future, even if he didn't know where it led.

XXXI

Jennyleu said we should try the chandlery this morning." Ayrlyn tied her mount to the stone post and then tethered the gray gelding.

"People do listen to her." Nylan gave a short laugh as he dismounted and tethered the mare, and then the gray. With Weryl in the carrypak, he stepped into the chandlery warily. Ayrlyn followed.

Unlike the inn, the trading establishment smelled faintly musty, of oil and old leather. Despite the large glazed front window, the room seemed dim. A row of leather goods lay on a long wooden trestle centered on the left wall.

A square-faced woman in faded blue stood by the counter at the rear. "You two must be the angels. Jennyleu said you would be seeking travel food, and cheese. That be in the case here."

"Thank you." Nylan stepped past the neatly arranged leather riding gear, noting a child's saddle, a pair of saddlebags so large than only a plow horse could have borne them, a folded square of what seemed to be oiled leather—a lowtech waterproof?

"I be Gerleu, and my consort is Jersen. Jennyleu said it might be best were I here for you."

"Gerleu? Does that mean you're related?" Nylan asked as he neared the brunette and the case beside her.

"We're all related, somewise. Jersen's a good man, but Jennyleu said he had to answer to the other menfolk. Store's from my pa, and I got the right to serve who I please. I'm pleased to serve angels. Might change some things." She smiled at Nylan. "Does me good to see a man carry a child. Jersen did, but not when folks watched." Her head turned toward the curtain to her right, which fluttered, although there was no wind. "That be you, Marleu? Come right on out. The angels are peaceable."

A girl with brown hair and wide brown eyes eased from behind the brown curtain and sidled toward Gerleu. Marleu's eyes darted over Nylan to Ayrlyn, and widened as she took in the flame-red hair.

Nylan smiled and slipped to the cheese case. All the cheeses were in cloth bags. He opened one, and found a layer of wax around the square lump.

"The top line—that's yellow brick. The next is white brick. The white is tastier, but the yellow lasts longer than any journey anyone in his right mind would take."

"How much?" asked Nylan.

"The white runs around three coppers for two, the yellow a copper each." Gerleu put an arm around her daughter, whose head barely reached past her waist, but who still looked at Ayrlyn.

The healer smiled gently. "We're just people, Marleu. It is Marleu, isn't it?"

The girl nodded solemnly. She opened her mouth, then closed it.

"I can't guess what you wanted to say." Ayrlyn's voice was soft. "Did you want to know about the Roof of the World?"

"It's . . . cold . . ."

"Very cold."

"Are . . . you . . . all women?"

Ayrlyn inclined her head toward Nylan. "Nylan is a man. He is a smith. The ship that brought us from the heavens had more women, but that was an accident. It could have had more men than women."

"Don't see men without beards here," observed Gerleu.

"Some of the other men had beards," Nylan said, pulling out four white cheese bags and two yellow. "I get too hot with a beard, and my skin itches, especially around the forge."

"Knew a smith like that years ago. Kerler . . . I think," said the chandler.

The smith paused before a glass jar and looked at Gerleu.

"Travel biscuits. Six for a copper."

"Four coppers' worth, then." Nylan thought they might be good for Weryl's emerging teeth, and they had gathered nearly a gold and a half in silvers and coppers from the bandits' purses, and from the two who had attacked the afternoon before.

Gerleu extracted two dozen of the biscuits and replaced the lid, then tied the biscuits into a worn scrap of cloth.

"You have two blades," said Marleu.

"That's so we can throw one if we have to, and still have one to defend ourselves."

"Jennyleu said your fellow threw his right through Buil . . . that so?"

Ayrlyn glanced at Marleu, then nodded. "He doesn't like to fight, but he had to."

"That's what she said." Gerleu shook her head. "Wish more men were like that. You be fortunate."

Nylan stepped up beside Ayrlyn and set the cheese on the counter, then quickly caught Weryl's hands before the boy grabbed at one of the short daggers laid out there. "Those are too sharp for you."

"Silver and two coppers," noted the chandler.

Nylan extracted three coins. He almost felt guilty that killing two men had more than paid for their stay in Henspa, but no one had complained about their taking the dead men's wallets, as though it were the accepted practice in Lornth. He still didn't feel guilty about the bandits.

Outside, under the clear green-blue sky and the sun that promised a hot day for travel, Nylan slipped the cheese into Weryl's food pack, now fastened to the docile gray, then all but one of the travel biscuits, which he tucked into his shirt pocket, adjusting the fabric so that neither the carrypak nor the shoulder harness for his second blade crushed it, although he had some doubts that anything could dent the biscuit.

Across the street, the cooper worked on another barrel, and two dogs trotted past the statue. The yellow dog paused and anointed the corner of the low wall before following the black and white mongrel eastward and down the street.

"Quiet," Nylan said as he guided the mare toward the inn . . . and the road that led out of Henspa.

"Most places are in the morning."

From the porch of the inn, broom in hand, Lessa waved.

Ayrlyn and Nylan waved back.

For a time, they rode without speaking toward the north-west end of the town, seeing only a handful of people—a woman struggling with laundry in two wooden tubs, a carter with barrels of something driving his wagon past them toward the square, and two children weeding a garden.

"Is it just male dominance," mused the healer, "that makes this place the way it is?"

Nylan wondered if he should even think about answering.

She turned in the saddle. "Well? You have that look that says you've thought about it, and you aren't about to answer unless someone hammers it out of you."

Nylan looked down sheepishly. Weryl looked up with a grin of gums and teeth.

"Out with it. I'm not like Ryba, and I won't let you hide your thoughts until we can't talk at all."

"Well . . ." Nylan swallowed. "Look at Henspa. One woman changed the town. She's remarkable, but I'd say that you, Ryba, Istril, Huldran, probably others from the *Winter-lance,* might have acted the same way. The culture here sup-presses women, but do they have to accept that degree of suppression?"

"That's a good question." Ayrlyn was silent as they rode past a cot where a woman in tattered gray trousers and a faded brown shirt hoed a garden, bearing a child in a backpack. "Then, look at how many women made for Westwind."

Nylan rubbed his chin, reminded again that he was still being taken for a woman from a distance because he had no beard. "Henspa's more isolated. Do you think that . . ." He wasn't quite sure what he thought.

"Oppression is usually less in any culture where people can leave. Maybe there's something we don't know. Maybe, ex-cept in places like Henspa, near the borders, there wasn't anywhere to go."

"Maybe . . ." There was something more, Nylan knew, but he couldn't get his scattered thoughts to focus.

They neared the northwest end of Henspa, where the dwellings thinned out, and then gave way to recently tilled fields on the downhill side of the road, and meadows interspersed with woodlots on the right side.

By a house where a thin line of smoke streamed from the chimney, a youth in brown trousers and a patched shirt stood beside a wood pile, ax in hand. His eyes took in the angels, and their hair, and he looked away, then spat on the ground.

"You see a lot of that. At least, I did before," said Ayrlyn.

"You think we ought to wear hats, or caps, like you did trading?" Nylan asked. "It's the hair." Absently, he let Weryl play with the fingers on his free hand.

Ayrlyn frowned, then shook her head. "I don't think so. It's not the same as trading. People would say we were trying to hide something."

Nylan glanced at Weryl. "When our hair-color sets people off—"

"That's just here. Once we get farther away from Westwind, they'll have heard of the angels, but I don't think the hair will be a problem."

Nylan wondered, but he wasn't going to argue with Ayrlyn's feelings. She was usually right, and she had much more experience in traveling Lornth than he did.

He fingered his chin, then swallowed. "Do you think that the bandits attacked because they thought we were both women, and maybe I was an old woman?"

"That would make sense. Unfortunately." Ayrlyn looked at the road ahead. "There are a lot of stereotypes in this culture, more than you'd expect to find, and I don't know why."

"Don't most low-tech cultures have stereotypes?"

"Not this many." Ayrlyn shook her head. "And it doesn't fit an open agrarian society, which is pretty much what Lornth is. So we're missing something, and that bothers me."

Nylan nodded. Missing anything else bothered him, too. It bothered him a lot, because that meant more problems down the road, and the last thing they needed was another set of problems, especially when he didn't know how long they'd be traveling or where they'd end up.

XXXII

WHITE PUFFY CLOUDS, intermittently spaced, scudded out of the north and across the green-blue sky, occasionally obscuring the mid-morning sun, but not enough to keep Nylan from perspiring.

The road had carried them farther westward, and it had been more than two days since they had left the hills covered with ironwoods that had flanked the eastern side of the road. At least, so far they hadn't seen any more ironwoods. A kay to the west of the road that generally wound northward was a line of trees that Nylan suspected followed a river. He blotted his forehead as the mare carried him over a low rise that overlooked a wide valley filled largely with cultivated fields.

On the right side of the road was a low stone pedestal bearing a kaystone. The ornate Anglorat lettering, surrounded by a chiseled frieze of grain sheaves, declared *Duevek*.

"Sculpted kaystones, now?" asked Nylan.

"Oooo . . ." murmured Weryl, drooling whitish fragments of travel biscuit across the front of the carrypak. Nylan was glad that Istril had sewed the pack from shipsuit synthetics, because it washed easily and dried quickly—both qualities a necessity to keep it from reeking.

Beyond the kaystone the road widened enough so that it would carry two wagons abreast, although it remained rutted and packed clay.

"Prosperous-looking town," Nylan said.

"They're the dangerous ones." Ayrlyn's eyes flicked ahead. On the low hillside on the northeast side of the town was a complex of white-walled buildings that resembled a Neorat villa—not that Nylan had ever seen one except on a screen.

"That has to be the local lord's place—or whatever they call them."

"Lords or holders—they're addressed as 'lord' or 'ser,' " said Ayrlyn.

Weryl waved a hand, and Nylan broke off another corner of the hard travel biscuit.

"You've given him a lot of biscuits."

"Not that much. They expand in his mouth, and he spits out about half. They keep him awake and happy. That means we get to sleep more—or haven't you noticed?"

"I've noticed him sleeping more at night. That doesn't go for his father, the lecherous cad." She grinned as she spoke.

"I haven't heard any complaints."

"Who would listen?"

Nylan tried not to grin. Best not to continue that conversation.

At the base of the hill, before entering Duevek proper, they rode past a white-plastered house with a red tile roof and a matching barn or stable. In the corral beside the stable were what looked to be hogs.

"Definitely prosperous," Nylan said.

Dark splotches in the road showed where potholes had been filled, and even the smaller cots had been recently painted or plastered.

Nylan absently provided the water bottle to Weryl as the mare carried them toward the square ahead—the first true square Nylan had seen, with buildings on all four sides around a walled section of green grass and bushes from the center of which rose a statue of an armed man on a horse brandishing a hand-and-a-half blade.

A green-framed sign of a huge golden cat hung from a green bracket outside the painted white inn. Unlike the first inn Nylan had seen—Essin's Black Bull—this sign had both the image and the name, if in old Anglorat, painted below in crisp green letters.

As they rode into the square proper, a thin man in a dark-green tunic peered out from the doorway of what appeared to be a cabinetmaker's shop. His eyes lighted first on Ayrlyn, and then upon Nylan. Abruptly, he stepped out and shut the door—quietly—and scurried down the brick walk to the next structure, a narrow building that featured a basket and a half-keg over the door. In turn, that door shut, and three figures—one of them the man in the green—fanned out across the square.

Three serving women darted from the Golden Cat and quickly fastened all the ground-level, dark green shutters before they disappeared back behind the firmly shut and iron-barred wooden door. Two women in brown bearing heavy baskets suddenly turned and ran back down a side street, leaving both baskets on the porch of the cooper's shop.

"Keep riding," said Ayrlyn.

"Are they always this friendly?" asked the smith.

"This is the polite way," said Ayrlyn. "Be thankful you don't have people with iron implements and torches marching toward you."

"Oh."

Out of the stable by the Golden Cat burst a rider who spurred his mount northward on the road ahead of the two angels. The rider never looked back, but rode as though a troop of angel lancers were chasing him.

"That's not good," Ayrlyn said. "Let's move a bit faster."

Nylan urged the mare to a fast walk, wondering why a single rider was not good after a whole town declared its rejection of them.

As the two rode out of the square, watching as doors and shutters closed as or before they passed, Nylan glanced to the sky as darkness fell across the road and left them in shadow. Were the clouds getting thicker?

"Was it like this last year?" he asked.

"Yes. In about half the towns."

Nylan patted Weryl's leg gently.

By the time they reached the end of the town proper, every shutter was closed, and the sun had come out again.

Ahead and on the right side of the road lay the villa.

Weryl squirmed in the carrypak, and Nylan smelled a certain familiar odor. Not now. Then he shrugged. Weryl didn't care if his timing was inconvenient.

Along the lane that led up to the Neorat villa rode nine men on horseback, all in brown. The squad rode through the arched gate and drew up in a single line, with one man in front.

"What now?" Nylan glanced at the healer.

"What do you think?"

"Keep riding. Ignore them. If they're serious they could ride us down anyway. Their mounts are fresh." Nylan's mouth felt dry, and he could smell both dust and his own sweat.

"We could string them out."

"That's plan B—if they attack," suggested Nylan. The memory of how awful he'd felt three days earlier in Henspa was still fresh in his mind, and he didn't want to think about the episode with the bandits.

He looked down at Weryl. Ayrlyn was right—he needed a better arrangement for his son.

The squad leader waited as Nylan and Ayrlyn neared the gate. The second mount in the row behind the leader *whuffed* and pawed the hard clay.

Nylan wanted to lick his lips or touch the blade hilt at his waist. He did neither, but kept riding, letting the mare's easy steps carry him toward the waiting armsmen.

"Angels . . . you're not wanted here," announced the blond squad leader, drawing his hand-and-a-half blade from the shoulder harness, but extending it downward until the tip touched the clay.

"We gathered that," said Ayrlyn. "We are not imposing on your lord's hospitality."

"The road is yours, as it is to all travelers," replied the armsman. "Yet, best you remain on the road until you are well clear of Duevek."

"We intend to do so, ser," answered the healer. "And we thank your lord for his respect for the way of the road."

"He respects the way of the road, but not angels who travel it." The armsman added, "You have been warned."

"We have been warned."

Nylan looked at the armsman, and smiled. "Those who would do violence because others are different. Those who would deny welcome to those who seek to treat all equally. Those who reject angels because angels have declared women and men are equal . . . all those also shall be warned." He could feel his eyes flash.

The blond officer started to raise the blade.

Nylan looked evenly at the man as the mare carried him almost abreast of the squad leader. "And any man who raises a blade against an empty-handed angel will die."

After a moment, the big blade dropped.

Nylan looked ahead, but let his senses follow the armsman. He had no desire to be spitted from behind.

None of the armsmen moved.

Not until they were a good half kay farther north along the road did Ayrlyn speak. "That was dangerous, Nylan. These boys are half crazy, and they think women are lower than horse manure."

"I'm just busy getting the word out," Nylan said lightly, trying to settle the slight queasiness in his stomach, and knowing his action had been foolhardy. "They'll remember, and they might even find out what happened in Henspa."

"Nerliat once said that unseen fires flowed from you. They do." She shook her head. "That man won't ever forget what you said. Of course, he may try to kill you on sight if he has an excuse, but he won't forget."

"I hope not." Nylan swallowed. Why was he essentially spreading the gospel of Ryba?

"Because it happens to be right," answered Ayrlyn.

He looked at her. "I didn't say anything."

"You felt it strongly enough that you might as well have. You were wondering why you were spouting the party line of a place that effectively kicked you out."

Nylan looked back over his shoulder, where the dust showed that the riders were returning to the villa. "I don't know which is scarier—that I said what I said, or you know what you know."

Ayrlyn laughed.

After a moment, so did he.

Overhead, the clouds thickened, and a distant roll of thunder announced a coming storm.

XXXIII

THEMPHI WALKED SLOWLY northward along the wall, his white boots gray, each step stirring ashes. Well ahead of him marched the peasants and a detachment of foot, each man bearing a pitch torch, each torch being applied to any trace of green that remained. After the torches came others, with once-sharp axes and mattocks. Behind Themphi followed teams of oxen with knife-edged but deep moldboard plows.

A rider in the green uniform and white sash of a Mirror Lancer rode across the field toward the wall and toward the white wizard.

"Ser wizard!" Jyncka's face was tight and pinched as the Mirror Lancer officer reined up.

Themphi stopped, glanced at the gray smoke that swirled everywhere in thin trails, then rubbed his forehead, trying to ease the throbbing in his temples. Slowly, he turned and looked up at the mounted officer. "Yes?"

"Forestnorth—you had me go there to enlist some of the younger peasants to help with pushing the forest back?"

"Yes," said the white wizard, tiredly. "I did. Do not repeat what I told you. I know what I said." He rubbed his forehead again, leaving ash smudges at his temples.

The officer moistened his lips. "There's no town, not now. Just forest, and the houses are already crumbling. We could not reach the wall. Some of the thickets, brambles now, are chest high."

"The people?" asked the wizard, his voice wooden.

Jyncka shrugged, his eyes going to the yoked oxen that turned the soil behind the white wizard. "There are stun lizards, forest cats, snakes—I lost one lancer. I didn't see any bones. One peasant woman—she was an old crone. I caught her hobbling away—she said that the people fled. They wouldn't fight the forest."

"Send men to ride the entire wall. Make sure they are the type that can remember and report what they have seen."

"The entire wall?"

"The entire wall. All ninety-nine kays of each side. I do not wish to repeat myself." Themphi started to lift his hands again, but stopped. "Take over here. Have them extinguish the torches, and return to Geliendra."

"Ah . . . yes, ser wizard."

"Don't you understand, Jyncka? We have not cleared an area half the size of Forestnorth, and we have a wizard and an apprentice, and fourscore men with torches and axes and mattocks and oxen and plows." The wizard turned. "Fissar!"

The thin youth in white tunic and trousers smeared with dark gray scurried up. "Ser?"

"Get our mounts."

"Yes, ser."

Themphi looked back to Jyncka. "I want a report on how much the forest has expanded."

"Would it not be faster—?"

"For me to use a glass?" Themphi laughed. "First, I am exhausted. Second, it takes time and energy to scree every cubit of the wall. I will use the glass once I have the reports from your men. Once I have regained some strength. Successful use of the white forces requires planning, not just spewing out power mindlessly. Some . . . even in power . . . have great difficulty understanding that." He walked slowly away from the cracking stones of the white wall toward the distant corner of the field where Fissar was untethering two mounts.

After a moment, Jyncka urged the horse forward, toward the torches.

XXXIV

NYLAN GLANCED AT the winding road that followed the eastern bank of the river and that looked almost identical to innumerable other stretches of winding road between the low hills of Lornth and along the river—or it would have looked similar except for the misting rain.

He blotted the combination of sweat and rain off his forehead and peered through the falling water. "I don't see any way stations, and our reception in most of the towns hasn't been the warmest."

"The weather's been good, at least for most of the time."

"Except for the first hamlet, and that other afternoon."

"Don't get picky with me, almighty smith."

"Sorry."

"Waaaaa . . . waa-daaa-daa!" said Weryl firmly. His silver hair was plastered to his skull, and he had squirmed almost continuously in the carrypak since the rain had drifted over the river from the northwest.

"There's a larger dwelling ahead, below that second rise, and some outbuildings. Maybe we can pay to get a shed or something over our heads."

"If they don't slam the shutters in our face." Nylan paused. "Are you still sure about this feeling you had? About Lornth being a better place?"

"I still have it." Ayrlyn wiped moisture away from her own face.

"I wouldn't want to be any place that you had a bad feeling about."

"Thank you, ser engineer."

Nylan winced. "Sorry."

"You should be. Again."

The chestnut whuffed and shook her head, sending more droplets across both Nylan and Weryl.

"Noooooooooo . . ." said Weryl, waving his hands, and wiggling his legs, almost drumming them on the damp leather of the saddle.

"I don't care about child psychology," said Ayrlyn. "He knows what 'no' means."

Nylan had the feeling she was right . . . perhaps about too many things.

They rode downhill and then back up the low rise to the holding, centered on a plaster-sided house that had once been white, but now appeared gray. A line of gray smoke swirled from the stone chimney.

"Hello . . . the house!" called Nylan.

"Hello the house?" asked Ayrlyn.

"What else could you say? Welcome, some angels?" Nylan shifted his weight in the saddle, wondering just how chafed he was going to be from riding in damp trousers.

A man with a red and gray beard opened the door and stepped onto the narrow porch. The rain rolling off the roof put a thin curtain of water between him and the angels.

"What ye be wanting?" His eyes went to Ayrlyn, then to Weryl. "Wet travel for a child."

"We had hoped you might have a dry place where we could stay," said Nylan.

"I be no inn," said the man. "Herder in a hard land."

"We're not asking for charity," Nylan said. "Nor even that you open your house—just a dry shed."

The man shrugged, then looked at Nylan intently. "You one of those angels?"

"I've been called that, but I'm a man who's had to travel with his son, and we're wet. I can offer you some coppers for a dry place—a shed, a barn."

"I don't know." The herder looked at Weryl, who looked back, somber-faced. "I suppose you would not harm the hay shed, and you could put the mounts in the animal shed. They be not nipping, do they?"

"They never have yet."

"Fine." The red-bearded herder looked at Weryl again.

"You get settled, and you can pay as you think is fit. A moment—need to get a waterproof."

When he ducked back into the house, Ayrlyn looked at Nylan. The healer looked back, raising her eyebrows.

The smith shrugged.

"Follow me." The herder stepped down onto the damp ground and into the rain. The angels followed him around the dwelling to a narrow structure, unpainted wood darkened by the dampness. The herder opened the door, little more than three planks fastened to two boards. "Hay shed." He pointed to a three-walled shed with a slanted roof. "Animals there. Plenty of room. Flock's up in the lower pasture. Like the rain."

Nylan dismounted and fumbled out three coppers. "Thank you."

The herder took the coins. "Well is there." He pointed to the stones mortared into a circular form midway between his house and the hay shed. Then, with a quick look at Weryl, he nodded, turned, and trudged back through the rain, now falling even more heavily.

Both Nylan and Ayrlyn were soaked by the time they had unsaddled the mounts and carried their gear, and Weryl, to the hay shed. The shed was still half filled with hay, stacked in small circular bales bound with straw braids. Dust swirled around them in the gusting winds that entered with them, despite the dampness of the air.

"At least, it has plank floors. And it's dry." Ayrlyn closed the plank door, leaving them in the gloom that was not too dark for Ayrlyn, nor any bother for Nylan, not with his night vision.

"Lots of splinters," added Nylan, pulling one from his finger. "Be careful when you put down things." He rubbed his nose, once, twice, then sneezed.

"Daaa—daaa!" Weryl windmilled his arms in response to the sneeze.

"You can drape the bedrolls over that beam there for a while. It's dry enough."

Nylan rubbed his nose again, this time holding back the sneeze, and then extracted Weryl from the carrypak, and then his son from soaking wet clothes. Once he had Weryl in a dry outfit, he straightened and looked to the bedrolls.

"I'll get some water, and hope it's not too bad. Trying to separate the chaos from it—I get tired." Ayrlyn wiped more water from her forehead as she looked at the door, almost as if she dreaded going into the rain.

Weryl sat in a pile of hay, and tried to chew on one of the pale yellow-brown stalks.

As he eased the second bedroll over the thick timber, Nylan looked from Ayrlyn to his son. "I'll get the water. I can do that. It's better than getting sick. You watch our friend, and make sure he doesn't eat too much straw."

The healer smiled faintly. "I need to get out of these clothes."

Nylan smiled. "I hope you do."

"You're impossible. You were impossible when you were wounded."

"I'll get the water." He eased open the door and hurried toward the well. Each impact of his boots sent mud flying.

After lifting the bucket, he took a deep breath and concentrated, trying to use the dark lines of force to separate out the unseen reddish-whiteness that was chaos—or infection—and trying not to think about the apparent engineering impossibility of what he did.

"Just think about different laws . . . . different laws, that's all."

The water didn't look that different when he poured it into the two bottles, except marginally clearer.

He headed back to the hay shed, closing the door behind him and then setting both water bottles on the plank floor. "The water wasn't too bad."

"Good." Ayrlyn, wearing only a dry shirt extracted from her pack, looked out the door before closing it. "It's raining hard."

"I'd say so." Nylan wiped water from his hair and face, then stripped off his shirt and walked to the corner where he wrung out a stream of liquid. Then he hung his shirt next to Ayrlyn's damp clothes. He pulled off his boots and did the same with the rest of his clothing, then extracted a shirt and trousers that were only marginally damp.

"Nice figure," commented Ayrlyn.

"I notice you changed while I was getting water. That wasn't fair."

"Some things aren't." Ayrlyn spread some straw on the planks beside Weryl and eased herself down, very carefully.

Weryl reached for her, and she picked him up. "In a moment. Daddy will get out the food."

Nylan pulled on the trousers. Then he emptied the food pack, taking out the last section of the yellow brick cheese that left an aftertaste of goats or . . . something, four travel biscuits, and three strips of dried venison. "Not much left to eat." He sat on the straw between Weryl and Ayrlyn. "We need more food."

"We should reach Lornth tomorrow."

"Will anyone sell us food?" He broke off a section of biscuit and handed it to the silver-haired boy.

"I don't know. We'll have to see." Ayrlyn sliced two thin slivers of the yellow cheese and handed one to Weryl, the second to Nylan. She cut another for herself.

"Tomorrow, let's see if we can buy anything from the herder. All he can say is no."

"He won't if he can spare it," Ayrlyn prophesied. "Hard coin is too hard to come by. It always is for agricultural types."

"I hope you're right."

They ate silently for a time. After that, in between chasing Weryl around the hay shed, Nylan packed away the remnants, remnants that were getting slimmer and slimmer. He paused. "It's still raining."

"I'm not tired . . . and neither is our little friend."

"Why don't you sing something," Nylan suggested, "something that you'd like."

"Do you think our friend would stand still long enough?"

"He's tired, but not sleepy."

"I'll try." Ayrlyn walked over to the lutar case and extracted the instrument before sitting on one of the hay bales.

Nylan picked up Weryl and sat on another bale across from her.

At the first sound of her fingers tuning, Weryl's eyes flicked toward the singer. "Ooooo . . ."

"I'm not that good, Weryl, but I appreciate the flattery." Her fingers crossed the strings. "How about something cheerful?"

"Fine with me," Nylan said, "and with Weryl, I'd guess."

Ayrlyn cleared her throat and began.

> *"When I was single, I looked at the skies.*
> *Now I've a consort, I listen to lies,*
> *lies about horses that speak in the darks,*
> *lies about cats and theories of quarks . . ."*

"Aaaalaaan . . . daa, daaa," said Weryl as she finished the tune.

"I think that translates as 'more.' " Nylan laughed.

"Well . . . we'll give him a song about you."

"Not that one."

"Why not?"

"It's awful."

"You'll just have to get used to it." The healer grinned in the gloom, and her flame hair glittered with a light of its own.

> *"Oh, Nylan was a smith, and a mighty mage was he.*
> *With lightning hammer and an anvil of night forged he,*
> *From the Westhorns tall came the blades and bows of the night,*
> *Their lightning edges gave the angels forever the height . . .*
>
> *"Oh, Nylan was a mage, and a mighty smith was he.*
> *With rock from the heights and a lightning blade built he.*
> *On the Westhorns tall stands a tower of blackest stone,*
> *And it holds back the winter's snows and storms all alone. . . ."*

"All right, all right," said Nylan as he picked up Weryl and began to rock the child. "Something softer?"

"You don't mind the Sybran song?"

He shook his head.

> *"When the snow drops on the stone*
> *When the wind song's all alone*
> *When the ice swords form in twain,*
> *Sing of the hearths where we've lain . . ."*

Midway through the second stanza, Weryl lurched in Nylan's arms, his fingers grasping, and for a moment, Nylan saw the chubby fingers actually touch the silvered note that hung in the gloom.

The smith blinked, and only silvered dust motes shimmered in the air—and vanished.

The child was oddly silent, an enigmatic smile across his lips.

Ayrlyn glanced toward Nylan. "He *saw* the notes."

"We saw the notes. Because of him?"

She shook her head. "Did we ever look?"

The question bothered Nylan. Where else had he failed to look? How much else was there that he had not seen because he had not realized it could be possible?

Ayrlyn's fingers flicked across the strings, and Weryl settled back as Nylan rocked him and the singer hummed gently.

Outside, the rain drummed on the shed roof.

XXXV

To THE LEFT of the highway, to the north beyond the flatter grasslands where grazed the herds of the Lord of Cyador, lay the grass hills, green enough in the winter, but brown by late spring, and sere and dusty by summer.

At times, Majer Piataphi could glimpse those hills, hills similar to those through which he must lead his force once they reached the terminus of the Great North Highway in Syadtar on the next day.

The wind that ruffled his hair was warm and far drier than the moist breezes that made Cyad and Fyrad so comfortable. He stood in the white saddle to stretch his legs and looked ahead to the white and green banners of the van.

A single steamwagon passed, its trailers loaded with sealed

barrels, hugging the north shoulder of the highway, headed west toward distant Cyad.

"I wish we were done and headed in that direction," said Miatorphi. "There's no honor in defeating barbarians."

"We have to defeat them and keep them defeated before we need concern ourselves about honor," answered the majer.

A messenger galloped up. "Majer!"

"What is it?" Piataphi eased his mount around Captain Azarphi's horse.

"Serjeant Funssa—he wants you to know that steamwagon seven is leaking, and that he has no more spare fittings."

"Watch the van, Miatorphi," ordered the majer. "I need to find out what seven's cargo is. They may need to shift things." He turned his mount westward and rode back toward the steamwagons that followed the first three divisions of Mirror Lancers.

"If it's not one thing with those damned wagons . . ." murmured Miatorphi to Azarphi.

"They carry a lot, though."

"When they work. Half the time they don't, and it's getting worse. Fewer of them, too. Once there were hundreds. Now . . . what? They've got a score that really work, and they run them all the time, and even more break down. Give me a good horse team any day."

The two captains looked to the banners that led the Cyadoran force. Neither glanced back to the trails of smoke that marked the steamwagons.

XXXVI

HIGH HAZY CLOUDS swirled slowly across the sky as the three horses plodded along the rutted clay road and northward toward Lornth. Nylan glanced to the east, but the trees on the hills above the scrubby meadow were deciduous, or what passed for it on this world, and they had, he suspected, finally left the thorny iron-woods behind.

"The herder's cheese wasn't bad," the smith said.

"For three coppers, it shouldn't be. The loaf of bread was better, and cheaper."

"We've got plenty of the cheese left."

In the swale to the left of the road, on a bluff overlooking the river were a deserted dwelling and a shed with a half-collapsed roof. Beyond the bluff and river to the west were neatly fenced and tilled plots of ground, regular in outline.

"Definitely on the wrong side of the sky," mused Nylan.

"This side of the river might be better. We haven't gotten the best reception in prosperous areas, and the west side is more prosperous. Even that rider this morning circled around us. He wore purple."

"Purple—that means he's something in Lornth. Some sort of lord or functionary or messenger. He had a sour look in his face. Are they all like that because those that have more dislike change? And we've brought change?"

"It could be, but I really don't know." Ayrlyn stood in her stirrups and peeled her damp trousers away from her body. "Don't laugh."

"I wasn't even thinking of it." Nylan made a show of studying the road, then frowned and glanced down it. "It looks like it barely rained here. The top of the ground is damp, but it's merely wetted the dust, and the hillside ahead looks dry."

"It doesn't rain everywhere."

"Only where we are. It's not as though we have that much in the way of clothing. Those leathers were like iron this morning."

"You didn't have to wear that pair."

"If I didn't, I'd never get into them again."

"Complain, complain," Ayrlyn chided him.

"You were the one just peeling your trousers away from your skin."

"They never dried, and my saddlebags leaked. The other set got even wetter."

"Someone's riding fast." Nylan pointed toward the line of

dust leading from the valley into which the road carried them. Above the crest of the second and lower hill to the right, he could see what appeared to be a stone tower, and the top of several white-faced buildings. "You think that's Lornth?"

"I don't know what else it could be, but I've never been there."

Halfway down the hill, the dust-creating riders appeared over the crest of the next rise, trotting quickly toward the travelers.

"If I didn't know better, I'd say that they were after us."

"That rider in purple this morning?" suggested Ayrlyn.

"A Lornian messenger, you think?" Nylan laughed wryly. "He must have been, and he's reported that two fearsome angels are on their way to assault mighty Lornth."

"You could."

"Not without the laser, and there's nothing left of it."

"I still wonder about how much was the laser, and how much was you."

So did Nylan, but it wasn't exactly the time to get into theoretical order engineering.

Out of the dust came a full squad of armsmen in the dark purple of Lornth, darker than that of Gallos.

"They don't look exactly friendly," Nylan observed, his hands going to one blade and then the other to check their readiness. The bow he left alone, wrapped and tied behind his saddle, because at longer ranges his aim was less than accurate.

"Keep riding," suggested Ayrlyn.

Nylan kept riding, but his eyes measured the armsmen, what looked to be a full squad led by a brown-haired and brown-bearded man with broad shoulders that seemed to burst out of his tunic. He wore no breastplate, and a small round shield remained fastened to his saddle, shielding his right knee.

The Lornians formed a wall across the road, dust settling around the legs of their mounts.

"Halt, angels!"

The angels reined up to avoid riding into the Lornian armsmen.

"With the hair of the sky demons, you must be the dark ones." The armsman's hand lifted as though to draw the huge blade in his shoulder harness. His eyes centered on Nylan.

"We're travelers." Nylan's hand rested on the black blade he had forged so far behind them, but he did not show steel.

"Da!" offered Weryl. "Da!"

Great help, reflected the smith.

"We come to Lornth in peace." On the mare beside Nylan, Ayrlyn's fingers touched the hilt of her blade as well.

The armsman's face relaxed slightly as he surveyed them. "A man and a woman . . . and an infant." He shook his head. "Never let it be said that Tonsar destroyed a family, even one from the heavens."

"Besides," Ayrlyn said quietly, "we are at peace, and both the people of Lornth and those of Westwind have paid dearly for that peace."

"Peace, it may be, but few love the angels," reflected Tonsar. "I am ordered to bring you to Lornth to meet the regents."

"Did the regents offer any message?" asked Nylan.

The burly armsman rolled his eyes. "Come." He turned his horse, and the armsmen of the squad split, as if to let Nylan and Ayrlyn join Tonsar.

Ayrlyn looked at Nylan and rolled her eyes.

"I was just asking," said the smith in a low voice to Ayrlyn, as he urged the mare forward and alongside the squad leader. Ayrlyn rode on Tonsar's other side, the gray trailing. The remaining armsmen eased their mounts behind the three.

They rode nearly a kay before Tonsar spoke. "Many from Lornth died on the Roof of the World."

"That's true," Nylan admitted, spreading his fingers for Weryl to grab, then trying not too hard to jerk away the index finger Weryl had seized. "But we never attacked first, and we had nowhere else to go."

"You could not return to Heaven?"

"No," answered Ayrlyn. "Our ship failed."

"You are angels. Angels," repeated Tonsar, as if that answered everything.

"Our ship was destroyed in crossing the stars, and we were lucky to land on the Roof of the World," Nylan explained. "Few of the angels can live for long where it is lower and hotter. Our worlds are colder."

"Hmmmm . . ." reflected Tonsar. "That be what Kurpat and Jegel said, 'fore they left for the last battle. Jegel—he was wearing heavy leathers and he near froze, and he said the angels were in thin clothes, and they all were sweating like it was high summer in the Grass Hills."

For a time, only the sound of hoofs was heard.

"Be true that most angels cannot live where it is hot, then why are you here?" asked the squad leader.

"I can live where it is warmer," Nylan admitted, "but it is not comfortable. The trader here is the only angel from a warmer place, and the Roof of the World is too chill for her. All the others would suffer greatly if they tried to live in Lornth." Nylan wondered whether he was right in concealing that Ayrlyn was a healer . . . but he hadn't lied.

"Yet many of our women fled to that cold. That I do not understand." Tonsar turned to Ayrlyn. "Can you tell me?"

Nylan was glad Ayrlyn had to explain.

"All who fled to Westwind—the Roof of the World—had been mistreated, often hurt badly, and they had no place else to go."

"A place for women and angels who have no other place—that be odd."

". . . odd indeed . . . for many fled to Lornth from Cyador years past . . ." came a murmur from an armsman who rode behind the three.

Nylan frowned. He didn't like the way Cyador kept coming up, or the business about Cyadoran women fleeing to Lornth. He wasn't getting the most favorable impression of Cyador. Now, the regents of Lornth wanted to meet them. Again, that might be good, and it might be the worst possible situation.

Weryl grabbed the front of the saddle and tugged again.

Nylan disengaged his son's fingers and looked ahead toward Lornth, no more than a fair-sized town from what he could see, then to Ayrlyn.

She smiled enigmatically, and shrugged.

Great insight, thought Nylan. *Great help.*

"Waa-daaa?" asked Weryl.

Nylan eased out the water bottle. Water he could provide.

XXXVII

THE BLACK-BEARDED man stepped into the long room.

From the rocking chair, Zeldyan held up a hand and shook her head, then patted Nesslek on the back as she continued rocking. Fornal closed the door gently, but stood, waiting, shifting his weight from one foot to the other and back again. His eyes were cold as he regarded the boy.

In time, Zeldyan slipped from the chair, carrying the child, and walked through the narrow door into the small adjoining room where she eased her son into his railed bed, then knelt and patted his back. The boy murmured softly, then gave a sigh.

Fornal watched from the doorway, still shifting his weight from one foot to the other.

Finally, Zeldyan stood and walked to the doorway to the adjoining sitting room. After listening for a moment, she closed the door, then crossed the antique Analerian carpet and reseated herself in the rocking chair. Fornal did not sit, but paced to the window.

"You got a message about these angels, and you didn't tell me?" he said, each word said precisely and separately.

"You were out with the lancers. How was I supposed to find you?" asked Zeldyan reasonably. She lifted her goblet and sipped.

"Genglois tells me that you intend to make them welcome. You didn't consult with me or father."

"Father is at Carpa. I sent him a message. I was going to talk to you as soon as I got Nesslek down—if you were back."

"I cannot believe you. You're going to receive them, when they killed your consort?" demanded Fornal. "How will the holders feel?"

"I don't care how they feel. Listening to the holders killed Sillek. Do you know, Fornal, that those women, and their mages or whatever, never attacked anyone first?" She smiled coolly. "Every time they were attacked they destroyed the attackers, but they never attacked. Besides, we have an agreement with them. What do you want me to do—give them real grounds for an attack?"

"You know I would not wish that." He frowned. "But . . . Relyn?"

"Relyn is alive . . . and if he happened to be misled, it wasn't by the angel women."

"There's no sense in starting on that again." Fornal turned to the window. "We can't undo what the Lady Ellindyja did."

"Fornal." She paused. "I think we can use them. The messenger said one is a man, and he looks like the mage Sillek described. The two have a small child."

"That could be deception. After all that has happened, I would be wary of any black angels." Fornal did not leave the window.

"That is possible, dear brother. But why would a mage bring a small angel child—the child has silver hair—into Lornth after he has expended so much effort to create Westwind? There's another thing, too. I talked with Terek's page. He says that the big armsman who led Hissl's attack on the Roof of the World was a male angel. There were only three men that came from Heaven, and Lord Nessil killed one. The second attacked his own folk and was killed, and the third, who has to be the mage, is traveling through Lornth with a consort and a child. What does that tell you?"

"He's going to try to get us to do something." Fornal turned and spread his hands. "How will we know until it's too late?"

"If he is the mage who destroyed three white wizards, why is he here?"

"Should I care, sister dear? Rather we should send them on their way, since we dare not kill them under our . . . agreement."

Zeldyan stood, and her eyes blazed. "If you do not care, Fornal, then you are a bigger fool than Hissl and all of the holders together. You and they are right about one thing. The angels do not like men. They have driven out one of the most powerful mages in Candar, or he has left because he does not wish to remain. We face a renewed Cyador, and we have little enough in the way of resources to withstand the white legions. We had three white wizards. We have none. Would it not be worth something to enlist the support of the mage who destroyed them?"

"My sister, I know you wish the best for Lornth and for Nesslek, but is it wise to bring in a dark angel whose folk have brought us naught but death and grief?"

Zeldyan pursed her lips, and her brows furrowed. "Can it harm us to talk to them? We know so little."

"There is some risk, but, so long as we have cold steel nearby, I would think not. Information is useful . . . if the cost prove not too great."

"Perhaps we can enlist their aid," she mused.

"How do you propose to do that? With your own great wizardry?"

"No. I will use common sense and kindness. At times they work as well as cold steel." She shrugged. "If not, your blade will be near. And Father's."

"What can I say?" Fornal shrugged. "We need armsmen and mercenaries and coins, and you would bring in an angel mage."

"We still need armsmen and coins," Zeldyan said. "But remember that angels also destroyed every small force set against them without magic and against greater numbers. Relyn had twice their number, and whatever his faults, he was a master blade. We need every aid we can employ, and perhaps we can devise some good from what these angels offer. I will not let the unreasoning hatred of the holders destroy Nesslek's future the way it destroyed Sillek's."

"I almost pity this angel mage." Fornal shook his head. "Then wring all you can from them. I do not like it, but . . . as you say, we have few choices." He paused, and added under his breath, "And I have even fewer."

Zeldyan frowned, but only said, "It cannot hurt to try to obtain with kindness what one cannot obtain with force."

In turn, Fornal frowned once more, but momentarily, before he smiled. "My blade will stand behind your efforts, sister dear."

XXXVIII

LORNTH WAS FARTHER than it looked, and larger. The sun broke through the hazy clouds and hung above the rolling hills to the west by the time the angels and their escort descended the last low hill leading into the town.

Like all the towns Nylan had seen in Candar, Lornth was not walled, and the houses went from a few widely spaced on large plots of ground to a point where they were nearly wall to wall, with occasional shops sandwiched between.

Tonsar guided them down the street that the highway had become, a street that pointed toward the tower Nylan had seen from a distance. At a closer glance, Nylan realized that the buildings he had thought were plastered white were a stucco or cement of a pinkish color, so pale as to appear white from a distance. Some few structures were stone, like the tower, a light red stone that resembled granite.

The streets were narrow, wide enough for perhaps three horses abreast, or a single wagon, and an unpleasant aroma rose from the ditch on the right side of the paving stones, a ditch that was an open sewer.

Nylan wrinkled his nose and looked at Ayrlyn.

She shook her head. "No lectures on deaths from poor sanitation."

A puzzled look crossed Tonsar's face. "Lornth is not poor."

"Nylan worries about open waste ditches," Ayrlyn explained.

"The people are required to wash them down every eight-day," said Tonsar. "There is a fine if they do not." He reined up as a cart half-filled with barrels rolled out of an alley, pulled by a single ox, and then slowed as the wheels dropped into the depression of the sewage ditch.

The squad waited as the cart lurched across the waste ditch, flinging dark slime onto the paving stones. Nylan winced, and then shrugged.

At the end of the row of houses was a wider area, with shops on each side and several pushcarts on the paving stones beyond the storefronts. A few handfuls of people, mostly women, turned as the squad rode into the small square.

"You are not exactly the most welcome of visitors," pointed out Tonsar.

"I can hear that." Nylan shifted his weight in the saddle, and studied those who stared at him, but none moved toward him as the party rode through the center of the small square and back into the narrower street.

Less than three hundred cubits farther, the street ended, and they faced an open green area, behind which stood the keep of Lornth. The keep was of the pale pink granite, as was the wall surrounding it, although the wall was low, not more than ten cubits high and only three cubits thick——a barrier more suited to a rural estate than the domain of a lord, Nylan would have thought.

The two heavy wooden gates were bound in iron and stood open, guarded by four armsmen on foot.

Tonsar reined up and nodded to the guards. "The angels to see the regents."

The small thin guard with a halberd of sorts nodded back. "The Regent Zeldyan left word that she would see them in the tower room as soon as they arrived."

Tonsar jerked his head in a quick nod, then urged his mount through the gates. The sound of hoofs echoed from the pale pink paving stones of the courtyard as the riders followed the lead armsman around the north side of the keep or palace.

Nylan noted the relative emptiness of the keep. Only a score or so of armsmen? Four gate guards?

The stables were in the rear of the keep, a separate building with a tile roof and swept clay floors that smelled more of straw and horses than of manure. Several *clucks, brawks,* and *cheeps* indicated chickens were located somewhere nearby, although the smith saw none.

Nylan gratefully dismounted from the mare, stretching his legs and shoulders, then his arms. His left shoulder got stiff more easily than the right. His hand brushed the weathered lintel beam, reminding him that ceilings were low indeed in low-tech cultures.

"You may leave your mounts here in the stable. Your things will be brought to your quarters."

Ayrlyn unfastened the lutar case. "I'll take this. It's an instrument."

"As you wish, angel," Tonsar said with a laugh.

Nylan worried about the metal composite bow, but saying anything would draw more attention, and there was no way the locals could duplicate it. Besides, wrapped in oiled leather, it looked much like any other bow.

Again, those few in the courtyard watched intently as the angels walked back across the stones toward the keep building itself.

The armsman led the three up a set of stone steps and then into what appeared to be an older tower, stopping outside a dark and polished wooden door, guarded by a broad-shouldered man wearing a decorative breastplate and a short-sword. The shorter blade made more sense for an interior guard. Beside him was a page.

"Announce the angels to the regent," requested the armsman.

The page slipped inside the door, but Nylan caught some of the words.

"Lady Zeldyan, the angels . . ."

Almost immediately, the door reopened.

"You may enter," said the page.

"Leave your blades outside the room," noted the guardsman.

"Do all warriors leave their weapons?" asked Nylan.

"If you prefer," answered the guard, "you may lay them on the table inside the door. No one will touch them."

"Thank you," said Nylan. "I'll have to draw the shoulder blade." He looked at Weryl, who looked up sleepily.

"Why . . . oh."

The page opened the dark door, and Nylan saw the table, dark and battered wood, waist-high. He placed both blades there, side by side, realizing that they could still be taken before he could ever reach them. Ayrlyn followed his example.

A slender blond woman with piercing green eyes stood waiting. She wore a purple tunic, trimmed in green, and green trousers. Her hair was swept back in a malachite hair band.

"I am the Lady Zeldyan. Please be seated." The blond woman gestured toward the circular conference table, and her eyes went to Weryl. "Your child? How old is—?"

"He's a little more than a year," Nylan said.

"They like to explore. You may let him crawl, if you like. He might prefer that."

"Thank you." Nylan eased Weryl out of the carrypak and set him on the ornate but worn carpet. He followed Zeldyan's gesture and sat, taking the chair closest to where his son sat.

Weryl's fingers ran over the fabric, and he looked back at Nylan.

"You can crawl around," the smith told the boy.

With a glance back at the now-closed wooden door, Ayrlyn eased herself into the chair beside Nylan.

The blond woman took the chair across from them, her eyes on Ayrlyn. "I was the consort of Lord Sillek. The holders were kind enough to confirm me, with my brother Fornal and my sire, as one of the regents for my son Nesslek." Zeldyan gestured toward the pair of pitchers and the goblets. "The gray pitcher has greenjuice, the brown, wine. Would you like some?"

"I'd definitely enjoy the greenjuice," Nylan replied.

"The wine," answered Ayrlyn nearly simultaneously.

They both laughed, and Zeldyan smiled faintly, but poured the wine first for Ayrlyn, then the juice into the two remaining goblets.

"I am Nylan," the smith said, as he realized he had never given his name, "and this is Ayrlyn. Weryl is the one crawling there." Nylan watched as Weryl crawled away from the table toward a low closed chest. The boy's fingers explored the brass fittings before he levered himself upright and stood, holding on to the chest for a moment before he sat down with a thump. Immediately, he began the process again.

What did Zeldyan want? Nylan had to wonder.

"Many would guess why two angels would choose to enter Lornth." Zeldyan took a slight sip of the juice, and continued. "I have my own thoughts, but I would be honored if you would tell me how you came here."

The two angels exchanged glances.

"Might as well," Nylan said. "We were the crew of a ship that crossed the skies, a warship, and we were in a battle with the . . . demons of light, I'd guess you'd call them. The forces were so great that they carried us to the skies above Candar, but our ship was destroyed, and we were forced to land on the Roof of the World. We had to land in a cold place because most of the angels come from places far colder than Candar. Only three of us can really live for any long period of time in the warmer parts of Candar. Ayrlyn comes from the warmest place, and she finds the Roof of the World in the winter nearly as inhospitable as you do. Almost as soon as we landed, people started attacking us, and we had to fight back. They kept attacking, and we kept defending, until the peace agreement after the big battle last fall." The smith shrugged. "Does that answer your question?"

"Our wizards had told me some of that, but it is good to know why you picked the Roof of the World. Still . . . why are you here? Do you bring some message, some demand?"

"Hardly." Nylan held in a sigh. "You must know that Ryba is Marshal of Westwind, and that she is a mighty warrior. You also must know that there are few men in Westwind."

"It is said you slaughtered most of those who tried to enter, although there were said to be some few from Lornth who survived," said Zeldyan.

Nylan decided against addressing the issue of slaughter. "There were two," said Nylan. "One was Nerliat, and he left and was killed when he returned with a wizard to attack Westwind. Ryba is not all that fond of men, and she has become less fond of them as time has passed. I am a man." He shrugged.

Zeldyan frowned. "And what of the other man? Did he suffer her displeasure as well? Was he slaughtered as well?"

"That was Relyn. He attacked Westwind also, but he survived." Nylan paused, sensing that Zeldyan's interest was more than passing. "He left last fall to head east."

"East? Why would he do that?" The regent sounded puzzled. "Why was he spared when others were not?"

Nylan wanted to wipe his forehead. "It's not exactly simple. When he attacked Westwind, he tried to kill Ryba. She took off his right hand." The smith paused.

"Nylan saved him from bleeding to death, and later made him an artificial hand, and helped teach him how to fight with a blade and a knife," added Ayrlyn.

Nylan wanted to clarify that, because he hadn't really done the teaching. He'd only made the hand/hook and the clamp that would hold a dagger and encouraged Relyn.

"Why did you do that?" asked the blond woman.

"It seemed like the right thing to do. He was pretty defeated. He said he'd never be able to return home, that he could never escape the humiliation of being defeated by a handful of women." Nylan's eyes turned to Weryl, who was working his way around the chest with tottering steps.

"Do you know why he left?" asked Zeldyan.

"I told him to," Nylan admitted. "I was afraid that Ryba might harm him after the battle." He took a sip of the sweet and sour juice.

"You could not protect him?"

"Nylan was injured in the battle," said Ayrlyn. "He could not have protected himself, let alone anyone else. Because he worried about Relyn, he advised him to slip away in the confusion after the battle."

"Scarcely honorable advice," said Zeldyan.

"I'm a little confused about the definition of honor," said Ayrlyn. "From what I've observed, it appears perfectly honorable to attack or try to enslave people who have nowhere to go. It appears perfectly honorable to offer rewards to have them destroyed, but it is dishonorable to admit that they are strong enough to defend themselves, and dishonorable to leave when the alternative is death at the blade of the greatest warrior in the world."

"The greatest warrior? Who might that be?"

"Ryba," said Nylan. "From what I've seen, no one comes close to her."

"She does not rule by blood?"

"No. She rules by ability, especially ability with weapons."

"Many in Lornth would find that disturbing." Zeldyan took another sip of juice. "Why did you advise Relyn to leave? I am also confused. Did you know that you would be injured? Are you some sort of mage to predict such matters?"

"People have called me a mage," Nylan admitted, "but I am a smith and an engineer first. I did not know that I would be injured, but we were greatly outnumbered, and it seemed possible that many would be injured. I told Relyn that, especially if I were injured, he should depart."

"That candle adds some light." Zeldyan paused, sipped her juice, and asked, "Are you the black mage that the wizards saw in their glasses? The one who defeated Hissl?"

"I don't think I am a black mage, but I did manage to stop the wizards."

"I would suggest, ser Nylan, that anyone who can defeat three white wizards is a black mage," said Zeldyan dryly. "If you are so powerful, and needs must leave this . . . Westwind, then the Marshal must be even more powerful."

"She is a mighty warrior," said Ayrlyn, "and at times she can see what will be, or might be."

"You, flame-angel." The regent turned to Ayrlyn. "Do you believe that the black mage saved Relyn?"

"Yes. He saved his life, and helped him to regain his skills and confidence. Before Relyn left, he was a better blade, even left-handed and with a dagger over his hook, than he was when he came."

Zeldyan was silent, then took another sip of the juice. "Why did you leave?"

"Because the Roof of the World was too cold for me, and because I love Nylan, and because he had to leave."

Nylan slipped out of the chair to steer Weryl away from the table with the blades upon it.

"Yet he carries the child. Is this an angel custom?"

"Weryl is his. Why shouldn't he carry his son?"

Zeldyan laughed, before a frown crossed her face. "I wish Sillek were yet here to listen to that. Still, you have done some good, not even knowing that you have."

It was Ayrlyn's and Nylan's turn to look puzzled.

"Relyn is my brother, and while I would wish he could return to Lornth, I fear his judgment is correct. He would have to fight every day of his life for seasons to prove his honor." She turned back to Ayrlyn. "Sillek shared some of your concerns about honor, with some justice."

Nylan cleared his throat. "If it is not too impertinent, Regent Zeldyan, might I ask why you wished to see us?"

"Because I wanted to meet those who are angels to see if they were indeed black demons."

"Why does everyone think of us that way?"

"How else would they, after all you have done?"

"And what do you want of us?" Ayrlyn's voice was edged.

"Have you heard of Cyador, the ancient white land?"

"Only recently. There was a scroll that mentioned an ancient land where the builders channeled the rivers and built white cities, and then a trader mentioned the name," said Ayrlyn. "He said traders from Cyador had bought enough wheat in Certis and Gallos to drive the price up. He also said they don't let outside traders in."

"They turn away all outsiders, and kill those they find within their borders." Zeldyan was matter-of-fact. "Once, it is said, they controlled much of what is Lornth, including the copper mines in Cerlyn. They have demanded the return of the mines, and our scouts say that a mighty force of Mirror Lancers advances toward the Grass Hills."

At the term "Mirror Lancers," Ayrlyn and Nylan exchanged glances.

"You know of this?" Zeldyan's voice sharpened.

"Not exactly. Those who destroyed our ship used Mirror Towers, and we've often wondered if the white demons of your legends were descended from the ancestors of our enemies."

"Can you read?"

Nylan repressed a smile and answered. "We can both read your tongue and ours."

"Scholars and angels and warriors—truly an odd combination."

"No more than you, lady," Nylan offered.

"Aye, and oddity pays a high price." Zeldyan coughed. "You are welcome, once you are settled, to study the old scrolls in the tower. Some deal with the white ones, and you may find some information of use—that is, if you choose to remain in Lornth and aid us against Cyador."

Nylan glanced at Ayrlyn, catching the tiniest nod. "We would be pleased to remain and offer what help as we can—"

"I would ask what assistance you might offer," interrupted Zeldyan, as though she had forgotten to ask, almost as though she knew the answer.

Nylan kept getting the impression that the blond woman knew far more than she revealed.

"That may be slight," Nylan said. "We have no destructive fireballs like the white wizards. I am a smith. Perhaps I can devise some weapons that might help, although I'm not too familiar with what you can do."

"You were well acquainted enough to destroy two armies. That should offer some reassurance." Zeldyan looked to Ayrlyn.

Nylan slipped from his chair again to redirect Weryl back to the chest, away from the blades.

"I offer less, lady. I am a healer and a singer, and I can defend myself with a blade." Ayrlyn dropped her head.

"Enough to have killed a score, no doubt?"

"Half that, perhaps," conceded Ayrlyn.

The blond regent laughed again. "Most armsmen do not slaughter that many in a life, yet you are apologetic." She shook her head. "And you, smith?"

Nylan swallowed. "With a blade, a few more than the healer."

"And how did you destroy the flower of Lornth? With what awful magic?"

Nylan decided to risk it and tell the truth. "With devices from the heavens that no longer work."

"So . . . another army could take Westwind?"

"Perhaps," Nylan said, "although the tower would withstand anything short of a large siege engine, and there are more guards at Westwind now than when we landed."

Zeldyan shook her head. "I would scarcely hazard a single armsman against your Westwind. We gain nothing, and lose everything." The piercing green eyes raked over the two. "Since you are here, will you aid us against Cyador?"

"Yes." The answer was simultaneous.

"Good. I had hoped you might. I had taken the liberty of installing you in a guest room in the south wing. It even has a bath chamber. The wizards said that baths were important to angels."

"You know far more than you reveal, Regent," Ayrlyn said.

"That is the business of regents, and, I perceive, of angels." Zeldyan rose. "Tonight, I will have a supper sent to your room. Tomorrow, you will join us—all the regents—for the evening meal. Lornth is open to you." The blonde paused. "For now, I would suggest remaining within the walls of the keep. Most within Lornth are not that charitable toward angels." Her lips quirked. "I have no doubts about your ability to defend yourselves, but I would rather not lose any more souls, and not all of our people have enough sense to understand the futility of crossing blades with you."

Ayrlyn followed the regent's example and stood, as did Nylan, but the engineer had to bend to reclaim Weryl, who had returned to the carved chest.

Both angels bowed.

Zeldyan rang a small bell, and the door opened. The page stepped inside.

"If you would escort the angels to their guest chamber—the one in the south wing."

"The big one?"

"The big one, Nistyr," Zeldyan affirmed.

"Thank you," Nylan said quietly.

"I fear, angel, that thanks will count for little enough once Cyador moves against us."

Nylan suspected she was right, but it was still good to have a solid roof and food—even if he still had no idea of where their future truly might lie.

XXXIX

DISDAINING THE ANGEL Ryba, the smith Nylan, knowing the fate of the once-mighty hunter Gerlich, made his way from Westwind, with all the stealth and craft that befitted the one who had re-created the fires of Heaven and the rains of death.

The soul-singer Ayrlyn accompanied him, and a child, and far more harm than mighty Ryba did these three portend for all of Candar, and all lands, even unto the ends of the world. . . .

The Angel and Marshal of Westwind was sore vexed, and sent she her guards after the three, but, against the dark arts of the smith and the singer, they could not prevail, and in time the three came to the ancient and powerful land of Lornth.

The people of Lornth closed their shutters as the angels passed, and feared as the dark shadows crossed their doors.

The leader of the council of Lornth was a woman, and guileless, and, beguiled by Nylan and the sweet songs of the dark singer and the seeming innocence of the child, she offered them respite, and opened her land unto these dark ones, despite the counsel of those who cautioned against what would come from the angels.

And there, for time, abided the mighty smith and the singer of dark songs, and the child.

> *Colors of White*
> (Manual of the Guild at Fairhaven)
> Preface

XL

AS HE COMPLETED dressing, Nylan glanced around the spacious room, taking in the pale pink stone walls, the two ornately carved dark wood wardrobes, and the matching wooden armchairs beside a game table that doubled as an in-chamber dining table.

Ayrlyn sat up in the bed and yawned. "Do we find breakfast?"

Nylan shrugged.

"All right." Ayrlyn set her feet on the carpet. "I'm outnumbered."

"Outnumbered, but never outvoted," answered the engineer.

"Voting doesn't count here, remember?" She rubbed her eyes.

"It doesn't, but what do you think?" Nylan sat and balanced Weryl on his knee, offering the boy leftover greenjuice from the covered cup.

"About what?" With another yawn, Ayrlyn padded toward the wash basin in the adjoining chamber.

"Zeldyan."

"She's pragmatic. Warm-hearted, but that won't get in her way of doing what she thinks is best." Ayrlyn looked at the wash basin. "She wants her son to have the best, and to live to inherit it. I'd guess that we'd have to have her on our side, but she already is. She needs us, although I don't know exactly why she thinks we can help Lornth with Cyador."

"We're angels," pointed out Nylan, deadpan.

"She's not that credulous. She wants us to *do* something."

"You would bring that up," said the engineer. "Such as defeating Cyador and retaining these copper mines?"

"Probably, if not worse." Ayrlyn struggled into her leathers. "I wish I had some outfits like hers. These are going to get too hot here."

"For you?" Nylan laughed.

Thrap! At the rap on the door, the two angels looked at each other.

"Yes?" said Nylan, loudly.

"Your breakfast, ser and lady," announced a voice from the door.

Ayrlyn unbolted the door for the square-faced serving girl.

Breakfast was piled on a single platter on a large tray— eggs cooked into a flattened mass with cheese, two long blackened sausages. Beside the platter on the tray were a loaf of black bread, two applelike fruits, two pitchers—one brown and one gray—and two empty green stoneware mugs.

"Visen had to guess, ser and lady," said the dark-haired girl. "If you would tell the pages or me if there's something you would like better, she would be pleased to cook it." She bowed again.

"Thank you. This is fine," said Ayrlyn.

With a nervous smile, the girl slipped toward the door and was gone.

"I haven't had service like this in years," murmured Nylan.

"I never had it." Ayrlyn eased herself into the chair across the table from Nylan and Weryl.

"Sausage is pretty rank," said Ayrlyn after a time, pouring greenjuice into her mug. "It feels all right, but it's . . . something."

"Blood sausage, I think," Nylan said after one bite. "It is rank." Try as he might, he managed only three bites. Weryl spat out his first morsel.

"The opinion is universal," Ayrlyn noted, swigging more greenjuice.

"The bread is good." Nylan offered Weryl the cup, and the boy grabbed it with both hands.

When the tray was empty—except for the uneaten black sausages—the engineer glanced at the flame-haired healer. "We're fed. What should we do?"

"Talk to people," suggested Ayrlyn. "Talk to as many as we can."

After they had washed their hands and taken care of other needs, including a quick change for Weryl, Nylan eased open the heavy wooden door. The two wore single blades, those at their belts, and Nylan carried Weryl in his left arm, rather than in the carrypak still damp from washing.

The hall was dim, despite the light pinkish color of the stone walls and floor tiles, and empty. With a shrug Nylan turned right. Their boots echoed on the tiles as they headed toward the cross-corridor at the end of the hall. Around the corner and at the archway that led to the old tower where they had met Zeldyan, they found a pair of guards.

"Off-limits?" asked Nylan with a smile.

"If you please, ser," answered the wiry guard. His taller companion remained silent, though both looked at the angels and then at Weryl. The boy smiled, and a ghost of a response creased the shorter guard's face.

"We're strangers here," the engineer began, "and you could help us by telling us a few things we don't know. No, I'm not after gossip, or anything like that. How old is Lornth? Do you know?"

The wiry guard frowned. "Can't say as I'd be knowing that, ser. Some say that Lord Sillek was the fifteenth lord of Lornth; others say he was only the eleventh. Don't know as that helps much."

"How big is Lornth?"

"Well . . . I'd not know how many kays from here to there, but now that Lord Sillek added Rulyarth, those that owe him allegiance hold lands that run from the headwaters of the river near Clynya all the way to the sea, and from the Westhorns least halfway through the grasslands. Clynya's a good eight-day's ride, maybe more, right up the river from Lornth. Berlitos—that's the nearest place you'd call a town in Jerans—it'd be a good seven days' ride west from Rohrn."

"Where's Rohrn?" asked Ayrlyn.

" 'Bout two days' ride upriver—on the west side. Pretty town. Older than Lornth, but the Jeranyi used to raid it a lot, back a hundred years or so. Least, that was what my da told me."

"Are the Jeranyi still a problem?"

"Not since Lord Sillek burned out their fort near Clynya and sent them packing. Lord Ildyrom even paid tribute last year." The wiry guard snorted. "This year might be another thing. Except we don't have to worry about the Suthyans or the Westhorns, and that means ser Gethen could send a force right after them. Ser Fornal's been out gathering armsmen, and I'd guess that means ser Gethen has no great faith in Lord Ildyrom's promises. Who would? His consort has a bigger mace than he does—begging your pardon, angels." The wiry guard flushed.

"What's expected at dinners here?" Nylan tried for a less controversial subject.

The two guards exchanged glances and shrugged.

"You might ask Genglois, ser," said the taller guard. "He's the seneschal, and he has a study at the base of the stairs, but you'll have to take the other steps—back up that way." His head inclined toward the other end of the cross-corridor.

Nylan got the impression that it was time to move on. "Thank you."

Ayrlyn smiled, and they retraced their steps back up the cross-corridor and down the steps, then back down the empty lower cross-corridor. No lamps or candles were lit, and the corridors were darker than early twilight.

The door to Genglois's chamber was open.

"You be the angels, I see," said the heavyset man in purple, looking up from the small table that served as a desk and, from the greasy shoulder joint and bread on the platter there, as a dining table as well. A single candle flickered in a wall sconce in the windowless room.

"The guards suggested you might be able to help us."

"Me? I can get the pages to bring you food and more water, or to empty the chamber pots, or direct you to the stablemaster or armsmaster. That sort of thing—not much more." The seneschal paused. "Fine child, there."

"Thank you," said Nylan.

"We don't know much about Lornth or the regents," offered Ayrlyn. "We'd rather not waste time when we meet with the regents asking questions about things everyone in Lornth knows."

"Some of that . . . some of that, I know." Genglois gestured to the two stools. "Not that I've much room, but stools are fine for pages, not for warriors like you." He paused, and the deep-set eyes centered on Ayrlyn. "You are all warriors, are you not?"

"Yes. Some are better than others, though." Nylan took the stool directly across from the seneschal.

Genglois took a gulp from the greasy goblet on the table. "Jegel said that the head angel—"

"The Marshal?" asked Ayrlyn.

"He said the Marshal threw her blade, and it went right through Lord Nessil's breastplate. That true?"

"Yes," Nylan said.

Genglois shook his head. "Jegel—he always said what was—but I wondered about that. Maybe . . . maybe you angels will keep old Karthanos in line, though. He be a devious one. Anything else you want to know?"

"The other regent, Zeldyan's sire?"

"Old Gethen, you mean? He and Sillek—they took Rulyarth, and he reorganized the whole port. Had it making coins when the Suthyans couldn't. Course, it took the two of them. That's how Sillek met Zeldyan, they say—went to Carpa to talk strategy with Gethen—he was a friend of Sillek's sire, too—and he met her there. Never saw a lord so in love with his lady. She still loves him, and it's been more than half a year."

"What about the Suthyans?" pursued Nylan, easing a piece of chalk from Weryl's hand, and looking at the characters on the slate—apparently a personal form of shorthand for a menu—that night's meal?

"The Suthyans—they're traders, and coin is all that matters to them. Had a big banquet last year—every year, almost—for Lygon of Bleyans, except that the regents said he would not be welcome in the keep again. Seemed all right for a trader, and he even paid his respects to Lady Ellindyja. But you wanted to know about the Suthyans. They have ships, and they sail everywhere. Bled us dry when they had Rulyarth, but matters are better now, thanks to Lord Sillek. Poor man—did so much, and got pushed into fighting you angels. You know"—Genglois lowered his voice—"he didn't want to. His holders pushed for it, and he was not ready to stand against them all—that's hard for a lord even as old and respected as ser Gethen. Had Sillek lived longer, he might have. Then who knows . . . matters might have been different."

"They could have been," Ayrlyn said. "We did not wish to fight, either. But there's nowhere to retreat on the Roof of the World."

"Told that to Koric, and he just laughed. He be dead, and that says much. An old seneschal, and I prattle too much." Genglois stopped and refilled the goblet with wine so vinegary that Nylan could smell it.

"How do the protocols work for dinners here?" Nylan asked.

"There be few indeed. No spitting at table, and no belching. Just follow the Regent Zeldyan. Most proper, she be, most proper without being all stiff like . . . anyway. Most bring their daggers, but I lay out some, dull ones. Eat hearty." The seneschal smiled. "Anything special you like?"

"Pastries," admitted Nylan. "We see few on the Roof of the World."

Genglois laughed. "I will tell Visen." He looked toward the empty hall behind the angels.

"What can you recall about Cyador?" Nylan asked, ignoring the seneschal's glance.

"Not a great deal, ser." Genglois shook his head, and his jowls wobbled ever so slightly. "The trouble with the mines—

that was in the time of Lord Sillek's grandsire or before."

"We're strangers, remember?" Ayrlyn explained. "Could you explain what the trouble with the mines was?"

"Oh . . . that was when Berphi was Lord of Cyador—must have been twoscore years back, maybe threescore. Lord Berphi asked for the return of the mines and the removal of all Lornians. Except he called us barbarians."

"What happened?"

The ample functionary shrugged. "Nothing. Lord Berphi went to his ancestors, and there was some disturbance in Cyador, and the whole matter vanished."

"Until now?" suggested Nylan.

"If you see troubles riding their pale horses toward you, angel lord, it often pays to wait to see how many actually cross the river bridge. Even I have found that few make it that far." Genglois stood. "If you will excuse me, ser, I needs must visit the kitchen."

"Of course."

From the seneschal's cramped place, they crossed the courtyard to the stables.

"Ser and ser?" A slight youth in scarred leathers met them even before they had put three steps inside the stables. From the depths of the structure came the *brawk*ing of chickens.

"We wanted to check our mounts," Nylan said.

"Good beasts," the youth said. "They are in the second row." He turned as if they would follow. "So is the gray you used as a pack animal."

Ayrlyn grinned. So did Nylan as they followed the dark-haired stable boy's quick steps.

"Here you be—the dark mare and the chestnut." The youth pointed to the stalls. "Not like some that come in, so thin you know the rider has only grazed 'em. Hoofs worn, and the dark mare, she be needing new shoes afore long, least that be what Edicat said. Chestnut be sound, shoes and all." The boy glanced from Nylan to Ayrlyn and back.

"Who are you?" asked Ayrlyn.

"Merthek. Second stable boy, leastwise till Kielmer joins the armsmen."

"Do you want to be an armsman?" asked Nylan, wondering about the phrasing the youth had used.

"Me? No, ser. Love the beasts, not cold iron. Cold iron loves none save blood, and that price is high." He looked boldly at the smith. "Especially if one must fight angels."

"The price is high for angels as well," Nylan answered dryly.

Merthek glanced at Nylan's blade. "A short blade, yet deadly."

"Deadly enough," Nylan admitted. "I would rather it weren't necessary."

"So long as men want what others have," offered the youth, "blades be necessary."

"Unfortunately," answered Ayrlyn. "Stick to your horses, Merthek."

"I will, ser and lady, and if you need anything here, ask for me. That is, if I do not find you first." He flashed a gap-toothed grin, then offered a bow. "If I am not here, the stablemaster is Guisanek, and he is a good man, and one who knows all about the beasts."

"We will." Nylan peered over the stall wall at the mare, who stood on clean straw and ate what looked to be grain from a wooden manger.

After Merthek escorted them back to the courtyard, Nylan took a deep breath. "I need a break. Let's go up that tower and check out the surrounding terrain." He pointed to the smaller tower that rose just to the south of where he thought their chamber was—not the larger square tower that held the room where they had met Zeldyan.

"You sound like the engineer again."

"What can I say?" Nylan shifted his weight to catch a lunging Weryl, who grasped toward a chicken that scurried into the shadows of the stable wall.

"Don't," she suggested as Nylan made his way toward the doorway at the base of the tower within the keep. There was no lock, only an iron latch that squeaked as he lifted it.

The circular stairs were narrow and steep, and the steps barely wide enough for one boot, even at the outside end. The pink stone walls were polished smooth by years of shoulders passing.

Half-surprised to find that he wasn't even panting by the time he reached the top and lifted the hammered wrought-iron latch, which also squeaked, Nylan stepped out onto the parapet, a circular space not much more than ten cubits square, with chest-high crenelated walls.

"Definitely for defense," he said, shifting Weryl from his left arm to his right and moving to the south side of the tower. To his right, the river wound gradually to the southwest, presumably back toward the marsh and the ironwoods. Beyond the river, he could see the neatly cultivated fields, eventually giving way to the more distant grasslands. The reddish-brown strip that was the road to the Westhorns and Westwind followed the east bank of the river. Farther to the east were the rolling hills that concealed the Westhorns, although Nylan had no real idea exactly how far the mountains were in a direct easterly direction, since the road had brought them from the southeast. Westwind itself was probably east-southeast from Lornth, but good maps seemed to be another item in short supply.

White puffy clouds dotted the green-blue sky overhead, but to the north the clouds were darker and thicker, with the sheeting gray beneath that bespoke rain.

Nylan sniffed, but didn't smell the rain, not yet. He did smell something else. Weryl grinned at him.

"Not until late afternoon or evening," Ayrlyn hazarded. "The rain, not Weryl."

"We need to go back to the room."

"I can smell that, too."

Nylan took the stairs carefully. A misstep would mean a long bounce downward, a very painful series of bounces off hard pink stones. They had to go into the courtyard and then back along the cross-corridor and up the steps to the third level.

As they neared their chamber, a shorter figure hurried toward them.

"Ser and lady . . . or is it ser and ser?" asked the blond page, looking from Nylan's smooth-shaven chin to Ayrlyn's face and back to Nylan.

"We both fight, and we both take care of Weryl," said Ayrlyn, "but ser Nylan is a man, and I a woman."

"Ser and ser," continued the page, "tonight, the Regent Zeldyan has offered to have her nurse take care of your son and hers in the room adjoining the hall." The youth bowed.

"We appreciate her consideration," Nylan said after a quick glance at Ayrlyn, "and we will bring Weryl with us."

"Your midday meal is on your table." The page bowed again.

After the page departed, Nylan looked to the healer. "It seems as though they're going to some effort for us."

"That bothers me."

"Because it means they've got big problems?" The engineer opened the door and stepped inside. The tray on the table held another heaping assortment of food, bread, cheese wedges, cold slices of meat, more fruit, and three pitchers, plus a small assortment of what appeared to be biscuits.

"I have that feeling." Ayrlyn took in the tray. "I keep eating like that, and I'll be as heavy as my mount."

"I doubt that." Nylan set Weryl on the carpet to close the door, and the boy immediately began to race on hands and knees toward the lutar case.

"It takes a lot of energy to keep warm on the Roof of the World, and now I don't have to."

"Lucky you. Unlucky me." Nylan reached down to steer Weryl away from the lutar.

"I'm still hungry, though," she admitted.

So was Nylan. Even as he reclaimed Weryl and carried him into the bath chamber, he wondered if he'd get over the worries about food that two lean winters on the Roof of the World had generated.

XLI

IN THE DIM light cast by the small oil lamp, the white wizard studied the scroll. Feeling the perspiration on his forehead, he quickly blotted his brow before the dampness beaded up and fell on the parchmentlike white paper.

The words swam before him in the close confines of the small room, a room barely large enough to hold a narrow bed and the work table and stool.

> . . . we have with great effort beaten the Accursed Forest back along the southern boundaries of the white wall. This has taken all of my resources, and those of the local company of white engineers, as well as the two companies of foot and conscription of all able-bodied souls in three villages. . . .
>
> . . . I can sense great forces at work, perhaps the greatest since the binding of the forest in ancient times. . . .
>
> . . . although we have recovered Geliendra and Forestnorth, for us to return the forest to its former boundaries will take more men and forces, and I am writing to request that you make known your desires in this matter. . . .

The lamp flickered as a slight whisper of moist air, bearing the damp smells of the resurgent forest, slipped through the open and unshuttered window.

Themphi massaged his forehead again, then blotted it once more before rolling the scroll, leaving it on the corner of the table for the morning. After a moment, he stood and stretched, then walked to the window that faced north.

He gazed in the general direction of the Accursed Forest, sensing the flickers of white and darkness that not even the ancients could untwist, the flickers of white and darkness that had grown ever so much stronger.

"You dare too much, Lephi, and no one can tell you otherwise." The low words were lost in the rustling of vegetation.

Then, in time, he took a deep breath and turned away from the window.

XLII

Ser Nylan and ser Ayrlyn," announced the page.

As Nylan walked into the small dining hall, Zeldyan stepped forward, wearing trousers and a doublet of sorts cut from a shimmering green cloth that resembled silk, yet did not.

"Might I escort you and your son to the nurse, and to meet Nesslek?"

"Thank you," said Nylan, very much aware that even their best leather trousers and light linen shirts were plain indeed compared to Zeldyan's finery. Even in the light shirt, he was hot, though he knew Ayrlyn was not.

Behind Zeldyan, by the cold hearth framed by a mantle of golden wood, stood two broad-shouldered men. Neither moved forward as Nylan followed the blond regent to a side door within the dining chamber. While the second room contained long trestle tables, they had been pushed aside, and two small beds placed within several yards of the door, a rocking chair between.

The white-haired nurse in the chair talked to the blond boy on her knee. "Ride a fine charger to Carpa and back . . ." She stopped. "My lady?"

"Secora, here are ser Nylan and his son Weryl."

The nurse shifted Nesslek to her hip and rose. "Your pardon, ser."

Nylan smiled. "I appreciate your taking care of Weryl while we eat."

"It happens seldom that one can hold two handsome gentlemen, silver and gold, so to speak," answered Secora. "Year from now, they'd hear nothing of it."

"I appreciate your arranging this," Nylan said to Zeldyan as they re-entered the smaller dining hall.

"I do not like to be that far from Nesslek," answered Zeldyan, "and often make arrangements such as this when we must have dinners for outsiders, or when they would take askance at his presence."

"We would not."

"I had gathered that, ser, but we have much to discuss."

Nylan was afraid of that.

"This is ser Gethen," Zeldyan offered as Ayrlyn joined Nylan and the three walked toward the two men by the cold hearth that flanked the table. "Ser Nylan and ser Ayrlyn."

Gethen had jet-black hair streaked with gray, a short-trimmed gray beard, and green eyes, though the green was not so deep as that of Zeldyan's eyes. He stepped forward with an easy grace. "Gethen of the Groves, sometime regent of Lornth, and sire of these two—when they admit it." His head inclined toward Zeldyan and then toward the other man. "My son Fornal," he added.

Fornal had the jet-black hair of his sire, without the gray, and his black beard was longer and fuller. "I have heard much of the angels, and I welcome the chance to hear more closer to the source."

"Let us be seated." Zeldyan gestured toward the table.

The places were set with two on one side and three on the other. A purpled linen cloth covered the trestlelike table, with a large oval platter and a crystal goblet for each diner. Light came from a single candelabra set at the head of the table and a half-dozen brass lamps set in sconces on the dark-paneled walls.

Zeldyan seated herself in the middle of one side, and Fornal sat on her right. Nylan found himself across the table from them, while Ayrlyn sat across from Zeldyan and Gethen. The engineer waited.

"You might try the wine," suggested Zeldyan.

Nylan poured some for the blond regent, then looked at Ayrlyn.

"Just a little."

He poured half a goblet for each of them, wondering just how much their systems could take after two years of short rations and little alcohol.

"Surely, you will drink more," insisted Fornal.

"A wine's excellence is not determined by how much is drunk," said Ayrlyn.

Fornal looked puzzled.

"A good weapon and good wine are used sparingly." Nylan lifted the goblet. "To the regents of Lornth."

Ayrlyn nodded and murmured, "To the regents."

"To our visitors," responded Gethen.

Nylan took the smallest sip of the wine. "It is excellent, almost better sipped than drunk."

Zeldyan turned and offered a fleeting smile to Fornal.

"Very good," added Ayrlyn.

Two serving women slipped into the room, each bearing platters. One bore meat smothered in a white sauce, and another meat smothered in a brown sauce. A third contained long white strips of something flanked by green leaves, while the last bore sections of the fruit called pearapples.

"The brown sauce is burkha, a hot mint," Zeldyan said. "The other is a spice cream."

Nylan took moderate portions. His eyes strayed toward the closed door behind which were the children. He didn't like trusting the regents, but . . . what choice did they have? He could sense Zeldyan's honesty, but Fornal and the older man were harder to read.

Fornal filled his platter with burkha, and little else, while Zeldyan and Gethen took moderate helpings of everything.

"You still do not like the quilla," observed Gethen to his daughter.

"I have not gained an appreciation of oiled woodchips, but I requested that Visen serve it because of your fondness for it." The blonde offered a smile to the two angels. "Please do not feel you must eat everything for fear of offending. I do not eat quilla, and Fornal has an aversion to anything that resembles fruit, unless it is fermented and comes from a cask."

"That is the only way to serve fruit," the younger man admitted.

After a single moderate mouthful of the sour-sweet minty-tasting meat and sauce, the engineer felt the heat on his forehead. Blynnal had obviously toned down what she had served on the Roof of the World—greatly.

"This is good burkha," Nylan said.

"You have had it before?" asked Gethen.

"A cook who joined the angels makes it, but a far less tasty version."

"Angels are not used to eating liquid fire," Ayrlyn said. "Our worlds are colder."

"So it has been said," Fornal said. "Yet you are here."

"We are two of the three who can live in this heat," Ayrlyn said.

"Even now, it is as hot as summer where I was born," Nylan added. "I do not look forward to real summer." He blotted his forehead—warm and damp from both the burkha and the stillness of the room, then took another small sip of the wine, enjoying the tang, but not wishing to let it creep up on him.

"I had thought the hall chilly," admitted Gethen, "but Zeldyan had suggested that a fire might prove uncomfortable for you."

"We thank you, lady," Nylan said. "At least, I do."

"Zeldyan has said you would help us against the Cyadorans," Gethen ventured after a moment of silence.

His mouth full, Nylan nodded, as did Ayrlyn.

"Can you bring the fires of the heavens against them?" asked Fornal.

"As I told the Regent Zeldyan," the engineer said, "those fires cannot be used any longer. All our skills are at your disposal."

"Any information you have on Cyador . . . that would be helpful," Ayrlyn said quietly. "What weapons they have . . . their tactics . . ."

"Their tactics are simple enough," said Fornal almost

drolly. "They line up endless legions, and like soulless men their armsmen cut down their enemies. Many of their lancers do not bear iron, but blades and lances made of a white bronze. Their wizards, as with all white wizards, cannot bear the touch of cold iron."

So that was why the white wizard who had accompanied Gerlich had almost disintegrated when Huldran's blade had barely touched him.

"Is there anything else?" Ayrlyn asked gently.

"I fear much is buried in the scrolls of the Great Library," said Gethen. "We have not had to cross blades with Cyador in generations."

"Where is that?" asked Ayrlyn.

"Here, off the old tower, but it is written, and in the old tongue of the white ones—at least some is."

"That shouldn't be a problem," said Nylan, again blotting his forehead.

"You read the old tongue?" asked Gethen.

"I read it and one or two others," the engineer admitted. "Ayrlyn reads six or seven languages, isn't it?" Behind his words, he was puzzled. Hadn't Zeldyan passed on what they had told her? Or was the blonde playing a deeper game?

"Five well," the redhead said. "I can make my way in four others."

Zeldyan offered another small smile to Fornal, but her brother did not respond, from what Nylan could see.

"You carry yourselves as warriors, yet you are scholars." Gethen touched his beard. "I do not believe there are nine different tongues on our world."

Nylan nodded to himself—clearly a planoformed and colonized world, not surprisingly. "Languages differ, but in any language people fight."

"Do the Cyadorans still use the old tongue?" asked Ayrlyn.

"So the traders say," answered Zeldyan. "The white ones remain within Cyador."

"Except when they decide they want our lands." Fornal punctuated his words with a hefty swallow from the goblet.

"We are barbarians to them. So are all outsiders," added Zeldyan.

Nylan tried a helping of the milder lemon-creamed meat, then asked, "Do they have any of the older weapons?"

"Who would know? No one who enters Cyador ever returns." Gethen shrugged. "The old tales tell of lances of fire and great wagons that move without horses or oxen, and ships that needed no sails."

"And now?" prompted the engineer, pleased that the lemon sauce was but mildly tangy, rather than liquid flame.

"The only ships that sail from Cyador are coastal traders, and they bear sails like any others."

"They may have lost those weapons," Nylan mused.

"That may be," countered Fornal, "but Cyador is large and has endless waves of lancers and foot. We do not. That is why my sister offers you our hospitality, in hopes that you can help."

"We will do what we can," affirmed Ayrlyn.

Nylan hoped that would be enough, but his guts twisted. Even the order-forged blades he had developed would probably be useless against the reputed hordes of Cyador, and he'd pledged not to forge them because they'd more likely be used against Westwind—and his other children. He held in a sigh, and added, "Perhaps the scrolls in the Great Library will also help."

Zeldyan nodded politely. "How was your journey?"

"We are here," answered Nylan. "We had a little trouble with bandits in the lower part of the Westhorns."

Fornal glanced at Gethen, then answered, "I had thought the angels would rid—"

"Those bandits will trouble no one," Ayrlyn said. "They are all dead."

"How many were there?" asked Gethen.

"Five."

"And they were all armed?"

"They had those large blades," said Nylan. His shoulder twinged sympathetically.

"You see," said Zeldyan, turning her head to Fornal. "Before long there will be few bandits indeed in the Westhorns."

Fornal picked up his goblet with a nod and took a deep swallow. "That was the agreement, I believe. Would that Cyador were so easily handled."

"There is some difference between an ancient land and bandits," Gethen said smoothly. "Any assistance you angels can provide would be most welcome, and we will talk of that after you study the Great Library." He smiled. "How have you found Lornth?"

Nylan got the message. "It seems a pleasant land, and some have been most hospitable. . . ."

XLIII

TURNING HIS HEAD from the dusty book, Nylan sneezed. Then, after rubbing his nose, he looked toward the high windows above the shelves, also dusty. The Great Library contained perhaps five hundred volumes—the older ones in scrolled form, the more recent ones in handbound volumes. He shook his head. Five hundred volumes for the greatest collection of written knowledge in the entire land—and most of it was history and myth, rather than an attempt at hard science. The books had been arranged by size and shape, not in any deeper order, and that meant at least thumbing through each one.

The engineer rubbed his forehead, and stifled another sneeze.

Ayrlyn had a pile of books beside her on the table and Weryl on her knee. Before long, Nylan reflected, he should reclaim his son.

The engineer's eyes went back to the title of the volume in his hand—*Concerning the Red Shield of Rohrn.* From what he could tell from a quick skimming, the volume centered on the reputed exploits of Rohrn—whose small round shield had turned permanent red from the blood of various miscreants who had attempted to eliminate Rohrn without success.

Nylan's only problem was that Rohrn seemed to have been

a thoroughly disagreeable fellow, who killed people if they even suggested that murder was hardly useful or noble or even, in one case, because an old woman had suggested that the ancient Ceryl might have been as great a warrior as Rohrn. There, Rohrn had been relatively merciful—he'd only killed the old woman and raped her daughter, rather than slaughtering the entire household in the name of his honor as a great warrior.

"How's it going?" he asked Ayrlyn as he lifted another volume, half-nodding as he saw the title—*The Founding of Fyrad and the White Lands*.

"Slow. Very slow." She set down one volume and rubbed her nose. "And dusty. No one's read some of these in years."

"Probably not since they were shelved." Nylan flipped through the opening illustrations, faded into pale outlines, and began to read.

"Some couldn't have been read *before* they were shelved," answered Ayrlyn. "Listen to this." She cleared her throat. " 'So when the time came, and that time was in the summer in the first year after the death of Ceryl, that being also the first year after the winter when the goats' milk froze in their udders, Dos betook himself down to the marsh, and he saw the five times five white-legged cranes, and each crane had a silver chain about its neck, except that the mesh of the chains was so fine that it be like spidersilk, and so strong that not even the chisel of a smith might break it, not even the hammers of Clueuntaggt . . .' " Ayrlyn smiled. "This is one of the more readable ones."

"I know."

"Wah-daaa?" asked Weryl.

"In a moment." Ayrlyn reached for another volume. "Do you think we'll find anything?"

"I don't know . . . hmmm." Nylan paused. "This is interesting." He coughed, cleared his throat, and began to read. "Before the white ones crossed the mighty western peaks, all the land was covered by the Great Forest, even unto the Western Ocean."

"So what's unusual about that?" Ayrlyn frowned, trying to juggle Weryl on her knee, as she studied the faded ink of the book before her. "Most places are either covered with trees or grass or something. Here it was forest—pretty standard for planoforming."

". . . and few indeed of the first white ones survived the Great Forest. And those who followed were wroth indeed, and turned their mirrors of fire unto the mighty trees that covered the skies, and there were ashes, and much of the Forest died—"

"That does seem odd," Ayrlyn admitted. "Burning an entire continent, or even a section of it after someone went to all the effort of planoforming it in the first place."

"How about this?" Nylan cleared his throat again. "Then the White Mightiness wrenched rivers from their courses. . . ." He kept reading. "In time, there were ships without sails, and wagons that rolled themselves from one end of Cyador to the other along the white stone ways that linked Fyrad and Cyad, and the multitude of cities raised from the ashes of the Accursed Forest." His eyes met Ayrlyn's.

"Anything about how they worked those wagons—or the ships—are we talking biotech or plain old steam?"

"It doesn't say. It does say—" He stopped as the library door creaked open.

Zeldyan, carrying Nesslek ôn her hip, stepped into the dim room.

"Greetings, Regent," Ayrlyn offered.

"Greetings." Zeldyan inclined her head to each angel in turn. "Greetings, young Weryl."

"Daaa . . ." answered Weryl.

". . . oooo . . ." suggested Nesslek.

"Have you discovered what you sought?" asked the blond regent.

"Perhaps." Nylan held up the slim volume. "I just found this one, and it talks about the White Mightiness and great wagons that move by themselves, and some mighty weapon that leveled whole forests. The writer calls it the Accursed Forest. So far, it doesn't say much more. Have you heard of an accursed forest anywhere?"

Zeldyan frowned. "I do not think so. I will ask my sire Gethen. If anyone would know, he might." She shifted

Nesslek to the other hip. "How long might your search through these volumes take?"

Ayrlyn shrugged.

"We can sift through the books today, and find the ones— if there are any—that might help." In turn, Nylan shrugged. "I couldn't say how long it would take to study any that have detailed information. No more than a few days, I would guess."

"A few days?"

"It does take time to read them in detail," Nylan explained.

"I see." Nesslek lurched in her arms toward Weryl, and the regent swung her son onto her shoulder before continuing. "I would appreciate your letting us know of what you may discover."

"We will," Ayrlyn promised.

After Zeldyan slipped back out of the dusty room, Nylan picked up Weryl.

"Thank you," said the healer. "It's hard to concentrate."

"I know." Nylan licked his lips. "There's another thing . . . you remember that tree dream?"

"What tree dream?" asked Ayrlyn.

"The one where the trees were mixed with both the dark flows—the order fields—and the white chaotic stuff?"

Ayrlyn nodded.

"Well . . . I had it again, and it seemed really important, almost urgent, but I couldn't possibly say why."

"You think the things about the Accursed Forest are linked to your dream? That seems far-fetched."

"I don't know. Just keep it in mind. We still haven't found anything very helpful. If this account is true, Cyador has— or had—higher-level technology, but I can't tell if it's myth, order-control, chaos channeling, or steam-powered low-tech."

"Myth and steam technology, with a bit of that white magic stuff," suggested Ayrlyn.

"Probably, but let's keep looking. It can't take that long to peruse five hundred volumes."

"It seems that long." Ayrlyn shook her head. "Most of this is awful. Awful," she repeated.

Nylan nodded.

XLIV

THE THREE REGENTS sat around the table in the old tower room. Zeldyan fed Nesslek, her chair pushed back from the old and battered wooden table that held little more than a pitcher of wine and three goblets. A warm breeze blew through the open window, stirring the few ashes remaining in the hearth, and the dust motes sparkled in the column of sunlight.

"I do not trust them," said Fornal lazily. "They have used the fires of heaven, but now they say they cannot call them forth. They do not say what they can do, but they can read many tongues. And while they bear those devil blades, neither has even raised one. Nor has anyone seen them do so."

"Would you that they had—as guests?" asked Zeldyan, shifting Nesslek's weight in her arms but not removing him from the breast where he nursed.

"They have the strange hair." Gethen's eyes went to the open window that provided the panoramic overlook of Lornth, his lips pursed. "And there is a strangeness to them both."

"And to their son," added Zeldyan.

"The leader of the angels had black hair. Perhaps the strange hair is as foreign to the true angels as to us. We can confirm so little." Fornal swallowed the rest of the wine in his goblet.

Zeldyan lifted Nesslek to her shoulder, hitched the loose tunic back in place, and patted her son on the back. "They sound as though they tell the truth."

"No one tries to sound like a liar." Fornal reached for the pitcher. "Where are they?"

"In the Great Library."

"What have they discovered? Or was reading another skill that no one has yet seen demonstrated?" Fornal refilled his goblet, splashing droplets of wine across the battered table.

"It would appear so," Zeldyan answered. "The silver-haired one—ser Nylan—was telling me what was in one of the scrolls—something about an accursed forest. He was most intrigued. I'd never heard of an accursed forest."

"The old legends say that the forest fought the old white demons, and that the white ones bound it behind eternal walls," said Gethen. "I'd forgotten that."

"What else have we forgotten?" Fornal shook his head. "Did they say anything else?"

"Ser Nylan said that they would be able to determine which books are important by the end of the day. And to find any knowledge they hold within a few days." Zeldyan paused. "There are hundreds of books and scrolls there. Not even Terek could have read them that quickly."

"The man bothers me," said Fornal. "There's something about him. I don't know. He speaks well, but fine words are only fine words."

Gethen frowned. "Did you see his hands? They are callused, and his arms, slender as he seems, are heavily muscled."

"Muscles alone do not make an armsman. Many of our better armsmen could chop him in two."

"I recall that more than a few armsmen have thought the same of the angels. They are all dead," said Gethen.

"You make the case that they are dangerous, my sire. I submit that a good ally is also one who would make a dangerous enemy. How far should we trust them? And how can we ensure they work to our benefit?"

"Fornal," pointed out Gethen, "they travel with a child, and few do so without great cause. That alone makes them far more vulnerable."

The black-bearded man lifted his goblet once more. "I still do not trust them. In time, if not immediately, I worry that the angels will be our undoing. Perhaps not this pair, but certainly those in the Westhorns."

"That may be, my son, but unless we can raise more coin and more armsmen, we could be back under the lord of

Cyador all too soon—or unless the angels can provide us with some assistance."

"I wish them well with those ancient scrolls." Fornal laughed. "I need armsmen and fire lances or the like, not words."

"They have some skills," said Zeldyan mildly. "Enough to destroy most of the armsmen who attacked them and to establish a presence where no others can even live. Let us see what they offer."

"True," added Gethen. "It will cost little enough."

"It will cost too much if we rely on them and they offer nothing," mused Fornal. "Perhaps we should have some proof of what they are."

"Proof?" Gethen raised his eyebrows. "You have something in mind?"

"I would like to spar, or practice with one of the angels. All I have heard is rumor and tale. Then we could see firsthand." He spread his hands. "I can see no harm in it. If they are as good as it is said, then word will pass, and those who would oppose my sister's allies will be quieted."

"Just spar?" asked Zeldyan.

"Of course." Fornal smiled. "With proof, everyone will be much happier when I leave the day after tomorrow for Rohrn."

Zeldyan frowned.

"What harm can sparring do?" asked Fornal.

"A great deal," answered Gethen, "if you provoke the angel into taking off your head."

"I would not wish to prove their abilities with my own wounds. I will be most careful."

"I would hope so," said Gethen.

"As you wish, brother." Zeldyan inclined her head.

Gethen smothered a frown with a cough.

XLV

NYLAN SAT ON the end of the bed in the darkness, his stomach growling from the heavily spiced dinner as he looked down at his sleeping son. "At least this way he's not up all night."

"No," answered Ayrlyn from the wash chamber. "He's on the go all day and leaves us exhausted." She stepped into the bedchamber, wearing only a thin cotton gown.

"I haven't seen that." Nylan's night vision remained as sharp as ever, if not, he reflected, having become even sharper with practice—and he still didn't know why, except that he suspected it was linked to his perceptions of the fields of order and chaos that seemed to surround everything, including dreams of trees he'd never seen.

"A gift from the regent."

"I like it, but I like the package more than the wrapping." Nylan eased off the bed.

"Good." Ayrlyn stepped around him and sat cross-legged on the other side of the bed.

"Are you upset at me?" he asked.

"Darkness no." She rubbed her forehead. "I just want to sit here for a bit. My head still aches."

"I'm sorry." Nylan repressed a sigh and sat back down.

"It's not your fault. Most of those books were pretty boring." She yawned.

"A dozen books or scrolls out of more than five hundred, and none of them say much except that the Old Rationalists had enough power to incinerate a magic forest, move rivers, and build horseless wagons and sailless ships."

"Well," mused Ayrlyn, "the legends will say that you had enough power to destroy two mighty armies and forge magic blades and enchanted bows, and no one who writes them down will have any understanding of what really happened."

"Great. Except that Cyador is still here, and not too long

ago, if you can believe Gethen, they still had the horseless wagons."

"If wagons are all that's left—"

"I'm not worried about the wagons. I'm worried about a culture that's retained enough technology to keep building steamwagons." Nylan shook his head. "I'm not a damned chemical engineer. Sure, I know that I could probably come up with some explosives—or blow us both up—if I could figure out a way to make nitric acid—but for it to be useful, I'd have to make a lot. Armies use a lot of explosives. That means an industry, and"—he gestured toward the open window that framed a Lornth showing but a handful of dim lamps—"what industry do we have here?"

"Not a lot," admitted Ayrlyn.

"Even simple black powder—that takes potassium nitrate—and supposedly you can get that from bat guano, under manure piles, or as crystals in some kinds of soil. Seen any lately?"

"Stop being so pessimistic," said Ayrlyn. "We'll figure out something."

They had to, Nylan reflected, but he still hadn't the faintest idea what that might be.

"It's not all a loss," she added. "Legends are useful, in a way, because they tell about the land and the people."

"What about trees?" asked Nylan.

"Those dreams must be pretty vivid."

"Not so vivid as other dreams," he said with a laugh.

"You have been deprived."

He looked down at Weryl again. "I'm learning more about parenthood. I think."

Ayrlyn took a slow deep breath.

"Your head still ache?" he asked.

"It's getting better."

Nylan looked at her and forced himself to take the same sort of long, slow deep breath she had. "So what do all these legends tell us about Cyador?" he asked, wondering whether she had a headache from reading in dim light or for some other reason.

"I'd say it's a very formal, hierarchial, and almost brittle structure. It's also stronger than anything else around and has been for a long time. That might help."

"Stronger, and that might help?"

"I'm guessing," the healer admitted, "but rigid societies often don't take much to topple."

Nylan laughed. "I'm worried about coming up with some tool or weapon so we don't get disgraced in handling a minor invasion, and you're talking about toppling what amounts to an empire."

"Why not think big?" Ayrlyn grinned.

He had to grin back.

"And besides, my head is feeling better."

Nylan decided to worry about the wagons, the dreams of trees, and empire-toppling later.

XLVI

NYLAN STEPPED OUT into the morning-shadowed courtyard, carrying Weryl. Ayrlyn followed, closing the heavy-timbered door with a dull *thunk* that echoed in the open space between the walls.

Across the courtyard, outside the stables, were the three regents, as well as a muscular sandy-bearded armsman.

Fornal was inspecting one of the big blades, but handed it back to the armsman as he caught sight of the angels. He stepped toward the two.

"Good morning," offered Nylan pleasantly.

"A good morning to you, ser angel. I was talking to my fellow regents. Some here in Lornth have said that the angels hold their domain by wizardry, and that they could not stand up to cold iron," declared the black-bearded man. "I would not dignify such a statement, yet in our positions as regents, we must act on what can be proven. It is regrettable." Fornal shrugged. "And it presents a . . . difficulty."

"I'm not certain I see the difficulty, ser Fornal," said Ayrlyn quietly. "I do recall that the angels have been quite successful with cold iron."

"So it is said," answered the black-bearded regent. "But all we have here in Lornth are words. Words are fine and necessary to us all, but our holders often find words less convincing than example." Fornal smiled politely, then added, "And the color of the hair of those claimed to be angels is unusual, but hair color does not a warrior make."

"That is true," Nylan said. "We never asserted that hair color made an angel."

"I myself believe you are an angel. But how am I to tell our holders and people that you are an angel?" Fornal shrugged. "As I said words are fair, but the holders hold to their belief in honor and cold iron."

"Words can be more deadly than iron if used properly." Nylan frowned, shifting Weryl from one shoulder to the other, and steering one of Weryl's fists away from his chin. "I take it that you would feel more easy about matters if some proof—beyond *mere* words—existed?"

"That would make our course easier, and your assistance would set easier with those who have lost much." The younger male regent shrugged.

"What do you wish, Regent?" asked Nylan, deciding to cut through the endless innuendoes.

Fornal stroked his beard, almost indifferently. "You might call it a demonstration, some indication of your skill with a blade. Your blade against mine. Sparring only, of course." He smiled. "To show some of our armsmen your skills."

Ayrlyn's eyes narrowed, and she looked to the impassive faces of Zeldyan and Gethen.

"Just sparring?" asked Nylan.

"With real blades?" asked Ayrlyn.

"Of course," said Fornal. "How else?"

The redhead glanced at Nylan.

The smith shrugged. "How else? That's one way of looking at it . . . if you choose."

"That is a curious statement, angel. How else would one spar?" Fornal's lips curled slightly.

"We spar with wooden wands. It allows greater flexibility in teaching. We can also can recover from mistakes more quickly." Nylan smiled. "When in Lornth, however, we shall do as the Lornians do."

"That might be for the best," replied Fornal. "Huruc, here, will act as referee."

The sandy-bearded armsman inclined his head. "As you wish, ser Fornal. I would suggest that head blows be avoided."

"No head blows," said Fornal.

Nylan nodded and handed Weryl to Ayrlyn.

"Think of him as Gerlich," Ayrlyn offered in a low voice, so low that Nylan had to strain to hear the words. "Ready to bend the rules to maim you at any opportunity."

"I got that idea," Nylan returned, shrugging his shoulders and stretching, scuffing his boots against the dusty pink paving stones of the courtyard, trying to gauge the footing. He glanced around the space, nearly three dozen cubits in width between the walls of the keep and the stable, and all in morning shadow. He wouldn't have to worry about the sun, at least.

Finally, he unsheathed the dark gray iron blade he had forged, stepped forward and inclined his head to the black-bearded regent.

Fornal lifted the big blade and held it before him. "Any time, angel."

"You may begin," said Huruc.

Nylan lifted his own blade, but did not move toward the taller man, just waited.

So did Fornal.

"A cautious angel," said the black-bearded regent, after a moment. "So cautious. So strange for someone with a reputation so fierce."

Nylan waited.

Fornal took another balanced step forward, leading with the big blade.

Nylan circled right, wishing the smoothed leather of his

boot soles offered better traction on the lightly sanded stone surface.

Fornal stamped a foot, dipped the big blade, and then attacked. The heavy blade whistled toward Nylan—like a gray streak designed to pulp the smaller angel.

As he had so many times with Ryba, Nylan slid the blade aside, but made no move to strike, stepping back, rather than moving forward, but keeping his full senses on the other.

"Ha! You missed that chance," said Fornal, recovering the big blade and edging forward again, with a half-thrust toward the angel.

Had Gethen frowned? Nylan forced his concentration onto Fornal, continuing to let the order field flow around him, focusing on sensing and melding with it, and letting his blade be guided.

". . . holds back . . . why . . ." murmured Zeldyan.

Ayrlyn held Weryl, brown eyes cold as they rested on Fornal.

Fornal brought the huge crowbarlike blade around in a tight arc, another whistling arc that could have bisected the smith—except that the smaller black blade blurred like lightning, as did Nylan, and his shortsword swept over Fornal's guard and slammed the crowbar into the ground.

Nylan's boot pinned the big blade against the stone, and the shortsword was at Fornal's neck.

"I think we've sparred enough, ser Fornal," Nylan said mildly.

"That was an accident."

Nylan held in a sigh and stepped back, letting Fornal lift the blade, knowing what would happen.

The black-bearded man swept the blade up and toward Nylan, trying to catch the engineer by surprise. For mere sparring, Nylan reflected absently, Fornal was putting in a lot of effort designed to kill Nylan.

Even as the thought crossed his mind, the engineer was already accelerating into full step-up. He slipped around the arc of the hand-and-a-half blade, caught the crowbarlike weapon on the trailing edge, forcing Fornal to stumble forward or lose his weapon. Then Nylan turned the hand-and-a-half blade into the ground again, pinning it immediately with his boot.

"Wizardry!" Fornal looked toward Huruc, who stood with his back before the stable door. "Did you see that?"

"Ser Fornal," said Huruc ponderously. "The angel struck only your blade, nor did he throw dirt or even spit."

"Fornal," added Gethen firmly. "Had this been a battle, or a back alley brawl, you would have been dead three times. The angel smith is better than you are; he is quicker; and he is being exceedingly generous. Were I you, I would not test his patience any longer."

"Nor I, ser Fornal," said Huruc slowly, as if the words were forced from his lips. "I would not willingly cross blades with him." A smile crossed his face momentarily. "Unless they were wooden."

Fornal's eyes traveled from Huruc to Zeldyan and then to Gethen. Zeldyan's eyes were cold and green as they met Fornal's, and the oldest regent shook his head.

Fornal took a deep breath and sheathed the big blade. "It appears, ser angel, that your blade skills are as reputed. We are indeed fortunate to have such allies." He beamed a broad smile that Nylan distrusted.

"You say that the leader of the angels is better?" asked Zeldyan, looking at Ayrlyn.

"Yes. Nylan can usually keep from getting hit too often when they practice, but she is better." Ayrlyn offered a faint smile.

"How many are as good as the smith?"

"Two," said the redhead, "but nearly a dozen are almost as good. Ryba is a very good instructor. So are Istril and Saryn."

"I am beginning to see why it might not be the wisest idea to cross blades with an angel," observed Gethen.

"Wooden wands . . ." mused Zeldyan.

"They are painful enough that those who fail realize their failures," Nylan said dryly, "but they also allow the better blade-handler to use full skill without as much restraint."

"Hummmmpphhh . . ." mumbled Fornal, barely loud enough for Nylan to hear.

Nylan turned. "Ser Fornal, perhaps blunted blades are better for those of Lornth, who have long experience in handling such massive weapons, but the angels have had success in training those less experienced with the wooden wands. Each force must find its own way." The engineer eased the short sword into the belt scabbard, almost awkwardly. He still preferred the shoulder harness.

"Well said, ser Nylan," offered Gethen quickly. "Traditions and skills rest on long experience, and what works on the Roof of the World may take longer to effect in Lornth."

"Fornal," said Zeldyan clearly. "We need to talk about your trip. Would you join me in the tower?"

"I thought—"

"The tower would be better," Zeldyan insisted. "Do accompany me, brother dear."

"If you would, Fornal," added Gethen, "I will join you both momentarily, after I talk to Guisanek about the roan."

Zeldyan took Fornal's arm, and the two started back toward the keep proper. Huruc vanished into the stable.

"Ser Nylan . . . you looked disturbed," said Gethen as the older man approached the smith. "You are scarcely the painting of an elated contestant. Might I ask why?"

"I don't care for fighting," answered Nylan. "It is often necessary, but I don't have to like it."

The older regent nodded. "I like that answer. Lord Sillek would have liked it as well. You are older than you appear, I suspect."

"I couldn't say how old I look." Nylan shrugged, almost embarrassed.

"Like a young man, perhaps in his early twenties."

"I'm a decade beyond that," the smith admitted.

"I thought as much. You have the look of a man who has seen too much death, the bored skill of self-preservation and the contempt for those who see glory in fighting." Gethen offered a wry smile. "We older ones must stick together to keep the youngsters from killing themselves off before they learn that fighting is both necessary and evil. And, of course, we can never mention that in any public place, where some fool will trumpet that we are cowards and not honorable." With another wry smile, Gethen nodded and turned toward the stable.

"Interesting," said Nylan.

"Very," added Ayrlyn. "He feels honest, all over. So does Zeldyan."

"Fornal doesn't."

"He probably wants to be lord, rather than just a regent." Ayrlyn shook her head. "He's a fool. You were gracious there at the end. I'm not sure I would have been," she said as they walked toward the rear of the courtyard.

"Gaaa . . . dah," added Weryl, thrusting a chubby fist toward Nylan.

"I wasn't good enough to make the fight look better," mused Nylan. "I didn't want to humiliate him, but when his pride is touched, he's as dense as a stone tower. Relyn was like that to start."

"All of them are, except the older man," replied Ayrlyn.

"Huruc seems to have some sense, too," offered Nylan.

"That's because he's no lord."

Nylan frowned. Now he had to worry about an offended regent, although it didn't seem as though he'd been given much of a choice. Then again, ever since they'd landed on this impossible world, it didn't seem like he'd had much in the way of choices, except trying to find the least damaging of a range of bad alternatives.

XLVII

THERE ISN'T ANYTHING here." Nylan closed the book and set it on the table, his eyes straying to the window and the white and puffy clouds that dotted the green-blue summer sky. "Nothing but rumors and implications, and none of those are very clear— except that a group of noble women once fled, and there was a lot of power involved once in creating Cyador. And that somehow, there was a magic and evil forest . . . and may still be."

"I've read a lot in a lot of languages, but I've never come across a forest that was treated so much like . . . an entity."

"Entity?" asked the smith.

"Wadah, da-da?" asked Weryl, tottering on both legs, while holding on to the side of the big bed's footboard.

The engineer stood and pushed the straight-backed chair from the writing table, then retrieved Weryl's cup from the sideboard that served as their meal table when they had not eaten with the regents. "Here you are."

"You know. The North Forest of Sybra—the poets say it's desolate . . . cold . . . terrible . . . but the dangers are from the yellowcats or the wind that sucks away life. The rain forests of Svenn—there it's the same thing. People talk about the knife lizards or the walking snakes or the rhombats. Here . . ."

Weryl took the covered cup, sat down on the hard stone floor with a *plop,* and slurped water from the spout, ignoring the stream that dribbled around the edges and out of his mouth.

"It's as though this Accursed Forest were alive?" asked Nylan after deciding to let Weryl slurp and dribble as he pleased for the moment. "Isn't that just low-tech superstition?"

"I don't think so. Besides, why are we both getting repetitive dreams about a forest, a forest filled with both order and chaos?"

Nylan wasn't sure he wanted to think about it. "So we have to go off and fight an enemy that we don't know that comes from a land where there's a magic forest that no one understands that's sending us dreams?"

"We don't have much choice," said Ayrlyn, shaking her head as she watched the silver-haired boy drink. "Do you think so?"

"Probably not, not unless we want to turn into fugitives unwelcome anywhere."

"So we'll go with Fornal and see what happens at the mines. Maybe we can figure out more as we travel."

"The whole business is shaping up as a mess," said Nylan. "Sillek lost most of the disciplined armsmen on the Roof of the World, and Fornal is one of those types that distrust all strangers. And I'm certainly not one of his favorite people—not now. Yet we're stuck with him. He isn't going to want us to go with him."

"He's only one of the three regents," Ayrlyn pointed out. "So we ask one of the other regents."

"Which one?"

"Gethen," said Ayrlyn. "Zeldyan has already stuck her neck out for us, and Fornal was ready to kill her when she hustled him out of the courtyard." Ayrlyn paused and frowned. "She was trying to keep him from making a complete public idiot of himself, and he didn't even see it."

"Some of us men don't." The engineer, his eyes half on Weryl, stood by the open window, where the hot afternoon breeze—bearing an unfamiliar fragrance, a combination of lemon, mint, and reisera—ruffled his hair.

"Should we approach Gethen right now?" Nylan carted Weryl into the bath chamber.

"There's something a smith told me about forging while the coals are hot." The healer grinned as she followed him.

Cleaning Weryl didn't take that long, and in time they stepped out of their chamber into the stone-walled inner corridor of the keep.

The inside hall was stuffy, and hotter than their chamber by far. Nylan was damp all over within a dozen steps toward the old part of the keep where he hoped to find the oldest regent.

Gethen wasn't in the old tower, nor in the armory. They did find him in the stable, beside the stall of a roan, talking to a square-faced but spare man with thinning mahogany hair.

Whufff . . . uuuufff . . . The big horse thumped against the side of the stall, edging away from the regent as he stepped into the stall, followed by Guisanek.

Nylan and Ayrlyn retreated to the shadows near the front doors, waiting not exactly silently, since Weryl continued to murmur, but far enough away from the two men that Nylan hoped they wouldn't seem too intrusive.

The odors of horses, straw, clay, and manure drifted up around them as they stood waiting.

A sandy-haired figure appeared and bowed. "Good day, angels. Your mounts are doing well," said Merthek. "I persuaded Edicat—he's the farrier—to reshoe the one mare, not the chestnut." The stable boy grinned. "Told him he could charge the merchant types more by telling them he'd shoed an angel mount. He growled at me, but he did it."

"Thank you," Nylan said.

"I did it for her, too, ser angel," Merthek pointed out. "She is a good mare, and deserves solid shoes." He paused. "Surely not just concern for your mounts brings you to the depths of our stables?" The boy wrinkled his nose suggestively.

"Your stable is far cleaner than most," Nylan said.

Merthek gave a short bow. "Master Guisanek insists upon it . . . but still—"

"We were waiting for ser Gethen," said Ayrlyn.

"He be talking with Guisanek, about the roan." Merthek shook his head. "The stallion limps, and they find nothing. Edicat knows it lies in the pastern, but he can do nothing. We have no animal healers here." His eyes flicked toward the stall where Guisanek and Gethen still studied the stallion's front leg. Then his voice lowered. "We had three wizards, and not a one could help a mount. Oh, they could cast fire and murder . . . and when all's said what good be that?"

"No good," answered Nylan, "but sometimes necessary."

"There be nothing . . . ser Gethen." Guisanek's voice drifted toward the angels and Merthek.

The stable boy bowed again to the angels and slipped away.

"He might make a good stable master some day," said Ayrlyn.

"He's too practical and caring," Nylan answered.

"Cynical man."

They both stepped forward as Gethen strode away from Guisanek. "Good day, Regent Gethen."

"Good day, angels." In scarred working leathers that could have passed for those of a stablemaster, Gethen surveyed the three. Then his eyes narrowed, and he focused on the redhead.

"They say you are a healer. Can you tell me what ails the roan?"

"I can look," Ayrlyn responded.

"Come then," said Gethen.

Nylan followed Ayrlyn, and Gethen frowned but said nothing as he turned back toward the stall.

Ayrlyn stood by the stall for a moment, and Nylan could feel the waves of calmness radiating from her before she slipped up beside the roan stallion.

The redhead ran her fingers across the roan's pastern. Even Nylan could sense the chaos there, and nodded. She stood and looked at him. "The two of us . . ."

Nylan set Weryl on a pile of straw. "Stay right here."

"Da?"

"Here," the smith said firmly, before he slipped into the stall.

As they knelt beside the injured forefoot, Nylan let Ayrlyn control the dark order flow while they channeled the chaos from the hoof.

Sweat beaded on Nylan's forehead almost immediately in the closeness of the stall, and his nose began to itch.

After a timeless period, they finally rose to their feet. Ayrlyn steadied herself on the stall wall for a moment. "Horses are big." Her voice was low.

"Makes it hard, even when the infection's small," Nylan agreed.

Ayrlyn patted the roan's shoulder, and the stallion whickered, tossing his head only slightly.

"You'll be all right, fellow," Nylan added, before easing out of the stall.

"A way with mounts you have," Gethen said, glancing at the redhead. "He has not been so quiet in days."

"The hoof will be tender for a day or two, I think," Ayrlyn told Gethen, "but he should stop limping before long."

Nylan reclaimed Weryl, blotting his forehead dry with the back of his forearm to keep the sweat from running into his eyes.

"That is all?" Gethen frowned. "All you did was stand there and touch his fetlock."

"There was an infection—chaos—where the bones met. I don't know what caused it, but it should heal now." Ayrlyn offered a faint smile, then wiped her forehead.

"I do not claim to understand your ways, angels, but we shall see." Gethen's lips tightened.

"We have a request of you . . ." Nylan offered as Gethen glanced toward the keep.

"What might that be, ser angel?" Gethen's voice was neutral.

"We have studied the scrolls and books in the Great Library, but they offer little insight into the ways of Cyador," Nylan admitted. "There are tales of what might have been, but no explanations. To help you, we need to learn more. We thought it might be best if we accompanied Fornal on his expedition to the mines."

"You would accompany Fornal to fight the Cyadorans?" Gethen's eyes widened. "And leave your son behind?"

"I hadn't planned to leave him, ser Gethen. I had hoped to beg your indulgence for the loan of a forge to craft a seat that would fit behind my saddle."

"The loan of a forge and fire might be accomplished, but children do not belong in the fray."

"Where else would he be any safer?" asked Nylan. "We wouldn't think of leaving him days away. An angel's child? In Lornth?" The smith wondered if he had gone too far, but he kept his lips firm.

The gray-haired regent stroked his beard, but said nothing. Nylan and Ayrlyn waited.

Then Gethen shook his head. "Times are such . . . many would wish you had not come. Like young Sillek, you ask the questions few would dare voice. Not asking such does not make them vanish. You learn that with gray hair. Some of us do, anywise. Others cling to the unspoken old ways like to a broken mount, fearing to change horses, even as the old horse falters." He paused. "Some of us talk too much without answering the questions put."

The older regent frowned. "There will be cooks and wagoners . . ." He shrugged. "One wet nurse . . . who could also assist the healer here . . . it might be done."

"What might be done?"

"I will have a wet nurse who can also help you, healer," said Gethen. "Or both of you. You are both healers, are you not?"

"Ayrlyn's better," Nylan said. "She has more experience."

"The smith is stronger," the redhead added. "That's why we work together."

"So you are warriors, scholars, and healers. And you are a singer, and he is a smith. What other talents lie hidden?" snorted the oldest regent.

"I can't think of any," Nylan admitted. "Except a knack for getting people upset when I don't mean to."

"Somehow, I have found that a widespread trait—from those who have done nothing to those who have done everything." Gethen shrugged. "Since doing anything or nothing upsets people, it is usually better to do something, if only for one's own self-respect." The oldest regent gave a wry smile. "And then they all call your self-respect putting on airs."

Both angels could not help smiling slightly.

"Times change, and I will change mounts as I can, hard as it seems." Gethen looked at Nylan. "I will talk to Husta, the holding smith, and you may borrow such as you need. I also will speak to Zeldyan and Fornal." He shrugged. "I am only one of three regents, but I would hope Fornal would see fit to use both your experience and your blades."

"Thank you." Nylan inclined his head.

"I suspect thanks be more due you two," Gethen answered. "Few benefit by riding against the white ones, or even nearing them." He nodded. "And if you can craft a saddle seat for your small one, Zeldyan might ask leave to have you craft one for her."

"I would be pleased to do so . . . if I can make it work," Nylan said.

"You make things work, angel. Of that I have no doubts." Gethen nodded again.

Nylan wished he were as sure as Gethen—or even half so sure.

XLVIII

NYLAN GLANCED OUT from the tower to the west. The thin clouds obscured the sun just enough that it was a golden ball hanging low over the green fields beyond the river. "We haven't heard anything."

"Matters of great import," replied Ayrlyn ironically, "take time to settle, usually over wine or strong spirits late in the evening."

"Ooooo . . ." offered Weryl from a sitting position by Nylan's feet, where he pawed at the sandy dust that had drifted up in the angled space where the stone blocks of the tower floor met those of the parapet.

"I hadn't thought that letting us fight their battles for them—or volunteer to help train or whatever—would be a matter of great import," responded Nylan. "It's not as though Lornth is exactly overflowing with trained blades."

"Ooo, da," concurred Weryl.

"Lornth is not exactly filled with love for angels, either, and it's pretty clear that the holders have some considerable influence over the regents."

Nylan nodded, recalling that those holders had apparently forced the late Lord Sillek into his ill-fated expedition against Westwind.

The sound of hurried feet on the stones of the tower steps rose from a murmur to a whisper-slapping rhythm. Then a young woman, black hair bound into a loose braid, burst out into the orangish afternoon light. Her eyes darted from Nylan to Ayrlyn.

"Healer! Please, it be young Nesslek."

Ayrlyn looked to Nylan, then back to the black-haired young woman. "Nesslek? The regent's son . . . what?"

"They say it be a fever." She shook her head. "It be more—

chaos fever—like as killed my Acora. Please . . . go to her. Go to the Lady Zeldyan afore it be too late."

"She sent you?"

"I did not wait to be sent."

Ayrlyn gave Nylan a wry smile. "It's nice to be needed for something."

Nylan scooped up Weryl and hoisted the boy up to his shoulder. "Lead on."

Despite the woman's urgency, the smith forced himself to take the narrow stairs carefully. The illness might only be a fever, but even if it weren't, there was no benefit to anyone if the would-be healers crashed down the treacherous and narrow stone steps.

Then, too, what exactly could they do? Localized infections caused by wounds were one thing, but Nylan wondered about a systemic infection. He'd been less than spectacularly successful in his one attempt—Ellysia had died, and he hadn't been in the best of shape for days afterward.

"This way," urged the woman, turning and scurrying down the dim hallway toward the end of the keep that held the apartments of the regents.

Still carrying Weryl, Nylan approached the guards, Ayrlyn matching him, step for step.

The black-haired woman halted before the guards. "The angels are healers, and the Lady Zeldyan has need of them."

The two guards in green-trimmed purple tunics exchanged glances, one looking to the blades at the angels' waists.

Nylan glanced down. "Oh . . . sorry. We hadn't planned to be here."

Ayrlyn unsheathed her blade and extended it, hilt first, then took Weryl as Nylan followed her example.

The heavy-set guard, now holding two shortswords, looked puzzled.

"Announce them," ordered the thinner guard.

The heavy guard rapped on the door. Muffled words issued from behind the heavy dark wood.

"The angel healers are here."

After a moment the three-paneled carved door swung open,

and a dark-bearded form stepped out into the corridor. "We have no need of angel healers."

"Your pardon, ser Fornal," Nylan said. "We did not wish to intrude, but we were summoned."

"There is no need—"

Zeldyan slipped out beside Fornal.

"Lady." Nylan bowed his head.

"I did not summon you, yet . . ." the regent began, her blond hair disarrayed—the first time Nylan had seen it so. Her eyes went to the black-haired woman. "Sylenia?"

"Your Grace . . . it be the chaos fever." Sylenia bent her head. "I know. I know."

"It be nothing," snorted Fornal. "The boy has but an unpleasantness. It happens to many young folk. It will pass. These matters do."

For a long moment, Zeldyan surveyed Fornal, the angels, the hallway, the guards, Sylenia, and finally Weryl.

"Ahhh?" asked the boy.

Zeldyan smiled faintly. "Angels . . . you may enter. Sylenia, you wait here with their child. If it be chaos fever indeed, he should not enter."

Nylan slowly eased his son into Sylenia's arms. "You be good." He couldn't dispute the validity of Zeldyan's point, especially in a culture without any real medical technology—but what was he doing in exposing himself—and Ayrlyn?

"He will be fine." Sylenia beamed down at Weryl. At her smile, the puzzled look on the boy's face faded into a wary acceptance.

Fornal scowled at Zeldyan. "Be you sure?"

"Fornal, Nesslek is my son. Angels, if you would follow me." Zeldyan turned, and the two angels followed the blond regent into the sitting room. Nylan nodded to himself at the quiet luxury—the matching and cushioned armchairs, the carved game or informal dining table, and the heavy purple and green carpet, worn enough, yet still thick, to indicate its age and considerable value. Beside the base of the candelabra was a malachite and silver hair band, lying there as if dropped or tossed carelessly.

"He is in the small bedchamber," the regent said, crossing the room and easing wide the already ajar door. "All children have their illnesses." Zeldyan paused. "Healers are for wounds and cuts, not for fevers and the fluxes within. Those healers I have known, they bleed and mix potions, and it matters not." The regent looked at Ayrlyn. "You would not cut or bleed him?"

"Bleeding? Why do . . . no. Never," the redhead added more strongly.

Nylan shook his head as well.

Nesslek lay on his back in the ornately carved bed of dark polished wood, his breathing labored, and his small forehead damp and flushed.

Even from cubits away, both angels could sense the white ugliness of chaos and infection.

Nylan knelt beside the small bed, his fingers going out past the silklike pillowcase with the green and purple embroidered edging to the forehead of the fevered child.

"Definitely some sort of infection—"

"No antibiotics, no anti-inflammatories . . ." whispered Ayrlyn.

"This is tough . . . like the stuff that got Ellysia."

Ayrlyn winced.

"Maybe we can . . . he's small," Nylan said in a low voice, all too conscious of the regent standing behind them.

"We can."

Nylan wasn't quite so sure, but could sense Ayrlyn's determination. So he extended his perceptions, trying to ignore the regent, the ornate carved furniture, the woven carpet under his knees—trying to twist the chaos in the small figure, turn it somehow into order. The sweat beaded on his forehead, his chest, his back, the dampness soaking through his clothes as he struggled.

Ayrlyn's hand touched his, adding some of the cool black order to their struggle, but the white ugliness seemed to be everywhere within the boy, with the dissonant redness of chaos shimmering dully, unseen.

Nylan wiped his forehead with the back of his forearm.

Although Nesslek breathed more easily, Nylan knew that respite was momentary, as it had been with Ellysia. They had done nothing to reach the cause of the infection.

"Rest for a moment," Ayrlyn suggested.

Zeldyan backed up a step, but continued to watch, her eyes moving from her son to the healers and back again. "He's better, isn't he? Isn't he?"

"For a bit, lady," Ayrlyn said gently. "We've gained some time, but we need to do more."

That much was true . . . but what?

For some reason, Nylan thought of trees, trees clustered in an ancient grove, surrounded and infused with an incredible *depth* of order—and of chaos almost as deep. Why? Why trees, for darkness's sake? He knew he'd never seen that grove.

Then he shrugged to himself. As seemed to be the case all too often in Candar, he was left with going with his feelings and senses, not his engineering-honed logic.

"What?" asked Ayrlyn.

"Trees," answered the smith cryptically. "Order. Patterns." Would it work? Who knew, but what he'd been doing hadn't worked with Ellysia, and it probably wouldn't work with poor young Nesslek.

He closed his eyes and tried to replicate the patterns, the flow of dark and light, trying not to eradicate that white chaos within the child, but to twist the flows, to contain the chaos within order, within the dark fields. As he struggled again, he tried to ignore the impossibilities, the feelings that everything was an elaborate illusion, that he might be just a fraud . . . but he kept ordering . . . and struggling . . . and patterning . . .

And beside him, so did Ayrlyn.

In the end, they locked order over chaos, fragilely, gently. And after that lock, a different darkness rose up and brought them down.

XLIX

YOU BRING ME a message such as this?" Lephi looked down from the white throne at the aging and balding figure.

"I bring what was written." The white wizard bowed.

"What use is a white wizard if he cannot contain the Accursed Forest? Why should I cosset and coddle you and your kind if you cannot even retain that monstrosity within its ancient borders? Now . . . even the wizard you have provided me sends messages, rather than face me."

The figure in white robes did not respond, but merely waited.

"No one will face me. Am I so terrible? Tell me, ancient Triendar. Am I so terrible?"

"Themphi is not here, Your Mightiness, because he spends all his efforts to contain the Accursed Forest. Should he leave Geliendra, it would spread ever more rapidly." Triendar bowed again, and a strand of wispy white hair drifted across his forehead, hair almost as white as the shimmering tiles on which he stood.

"He dare not leave? Then why did no one notice the power of the forest rebuilding? That is your task, is it not?"

"It is, and we are sending the young wizards to assist Themphi, those who are not already assigned to the Mirror Lancers, the sea watches . . . or the fireship. You have laid many tasks on few of us."

"You did not answer my question." Lephi glared at the older wizard.

"Until it occurred, Your Mightiness, there was no increase in the power of the forest."

"How could that happen?"

"Do you recall, Lord of Cyador, when we told you of the surge of white power that came from the Westhorns last fall?"

Lephi rubbed his chin and squinted. "That I recall vaguely."

"We believe that power helped the forest subvert the wards, but the dark forces were sly, and did not show their renewed might until the spring growing season. We did not sense the forces, because, until now, there were no new forces." Triendar bowed yet again.

"There were no forces? Then from whence came the white blasts from the Westhorns?"

"We know not, save by rumor and glass. The glass shows a dark hold, a small hold, on the Roof of the World, and the rumors from the traders talk of dark angels who have pushed back the barbarians."

"Pushed back the barbarians? That takes little skill. Nor to build a small hold on a mountain—as if any would choose to live there willingly. Talk to me not of distant and tiny holds." Lephi snorted and stared at Triendar.

The white wizard waited silently.

"Come! What is your advice, ancient one?" Lephi finally asked. "Do I send every spare lancer and foot company, and every white wizard to Geliendra? Just because a forest has decided to grow outside its boundaries? Just because of rumors of dark angels on distant mountains?"

"In the ancient books, and in the tablets of gold, it was written that the wards would not last forever, not even until twenty generations. Yet it has been nigh on thirty generations since the white walls were laid and the wards set, and the Accursed Forest has abided."

"I know my history. Tell me what you advise."

Triendar nodded. "Let us provide the wizards, and you a few more companies of foot. Themphi has beaten back the side of the forest that would threaten Cyador, almost alone. We will contain the forest."

"And the wards?"

"Those were from beyond the heavens, and we cannot rebuild or replace them." Triendar shook his head slowly. "We are having difficulties, as you know, with the chaos-engines for the fireship, and we have the plans for those."

"Let us not speak of the fireships. We must have them to teach the coastal traders a lesson. And the eastern barbarians.

For too long, the people of Cyad have let their heritage lapse into laziness and dust. It will not continue." Lephi took a perfumed towel and daubed his forehead. "I suppose this means that we must fight the forest each year from henceforth."

"Yes, Your Mightiness."

Lephi's hand jerked as if to summon the arrows of light, but, instead, he lowered it, the gesture incomplete. "Find me a better solution, Triendar. There must be a better solution."

"We will seek such, Your Mightiness."

"Best you find it. You may depart."

Triendar bowed and walked slowly across the shimmering tiles.

L

NYLAN WOKE IN the bed he shared with Ayrlyn, damp cloths on his forehead. His head throbbed, but he nearly bolted erect. "Nesslek?" His voice rasped, and his eyes burned at the early morning light. Wasn't it morning?

"He'll be fine," said Ayrlyn. "You almost weren't."

"What about you? You were there with me." Nylan could sense more pain in the wide bed than could be his alone. "How do you know?"

"Sylenia's been in and out with Weryl. She was in charge of getting us dragged back here and laid out."

"How's Weryl?" Nylan closed his eyes, resting his head in his hands. Everything he wore smelled. Was healing getting more difficult?

"He's fine. She fed him and kept him last night." Ayrlyn shifted her weight on the bed and eased a pillow behind her back. "You need something to drink. You're dehydrated."

"What about you?" he asked again, opening his eyes for a moment, then closing them at the glare. Slowly he lifted the damp cloth off his forehead, and laid it over the edge of the carved headboard. He squinted into the mid-morning light. His nose felt dry, and dusty, and the murmurs of voices from the courtyard below and outside the room seemed to rise and fall, rise and fall.

"My head aches, and I feel like several horses rolled on me." Ayrlyn lifted the mug and drank, then extended it to him. "Pardon me, but I'd rather not get up and pour another."

The smith understood. He took a long swallow, leaving some water in the mug and returning it to her.

There was a gentle rap on the door.

Ayrlyn and Nylan exchanged glances. He started to turn to put his feet on the floor, but the room seemed to tilt as he did.

"My balance is better right now." Ayrlyn handed him the mug, then eased her way onto the stone floor and walked slowly toward the door, each foot placed carefully one before the other.

"Not much . . ." murmured the smith. Still, Ayrlyn seemed to have greater resilience in recovering from excesses in dealing with the order fields that permeated Candar, certainly greater recuperative powers than he did.

"Yes?" asked Ayrlyn, before opening the door.

Zeldyan slipped inside the room, the malachite and silver hair band in place, her garments fresh. Only the circles under her eyes marred the impression of perfection. She inclined her head to Nylan, then to Ayrlyn, who had propped herself up on the back of one of the chairs.

"No one has ever healed a child of the chaos fever. You are angels." The regent's eyes were bright. "Life balances. You took my consort, and you saved my son."

"We would not have taken your consort . . ." Nylan rasped, stifling a cough, and trying to ignore the headache that resembled a battle axe cleaving his skull.

"No, mage. I know that. He knew that. He was forced . . . into that battle. Had he ruled longer, he might have avoided it." Zeldyan smiled sadly. "Were things other than they are . . . we always hope, but they are not. This time, you were there, and Nesslek is already better, and drinking." She paused. "This took all your strength—from two of you?"

"Pretty much," Nylan admitted.

"I will not trouble you more, but I would thank you both." Her eyes went to Ayrlyn. "In time, all Lornth may be grateful."

"We're glad Nesslek's better," answered Ayrlyn.

Nylan nodded in assent.

"So am I. So are we all." With a wide smile, the regent inclined her head. Then she opened the door, and slipped out.

"It's hard to believe." As the door thudded shut, Ayrlyn sat in the chair, heavily, with a deep breath.

Were her legs shaking? Did that mean she just exerted more willpower? Nylan felt almost ashamed. Ayrlyn had to be hurting as much as he was, or more. They'd shared the energy drain.

"What? That he's better, or that it took so much out of us?" asked Nylan.

"Both."

"I tried just as hard with Ellysia. It didn't work. This time, you were here, and it did." He closed his eyes for a moment. It didn't really help. His head still pounded. He opened his eyes.

Ayrlyn frowned. "I'd like to think that was the difference, but it wasn't. You handled the order flows differently, somehow."

"Different how?"

"It was as though you weren't forcing things . . . weren't fighting them . . ." Ayrlyn laughed softly. "You said something about trees."

The tree images . . . how would they have helped? He remembered, vaguely, the feel. "I tried, I think, not so much to push out the chaos, but to wrap order around it, to contain it."

"It felt different," Ayrlyn repeated.

Had that been the difference? He rubbed his forehead. "Feel like road dung under a wagon—"

"Have some more water. You're still dehydrated."

"So sympathetic you are."

"Healers help those who help themselves." Ayrlyn grinned,

crookedly. "I hurt, too." She rose slowly and lifted the water pitcher from the table, edging toward the bed.

Some water splashed on Nylan's hands as she refilled the mug, but he had enough sense to keep his mouth shut, and to start drinking.

Still . . . he wondered about the trees and the business of binding chaos. He shivered as he swallowed, almost choking.

"Careful . . ."

Did he have to be careful in everything? In every little thing?

"Probably," said Ayrlyn.

He stifled a sigh, carefully, then swallowed more of the water he needed.

LI

WE MEET AGAIN." Fornal glanced around the tower room, pacing from the table to the open window and back again. "Have we new information? I need to be on the road if we are to gather forces and stop the white ones."

"There is a good chance that the Cyadorans will seize the mines before you reach there," Gethen said deliberately, fingering the goblet on the table before him.

"Yet you did not bid me hasten? Might I inquire of you your thoughts on this?" Fornal's words were almost languid under his cold eyes.

Zeldyan glanced down at Nesslek and shifted him in her arms, cradling him a shade more possessively.

"Zeldyan had some other pressing concerns," Gethen offered mildly. "Besides, were you at the mines, you would be dead, and for no purpose."

"You feel that the white demons' forces will be overwhelming?" asked Fornal.

"Were you at the mines before the Cyadorans, as regent,

you would be bound to defend Lornth, even to the last man, and neither the holders nor your honor would let you act otherwise. We do not have the forces to withstand the massed forces of the white ones." Gethen smiled ironically. "In attempting to reclaim the mines, however, you may use any stratagem you wish, so long as it kills whites and proceeds toward reclaiming our lands."

"Do you think the holders will see my delay as self-preservation or as wisdom?" Fornal pursed his lips.

"No one would expect you to depart without the most armsmen you could raise." Gethen extended an arm toward the window. "Even the most honor-bound of holders. And you, certainly, are considered honorable and direct."

Fornal laughed. "You find my methods too direct, my sire?"

"Often directness is laudable. Sometimes it leads equally directly to disaster. Wisdom is knowing when to be direct and when not to be." Gethen gave a twisted smile. "And sometimes, events do not allow wisdom. At the moment, we have the time to exercise wisdom."

"You suggest that we may not always have that luxury." Fornal paced back to the window.

"Sillek did not," said Zeldyan bluntly.

"Before long, we may not either, sister." Fornal paused and looked at Gethen. "How do you recommend I use this . . . luxury?"

"I would suggest that you set up a garrison in Kula. The white demons will not risk their entire force once they hold the mines, but will try to raid and level the countryside. You could deploy your men to reduce their numbers with each raid. You can continue until you can retake the mines." Gethen held up a hand. "I have talked with the angels. They will accompany you. Use the angels as much as you can. They boast of their training—give them the least trained and see what they can do—always in situations where their failure cannot affect you."

"I am a plain man, and I cannot use fancy words to explain. I cannot make people believe white is black or black white. I mistrust the angels—or what they portend—and I cannot explain why. I know what I feel." Fornal turned to the tower window. "Yet their blades are sharp, and they can kill white demons." He touched his beard. "All the same, I fear mixing angels with armsmen will bring no good."

"You avoid mixing them," Gethen pointed out. "Give them the riskier tasks."

"What of their child?" asked Zeldyan.

"They will have the child with them," Gethen answered.

"I would have offered to take care of him," the blond regent said.

"Ser Nylan asked for the loan of a forge to make a seat for the boy—one that would fit behind a saddle."

"And?" said Fornal, an amused smile on his lips.

"I asked Husta to accommodate him, and to learn how good a smith he is, and anything else he could."

"At times, my father, you are as cunning as a serpent, and at others . . . I do not understand. How can the angels be other than useless with their child riding with them?"

"I thought they should be able to bring their blades in support of you. As you say, those blades are sharp and deadly. Secora's daughter Sylenia will ride with them as a wet nurse. She also has some experience in dressing battle wounds."

"That would help." Zeldyan smiled.

"I suppose the armsmen would welcome more healers, especially far from Lornth." Fornal nodded. "But what of the safety of the wet nurse? We have few enough armsmen."

"You have cooks and wagoners—and do you really think that your armsmen will touch the nursemaid of an angel—or live if they did?" asked Gethen. "And the angels will fight more fiercely if their child is with your force. What happens to him if you are overrun? Do you see how fierce your sister becomes in defense of Nesslek?"

Fornal's smile broadened momentarily, then vanished.

"They will meet you in Rohrn in less than an eight-day. Their efforts in saving Nesslek have exhausted them, and the smith has not been able to forge yet."

"Do you believe that such healing was necessary? I would not wish any ill for Nesslek, but how do we know—"

"Fornal," interrupted Zeldyan, "have you known any child to survive chaos fever?"

"Then it may not have been that." The black-bearded man's tone was casually careful. "As I said, I wish the best for Nesslek, but after all the destruction the angels have created, you must pardon me if I am not fully trusting of their aims."

"It was chaos fever." Zeldyan's eyes flashed.

"Then we are blessed, and can thank darkness for his deliverance," Fornal added smoothly. "Yet, I still caution against trusting completely those of whom we know so little."

"We will see."

"That we will, sister, and I hope most deeply that your insights are correct, as so often they have been. Please pardon my caution, but one cannot undo a blade in the back, and the angels have shown no great affection for Lornth in the past."

"Then keep them before you," said Gethen.

"I will, my father. That I will." Fornal shrugged. "And I pray that their blades will bring down many of the white demons."

"I will send the angels with the force from the keep here," suggested Gethen. "As we know, they are warriors. Let us see what they can do in training the worst of your force." Gethen smiled. "You lose nothing."

"Except time and men."

"Even then, you win." Gethen shakes his head. "If they are successful, then you take the credit for giving them the opportunity and testing untried techniques on a small group." He paused. "If they fail, you point out that you were giving them every opportunity in a way that jeopardized the fewest armsmen."

A smile cracked Fornal's face. "That would work. I can appear generous no matter what. I can even say that the failures got two chances, and that will blunt some of the levies' mutters." The smile vanished. "Yet what we have learned so far troubles me." Fornal looked toward the two others, then lifted his hands. "They are warriors and healers and scholars . . . and a singer and a smith. Does it not seem strange that two so skilled arrived when we need so much?"

A faint frown crossed Gethen's brow. "I have thought on that. They healed Nesslek, and they healed the roan's foot. The flame-hair said it would be a day or two before he stopped limping, but Guisanek came over to tell me that he seems totally healed." Gethen paused. "Still, they are healers, and that will help you."

"Wizardry . . . how do we know it will last?" mused Fornal.

"Everything they have done so far has lasted," said Zeldyan. "Everything." She shivered, and her green eyes were deep as they fixed Fornal's.

Slowly, slowly . . . he looked away.

Gethen nodded to himself, almost imperceptibly.

LII

AFTER LEAVING AYRLYN with Weryl, Nylan slipped out of their chamber, glad that the coolness of the night before remained into the morning, and down the stone steps and out into the courtyard.

He followed the sound of the hammer to the southwest corner of the keep, where, against the outer walls, rested a small square building beside a small open gate. Although the gate would be necessary for deliveries of charcoal and iron stock, he reflected, there was no guard at the smithy gate. Was the lack of guards a reflection of the high esteem in which the regents were held or a reflection of the sad state of the armsmen and the treasury of Lornth—or both?

The angel smith turned from the gate toward the sounds of the hammer and anvil. A battered and unpainted sliding door was pulled open, revealing the smithy inside, where the smith and his striker already worked. For a time, Nylan watched the burly smith. With shoulders as broad as a wine barrel and arms like tree limbs, the smith's hammer seemed more like a toy in his huge fist as he forge-welded a ring together on the anvil horn.

The odor of hot metal, quench oils, and forge coals drifted around Nylan, and he rubbed his nose gently as he watched.

Abruptly, the dark-bearded smith set the hammer aside, used the tongs to place what looked like a harness hame ring on the forge bricks, and nodded to the striker at the bellows. Then he stepped away from the anvil and toward Nylan.

"You be the angel?" His voice was high-pitched, surprisingly for such a big man.

"That seems to be what everyone calls me," Nylan admitted. "I'm Nylan."

"They say you're a smith. I'm Husta. Regents asked if I'd mind lending fire and an anvil." Husta inclined his head and grinned wryly. "No smith likes to be told. But they been good to me."

"I had to learn it alone," Nylan said. "I'm probably a poor smith, compared to you."

"Got any work?"

Nylan looked around, then eased out the blade. "I had to do weapons, mostly."

Husta extended his huge hand, then touched the blade, studied it, and slowly shook his head. "Be not three men in all Candar could match that." He grinned. "You use the dark forces and the fire, do you not?"

Nylan nodded.

"An honest mage. One who doesn't mind using his hands." Husta laughed. "You be doing blades here?"

"No. It's an idea I told ser Gethen about, and he said he would talk to you."

"Aye. He did." The burly man shook his head. "Good man, and lucky we are that he be one of the regents. Sure be wishing that poor Lord Sillek had lived—talk was he didn't want to fight the angels, begging' your pardon, ser Nylan. But those stiff-necked holders . . . they worried about a bunch of women on a mountaintop. Ha! My Cethany'll have told 'em not to mess with 'em, she would. Women are tougher than men most ways, even if they can't heft a big blade or a hammer." Without a pause in his words, Husta nodded at Nylan, motioning him toward the striker who stood by the great bellows. "Corin, this is the angel smith. Work the bellows for him like you would for me, 'less he tells you otherwise." Husta glanced at Nylan. "That be all right?"

"That's fine, and I appreciate the help." Nylan stripped off his shirt.

Husta gestured to an old leather apron hanging in the corner. "Use that. Old, but it stops sparks."

"Thank you." Nylan hung his shirt on the peg from which the apron had come.

"If you do not mind, angel, I'd lief watch as you work."

"As you please," Nylan answered pleasantly, knowing that, once again, he faced some skepticism.

Husta grinned, not unpleasantly.

Nylan wandered over to the dark inside corner where the rod stock was heaped, then looked at the scrap bin. For a moment, he stood in thought, trying to assemble mentally what he had in mind. Finally, he selected a length of the narrowest stock. "This—and perhaps some cuts from the scrap plate there—they should be enough."

"Lord Gethen pays for the stock. So long as you waste none, it's no matter." Husta laughed, again a high-pitched sound.

The silver-haired smith nodded and pointed to the hammer. "Might I use that, or would you prefer I use another?"

"Use it you may, and I thank you for asking."

Nylan nodded and hefted the hammer, fractionally heavier than the one he had used on the Roof of the World, though not by too much, then set it down while he set out the rod stock beside the anvil and found a pair of tongs. He looked at Husta.

The big smith nodded, and Nylan took the tongs, using them to ease the first section of rod stock onto the coals.

Once laid on the forge coals, the iron heated quickly—at least compared to the finished blades and higher-tech alloys he had been working. With the tongs he slipped the cherry-red rod onto the big anvil and, using firm strokes of the hammer, began to fuller it into the thinner strips he would need, sensing the grain of the metal and the tiny fluxes and the unseen white shimmers that told of impurities and weaknesses.

Compared to what Nylan had used on the Roof of the World, the smith's stock was soft iron.

"See . . ." bellowed Husta to the striker. "He's worked out that bubble there. Have to learn to know the metal, like a lover, know where the hidden rough places are. You can see if you look hard enough."

Nylan almost felt guilty, because he couldn't see half of what he sensed, and clearly Husta had learned to use his eyes far better than Nylan. The angel smith held back a shrug. He had to use what senses and skills he had, and he was glad he had them.

Still, in three heats, he had the first long strip rough-finished.

Three more finished the second, and another three the third.

"Ah . . ." Husta cleared his throat and glanced at the sky.

Nylan blotted his sweating forehead with the back of his forearm and lowered the hammer. His eyes took in the lack of shadows, and he realized it was nearly midday. Had he been working that long?

"Would you join us for bite?" asked Husta. "Bread and cheese, and some ale—and pale sausage—meat stuff, not that blood crap."

"I'd be pleased." After setting the hammer aside, Nylan had to blot his forehead again. In the comparative heat of the low-lands, sweat seemed to flow from every pore of his body—and it was spring, not summer.

"Over here."

The bigger man hoisted a long bench out of the back of the smithy and set it in the shade outside. "Cooler here. Can see you're used to a colder place."

"The Roof of the World is a lot cooler," Nylan admitted.

Husta poured the pale liquid into a tin mug, then into a wooden cup. He handed the cup to Nylan. "Good ale. Got it from Gherac for some piping. Pipes are a friggin' pain."

The angel smith nodded. He hadn't even tried something like piping, although he supposed he could. It would involve bending thin sheet around a rod or cylinder, not that difficult compared to ensuring that the welds were tight.

"You work hard," the big smith said. "Good rhythm, too. Got to have rhythm in this craft."

Nylan took a sip of the ale, which was surprisingly cool and bitter, and sat, straddling the end of the bench clearly reserved for him.

"He strikes hard," observed Corin, as if Nylan were not present, as he pulled up a battered stool. "Wouldn't think it, but he never stopped."

"Good smiths don't be stopping, Corin, except when they choose. And plenty of smiths I've seen aren't all that big— good ones, too. Mikersa, he wasn't even up to ser Nylan's shoulder—seems strange that a smith be a warrior, too, but like no one's seen an angel smith." Husta took a long pull from the battered mug, then shoved the platter from his end of the bench toward Nylan.

The silver-haired man broke off a chunk of the dark bread, then used his belt dagger to carve off slices of sausage and cheese, almost creating a sandwich. He wolfed through three bites, then almost laughed. He'd forgotten how much energy smithing took, especially when he'd barely recovered from the costs of healing young Nesslek.

"He eats like a smith, not like some fancy lord!"

"They all call him 'ser,'" pointed out Corin.

Nylan shook his head. He was really closer to the professional armsmen, those who were officers, than to the lords of Lornth, if he equated his past position in the U.F.A. to the equivalent in Candarian society.

"You look thoughtful, ser Nylan," observed Husta.

"I was thinking," he admitted. "I was more like . . . I don't know . . . there's nothing quite like it here . . . but someone who leads a special kind of armsman. I certainly wasn't a lord."

"They call him 'ser,'" Husta continued, " 'cause he's a right good blade and a mage. Huruc told me he pinned Lord Fornal's blade twice so quick that Fornal couldn't believe it."

"Is that true?" asked Corin.

"Unfortunately," Nylan mumbled. He took another mouthful of cheese, sausage, and bread. The headache he had ignored was beginning to subside.

Corin glanced to Husta.

"It's risky showing a lord up. If you don't, you could get hurt, and if you do, they don't forget."

Nylan nodded. The big smith had that right.

After he went back to the forge, Nylan had to hot-cut the strips and then bend and weld the framework together—quenching it in sections. That took most of the afternoon, and Husta watched and puttered, watched and puttered.

In the end, Nylan still had to make the equivalent of two low-tech cotter pins, and punch four holes in the attachment brackets. The pins took almost as much time as the bracket, and he had to fish one out of the quench tank when it slipped out of the tongs.

By the time the sun hung just above the walls, what he had was a cantilevered framework that needed to be covered with leather or cloth or both, forge-welded all the way around. Rivets would have been faster, but he saw none, and making them would have taken other stock, and he still wasn't so proficient as he would have liked in making small items.

"Nice work," said Husta. "Smooth, but I cannot see its use."

"Once it's covered in leather or cloth, I'll fasten it to a saddle—one of those with a high back." Nylan sketched with his hands. "That way you can carry a child too small to ride, but too big to carry."

"Don't know as many would want that—except you and the regent. They say she's loath to leave her son—and she likes to ride. Most folks would use a wagon or a carriage."

"Wagons don't go everywhere," Nylan pointed out.

"They go everywhere I want to go," laughed the big man. "People who ride end up in bad places."

Nylan hadn't thought of it in such a fashion, but Husta was probably right about where riding often led.

LIII

THE THIN, LONG-FACED young woman looked down at the pink floor stones. "Lord Gethen said you needed a nursemaid for your son. He and me, we got on well enough while you were ill." A gust of hot air from the open chamber window fluffed her shoulder-length black hair, drawing a strand across her left eye, but she made no move to brush it back.

"You did," said Nylan. "You were good to him, and I appreciate it. We are looking for someone to ride with us and to take care of Weryl. It won't be all that easy, not like it was here." Nylan paused. "Do you ride?"

"Yes, ser. My father, he works for Edicat, and they let me ride when I was a girl."

The engineer suspected that it hadn't been that long since Sylenia had stopped being a girl, although some women looked girlish forever. He reclaimed Weryl from the brass-bound chest where the boy tottered on unsteady legs, holding himself erect with one hand on the brass handle at the end while trying to step away.

Nylan carried his son over to the young woman. "Would you like Sylenia to be your nursemaid?"

Sylenia raised her eyes to the silver-haired boy and smiled. "A handsome child."

"You lost a child?" asked Ayrlyn. "That was Acora?"

Sylenia nodded, then added slowly. "My girl. Only child."

"Are you sure you want to do this?" asked Nylan. "It's a long ride to Clynya and the copper mines."

"I am at your bidding, ser." The slightest of shivers passed over the thin girl.

"Sylenia," said Ayrlyn softly. "You are under our protection." Her voice turned dry. "Such as it may be."

"Lord Gethen . . . he said none of the soldiers—"

"They won't," Nylan affirmed.

"He said you were both mighty warriors . . . and that you would not leave your child behind."

"That's true."

Sylenia looked at Weryl again, solemnly.

". . . aaaahhh-raaa . . ." Weryl gurgled and smiled, thrusting a chubby hand toward the dark-haired woman. ". . . aaahhh . . ."

Nylan stepped closer to Sylenia, and Weryl's fingers brushed her cheek, exploring with a gentleness that surprised his father.

"I would . . . take care of him . . . like my own," the dark-haired woman said, her thin fingers touching Weryl's. "Could . . . I?"

"Ahhh . . . daaa . . ." interjected Weryl, squirming in Nylan's arms.

"Leaving Lornth . . . ?" began Ayrlyn.

"I would as soon leave Lornth for a time." Sylenia's words were firm.

"Good. That seems to be settled," Nylan said. "We won't be leaving for a few days, but it might be better if we arranged some times for you to spend with Weryl and to show you how we do some things."

"As you wish." She inclined her head.

After Sylenia finally left, Nylan closed the door, then set Weryl back by the chest. The boy promptly grasped the hand-tarnished handle and pulled himself erect. "Daa-da!"

"Yes, you're standing, and it won't be that long before you're running everywhere." He shook his head slowly as he turned toward the window, gazing out to the southwest. Clynya and the copper mines lay there—somewhere—and so did the white troops and Cyador.

"She's basically sweet," Ayrlyn said, "and she likes children."

"She's been ordered into being Weryl's nurse or whatever," said Nylan, after a moment.

"That's obvious."

"Zeldyan and Gethen, you think?"

"I'd suspect so." Ayrlyn shrugged. "They're not happy with Fornal."

"And they can't do anything about it?" Nylan blotted his forehead. He already was sweating all the time, guzzling liquids, and was generally miserable with the heat—and everyone told him that summer hadn't really started. He could hardly wait.

"What? Zeldyan's a woman, and no one in this culture thinks much of women as leaders. She's only a regent because she's Nesslek's mother, and because her family is strong. Gethen would be the logical candidate, from what I can figure, to be the lord if anything happened to Nesslek, but since Nesslek's his grandson, that sort of balances. But . . . Fornal would be heir if Nesslek died, and that means that any effort Zeldyan and Gethen made to get Fornal off the regency council would be viewed with skepticism. Besides, they can watch him more closely if he is a regent—"

"And that's where we come in?" asked Nylan. "We're supposed to keep him out of trouble?"

"Something like that."

"It's never simple, is it?"

"Death's the only simple thing, and it usually leaves behind a mess for the living."

Nylan smiled wryly. "You're so cheerful. Accurate, but so full of good cheer."

"And you're not?" She grinned at him.

"Daaa!" added Weryl. For a moment, he looked like Istril, and Nylan swallowed. Was this how he was protecting her son? By taking him into danger? Except who else could protect him better?

Ayrlyn nodded.

Nylan shrugged.

LIV

GETHEN ROSE AS Nylan and Ayrlyn approached the table in the small dining room. Zeldyan, wearing yet another tasteful green and gray outfit, smiled. Her blond hair was perfectly in place, held there by another hair band, this one of silver and malachite.

Following Gethen's gestures, Nylan seated Ayrlyn directly across the circular table, covered in a pale green linen, from Zeldyan, then took his seat across from Gethen, with Ayrlyn to his right.

Two twin-branched candelabra provided the light, and, thankfully, the small hearth was cold, and the high rear windows were open, providing a light breeze.

Nylan hoped Weryl and Sylenia were getting along, but he was glad for some time when neither he nor Ayrlyn was worrying about his son. He took a slow deep breath as he settled into the straight-backed chair at the table.

"The wine is one of Father's best," Zeldyan said brightly. "The brown pitcher."

Nylan took the hint and poured some for each of them, although he had to lean forward and stretch to reach Ayrlyn's goblet.

"This is very good," the redhead said after her first sip.

"Thank you," answered the oldest regent.

"Excellent," added Nylan.

Two serving women entered with the heaping platters of food. Nylan could smell the spices before they reached the table.

"Wintermint all-curry," Zeldyan said with a smile, "and no quilla tonight." He glanced at her father. "Next time."

The gray-haired Gethen smiled back.

One of the serving women returned with a basket filled with two hot loaves of dark bread, fueling Nylan's suspicions that the all-curry was spicy indeed.

"You leave tomorrow?" asked Gethen rhetorically. "A long ride, as long as riding to Rulyarth."

"The port?" asked Nylan politely.

"Such as it be," said Gethen with a laugh.

"Father, you are too modest." Zeldyan turned her head to Nylan. "My sire has practically rebuilt the entire port, and city, and we could not survive without the revenues from the traders there. The Suthyans are jealous." She shrugged. "But they neglected the port when they held it, in favor of Armat. Now they wish they had not."

"Lord Sillek—he acquired the port?" asked Ayrlyn.

"He had little choice. Lornth was beset on all sides. Ildyrom—the lord of Jerans and the grasslands to the west—had established a fort just across the river from Clynya. The traders were squeezing us because they controlled all the ports, and . . ." Zeldyan gave an embarrassed smile. "That be history."

"Zeldyan speaks truth," continued Gethen. "Lord Sillek needed security and coins. He drove the Jeranyi out of the grasslands west of Clynya, and then was successful in taking Rulyarth. He had hoped that the revenues from Rulyarth and the expanded trade would strengthen Lornth." Gethen paused and took a sip of wine. "They did, except that the older holder families insisted that he take on Westwind before Lornth was strong enough. Both Karthanos of Gallos and Ildyrom sent thousands of golds to support the Westwind campaign, and made sure the older holders knew it."

"It sounds as though they forced Lord Sillek to overreach himself," Nylan said.

"Everyone only wanted him to do the honorable thing." Zeldyan's voice was overly sweet.

Gethen cleared his throat.

"We are sorry . . ." began Ayrlyn. "It must be painful . . ."

Nylan recalled his speculations about Sillek—that the man had been too decent for his own good and forced into an impossible situation. It appeared those speculations had been closer to truth than he had realized. Was trying to be good, decent, and even-handed always a formula for failure in government? Ryba would have said so.

"We cannot change the past," Zeldyan said, "even if it be painful."

"The future be the question," Gethen added.

"Do you know where the Cyadorans are?" Nylan asked, his fingers on the goblet.

"The white demons have taken the mines," Gethen said, "as I thought they would. We received the message yesterday from Fornal in Rohrn. He writes of his concerns. They crossed the Grass Hills and brought more lancers and foot than have been seen in Lornth in generations."

"I believe I'd be concerned also," said Nylan. "Did they bring any of their horseless wagons or anything like that?"

"No. They brought no strange devices, not that our scouts have reported." Zeldyan served herself some of the creamy curry, filled with chunks of meat, before passing the platter to Nylan. Then she broke off the end of one loaf of bread and passed that.

Nylan's eyes watered from the aroma of the curry as he served himself.

"How are you finding Sylenia?" asked the older regent.

"She seems very nice," answered Nylan. "She and Weryl get along."

"You would not consider leaving him in my care?" asked Zeldyan. "I would treat him as my own."

"You are most kind," Nylan said, "but who knows how long we will be wherever we end up?"

"I understand." Zeldyan nodded. "I do not like leaving Nesslek. I am glad I am not in your boots." She turned to Ayrlyn. "Have you any ideas how you might assist us in removing the white demons?"

"Well," answered the redhead, with a slight laugh, "since it appears unlikely they will leave voluntarily, we'll have to find a way to make life unpleasant. That usually means a better way to slaughter people. I don't look forward to it."

"For people reputed to be so warlike, you seem to dislike killing," said Gethen.

"Most people respond only to force," Nylan said. "That's

the way it is, and I'd be a fool not to accept that. I don't have to like it."

"That is why you are so dangerous." Gethen shook his head. "That is why Sillek would have been a great lord."

A faint smile crooked Zeldyan's lips.

"Perhaps he was," suggested Ayrlyn. "Most great leaders die before their greatness is known, or they're hated while they're alive because they want to change things."

An awkward silence settled over the table.

"How effective has Fornal been in raising armsmen?" asked Nylan, abruptly, breaking off another chunk of the dark bread, and refraining from wiping his damp forehead.

"He will have twenty score in levies, and a quarter of that more in true armsmen," said Gethen.

"And how many Cyadorans are there?" asked the engineer.

"We do not know for certain, but between five and ten times that number." The gray-haired regent smiled grimly. "That is why we had hoped you might help."

Nylan nodded. Gethen didn't want help; he wanted divine intervention, and Nylan hadn't the faintest idea of how to get it, only that he and Ayrlyn had to figure out something.

He glanced to his right and saw Ayrlyn nod, ever so slightly.

"It could be an interesting year," she said quietly.

Gethen and Zeldyan exchanged glances, before Zeldyan lifted the brown pitcher. "Would you like some more of the wine?"

"A little," answered Nylan.

"Please," followed Ayrlyn.

The smith took another sip, wondering how a land that could create such good wine had gotten itself in such a mess.

LV

THRAP!

In the gray light of predawn, Nylan lowered the wide-bladed razor he was using to shave and glanced over his shoulder toward the bedchamber, catching sight of Weryl. The boy stood and held on to the brass-bound chest, rocking his weight back and forth as though he wanted to take a step.

"Ah dah dah ah . . ."

A slight breeze stirred the room, bearing the odor of damp grass and the slight fragrance of some unknown flower—both sharp in the air cleaned by the night's thunderstorms. A small puddle of water lay beneath the open window.

Thrap!

"Can you get that?" he asked.

"I'm throwing something on, master of the bath chamber," snapped Ayrlyn.

"Sorry. Do you want me . . ."

"I'll get it."

At the sound of the door opening, Nylan lifted the crude razor to finish shaving, concentrating on not slashing himself. He finished as quickly as he could and washed hastily, trying to ignore the cock with the off-key crowing that seemed perched on the wall directly below their open window.

"Zeldyan sent these up with breakfast," Ayrlyn said as Nylan stumbled from the washroom. She held up trousers, shirt, and tunic, all in dark gray. "There's a set for me as well. They seem to be to our measurements."

The smith shook his head. "Why now?"

"So we couldn't exactly refuse. It also reflects on the regents, I suspect, if we're poorly clothed." Ayrlyn offered a tight smile. "I'm sure we'll pay for the garments."

"You would put it that way." Nylan lifted the trousers and slipped them on.

"They do fit nicely," Ayrlyn observed. "I like them on you."
Nylan flushed.

By the time they were dressed, had wolfed down the eggs and cheese and slabs of something Nylan hoped was ham, and had all their gear in the appropriate bags, the edge of the sun was peering over the eastern horizon, casting a flat glare into the room.

"Huruc did say dawn," Ayrlyn said.

"We're a little behind." Nylan hoisted saddlebags into his arms, trying not to get them caught on either his shoulder harness or the hilt of the blade in his waist scabbard.

"Not so that it would matter. In case you haven't noticed, this isn't the most punctual of cultures." Ayrlyn reclaimed Weryl from his exercises with the trunk.

"No exact timepieces," observed Nylan, struggling toward the door, then waiting for the other two.

"It's hard to make anything exact in a low-tech culture."

As Ayrlyn opened the heavy door, Sylenia rushed down the stones of the corridor toward them. On her back was a thin pack, but she also wore new grays, trimmed with purple, unlike those of Ayrlyn and Nylan.

"Oh, sers, let me take Weryl."

"Be my guest," said Ayrlyn.

"You look so handsome this morning," the nursemaid cooed at the boy. "One day all the girls will think so."

"Not too soon," said Nylan.

"You don't want to stop lugging him around?" asked Ayrlyn as they started down the steps to the courtyard door.

"That would be nice, but I've noticed that the older children get, the more problems they have."

"Since you've never had children before, that has to come from your own upbringing." The flame-haired angel shook her head. "I pity your poor parents."

Horses and their riders milled around in the shadows of the courtyard as the three adults and Weryl made their way toward the stables. Nylan dodged a fresh horse dropping, slipped slightly on the damp paving stones, and jarred Ayrlyn's arm. "Sorry."

"Walking is hazardous to your health here," she said wryly.

"Just about everything is."

Merthek was waiting just inside the stable door, with the four horses lined up. "I have your mounts saddled, sers, but I didn't know about the seat." His head went to the leather-covered framework by his feet.

Nylan shifted the bags in his arms. "I'll attach it to my saddle, but it works better after the saddlebags are in place—one set anyway. The others will go on the gray." Nylan had drilled holes in all three saddles—his, Ayrlyn's, and Sylenia's—so that Weryl's seat could be moved from one mount to the other, as necessary. Weryl faced backward, seeing where they had been.

After setting Weryl in the seat, and fastening him in place with the wide leather strap, Nylan stepped back and asked Ayrlyn, "How does he look?"

"Happier than when he was in the carrypak."

"I think I'll be happier, too."

"You mean you don't want to fight off bandits with your son strapped to your chest?"

Sylenia, wearing her new long-sleeved gray shirt, glanced from Nylan to Ayrlyn, and then to the array of armsmen mounted in the open space of the courtyard to the north of Huruc.

Nylan swung into his saddle, then checked the shoulder harness, before looking to Ayrlyn and Sylenia. As he did, the purple-cloaked Huruc rode slowly across the damp stones of the courtyard.

"Are you ready, angels?" asked the burly armsman.

"We're ready," answered Nylan.

Huruc guided his mount across the paving stones, each step clicking and echoing from the keep walls. "If you do not mind, we should ride at the head of the column."

Nylan flicked the dark brown mare's reins, urging her after Huruc. Ayrlyn eased the chestnut beside Nylan, and Sylenia, seated easily in her saddle, followed.

". . . get that nag moving, Nuorr!"

". . . in line . . . know where you belong! Keep it that way."

Nylan looked back over his shoulder at the still-shadowed walls, whitish-pink and splotched with irregular patches of moisture from the night's rain. Neither Gethen nor Zeldyan had appeared.

Again, Nylan noted, there were four guards in gray and purple at the gate to the keep. While the four stood stiffly as the column moved past, none looked up. Slowly, slowly, the column clopped out the open gate and turned southward, away from the river, back along the road that had brought Nylan and Ayrlyn to Lornth, less than a handful of eight-days earlier.

LVI

THE THREE OFFICERS remained mounted, watching on the hillock, as the engineers struggled below to lift walls around the mining camp, each wall a rampart of earth piled between walls of stone. A deep pit gaped on the eastern side of the camp, where stones were being mined. Only the wall facing the road to Clynya had been completed, and it rose less than six cubits. Other engineers worked on the additional earthen-walled barracks.

"I don't like it," muttered Captain Azarphi. "They all just scattered, not a single arrow."

"You want arrows." Captain Miatorphi laughed. "We'll see them soon enough. Why do you think we need barracks and not tents?"

Majer Piataphi did not take his eyes from the horse teams that dragged stone boats full of red earth from the back side of the hill.

"What do you think, Majer?" asked Azarphi.

"I'll be happier when we're dug in properly."

"Maybe we should keep the locals busy," suggested Miatorphi.

The majer nodded. "According to the old maps, there's a town a half day west of here. It's called something like Derlya. Take a detachment and scout it out." The majer paused, without looking at either officer, then added, "You, Azarphi."

"There are a couple of hamlets closer than that, small places," ventured Miatorphi.

"You take care of them," answered the majer. "Not personally. Send a force leader with a few scouts to each, but try not to be seen."

"Those miners, they didn't even know we were coming," repeated Azarphi. "They ran, like no one had told them." He shook his head, squinting slightly against the bright morning sun.

"You asked me what I thought," said Piataphi abruptly. "I don't like it either. Those Lornian barbarians, they had to know we'd send a force. Their messages were stalling for time."

"You think they're headed this way with lots of those half-assed warriors?" asked Azarphi.

"Not yet. They were stalling, and that means they need time. It also means they think they can do something. We need to know when they're coming and from where." Piataphi turned in the saddle to face Azarphi. "Try not to let them see you."

"What can they do, really do?" inquired Miatorphi.

"Very little, if we set up our base right and carry out His Mightiness's orders. That is, if we're careful, and I intend to be very careful."

LVII

THERE BE ROHRN," announced Huruc.

Nylan's eyes followed the armsman's gesture, although he had to squint into the sun that hung low in the western sky.

Rohrn lay where the river forked, a town perhaps three-quarters the size of Lornth lying on the west side of the western fork, rather than on the triangle of land formed by the fork. The eastern fork seemed barely a third the size of the western branch, but the road led to a bridge over the eastern fork and then across the triangle to a second and larger stone bridge across the larger fork to Rohrn itself.

"Daaaa . . ."

At Weryl's semi-words, Nylan looked at the road ahead, not quite muddy, but slippery in places from the previous day's rain, and at the gentle slope down to the first bridge. Deep ruts filled the center of the road, and the riders all took one shoulder or the other.

The road had followed the east side of the river all the way from Lornth, if often more than a kay or more from the river itself, because of the frequent marshes and swamps, at times even climbing the low hills east of the river to avoid the wetlands beside the water.

As he rode down toward the eastern fork and the smaller bridge, Nylan noted that thickets and low trees bordered the narrow strip of brown water from the fork all the way back to where it vanished into the rolling hills to the southeast.

Huruc reined up at the approach to the bridge and turned his mount. "You lead 'em across, angels, if you would."

"All right." Ayrlyn nodded, as did Nylan.

The timbered bridge was perhaps six cubits wide and almost a hundred cubits long, with log piers planted at each end and on each side of the actual stream. It had a planked roadbed and a single railing on each side, scarcely sturdy enough to halt a running horse or a heavy cart. The thickets below the approach rose from the streambed to nearly the height of the waist-high railing, and only the center of the span, that part over the water itself, was clear of flanking growth.

Nylan urged the mare onto the planks, and her hoofs clunked on the wood.

"Two abreast," ordered Huruc, from behind them, as the armsmen neared the span. "More spaces between your mounts. Two abreast. Not so close."

Even with the spacing, Nylan could sense the bridge flexing as they neared the far side. No wonder the chief armsman wanted them spaced out.

Nylan drew up short of the second bridge, a wider stone span, with two stone piers anchored in the river itself. Despite the raised causeway approach to the eastern side, the bridge still sloped slightly upward to the bluff on the western side where it entered the city.

As he waited for the rest of the column to cross the first bridge and for Huruc to arrive, the engineer noted that the center section of the larger span, between the piers, also had a planked roadbed and wooden side walls.

Rohrn seemed to be a trading town, with a scattering of empty wharves on the western side of the river, just north of the stone bridge. Part of the bluff had been terraced to allow access to the wharves. Most of the town sat on a bluff a good ten cubits above the river. The river was flowing more fully than normal, Nylan could see, because the bushes and trees on the eastern side were partly submerged in the churning brownish water, and the water on the western side lapped at the top of the wooden piers.

"Da . . . wahdah, wahdah," called Weryl from behind the saddle.

"Yes, there's water there. Lots and lots of water." Nylan turned his mount to watch the last of the armsmen cross the first bridge, followed by Huruc.

Another face caught his eyes—a brown-haired and burly man who appeared to be a squad leader. The subofficer looked at Nylan and smiled. "Ser angel, I did not think to see you bearing arms for Lornth."

"Stranger things have happened," answered the smith, still trying to wrack his brain for the other's identity.

"Tonsar," whispered Ayrlyn.

"You want to fight the Cyadorans, Tonsar?" asked Nylan, glad for the reminder from Ayrlyn.

"I would not say that it's something anyone would wish." Tonsar grinned. "My boys and me, we will do our best."

"Just make sure you do," rumbled Huruc as he rode up. "Lead on, angels. Two abreast." The force leader gestured toward the second bridge. "Just follow the main street to the other side of the town. The barracks are there, but I'll catch you before you get that far."

The near-setting sun beat right into Nylan's eyes as he urged the mare onto the bridge. The echo of her hoofs reverberated from the paving stones of the approach and the first section of the bridge proper.

He leaned toward Ayrlyn. "Thank you. I knew he was the one who escorted us to Lornth, but I just couldn't remember his name."

"Tonsar? Who would never let it be said that he slaughtered a family? And you couldn't remember that?" Ayrlyn grinned.

"No," said Nylan sheepishly. "I never was good with names. I guess I'm still not."

The mare's hoofs thudded on the planks of the bridge's center section, then clopped again on the stones on the far side, where Nylan headed down the fractionally wider street that seemed to lead toward a square a few hundred cubits westward.

Rohrn was a smaller version of Lornth, with a scattering of buildings constructed of the pinkish granite, and the others of stone and plastered—except that Rohrn seemed older, with patches on the plaster. Nylan guided the mare around a long series of potholes that dotted the cracked paving stones of the main street, some of which were deep enough to hold stagnant water. The houses, some shuttered and some unshuttered, were plaster-finished in various shades of white, tinged pink by the red dust and gray by age.

A mosquito whined out of the shadows cast by a shuttered house, and Nylan brushed it away, still squinting into the low sun.

"There's a square ahead," Ayrlyn observed.

Nylan nodded and turned at the sound of faster hoofbeats to see Huruc squeezing his mount past the left side of the column.

"Be not long now," said the armsmaster as he reined back his mount and took a deep breath. "Hate riding narrow streets."

Three women in brown trousers, with baskets at their feet, watched from the porch of the chandlery as Nylan and Ayrlyn led the column into the square.

". . . sad sight . . . old man and a woman leadin' Lornth . . . and a child behind them . . . sad it be . . . ."

". . . ser Gethen, mayhap . . ."

". . . say he's a big man, and that old fellow's not that big . . . Gethen's bairns . . . all growed . . ."

Nylan snorted. "If I'm not a woman, then I'm an old man."

"I know better."

"So do I," said Huruc.

A charred signboard swung from a chain before a burned-out shell that might have once been an inn. Large clumps of browned grass, interspersed with pale green stems, grew around the base of the empty stone pedestal in the square.

Rohrn had clearly seen better days, but Nylan said nothing as Huruc trotted up.

"You can see the barracks ahead," announced the head armsman.

The space between the houses widened, and then there were no more houses, but an open field. The ground before the barracks was churned mud, as was the soil inside the large corral to the right of the stable building. The corral held more than a hundred mounts. The entrance to the stable had been strewn with straw in an apparent effort to firm up the reddish ooze.

From the odor, Nylan decided that the ooze had mixed thoroughly with horse droppings and less savory other items. His nose wrinkled.

"Thinking about sanitation again?" asked Ayrlyn.

"Was it that obvious?"

"Only to me."

Huruc whipped out the big blade and stood in the saddle. "Hold up! Hold here!"

As the column jostled to a halt, another group of horsemen rode awkwardly toward the stable and then toward the corral. While all wore blades, the blades were far from uniform, and one youth carried his without even a scabbard.

"Levies . . . some not much good," said Tonsar in a low voice that barely carried to the angels.

A black-bearded figure rode across the muddy ground.

"Here comes Fornal." Nylan glanced back at Sylenia, but the nursemaid's face was calm, impassive, as it had been for most of the trip.

"Greetings. I am glad to see you have arrived as announced." Fornal inclined his head. "The angels and you, Huruc, have quarters on the upper level, and you many stable your mounts within the stables. Your men have the south end of the barracks," he added to Huruc, "and they will have to use the smaller corral behind the stable."

"Yes, ser." Huruc stood and waved the blade. "This way!" he bellowed.

As Huruc led the others away, the black-bearded regent eased the roan toward the angels. "Besides your blades, deadly as they are, did you bring any magical weapons?"

"Not many battles are won with magic," Nylan said calmly.

"I am glad to hear you say that, mage." Fornal smiled openly. "Few seem to understand that simple truth."

Nylan waited.

"Have you thought of a nonmagical way to aid us, besides your own considerable prowess?"

"Some of your levies don't know how to hold a blade, much less use it," suggested Ayrlyn. "You cannot afford to spend time training them. That's something we've had a little experience with."

"My sire had mentioned such." Fornal's fingers stroked his dark beard. "There are two squads and a few others—not a large number perchance—but," the young regent shrugged, "as you say, they might well be armed with pitchforks as blades for all that they know of either. I would be indebted if you would undertake to turn them into a fighting force. Or at least a force that will not mill or turn at the first charge or arrow."

"Do we have your leave to use what methods we see fit?" asked Nylan politely.

"Any such method as you know that will leave most of them intact to fight." Fornal smiled more broadly. "I will introduce you two as their force leaders before we ride in the morning. We can discuss the details when we eat this evening." He inclined his head. "I will leave you to make ready."

"By the way," the smith asked, "do we know how much armor these Cyadorans wear?"

"A breastplate and a small glittering shield—that is what the reports tell." Fornal frowned momentarily. "Why ask you?"

"We can discuss it later, but I would like to request that we bring an anvil and some hammers."

Fornal nodded. "You would use your skill to repair weapons, ser angel?"

"That is one thing I can do. A grindstone would also help."

"Those . . . those we can find."

"Thank you."

Fornal inclined his head politely, then turned the roan to follow Huruc.

"What was that all about? The armor business?" asked Ayrlyn. "You said you wouldn't forge better blades—"

"Repairs won't be that, but if I need to forge something, once we get in the middle of nowhere, where will I find an anvil or tools?"

Ayrlyn nodded, then smiled faintly. "Here we go again."

"Probably." Nylan took a deep breath. "We'll also need coal or charcoal, and some oil. Most of these blades are dull and nicked. They use them like crowbars, to knock people off their mounts."

"That won't go over well with the professionals," Ayrlyn predicted.

"No, but since nothing will," Nylan answered, "we might as well do it our way." He flicked the reins. "We need to get off these mounts. I can smell Weryl even above the local sanitation."

Behind them, Sylenia's mount and the gray squushed through the mud as the four horses headed for the weathered stable. In the rank behind Sylenia, a squat levy watched the nursemaid, nervously running one hand through his brown beard.

Nylan frowned, but he could not stop a man from looking.

LVIII

IN THE MIGHTY city of Cyad dwelt the mages of the white rainbow, whose ships fueled on fire and spanned the seas, whose white marble palaces glittered in the sun of contentment, and who pursued the knowledge of the distant stars.

Horseless wagons, harnessing the power of chaos to the will of man and mage, traversed the polished stone roadways smoother than glass. Those great firewagons sped more swiftly than the wind, bringing crops and goods and wealth to all of Cyador.

All were content in the order kept by the white mages, and seldom were necessary the shimmering shields and burnished blades of the mighty Mirror Lancers, for there was peace.

In those days had Cyador allowed Lornth privileges in the Grass Hills, among them the privilege to remove metals from the earth. Seeing this privilege, the smith Nylan, in his guile, asked of the regents of Lornth why they existed upon the suffrage of Cyad, when for generations they had slaved and the mages of Cyad had done nothing with the bright copper buried in the Grass Hills.

Those of Lornth pondered his words long into the deeps of the night and recalled that the Grass Hills were yet those of the Lord of Cyad.

As they pondered, then sang Ayrlyn the soul-singer of that darkness of despair that would follow when Cyad asked back what was its due, and when Lornth could no longer mine the bright copper of the Grass Hills.

What can be done, asked the leader of the Lornians, for she was a woman and trusting. How shall we hold to the delvings of our fathers and forefathers that have sustained us through the years?

In response to such questions, the dark angel Nylan offered a great wizardry against which the might of Cyador and her mages would not prevail, and, persuaded by the wily Nylan, the council of Lornth said, it shall be so, and they turned their eyes from the evil that Nylan proposed.

> *Colors of White*
> (Manual of the Guild at Fairhaven)
> Preface

LIX

THE ROAD DUST raised by the column of armsmen riding ahead was everywhere, rising shoulder high, sometimes higher, coating Nylan's and Ayrlyn's new grays with fine red powder. Tonsar rode to Nylan's left, Ayrlyn to his right.

In the hot afternoon sun, every time Nylan blotted away sweat, his forearm came away coated with a thin later of reddish mud. If it rained, it would settle the dust, but with much rain, then they'd have to slop through mud. Nylan took a deep breath. His mount looked like a roan, and his nose itched. He rubbed it, but it did no good. He sneezed—once, twice.

Then the engineer glanced back toward Sylenia, since Weryl's seat was mounted behind her saddle, and had been from the morning after Fornal had put all the troublemakers and trainees under Nylan's and Ayrlyn's command. Nylan wasn't quite sure what to expect, except trouble sooner or later. Happily, he did not see the squat armsman who had leered at the nursemaid earlier.

The current trouble was that their "command" got to eat Fornal's armsmen's dust. Only the supply wagons were farther to the rear. The last one had a small anvil, probably what passed for a weapons anvil, and an antique bellows, hammers and tongs, even ten stone worth of coal in bags. Where Fornal had gotten them Nylan hadn't asked, though he hoped the coregent had paid for it, rather than seized it. Somehow, though, he wasn't that hopeful, and it bothered him, not that he could afford to do much about it, not at the moment.

Weryl seemed to be dozing, with muddy streaks running from the corners of his mouth where drool and dust had combined. Nylan smiled faintly, then looked through the dust at the line of trees a half kay to the right that bordered the river. Was the entire east bank nothing but marsh, swamp, and thicket? While the road on the west bank was level and faster traveling than the section from Lornth to Rohrn, the way was dry and hot, although the rolling fields to the left of the road beyond the fences showed healthy green shoots.

"Dust and more dust." Ayrlyn coughed, then glanced over her shoulder. "If they fight the way they ride, we're in trouble. They'll need a lot of training."

"What do you think, Tonsar?" asked Nylan.

The subofficer shrugged.

"You'll have to lead some of them," Ayrlyn prompted.

Nylan could see her smile, but the brown-bearded armsman looked stolidly ahead, as if he were riding to his doom.

After they had covered perhaps a hundred cubits, the armsman sighed, loudly. "I have been faithful and I have worked hard. And begging your pardons, angels, I do not see why the regent insisted I must be your subofficer. I will do what I can, and that be little enough with these."

Nylan understood. Tonsar had brought them to Lornth, and Fornal was the type to blame the messenger.

"Begging your pardons, again, sers," the subofficer continued, "but, if I lead them, they will not follow, and one cannot lead from the rear." He pursed his lips. "I would march all of them against the white demons at the first chance and be rid of them."

"We don't have that choice," pointed out Nylan. "There is no one to replace them."

"Would you send them against the white demons?" Tonsar looked hopefully to Ayrlyn. "Could we not find others . . . somewhere?"

"Where?" Ayrlyn raised her eyebrows. "Fornal had to beat the bushes to get this crop—or so we were told."

"That be true." Tonsar sighed again.

Over dull murmurs of conversation and the dust-muffled steps of the horses, two voices rose.

". . . worthless hunk of dog meat . . ."

"You should talk . . ."

At the yelling, Nylan turned in the saddle and looked back to where two riders had pulled off to the side of the road.

"Now what?" asked the flame-haired angel.

"Two of them are arguing about something." He shook his head and looked at Tonsar. "Any suggestions?"

"Most are hopeless. Some are troublemakers. The others are mad." Tonsar frowned. "You could kill one. Fornal would."

"Remember Ryba," said Ayrlyn. "This isn't the time for kindness."

"You think . . . ?" Nylan's guts tightened.

"Yes."

Nylan wheeled the mare and urged her toward the two troublemakers, where three other riders lagged, clearly trying to hear what was going on with the arguing pair. Refraining from shaking his head, the engineer urged the mare toward the five.

". . . wouldn't know a bow from a hoe . . ."

". . . never worked an honest day . . . or a dishonest one . . ."

The engineer wondered if both he and Ayrlyn should have intervened together. No, he decided. Each had to handle things alone, or there would be even more trouble.

"Owara is so small that a hare would miss it, except it smells so bad that even a hare wouldn't hop through it." The man with the braided black hair laughed cruelly.

"You must be the only man in Runnel," called the thin-faced blond, "and the last, for your mother would have expired immediately on seeing you, and no woman could—"

"Knock it off!"

Both men looked up, but just waited as Nylan rode up. Both sneered, the black-haired man openly, the blond with his eyes.

"For the moment, I don't care how you two insult each other, so long as you keep in formation. You're slowing things down. Now, get moving."

"And if I don't want to?" asked the black-haired man.

"Well . . ." mused Nylan. "I suppose the generous thing would be to wound you, but that would either get you out of the fighting or a pension. I could beat the manure out of you, but I might end up just disabling you for life, and that would create the same sort of problems." He shrugged and offered a smile. "So . . . take your choice. Leading the first charge against the Cyadorans, or getting a blade through your chest right now."

"You talk big, but you're just another little lord," snapped the black-haired man. "I'll do as I please."

"You'll get back in formation," Nylan said coldly, triggering his step-up as he spoke, knowing what he would have to do.

"Make me."

In a single flowing motion, Nylan drew the shortsword from the shoulder harness and released it.

The blade went into the other's chest hilt-deep. The man tried to reach for the big blade, but after an initial twitch, slumped over the mount's neck.

Ignoring the white wave of death and agony that washed over him, and the daggers that knifed through his eyes, Nylan had the second blade in his hand even before the other four looked to him. All four mouths were open. "The regent wouldn't take that, and we don't either."

The engineer rode up next to the sagging body, and yanked out the blade, then turned to the blond man. "You! Your name?"

"Wuerek, ser."

"You strap his body to the mount, and when we get to Clynya tonight, you bury it. We don't have time right now. You understand?"

"Yes, ser." Wuerek looked down.

"I'll do my best to get you all through this, but your part is to do your best, and that means following orders." He eased the mare back through the dust raised by Fornal's armsmen. "Ride in pairs!" snapped Nylan. "This isn't a jaunt to the tavern."

As he rode, the levies looked away.

". . . black angel . . . mean bastard . . ."

". . . gave Gisyl a chance . . . .idiot . . . don't mess with pros . . ."

The smith wanted to shake his head. It didn't seem to matter where he was. There was always some idiot who would respond only to force. To such, forbearance, reason, or common sense meant nothing. He took a deep breath. How many more such would there be?

He rode along the shoulder of the road, passing their command—four squads roughly, except that it was hard to tell because, even when the men did attempt to approximate a column, about half couldn't figure out how to get their mounts to match pace with their partner.

He wanted to rub his throbbing forehead, but didn't dare, not immediately, since that would send the wrong signal.

"What happened?" asked Ayrlyn. "I could feel—"

"Idiot dared me to make him follow orders." Nylan shook his head. "Makes me think of Mran—and Ryba. I guess I'm no different. I thought I was, but—" He shrugged.

"They'd have torn you apart if you hadn't," Ayrlyn said.

"Sad, isn't it?" Nylan rubbed his forehead, trying to ease the throbbing there.

"It's life."

"Begging your pardon, ser?" asked Tonsar.

"Some troublemaker, big black-haired fellow, Gisyl, I think, wanted to stage a mutiny. He dared me to make him obey. I told him he could obey or die. He didn't believe me."

"And what happened?" asked the armsman.

"He's dead."

Tonsar's mouth opened, then shut. "So . . . so quickly?"

"If you're going to kill someone, it's better to make it quick. Then they can't hurt you threshing around."

Tonsar swallowed, then looked over his shoulder. "You didn't leave the body?"

"No. I made the other troublemaker strap it on the mount. He'll have to bury it when we get to Clynya."

Tonsar swallowed again. "No one would have minded—"

"If they have to clean up afterwards," said Nylan, "maybe they won't be quite so ready to quarrel."

"Yet . . . yet . . ." Tonsar stammered.

"You think they'll just blame me?" Nylan shrugged. "Troops always do, but that's all right so long as they get in the habit of obeying and not doing stupid things."

Tonsar closed his mouth, and beyond him Ayrlyn nodded thoughtfully. Sylenia busied herself with checking the sleeping boy.

Nylan noticed that the line of trees that had marked the east side of the river had vanished, and only a low line of bushes followed the watercourse. On the west side, between the road and the bluff that ran down to the river, was only grass.

A shadow slipped across the road, from the thickening clouds blowing out of the Westhorns to the east.

"Be not too long afore we make Clynya," observed Tonsar. "And a good thing, with the rain coming in. A good rain will lay the road dust for the journey south."

"Too good a rain will turn the road into mud soup," ventured Ayrlyn.

"Ah, lady angel, the rain in the south here, it never falls for long."

Nylan hoped he was right, but the relief from the direct sun provided by the clouds was welcome, more than welcome. He turned to Ayrlyn. "Your turn."

"Right." With a grim smile, she turned her mount and began to ride back along the part of the column that contained their two squads plus of trainees and troublemakers.

The sun hung just above the western hills when they reached a ridge crest. On the other side, the road swung down in an arc into a gentle valley cut by the river. There were no bridges, just what appeared to be a flat sloping ford.

"Clynya . . . Clynya . . ."

The mutterings that came back through the road dust confirmed to Nylan that they were nearing their immediate destination.

"It is not even sunset," proclaimed Tonsar.

"Good," murmured Sylenia.

Nylan just wiped away more muddy sweat, and glanced up at the still-dark clouds that covered two-thirds of the sky. They felt like rain, but there hadn't been any, not even a hint of moisture on the light breeze out of the east that had done little to cool him on the afternoon's ride.

He studied the valley as they began to ride down toward the ford. Unlike Rohrn, Clynya was on the eastern side of the river, on a slight hill nearly two kays north of the ford itself. Was that because the greater threat happened to be the Jeranyi? Using the river as a defense made sense to Nylan, but he wondered if towns and cities were located for such sensible reasons. The plateau he had picked out as a possible city site made more sense than Lornth's location, but there wasn't even a town on the plateau.

Just across the ford, less than a kay from the river, and to the left of the road, were a series of earthworks, and behind them, blackened timbers. The grass reached halfway up the earthen barrier, but had not covered all the blackened ground or ashes.

"What was that?" asked Ayrlyn.

"I believe that must be the Jeranyi fort—the one that Lord Sillek destroyed. I have not been this far south, but Huruc was, and he said that Lord Sillek had destroyed the fort and driven the Jeranyi back across the grasslands." Tonsar shrugged. "They will try again. They always have."

"Wasn't there some sort of agreement?" Ayrlyn pursued.

Nylan looked toward Sylenia, who was turned in her saddle and trying to give Weryl a drink of water.

"Ildyrom cannot be trusted. He is a Jeranyi." Tonsar shrugged. "They will be back."

Nylan frowned. For the Jeranyi to have built a fort on the Lornian side of the river . . . Sillek had indeed had his troubles. To have succeeded in pushing the Jeranyi back across the grasslands, and then still having been forced to fight Westwind—the engineer shook his head. The Lornian holders appeared singularly stupid, but, maybe, there was something he and Ayrlyn didn't know. Maybe.

"There aren't many trees," said Ayrlyn, breaking into his thoughts, "even near the river."

"The sheep like the green shoots, and," Tonsar shrugged, "there is not that much rain."

Nylan glanced up at the clouds. "This doesn't make sense. There's enough rain here for there to be trees."

"Unless the summer is very dry and long and hot," suggested Ayrlyn.

"Hot . . . very hot," agreed Tonsar. "Rain. It rains seldom."

The engineer did not even want to think about a summer that hot and dry.

A line of rain gusted over the low thatched roofs of Clynya and swept westward down the road toward the column of armsmen, down toward the ford, the West Fork, the grass-lands, and Jerans. Almost as the sprinkling of rain had come, it was gone.

Yet after the splattering of rain, all that was left were dark spots on the road, and a hint of dampness in the air.

Nylan stood in the saddle as the column ahead slowed in an open space before several buildings. While the timbered two-storied barracks had a rough plank roof, the stable was roofed with sod, and long streamers of brown grass hung over the thick eaves. Some sections of the roof sported new growth.

Still, the barracks and the stable were large, large enough for the several hundred levies.

Nylan turned to Tonsar. "You get to make sure that Wuerek buries that body—and deep."

"Yes, ser angel." Tonsar's voice was weary.

"If he gives you *any* trouble, tell him I'll bury him next to it."

"Yes, ser." A faint smile crossed Tonsar's lips.

"Tonsar . . ." suggested Ayrlyn. "Don't invent trouble."

Nylan thought the subofficer was going to roll his eyes, but the man only nodded. As Tonsar rode toward the rear of the group, one word escaped his lips, loud enough for the two to hear. ". . . angels . . ."

"He's not used to being understood," said Ayrlyn dryly.

"Thanks to you," Nylan answered.

Sylenia glanced from Nylan to Ayrlyn. The nursemaid opened her mouth, then closed it as another rider neared.

"The front stalls of the stables are for us. You angels have the upper middle quarters," Fornal said smoothly, gesturing toward the wooden outside steps. "They are large enough for your needs. We all eat in the barracks hall after the two bells ring."

"Thank you." Nylan smiled politely. "Where are the sub-officers billeted in case we need to find Tonsar?"

"At the end in the rear." Fornal gestured vaguely in the direction of the long building. "They each have a small room."

After the coregent rode toward the stables, the two angels followed, trailed by Sylenia and Weryl, letting Fornal enter the stables first. A handful of chickens skittered away from all the horses, flocking toward a gap-planked and tilting structure to the south of the stable. Some form of hen house, Nylan guessed, both from the low roof line and the smell.

"This way, sers," called a grimy youth. "Officers at the front here."

The stalls were small, smelly, and the clay underfoot slimy.

Nylan raised his eyebrows and glanced across the stall wall at Ayrlyn. She shrugged. What could they do—except share a wry smile?

After stabling their mounts, and grooming them, the three walked toward the barracks building, where they climbed the outside steps to the central rooms.

Nylan opened the door, and a faint wave of dust—and something else—roiled up around him. There were two rooms, consisting of a small bedchamber with a double-wide bed, and a main front room with two couch beds, and a small hearth. There was no wood for the hearth, not that they needed a fire in the early summer heat. An open area before the windows showed marks on the wide-planked floor where other furniture had been removed.

"It's not too bad, but there's something . . ." Ayrlyn frowned.

So did Nylan. "Chaos. Some time back, though. It's gone, except it's not."

Sylenia, juggling a squirming Weryl, glanced from one angel to the other.

"One of Sillek's wizards?" suggested Ayrlyn.

"Probably—there was one out here in the grasslands to hold off the Jeranyi. Someone told us that. He's probably the one that burned out the Jeranyi fort we passed."

"Sillek was resourceful . . ." Ayrlyn paused and turned to Sylenia. "You can put Weryl down and let him totter around. There's nothing here that can hurt him."

"But you said—" began the black-haired woman-girl.

"There's nothing here now," Nylan said, forcing a smile. "We could just tell that a wizard had lived here."

"You are wizards," pointed out Sylenia.

"Not exactly, and not the same kind," answered the engineer.

A faint frown crossed the nursemaid's forehead.

"Not all wizards are the same," added Ayrlyn. "Healers and mages are not like white wizards. We cannot throw fireballs; they cannot heal."

Slowly, Sylenia lowered Weryl. The boy sat down in a heap beside one of the couch-beds, then pulled himself erect and tottered toward Nylan.

"Daaaa . . ."

The engineer scooped up his son. "Long day? It's not over yet. We still have to find supper."

"Wahdah!"

"And water, too." Nylan laughed.

"Especially water," added Ayrlyn. "I feel like I'm wearing more dust than clothes."

Nylan nodded, thinking it would get worse, with another three days before they reached the area of the copper mines. Had it been a good idea to bring Weryl? Probably not, if there had been any alternative. "There are buckets over there. I'll find a pump or well." He set his son back on the plank floor.

LX

NYLAN SNEEZED TWICE, sharply, wishing that the rain squalls of the days previous had been heavier, at least heavy enough to hold down the road dust, but all they had done was leave dark splotches on the ground, splotches that vanished quickly in the sunlight.

"Kula lies five kays ahead," said Tonsar. "That be where the regent says we will make our outpost. I would rather we had remained in Clynya."

"It might have been more comfortable," said Ayrlyn, "but it's too far away from the mines."

"Besides," added Nylan, "with fewer distractions, we just might get this bunch into shape." He tried to think positively, ignoring the ever-browner grass that flanked the dusty road, and the heat, and the sun that beat all too strongly on his right side.

"You think so?" said Tonsar.

"We can hope," added Ayrlyn.

With each kay south from Clynya, the trees had gotten lower and more widely separated. One rolling hill looked much like another, the grass hanging limply in the hot sun. Scattered patches of weedy growth, amid the grasses, had already begun to brown, and the once-intermittent patches of bare ground had become more and more common, almost joining in places to form a patchwork of red clay.

Wondering if the whole area would be brown and sere before mid-summer, Nylan looked at Sylenia. "Have you ever been this far south?"

"No, ser. I have been to Rohrn, but no farther." She frowned. "It be dry here."

"And it gets drier, I am told," said Tonsar. "No great life being a miner in these parts. My sister's man was, once, but he walked away. Two coppers a day, a pallet, and meals, and it was not near enough, not even for the young ram he was then." He offered a broad smile to Sylenia.

"How long ago was that?" Ayrlyn rubbed her nose.

"Must have been, oh, ten years back. Nuria was the oldest. She died of the chaos fever two winters past." Tonsar shrugged. "Even that, and Wesay wouldn't go back to the mines." He gestured toward the long gentle slope ahead. "Late summer, he said, dust rolled in like rain."

Nylan winced. More heat and dust were the last things they needed.

Out of the dust before them emerged a rider, skirting the edge of the road, peering at faces as he rode, before pulling his horse around and up beside Ayrlyn.

The healer looked at him and waited.

"Ser Fornal would request your presence," stammered the young armsman. "Both of the angel leaders."

"You've got our levies, Tonsar," Nylan said with a laugh. "Alas . . ."

Sylenia smiled shyly, past Nylan at the burly armsman, as Nylan flicked the reins and urged the mare forward.

"Do you feel we have a romance budding there?" asked Ayrlyn.

"I hadn't thought about it," Nylan confessed. "I don't even know if Tonsar has a consort."

"I don't think so, but, out here, does it matter?" The redhead's smile was wry.

If Sylenia were interested in anyone, Nylan preferred Tonsar to most of the levies or scarred professionals. He hoped she wouldn't get hurt, but there wasn't that much that he could do. Forbidding the romance would make it worse, and might jeopardize Weryl. He sighed.

The messenger followed them, just far enough that Fornal could see the youth had carried out his orders, before easing into the column behind the lead riders.

"Kula lies ahead," announced Fornal. "The scouts say that the white ones have burned some of the holdings, some days back, but have left, and there is enough for us to use."

"I assume they will be back," said Ayrlyn.

"They will return anywhere, but Kula is the most distant of the near hamlets, nearly ten kays from the mine, and it has water through the summer from the stream." Fornal scratched his dusty beard. "Derlya offers more, but it is twenty kays to the northwest of the mines, and too close to Jerans for my taste. Choosing between the Jeranyi and the white demons, that is not to my liking, but the Jeranyi sneak up, and the demons do not. So—"

"We camp in Kula," finished Ayrlyn.

"Exactly."

They rode up the long hill in silence, until another valley stretched out before them, more a depression between low rises than a valley. Kula itself consisted of a half-dozen holdings bordering a narrow stream. Nylan scanned the valley, catching the traces of past Cyadoran presence.

One holding held three buildings—house, barn, and shed—and all were charred, roofless. The ground around was burned and black, the black running until it stopped at bare ground, creating a dark blotched effect.

"The white devils," noted Fornal. "They burn enough to drive people out, then take or slaughter the stock." The coregent gestured toward the far side of the valley. "We'll use the large holding. They burned not that. There will be room in the house for us and the senior armsmen, and three sheds and barns." He smiled, faintly. "And plenty of space for you to whip your trainees into shape."

"How far are the mines?" asked Ayrlyn.

"Ten, perhaps twelve kays to the south, over the ridge hills there."

The road wound down and past the burned-out holding and then across the stream. As the mare crossed the crude stone span, Nylan glanced down at the water, a brook surrounded by sheep-cropped grass less than two cubits wide and half that in depth. He saw no animals, unless the white dots on the hill beyond their destination were sheep. Had the Cyadorans taken or slaughtered them all? Or had the holders driven them with them in fleeing Kula?

As they neared the house, Nylan studied the holding. A broken chair lay on the stone stoop, and the door hung on a single iron hinge. Dark splatters stained the gray-white plaster beside the door. The shutters remained closed.

Nylan extended his senses, but could find no trace of life behind the silent walls. From her mount beside him, Ayrlyn shook her head.

In the hillside fields to the south were scattered handfuls of sheep.

"Ha! Some forage food," exclaimed Fornal. "The white demons did not destroy everything."

Nylan sniffed, and his nose wrinkled.

"We'll need to bury the ones they left," Fornal continued. "Huruc?"

"Ser. We'll take care of it."

"Away from the stream," Nylan added.

"Yes, ser."

"We will use the house. The larger squads will turn the barn into a barracks," suggested Fornal. "The shed there—that should work for your squads."

Nylan glanced toward the long shed—gap-planked, like half the outbuildings he'd seen in Lornth—but the woven-grass-thatchlike roof seemed relatively sound. If they remained in Kula into the winter, the ventilated planks would need work, but were probably an advantage in the summer.

Ayrlyn raised her eyebrows, and she and Nylan exchanged glances, before she answered. "It needs some work."

"Everything will need work," answered the coregent. "Best we start now." He turned in the saddle. "Huruc!"

"Ser?"

"Have them clear out the barn. The angels are taking the shed for their . . . squads. The four—five—of us will share the house."

Fornal turned his mount toward the barn, directly behind and to the west of the dwelling. Nylan and Ayrlyn, with Sylenia following, rode toward the shed to the right rear of the house.

Beside the shed were three bodies, bloated. Nylan swallowed. No wonder Fornal didn't worry about the holders returning.

He turned in the saddle. "Sylenia?"

"Sers?"

"You find which room in the holding we get and do what you can to make it habitable. Take Weryl with you. All right?"

"Yes, ser." The black-haired woman nodded.

"We'll be out here, trying to get the squads settled." *And taking care of some basic sanitation problems. Very basic.* "Just tie your mount near the house for now."

As the nursemaid turned her mount, Ayrlyn said in a low voice, "This is just getting worse."

"You had that feeling, didn't you?"

"Degraded Rationalist superiority complex, but I'd hoped otherwise."

"They haven't changed. Anyone else is less than human." That was the problem with the Rats, Nylan reflected, always misusing logic to prove their superiority, and to justify their attempts to eliminate any competition. Somehow, he'd hoped that he and Ayrlyn wouldn't keep having to fight the *Winterlance*'s battles again in Candar, but it looked like the same problem occurred everywhere there were humans.

"No. They haven't changed. They won't." Ayrlyn's voice was heavy. "And you know what that means."

Nylan did. Again . . . people who respected only superior force. His nose itched. Ayrlyn rubbed her nose, swallowed, and tried to stop a sneeze simultaneously. He still sneezed.

After tying their mounts to a well-kept rail fence by the shed, Nylan and Ayrlyn stepped into the sheep shed. Nylan's boots sank into the combination of animal waste and dust.

"Darkness—"

"Not too bad. Seen worse," offered Tonsar as he neared on foot, leading his mount. The thirty-odd trainees and troublemakers remained mounted, well back from the shed.

"Let's get this mess cleaned out," Nylan said quietly. "Use whatever it takes to get the floor down to bare earth, and then sweep it clean before anyone puts a pallet down. Oh, there are three bodies behind the shed, and a couple of dead sheep. They need to be buried—at least a hundred cubits from the stream—downhill."

Tonsar glanced at Nylan. "The men, they likely be tired."

"Better tired than sick in two days, and they will be if they try to sleep in that muck. Or with decomposing bodies within a score of cubits."

A faint sigh escaped Tonsar's lips. "Yes, ser."

"Tonsar . . . we're not . . ." Nylan shook his head. "More men die from sickness than from enemy blades. I can't stop a lot of the blades, but I do know some things to do to keep them from getting sick."

"We'll also make sure that they get clean water," added Ayrlyn. "So they don't get the flux."

Tonsar looked skeptical.

"We are healers, remember?" said the flame-haired angel. "And if that doesn't convince them . . . well . . . does someone else want a blade through his chest?" Her words were bitter, and Nylan understood why. He felt the same way.

"No, ser angels. It will be done." His voice was tired.

"We'll be working here, too," Nylan said. "I'll set up the anvil and a temporary forge under that overhang there. I'll need some stones or bricks—"

"Yes, sers . . ." Tonsar repeated.

"If I'm repairing and sharpening blades, Tonsar, they can carry stones."

Ayrlyn nodded. They both knew there were times to lead by force, and by example. He hoped they'd picked the right times.

LXI

As the morning cookfires were being banked, Nylan swallowed the last of the bread, then stood. The bench was hard. He was still amazed that someone could bake even half-decent bread over a cookfire. Certainly, poor Kadran hadn't been able to.

"The bread's not bad." As he followed Ayrlyn toward the shed where Tonsar would be mustering their would-be armsmen, his eyes went back to the front stoop of the dwelling where Sylenia continued to feed Weryl, then to the spot under the sheep shed's eaves where stones and broken bricks formed a rough forge. Nylan hoped it wasn't too rough, but he'd not had a chance to even think about forging, not yet. And he'd dreamed about trees again, ancient trees filled with both order and chaos.

"So far, the cheese isn't, either." Ayrlyn paused. "What's bothering you? You've been star-systems away ever since you woke."

"Trees . . ." Nylan admitted.

Ayrlyn turned to face Nylan. "Trees filled with whiteness and darkness?"

"Order and chaos?" The smith nodded.

"Strange . . . so did I. I wonder . . ." She shook her head, then looked toward the dying cookfires. "Well . . . our charges are waiting."

Nylan followed her eyes to the cooking area set up between the shed and the barn. Then he looked back to the group of would-be armsmen who stood outside the partly converted sheep shed, most still finishing off their bread, hard cheese, and spiced mutton stew. The engineer had trouble with hot mutton for breakfast, but all the Lornians seemed to relish it.

"I know," Ayrlyn continued. "Mutton for breakfast. Does it cause strange dreams?"

"It is a good and filling breakfast," offered Tonsar cheerfully. "No one dreams badly on mutton."

The engineer shook his head as Tonsar walked closer. "Ready to start the training? You have them organized into groups, like we asked?"

"Yes, ser." Tonsar frowned. "They be not happy with the idea of wooden blades."

"They'd be a lot less happy if we used cold iron," said Ayrlyn.

"Wood is for young children . . . they think."

"Darkness save us—and them—from stupid male vanity," muttered the redhead. "They'd rather play with iron and die."

Tonsar gulped.

"Most don't want to be here, and the rest hate everyone." Ayrlyn looked at the ragged grouping. Already, although the sun had barely cleared the horizon, heat waves were shimmering off the dust-covered clay.

"That is true," admitted Tonsar, "save they fear you both."

"Better to be feared than loved," quipped Ayrlyn.

"I guess."

"Don't guess," said Ayrlyn soberly. "Remember Ryba. This isn't the time for kindness."

"It doesn't seem like many times are," answered Nylan. "Not here in Candar anyway."

"I'll be watching your back," Ayrlyn continued.

"You get to do the second set," Nylan said. "We have to get the point across that either one of us is deadly."

"You could kill one a piece," said Tonsar.

Nylan wasn't sure he was jesting. "No. That lets them off too easily. They need to suffer."

As Tonsar studied Nylan to see if he were joking, Ayrlyn rolled her eyes.

The silver-haired angel managed to keep a straight face.

When it appeared as though most of the armsmen, save the obvious stallers, had finished eating, he nodded to Tonsar. "Line them up."

"Line up!" bellowed the burly subofficer. "Now. Dersio! That be you! And you, Ungit!"

"He sounds like every other noncom," said Ayrlyn.

"But they're worse," answered Nylan, almost under his breath. "This will be worse than a dozen Mrans."

"I hope not. We can't afford to kill that many."

Nylan took a slow breath and walked toward the group, his eyes focusing on the front row. He stopped and took another long look before he spoke. "I'm not one for beating around the bushes." Nylan glanced across the score of dubious and unfriendly faces. "You've all been assigned to Ayrlyn and me because you've been judged as untrained or as troublemakers. I frankly don't care about what others think. If you follow instructions and work hard, I can give you a much better chance to survive and go home." He shrugged. "If you don't want to, fine. You'll be dead meat for the Cyadorans in the first skirmish, and I won't have to worry about your being a problem."

He took one of the wooden wands from Tonsar. He and Ayrlyn had managed to rough-craft eleven, and he wished they had more. There was no safe way to train this lot with real weapons, not without killing or maiming most. "This is a training blade. Why do we use wood? Because you live through your mistakes. It stings. Sometimes, it even hurts, and once in a while you still might get injured. Hopefully, the pain will help you improve."

"Easy for him to say . . ."

Nylan looked across the red dirt toward the big rawboned youth with the scraggly beard. "You said something?"

"Begging your pardon, ser, but you're not all that tough, ser."

Ayrlyn glanced at Nylan and shook her head. The engineer knew what she was thinking, and agreed, even though he hated what would come next. Some people never learned until it was beaten into them or they were killed.

"Fuera—it is Fuera, isn't it? Take the wand and see how you do with it, then." Nylan tossed the wooden wand to the youth.

Fuera scooped the wand up and started toward Nylan, waving it wildly.

The smith edged aside, easily avoiding most of the wild slashes, parrying a few, before knocking the wand out of the man's hand.

"Pick it up."

Fuera glared, but picked up the wand and charged toward Nylan.

Nylan cracked him across the back of his wrist, and the wand dropped a second time.

Fuera turned with a bellow and charged Nylan.

The engineer, triggering full step-up almost unconsciously, dropped his own wand and blurred, ducking aside, and letting the few moves he knew nearly automatically take hold.

The youth went over Nylan, almost in an arc, and hit

the ground with a dull thud. He lay still for a long moment.

Nylan bent and picked his own wand back up, then walked over and tapped Fuera on the shoulder, hard enough for it to smart. "Get up and pick up that wand. You don't get to quit because your pride's hurt. If I'd been using those crowbars the professionals in Lornth use, you'd be dead or maimed for life."

The youth glared at Nylan, then scrambled to his knees, gathering his strength for another charge.

Nylan forced a smile, waiting in step-up.

With a bellow, Fuera charged again.

The score of recruits stood silently.

Nylan flashed aside, using his elbow to club the youth into the ground, then he stood, waiting, as the brown-haired would-be armsman rose drunkenly to his feet.

"Pick up the wand, or not, as you please," Nylan said. "I'm trying to teach you enough to keep you alive. You seem to want to die young."

Snickers ran through the onlookers.

Fuera charged Nylan. This time the smith stepped inside the bearlike rush, and using open palms, dropped the youth onto the clay with two quick blows.

Fuera did not rise.

". . . never saw . . . so fast . . ."

". . . coulda killed him easy . . ."

". . . friggin' mean bastard . . ."

Nylan let the murmurs die away before he turned to the others. "I would prefer not to keep making this point. In a fight, I wouldn't have bothered. Fuera would have been dead with about one blow." He looked at the unconscious man, then at the others. "One reason why he's still alive is that we're short of fighters. Now . . . is there anyone else here who would like to prove that he's the toughest, meanest, and nastiest idiot in Lornth?" Nylan's green eyes raked across the group of the nearest nineteen arrayed in a rough arc.

Each man looked away as Nylan fixed his eyes on each in turn.

LXII

LEPHI LEANED FORWARD in the silver-trimmed malachite chair. His brown eyes were flat as the slim, balding, and white-haired wizard walked across the polished white stones, then bowed.

"You summoned me, Your Mightiness?"

"I did. Have you a solution for the Accursed Forest, Triendar? One that does not cost me the double handful of white mages remaining? Or more troops that I do not have?"

"Has Your Mightiness rediscovered the secrets of the iron birds? Or how to make iron feathers that reflect the sun? Or perhaps you have found the means to create the ice lances of the ancient angels to place upon your fireship?" Triendar's voice was mild, even.

Lephi raised his hand. "Do not mock me, Triendar, unless you wish . . ."

The white-haired wizard bowed again. "I do not mock Your Mightiness. What you have asked of me is as easy as what I have asked of you."

"You are the wizard, not I."

"Can I lift myself into the sky, Sire? Can I turn the Great Western Ocean into steam and leave the fishes gasping on dry sands and seaweed?" Triendar bowed once more.

"I set you a task, and I bid you leave until you can return and tell me it is done." Lephi's voice was hard and flat, but his hands gripped the armrests of the malachite throne so hard that they trembled.

"Very well, Your Mightiness. I shall not return." Triendar bowed once again.

Lephi raised his right hand, then lowered it. "What mean you that you will not return?"

"Your Mightiness," offered the white wizard. "All of us are bound. You cannot fly. I cannot turn all the seas to steam nor hold back the Accursed Forest without white wizards and fire and men with torches and mattocks. You can bid and command all that you desire. You can have the Archers of the Rational Stars turn me into a target, but I cannot do what I cannot do, and I will not deceive you into thinking it is so."

Lephi's hands gripped the armrests again, tightly, and for long moments there was silence. Not even a whisper nor a sigh caressed the cold white polished stones.

Finally, the Lord of Cyador spoke. "You have always been honest, and you risk your life to be honest. I cannot say I am pleased, but I cannot ask more of any man nor wizard." Lephi paused. "Bring me a plan. Tell me what you can do with how many wizards and how many men. Tell me how many it will take—forever, is it not—to keep the forest in check?"

Triendar bowed a last time. "It will be done, Your Mightiness."

After the white mage left, Lephi wiped his forehead, then crumpled the perfumed white towel and dropped it beside the chair, where a girl in white silently retrieved it.

"At least . . . I will bring back the fireships . . . and the fire cannon." He smiled. "Then, then they will *all* fear great Cyad again."

LXIII

NYLAN RESET THE last stone in the forge bed, then paused and wiped his forehead with the back of his forearm, glancing out at the training yard.

"Rather be here than there, ser," said the lanky blond barely into manhood from where he pedaled the grindstone.

"You get a chance at both, Sias," Nylan told his semivolunteer apprentice. "Tomorrow, you get to try it all on horseback."

Sias groaned.

"Watch the blade," the engineer cautioned. "Even a healer can't grow back missing fingers."

Between the two of them, they'd managed to sharpen and clean most of the ill-assorted blades belonging to the two-plus squads of levies that he and Ayrlyn had been assigned. If only upgrading blade skills and horsemanship were that easy!

Still, it had to be possible. Nylan had learned both—albeit with the help of order-field skills and hard-wired reflex speed-ups the locals didn't have. So had the refugee women of West-wind, without his hard-wired advantages or the strength or the conditioning of the levies.

"Are the white demons really six cubits tall?" asked Sias innocently.

"You know they're not, unless you mean on horseback on top of a dwelling. Who's been spreading that nonsense?"

"At night . . . there are whispers." Sias took the blade and carefully wiped it with an oiled cloth, before returning it to its scabbard and picking up another.

The drum of hoofbeats drowned out Ayrlyn's orders for a moment as two squads of levies and a squad of the professional armsmen followed Fornal down the lane and toward the road to the south.

Nylan coughed. As usual, the light summer breeze was just strong enough to lift the ubiquitous grit and red dust—this time from Fornal's departing force—across the training yard, but not strong enough to cool anything.

The coregent's scouts had reported in the night before. The Cyadorans had built a rock and earth barrier around the mines, with reinforced gates, and a tall watchtower on the highest point of the hill. Most of the Cyadoran troops were already housed in earth-walled barracks. Cooler than tents, no doubt, reflected the seated smith.

So far, the white forces remained within the compound, except for scouting, raiding, or foraging missions. And they had begun to produce copper again, if the smoke and fires from the furnaces were any indication.

Fornal hoped to confirm that—and pick off any Cyadoran forces that he could. Nylan hoped the Cyadorans didn't pick off Fornal.

A burly figure walked from the barn toward the makeshift

smithy, and Nylan nodded to himself as he straightened and walked from behind what would be the forge bed.

Huruc surveyed the makeshift forge, his eyes dropping to the anvil wedged in place between two timbers sunk into the clay. "Your smithy looks ready." He gestured toward the dust on the hillside. "Let us hope ser Fornal brings back only nicked and damaged blades."

"As opposed to empty mounts?" asked Nylan.

Huruc nodded, then glanced toward the training yard where Ayrlyn walked from practicing pair to pair.

"Get that wrist stiff, Meresat! Keep your blade up! Up!" The redhead's voice was hard, sharp, yet impersonal.

"They look better already," observed the armsman. He lowered his voice. "Is it true that you let that young cock Fuera charge you and then cold-cocked him three times in a row?"

Nylan nodded. "I either had to destroy him or kill him, and I don't have enough armsmen to kill one out of hand."

"They say you have eyes in the back of your head. Both of you."

"I'm glad they think so." The engineer laughed.

"You're putting edges and points on the blades."

"Yes," answered Nylan neutrally.

Huruc shook his head ever so slightly, and Nylan understood. Good edged weapons—and the idea behind them—could be a danger to an overbearing Lornian lord.

"We need every edge possible against the Cyadorans," the angel smith added, wondering if Huruc would get the pun.

"Keep your friggin' feet apart!" snapped Ayrlyn from behind Huruc. "A two-year-old could push you over."

Sias grinned and resumed pedaling the grindstone.

The burly armsman just shook his head.

LXIV

CLANG! CLANG! THE armsman on watch on the second level of the converted barn rang the alarm chime.

"Stand down," snapped Nylan to the levies, glancing up at the watch post where a bearded armsman in purple stood and scanned the horizon. The angel engineer stood in the saddle and peered south, but could see nothing but the dust of riders. "But stand ready!"

"Ser . . ." murmured the mounted squad.

The engineer turned to Tonsar, on a roan beside him. "It's probably Fornal, but hold until we know. If it is, we'll meet him, and you take them through it again."

"Yes, ser." The brown-bearded subofficer took a deep breath, then studied the squad. "Stand fast!"

Ayrlyn eased her chestnut toward Nylan as he guided his mount away from the flat area behind the converted sheep shed.

"They still just fling up a blade," he said.

"They're getting better," she answered, nodding her head toward the south. "Fornal, you think?"

"I hope," muttered Nylan as he reined up before the dwelling, his eyes focusing on the road to the south, the late afternoon sun uncomfortably hot on his back.

Ayrlyn reined up beside him. His eyes flicked to the corral where the remaining horses, mostly the Lornian draft animals, gathered at one end.

"Ser Fornal! It be ser Fornal!" called the watch.

Behind him, Tonsar began to speak to the arrayed levies. "You are a miserable excuse for armsmen. Let us begin again. Do not hold your wands like brooms or I will chop them up with real cold iron. . . ."

With a half-smile, Nylan eased the mare into a slow walk out toward the road. "I'd like to see how he did before the men do."

"You're afraid he didn't do all that well?"

"Who knows? Early success could be as dangerous as failure." Nylan flicked the reins to urge the mare into a faster walk.

Fornal wore dust like a second skin, as did the older armsmen who flanked him, and who reined back as the angels neared.

"Greetings, ser Fornal," Nylan offered.

Fornal nodded brusquely, but offered no objection as Nylan eased his mount up beside the coregent. Ayrlyn slipped hers beside Nylan's.

Fornal had left with three full squads, one of hardened armsmen, and two of the better levies. Half a dozen saddles were empty, and blood splattered across twice that many riders. Just from the residual chaos oozing from the armsmen, Nylan could tell that most of that blood had not come from the Lornians, but more than enough had.

Beside the half-dozen mounts with gray blankets under the empty saddles, or saddles with bodies strapped over them, there were nearly a dozen with blood-splattered white blankets, and two were piled with blades and another pair with various saddlebags, roped haphazardly in place.

"You had some success, it appears," ventured Nylan.

"Better than I had hoped for a first skirmish," admitted the black-haired regent. "They were surprised." He slowed his mount to a walk as they neared where the lane split between the ways to the dwelling and the converted barn, then turned in the saddle. "Take care of the mounts first, except for the wounded. Put the wounded in the front bay." Fornal turned and let his mount carry him toward the quarters of the converted barn.

"You will heal them? The wounded? You are healers." Fornal's dark eyes went from Nylan to Ayrlyn.

Nylan glanced at Ayrlyn before answering. "We'll do what we can. It depends. We'll have to look at each."

Fornal nodded to see the two lines of mounted levies that Tonsar had drawn up. "They look more like armsmen. We will need every one. The white ones are thick as flies." He reined up under the watch post, and, after a moment, looked at

Huruc, who stood waiting, impassively. "You have a burial detail?"

The senior armsman nodded.

"We lost a half-dozen—more than I would have wished, but it happens." Fornal inclined his head to Huruc, then eased his mount toward the right, and the corral. The angels let their mounts follow. Fornal reined up by the unwalled but roofed shelter at the north end of the corral where the mounts of the senior armsmen and officers were kept.

Nylan and Ayrlyn dismounted as well, tying their mounts. They could unsaddle and groom them later.

"We'll start on the wounded immediately," Nylan said to Fornal.

"Each one you save will live to kill another white demon," said the regent. "I have heard that your healing is without peer in Candar. Let us trust you can heal many."

"That depends on their wounds," Ayrlyn answered.

"Do what you must."

Neither angel said anything as they recrossed the practice yard.

"Tonsar?" Nylan said quietly, stopping for a moment and looking up at the mounted subofficer.

"Ser?"

"That was very thoughtful of you to draw up the men to welcome ser Fornal. I should have thought of it, but I am glad you did."

"I would be a poor subofficer, ser, if there were some matters I did not know more of than you." Tonsar grinned.

"All right." Nylan had to grin back. The grin vanished as he thought about the wounded. "Run them through the last exercise again. Then, have them groom their mounts before dinner. We're going to be busy doing some healing."

The burly subofficer nodded.

As they neared the barn, Ayrlyn reached out and squeezed Nylan's hand. "I know you wanted to kill Fornal, but thank you."

"For what? Being sensible? For ignoring his setup? If we don't save them all, we've failed?"

"Of course."

The six wounded armsmen lay on pallets barely raised off the dirt floor by worn and filthy planks.

The first man sat on his pallet cradling an arm. Another man stood beside him, shaking his head. "He won't let us touch him."

"No butchery! No . . ." Sweat poured off the dusty and muddy forehead, but the armsman did not look up.

"Do we have splints?" Nylan murmured. "Or something like them?"

"Haven't seen any." Ayrlyn turned to the uninjured man. "Get us two lengths of straight wood, about the width of a blade and no longer than his forearm—and some strips of cloth." She paused. "Actually, get us about a dozen lengths of wood like that."

"Yes . . . ser." The man scurried away.

"We're not—" began Nylan.

"You're not cutting off my arm! I'll die first."

"We're not cutting off anything," Nylan said gently.

"Then you be no healers I know."

"No, we're not. We'll be back in a bit. And you'll keep your arm." Nylan could sense that the break was a compound sort of thing, but within the capabilities of healing through the fields—if done soon.

They moved to the second man—young, with a scraggly blond beard and rosy cheeks. A dirty bandage covered a deep gash in his shoulder, and the slump of his body and the pain in his eyes warned Nylan.

"Deep thrust and some broken bones," murmured Ayrlyn.

Nylan could feel the chaos of infection, although it was not great, not yet.

"Two of us," said Ayrlyn, "but we can do it. Let's check the others first, quickly."

The third man was already dead from internal bleeding of some sort.

They exchanged glances, then moved to the next.

"Crushed bones in the hand" was Ayrlyn's verdict. "Maybe we can get back some function."

The fifth patient looked blindly past them, his breathing

ragged, the white of chaos already filling most of his body.

The sixth man had a deep bruise/cut/gash across the top of his right thigh, open almost to the bone. An older armsman waited there, holding loops of gut or thread or something, and a needle in his hand.

"I can close it, but the chaos would kill him."

Nylan smiled. "This one—this will be easy."

"Such a deep wound . . ." The voice lowered. "Most die."

"He'll live," Ayrlyn said.

"He is my sister's consort."

"Shouldn't we try . . . the way you did with Nesslek?" the redhead asked Nylan.

"For around the infection, but it's not quite the same."

She nodded. "Still . . ."

Nylan extended his perceptions, joining them with Ayrlyn's, and discovered some infection/chaos, but had no trouble in forcing it out, knitting a sort of barrier that bound the white chaos away and around the wound. The young man looked at them stolidly.

Ayrlyn touched his forehead, and the armsman's eyes closed. "Now . . . stitch up the wound."

"Yes, lady healer."

Again, after the stitches were knotted, the two pushed away the remaining chaos in the wound and stitched area.

"We'll have to keep doing this," she pointed out.

"If we do it daily, it won't take much."

They straightened. A man stood in the shadows, holding lengths of wood.

"Now . . . for the broken bones." They walked back toward the first man, who watched them, fear and sweat pouring from him.

In the end, they staggered out of the makeshift infirmary.

"Four out of six . . . not too bad," mumbled Ayrlyn.

"That's malpractice . . . on Heaven," said Nylan.

"Miracle . . . here." Ayrlyn coughed, pushing Nylan toward the cookfires. "We need to eat."

Nylan agreed, and he followed Ayrlyn's steps toward the small fire at the end where the officers got served.

"Did you heal Gerrit, ser angel?" asked the cook, who thrust half a loaf of black bread on Ayrlyn's trencher.

Ayrlyn looked blankly at the red-bearded man.

"Blond fellow. Looked like his forearm was smashed."

"He'll heal. Be some eight-days, but he'll be fine."

Another man, balding and breathing heavily, stepped up. "What about Giste? He was the big fellow."

"I'm sorry." Nylan took a deep breath. "He was dead before we even got there."

"How many will live? Any of them?" asked the balding man.

"Four. The one with the smashed hand probably won't hold a blade well, but he'll keep the hand." Ayrlyn turned and walked unsteadily toward the dwelling that served as quarters and headquarters.

"Why not Giste?" pursued the armsman behind Nylan.

"Because the damned blade shredded his guts, and even the best healer can't unshred a chopped intestine." Nylan turned to follow Ayrlyn.

"Don't push it, Delman," cautioned a voice behind the angel. "We're darkness lucky we got any healers at all."

Nylan carried his wooden trencher toward the dwelling, and the shaded side porch on the east side.

Fornal already sat on one of the stools on the side porch and chewed on a chunk of greasy mutton—all the meat was mutton, and the animals were slowly vanishing, Nylan reflected, doubting if the remaining strays and abandoned flocks would be enough to last the summer. Then, would they and the Lornians survive the summer, once the Cyadorans decided to act?

Huruc just sat on the top step, chewing noisily.

The angel smith stepped around the senior armsman and sat down on the other end of the bench from Ayrlyn, and after a bite of the tough bread, forced himself to take a bite of the mutton. It was greasy—and strong.

"It's pretty fierce," Ayrlyn said with a smile. "But it helps."

"These are good rations," suggested Huruc. "Times have been, in the grasslands, where we had only moldy cheese and roots—the wild onions."

"I'd prefer they not get any worse," answered Nylan.

"So would all the men," said Huruc, his mouth half-full. He swallowed and asked, "How did your healing go, angels?"

"Four of them should live, three to carry a blade," answered Ayrlyn.

"That's good," said Huruc. "Most usually die."

"I had heard that the angel healers could heal almost all," said Fornal mildly.

"I'm sure the Marshal of Westwind wishes that were true," Nylan answered blandly, after too long a pause to think of a suitable answer. "There would be three times as many guards there, if it were so."

"What about the blond?" asked Huruc.

Nylan smiled. "He should live. We stopped the chaos early enough. Even so, he won't lift a blade for seasons. Not until the bones knit. You'll have to make him a cook's helper or something. It'll free someone else to fight."

Ayrlyn asked politely, "What happened?"

"We ran into one of their raiding parties. They didn't expect us." Fornal smiled. "Not many escaped."

"How many in the party?"

"A score and a half, I'd guess."

Nylan held back a frown. His guess was that Fornal had caught a scouting group of sorts, not that Nylan had any problems with the coregent's decision to take them on—not after he'd seen the bodies of innocent Lornians scattered across Kula. "A few more times, and they may wish they'd picked on some other land."

"Not the white demons. They will stay until the last man."

"Then, we'll have to get rid of them to the last man—even if we do it one at a time."

Huruc laughed gently. "A merchant's approach to fighting."

"No," answered Nylan, after swallowing another mouthful of bread and mutton, "one that works."

"You angels did not do such," pointed out Fornal.

"We didn't have much choice, and where we could follow that doctrine we had almost no losses. Westwind lost two-thirds of its original forces in pitched battles against more numerous opponents." Nylan frowned at the twinge through his skull. He should have remembered that the order forces of the damned planet never let him exaggerate without reminding him—often painfully. Still, the point was basically true.

"Because we have not attacked the enemy encampment, some holders would claim I have lost honor." Fornal shrugged. "I would not regain it by dying in battle."

Nylan wasn't sure if that were an apology of sorts, or an observation. "If you drive out the Cyadorans, won't that suffice?"

"For some. For others . . . they would find some other reason to find fault." Fornal shook his head with a sad smile and then stuffed a large chunk of bread into his mouth. He did not look back at Nylan.

After eating, Nylan walked around to the front porch where Sylenia held Weryl.

"Weryl!" Nylan held out his arms.

"Daaa!" The boy lurched from the nursemaid's arms and across the planks.

Nylan scooped him up, and, for a time, just held the silver-haired boy, letting himself feel the warmth, the aliveness. Weryl finally began to squirm.

"Sorry, son. You felt so good." Nylan eased himself down onto the plank floor and set Weryl on the planks beside him. "So good." He still asked himself at times if he were carrying out Istril's charge as well as he could. He supposed he always would.

"Ser Nylan?" asked Sylenia.

"Yes?"

"Might I depart for a time?"

"Of course." He paused. "Try not to get into too much trouble with your armsman."

Sylenia blushed as she rose from the bench.

"That was unfair, Nylan," said Ayrlyn from the doorway.

"I apologize, Sylenia."

The nursemaid blushed again, but smiled shyly as she slipped past the angel smith.

Ayrlyn sat on the bench.

"Ah-yah!" Weryl tottered toward the redhead. "Ah-yah!"

Nylan followed the nursemaid's progress toward the makeshift barracks.

A squat armsman eased his mount toward Sylenia, then spurred the horse away after she spoke. The smith frowned and glanced at Ayrlyn.

"We'll need to watch that."

He nodded slowly. Along with how much else, he wondered.

LXV

I WASN'T READY for my first fight." Nylan offered a grim smile to the levies ranked in three lines before the sheep-shed barracks. "That's one reason why we've pushed you. I was lucky, but that's not something you can always count on." He nodded to Tonsar. "Have them mount up, and check each man's gear. Then I will."

". . . never lets anything past him . . ."

". . . he talks . . . she looks through you . . . and they say she's warm, compared to most angels . . ."

Always the stereotypes—Nylan glanced at Ayrlyn as they walked toward the corral and their waiting mounts. "And they think you're cold," he said with a low laugh, thinking about Ryba.

"For them . . . I am. Ryba wasn't far off about the men in Candar." She shook her head. "If I appeared at all human, they wouldn't respect me. It's the same for you, except you're a mean bastard and I'm just a cold bitch. Bastards get more respect than bitches."

"Both earned with force."

"Unfortunate, but true. Then, that was true in the U.F.A. It just wasn't quite so blatant." Ayrlyn checked her gear, then swung up into the saddle with a fluid grace that Nylan knew had been hard-earned.

The saddled mounts at the other end of the corral circled uneasily, as if they knew the day were different.

Nylan refocused on his mare and mounted. With a glance at the levies as they moved toward the corral, he guided his mount toward the dwelling where Sylenia stood on the front stoop holding Weryl. He reined up at the edge of the lane, beside Ayrlyn, then looked at Weryl and Sylenia. He eased the mare closer to the porch/stoop, until he was less than ten cubits from them.

"Just take care of him," he finally said.

"I will, ser. I will." Sylenia met the smith's eyes.

"Take care of yourself, too." Nylan nodded and forced a smile to Weryl.

"Daaa."

"Be good to Sylenia, Weryl." With a last smile, he turned the mare back toward the space to the north of the sheep shed where the levies were mounting and sorting themselves into ranks. He had to squint momentarily as he looked east, where the sun had barely cleared the low hills.

"Children make it harder," said Ayrlyn. "Even for me."

He looked at the redhead riding beside him.

"He's sweet, like you must have been," she said, the corners of her mouth not quite smiling.

"Me? The terrible angel?"

"To fight at all, gentle souls often have to be the most terrible, to overcome their nature."

Did they, Nylan wondered, or were gentle souls really gentle at all? He looked toward the space before the sheep-shed barracks, where men and mounts milled.

"Form up!" ordered Tonsar as he glanced over his shoulder toward Nylan and Ayrlyn. "Nesru! You be the one I'm talking to!"

"Ser!"

Nylan repressed a smile as a single chicken skittered along the planks of the former sheep shed, snapping its beak down to retrieve the smallest of dark bread crusts discarded by some levy. How had it survived? Or were they the equivalent of wild chickens?

"Give them a last chance to make sure every man's water bottle is full," Nylan suggested in a low voice as he eased the mare up beside the subofficer. "That's if you haven't already."

"Told 'em twice, ser."

"That's once more than they deserve," said Ayrlyn, "but they're new at this."

Even newer than we are, Nylan reflected, holding in a smile as he caught the grin in Ayrlyn's brown eyes.

Slowly, he rode down the line of levies.

"Mearet . . . where's your water bottle?"

". . . check that rear girth . . ."

Finally, he nodded at Tonsar. "We'll wait for the regent."

"You ready, angels?" came the call—seemingly within moments.

"Ready," Nylan confirmed.

With a last look at the dwelling where Sylenia and Weryl still stood watching the riders, Nylan forced his concentration away from his son and onto the ride to Hesra—supposedly the next target of the Cyadorans, if Huruc's scouts were correct, although it didn't take much guessing. After their initial swift raids, the Cyadorans seemed to be moving from the nearest target to each hamlet successively more distant from the copper mines.

Dust swirled up around the angels before the column even had left the holding that had become the Lornian camp, and sweat had begun to trickle down the engineer's neck.

From out of the dust ahead, Fornal gestured.

"I think the regent wishes our presence," said Ayrlyn.

"I get that impression." Nylan leaned toward Tonsar. "I don't know how long we'll be, but I'm sure you can keep them in order."

"All I have to do is tell them what you'll do if the regent sees them acting up while you're talking." Tonsar offered a broad grin.

"There is that," said Ayrlyn with a straight face, "but we will need to leave some alive for the Cyadorans."

The burly subofficer was still shaking his head as the two angels eased their mounts onto the shoulder of the narrow road and up a column of levies, and then past Fornal's squad of professionals.

The dark-bearded regent continued to look at the road ahead to the south for several moments after Nylan and Ayrlyn joined him, and the three rode silently.

"Your training has been good, but we'll see how well they recall it when blades fly." Fornal glanced back toward the three squads that trailed his professionals, the last two being those of the angels.

Nylan could sense one thing—his levies rode better, in better order, and more quietly than they had on the way to Kula.

"Look like armsmen now, anyway," observed the red-headed subofficer riding to the left of Fornal.

Nylan glanced at the man, recalling the face but not the name, wishing he were better with names.

"This is Lewa, next senior to Huruc," offered Fornal pleasantly. "He has the Rohrn levies."

"I've seen him, but I'm not good with names," admitted the engineer.

"Not me, either, ser," returned Lewa. "But angels are easier to pick out."

"How far to Hesra?" asked Nylan.

"Mid-morning. The Cyadorans will show after that. They don't move that early." Lewa snorted. "They only ride in perfect order, and each one carries a white-bronze toothpick just like the rider before him and the one behind."

"Does it work?" asked Ayrlyn.

"As long as there are more of them than us . . . yes." Lewa ran a hand through his short red hair.

One rolling hill followed another, with the dust growing with the day, and the grass getting sparser and browner with each hill. Whether they rode through the depressions between hills, or along the ridge lines, as the road wandered southward, each hill revealed yet another hill similar to the last.

Just past mid-morning, at the crest of one hill not markedly different from any other, Lewa nodded to Fornal and announced, "Hesra is over the next line of hills."

Fornal grunted. When the road had carried them to another

valley and turned east toward a gap between the hills, the regent gestured. "We'll leave the road here, angle up to the south."

"That will be a better position on the road from the mines," Lewa explained.

A good two hundred cubits short of the browned grasses that covered the ridge line ahead, grasses that hung limply in the morning light, Fornal slowed his mount, then nodded to the subofficer.

"Rein up!" snapped Lewa. Both the Rohrn levies and the more professional armsmen halted.

Nylan slowed his mount on the dusty grass and stood in his stirrups, echoing the command.

"Rein up!" repeated Tonsar.

With little more than a ghost of a breeze, the dust began to settle immediately once the horses stopped.

Fornal eased his mount toward the angels. "We'll ride over the top and out along the ridge. You ought to be able to get a good view from there," said Fornal. "The white demons will branch from the road—they have so far anyway. If they see us, they'll think we're scouts."

Nylan wondered, but said nothing as he flicked the reins for the mare to follow Fornal. Sweat poured down his neck, and the space between his shoulder blades itched—and it wasn't all that far past mid-morning.

Several flies buzzed past his sweat-dampened forehead, and he brushed them away, wishing absently for the cool of the Westhorns.

"Hot already," Ayrlyn observed.

"Cool compared to late summer, angels," answered Lewa.

The ridge was covered with browning grass, with only two low trees breaking the grass line, and one of them was dead. Neither tree was much higher than the head of a mounted rider.

Fornal reined up at the crest, then inclined his head toward the redheaded subofficer.

"Hesra's at the head of the valley where the stream turns. There's an earthen dam there." Lewa pointed toward a blue oval and a dark splotch to the left. "They use that for ground crops, and for stock water." The redhead turned in the saddle.

"That's the road from the mines, and it won't be long now, I'd say."

The empty road from the southwest entered the valley at the west end, traversed the flat, and met up with the section they had taken at the gap on the northeast end, less than a kay from the dark splotch that Lewa had called Hesra. Where the road from the mines entered the valley, it was a line of reddish brown that angled down a brown-grassed hillside steep enough that the parts of the lower section of the hill were still in shadow, even late in the morning.

Was the haze beyond the hill a cloud? Nylan shook his head as the dust began to rise over the top of the hillside.

"We'll wait until they're on the lower part of the road," Fornal said. "Then we'll hit them. Lewa and I will take the lead. Your job, angels, is to seal off their rear."

The four eased their mounts back beyond the ridge crest, far enough that they could still see the road, but so the Cyadorans would have difficulty seeing them.

Amid the dust came the shimmer of white, and the glinting of sun on polished shields, as the white lancers rode downhill. The van was less than a kay before the main body, and Nylan saw no scout—perhaps because Fornal had been more than effective over the past days in picking off scouts.

Nylan studied the precise column of white lancers, absently estimating the group—three score, in all—compared to perhaps four and a half for the Lornians, but the score and a half of his troops were greener than the hillside grasses had been a season earlier, and the engineer wasn't too certain that the grasses still didn't have more seasoning.

"Seen enough?" asked Fornal. "Let's get them ready."

"The Cyadorans are professionals," Ayrlyn said to Nylan in a low voice as they rode back to where Tonsar and their levies waited.

"They're well-drilled. That doesn't make them professionals. If Gethen and the scrolls are right, we and Fornal have more experience than they do. I also didn't see any archers."

"Why doesn't that comfort me much?" asked the flame-haired angel.

"Because their good drilling could still kill a bunch of our hotheads?"

"That thought had crossed my mind."

"And because archers aren't that effective when you've got two bodies of forces on horseback?"

"That, too." Ayrlyn, slightly ahead of Nylan, reined up first.

Tonsar and the levies watched, silently, waiting for the angels to speak.

"The Cyadorans are about to enter the valley on the other side of this hill," began Nylan. "They'll be on the road. Our job is to hit the end of the column and seal off their line of retreat." The engineer looked around. "We have more armsmen than they do. So I don't expect either problems or complaints."

Several of the levies swallowed, including Fuera and Wuerek, both of whom would be in Nylan's squad.

"We'll each take a squad, like we practiced," Nylan said. "Tonsar, your group will be on the left, and Ayrlyn's will be on the right, and we'll make this simple. Just hit the column straight-on from the side and chop down anyone you can."

". . . just?" came a murmur from somewhere.

"Just," affirmed Ayrlyn.

"Fighting is simple," added Nylan. "You hit them and kill them before they hit you. You can do it, and I expect you to." He looked around, and saw that the other squads were riding uphill.

"Let's go." The mare followed his flick of the reins, and he found himself leading the trot uphill.

Ayrlyn crossed behind him to take the lead of the right squad, and Tonsar flashed a grin as he lifted his blade.

Blade? Nylan wanted to kick himself as he crossed the ridge and started downhill, toward the white forces that had still not even looked up—or so it seemed. The engineer eased the dark blade from his shoulder harness. Did he wave it? The business of leading armed charges was something new to him.

His lips curled for a moment, and he made a brusque flick of the shortsword—no waves or flourishes. "Blades out!" he ordered, just in case someone else had made his mistake, but he did not look back, concentrating on the grass ahead, trying to see if there were potholes or the like in the grass.

If there were, the mare avoided them. Nylan's squad trailed the others by nearly fifty cubits when they hit the flat before the road, but it wouldn't matter.

Three doublets sounded from some sort of horn, and the lancers swung toward the charging Lornians, not turning to retreat, but dressing ranks, almost automatically, as the Lornians bore down on them. Glittering reflections splayed from the small polished shields, making it difficult for Nylan to concentrate on an individual lancer.

A faint white mist surrounded the detachment, similar to, but subtly different from, the whiteness that had enfolded the white wizards who had attacked Westwind. The whiteness around the lancers was more . . . ordered, for all the lances of light that played from the small and heavy mirror shields.

Nylan focused on a Cyadoran who seemed to lead one section, but a tall man in glittering white beside the officer or sub-officer had pivoted in his saddle and a long length of metal flicked—impossibly swiftly—toward the angel—too swiftly for Nylan to turn the mare.

"That's why they're called lancers, idiot," he murmured to himself as he twisted in the saddle, and beat aside the glittering lance with the dark blade that seemed so short.

The lance shattered, as though it had been made of glass, but another lancer spurred toward Nylan, a sabre glittering in the midday sun, held low and angled to bisect the engineer, more light glaring into Nylan's eyes.

Nylan flung his blade—almost blindly against the mirror shield's light and nearly point blank—and threw himself sideways in the saddle, feeling the sabre catch the edge of his shirt, before the lancer slumped in the saddle, grasping at the short sword buried to its hilt in his chest.

Nylan brought up the second blade, struggling to get it out of the waist scabbard, and absently noting that he should have used the blade at his waist first, because the shoulder harness was easier to get to. He forced his thoughts away from the white pain of death that flowed around him, knowing that he had to get back to Weryl.

His eyes flickered to the scattered individual skirmishes on his right. Only Ayrlyn had cut through the column, as he had, and she was surrounded by three of the white-clad Cyadorans. He turned and spurred the mare toward the three lancers around Ayrlyn.

The healer's blade wove a web of gray, and as Nylan drew nearer, one of the white-bronze sabres snapped, the blade streaking toward the trampled reddish soil like a crippled lander. The disarmed lancer backed off, then spurred his mount downhill at the sight of Nylan.

Neither of Ayrlyn's two remaining attackers budged, despite the hoofbeats of Nylan's mare, hoofbeats that sounded thunderous to the angel. The attackers were spreading, to catch the healer from each side.

Nylan winced even as his blade flashed, cleaving through the unprotected neck of the lancer to the right. The engineer staggered in his saddle, half-blind again, from the white knives that slammed through his eyes and skull with each killing, but instinctively, he raised his blade, though he felt blind.

At that, the remaining lancer ducked, and pulled his mount away.

While Ayrlyn could have slaughtered the Cyadoran, she held her blade, then slowly sheathed it as the handful of lancers retreated through the grasslands, circling back to catch the road.

For a moment, the silver-haired angel and the flame-haired angel just looked at each other—almost blankly—before Nylan squinted through the burning in his skull to survey the field.

To his left, Tonsar chevied a group back toward Nylan.

"You let him go," wondered the subofficer. His mount's muzzle was smeared with foam.

"I had to," said the healer tiredly.

Tonsar glanced from one angel to the other, then shrugged. "Holding off three apiece and killing two each. That is not bad."

"Not bad . . . who's he jesting?" came across the space from where a handful of Nylan's and Ayrlyn's levies had drawn up.

Nylan wanted to grin, despite his throbbing headache, but managed to keep a straight face.

The dust on the hillside road faded, as the handful of Cyadoran lancers rode back south toward the mines.

Nylan's urge to grin faded abruptly as the pounding in his skull continued and as he surveyed the trampled and dust-swept road and the fields that flanked it, looking at the white lumps and the handful of dark-clad figures strewn across the grasslands, and shields that still caught and threw the light.

Was it over? Nylan took one deep breath and then another, trying to slow the pounding in his chest. His palms were sweating, and, in addition to his throbbing headache and the sharp knives in his eyes, the corners of his eyes also stung from the salty sweat that had run into them.

He took another breath, swallowed, and looked around.

Fornal's men were already stripping the dead, and only a faint cloud of dust showed on the south road.

A short skirmish, and . . . what? Thirty-five Cyadorans dead, and more than a dozen Lornians, and who knew how many cut and wounded?

Ayrlyn had already dismounted beside a moaning figure, and the engineer rubbed his forehead as he urged his mare toward her. Sooner or later he had to reclaim his first blade—if someone hadn't already—from the dead lancer.

These killings were just the beginning. That was all too clear.

LXVI

FORNAL TOOK A small sip, as if he were trying to make the vinegary wine last, then set the earthenware mug on the rickety table that had once been the dining table for the Kulan holding.

Nylan took a sip of his ordered water, watching the shifting shadow profile of Ayrlyn cast by the candle. The healer

302 ◊ L. E. Modesitt, Jr.

sipped wine, even more infrequently than Fornal, the circles under her eyes even deeper than those under Nylan's eyes.

Lewa coughed, once.

Nylan tried not to breathe too deeply of sweat and grime and dust.

All four looked through the dim light at Huruc, who used a whittled stick as a pointer on the crude map spread beside the candle lamp.

"The scouts say that they'll head for a little place called Yasira," the subofficer said. "They were setting up for nearly fifteen score, just like they did for the second attack on Hesra."

Lewa looked down at the battered plank floor.

Nylan didn't like the reminder. Every time the Cyadorans ran into trouble, they just increased their forces. Before long, they'd only be using five or sixscore lancers—or more.

"Too many for us now?" suggested Ayrlyn.

"We have score six, with another score or so coming from the Carpa area in an eight-day or so." Fornal shrugged and fingered the mug. "We cannot attack or defend against score fifteen."

"So why don't we take a troop and warn the locals?" asked Nylan.

Fornal frowned.

"Our men could use the exercise, and it will make life harder for the white demons. They wouldn't get any supplies—or fewer—that way."

"We don't know it's Yasira," said Huruc slowly. "And the people might not listen anyway."

Nylan thought. They might not. The peasants weren't fond of anyone's armsmen, but he could try, and it should make the locals more likely to hide food or move it, and that would cut into the Cyadorans' foraging efforts.

The candle flickered behind the sooty mantle with a sharper gust of hot wind that slipped through the half-open rear door to the main room of the dwelling.

The black-bearded regent fingered the earthenware mug and waited.

Nylan swallowed, trying not to burp mutton.

"Fine," Ayrlyn said after a moment. "We'll watch, and if it is, we can move faster, and we'll warn whoever it is. If they get a warning, maybe they can move out for a time. That should frustrate the Cyadorans some."

"This would be a good exercise for your levies," suggested Fornal. "We would stop any scouts, of course, and oppose any other . . . attacks." He finally took another sip from the mug.

"It might at that," Nylan agreed, understanding all too well Fornal's meaning. The regent wasn't about to admit to inability. The angels could, and that would tarnish their reputation, but Fornal was going to remain the image of Lornian nobility—or whatever.

"What other ideas do you have that might reduce their numbers? We cannot prevail against endless lines of lancers, but"—Fornal frowned—"many of the holders of Lornth will doubtless find fault if we do not show results quickly. They would fault any commander who told villagers that he could not protect them."

"There are always some in power like that. Anywhere," Nylan said.

"True that may be, but with a regency council, we are more vulnerable. So, angels, any thoughts you might have would be most welcome."

Nylan tried to concentrate. The white soldiers used lighter weapons—hand to hand the Lornians always won—but it seldom got to one-on-one. Why? Because there were far more Cyadorans and because they generally operated in large formations?

"We need to set traps of some sort. Let me think about that, and I'll let you know after we get back." As if he didn't have enough to think about. His eyes went toward the closed door in the rear corner of the room, behind which, in the evenings, Sylenia either knitted or watched Weryl or did stitchery or all three—especially when Nylan couldn't even spend time with his son. He wanted to shake his head, but didn't.

"I will be waiting with interest," said the regent with a faint smile, before lifting the mug and draining the dregs.

LXVII

IN THE GRAY light that was neither night nor dawn, Ayrlyn and Nylan studied the walls around the mining camp from the hills to the north. Already thin wisps of smoke drifted upward from the various chimneys behind the walls.

"Despite Fornal's slights on the rising habits of the Cyadorans, someone is up early," whispered the redhead. "A lot of someones."

"Makes sense. It gets hotter here than anywhere we've been so far." Nylan blotted away the sweat that threatened to run into the corners of his eyes. "Today's going to blister me."

"Here they come," said Ayrlyn.

Nylan shifted his eyes to the mining compound where the gates opened with a screeching that carried the several kays to their hilltop vantage point. Two long columns of white lancers trotted out from the gates. Behind them even more smoke swelled from the chimneys of the older buildings, presumably from the smelting furnaces or whatever they used to melt the copper out of the crushed ore.

"That's enough." Nylan nodded, and the two crept back toward their mounts, the drying grass rustling with their passage.

Behind them, the sun peered over the hills of the eastern horizon, and began to glitter off the small mirror shields of the lancers.

They rejoined the squad another three kays down the road.

"Won't they see our tracks?" asked Tonsar.

"Of course," answered Ayrlyn. "That's the point, this time. We want them to feel watched."

Finally, Tonsar nodded.

Nylan turned toward the two men he and Ayrlyn had picked as scouts. "Diess, Restr, once we get to the first crossroads, you'll wait there. If it looks like they're *not* going to Yisara,

Diess, you ride and tell us. We'll be outside Yisara. Restr, you follow them—at a safe distance to see if you can see where they are going. If they seem to go straight, right toward Yisara, just stay in front of them, Restr, like we discussed, until you get closer to the town. Then break off and head for the grove. Do you understand?"

Whether they did or not, both men nodded.

Nylan looked back, twice, before the two disappeared behind the hill crest overlooking the road. He hoped that they had understood, but that was another problem in an honor-bound culture. No idiot wanted to appear cowardly—or stupid—even if the results were disaster.

Once the scouts were out of sight, Nylan exchanged glances with Ayrlyn, and the squad began the ride to Yisara.

It was past mid-morning when Diess cantered up to the small grove of trees—Nylan didn't know what kind, except that they weren't olives—that marked the crossroads outside Yisara and provided the only shade in kays.

Nylan stretched, blotted his forehead again, and walked toward the armsman. The angel engineer seemed to sweat all the time, while his levies seemed comfortable in long-sleeved shirts.

"They're . . . coming," gasped the armsman as he reined up.

"You have a moment. Drink something," suggested Ayrlyn.

Diess glanced at Nylan, who forced himself not to second Ayrlyn's suggestion. Finally, Diess unstrapped the bottle and uncorked it and took a quick gulp. "They still march straight for Yisara, sers. More than tenscore." The scout coughed, then took another swig. "The dust . . . it makes it hard."

"How long before they get here?" asked Ayrlyn, with a glance toward the scattered dwellings and outbuildings in the brown-grassed vale a kay west of where Nylan's and her squads were drawn up.

"Midday, ser. Could be later."

Nylan blotted his dripping forehead. His face kept getting red and burned, and he was going to have to wear some sort of hat if the days got any hotter—if he wanted any skin left on his face.

"Mount up!" ordered the redhead.

"What said the scout?" asked Tonsar, looking at Nylan.

"They're making a good pace toward Yisara, and it can't be any place else." The angel engineer coughed to clear some of the dust from his throat, then swung up into the saddle.

Once mounted, he glanced toward Ayrlyn, and then around the grove. Two men still straggled.

"Move it!" snapped the redhead, and Nylan grinned, then wiped the grin away as she turned the mare.

As they headed toward the center of Yisara, Tonsar, Nylan, and Ayrlyn rode abreast—the road was barely wide enough for three mounts.

"Too bad we don't have any ways to stop them, something besides blades." Nylan shifted his weight in the saddle, trying to relieve what was becoming continual soreness. "But everything . . . everything has to be made from scratch, even wire. Wire would help in setting blades and a bunch of things. Some nails are made from wire." He was rambling, but sometimes it helped. Most times it didn't.

"Wire?" asked Tonsar, as if he had never heard of the material.

"Metal drawn so thin that it's not much bigger around than a thread," Nylan said.

"Jewelers use it," said the subofficer, "but why would you want wire?"

"Iron wire," Nylan said futilely, shifting his weight in the saddle. "Does anyone make it?"

"I have never heard of such."

Ayrlyn offered a faint grim smile, and, in turn, shifted her weight in the chestnut's saddle.

The smith shrugged. Probably iron wire was something he could create—that required a drawing wheel and a precut die through which the metal could be drawn. But how useful would it be for the effort it took? Maybe it would be better to set up pikes in trenches or something.

Nylan reined up in what seemed to be the rough center of the village, beside an empty building, one without shutters or doors. He glanced around as the squad behind him reined up as well.

The inhabitants of Yisara couldn't have numbered more than a hundred, not with only a score of homes, and twice that many outbuildings. As in Clynya, the outbuildings were sod-roofed, for the most part, and the dwellings were plaster or stucco walled with light-colored paint that was either peeling or sun-faded and stained into pink by the ever-present red dust. "Now where?"

"The biggest dwelling?" suggested Ayrlyn.

"Since the owner has the most to lose? Why not?" Nylan turned his mount north, toward the sole two-story dwelling, one laid out in a square, apparently around a central courtyard.

As the riders neared, the shutters slammed shut, and a single face peered from the half-opened front door.

"Hello!" called the angel.

"What want you?" asked a stocky man in a graying shirt.

"To warn you that the Cyadorans—the white demons—are riding toward Yisara. They intend to take everything they can, and kill all they find."

"Why should we listen?" asked the gray-haired man. "Why should you care? Both Lornth and Cyad are far. You lords of Lornth have cared little, except that we provide levies for your wars and food for the miners."

The man probably had a point. Still . . .

The angel shrugged. "We don't kill everyone in the town. That's what the Cyadorans did where people didn't leave."

"And you will not protect us?"

Nylan gestured to the mounted squad behind him. "We do as we can. Will these stop score-fifteen lancers?"

"Then why do you tell us when you can offer nothing?" The man squared his shoulders and shrugged.

Nylan took a deep breath. "There is nothing stopping you from leaving the town and hiding—if you want to live."

"And what life will we have if our houses and grain are gone?"

"What life will you have if your head is gone?" countered Nylan. "You have time to move your stock and families."

"Far enough to outrun the white demons?" The man shrugged. "I think not."

"Fine," said Nylan. "You have been warned. If you choose to stand here and wait for the white death, then it is on your head."

"And on yours, lord of Lornth, for you have no honor if you will not protect your lands."

"In the end, we will drive out the Cyadorans," Nylan said quietly, "but Lornth was not built in a day. Nor was Cyad."

"As darkness wills." The man walked into the house.

"See? And what good was this day?" asked Tonsar.

"Some of the peasants are worse than Fornal," muttered Nylan.

"I'll bet most of them hide or leave," said Ayrlyn. "They just wouldn't give you that satisfaction."

"I hope so. I hope so."

"They will stay and be slaughtered like the hogs they are," predicted Tonsar.

Nylan and Ayrlyn exchanged glances.

"That may be," she finally said.

"We need to find another way to stop them," murmured Nylan, more to himself than to the others. "There has to be a way . . . has to be."

LXVIII

NYLAN TURNED THE heavy blade with the tongs, then brought the smaller hammer down behind the edge of the cherry-red metal, once, twice.

Clunnng! Clunng!

Although the sun had barely cleared the eastern hills and the dawn breeze had not quite died out, sweat poured from Nylan, even while he worked in only trousers and a leather apron.

He raised the hammer again, using each blow to narrow the base of the blade edge. Should he add a blood gutter?

No. Too much time involved, and that would involve totally reforging each blade.

"What do you think you're already doing?" he murmured.

"Ser?" asked Sias, pausing in pumping the bellows.

"Nothing. Nothing." Nylan turned the blade again, checking the heat in the metal, both by eye and with his order senses.

Dust rose from the broader fields to the west of the corral where Ayrlyn and Tonsar worked the squads through a series of mounted drills, trying to drill the levies into anticipating the Mirror Lancer moves and developing quicker responses.

"So . . . the angel smith works blades, and the angel healer works men?"

Nylan glanced up from the anvil to see Fornal, mounted, looking at the coals and then at the darkening iron of the blade Nylan worked.

Sias, hands on the bellows, looked imploringly at the smith.

"You can get some water. Take a quick break," Nylan told the armsman/apprentice. The lanky blond man bowed to Fornal and eased off toward the well behind the dwelling.

"You train them well in discretion, too, I see."

Knowing Fornal would take awhile to get to the point, the smith eased the blade back onto the forge coals.

"What are you doing to that blade?"

"Fullering the edge and case-hardening it." At least, that's what Nylan thought smiths called narrowing the cutting edge and adding a thin layer of hardened iron/crude steel.

"I would have said that was a waste two eight-days ago." Fornal frowned, and the stallion sidestepped. "But none of your levies broke. Some died, but they didn't run." The black-bearded regent forced a smile. "You will give me trained armsmen . . . but they will never attack Westwind, will they?"

It was Nylan's turn to frown in puzzlement.

"They see what two of you do, and the word is already out. They say, 'Best leave the angels alone.' Or 'Better on our side than the other.' "

Nylan shrugged and wiped the streaming sweat out of his eyes. "We're trying to throw the Cyadorans back."

The regent nodded. "You may well, but Lornth will never be the same. For that, angel, I cannot say I am pleased." Fornal's lips curled. "We must choose between black angels and white demons, and neither is to my liking. Still, for better or worse, you keep your word, and that is far more than one can say about the white demons."

After a moment, Nylan asked, "Where are you headed?"

"We think they will scout out Jirec. The locals have followed your example in Yisara, but . . . if we take out the scouting party, that will incline them in that direction—and remove more of the demons." Fornal smiled briefly. "Your levies will go out tomorrow."

"We'll be ready."

"Good." Fornal gave a quick nod and turned his mount back toward the mounted squads that gathered by the barn barracks.

Nylan eased the blade off the coals. He could harden at least a handful, perhaps more, and that would help, maybe make then strong enough to shatter a few more of the white lances.

LXIX

A SINGLE CYADORAN scout wheeled his mount off the road and began a headlong gallop toward the right side of the Lornian line—and Nylan. The dust from the Cyadoran's mount's hoofs rose like a brown thunderstorm, blocking the angel's sight of the rest of the squads farther to the left and around the gentle curve of the road. Light reflected from the round shield, glittering and making Nylan squint.

The angel raised his second blade to throw, but he didn't have to because Ungit and Wuerek, trailed by Meresat, swept toward the lancer. The white's sabre slashed at Ungit, and red prayed across the levy's upper arm, even as his blade spiraled into the red dust. Wuerek's heavier steel-edged blade smashed the lighter sabre aside, and Meresat's edged crowbar crushed through the comparatively thin burnished armor. The circular polished shield bounced along the grass, reflective side down.

"Frig!" Ungit held his arm, sweat beading quickly on his forehead. "Frig . . . frig."

"Wuerek! Help Ungit get that arm bound," Nylan said. "We don't need anyone surviving the Cyadorans and bleeding to death."

"Ser." Wuerek eased his mount up beside the balding Ungit.

The dust settled as quickly as it had risen in the hot and still air, except for what coated the Lornians and Nylan—and the scattered bodies. Nylan's neck itched, and so did his damp hair. His ears hurt and itched where the flaking and sunburned skin had begun to peel.

Nylan surveyed the road—no dust, no fleeing riders—just ten riderless mounts. And one wounded armsman—Ungit—and one dead. Nylan didn't even remember the fellow's name, just that he'd been clumsy in practice. A handful of the armsmen—Nylan guessed they rated the term as much as some of Fornal's men—had dismounted and were looting the bodies of the Cyadoran scouts.

"Make it quick!" bellowed Tonsar. "Cuplek! You get Fienc's body on his mount."

"Me?"

"You! Unless you want me and the angels to help you join Fienc."

"Yes, ser."

"Siplor—you and Meresat get the mount detail. We can always use more mounts, one way or another."

Nylan turned his mare back to the place where he'd thrown his first blade, sheathing the second in the shoulder harness.

An armsman, already looting the corpse, looked up, then quickly extracted the dark gray blade. "Yours, ser?" Nesru extended it sheepishly, hilt first. "You get his purse . . ."

"You can keep it." Nylan took the blade and wiped it on

the cloth tied to his saddle, then sheathed it and massaged hi forehead. The one man he'd killed had been enough.

Then he eased the mare toward the burly subofficer who had reined up on the center of the road. Ayrlyn was guiding her squad from the east toward the rest of the group.

"We got them all," she said, just loudly enough for he voice to carry. Dark blotches stained her vest.

Nylan looked closely at the stains.

"Not mine. He got closer than I'd like. Those damne shields are distracting."

"I see." He raised his eyebrows.

"I'm not as good at throwing blades as you are. That mean they get closer."

"The shields give me trouble. That was why I threw th blade. I only do that when I'm in real trouble," Nylan con fessed, turning his mount and nodding to Tonsar.

"We're always in real trouble . . . anymore," she murmured

With that, he had to agree.

"Form up!" Tonsar ordered.

For a time they rode quietly through the mid-afternoon, th road dust muffling the clopping of hoofs, but sifting throug every opening in Nylan's garments, or so it seemed. He trie not to scratch too much, and concentrated on listening to th low comments that drifted forward from the squads behin them.

"How did the angels know they were there?"

". . . we didn't have any scouts . . ."

". . . you want to be a scout? White demons don't take pris oners . . ."

". . . don't care how they do it . . ."

Nylan glanced at Ayrlyn. Despite the furrowed brow tha indicated the same kind of splitting headache he suffered, h could see a glint in her eyes.

"You're getting better at sensing people," he said quietly.

"The weather's easier." She nodded. "I can almost ride th winds sometimes."

Nylan shook his head. "How you do that . . ."

"To each her own—or in your case, his own. You can fee

the grain of those metals you forge, and they feel like opaque blackness to me."

Nylan took a square of worn gray cloth from his belt and blotted away sweat and mud from his forehead and cheeks, then replaced it, and shifted his weight in the saddle. The mare whickered, but did not increase her measured pace northward.

Nylan looked back southward.

"There's no one close," Ayrlyn confirmed. "They won't keep letting us do this, you know."

"The Cyadorans?"

"We've been getting most of their smaller parties. Life may be cheap here in Candar, but even the Cyadorans are going to stop traveling or scouting in small groups." The healer stood in her stirrups and massaged one hip. "Won't ever get used to this."

"You already are."

"Not really."

"You think they'll start attacking in force?" the smith asked. "Just in force."

"That's what I'd do. I'd have started sooner." Ayrlyn closed her eyes for a long moment, and Nylan could almost feel the relief across the few cubits that separated their mounts.

"Why don't they use white wizards?"

"Maybe there aren't too many."

"Even mighty Cyador has but few of the white mages," confirmed Tonsar. "They do not wish to send them beyond the white walls. That is what my sister's man said, and he once guarded the great Hissl."

"Could it be that there are limits to white wizardry?" Nylan's tone was mocking.

"Why not? There are limits to everything else."

Nylan nodded. But what were the limits to wizardry, or magery, or whatever it was called, whether white or black? He looked at the dusty road northward, leading back to Kula . . . and Weryl.

LXX

YESTERDAY, YOU BROUGHT back ten mounts and left ten dead scouts. Three days ago, we slaughtered twenty. For nearly three eight-days, we have bled them, yet they have not left Lornth." Fornal raised his eyebrows as his eyes went from Lewa to Huruc, and then to Nylan and Ayrlyn.

The candle stub behind the glass mantle flickered. Lewa cupped an empty mug between his hands, his eyes darting from the regent to the angels and back to the regent.

"If we had attacked them three eight-days ago," Nylan answered slowly, "you would have few armsmen left, and the Cyadorans would be marching toward Clynya. If they didn't hold it already."

Fornal looked at the mug. "Hot . . . and sour, like your truths." He set it on the rickety table, which wobbled. The shadows on the dingy wall wobbled as well. "So we have preserved Lornth—for now. The Cyadorans will do something. What think you, angels?"

"Sooner or later, they'll send a big force after us," Nylan predicted. "They'll have to." The wine in his mug was almost untouched. One sip of near-vinegar had been enough, even if it deadened the smell of sweat and blood.

Huruc took a quick and small sip, his eyes never leaving Nylan's face.

"I would have acted. You would have, I think, yet they have not. What do you judge they will do, and when?" Fornal took another sip from the mug, made another face, and set it down.

"If you were the . . . lord of the Cyadoran forces, how would you explain how you keep losing men and mounts to a bunch of barbarians?" asked Ayrlyn. "They think we're barbarians—that's their attitude—and they have to do something."

"You think so?" asked Huruc.

"What did they do to the people in Kula?" Ayrlyn raised her eyebrows, her hair glinting in the light from the single candle, despite the soot on the chipped glass mantle.

"Killed them."

"They mutilated them," added Nylan. "Even the children. Remember the lord of Cyador's response to your scrolls?"

"There is that," mused Fornal.

"When they send out large parties, we've managed to warn the locals, and we don't attack. So they don't get much. We've been pretty successful picking off their scouts and smaller forage parties. How would you feel?" pursued Ayrlyn.

"I would be angry," admitted the coregent. "You did the warning, though. Did the locals heed you?"

"They said it wasn't honorable," admitted Ayrlyn, "but as soon as we left, so did they."

"Peasants . . . they talk . . ." Fornal took another swig of the wine, followed by another face. "You ask questions, angel. Why do you not say what you mean?"

"Would you keep sending out smaller groups of lancers and armsmen if you had more armsmen than your enemy?"

Fornal frowned, and Nylan wanted to grin. Ayrlyn, without making a direct point of it, was refusing to be intimidated by the big young noble.

"Why . . ." Fornal nodded. "I see your point. What would you have me do?"

"Be ready to move," Nylan said, "to another base. They can't keep sending out their entire army. If they try it again, then perhaps—I may have some ideas—we can create some damage at the mines while they're trying to sweep the countryside."

"Some holders would call that a retreat, at least behind my back," Fornal pointed out.

"Moving is not retreating. There is a difference. We take another position and keep fighting."

"I will think about how I must report this so that our actions are not mistaken." The black-bearded regent stood and stretched. "Thinking and hot wine—enough to spoil anything for an armsman." He offered a quick grin before he strolled out of the dwelling's main room and into the warm night.

"Good eve, angels," added Lewa as he stood and followed Fornal.

Huruc sat and looked down at the mug. After a moment, he turned his head toward Ayrlyn. "What you say makes sense, but I fear it." He paused. "Tell me, angel healer, why I fear your counsel."

Nylan and Ayrlyn exchanged quick looks.

"It appears I am right to fear," added the armsman with a laugh.

Ayrlyn nodded. "What we do has been effective, has it not? And it will become more effective. That will sting the lord of Cyador, and he will send more armsmen. It's always that way." She took a deep breath. "Then we will have to find out how to kill those men, and, if we succeed, he will send more. In the end, either Lornth or Cyador will fall."

"That was fated from the beginning," Nylan said softly. "The mines were only a game for the lord of Cyador to see how he could conquer Lornth. Cyador is not ruled by grass-land bandits like Lord Ildyrom. And Cyador does not believe in honor as Lord Fornal does."

"I have known that," Huruc answered, "and it gives me no comfort." He rose. "I thank you for your straight words, though many would not, if they knew them. Best they do not. Good night."

After the older armsman left, Nylan stood, as did Ayrlyn. "Now what?" he asked.

"We figure out how to change the world—or we die." Her words were cold, and so were her hands, despite the evening heat.

LXXI

THEY SKULK AROUND and watch," snapped Miatorphi. "If we ride out with less than twoscore lancers, they wait, and then they attack, and run. We've lost half our scouts, ten at a crack, twice, and more than a few in some skirmishes, and that one time where we lost nearly a half company." He scowled. "Three men left."

"They only attack when they have an advantage in numbers," added Azarphi, his narrow face shimmering in sweat. "If we ride out with more, nothing happens."

"One on one, they're no match for a Mirror Lancer," said Miatorphi.

Majer Piataphi frowned. "Some must be. One of their war leaders sliced right through a blade and a shield. Funssa brought back the shield. Another shattered a lance and a sabre with a short blade."

"So . . . we move in larger groups."

"That's not the point," countered Piataphi. "That means they're using blades with sharp edges, and not just those metal bars they call swords."

The two captains waited.

After a moment, the majer continued. "The sooner we get rid of them the better. Have you located their camp?"

"It's here, we think." Azarphi pointed to the map. "One of the smaller hamlets where we removed all the contraries in the first sweep."

"Take the entire Fourth and Sixth Lancers." Majer Piataphi frowned. "And the Eighth. Attack their base. Their 'honor' will make them defend it if we attack—and that will be the end of them."

"What if they show some common sense and retreat?" asked Miatorphi.

"We lose nothing. Destroy the camp. Raze it to the ground. Then they will have a less suitable base. We will keep doing that until they have no place suitable." The majer smiled grimly. "And we only move in forces of two companies or more. That should put an end to these efforts to whittle away our men."

LXXII

NYLAN LOWERED THE hammer and turned the cooling blade, but it looked and felt right. From the partial shade under the eaves, his eyes strayed toward the trampled grasslands beyond the corral, where Ayrlyn again worked the levies in the already hot mid-morning sun.

He smiled. No longer, not after the skirmishes, was there such reluctance to the drills. Some of that was doubtless because several of those who had been clumsy or reluctant were dead or wounded. Still, neither the other levies nor the professionals drilled, and, after a while, it might be a problem to keep upgrading the skills of the angel-led squads.

"You can stop pumping," the smith added to Sias. "Take a *quick* break."

Fornal strolled toward the makeshift smithy as the apprentice trotted toward the well and as Nylan slipped the blade into the cooling tank, not much more than brackish water, and not nearly so effective as what he had used on the Roof of the World.

"I see why you didn't allow your trainees to practice with blades," said Fornal. "Don't the narrow blades break more often, though?"

Nylan set the blade on the forge stones to anneal before turning to face the black-bearded regent. "They might. We work on how to avoid taking a big blade straight-on. That's hard on both the armsman and a blade. Besides, the point is to take out your enemy, not bang up his blade."

Fornal nodded. "You have a different view of arms."

"I suppose so. We don't like to fight." The smith shrugged. "If we have to, we want to get it over as quickly as possible, with as little injury to us or to our armsmen as possible."

"Are all angels that way?"

"Most of them. Ryba likes to humiliate her personal opponents as quickly as possible, I think. She's good enough that it's never been a problem." Looking over Fornal's shoulder, Nylan could see a line of dust on the south road. "Do you have scouts out? Someone's riding hard."

The dark-haired regent glanced south for a minute, then back at Nylan. "Ours. Perhaps the Cyadorans are on the move."

"I'd be surprised if they weren't. Empires don't like being stung by wasps, especially barbarian wasps." Nylan grinned.

"You are pleased to think of yourself as an insect?"

"Fornal . . . as you pointed out, I'm more interested in what works than in how I look." *Except that you like to be well thought of as much as the next person.* Nylan repressed a frown at the inadvertent self-correction. Whatever it was about Candar, he was having more and more trouble deceiving himself—about much of anything. "Not that I mind looking good," he added to quiet the twinges in his skull.

"It is good to know that a terrible angel has some vanity." Fornal did not quite grin as he waited.

"More than some," Nylan admitted.

Fornal did offer a faint smile.

The rider guided his dust-streaked mount straight to Fornal, reining up, then swallowing as he looked at the regent. "Must be more than score twenty riding this way—still more than ten kays south, though," panted the scout.

"Score twenty? All mounted?"

"Yes, ser."

"Go," snapped Fornal. "Send Huruc, Lewa, and the other angel here."

The scout flicked the reins and turned his mount toward the barn.

"Should we fight?" asked the regent after the sweating scout trotted toward the barn barracks.

"Against that many? Why? We can keep picking them off,

bit by bit. This attack just points out that what we're doing is right." Nylan paused as Ayrlyn rode up and dismounted.

She tied the chestnut to a corner post and stepped toward the two men, her face impassive. "Bad news? A big Cyadoran force?"

"Gifrac says there are score twenty," answered Fornal.

"We must have upset them," observed Ayrlyn.

"I don't think it takes much," said Nylan.

The three waited as Huruc and Lewa strode across the dusty ground toward them. The sole chicken pecked at the ground along the east side of the old barn, ignoring the hurrying humans and the armsmen who gathered and watched the five.

"Gifrac said the white demons were bringing score twenty against us." Huruc's voice was neutral.

Lewa just bobbed his head and waited.

"I do not like to retreat," Fornal said. "You know that. But a dead commander does not fight again, nor does one without many armsmen." He offered a grim smile. "We move to Syskar, and then . . . then we kill more white demons."

"I'd better get the men loaded out," said Huruc.

Lewa nodded once more and turned to follow the senior armsman.

"Ours are mostly mounted already, because of the drills this morning, but they'll have to get gear." Ayrlyn inclined her head to the regent, then turned and untied her mare.

As Fornal walked toward the dwelling, presumably to gather his own gear, Nylan turned back toward the smithy and an open-mouthed Sias.

"Sias! Unfasten the anvil—knock it loose if you have to. We don't have time to waste. Dump the anvil, the bellows, and the tools in the wagon. Any of the bagged coal. Forget the loose coal."

"We aren't holding here?" A puzzled look crossed the face of the lank blond man, and he brushed back a lock of sweat-stained hair.

"Not this time."

Sias shook his head. "I thought you angels . . ."

Nylan paused. "Sias . . . we're not gods. We're people, and the Cyadorans have about twentyscore troops marching this way. If I got lucky and wanted to commit suicide, maybe I could stop a dozen—individuals, not scores. How many could you stop?"

The armsman/apprentice looked down at the dusty clay. ". . . hoped . . ."

"We're not giving up, damn it! In a couple of days, we'll be back killing Cyadorans." *Unfortunately.* "Now, let's get this packed up so that we have the gear to keep giving them fits."

He glanced toward the dwelling where Sylenia stood, Weryl in her arms. Her entire body posture reflected concern and confusion. "I'll be right back. I need to get Sylenia moving, too. Start with the anvil and the tools. . . ."

LXXIII

NYLAN LOOKED DOWN at the line of bricks and stone. This time his makeshift smithy was in the remnants of a chicken coop—but he needed some sort of roof as protection from a sun that kept getting hotter with each passing day. His eyes went to the tile-roofed and heavy-walled house that quartered two subofficers, the regent, two angels, and a nursemaid and child. The thick walls kept the dwelling from getting more than hot enough to roast meat during the day, but the place was dark and smelled moldy, although how any place that warm could smell moldy was beyond the smith's knowledge.

Syskar was a few kays farther from the mines than Kula had been, and ten kays farther west, and ten kays more distant from Lornth. The hamlet was smaller even than Kula, and the stream was a mere trickle that barely sufficed for the more than a hundred horses. Nylan snorted. More like a hundred and several score. Before long, the way things were going with the captured mounts, they might have spare mounts for every Lornian.

In the afternoon heat, half the squad sat under the eastern eaves of the long roof of what had been the winter sheep barn. It was too hot in the still air to rest inside the heavy planked walls. Ayrlyn had the other half with her, scouting the area, and seeing where watchposts should be established.

The sound of hoofs broke the hot stillness as Sias drove the team toward the holding. The wagon shuddered to a stop less than ten cubits from the chicken house smithy, and a black-faced Sias set the brake, then clambered down. The one thing that Syskar did have was a small seam of coal, almost played out, but with enough to feed Nylan's forge—once Sias chipped the dark rock away from the walls of the near-abandoned pit trench.

"There should be enough for an eight-day, ser."

"You don't know how fast a forge can go through coal."

The lanky armsman slowly shook his head.

"Let's get it unloaded. Then you can take care of the horses."

After the two shoveled the rough chunks of coal into a pile, and Sias led the team toward the corral, Nylan stepped toward the forge and looked at the short heap of white-bronze blades. He needed a closed container first—the tubing would come later.

The white-bronze blades held some order, like his own dark iron blades—something he had not anticipated, not after sensing the whitish chaos that seemed to mist around the Cyadoran forces. After studying the top blade, turning it, and letting his perceptions range across and through it, he set it back on the pile, and took his own blade from the scabbard hung in the corner, and gave it the same scrutiny.

He frowned. There was definitely whiteness within his blade, almost as though he had inadvertently wrapped order around chaos to bind it—but he had never even thought about that, not before the tree dreams and his binding order with chaos in healing Nesslek. Finally, he replaced the blade. Speculations weren't going to solve his technical problems.

By the time the cookfires had added smoke and grit to the dusty air, as well as the odor of burned fat and strong mutton, and the chime had rung, Nylan had little more than two sheets of bronze—or was it brass? No, brass was softer, he thought, and used zinc as an alloy.

"Let's bank it," he told Sias. "Enough for tonight. The bronze is harder to work, and . . . never mind."

"Harder?"

"You have to be more gentle. I punched through more than once, and you saw the problems that caused." The smith racked the tools. Once he was satisfied the smithy was as neat as possible and the coals were safely banked, he headed for the well. He needed to wash up—badly—before he ate.

The evening meal was as strong as the odors had suggested, and eating around the battered trestle table in the dwelling with Fornal, Lewa, and Tonsar—none of whom placed bathing high on the list of daily rituals—didn't help the offenses to Nylan's olfactory system. Nor to Ayrlyn's. She excused herself even before Nylan, and Fornal only grunted.

After forcing himself to eat and finishing what he could, Nylan escaped the hot table in the main room of the dwelling by following Ayrlyn's example and heading for the shadowed front stoop on the north side of the structure.

He paused in the doorway, listening to Sylenia and Ayrlyn singing.

"Oh, Nylan was a mage, and a mighty smith was he.
With rock from the heights and a lightning blade built he . . ."

The smith held in a groan and stepped out onto the stoop, keeping a smile on his face, mainly for Weryl, since Ayrlyn wasn't deceived by such.

Ayrlyn continued to strum the lutar, but her eyes smiled as she wound up the song. Then she turned to Sylenia. "You need time to yourself, whatever . . . but don't believe everything that Tonsar says."

The nursemaid flushed.

Nylan scooped up his silver-haired son and hugged him, just holding him for a long time, until Weryl began to squirm.

"All right . . . all right." Nylan sat down in the shade on the fired mud tiles of the stoop, setting Weryl so that the boy stood between his knees.

"Enyah . . ." Weryl jabbed a hand toward the black-haired nursemaid as she walked through the long shadows that presaged twilight toward the well, toward the long and low former sheep shed that served as the barracks for all the armsmen. "Enyah."

"That's Sylenia. She's good to you." *And good to us.*

"Does it bother you?" asked Ayrlyn from where she sat propped up beside the door Nylan had rehung with a crude strap hinge he had forged.

"That he's taken to her?" Nylan shrugged. "I don't know. If he'd stayed with Zeldyan, he'd be fond of her, too. It's better this way in some ways—but he's had rashes, and sunburn, and that insect bite. It's a good thing you're a healer."

"You've healed as many minor injuries as I have. More probably." Ayrlyn offered a faint smile. "Why don't you think of yourself as a healer? Does identifying yourself as a smith and engineer mean you can't be a healer?"

The silver-haired angel rubbed a stubbly chin, extending an arm that Weryl promptly grabbed.

"Daaa!"

Nylan smiled at his son.

"Well?" prodded the redhead gently. "Why don't you want to think of yourself as a healer?"

Was it that he thought healers were somehow . . . unmanly? No . . . not exactly, because he'd certainly tried to heal enough people in Westwind after discovering the innate talent. Did he fear that being labeled as a healer would force him to prove more? Or was it that he thought being a smith and engineer was more valuable . . . more prestigious?

"I'm not sure . . . probably a combination of a lot of things." He eased himself down a step to follow Weryl as the toddler climbed down the steps.

Nylan's eyes caught a movement, and he paused as the

squat brown-bearded levy stepped toward Sylenia. She shook her head, her face set.

Nylan's fingers reached for the blade at his hip, but relaxed as Tonsar strolled from the de facto barracks toward the woman. The levy backed away.

The shadows did not hide what seemed to be a wide and shy smile from Sylenia as the subofficer neared.

"Tonsar seems well-meaning enough, for all the bluster." Nylan paused. "Think we ought to talk to him about Sylenia?"

"Like your engineer self-definition, his bluster protects him. And yes, we should."

"Do you know who that levy is?"

"Tregva or Tregvo, something like that."

"He's been watching her."

"I told Tonsar," Ayrlyn said. "He said that no one would bother her."

"Enyah!" Weryl began to totter toward the well.

The smith found himself walking after the boy and scooping him up. "Let her be, young man." He lifted the boy to his shoulder and turned back toward the dwelling where he set Weryl on the stoop, seating himself so that his body and legs blocked the steps.

"Enyah?"

"Later." Twilight or not, Nylan found his forehead dripping. "Darkness, it's hot. These people really are descendants of the Old Rat demons."

"It's not even the hottest part of the summer, yet." The corners of Ayrlyn's mouth turned up in the dimness of the covered stoop. "They think we're descendants of the ice angels, remember?"

"Crazy universe . . ."

"I don't think we've found out how crazy," Ayrlyn said.

Despite the heat, Nylan shivered at the certainty in her voice.

LXXIV

FORNAL SAT ON the sole stool at the end of the trestle table, next to the mug and uncorked bottle of vinegary amber wine. He picked up the bottle and filled the mug. "Hope this has fared better than the last."

"It should." Nylan had tried to sense the handful of wine bottles and had picked what felt the least disordered.

After a swallow, Fornal wiped his mouth with the back of his hand. "Best of a bad lot. Too hot here for good wine." He took another swallow. "You wanted to talk."

On the bench across the table from the one on which the angels sat, Huruc and Lewa nodded in turn, the candle throwing exaggerated shadows of their motions on the blotched wall behind them.

"We should make Jirec our 'official' camp," suggested Ayrlyn, taking a swallow of water from her mug.

"Even I know Jirec is not a good place for our camp," said Huruc. "The stream is drying up, and the wells are brackish."

"Brackish," echoed Lewa. "It is too close to the camp of the white demons."

"Say on," said Fornal mildly, refilling the mug before him.

"We build some large cookfires, spend a day or so there, clang a few chimes, and get our friends to come visit. And we give them a surprise party."

Fornal and Lewa exchanged puzzled glances. Huruc and Nylan grinned.

"What sort of surprise?" asked Fornal cautiously.

"We set up a trap. So far, we've been fairly straightforward. Barbarians don't do sneaky things," Nylan explained. "The Cyadorans know you wouldn't consider such a devious scheme." He wanted to add something to the effect that honor forbade it, but decided against pressing Fornal.

"If you wish to attempt such a . . . a scheme," Fornal finally said, "I wish you and your levies well." He drained the mug in a single gulp—admirable restraint, Nylan suspected, for the young regent.

At least he hadn't openly called it dishonorable, Nylan reflected as he answered. "We should be able to kill more than a few if we set it up right." He smiled at Fornal. "That way you will have fewer to face in open battle." His guts twisted—the order fields didn't like deception, not in him, anyway, and the discomfort was continually getting worse.

"I am becoming more glad that you fight for Lornth," Fornal said slowly. "I do not like this dodging and plotting, but the white demons have not been honorable. While you undertake this, I will return to Clynya to raise more armsmen to replace those we have lost. I trust that will not be a problem?"

"No," said Nylan. "We will work to ensure you return to face fewer of the Cyadorans. We will have to gather a few things, like mattocks and shovels and picks, and I will have to forge a few items."

"Do what you must." Fornal picked up the bottle as he stood. "This was almost decent, angels." He nodded stiffly. "Good eve." Then he carried the bottle to his room. The door shut firmly.

"I must go. To the barracks." Lewa rose.

Only after the other suboffi cer left did Huruc shake his head. "You angels make them uncomfortable," he said in a low voice. "Ser Fornal knows he must win, but he struggles against the old traditions. Lewa—he cannot see beyond what has always been."

"And what of you, Huruc?" asked Nylan.

"The world is changing. A handful of women and a single mage have destroyed the mightiest gathering of armsmen in my lifetime. Three mighty white wizards perished. A smith and a mage takes a small heavy blade and disarms the mighty and apologizes for his skill." Huruc smiled ruefully. "Yet . . . honor should serve men, not destroy them." He rose. "I, too, must check my men."

At the door, the armsman turned. "I hope you are as successful against the white demons as you have been against

Lornth." Then the subofficer disappeared into the darkness.

"I do, too," offered Nylan, watching the flicker of the candle change the size of Ayrlyn's shadow on the wall.

"We will be." Then Ayrlyn's fingers reached across the table and twined with his. "We can't do anything more tonight. Success or not, life is short. And Sylenia is meeting Tonsar in the old hayloft, and Weryl is asleep."

Nylan squeezed her fingers in return. They rose, side by side, and eased toward the door to their room.

The smith hoped that, later, he did not dream once more of trees filled with both order and chaos. His daytime existence had far too much of each . . . and yet . . . yet . . . he knew he needed to explore whatever the tree dream—or message—meant. He just didn't know when he had time.

"Later," Ayrlyn whispered.

LXXV

. . . AND SO IT came to pass that Ryba was the last of the angels to rule the heavens and the angel who set forth the Legend for all to heed. Yet Ryba did not wish the Legend to leave Westwind.

For with the going forth of the prophet Relyn, who told all east of the mighty Westhorns about the Legend and the triumph of order, Ryba became more displeased, and called unto her all those of her guards.

And from that day did the new angels accept no man fullgrown, no matter how ill or disabled, leaving any man found in the domain of Westwind to make his own way or to perish upon the Roof of the World.

Nor was any man raised in Westwind allowed to lift a blade, for it was foretold that when a man next lifted a blade would Westwind soon fall, but until then would Tower Black hold against all Candar, east and west, and even against all the mages of the world.

When word carried to Tower Black that the smith Nylan

forged mighty blades again, and that those of Lornth warred with ancient Cyador, the black stones shivered with the foresight of the Angel.

Then did Ryba announce that Lornth would rue the day it put its trust in the iron of Nylan and the songs of Ayrlyn, for all that a man builds with iron will fall to iron, and the songs that a man finds sweet can carry no truth.

And the guards of Westwind hardened their hearts, as cold and terrible as the ice that never leaves Freyja. . . .

Book of Ayrlyn
Section I
(Restricted Text)

LXXVI

NYLAN PATTED THE mare's neck, easing her into a wide turn, and rode slowly back toward the south end of Jirec, trying to see the approach to the abandoned hamlet as the Cyadorans might. On the right side of the road were the remnants of a long animal shed, the west end collapsed, so that the ruins looked like an earthen ramp. Beyond the sod-roofed shed were the blackened walls of a dwelling that had been fired by the Cyadoran sweep of the hamlet eight-days earlier.

Thin plumes of gray smoke—cookfires for the "Lornian camp"—rose from the far end of the rough oval of dwellings that clustered around the seasonal and now dried-up watercourse.

If Kula and Syskar were ovens, Nylan reflected, Jirec was an antique blast furnace where a low wind carried gray grit everywhere, pitting building walls and removing all color, roughing exposed skin and faces, irritating already overstressed eyes, shortening tempers, and turning every scrap of food into something resembling internal sandpaper.

He blinked, trying to let his tears dislodge another fragment of wind-blown grit, as he rode slowly along the rutted way until he neared the small olive grove where eight armsmen—and Ayrlyn—labored.

"I am not a laborer," said Fuera, under his breath, looking up from the thigh-deep trench, then looking away from Ayrlyn, whose eyes flashed.

Nylan turned in the saddle. "Ayrlyn didn't want to hear your complaints, Fuera, and now you're bitching to me. Neither of us wants to hear it. We've been doing our best to keep you alive, and you keep complaining. Do you think Ayrlyn likes plaiting grass? Or that I liked sharpening poles?" His arms went to the scratches across his uncovered forearms. "Your bladework has gotten good enough that you could rejoin Huruc's squad. If you keep it up, I just might let you. Besides, why complain now? You're almost done."

Fuera looked down at the shovel and resumed digging.

". . . may be tough, Fuera, but most'd have flogged you or killed you . . ."

". . . poor Fuera doesn't want to get his white hands dirty . . ."

Ayrlyn continued to rough-plait weed stalks and grasses into mats which she had stacked along the trenches. Meresat laid sticks across the completed trenches, then set the mats over them, concealing the lines of sharpened poles that angled up, before gently covering the mats with a thin layer of gravel and dirt—some of which blew away even before touching the mats.

Nylan guided the mare around the road. He glanced toward the trenches opposite the olive grove. That part had already been completed. "You have that nasty look in your eyes again," he said as he drew up beside Ayrlyn and looked down at the redhead. "The one that says people are going to get hurt."

"If I have to go back to basket-weaving, someone is going to pay for it. I don't get to ride around looking important."

"I did cut and sharpen most of those poles," he pointed out. "And I was lugging stones for a barrier."

"Let's hope this works."

"It should. The Cyadorans are arrogant enough to ignore most of the details. They always attack later in the day." He pointed. "The shadows from the olives—I think they're olives, anyway—they're already hitting on the covered trenches."

"You're sure they won't see them?"

"That's where the archers come in. You don't look at the ground when people are firing arrows at you, particularly dumb barbarians."

"So . . . they'll keep moving?"

"That's the general idea."

Ayrlyn tossed out another mat and stretched. "That should do it." She walked back across the road and toward the side of the grove farthest from the road to where she had tied the chestnut. She eased her water bottle from the holder, uncorked it, and took several long swallows.

"That's better. This place is dusty."

"Let's take a look at where we set up for the archers, and then check and make sure Tonsar has everything ready to bring to the diggers if the Cyadorans show up." Nylan waited as Ayrlyn mounted, then let his mare walk slowly away from where the eight men completed the last trench. If the Cyadorans didn't show, then they'd start adding another trench or so at twilight and finish early in the morning.

North of the olive grove were more burned-out buildings—a dwelling, two sheds, and the earth-banked and stone-walled ruins of a long barn. The faint odors of death and charcoal swirled together with the grit of the hot light wind.

Nylan swallowed and pointed. "We can hold all the mounts here. You can't see them from the grove or the road."

"This is the third time you've told me," Ayrlyn answered with a hoarse laugh. "I believed you the first time."

Nylan grinned sheepishly. "Sorry."

They rode past the back of the burned-out dwelling where Nylan had built a ten-cubit-long stone barrier from behind which they would be able to use their bows. He hoped his skills with his composite bow hadn't deteriorated too much.

Then they headed north, toward their temporary quarters and the mock "Lornian" camp that consisted mainly of outsized cookfires and all-too-rustic quarters in a mostly roofless barn.

Tonsar paced toward the two as they reined up, swinging a short length of rusty chain, almost idly.

"How much longer might we be here?" asked Tonsar. Behind him, in the shade of the half-burned barn-stable, were ranked the armsmen's mounts, saddled and ready. Most of the armsmen sat or stood under those undamaged parts of the roof that provided shade from the unforgiving sun. Ayrlyn and Nylan had been rotating the diggers and trap-builders, so that no more than a third of their force was laboring at one time. "Been near three days . . . and no one comes."

"They'll be here," Nylan said, shifting his weight in the saddle and blotting his forehead. "They'll be here."

"You may not have to wait that much longer." Ayrlyn pointed to the southeast, where a single rider galloped along the dusty road through Jirec, skirting the olive groves, much as Nylan had.

"He be riding like the white ones are behind him," agreed the burly subofficer.

The three watched as the rider pulled into the holding, glancing from one end of the former barnyard to the other before seeing the angels and heading toward them.

"They're coming! Scores of them! They got those long stickers," gasped the slender armsman.

"How far back?" asked Ayrlyn.

"Not more than five kays."

"Are they riding hard?" Nylan pursued.

"No, ser." The scout swallowed. "Measured pace, like always."

"We've got enough time to do it right," Ayrlyn said, nodding to Tonsar.

"Siplor! Get out there to the traps, and tell 'em to clean up and mount up!" Tonsar gestured, then marched toward the half-walled quarters, tossing the chain over the end of a charred timber. "Form up!"

"Buretek! Ailsor! Get your bows!" Ayrlyn's voice cracked across the compound like a whip. "We need to set up."

The other two archers scrambled across the barnyard toward their mounts, and Ayrlyn swung the chestnut and began to head back toward the ambush point.

Under the hot sun and clear sky, Nylan waited, his skin itching from sweat and dust, his face burning from the same. He forced himself to watch, then eased out his water bottle and took several long swallows. Commanders were supposed to be calm, even when their hearts were pounding. He replaced the water bottle slowly, deliberately, then shifted his weight in the saddle slightly.

Although the armsmen seemed frozen in molasses, Ayrlyn was less than half a kay ahead of Nylan when the remaining armsmen had mounted up, and the smith flicked the reins.

"Let's go."

"I see no dust," said Tonsar.

"Good."

When they had crossed the center of the loose grouping of devastated structures and reined up behind the long shed that would shield them from the view of the Cyadorans as the white lancers entered Jirec, Nylan turned his mount, raising his hand for quiet. Siplor and the diggers were already mounted and waiting. Meresat grinned, but Fuera avoided looking at the angel smith.

"I've told you, and Tonsar's told you, but I'll say it again. Whether you live could rest on how quiet you are. So don't say anything. We'll be back to lead you against the demons." He gestured toward the other side of the ruined shed/barn. "The four of us will be less than two hundred cubits away, and we'll be getting the whites as confused as we can. Then, it will be up to you to finish the job." He nodded curtly, and turned his mount.

Ayrlyn and the two archers had their bows out and arrows set up for easy reach by the time Nylan had tethered his mount and carried his own composite bow and shafts behind the barricade on the south side of the ruined dwelling.

"Tonsar got them moving fairly quickly," said Ayrlyn, moving to make room for Nylan behind the planks.

"He wants to get back to Syskar."

"I wonder why."

They both laughed.

The silence, broken only by the hiss of the hot breeze, dragged out.

"Still no sign of them," murmured Buretek.

Ailsor nodded.

Stillness descended again.

"What are you thinking?" Ayrlyn asked.

"I still wonder why they don't use archers more."

"After all the effort it took to make those arrows for Westwind, you wonder?" Ayrlyn laughed softly. "Arrows take effort; they get lost, and a lot don't ever hit a target, and it takes time and effort to train an archer. Swords don't get lost, and anyone can sort of swing one."

"Oh . . . in a way it makes sense, but bows are about the only standoff capability in a low-tech culture."

"You're also assuming that those who fight want a standoff capability."

Nylan nodded. Fornal—or the anonymous holders he always quoted—didn't seem to like it—that was certain.

Another stretch of quiet fell.

"You can just see the dust rising above the road," said Ayrlyn in a low voice. "There."

The dust continued to rise, as the first white-clad riders appeared, moving at the measured pace that all Cyadoran forces affected. Glints of light flickered from the mirrored shields and burnished blades.

When the lancers were almost a kay short of the first dwelling in the hamlet, a series of triplets sounded—on-key. The entire column seemed to stop, then thicken, before flowing out on each side of the row to form three-deep ranks of the lancers.

The first line of lancers moved at a quick trot, the small shimmering shields worn on their left arms, the long white lances all resting on the lance guides at the same precise angle.

The Cyadoran lines passed the ruined ramplike shed, the hoofs of their mounts almost drumlike on the dry ground, and swung toward the olive grove and the smoke of the "cookfires" beyond. Not a word passed the lancers' lips, and the hoofs continued to drum the hard dry ground.

"All right," Nylan ordered. "Let's start the fun." He raised the composite bow and released the shaft.

Not a single lancer even blinked, from what Nylan could tell, as the shaft whizzed through the ranks. Nor did his second shaft hit.

Frig it! Sure, it'll hurt if you kill someone, but you'll be dead if you don't and that'll hurt more! His third shaft struck true, and a lancer staggered in his stirrups.

Ayrlyn released a shaft. "Not as good as your bow."

Buretek followed Ayrlyn's example.

Before the Cyadoran lancers reached the flat before the olives, the four with bows had loosened nearly twoscore shafts, and perhaps eight or ten lancers had fallen, mostly wounded, although wounds tended to be fatal eventually in low-tech cultures, Nylan suspected.

"Faster! Now!" he ordered, as the lancers neared the concealed trenches. Arrows sleeted toward the white forces for several moments.

Then, abruptly, more than a dozen mounts went down where the weakened road caved in, and even more when those who followed, dodging the fallen horses and lancers, ran afoul of the staked trenches and struggling downed mounts. The glittering reflections from the mirror shields sprayed in all directions.

The screams of the horses bothered Nylan, but he pushed them out of his mind. "Keep firing!"

With barely moving targets, the four were far more effective than earlier, but the massed lancers still began to move across and around the trapped area.

"Let's go." He touched Ayrlyn's arm. She jabbed Buretek, who nudged Ailsor.

The angel smith and Ayrlyn pulled themselves onto the mounts waiting behind the burned-out house. So did Buretek and Ailsor.

As Nylan rode around behind the ruined barn, with Ayrlyn beside him and the others behind him, he lifted the blade—

the one from the waist scabbard. He looked at Tonsar. "Now!"

Slowly, too slowly, the double squad that had formed behind the low walls of the ruined structure began to follow him westward, as if fleeing—until they reached the gentle hill that concealed them from any who might watch or follow. Then, they turned back south and began to parallel the incoming road.

If the lancers saw the dust, he hoped that they would believe the Lornians were still retreating. But no one followed—the Cyadorans were disciplined—perhaps too disciplined for their own good.

Nylan mentally filed that datum for future consideration and concentrated on the rough side road that led back to the main road—behind the Cyadorans. There wasn't much cover, but if the lancers were prepared, well . . . the Lornians had everything with them and they could head back to Syskar, with virtually no losses. Even the tools had been parceled out among the squads.

The Lornian force quick-trotted toward the rear of the lancers, the last squads or companies still jammed up by the confusion of trenches before the olive trees, their eyes forward and focused on the commotion ahead of them.

Nylan hated leading charges. His riding skills were newly acquired enough that he still feared bouncing off the mare or some other probable occurrence. But if he or Ayrlyn didn't lead, who would follow?

Only a single Cyadoran looked back, his mouth opening, as if in slow motion, and the rearmost dozen of the white lancers fell before the others understood what had happened.

Then lances began to swing, and shimmering round shields, and white bronze sabres to rise and fall as the rear of the white forces began to respond to the attack.

Nylan forced his own blade against a lancer whose lance tangled in the stirrup of the flanking lancer. The man dropped the long shaft and grabbed for his sabre, but the angel's sword was quicker.

Nylan willed himself to hold on to his blade as the inevitable wave of whiteness and pain swept across him, trying to keep his guard up even as he shivered in the saddle from the impacts of the currents of chaos and death.

From the corner of his eyes, while fending off a lance that seemed a kay long, the smith could sense one . . . two . . . three . . . purple-clad figures tumbling. It was time to cut their losses.

"Back! Now!" His voice seemed lost in the grunts and swirling dust, but Tonsar repeated the command, and slowly the Lornian armsmen disengaged, straggling away in groups.

Only the tops of the grayish olive trees were visible clearly, with all the dust that swirled across and around the road.

"Back to Lornth!" Nylan ordered again, lifting his blade and blocking the thrust of another long lance, before driving the shortsword across and severing the wood. The lancer urged his mount away from the angel; Nylan let him go and, after scanning the intermixed purple and white figures, pulled the mare back from the fray.

A gleam of red caught his eyes, as Ayrlyn's blade came around in a short arc. Another lancer swayed in his saddle, and both Ayrlyn and Nylan shuddered.

"Back . . ." he half-yelled, half-gasped.

"You . . . first . . ." She followed the retort with a savage grin.

". . . fine . . ." He half-guided, half-willed his mount back to the road, gesturing to the others with the shortsword as he did. "Break it off . . . now! Now, frig it!"

A handful, including Wuerek, turned toward him, followed by another group.

As he led the retreat, Nylan kept looking over his shoulder as yet another three armsmen pushed their mounts to rejoin the retreating Lornians he and Ayrlyn led back toward Syskar. His head throbbed; his fingers ached; and both forearms were a welter of cuts and scrapes, none deep, but all blood-streaked.

"We could have made another pass," said Drossa from behind Tonsar, his raspy voice carrying above the clop of hoofs. "We had 'em."

"How many of us would a last pass have killed?" asked Ayrlyn, rubbing her forehead. "We lost too many anyway."

Nylan stood in the saddle and looked back toward Jirec, where the dust still swirled as the Cyadoran force rode toward the still-burning cookfires. He made a count of their force, but it took several attempts because his vision flickered with the headache. Nineteen, besides the two of them and Tonsar. He'd only seen six to eight Lornians fall. Maybe a few of the missing armsmen would find their way back to Syskar. Maybe not.

"We lost eight—maybe as many as twelve," Nylan said as he returned his concentration to the road ahead, inadvertently massaging his forehead. "How many did they lose?"

"Forty—twoscore, I'd guess," Ayrlyn said. "Could be more."

"Twoscore," said Tonsar with a laugh. "Not even ser Fornal has taken that many with all his men."

Nylan almost winced. That wouldn't set all that well with the touchy regent, although he was sure Fornal would dismiss the results because they arose from dishonesty and deceit.

His head ached, and his vision strobed, as if flicked with the reflections from the damned Cyadoran shields, but he managed to keep riding. In most ways, they'd barely started their campaign against the Cyadorans, and he was wondering how much longer he could keep it up.

"As long as we have to," said Ayrlyn quietly.

Nylan still wondered.

LXXVII

IN THE HOT night that baked Syskar, Nylan lay back on the lumpy straw-filled mattress, rubbing his temples, and trying to massage away the headache that still hammered through his skull.

"Ooooo . . ." Weryl turned on his own small pallet, and Nylan could sense his discomfort with the heat—or was Weryl picking up what they felt?

"We can't do that again," Nylan repeated to himself in a low voice. He almost grinned as he looked at Sylenia's empty pallet, but he also hoped that she wouldn't regret giving herself to Tonsar—or get left with a child.

"You've said that three times," Ayrlyn whispered. "We did what we could. We lost nine out of thirty-five. We destroyed four, five times that number."

"They have a lot more troops. Overall, I figure that we've lost a score and a half in less than four eight-days. The Cyadorans have lost at least score seven, could be score nine, but they started out with something like score twenty, and they can probably get reinforcements more easily."

"I wonder. Fornal brought back almost a score of raw trainees for us."

"Great. Back to the basic drills."

"Tonsar can do some of that."

Nylan shrugged, then asked, "Now what? What other trick can we pull out of subspace or the low-tech equivalent?" He shook his head. "Not gunpowder . . . we don't have the industry . . . or the chemistry to refine the raw materials. At least, I don't."

"How about incendiary grenades or something like that?" asked Ayrlyn. "Couldn't we figure a way to lob or fire them into their bases?"

"That might work, but what burns in this society?" mused Nylan. "Oils, pitch, but I haven't seen any around here . . . grease, tallow, I suppose."

"Coal gases?" asked the redhead.

"How do you get them? If I could figure out a way to heat coal in an airtight oven—that's destructive distillation, but that takes too much technology. I might be able to make the gas, but how could I store it or transport it? That leaves natural stuff—like pitch or asphalt, but you asked Fornal and Huruc about that, didn't you?"

"There's an asphalt lake somewhere in Cyador, according to rumor, and some in eastern Candar," Ayrlyn said. "None around here."

"That leaves me where I started, with a crude distillery. I asked Sias about what people fermented around here. He stammered for a while, but it's the same as anywhere—stuff with high sugar content—fruits, berries, grapes, and, around here, there's a tuber—they call it fat grass—"

"Oh . . . was that what they were digging up?" Ayrlyn made a face. "Tonsar insisted I chew a little of it. It tastes like glue laced with solvents."

"You got it—it's more starch than sugar, but there's a lot of it." Nylan sighed. "Ferment and distill it. Maybe mix a little wax with it . . . I don't know. And we still have the delivery problem. They used to shoot flaming arrows at things, I read somewhere, but that wouldn't work against someone as disciplined as the Cyadorans. They'd have a fire brigade out before the second arrow hit."

"Incendiary grenades," Ayrlyn repeated, a touch of asperity in her voice. "Alcohol in glass bottles. I could build a catapult."

"Could you get it to throw something far enough? I thought catapults were big heavy things that it took teams of horses to drag into place."

She smiled. "What about one portable enough to break down and reassemble in moments? We could sneak up at night and drop in a dozen incendiary packages and scoot off."

"Ooooo . . ." Weryl turned on his pallet.

Nylan reached out and patted his back gently, then looked through the darkness at Ayrlyn. "Can you?"

"I can try."

The smith tried to repress a frown.

"I can," snapped Ayrlyn.

"Sorry . . . I was thinking about something else. This honor bit. We're better off avoiding combat, stretching them out, destroying equipment and supplies. Half the armsmen—not to mention Fornal—think that's cowardly. So we'll probably have to keep raiding some, and try to avoid big detachments of Cyadorans." The smith snorted. "Of course, they'll be trying to avoid sending out small groups. Before long, if Fornal's right, about half the holders in Lornth will want to chop us into little pieces for being cowardly."

"The faster we start destroying Cyadoran material and supplies, the more time we get."

"Oh, because they aren't as likely to come running after us if they're on the defensive?"

"Right. Also, the locals will understand that we're doing *something.*" Ayrlyn was the one who frowned. "What if the Cyadorans start really reinforcing the mines?"

"That won't happen right away. First, no commander who supposedly has superior forces wants to go running home to Daddy immediately. At least, I've never met one—here or in the U.F.F. And second—"

"No one who's not there is going to believe him immediately?"

"Exactly."

"But when they do . . . what do we do?"

"We dig up something else cowardly," Nylan said. "Assuming Fornal doesn't insist on waging war in the traditional—and sure to lose—manner."

"Each time we bring in something new, he'll have more difficulty accepting it," predicted Ayrlyn.

"You have that right . . . and how." Nylan shifted his weight on the lumpy mattress again, rolling into Ayrlyn.

"Careful there."

"Sorry."

"Pleasant dreams."

In the darkness, the smith shrugged. "I don't know. I keep dreaming about trees."

"You, too? Still?"

"I take it that trees also infest your dreams?"

"They aren't dreams, exactly," Ayrlyn said slowly. "They don't feel like dreams. It's more like I'm seeing something in a new way."

"A way? That has to mean something."

"It has already," she pointed out, half-yawning. "It's helped with Nesslek and the healing. Maybe there's something else about the trees that will help."

"Trees are going to solve our problem?" The smith shook his head. "Hardly. I just wish I knew what it meant." He shifted his weight, more gently, and squeezed her shoulder.

Her lips brushed his neck. "Good night."

LXXVIII

NYLAN PUSHED BACK the floppy hat he'd taken to wearing when working in the sun—except for drilling or riding on patrol with the squads. Already, it was sweat-soaked, and mid-morning had yet to arrive.

He stirred the mess in the second crock, quickly replacing the earthenware top, and moved to the third crock, where dampness around the base told him that yet another example of his copper work was failing. He forced himself to take a long, slow, deep breath. Why did he always have to learn through his mistakes?

Because you don't learn any other way, stupid. He took another long breath, trying to relax tight muscles that seemed to grip him from neck to toe.

Sylenia, holding Weryl's hand, slowly walked with the boy along the line of clay crocks toward the well beyond. The yellow-gray dust puffed around her sandaled feet, and her nose wrinkled as she glanced at Nylan. "It smells terrible. Worse than the beer vats in Niset."

"Smee . . . tah . . ." Weryl affirmed, abruptly sitting down in the dust.

"It won't get better soon." Nylan eased the crock's cover back in place. At least, in the summer heat of southern Lornth, things fermented quickly.

Sylenia bent and took Weryl's hand, half-urging, half-dragging him to his feet. "Come on. We need to get the water."

"Wadah."

"Yes, water," Sylenia agreed.

Nylan moved to the next crock. He had two bronze-brass distilling containers ready. One needed repairs—a pinhole leak he hadn't seen or sensed—and the second had no cover. He'd put off finishing that until he saw whether he could even form enough of the tubing he needed.

The hot wind swept across the yellowed ground, picking up and carrying grit that, day after day, ground itself into all of their skins. Nylan blinked away more grit as the gust of wind died.

Lewa wrinkled his nose as he approached. "You cook up a demon's brew, ser Nylan."

"It's just the beginning, Lewa." Nylan readjusted the soggy hat. "We'll need a lot more crocks. Or brass containers. I'm really just testing the fermentation with these."

"Begging your pardon, ser . . . for what reason do you stew the fat grass?"

"Let's just say that we're working on another way to get rid of more Cyadorans, a way that doesn't involve killing as many of our people."

"Ah . . . hmmmm."

Nylan answered the expression, and the question that Lewa had not asked, with a friendly smile. "Don't you think most of the men would rather face fewer of the Cyadorans and have a better chance to prevail?"

"Ah . . . yes, ser." Lewa nodded.

As Lewa left, Nylan could sense the purposeful steps were headed straight for the regent, with yet another tale of the strangeness of the angels. He took a deep breath and turned from the crocks. Before long, Fornal would be at his elbow, but Nylan hated explaining anything to Lewa, because the armsman invariably got the explanation scrambled.

As he crossed the dusty ground toward the former chicken coop where Sias shoveled more coal into the crude forge, Nylan looked back at the line of crocks that Sylenia and Ayrlyn and a half squad of levies had gathered from around Syskar.

He still needed to create tops with tubes in them and tubing and collection systems—if he could.

"The white blades, ser?" asked Sias when he saw the smith nearing.

"Unless someone's broken a blade. Those come first."

"No, ser."

Grateful for the shade offered even by the rough and split

planks of the former chicken coop roof, Nylan set aside the soggy hat and blotted his forehead. Syskar was so hot that there weren't even any stray chickens—just sand rats and snakes and scattered goats.

Nylan wondered about the goats. They weren't supposed to be good for dry grasslands, from what he recalled. He studied the anvil for a moment, then eased the broken Cyadoran blade onto the coals. The hardened bronze had proven easier to work than iron, but also easier to damage and rip.

"A little more with the bellows," he called to Sias.

The armsman began to pump as Nylan extended his senses to the heating blade. After a time, the angel smith extracted the blade section and began to hammer the softer metal around the thin iron rod he had forged from leftover scraps of metal gathered from both Jirec and Kula. He continued to extend his order senses to ensure there were no holes in the metal as a short length of tubing began to emerge.

There was probably a better way to form copper, bronze, whatever the copper alloy was. The problem was that he didn't know what it was. His attempts with molds had been a disaster, and he'd tried cold hammering, and hammering out the metal when it was hot, but not hot enough to be easily malleable—and ended up with an uneven sheet, with things like pinhole leaks.

He had finished not quite a cubit of bronze tubing when the dark figure of Fornal emerged from the squat dwelling that served as lodging for the command staff—such as it was—and strategy center for the Lornian force.

"Sias, take a break."

"Yes, ser." Sias glanced toward the oncoming regent and circled away from Fornal in making his way to the well.

Nylan blotted his forehead and waited.

"What is that for?" asked Fornal, even before he stopped and looked at the tubing.

"Tubing for a still."

The armsleader and regent waited, as if it were Nylan's patent duty to explain everything.

"A still. It should turn that glop in a covered copper kettle into something sort of like wine, except we'll start heating it after that and trying to get it pure enough to burn."

"Burn?" Fornal's eyebrows lifted. "Why would one burn even bad wine?"

"Incendiary devices. Do you know if any of our levies know anything about glass-blowing? Ayrlyn's been working on that, but the containers are crude and heavy. It's a good thing we've got most of the materials here . . . sand, lime . . ." Nylan stopped as he caught the glazed look in Fornal's eyes. *Too bad everything new gives him that expression.*

"Ser angel . . . would you explain?"

"Oh . . . we're going to make it hot for the Cyadorans. Very hot. Especially at night."

"Ser Nylan," Fornal said slowly, "I am most glad we are not near the old holders of Lornth. Some were not pleased when Sillek attacked the Jeranyi at night, but burning . . . they would find that . . . less than honorable."

"I'm not terribly honorable, Fornal," Nylan said quietly. "I'm interested in doing what I promised, and that means destroying the Cyadoran troops by whatever means I can with as few casualties as possible for us."

"You sound like Lord Sillek." Fornal's fingers touched his beard.

Nylan understood. Sillek had lost the conflict with the holders over honor. "I only saw Lord Sillek once, across a battlefield. Perhaps we had some similarities, but I don't know. I think I might have liked him, but that's not something I'm likely to find out."

A ghost of a frown crossed Fornal's face, then vanished. "As long as you kill the white demons—that is what we must do to reclaim all of Lornth."

"We're working on it." *But not precisely in a way to make you happy. Not in a way to make us happy, either.*

After Fornal had crossed the yard and reentered the dwelling, Nylan lifted the hammer again. Sias resumed pumping the bellows without a word or a question, for which Nylan was glad.

They managed to extend the tubing to two cubits before the next interruption.

"Ser?" asked a heavyset armsman whom Nylan did not know. "Ser Ayrlyn asked if you could spare a moment to watch her device."

"Tell her I'll be there in a moment." Nylan continued to hammer the hot copper around the iron rod.

"Yes, ser." The armsman left, but Nylan did not look up, concentrating on the metal before him on the anvil.

When he finished and racked his hammer in the crude holder, he nodded to Sias. "Add some coal, but don't use the bellows, and then take a break. Don't go too far, and watch for me to return."

The lanky blond nodded. "Ser."

The angel smith turned, grabbed the floppy hat, no longer soggy, not after the time spent in the dry furnace that was Syskar, pulled it on, and walked quickly past the shed barracks.

In the flat expanse to the north of the corral, well away from where the nearest group of horses—joined on a communal tieline—grazed the sparse and browning grass, Ayrlyn waited beside a spindly contrivance that looked like the wooden framework for a cube with two long poles that joined in a half-basket sticking out behind. In the half-basket rested a roughly cylindrical container that shimmered in the pitiless summer sun.

"Sorry," Nylan apologized as he hurried up. "You caught me in the middle of a section of tubing."

"I figured that." Ayrlyn offered a smile. "So I sent off Jinwer before we were quite ready. We just got the stones set on the frame base."

"What's in the . . . the . . ."

"Grenade case? Just brackish water. It's heavier than the alcohol would be, but not that much for something this size. Juusa's father was a potter. We gave up on glass-blowing. I think it's probably too thick-walled, but it's easier to let him see that." The flame-haired angel gave Nylan a twisted smile.

The smith understood all too well. "Experts" always knew

better—even when they weren't the ones who flew the ships or rode the power fluxes—or built the stills and catapults.

Ayrlyn turned. "Ready?"

"Yes, ser," answered the two armsmen by the base of the catapult.

"Fire it."

Sprung! The catapult arm straightened, and the clay container flew perhaps eighty cubits, barely getting as high as Nylan's head. It dropped onto the dusty ground, then bounced along another twenty cubits before coming to rest against a clump of already-browning grass.

"It's back to the drawing board," Ayrlyn said dryly.

Nylan turned. The catapult had flung itself forward.

"I need a better way to anchor the back legs. We can't carry heavy stones around."

"The container didn't break, either, and it has to. Fornal thought I was crazy when I asked about glassblowers. Maybe we are." The smith shrugged.

So did Ayrlyn.

Then, they both grinned at each other.

LXXIX

AS THE SQUADS rode southward, following the back trail, the sun poured its heat through the green-blue sky.

Nylan took another long swallow, finishing the water in the second bottle, then recorked it and replaced the bottle in the holder. The heat just baked the moisture out of him, and he was always facing dehydration. He blotted his forehead with his forearm, then half-stood in the saddle, trying to stretch the muscles in his thighs and legs.

He turned in the saddle. With no breeze, the yellow-gray dust raised by the single squad they had brought died away quickly, and he could see no signs of other riders, such as white lancers. In fact, he saw little except hills covered with browning grass, grass that got sparser with each key they rode southward.

Riding to his right, Ayrlyn juggled the crude map, her eyes going from map to trail and back again.

"How are we doing?"

"If the map and the scouts are right, we should be reaching a stream before too long."

"Hope so." His eyes dropped to the two empty water bottles. A third—still full—was fastened to his saddlebags.

Ahead, the trail seemed to wind over and around yet another set of brown-grassed hills. With each hill they passed, another set appeared, almost as if they stretched to a horizon they would never reach. The last tree had been kays behind them, not all that far from Syskar.

"Have faith," Ayrlyn said with a laugh.

"I have faith. Faith that everything will work out in the most difficult manner possible."

"That's skepticism, not faith."

"I have faith in skepticism."

Tonsar cleared his throat but said nothing.

From the riders behind came a low hum of words barely above a mumble, words their speakers did not wish to reach their leaders. Nylan could guess at the general tone and content.

Nylan had drunk a third of the last water bottle, and the sun hung nearly overhead when the trail suddenly dipped into a depression, not quite a gorge because the slopes remained mostly grass-covered, with some smooth boulders protruding in places where the narrow and winding stream had undercut the ground.

"See?" Ayrlyn grinned at Nylan.

"So Siplor, he was right," said Tonsar.

"Good." Nylan glanced south and then west, but nothing moved. There were only the brown-covered hills and the sun—and them.

"Make sure that all the water bottles are filled—upstream from here—and all the mounts fully watered," ordered Ayrlyn.

"It's going to take awhile," noted Nylan, with a glance at the stream, not more than a cubit wide. "And we'd better use whatever you call that water ordering."

"I'd planned to."

Tonsar turned his mount and stood in his stirrups. "Watering time! Take turns! Do not foul the water, and fill your bottles upstream. Keep your mounts' hoofs out of the stream!"

A low murmuring rose and faded. The burly armsman eased his mount back toward the two angels.

"This is the last stream, then?" Nylan dismounted and stood on the dusty bank beside a scrubby gray-leafed bush while the mare drank.

"That's what the map says," Ayrlyn said after dismounting. "It vanishes a few kays south of here, and the trail turns west and intersects the main road from Lornth to someplace called Syadtar. The mines are on the road, and I'd guess it was once a trading road before the Cyadorans closed off free trading."

Nylan looked at Tonsar.

The armsman spread both hands. "I do not know. I am from north of Lornth, closer to Carpa. Siplor, he be from a hamlet east of Clynya, and he says that there are no more streams, but . . ."

Nylan unstrapped his three water bottles and glanced toward Ayrlyn. "You want to watch the mounts while I refill ours?"

"You can carry six?"

"I'll manage."

"Three water bottles each?" Tonsar balanced on a thin strip of gravel beside where his gray slurped up the stream.

"It's cooler where we come from," said Nylan. "Remember?"

"But this . . . this is not even full summer."

"I can't wait," said Ayrlyn dryly.

Nylan carried the bottles southward, upstream, trying to ignore the commotion behind him.

"Stop mucking the water, Ungit . . ."

". . . keep that beast's ass away from the water . . ."

". . . take the reins . . . get water for us both . . ."

Whhheeeeee . . . eeeee . . .

Nylan shut out the noise and concentrated on filling each water bottle and using his control of the order fields to ease the residual chaos—bacteria?—from each.

When they resumed riding, heading westward, Tonsar began to study the horizon, then the trail behind, then the trail ahead, then to stand in the stirrups and peer ahead again.

"Settle down, Tonsar," Ayrlyn suggested mildly.

"South of the mines, that is where we will end up," predicted Tonsar as the short column continued westward on the trail that might have once been a road. "And there will be white demons everywhere."

"We're already south of the copper mines," Ayrlyn answered, "and we haven't seen a single white demon. We won't, either. Not unless we see a huge cloud of dust, and if they have that many riders, they won't be able to keep up with us."

Tonsar pointed westward, toward a spiral of dust. "The white demons . . . at least we will perish with honor."

Ayrlyn's eyes semiglazed, and she swayed in the saddle as the mare carried her westward and as Nylan eased closer to her. He always worried when she did that.

After a time, she straightened and turned to the burly armsman. "Tonsar, that's just a dust devil. Besides, with what we're working on, if the Cyadorans aren't afraid of us yet, they will be."

Despite the heat, Nylan almost shivered at the healer's words, words uncharacteristic of a healer, but getting to be more characteristic of Ayrlyn. Was that what Candar was doing to them—turning them harder and colder? Did they have much choice if they wanted to survive?

He wondered about Istril's visions . . . and her faith that Nylan could provide a better life for Weryl. So far . . . Weryl probably would have been better off in Westwind—but that hadn't ever been the question. It was what would have happened as the silver-haired boy grew older. But how often did people sacrifice the present for the future? And how wise was that when there might not be a future?

Forcing his thoughts back to the road and what they needed

to find, he glanced at Ayrlyn. "There's scarcely any wind. Why . . ."

"A dust devil?"

He nodded.

"You get swirls out of the air above, because of the heating and some of the colder winds out of the Westhorns. I'm guessing, but it's sometimes like an inversion, and the colder air presses through . . . or something. I'd guess that the winter winds here are something. Probably not too cold, but strong, and then there are drenching thunderstorms in the spring. That's what supports the grass. Then it dries, and"— Ayrlyn smiled brightly—"it starts all over again."

"The horse nomads left because of the winds. That was what my grandmother said," Tonsar volunteered.

Almost as suddenly as it had appeared, the distant dust devil vanished.

"I have a question, Tonsar," Nylan said quietly.

"Ser?"

"About Sylenia. How do you feel about her?"

Tonsar swallowed again. After a moment, he coughed, then shrugged. "I like her. I like her very much. Is that wrong?"

"She seems like a good young woman."

"Her man was Yusek. He died on the Roof of the World. Her little girl died of the chaos fever. That is why she can be a nursemaid." Tonsar wiped his forehead, something Nylan hadn't seen from the burly armsman before. "She was close to Enyka."

"Enyka?" asked Ayrlyn.

"My sister. She went to Rulyarth with Gidser when ser Gethen and Lord Sillek opened the port to our traders." Tonsar swallowed. "Gidser says that trading is easier there."

"Do you have a consort?" Nylan asked bluntly.

"Me? No, ser. It is a long tale, and once I almost did, but she left me for a merchant, like Enyka took Gidser. Armsmen, they do not find consorts easily." Tonsar offered a wary smile.

Nylan could sense the other's apprehension, but not the chaos that seemed to go with deceit. His eyes crossed Ayrlyn's, and she nodded.

"Are you interested in asking Sylenia to be your consort?"

Tonsar looked down at the mane of his mount. "I would . . . but I do not know . . . she has lost one who was . . . an arms-man."

Nylan wanted to laugh. The outgoing, almost boastful, armsman was timid, or worried, or self-conscious.

"I think she would have you, Tonsar," Ayrlyn said. "If you do not wait too long to ask her."

"And you, angels?"

"We have no problems with her being your consort, if that's her wish," answered the healer.

"If you treat her well," Nylan added.

After a long look at Nylan, Tonsar finally grinned. "I worried. I worried many nights, and she said all would be well. But I worried."

"Trust her." Ayrlyn's tone was both dry and prophetic.

Tonsar's grin got wider.

In the silence that followed, Nylan studied the browned hills, and he could almost sense the rockiness beneath, as though the soil had been laid over rocks without the depth that natural processes would have created. He frowned. There was also *something* else, an orderliness, a thin line of order that separated the topsoil and the topmost subsoil from the underlying stones, stones that his order senses registered as preternaturally smooth.

"There's a funny line of order under the soil," he finally said.

"I do better with clouds," Ayrlyn said. "Unless I'm lying on it, the ground is just ground. Even then it's hard to sense much."

Nylan felt just the opposite—sensing order in metals and earth was far easier than in the swirling currents of the atmosphere.

"It has to be sloppy planoforming," Ayrlyn added. "Even without your senses, I can tell it's not going to hold that much longer. The rocks are beginning to show through. If there were a lot of rain, the erosion would be fierce. As it is, there's some grassland stability, but it won't last much longer."

"Grassland stability?" asked the engineer.

"There's a thin line between grasslands of this type and desert. Grasslands can actually create rain that wouldn't be there otherwise." Ayrlyn shook her head, still surveying the area ahead.

"So can trees." Nylan lowered his voice. "I'm still dreaming about them. Is that because we never see any?"

"Could be. Except . . . what are you dreaming? Is it the same stuff about dark and white flows?"

"It's never been anything else."

"Not for me, either, and that's beginning to bother me."

Just beginning? Nylan questioned silently.

Surprisingly, it was not that long after midday when the trail turned along a ridge line and began to parallel a wider track just to the west.

"Is that the road you want?" asked Ayrlyn.

"That's it. We need to find some ambush spots, places where they couldn't see if the road were blocked, and where they couldn't drive a wagon around the barricade. We'll also need stones—big ones—nearby."

"You don't want much, do you?"

Nylan shrugged. "If we can't find everything, we'll work out something else." In some ways, that was exactly what he feared.

LXXX

THE CYADORAN MAGE walked slowly toward the ash-covered wall. His once-white boots were gray and matched trousers that were so ash-encrusted that they would never be white again.

Behind him walked Fissar, trimming his longer steps to remain behind the mage.

Themphi stopped a good hundred cubits short of the line

of white stone and turned to the lanky apprentice. "You have the case?"

"Yes, mage Themphi." Fissar extended the whitened leather container. His eyes flickered from the gaunt visage of the mage to the knee-high green shoots that rose from the ashes. Those ashes stretched nearly a half kay away from the white stone wall that once had marked the definitive south border of the Accursed Forest. The latest set of shoots remained confined to a space one hundred cubits from the wall.

Themphi eased the glass from the soft leather, careful to touch only the edges as he slowly lifted the glass and turned it to catch the sun. Covered with soot, his hands shook. His brows furrowed, but his eyes flashed.

The air around the white mage seemed to twist, and scattered shadows flickered through the cloudless sky.

From the glass poured a line of fire that struck the greenery. Ashes exploded like water striking cherry-red iron from a forge, sparking and spraying away from the sunflame that Themphi played across the ground.

In time, he lowered the glass.

Fissar took it from his shaking hands, and offered him a silver flagon.

The mage drank, deeply, then relinquished it to his apprentice.

Beyond the haze, Themphi could see the line of white stone, fissured and cracked. He also sensed fresh shoots of green ready to edge upward through the ashes, as they did in all places along the southern walls when the mages were not present. He tried not to think of the kay-wide stretch of new forest, more than waist high, sometimes man tall, that had grown along the north wall. All that despite the redoubled efforts provided by two journeymen and two apprentices, and three more companies of Mirror Foot. Despite his efforts and theirs, the Accursed Forest continued to threaten. If not for his efforts, would it reclaim all of eastern Cyador?

"Not while I am here," he murmured. "No."

Fissar opened his mouth, then closed it.

The white mage sighed and closed his eyes, standing silent in the sun for a time before reopening those tired orbs and starting to walk westward toward the next section of green-infested ash.

LXXXI

HANGING JUST ABOVE the western horizon, the sun beat against the right side of Nylan's face in the stillness that came with late afternoon or early evening—not that there was any real difference between the two in southern Lornth. Both were hot.

Beneath him, the mare half-panted, half-*whuffed*.

Swaying with the motion of the dark mare, the engineer rubbed his nose gently, trying to take away the itching from the gritty yellow dust—without rubbing it raw and bloody. Finally, nose still itching, he forced his fingers away and looked eastward to rest his eyes and face from the glare of the sun, rather than in hopes of seeing anything.

"Grass and more grass."

"Real grass is green, not faded brown," suggested Ayrlyn as she rode to his right.

On his left, Tonsar grunted or mumbled, but the engineer made no attempt to decipher the sound.

A dozen of the more able levies rode behind the three, the last two leading the pair of packhorses bearing the catapult and the clay fire grenades. All rode quietly enough that the loudest sound was that of hoofs on the hard surface of the trail, a surface so dry and hard that not even the dust muffled the hoof impacts.

Ayrlyn's eyes glazed over, as they did periodically when she resorted to using the infrequent breezes and the upper winds to scout the land ahead.

"That way," she said abruptly, pointing to the right and toward a hill slightly higher than those around it.

"The mines are ahead," said Tonsar.

"So is a Cyadoran patrol," answered Ayrlyn.

Nylan turned in the saddle. "Toward the hill there. Follow us."

A chorus of "yes, ser" followed the order. Nylan ignored Tonsar's frown, even as he squinted into the almost-setting sun. At times, he didn't feel like explaining, and Tonsar needed to realize that.

The hill was farther than Nylan realized, and he began to look over his shoulder, but he saw neither dust nor riders. His eyes watered with the shift in vision from the glaring orange sun and the long shadows.

As the levies reached the depression between the hills that led to the western side of the designated hill, a cloud of dust appeared on the southern horizon where the trail disappeared over a ridge.

"A great many horses," murmured Tonsar, "a great many."

"Discretion is the better part of valor," said Ayrlyn, with a half-laugh.

Nylan blotted his forehead, perpetually burned and raw, it seemed. At least the Grass Hills harbored few flying insects. Dust and grit and heat, but not much in the way of flies, mosquitoes, or the like.

After having the levies dismount behind the hill, the three left their mounts and walked up the slope, a slope offering uncertain footing with dry slick grass and crumbling soil. From just behind the crest of the hill, the angels and Tonsar lay in the grass and watched as the dust rose out of the south along the trail they had been taking. The cloud of dust was a detachment of Cyadoran lancers—if as many as threescore riders could be called a detachment.

Yet, even before the white forces reached the flat expanse where Ayrlyn had waved the squad off the road, the Cyadorans reined up, remaining stationary for some time, their white banners hanging limply in the windless afternoon heat.

"What do they do?" whispered Tonsar. "If they rode a half kay farther, our tracks—"

"Patrolling a perimeter of sorts—just to check things out,"

Ayrlyn said. "They really don't want to find anything—at least the officers leading this group don't."

Nylan smiled faintly, wondering in how many times and places patrols and scouts had avoided discovering the unpleasant. He bet that the entire group had remained within a few kays of the mines—a perimeter patrol.

"I wouldn't want them after us," Tonsar muttered. "With not even two squads here."

"Numbers won't help us," Nylan pointed out. "Not with something like score-fifteen or twenty mounted armsmen inside those walls. And all of them bunked behind earthen walls."

Tonsar looked back toward the pack animals and frowned.

After a time, almost as abruptly as they had appeared, the white troopers turned and rode back southward.

"It is strange," observed Tonsar. "Even Lewa would not be such a fool." He looked at Nylan guiltily.

"I won't say anything, Tonsar, but I'd be careful around ser Fornal."

"Yes, ser."

"We're less than four kays from the mines." Ayrlyn stood and stretched after the last of the Cyadorans had vanished to the south. "We can move in slowly to the last line of hills before the mines, so long as we stay out of sight. Then we'll set up, and after dark, the catapult team will ride down into that gully to the south of the walls. They won't be looking at the south, not so much anyway. Tonsar, you'll keep the rest of the squad ready to ride out at a moment's notice."

"They may not even want to chase us, but we can't count on that," Nylan added. *After dropping incendiary canisters where you intend to drop them? Are you deluding yourself? Even Fornal will be furious . . . but there isn't any choice.*

Ayrlyn only raised her eyebrows, and Tonsar actually nodded.

The three eased their way over the dry and slick grass and back to the rear of the hill and the waiting levies.

"The whites turned back to the mines. It was just a patrol," Nylan said.

"We'll head for where we'll leave most of the armsmen,"

Ayrlyn explained as she mounted. "It's no more than four kays, if that."

A low groan, almost inaudible, greeted her announcement, but both angels ignored the sound, watching as the levies who were becoming armsmen mounted.

Before they reached the base of the hills flanking the mines, the sun touched the horizon. As it dropped behind the western hills, a reddish orange glow spread across the brown of the grass hills, creating the impression that the hills were smoldering, like the banked coals of a forge.

"Some day, this will be that hot," predicted Ayrlyn, "like a forge or a furnace."

"It is already," protested Nylan, half-standing in the stirrups and stretching his legs. His knees creaked. At least, that was the way they felt.

"The ecology's fading, and it'll get worse."

Was she seeing visions, too, like Ryba? Nylan moistened his lips.

"Not visions. Common sense."

"Sorry."

"It is hot," Ayrlyn said. "Makes us jumpy."

After riding into a lower spot, sheltered from both the mines and the road, Ayrlyn reined up. "This is as good a spot as any." Her voice was flat.

"Stand down," ordered Tonsar, his voice low, but firm. "And keep it quiet. The noise—it carries across the grass."

Reins still in one hand—there was nothing to tether the mare to—Nylan stretched out on the hard and dusty ground, ground that the dried grass did little to soften.

Ayrlyn sat beside him. "You're worried."

"Wouldn't you be? We can't reach most of their troops, not behind earth walls. What I'm planning won't set well with *anyone.*" He sat up and shook his head. "But not doing it will ensure we lose, and before long. Damn honor, anyway."

"Do you ever think we'll get away from this?" she asked.

"I hope so, but I have my doubts. I've been thinking. It takes strength and power to manage a comfortable living away from society."

"But people make it harder," she observed.

"Do they? That assumes people are different from nature in a fundamental way, and I'm not so sure we are. Trees—"

"Trees again?"

"Trees want to grow and survive—or they act that way," the smith continued. "So do animals. And when resources are limited, and they always are, those who have greater control of their environment survive. That's usually power of some sort. I don't know that you can escape it."

"So you want to be world ruler?" she asked dryly.

"Hardly. Civilization has a tendency to smooth things out, where power isn't so direct for people—but sometimes it's even harder on the rest of the ecology. I wonder if there's a way to get that smoothness, that balance, across the ecology without reducing people back to animals—"

"It's an interesting thought," Ayrlyn said.

"I know. But for now, we've got to reduce the power of a self-centered xenophobic culture that believes all other humans are barbarians and animals, and we'll do it by becoming even more savage in warfare." He sat up and shook his head. "Is it time to do the nasty deed?"

"Almost." She reached out and squeezed his hand. "I do love you, you know. Part of that is because you are an engineer. You do try to find answers, even when it seems impossible. And you still care." She gave his fingers a last squeeze and stood.

He squeezed her hand back, then rolled over and up, brushing the dust off his trousers and shirt, far more stained than when Zeldyan had presented them.

"Borsa, Vula? Do you have the pack animals ready?" Ayrlyn glanced at Nylan, who nodded in the dimness that was not quite full night.

"Yes, ser."

"The canisters are ready, and so are the fuses and the striker," added Nylan.

"Let's mount up, then," ordered the redhead.

"Tonsar," Nylan said. "Stand by. When we head back here, we'll need to be moving—immediately."

"Yes, ser."

Nylan swung into the saddle and glanced toward Ayrlyn.

"You ready?" she asked in a lower voice. "I can see a bit, but—"

"Ready." Nylan's night vision—another result of the *Winterlance*'s involuntary subspace transition from one universe to another—gave him a small advantage as he led the other three riders and the pack animals downhill toward the swale between the two hills. Beyond the swale was a narrow depression that might have been a stream or runoff channel in wetter years, and that channel led in a circling way around the west side of the semiplateau on which the mine complex stood, getting closer to the walls as it meandered south.

An acrid odor drifted over the riders, and Nylan wrinkled his nose. The Cyadorans were clearly doing something with the mines. He glanced upward at the still unfamiliar pattern of stars—cold and clear even in the summer night's heat.

Once clear of the hills' cover, the smith could see the yellow flickers of some type of watch lanterns on the walls, but their light only illuminated a few cubits of ground beyond the outer walls, and dimly at that.

Slowly, slowly, the six horses walked through the darkness, carrying their four riders along the gully that circled south of the mine's walls. Nylan could sense an occasional trembling of the ground. Were the Cyadorans working the mine shafts at night as well?

He studied the ground. They were almost due south of the walls, walls still but barely lighted in places, and seemed to be opposite the corrals and stock area, from what Nylan could tell. He glanced at Ayrlyn.

"Looks good here," Ayrlyn murmured, and, with a gesture to the two other members of the catapult team, she dismounted.

So did Nylan.

In the comparative silence of the gully, Borsa and Vula began to assemble the catapult with quick, practiced motions, slipping the pegs into place, while Nylan took the first canister from those strapped to the second packhorse. The animal stepped sideways, and the engineer patted her shoulder, trying to project some reassurance, and saying, "Easy there, easy."

An occasional horse noise *might* not alert the sentries, but the more time before they were discovered the better. The engineer kept glancing at the mine walls, but the lanterns did not move.

Nylan laid out several rows of the alcohol-filled canisters. He wrinkled his nose again. The semidistilled liquid still smelled like places he'd rather never visit, but he doubted the odor would carry, or prevail above the stench of the mineworks.

"It's ready, sers."

Ayrlyn glanced through the darkness at the silver-haired smith.

"Can you sense where the few tents are? We'll start there."

"There are only a few."

Nylan sighed softly. "We'll hit the tents first, then the corrals. I don't like it, but . . . a lancer on foot . . ."

The healer nodded in agreement, but Nylan could sense the sadness. He just couldn't do that much about it, not the way matters were playing out. If the choice were between Lornth's survival and Cyador's horses, the horses had to lose. He didn't like it, but war wasn't exactly a matter of what one liked.

"What about the wagons?" he asked.

"They're more scattered."

"Is there any place where there are a couple together? And hay or fodder. That should burn easily and make life harder for them," Nylan added.

Silence followed while Ayrlyn sent her senses out on the light breeze that had risen with the night.

Nylan tried to follow her perceptions with his, but he was far more aware of the strange wrongness of the ground beneath, and the time-smoothed boulders that lay not that far beneath the drying grass and soil.

"Wind it up," ordered Ayrlyn, her voice low.

"Ser," agreed Borsa. The faintest creaks followed his efforts. "Set, ser."

The angel engineer eased the fuse into place in the canister tube, then placed the canister in the catapult cradle. He took the striker. "You ready?"

"Ready, ser."

Whhsst-click. The fuse caught, and Nylan let his senses check to make sure the flame was solid.

Ayrlyn did something to the frame angle, then tripped the catch.

Thunk! The release of the catapult echoed dully along the shallow gully.

Nylan could feel Ayrlyn's order senses doing . . . something . . . although what he couldn't tell.

A flash of light flared from behind the stone and earthen walls that loomed uphill from them.

"Wind it up!" hissed Ayrlyn to Borsa. "Don't wait for me to tell you."

Nylan slipped another grenade from the pack and roughened the fuse, holding the striker ready. When the arm was back and the catch clicked, he flicked the striker again, using his own senses to strengthen the flame as he placed the next canister in the fitted cradle.

"Now!" Ayrlyn ordered.

Thunk!

Borsa began to wind the wheel as soon as the throwing arm stopped vibrating, and Nylan had another grenade ready, feeling that the catapult was slow, too slow. Ayrlyn made another adjustment.

Thunk!

Yet . . . five grenades went over the wall before a series of ragged horn calls echoed into the hot night.

Thunk!

Was that smoke oozing downhill from the Cyadoran walls? Nylan readied another canister and fuse, trying to be precise, despite the increasing pain and pressure in his skull.

Thunk!

The screams of horses began to fill the hot darkness, competing with intermittent trumpet blasts and shouts, and the white chaos of death flowed down into the gully with the smoke from burning hay, and the stench of charred meat.

Nylan forced down the bile in his throat, knowing that Ayrlyn had to do the same, as she sensed, watched, and adjusted the catapult.

Thunk!

Additional watch lanterns flared up, and the four continued to aim, load, and fire the canisters over the wall less than a hundred cubits away. The smoke thickened, and the smell of burned flesh enfolded the gully. Borsa retched, but kept rewinding the catapult.

Thunk!

Before long, yellow and red flames licked into the dark sky, well above the walls, and Nylan's head throbbed from the screaming of the horses and from the handful of armsmen who had perished in the flames.

Thunk!

"Time to go!" ordered Ayrlyn. "Someone's gathering a force together, and we don't need to stay and get discovered. Besides, we don't have that many canisters left."

Fighting the stabbing pain in his eyes and skull, Nylan slipped the remaining grenade canisters back into the half-quilted pockets on the pack mare, then handed the hammer to Ayrlyn, who knocked out the pegs—the low-tech equivalent of massive cotter pins—while Borsa and Vula tied the framework together and strapped it on the other packhorse in swift movements.

Ayrlyn's insistence on practicing in the dark in Syskar had clearly paid off, Nylan reflected as they rode back down the gully and up toward the swale where the rest of the squad waited.

As he rode, trying to ignore the pounding in his skull, Nylan remained absently bemused, simultaneously horrified, that in such a short span of time, they had created such a mess, and were leaving before the Cyadorans were even really organized. Then, how could they fight fires in what was nearly a desert?

He jerked in the saddle as he sensed the Lornians ahead, realizing that pain was fogging his senses.

". . . that them?"

". . . four riders . . . silver hair . . ."

"It's the catapult party," he announced, not knowing what else to say. "We're back."

Tonsar had the ten others mounted and waiting. "The flames, they reach the stars."

"Hardly," answered Nylan, "but let's go. Before they send out lots of riders."

"You're leading," Ayrlyn pointed out. "You're the one with the night vision."

Nylan turned his mount, easing her into a fast walk, resisting the temptation to trot or canter.

"Is anyone coming?" he asked Ayrlyn.

"I can't sense anyone. They've sent some patrols out to where we were, but nothing on the road to the north."

Nylan nodded. Maybe, just maybe, the Cyadorans were afraid of some sort of night ambush. He hoped so.

While he kept looking back, and while Ayrlyn rubbed her forehead and cast her senses on the evening breezes, no one followed. No one at all, and that bothered Nylan . . . somehow.

The glow on the southern horizon had faded into a blurred smudge of light, and the crunching of hoofs on the dusty trail had taken on a monotonous rhythm before anyone spoke again.

"The white ones—they will be most angry," ventured Tonsar.

"That's generally what happens to whoever takes the damage in war," Nylan said, one hand massaging the back of his neck, hoping that easing the tightness would help his headache. Why did the death of horses create the white-based chaotic pain? It wasn't so bad as that of the soldiers that had died, but it still hurt. He took a deep breath.

"You angels have won another victory," said Tonsar. "Yet you are not pleased."

"We killed soldiers and horses, and killing horses isn't exactly a glorious victory," Nylan pointed out tiredly. "Not the way anyone would prefer to fight. We just don't have many choices."

"You were not happy about sending your mage-fire at the horses, but you did," said Tonsar.

"We also fired the hay they had collected," Ayrlyn said with a sigh. "And a few wagons. It's all the same thing." She shifted her weight in the saddle.

Nylan concentrated on the trail, trying to sense if it were as empty as it seemed to his night vision, trying to ignore the white agony that blanketed both of the angels.

"But why?" pressed the burly subofficer.

"Tonsar, we killed close to twoscore soldiers and twice that in mounts, I think," answered the redhead. Nylan could sense the pain in her voice, and his own head still ached. "Even with the men they lost, the Cyadorans will be short of mounts and fodder for those they have left. Where will they find it now?"

"Our camp, I would say. Or the hamlets. Somewhere."

"Fornal won't leave it for them. Besides, how will they get there? And will they want to leave a third of their force behind—without mounts?"

"No," predicted Nylan. "They'll take it out on someone else. That's usually the way it works."

He turned his eyes to the long road northward, a road that seemed to stretch forever. Even the thought of Ayrlyn beside him and Weryl waiting in Syskar offered little comfort.

LXXXII

So much for honor among barbarians," snapped Azarphi. A long red welt covered his forearm, and scattered burn marks dotted his forehead.

"The lack of honor was to be expected," answered Majer Piataphi. "The fireballs were not. Where did they learn about those?" He turned to the third officer.

"It's hard to tell, ser." Miatorphi frowned, then winced.

Like the others, he sported scattered burns. "They couldn't burn the buildings, not with all the earth, but they got those few still in tents. Then they went for the horses, the wagons, and the hay."

"Even with all the earthworks, they got one of the barracks and the small mill building, too," added the majer.

"That took awhile. Most got out. The horses weren't so lucky." Miatorphi lifted his tunic away from the burn on his arm.

"Those aren't barbarian tactics," pointed out Azarphi. "Not any barbarians we've heard about. There must have been scores of them."

"No," answered Miatorphi slowly. "There were less than a score. There were no wagons, either. We found tracks. The fireballs came from down in the south gully. They had to get close."

"White magic?" asked the majer. "I don't see how. You can follow a white fireball, the magely kind. These just flared up when they hit."

"There were clay fragments," Miatorphi added.

"So . . ." Piataphi pursed his lips. "A disciplined night attack, and the barbarians have never done that. Targeted fireballs, no wagons, no wizards, and less than a score of barbarians. Yet we lost nearly fourscore mounts, between those that went over the wall or were burned or so badly injured that they had to be destroyed. There's not much fodder, and three supply wagons are charcoal. That doesn't count the eighteen men who were burned, the barracks, and the mill. How do you suggest I explain this to His Mightiness?"

Both the captains swallowed. Miatorphi looked at the ashes that had once been a corral.

Azarphi grinned nervously. "Could you blame it on those angels?"

"Where did you hear about them?" asked the majer.

The younger captain shrugged. "You hear things, ser. Could be that some are helping the barbarians."

"How likely would that be? Supposedly, the barbarians

fought a war with the angels last fall. Why would the angels help them against us?"

"Stranger things have happened. Besides, ser, you don't have to say that it was the angels. You could sort of hint . . . I mean, where would barbarians come up with fireballs? And they really like horses . . . the barbarians do. You've heard the joke. You know, what's a barbarian sodomite?" Azarphi paused. "He's one who likes his woman better than his mount."

Miatorphi shook his head.

The majer touched his chin absently, stifled a wince, and frowned. "I had not thought of it in that way. Yes . . . we could raise those points." He smiled a hard smile. "We also need to strike back. It does not have to be at their warriors. But we will show that Cyador is not mocked."

The other two nodded.

LXXXIII

THE CANDLE WAVERED behind the sooty mantle, adding its own infinitesimal heat to that of the dwelling's main room.

Nylan wished he could put it out. Any relief, however little, from the heat would have been welcome. Instead, he finished the water in his mug and refilled it, then looked at Ayrlyn, who nodded. He refilled her mug as well.

Across the table, Fornal took a small sip of the near-spoiling wine and winced, but took another sip before setting the mug down hard enough to shake the wobbly table.

"For an eight-day, they have done nothing. And we have done nothing except watch them," said the regent. "Nothing. The armsmen are getting restless."

"So . . . they want to die sooner?" asked Ayrlyn.

Fornal's eyes hardened as he turned toward the redhead.

"The Cyadorans won't attack directly. That means you have to attack them behind their walls. Do you want to guess how many armsmen you'd lose?"

"They just squat there," protested Fornal.

"They'll retaliate," Nylan predicted, "but not against arms-men. They'll lash out at some hamlet or town."

"Cowards."

"What else would you expect?" Nylan asked. "They lost probably a score of troops and a quarter of their mounts."

Lewa frowned and nervously moistened his lips. Huruc watched Lewa stolidly for a moment before returning his attention to the black-bearded regent.

"A waste. Nearly score-five horses." Fornal shook his head. "For what?"

"That will keep a good hundred of their armsmen from mounting up and trying to kill you," suggested Nylan, not bothering to correct Fornal's exaggeration. They might have killed or maimed eighty mounts—bad enough considering the horses weren't at fault. Then, probably the lancers weren't either, but seldom did the consequences of fighting get visited upon the leaders. Horses, ignorant soldiers, bystanders—they all took the brunt of war. He almost snorted, thinking of poor Lord Sillek—who had cared, and had been one of the few leaders Nylan had ever seen get destroyed. "Your enemy can't fight you when he can't get to you."

Huruc offered a faint and ironic smile.

"Why can you not attack again tonight or tomorrow?" asked the regent. "The same way you did before? Perhaps you could aim more fireballs at the soldiers," Fornal added lazily.

"Because the last attack took all the alcohol we'd made, and I won't have enough even for a small attack, for another eight-day." Nylan's head throbbed, and he added, "It might be a few days earlier. Besides, the Cyadorans will be expecting that. We'll have to try something different."

"This . . . this kind . . . of fighting . . ." Fornal shook his head again. "I am most glad the older holders are distant."

"It's what you have to do when the other fellow has more equipment and people. You make his strengths work against him. How do you think those horseless lancers feel right now?"

"Angry," suggested Huruc. "Some will be asking why their

leaders cannot protect their mounts. It will get worse, if their armsmen are like those I know."

"Then they will murder more innocent peasants. Peasants are not supposed to die in war. Armsmen are." Fornal shook his head. "Leaders are supposed to protect their people."

Lewa nodded sagely in agreement, his ears wiggling as he did so.

"How much protection will they have if the Cyadorans don't have to worry about you?" asked Nylan gently.

"You . . . you are worse than a white mage, angel." Fornal took another sip of wine. "The peasants, they are better for my presence. That is why I must suffer your tactics, but I do not have to be happy that I must act like a snake and creep through the grass, or a mountain cat and attack in the night."

"I wish it were easier," Nylan said, "but we are doing our best to stop them."

"No one faults your courage, angels." Fornal stood. "I, too, wish there were another way. But I cannot see it. Nor can anyone else, and that angers me. And I do not have to like the death of good horses, however . . . useful it may have been." He took a last gulp of wine—and winced as he set down the mug. "Still hot and sour."

Without another word, Fornal walked to his chamber and shut the door, hard enough that the table wobbled again.

Slowly, stolidly, Lewa rose and nodded to the three. "We patrol tomorrow." He left by the open front door, and a moth circled in toward the candle—fluttering around the sooty mantle after the subofficer disappeared into the darkness beyond the front stoop.

"They have no answers," Huruc said. "Nor do I. I fear many more will die before this ends." His eyes fell on Ayrlyn. "You are a seer. Is this not so?"

"Many would die no matter what happened," Ayrlyn said slowly. "All we can do is try to change who dies."

Again, her words left Nylan cold. Was that all life was—rearranging the names and dates of death, because everyone died, and it was only a question of where and when?

"You offer cold comfort, angel." Huruc stood. "Yet your

words ring true, and I would have truth over comfort. Comfort has all too often killed armsmen before their time." He nodded and was gone.

For a moment, neither Nylan nor Ayrlyn spoke. Then Nylan blew out the candle, and they sat in the darkness. "Nobody likes seers or truth," he finally murmured. "I'm not even sure we're either, just the next best thing."

"Is what we're doing right?"

"I hope so." At least that answer didn't start the headaches that followed what he recognized as deception or self-deception.

"You've changed. So have I."

"Everyone changes," he temporized.

"You offer what you think is truth more often. On the Roof of the World, you kept that to yourself."

"Ryba would have sliced me in two," he protested.

"No. I don't think so. You risk having Fornal or Gethen or whoever send an army against you now."

"So do you, even more than me. And it costs you in other ways. You don't pick up the lutar anymore. That bothers me."

"It bothers me, too, but that will pass."

"You're sure?"

"I'm sure. I *know,* and that's scary sometimes."

Nylan swallowed.

"It's not like Ryba, with visions, just a solid feeling," she explained.

"That's scary to me." He forced a half-laugh.

"Scary or not," she yawned, "I'm tired."

Nylan stood and extended a hand, then led the way to their room—hot and still despite the open shutters on the small window.

Weryl lay sprawled on his back on his small pallet, his arms wide, a faint smile on his open mouth. Sylenia snored softly, her back to the door.

"Sylenia is worried about Tregvo," Ayrlyn whispered as she leaned closer to Nylan.

"Who?"

"That armsman who keeps making advances. She told me that she feared none of us would return."

Now they had to worry about the nursemaid they'd brought so that they wouldn't have to worry as much about Weryl.

Darkness, if it weren't one thing, it was another. But that seemed to be life. Nylan took a deep breath, then slipped off his damp shirt, trying to relax in the hot still air of the room.

Ayrlyn slipped her arms around his waist, her lips brushing his neck for a moment before she released him. He could feel the dampness of her shirt. What were they doing in the sweatbox that was southern Lornth?

He grinned to himself for a moment.

"You're smiling," whispered Ayrlyn.

"Just thinking that everything that got us here seemed to be a good idea at the time. Probably be my epitaph—'He thought it was a good idea at the time.' "

Ayrlyn kissed him again, and it was all almost worth it. Nylan smiled inside.

LXXXIV

THE SMALL LORNIAN scouting squad reined up along the ridge line. To the west, the road curved halfway down the gentle hill, not too sharply, but tightly enough that the Cyadoran wagon drivers would have to slow as they climbed. Those drivers, already on the road from Syadtar, according to Ayrlyn's air scouting, would not be able to see around the next curve where the road began to wind between the hills until it reached the straight stretch that began the long haul to Syadtar.

"Well . . . will this do?" asked Ayrlyn. She glanced over her shoulder toward the northwest—in the general direction of the mines—and the Cyadoran lancers that they had avoided earlier in the day.

"They weren't headed in our direction," Nylan said, responding to her look, and not her inquiry. "Not even toward Fornal."

"They rode toward Jerans," said Tonsar. "That will not please Ildyrom."

"Better Ildyrom than Fornal right now." Nylan surveyed the site and nodded. The Cyadoran supply wagons would have to come nearly to a halt as they climbed toward the mines. "This looks very good."

"Good," grunted Ayrlyn. She massaged her forehead.

"What are we doing?" asked Tonsar. "We scouted the other part of the road an eight-day ago, and you said that was good. Now this is good. Will we not use the other place, or . . ." The burly armsman's hands and arms completed the question.

"That was good, and so is this. That was for one set of wagons. This is for another."

Ayrlyn shook her head at Nylan's obfuscation.

"The Cyadorans can't live off the land. There are too many of them. Even we have to get some supplies by wagon. So, what happens if they start getting short on supplies?"

"But the lord of Cyador will send more—"

"Which we will take right here," explained Nylan.

"That's not—"

"It's not honorable. War isn't honorable, and the Cyadorans certainly aren't. Is slaughtering children honorable?" He tried not to think about what would happen when the Cyadoran troops they had circled arrived in Jerans. Or what might happen all over southern Lornth and Jerans as the angel tactics became more successful.

After a moment, he rubbed his forehead. Even considering it gave him the echo of a headache. Was he becoming more and more like Ryba? Willing to do whatever was necessary to survive?

He winced again as his head throbbed, then closed his eyes for a moment and took a deep breath.

LXXXV

Daughter." Gethan bowed, slipping the scroll behind his back. "How is my young friend Nesslek?"

"Asleep, thank darkness." Zeldyan offered a gentle laugh as she closed the door to the sitting room behind her sire. A gentle light and shifting shadows from the candelabra on the low table suffused the room. "He has the energy of three boys, but only a single mother." Her voice lowered. "It is so hard to believe . . . the chaos fever . . . and now . . ."

"Was it chaos fever?" asked Gethen. "Fornal seemed to think otherwise."

"Fornal . . . he . . . It was. Several children died in the town. You did not see what happened to the angels." She gestured toward the larger armchair.

"Thank you." He paused by the armchair. "They seem to be what they claim, and they have done only good for us. Yet . . ." He extended the scroll to her before seating himself. "I would like your thoughts."

Zeldyan took the straight-backed chair and pulled it closer to the candles, then sat. Absently, she adjusted the malachite hair band before beginning to peruse the scroll, murmuring as she read. "The lord of the grasslands, the great Ildyrom, is unhappy . . . he claims that Fornal's barbaric actions in destroying good horses—even if they were Cyadoran horses—prompted the white demons to fire and raze Bestayna." Zeldyan swallowed. "The whites mutilated all the bodies—before they were dead." After a pause, she asked, "Have you any word from Fornal?"

"None, but he has never been overly concerned to inform others." Gethen's tone was dry. "Especially his sire. I had thought you might have heard."

"Not a scroll or a messenger." The blond regent shook her head. After a moment she resumed reading.

"Lornth's unwise actions . . . bring down the white empire on all of northwest Candar . . . must insist that Lornth reach an agreement with Cyador . . . or face not only the wrath of the Protector of Paradise but the undying enmity of Jerans . . ." She laughed harshly. "Sillek was right there, too."

"Your consort and lord was right about much. He was better than the holders deserved, and many understand that now."

"I am so pleased." Her tone was icy.

"Zeldyan—"

"I know . . . I know, but who else will understand? Fornal does not. Like Lady Ellindyja, he is filled with the idea of an honor that will destroy us, much as he dissembles around us." She stopped and returned her eyes to the words on the parchment.

"What think you?" asked Gethen when she lifted her eyes.

"Ildyrom is worried, but he wants us to face Cyador alone. If we weaken, he will take back the grasslands."

Gethen nodded. "I am still bothered about the horses . . . that does not sound like Fornal."

"No. That had to be the angels." Zeldyan frowned, then asked, "Can a lancer ride without a mount? And can a mount be found in the Grass Hills of summer?"

Gethen pulled at his chin. "You think the angels destroyed the mounts to stop the white demons?"

"I do not know, but they would not stop if they felt it would work."

"Perhaps Fornal was correct in one thing," suggested Gethen. "These angels seek results."

"You wonder if the price will be too high? Ask Sillek . . . if you can."

"Zeldyan—"

"I am not fair, my sire. Sillek was fair, and tried to make his holders happy. He is dead."

A gust of warm air puffed through the open shutters, and the candles flickered, and one almost guttered out before flaming up again.

The older regent sighed and touched his mostly gray beard. "The angels do their best to save our armsmen and your brother, and he doubtless finds fault with their methods each and every day. Ildyrom wants us to stop the white demons, but not if it carries the fight to his door, though it cost him not a single armsman or grassland raider." He took a slow breath. "We have just begun, and Fornal was right. Lornth will change because of the angels."

"Lornth would change without them, and not for the better, either. What other can we do?"

"I do not know. How would you answer Ildyrom?"

"You ask me?" Zeldyan laughed. After a moment of silence, she added, "I would suggest that the mighty lord of the grasslands *far* to the west of Clynya is welcome to join the fight against the white demons. Until then, he should not suggest conditions for those who fight and protect his borders."

"He will not like that."

"He will not like any course that is prudent for us."

Gethen smiled. "You have a fair hand. Will you write such? I will sign and seal it with you."

"Of course, my sire."

"And let us hope that the angels can deliver us."

Zeldyan nodded, but she did not smile.

LXXXVI

IN THE LATE-MORNING sun, Nylan studied the dust rising on the straight stretch of road to the south, the road from Syadtar. Ayrlyn sat in her saddle, glassy-eyed, her senses in the hot and still air somewhere over the source of the dust.

Tonsar glanced from one angel to the other. "Will stopping their wagons help that much?"

"They can't live off the land. There are too many of them. Even we have to get some supplies by wagon. So what happens if they start getting short on supplies?" asked Nylan.

"They send for more supplies?"

"And if their messengers don't get through?"

"They must forage."

"And if we keep shooting arrows at their foragers?" asked Ayrlyn, picking up the thread of the argument.

"Ah . . . and if they send more supplies, we do this again?" Tonsar beamed, then frowned. "But they will send more lancers the next time."

"More lancers eat more," Nylan said dryly.

Tonsar scratched his head.

Ayrlyn shook herself, then coughed. Her mount side-stepped on the mixture of grass and dirt that capped the hilltop, raising puffs of dust that added to the dust already coating the chestnut's lower legs. The redhead reined up the chestnut and looked to Nylan. "There are three supply wagons. From what I can tell, there are less than a score in guards, and they're not paying much attention."

"Any archers?"

"I didn't see any," answered Ayrlyn.

The silver-haired angel nodded.

"With a glass, I have seen such screeing, but never without. Truly, she is a dark angel." The subofficer on the mount beside Nylan coughed after he spoke.

"Thanks, Tonsar, but I'm just a healer who can sense the winds and use them to see things that aren't too far away." She raised herself slightly in the saddle and readjusted her position. "We need to set up."

"Positions," said Nylan.

"Positions for the attack! For the attack!" ordered Tonsar. "We will destroy these white demons."

The angels eased their mounts downhill toward the curve in the road, and toward the hill that held the concealed archery blind overlooking the ambush point. Tonsar turned his mount toward the curving swale from where the rest of the squad would attack.

Two other riders—Ailsor and Buretek—eased their mounts from Tonsar's group and drew up behind the angels. The four rode downhill to the Lornth-Syadtar road.

Nylan took a last look at the waist-high jumble of smooth

boulders that had been pried laboriously from beneath the earth—a barrier that left no room at all for passage on the uphill side of the road and a steep incline on the downhill shoulder. "No wagon will pass that."

"Especially not one driven by a white demon," ventured Buretek.

"It wouldn't matter if a black angel drove it," Nylan answered.

Buretek and Ailsor exchanged quizzical glances, and the engineer repressed a sigh. A barrier was a barrier. Why did so much get personalized in Candar?

"Because," answered Ayrlyn quietly, "everything is personal in lower-tech cultures. Patterns are obscured by the strength of personalities and by the seemingly random operation of natural forces."

"How did you know—"

"I just did." A faint smile followed the redhead's shrug.

All too often Ayrlyn seemed to read his thoughts. Another aspect of order-field mastery?

The redhead turned her mount to the left and rode up the dusty road for another three hundred cubits until she came to the grassy depression that led to the rear of the hill.

The three men rode silently behind her, up the slope to the back of the hill the road climbed, to a flatter area shielded from the southern road and the ambush site.

Ayrlyn paused before dismounting, her eyes glazing momentarily. "They're still on the road. Not any scouts out."

"Stupid," suggested Buretek.

"Not really," said Ayrlyn mildly. "Who has ever challenged the might of Cyador, or attacked a supply wagon? You don't guard against things that don't usually happen—not the first time. Some people never do." She swung out of the saddle and led the chestnut toward the tieline.

". . . still seems stupid . . ." murmured the square-jawed archer as he tethered his own mount and then started up the slope.

What sort of monster are you creating by bringing the total warfare concept to Candar? One you can survive? And how many will pay for how long? Nylan winced as he dismounted and tethered his mare to the tieline that ran between two stakes he had anchored earlier. Pushing away the words in his thoughts, he hoped the anchors held, although, supposedly, a well-broken mount would not break away. He glanced at the brown mare, half-chewing on the sparse brown grass. She was certainly strong enough to break the line if she put an effort into the attempt, but hadn't tried anything like that. Were even animals conditioned by patterns not to see the obvious? And what was he missing?

"We need to get in position," suggested Ayrlyn.

"Oh . . . sorry." Nylan unfastened the composite bow and his blades and followed her up the rise and down the slope to the trench behind the grass-and-brush screen.

Buretek and Ailsor were already waiting, one at each end of the blind, setting out their shafts.

"I didn't see any dust from the hilltop," said Ailsor.

"They're taking their time," answered Ayrlyn. "You don't raise as much dust when you plod. They'll get here soon enough."

Nylan wanted to nod at that. He wasn't looking forward to the ambush, successful though he hoped it would be.

"Wish we could do this on horse," offered Buretek after a period of silence. "It could be chancy getting out of here if something goes wrong."

"It won't," Nylan answered.

"It won't," Ayrlyn added, "but I'm not happy either to be on foot in the middle of nowhere." She sat in the bottom of the narrow trench and checked her bow for the fourth time, ignoring the minute cuts on her fingers and hands from plaiting the grass-and-brush screen that cloaked the blind.

Nylan looked at his hands—fewer cuts, but he'd both dug and plaited. "The horses will be secure enough tied to those stakes."

"Hoping it is so, ser . . ." murmured Ailsor from beside Nylan. Unlike Ayrlyn, the three men knelt, rather than sat. Ailsor's hands, like Ayrlyn's and Nylan's, bore cuts.

Ayrlyn's eyes glazed over again, briefly. "They're at the bottom of the hill now."

"Quiet . . ." Nylan said.

The four waited.

". . . at the turn . . . get ready . . ."

Ayrlyn's eyes cleared, and the four rose and nocked arrows, waiting, concealed by the grass and brush screen.

The creak of wagons and the low murmur of voices drifted uphill.

"Darkness! Not a rock demon-near everywhere . . . and then this!"

". . . didn't expect this . . ."

Nylan waited as the voices echoed uphill until all three wagons had stopped, and until the squad of a dozen lancers or so pushed toward the apparent landslide—although Nylan hoped none of them thought about the fact that the Grass Hills weren't especially rocky!

"All right, fire!" hissed Nylan.

Buretek and Ailsor began to pump shafts into the close-knit Cyadorans, followed by Ayrlyn and Nylan.

"Ambush!"

". . . a trap!"

"Ride toward those bushes. That's where . . ."

Nylan calculated. "Drop the stones, Tonsar!"

Half a dozen more boulders, dug from just beneath the hillside's surface, rolled down into the confined area of the road filled with riders and wagons, one after the other, and a dusty cloud rolled downhill behind the rocks.

Wheeeeee . . . . . . The scream of an injured horse rose above the voices.

"Move it!"

". . . where . . ."

The first half-squad, led by Fuera, the blond hothead, pounded up from the south behind the confused Cyadorans. With their sharp-edged blades out and ready, the Lornians took out the first of the white riders before the Cyadorans realized they were under attack from both sides.

Nylan forced his eyes back on the white teamsters and the

forward white guards, loosing another black iron shaft from his composite bow.

The shaft struck—a lancer with a green sash—and exploded. Nylan staggered as the white chaos force recoiled back up the hillside.

"What was that?" hissed Ailsor.

"Order-chaos collision," snapped Ayrlyn. "Keep firing, demon—damn-it!"

Nylan loosed three more shafts before another hit, with a smaller explosion, but enough of one that the white-recoil jarred his fingers, and he staggered in his tracks.

He swayed for a moment, putting down a hand to steady himself, since white stars seemed to be exploding in his eyes.

". . . frig . . . frig . . ." muttered Ayrlyn. "Damned recoils . . ."

By the time Nylan could begin to pick up images, most of the whites were down, sprawled on the wagons or the ground.

The last of the Cyadoran armsmen turned his mount back toward distant Syadtar.

Despite the fire white in his head, Nylan croaked out: "Get him, Buretek."

It took the young archer three shafts, but the armsman fell, as the others had.

Ailsor looked tiredly at Nylan, his bow almost hanging in his hands. "That . . . well . . . it wasn't really a fight, was it?"

"No," Nylan admitted with a shrug. "It wasn't." He coughed, trying to clear his throat. "And it's not honorable. War isn't honorable, and the Cyadorans certainly aren't. Is slaughtering children honorable?"

Ailsor looked dumbly at the engineer.

"What harm would it have done to let a few escape? Is that what you wanted to know, Ailsor?" asked Nylan.

The archer looked down at the tumbled plaited-grass screen.

"It would have destroyed the effect," Ayrlyn answered, her voice hoarse and tired. "We don't want them knowing what happened." She set aside the bow. "Go get the shovels. We need to fill this in. Buretek can stay here. You get his mount, too."

After a moment, Ailsor nodded.

"I'll get them and bring back your mount," the engineer told Ayrlyn, who nodded wearily. Nylan followed the archer, concentrating on putting one foot in front of the other.

After untethering both mounts, Nylan worked loose one stake, then the other, and rolled the rope around the two before slipping them into a saddlebag. By then, Ailsor had disappeared, riding back to the ambush site leading Buretek's mount.

The engineer mounted and led Ayrlyn's mount around the hill and down the road to just below where the redhead stood, dismantling the screen and tossing the pieces into the trench. She reached up for the shovel before Nylan extended it.

"Are you sure you should be digging?"

"It's not digging, just pushing stuff back in the trench. Besides, physical work helps, somehow." She glanced up. "Drop the reins. She'll stay."

With the redhead's tone, Nylan would have stayed put too, if he'd been the mare. He eased his mount down the slope, slowly picking his way above the rock barricade.

Tonsar waited on his horse on the far side. "It worked. You were right, ser angel."

"How many did we lose?"

"Three. Winse, Ungit, and Duira. Ungit . . ." Tonsar shook his head. "He did not listen."

"There's always someone who doesn't get the word." The engineer turned the mare. "Siplor, you take over that first wagon. Meresat . . . you've got the second. You'll need to replace that snapped wheel. Use the spare on the rear."

Nylan edged the mare up to the first wagon, mostly filled with kegs.

"That's real Cyad beer!" Siplor grinned at the angel. "And biscuits, and two wheels of cheese."

"We'll share it with the others at camp, but you get to dole it out." Nylan forced a smile, flicking the reins gently to ease the mare to the second heavy wagon, filled mostly with barrels stacked on end. The white-brown powder around the waxed end-ropes indicated that some had to be flour.

Meresat looked glumly at the broken left front wheel.

"You can do it," Nylan encouraged him, ignoring his own headache and the white flashes that blocked his vision intermittently. "Or would you rather dig burial trenches?"

"No, ser." Meresat slowly trudged to the spare wheel mounted on the rear of the wagon.

From above the barricade, Ayrlyn cleared her throat, then ordered, "Wuerek, you and your group—let's get those bodies buried. Over there out of sight of the road, and deep enough that scavengers don't dig them up."

Nylan could sense—somehow—that they shared the same, or similar, headaches and intermittent vision. Buretek and Ailsor shifted the shovel between themselves and were finishing the work of filling in the archery blind.

Ayrlyn mounted the chestnut, but remained on the uphill part of the road above the barrier.

"Fuera—the rest of you," rasped the engineer, "get the rocks back in the places we set."

"Why are we moving the rocks off the road?"

Nylan glanced around, but couldn't identify the speaker, not when he had to concentrate even to see. He took a deep breath before answering. "We want the Cyadorans not to know what happened. If armsmen and lancers just disappear, that'll make a lot of their people unhappy, hopefully with their commanders. How would you feel if your supply wagons and some reinforcements disappeared without a trace?"

". . . nasty thoughts, he has . . ."

". . . keep telling you that you don't mess with angels . . ."

". . . ways of the angels . . ."

Tonsar glanced at Ayrlyn, then at Nylan, and shook his head.

Nylan was afraid a lot more head-shaking would be going on before the fighting was all over—if it were ever all over. Somehow one battle just led to another. Was that human history on every planet in every universe?

". . . the regent . . . call it dishonorable . . ."

". . . ha . . . rather be dishonorable than dead . . ."

Fornal might not like Nylan's tactics, but he wouldn't mind

the food—or the beer. Neither would the armsmen mind the improved fare.

With his left hand, Nylan rubbed the back of his neck, then his temples, but the headache still pounded through his skull.

Ayrlyn rode around the road barrier on the uphill side where most of the stones had been removed and placed in scattered locales along the uphill side of the road.

"The headaches just get worse," the redhead said as she reined up beside Nylan.

"It seems that way."

After a moment, Ayrlyn added, "Think about those dream trees, about both order and chaos. It helps a little."

"Dream trees?" How could mentally re-creating dream trees help? Then again, there was a lot he still didn't understand about Candar. Dutifully, he tried to turn his thoughts to the dark trees with their flows of both order and chaos.

Beside him, Ayrlyn smiled faintly as Fuera and his detail removed the last of the road barrier rocks, and as one of the newer levies began to sweep the road with a makeshift broom.

LXXXVII

THE HAMLET OF Syskar crouched two kays away, under the late afternoon's hot sun, under the blistering green-blue sky, and a cloud of yellow-gray dust rose from under the hoofs of the Lornian armsmen approaching Nylan and the captured wagons.

Fornal reined up, the squad behind him slowing even more abruptly, then reluctantly sheathing unneeded blades.

"Greetings," offered Nylan. "We've brought a few supplies."

For a long moment, the regent glanced at the three heavy-laden wagons. "Supplies are welcome, yet . . ." He paused, then added, "Our holders would not expect us to stoop to becoming highwaymen. They would suggest that our mission was to destroy the white demons."

"We did," said Ayrlyn, her mouth turning up, although her eyes did not smile. "We eliminated almost a score of white armsmen. It seemed a shame not to bring back what they wouldn't need."

"The Cyadorans will call it dishonorable, and it will cost us more than you cost the demons. What will keep them from raiding our supply wagons now?" Fornal turned his mount as if to ride back to Syskar ahead of the returning force.

"How?" asked Nylan. "If they take a small raiding party, you can destroy it. A large one can't move that quickly. Besides, if we keep whittling them down, they won't have enough men to do raids and hold the mines."

"Will we have enough men left to attack, or defend against their attacks?" asked Fornal. "How many men did you lose to get those wagons?"

"Three. One was because the damned fool didn't listen. We killed nearly a score of theirs once they stalled at the barricade."

"A score?"

"Sixteen," reaffirmed Ayrlyn. "The archers got about half when they got tangled up. Then Tonsar dropped rocks on them and brought the mounted armsmen in from behind."

"It was like slaughtering trapped goats, ser regent. For once, the white demons were penned up—"

"They were penned up, and you killed them?"

"Do . . . the great and beloved holders of Lornth . . . want a score of reinforcements at the mines?" Nylan asked tiredly. "They want you to defeat the Cyadorans. Isn't that what we're doing?"

"I admit, angels, you have killed many white demons. Perhaps it takes one to kill one." Fornal looked to Nylan for a moment, then at Ayrlyn, whose brown eyes flashed blue. Finally, he glared at Tonsar, but the burly armsman merely met the regent's gaze evenly. After a moment, Fornal continued. "You have done so well, angels, that it is only right that you should have the honor of being the first to meet their massed might." Fornal smiled lazily, then flicked the reins and rode toward the shed barracks, his mount raising dust that fell almost as it rose.

Tonsar slowly moved his head from side to side. "If we keep killing them, they will not have that many armsmen. If we do not, then . . ."

Nylan wished Fornal could understand that simple argument. Or was Fornal merely preparing the way for their removal? Nylan took a deep breath. He wished he hadn't. He smelled; his clothes smelled; and even finding enough water to wash either was going to be a chore.

Everything was getting to be a chore.

"It always is," said Ayrlyn.

Nylan nodded.

LXXXVIII

THE BLOND WOMAN cooled herself with a narrow, bone-backed feather fan, then took a sip of greenjuice from the goblet on the table. The air in the sitting room hung so heavy that none of the candles even flickered, and the silhouetted shadows on the wall appeared painted there as the two regents sat motionless for a lingering moment.

"Your brother is most upset," Gethen began slowly. "I have never seen such words on a message scroll."

"The words must be terrible," offered Zeldyan with a smile, fanning herself once more.

Gethen eased the scroll across the table to his daughter. "I would not try to repeat them."

Zeldyan set aside the fan and began to read, while Gethen refilled his goblet, then half-drained it with a single long swallow. He blotted his forehead as she read.

"It is hot, too hot," he finally said into the silence.

His daughter nodded and continued reading.

Gethen refilled his goblet once more.

"He sounds like Lady Ellindyja," mused the blonde as she set down the scroll, "with all the talk of honor. And his concerns about the holders."

"He does, but we cannot ignore them." Gethen lifted his goblet, but lowered it down without drinking. "What the angels do disturbs me as well. They teach levies to be armsmen, and that is well. But their tactics . . . they will do anything to win."

Zeldyan touched her chin, then frowned. "Is it so terrible that they have found a way to destroy more of the white demons? Or to keep them from raiding our hamlets?"

"What will happen if the angels are successful?"

"And you think that our levies will learn that also?" asked Zeldyan.

"There is that possibility."

"And there will be revolts against bad holders?"

"Fornal was right. The angels will change Lornth. They are already doing so." Gethen pursed his lips, then scratched his right ear. "Their actions will bring all the white demons in Cyador to our doorstep. And with what will we stop them, then?" asked the older regent.

"They would take Lornth piecemeal without the angels." Zeldyan stood and walked to the doorway to the adjoining sleeping chamber, where she listened for a time before returning. "He's sleeping, but I thought I heard something." She lifted the goblet, sipped, and walked to the open window, so smoothly that the candles did not flicker as she passed. "You are right, my sire. Yet what choice have we? With the angels, Lornth will change, and much we hold dear will vanish. Without them, all will be destroyed."

"Then let us hope the angels have a way to stop tens of thousands of white demons. For that is what it will come to."

Zeldyan looked down on the few scattered lights that were Lornth for a time before turning. "Must it always come to that? If we defend ourselves adequately, then we face greater force and hatred, not only from without, but from our holders. If we do not, we face death or becoming vassals. Be those not the choices you pose, my sire?"

Gethen took a deep breath, deep enough that the candles wavered, but did not answer.

"Have I not stated what choices there be, my father?" asked Zeldyan more softly.

Gethen looked into the goblet, but found no answers, and lifted his eyes to meet hers. "You have seen what your lord saw, and that bodes ill. Mayhap, the angels can stop the white demons . . . mayhap. But I like not trusting in strangers and stranger magery. And I like not a land where holders may be questioned by peasants. For it will come to that."

"Nor I. Nor I." She paused. "Yet . . . better Lornth than no Lornth."

The faintest breath of hot air seeped into the room, so faint that it did not move the silhouetted shadows that again appeared painted on the sitting room walls.

LXXXIX

NYLAN SET THE hammer on the crude bench closest to the anvil, squinting as he walked out of the shade and into full morning sun to meet Tonsar. The brown-bearded armsman remained mounted and looked down at the smith.

"We are ready to leave, ser Nylan." Tonsar gestured vaguely southward.

"Just keep an eye on the mines. If there's any sign the Cyadorans are getting anything ready that deals with wagons, I want to know—immediately!" Nylan cleared his throat. "Avoid any fighting. Right now we've lost enough men. If they happen to see you—and try not to be seen—but if you are, seeing you will upset them enough."

Tonsar frowned.

"Believe me . . . it will." *Besides, we'll need every man we've got for the next trick.*

"You follow the wagons again?" asked Tonsar after another awkward silence. "It will be eight-days or longer before more come from Cyador."

"There's another way to make them pay." Nylan offered a crooked smile. "A quicker one, I suspect."

The armsman scratched the back of his head.

"Take their copper when they try to send it home."

"They will not like that. No, they will not. But will they risk sending wagons back to Cyad after . . . ?" The armsman paused, and his mount whuffed and took a step sideways.

"Now, you see why I didn't want anyone to escape? The whites don't know that we took out their supply wagons. They might guess, but they don't know." *But you do. And you know that most of the men you had killed were innocents.* Nylan rubbed his forehead.

"I would not wish to be your enemy." Tonsar grinned. "But I am not, and we are ready."

"Go . . ." Nylan forced a smile and watched for a time as the small squad trotted southward out of Syskar, raising a low cloud of yellow-gray dust that settled quickly in the still hot air.

He walked along the sunny side of the shed barracks, trying not to choke at the smells rising from his crude distilling apparatus. Two more of the tubes had sprung leaks. He wrapped each leak with a rag and then plastered it with the moistened clay from within the broken pot set aside for the purpose.

Then he walked to the well and washed his hands— twice—and then his face, not that the effect would last.

The smith's forehead was dripping again by the time he stepped back into the comparatively more shaded space under the chicken coop roof and blotted away the sweat.

Sias glanced up from the bellows and looked at the half-barrel serving as a quench tank. "You need more water, ser?"

"Just a bucket, Sias." Nylan reached for the tongs to slip the metal on the anvil back on the coals. He'd never promised he wouldn't forge black iron arrowheads for himself or Ayrlyn. Still, even looking at the metal almost turned his stomach.

He grimaced as he waited for the iron to heat to the necessary cherry red. The longer the war or conflict or whatever it was went on, the more squeamish he felt. What a great warrior and commander that made for!

How could he deny what he felt? Those in power made decisions, generally to preserve their power, and those who carried out the decisions suffered—or died. Yet he *felt* that the growth of Cyador was wrong, but so was Fornal's view of the world. Both imposed order of sorts through absolute force—just different kinds of order.

Was that why he dreamed about the damned trees—and their chaos and order flows? Did they represent an answer his subconscious was trying to formulate? Or were they something real his unconscious was trying to reach?

Do you want to know? Really know?

Despite the heat in the chicken coop smithy, he shivered. Engineering background or not, he lacked the cold rationality of a Ryba—or a Zeldyan—and even the callousness of a Fornal.

"You all right, ser?" asked Sias, returning with the bucket. "I thought this was too hot for you."

"It is." Nylan didn't bother to explain as he took the heated iron and slipped it onto the anvil. "Can you add some more coal to the fire?"

"Yes, ser." Sias added the brackish water to the quench barrel and then used a wooden scoop to add the brownish black coal to the forge coals.

The engineer raised the hammer, and then struck.

Cluunnggg . . . clunggg . . .

A half-dozen deadly arrowheads later, Nylan set aside the hammer, let Sias bank the forge coals, and walked to the shaded stoop of the dwelling, from where Ayrlyn had waved—presumably to indicate she had something resembling a midday meal. The Lornian cooks only prepared breakfast and the evening meal.

"Daaa! Daa!" Weryl tottered down the dusty path toward Nylan.

Sylenia followed, more slowly, a shy smile on her face, her eyes on the toddler.

"It's good to see you, too." Nylan grinned as he hoisted Weryl to his shoulder and walked toward the dwelling and

Ayrlyn. "And thank you, too, Sylenia. I probably don't tell you that enough, but we're glad you're here."

"So am I, ser. It has been good to get away from Lornth, from the sadness." She brushed back a strand of black hair, and, it seemed to Nylan, something dark within, before giving him another shy smile.

Nylan patted Weryl on the back. "Stronger and faster, every day."

"Faster," agreed Sylenia.

Nylan bent and set Weryl on the stoop, then took the two stairs onto the stoop itself. But he hadn't even stepped into the shade before Weryl threw both arms around his left leg.

Sylenia scooped up Weryl. "Let your daddy eat. He has been working. Smithing be hard work." She sat on the edge of the stoop, her legs dangling in the sunlight, one arm loosely around the silver-haired child.

"Daa woo haaah."

"Yes, I've been working hard." Nylan laughed. "Not that hard. It's better than riding all over southern Lornth." *Far better than killing . . . far better.* His eyes went to Ayrlyn, sitting in the shade, and he smiled at the sparkle in those brown orbs, and the warmth behind them.

She gestured toward a small block of cheese and a dark loaf resting on a square of waxed cloth beside her on the bench. "Have some. You're more hungry than you think."

"Thank you."

"It's just bread and cheese, and some cold water," Ayrlyn explained.

"Daaa!" Weryl twisted out of Sylenia's grasp and charged across the stones toward Nylan before he could even sit.

"Weryl . . ." Nylan hoisted his son again. "Determined, aren't you?"

"And who does he take after?" asked Ayrlyn.

"You would ask." Nylan sat on the shaded end of the bench, holding Weryl on his right knee, the one away from the bread and cheese, with one arm. With the other he reached for the bread.

"Wedd, daa?" Weryl lurched toward the chunk of bread the smith held.

Nylan frowned. "You've eaten. I haven't."

"Wedd!"

Sylenia stepped forward. "We'll take a walk, young man," the nursemaid insisted, "long enough for your father to eat."

Nylan slowly ate several mouthfuls of the dark bread, then glanced up, his eyes following Ayrlyn's.

Sylenia held Weryl in her arms, but a squat armsman—Tregvo—stood opposite her, talking loudly. ". . . you . . . up to the subofficer . . . he be a clown . . ."

Nylan started to rise, but Ayrlyn touched his arm.

"Do you wish I call the angels, Tregvo? Or Tonsar? Go, and trouble me no more." Sylenia's voice was cool, firm.

"Some day . . . you will be mine . . ."

Sylenia's cold eyes just burned, and Tregvo stepped back. After a moment, the armsman walked toward the barracks, looking back over his shoulder once.

Sylenia set Weryl down, and the two ambled toward the well.

"I don't like that," Nylan said quietly.

"She handled it all right."

"What if we're not around?"

"Even Fornal wouldn't tolerate his actually forcing himself on her." Ayrlyn took a swig from the water bottle. "The other thing that bothers me is the masculine assumption that women appreciate force and crudeness—or that they respond to it."

"Force again . . ." mused the smith, accepting the water bottle from the healer, then drinking. He ate several more mouthfuls of bread before speaking. "Dear?"

"What, dear scheming consort?" Ayrlyn's eyes sparkled for a moment.

"Me?"

"You. When you ask like that, it's trouble."

Nylan laughed. "Maybe. I have a really strange request. Can you do one of your searches on the winds? I mean, I know you can, but I wanted to know if some night you could try to find a sort of oasis—trees filled with order and chaos that are balanced? Maybe some place not too far away?"

"Those dreams are getting to you." She smiled. "Yes. I'd already thought about it."

"They're getting to you?"

"Something like that." She paused. "I can't sing anymore. The notes feel like they're copper . . . or lead. Even Weryl winces."

"All the deaths, you think?"

She nodded.

What was it coming to? If they didn't stop the relatively small Cyadoran expeditionary force, then Lornth would fall for nothing—and he and Ayrlyn and Weryl would be on the run in even more hostile lands, from what he could figure, and still required to survive by force of arms. Westwind would be surrounded as well. Yet stopping and destroying the Cyadoran force, as he knew from experience, would result in more massive retaliation.

"It's the proverbial no-win situation," Ayrlyn confirmed.

More and more, Nylan thought, she knew what he felt even when he did not speak his mind, and that, too, was strange.

"You could, too. You just don't look."

Nylan swallowed. Why didn't he? Because . . . because he feared what he might see?

"Go ahead . . . look at me . . ."

He swallowed again, but he let his eyes and senses rest on the redheaded healer and fighter, singer and lover. Besides the patterns of dark and light, almost like the dreams of his dreams and subconscious, besides the flame of song . . . there was something else.

"I'm not fragile, not that way," she said. *I love you, smith and engineer . . . won't lose me except by turning away . . . and I love your son . . . because he's you . . . and himself. . . .*

The engineer's eyes burned. . . . *hardly good enough for you . . . fumble through everything . . . can't really even protect you half the time . . .*

"I don't need protecting. I need you." Her hand grasped his, gently, but firmly . . . *and I need you to see me as I am . . .*

*fumble, too . . . get angry . . . impatient . . . don't turn away
. . . it's hard, but . . . fear you'll leave when you know me . . .
really know me . . .*

"That's what . . . I worried about all along." *How could
anyone love me . . . if they knew . . .*

Her laugh was gentle, and her other hand touched his cheek.
"I've known all along."

"All along . . ." and he hadn't seen it, or wanted to. *Some
mage . . .*

Some healer . . .

They both laughed, tears in their eyes.

XC

NO MORE BEER?" asked the thin-faced captain.

"No, ser," offered Serjeant Funssa from the gloomy back
of the narrow room. Despite the open windows, and the faint
twilight breeze, he wiped his forehead before continuing,
"But the supply wagons should be here afore long."

"They should have been here an eight-day ago," snapped
Miatorphi, looking glumly at his mug full of almost-brackish
water.

"They won't be here," said Piataphi in a low voice, low
enough not to carry outside the staff room. "The lancers operate on schedule, even in places like Syadtar."

"What happened?" asked Funssa, his eyes searching
through the gloom, going from one shadowed officer's face
to the next.

"Exactly? I don't know." The majer coughed. "Angel-
damned dust. The barbarians got them—the smart one, probably."

This time Azarphi and Miatorphi exchanged looks. Funssa
pulled at his short ginger beard.

"There have to be two barbarian groups out there," the
majer explained slowly, picking his words as though he had

drunk far too much beer. "Nothing else makes sense. There were two camps. They don't even act the same. One is the same old barbarian tactics—hit and run, but some semblance of honor. The other one avoids any skirmish except where he can destroy our force totally, or pick off a lot of our lancers with almost no losses. He's the one who dumped the fireballs on the corrals. Did you notice that he went for the fodder, too? What barbarian thinks about fodder, for darkness's sake?"

"A barbarian is a barbarian," offered Miatorphi.

"Your shafts were closer than you thought, Azarphi," continued Piataphi, as though Miatorphi had not spoken. "A barbarian would not think of fodder, but an angel might. And an angel would think of supply wagons."

"What do we do now?" asked Azarphi. "We can't exactly beg for more lancers and a bunch of foot."

"No. We can make His Mightiness force them on us."

The other three looked dubious.

"Trade and gold—that is all those in Cyad value. Pah . . . they talk of honor, but we have no fleet because it would have cost many golds to rebuild it. Even His Mightiness builds but one fireship, when we need many. The steamwagons fail because it takes too many golds to replace them, and with only barbarians around, why need we such devices?" Piataphi looked owlishly through the twilight. "So . . . we are going to send all the copper we have mined back to Syadtar. And we are going to do everything that we can to ensure that the barbarians know this."

Funssa swallowed. "Ser . . . the men?"

"I am most certain that you will pick the men most suited for such a mission, Funssa, as well as a messenger and a scout that could ride like skyfire if anything untoward happened." Piataphi looked soberly around the staff room. "His Mightiness would wish to know if anything happened to his precious copper, and so would the white mages."

"I do not understand," protested Funssa.

"Am I supposed to sacrifice good lancers and foot to protect mere copper?" asked Piataphi. "And with the losses we have had, because our forces are not adequate to fight two barbarian lands—or is it three with the dark angels?—I cannot spare more lancers and still hold the copper mines that His Mightiness has entrusted to our care. So . . ." The majer shrugged and stood. "We do what we can."

"Ser." Funssa swallowed once more.

"Good," replied Piataphi ambiguously. "Good evening, captains." He turned and walked out the half-open door, each step taken with exaggerated care.

Funssa looked at Azarphi and Miatorphi. "Sers?"

"You heard the majer," said Miatorphi.

With a deep breath, the serjeant departed.

"He must have been hoarding the beer for himself," Azarphi muttered.

"Wouldn't you? Do you know what his life is worth right now? Or ours?"

"Why is he doing this?" asked the thin-faced captain.

"To get all the merchants roused up, I suppose, and His Mightiness to send more lancers, before we get whittled down to nothing and killed."

"We've still got more horsemen than they do, lots more."

"For how long?" asked Miatorphi. "We're getting picked off. They aren't. Besides, they don't seem to care if they die, just so long as they die honorably. I do."

Azarphi shook his head in the dark.

XCI

A LIGHT BREEZE whispered across the sun-browned and dusty grass. The two angels remained mounted at the head of their three squads on the back side of a low hill. On the west side of the hill, one indistinguishable from the other Grass Hills, ran the rutted road between the mines and Syadtar, although the mines—and the bulk of the Cyadoran troops—were a good fifteen kays north of where the Lornian force waited.

A single man rode from the north, puffs of dust and bits of brown grass tossed up by his mount's hoofs.

The angels waited until the rider reined up. Both man and mount were breathing hard.

"The wagons are coming!" exclaimed Wuerek, his eyes going to Ayrlyn. "They've got less than a squad guarding them. And slow . . . I could hear the groaning from up in the grass."

As her eyes unglazed, Ayrlyn smiled to herself.

"Those wagons, they're not rolling faster than a walk, with mayhap fifteen lancers," Wuerek repeated.

Nylan and Ayrlyn exchanged glances. It made a sort of sense. No military commander wanted to denude himself of resources—wagons, horses, or whatever—merely to supply goods to civilians. So the wagons carrying the copper ingots back to Cyador were heavy laden and—this first time—lightly guarded.

"We'll set up below the next hill, as we planned," Ayrlyn said. "At the turn before the climb." She turned in the saddle and glanced at Tonsar, who nodded slowly.

The setup was straightforward. Accompanied by one squad, the two archers—Buretek and Ailsor—would wait until the supply convoy reached the turn where the road rose. Then they would begin shooting, and keep shooting their shafts until they ran out—or until the lancers reacted.

At that point, Nylan would bring the squad with the archers down, while Ayrlyn and Tonsar would strike from behind.

It was, Nylan reflected, simple enough, if it worked. Simple enough to get a few more armsmen killed, but he needed the wagons close enough to a side road or trail that would allow him to circle back to Syskar far east of the mines—and that meant a locale where digging up more boulders wasn't feasible.

If things went the way they usually did, he'd probably pay for not doing the hard work with something else—like lives. As he flicked the mare's reins and began to lead his squad to the southwest side of the hill, just out of sight of the road and the oncoming wagons, he hoped one of those lives didn't happen to be his—or Ayrlyn's.

Fuera eased his mount up beside Nylan's. "You still want me to take the second group, ser?"

"Yes," answered the angel. "Why wouldn't you?"

The blond shrugged.

"You're impatient," Nylan added, shifting his weight as the mare continued onward, "but I need someone who will lead, not talk. Just wait until I give the order. That's all."

"What if—"

"Fuera, you wait until I give the order. The only reason you shouldn't wait is if lightning or something knocks me dead. Then you're in charge. If that happens, I wouldn't charge. I'd turn those left alive and ride out of here as fast as you can."

Fuera's heavy blond eyebrows furrowed.

"Look," Nylan explained slowly. "Anything that can take out a force's commander even before the fight starts can probably do worse to all of you. If that happens, look to Ayrlyn or Tonsar. Follow their orders. If they're out," he shrugged, "you can do as you think best."

The blond nodded. "You think we can take out these lancers?"

"We should be able to—if we follow the plan. Let the archers get rid of some of them first."

"It doesn't seem . . . exactly . . . fair . . ."

"War isn't fair. It wasn't fair of the whites to slaughter the children in Kula or Syskar, or in those Jeranyi hamlets, either. We're not in this to be fair. We're in it to win." Inside, Nylan winced. How much had he come to take on the characteristics he'd deplored in Ryba? Did war do that to everyone who wanted to survive?

As his squad rounded the side of the hill, he looked northward to where the road ran downhill and to the south. A low rise still blocked the more northern section of the road from view. "All right. Rein up. We'll wait here."

Ayrlyn and Tonsar would be farther north, waiting behind the hill crest until the wagons passed, until the archers began to shoot.

Leather creaked; harnesses jingled; horses *whuffed* gently. The brown grass hung limply in the hot midday sun. A low drone seemed to come from the north—the conversations of bored lancers?

Nylan turned in the saddle and motioned to the archers. "Buretek . . . Ailsor."

The two eased their mounts around Fuera's gray and reined up.

"They're on the way. Get your bows ready."

Buretek gave a single sharp nod, Ailsor a sad and faint smile. Both unwrapped the longbows and took the covers off their quivers.

The low droning continued, accompanied by an intermittent series of creaks and sharper voices.

Nylan wiped his forehead with the back of his forearm, and bits of dried and sunburned skin stuck to the silver hair on the uncovered part of his arm. Sunburn—another occupational hazard.

The sound of the wagons increased, and Nylan stood in his stirrups, then motioned the archers forward, up beside him. "Won't be long now."

"Ser," said Ailsor quietly.

The sun continued to burn into Nylan's neck as they waited, as the white lancers neared the turn in the road.

He eased his mount forward to where Ailsor and Buretek would have a clear shot, wondering how long before they were seen. The two reined up and looked at him. Still, the lancers did not look uphill.

"Fire!" commanded Nylan.

Buretek and Ailsor began to loose their shafts. Several passed by the lancers unnoticed—until the first buried itself in a stained and soiled cream tunic. Even the civilized white lancers were having trouble with laundry, Nylan noted absently, wondering as he did why he'd noticed that.

"Barbarians!"

"Where?"

A Cyadoran stood up on one of the wagons and pointed toward the three Lornians. "There! After them!"

Nylan watched as the squad of lancers milled, then slowly formed, and began to ride toward the hilly rise.

"Just keep firing," the silver-haired angel said. "Hold your mounts!" he ordered as he turned and looked back at Fuera, and those behind the young hothead, still half-concealed from the oncoming lancers. Couldn't the idiot see that every shaft that struck left one less lancer able to fight—or fight well?

Dust rose from the north as Ayrlyn led the other two squads down on the three wagons from behind. Four of the remaining lancers turned toward the new threat, almost in slow motion, it seemed to Nylan. The fifth lancer reined up and studied the attack, and then spurred his mount out across the flat to the southeast—the only area where there were no Lornians.

"I'll get him! I can get him," said Fuera.

"Hold it!" Nylan snapped at the blond armsman. "The whites right in front of us."

Fuera bared his teeth, but held his mount.

Nylan waited. Let the whites do some of the riding— uphill.

White lances out, the Cyadorans continued to canter toward the Lornian group, although three lancers had gone down, and another clutched his arm and trailed his squad, as if uncertain what to do.

A fifth looked stupidly down as an arrow slammed through his chest.

"Bows away!" Nylan told the two archers. "Fuera, you take the left; I'll lead the right. Remember, angle from the sides. From the sides. They can't move those lances like a blade." He shut his mouth, realizing he was talking too much. If the training hadn't taught them, talking right now wouldn't do anything.

As soon as the silver-haired angel saw the two archers had sheathed their bows, he took the blade from his waist scabbard and lifted it. "Now!"

The mare jumped forward, and he lurched in the saddle before catching himself. A wry smile crossed his face—he still wasn't totally used to leading charges while bouncing around in a saddle with a heavy iron blade in his hand.

Reflections and shimmers of light—always reflections—

wavered off the small polished shields of the white lancers as they rode forward.

Nylan swung his group to the left so that they remained well uphill of the white lancers. He wanted to force the Cyadorans to look into the sun as well as climb to meet the Lornians. He hoped that would further tire the white mounts—but that meant that the glare from the damned shields would be even greater.

The smith glanced to his right and downhill where Fuera was almost level with the road and heading into the flat to the east.

With another gesture of the blade, Nylan turned downhill, and his half-squad followed.

Onward, on to another round of death . . .

The whites slowed, as if puzzled by attacks from two sides, and half the lances swung slowly uphill.

Before he really knew it, Nylan could see a long white lance seemingly moving toward him. He slipped aside the white lance with his short heavy blade, his eyes watering from the blast of reflected light from the shield—his success due to the "feel" that had come from Ryba's intensive training—then struck laterally underneath the shaft. The blade sheared through the lancer's torso and stuck, nearly wrenching the angel from the saddle before coming free.

Whhsttt . . .

The next lancer had dropped his lance, and Nylan had to flatten himself to avoid the sabre that threatened to take his arm. Before he could get his own blade up, he was through the column.

His head had begun to ache, his eyes to burn, and he had to guide the mare into a turn and back toward the fighting.

Another white shoved a jagged-tipped and shattered lance toward the angel, but Fuera's blade knocked it down as the blond galloped past.

Nylan's heavy short blade cut deeply into the white lancer's shoulder near the neck. Blood seemed to fountain everywhere, momentarily, followed by the unseen rush of whiteness and pain that accompanied every death Nylan created.

The smith, half-blind and fighting the knives in his eyes and the pounding in his skull, kept his own blade in a semiguard position, and let the mare carry him back through the scramble to the uphill side of the road, where he reined up, temporarily alone.

Two deaths is enough . . . more than you can keep taking . . . But he felt guilty, even as he forced his eyes open, burning from both deaths and pitiless sunlight.

Most of the white lancers were down, and the white haze that only he and Ayrlyn seemed to see flooded the low area around the wagons and the remaining mounts of the Cyadorans.

A second white lancer galloped south as if his life depended on headlong flight, which it did, Nylan thought.

He turned and studied the area around the wagons, taking a deep breath of relief to see that Ayrlyn had reined up beside one of the stopped wagons.

After all the waiting and planning . . . and the skirmish seemed almost over before it had begun. He turned his mount downhill and northward, toward the three big wagons and their six horse teams.

"Ser?" The words were croaked, rather than spoken.

Nylan turned in the saddle.

Ailsor rode slowly toward Nylan, weaponless, blood streaking the right arm that held his left. "Ser . . . ?"

Nylan reined up.

The archer's face paled, and blanked, and he slumped across the neck of his mount.

Awkwardly, the angel sheathed his own blade, not bothering to clean it, and eased his mount beside Ailsor's—too late. The archer was dead, his tunic soaked with blood. Nylan took a deep breath, knowing that he couldn't have healed the other, not even had he reacted more quickly.

How many other Lornians had died? He surveyed the road and the grass flats. Only one other Lornian mount seemed riderless. Fuera and the others were stripping the bodies of weapons and anything else of value.

"Ser?" asked Wuerek, riding up and slowing, but not stopping. "Do we need to do graves?"

"No. At least two escaped, and we need to get out of here. Take all the spare mounts."

"Good."

"We need to bring back the bodies of our dead." Nylan gestured toward the dead Ailsor.

"Yes, ser." Wuerek's voice was decidedly less enthusiastic, but Nylan didn't care.

"Tell Fuera." Nylan chucked the reins and eased the mare toward where Ayrlyn had reined up beside the first wagon. He massaged his neck, hoping that would relieve the pressure in his skull. It didn't.

Should he think of trees? Who had time? He snorted.

Tonsar arrived beside Ayrlyn at the same time Nylan did, reining up with a flourish. "These fellows"—the burly armsman jerked his head toward the bodies sprawled in the wagon seat—"they weren't very good. Some of ours were better after the first eight-day you had them."

Ayrlyn and Nylan exchanged glances.

Had it been a ruse? Nylan wondered. "What's in the wagons?"

"Oh, it is copper, many ingots of copper." Tonsar smiled broadly. "Big ingots."

The smith eased the mare over beside the wagon, then dismounted. He pulled back the dusty canvas, ignoring the few dark splotches of blood on the heavy fabric, realizing that his own shirt was equally splotched. As the dust rose around him, he tried to rub his nose one-handed, but failed to stop the sneezes. *Aaaa . . . chew . . . cheww!*

Finally, he rubbed his nose again and surveyed the wagon bed—filled with bronzish ingots, some already bearing a faint greenish sheen.

Ayrlyn sat on her mount, motionless, eyes glazed over.

Nylan re-covered the ingots, sneezing again and again. "Demon-damned dust." He rubbed his nose once more, then remounted, waiting until Ayrlyn's eyes refocused.

"You think it was a little too easy?" asked Ayrlyn, squinting as if the sunlight had suddenly brightened.

"I had that thought." Nylan nodded. "Let's get the Cyadoran gear rounded up and get out of here."

"I've already checked on the breezes—such as they are. There aren't any Cyadorans around. There might be a scout." Ayrlyn closed her eyes and massaged her neck and forehead with her right hand.

"I think one got away. Two actually, but one didn't even try to fight," said Nylan. "That seemed strange." He looked at Tonsar. "We can talk about that later. Let's get some drivers up here, and get these wagons moving. The sooner we're north of the mines and back in Syskar, the happier I'll be."

Ayrlyn nodded in agreement.

XCII

LEPHI STOOD ON the balcony, facing the harbor, his light silvered robes billowing in the gentle breeze rising off the blue of the water to the south, the scent of leydar and orange mixing in the salt air.

The late-afternoon sun cast the long shadow of the palace almost as far as the stone wharfs that had sparkled spotless white for all the centuries Cyad had stood, for all the generations of lords of Cyador. Each of the score of wharfs extended more than five hundred cubits out into the deep harbor waters; each was twice that from its neighbor. Beyond the wharves the harbor's greenish blue darkened into the far deeper blue of the Great Western Ocean.

The Protector of the Steps to Paradise took in the white clouds rising over the ocean to the south, with their promise of rain, and then the wharfs again, where the seemingly endless expanse of white stone dwarfed the dozen small coasters seemingly tied at random.

"Cyad will again be as mighty as . . . even more mighty than before . . ." he murmured. "No barbarians, no forests, no love of luxury . . . no . . ."

Although the shadow of the palace covered the Great Avenue, all the way down to the wharfs, the white paving stones and curbs glistened with a whiteness that leapt out of the shadow, out of the dark green of trees and grass. Indeed, Lephi knew, without looking, that every avenue in Cyad was white, spotless and shimmering in late afternoon, in twilight, even through the nights under the glittering lamps of the avenues. And every avenue was safe, clean, pure.

His eyes dropped closer to the palace, toward the hexagonal white market square to the southwest of his balcony. He frowned at the single blue awning among the green and white canvases.

"Blue? Blue . . . it will go, like the barbarians."

Lephi nodded, his eyes returning to the wharfs, and to the shipworks beyond where the superstructure of the first fireship in generations rose above the waves.

"Cyad . . . forever."

The Protector of the Steps to Paradise smiled.

XCIII

THE STILLNESS OF late afternoon had faded into the chirpings of twilight, and a light breeze swept out of the north, with the slightest hint of moisture. The insect chorus melded with the sounds of hoofs, clanking harnesses, and low voices.

In the dimness of early evening, Nylan rubbed his neck, then his temples, as he rode at the head of the column beside Ayrlyn. Behind them rode the three squads of armsmen, followed by five riderless mounts, two bearing bodies, a dozen lancer mounts, and the three heavy wagons, which creaked and squeaked loudly enough that each squeak sent another shiver through Nylan's skull. Ayrlyn merely winced, although Nylan knew that her less severe reaction reflected better self-discipline, not less pain.

"We can't keep doing this," he finally said in a low voice.

"No."

"Did you have any luck with the trees?"

He got the sense of a shrug, and waited.

"The trees we seem to dream about—they're a long ways south. There's a small grove to the northwest of Syskar— thirty kays, I'd guess—that feels somewhat like that."

The smith could feel Tonsar's puzzlement.

"We have to do something," Ayrlyn said. "You can't go out and fight another battle right now."

"Neither can you."

"No."

"Do we go to the closer grove?" he asked.

"Do we have much to lose?"

Ayrlyn was probably right. Had the lancers who had defended the wagons been first-rate, both he and Ayrlyn would have been dead or wounded during their increasingly violent reactions to the deaths they caused. Another skirmish, battle, fight, would have the same result. Yet they had everything to lose. How could they just ride away on the hope that a series of dreams, a sense of order, and a grove of trees *might* provide an answer, some sort of answer? Especially when Nylan wasn't even sure what the problem was.

Overhead, the emerging stars, unfamiliar as ever to the angels, shone clearly, coldly, across the hilly grasslands, grasslands bleached into a faint white even to Nylan's night vision.

"Will going to this . . . grove help?" he asked after a time.

"I don't know. You want certainty at a time like this? It's certain we won't make it if we don't change something."

That made too much sense, so much sense he didn't bother answering, knowing that Ayrlyn understood. He massaged his temples again.

The night darkened; the stars brightened; and the wagons kept squeaking and creaking.

"That's Syskar," Ayrlyn said.

Nylan looked out into the darkness, catching the few glimmers of light ahead. "Tonsar . . . send a messenger to the camp. Let ser Fornal, Lewa, Huruc know that we're coming in, and that we've got copper and some more supplies." Nylan rubbed his temples again, wishing the aching would subside.

"Yes, ser." The subofficer turned and called, "Kysta! Up here."

The angels rode silently as Tonsar explained the message to Kysta and sent the red-bearded young levy off at a canter.

"You will not be gone long . . . on this journey?" Tonsar ventured once Kysta had left.

"It shouldn't take long," Ayrlyn said.

One way or the other, thought Nylan.

"The men . . . they feel better when you lead them," confessed the subofficer. "No one can stand against an angel."

"Right now, a one-armed Cyadoran could knock me off this mare," Nylan said.

"That is why you must—?"

"Something like that," Ayrlyn answered ambiguously.

Tonsar nodded to himself as they neared the encampment.

Torches burned on the stoop of the officers' dwelling and from the front of the shed barracks, adding a dim light to the area.

"Fornal's over there," said Ayrlyn, half-gesturing toward the left.

The two rode toward the house and reined up, not bothering to dismount.

"More banditry and murder, angels?" asked the coregent pleasantly.

"Copper and supplies, and we got rid of another score of white lancers," Nylan answered tiredly.

"How many did you lose?"

"Two," said Ayrlyn.

"We just filled the air with arrows and then charged. Very Lornian attack, ser Fornal." Nylan could sense two figures in the shadows of the stoop—Huruc and Lewa.

"Why . . . the holders would be most pleased. You actually fought . . . directly."

"Yes, we did." Nylan forced himself erect. "You'll need to detach some guards to accompany the wagons back to Lornth."

"Guards for what?" asked Fornal. "I had thought you brought more supplies."

"The wagons are filled with copper ingots. We'll keep the supplies here, not that there were a lot. But I assume you don't want to lose the copper to brigands, and the wagons themselves are worth something."

"You would not wish to take the wagons to Lornth yourself?"

"Not particularly," Nylan answered.

"Even with the transfers from Huruc's forces, we still only have a score and a half," added Ayrlyn tiredly. "The copper wagons need at least a squad as an escort."

"Guards for copper. That would make us like merchants, not warriors."

Fornal was more than that, reflected Nylan, more of a warring pain in the ass with his pomposity. No wonder Gethen kept his son at arm's length and then some. The engineer still wondered about heredity. How could one man have a daughter so bright and a son so dense? Or did the cultural imperatives stifle male intelligence?

"Ser Fornal," the engineer said slowly, "the copper on these wagons is worth several dozen golds, maybe more. Your sister and your sire need those golds to supply you. They also need to claim some victory to the holders, as you have pointed out. Sending the wagons to Lornth will do both." Nylan paused and added. "Especially with your armsmen guarding them."

After a moment, Fornal nodded, slowly. "That does make sense, ser angel, and I could send a request for more armsmen to replace our losses, also."

Nylan could sense both the anger and discomfort from Ayrlyn, as well as a feeling of grim amusement.

"The other thing is that we're going off for a few days—call it a magely quest." Nylan held up his hand. "It's important, but I can't tell you why."

"You will be taking your squads?"

"No. I'd thought perhaps three men, and, of course, Sylenia and Weryl. Three would not make a difference here."

"A magely quest—that I could scarcely deny. Not after such a handsome result from your arms."

And you'll need us more than ever when the whites finally react. Which they will. Nylan locked eyes with Fornal, until the regent looked away. Then he turned his mount toward the corral.

Ayrlyn followed, chill still radiating from her.

XCIV

. . . AND WHEN THE white lancers of Cyad had come at last to the copper mines of the north, those of Lornth threw down their picks and shovels and their blades, and fled into the Grass Hills, for they well knew that the copper mines were not theirs, and they were sore afraid of the righteous wrath of the Lord of Cyador.

The white lancers rebuilt and refurbished the mines, and brought order and discipline back into the Hills of Grass, nor did they afflict the peoples nor their hamlets.

The wily Nylan, like the mountain cat who cannot face the well-prepared hunter in the light of day, advised the guileless council of Lornth behind heavy doors, saying, If the Cyadorans cannot eat and they cannot sleep, they will not hold to the mines that your fathers and forefathers have worked. And they will depart.

The delvers and diggers of Cyad labored long and with great effort to bring forth the copper from the mines, trusting in the honor of the Lornians and in the forces of the most honorable white lancers.

For in that time, none believed that even the wily Nylan would stoop to slaughtering innocent horses, nor to murdering hapless wagoners, nor to raising fireballs in the night and dropping them upon lancer and digger alike while they slept. All this did Nylan, and more, terrible and dishonorable deeds

better lost in tumult of time. Yet remember we must, for this
is how the dark angels came to power in Candar. . . .

> *Colors of White*
> (Manual of the Guild at Fairhaven)
> Preface

XCV

THE ANGELS REINED up at the crest of the low hill, where Nylan
unfastened his water bottle and took a deep swallow. Sylenia
twisted in the saddle and offered water to Weryl, who swallowed, splashed water across his tanned legs, and then thrust the
bottle back before Sylenia was ready. The bottle slid off the saddlebags and bounced into the dust of the road.

Even before Nylan could put down his own water bottle,
Fuera had vaulted from his saddle and recovered the water
bottle, handing it up to Sylenia. A dark splotch remained in
the road.

"Thank you." The black-haired nursemaid smiled.

"Just tell Tonsar that we looked out for you." Fuera flashed
an openly charming grin.

Sylenia shook her head, but the smile remained as Fuera
remounted with the same dash.

Ayrlyn offered the faintest of ironic smiles. Nylan smothered his own smile, then looked at the vista before them.

Under the mid-afternoon sun, and a green-blue sky with a
few scattered and puffy white clouds, the road wound down
the hill to the right, and then angled up yet another grass-
covered hill, topped by a small grove of low trees. A flock of
sheep grazed on the mostly green meadow west of the road,
and beyond the animals were several low buildings and a
sod-roofed dwelling.

"Still that way?" asked Nylan, inclining his head in the general direction of the road ahead.

"There's a hint of order. It's stronger that way," suggested Ayrlyn.

Nylan let his own order senses follow hers, feeling a thread of order, and something more, still to the northwest.

"It's stronger now."

He nodded, restowing the water bottle and wondering if they would reach the order grove, if that was what it was, before sunset.

Perhaps ten kays and three lines of hills later, the group reined up at the top of another low hill, looking out over the patchwork of continuing meadows and scattered flocks of sheep.

"We're close," Ayrlyn said.

Nylan glanced downhill, and his eyes wandered back to the opposite hill crest. He frowned. He'd meant to look downhill.

Rather than look, he listened in the stillness broken only by the hint of a breeze. Was that the gurgling of a brook or stream?

He started to look downhill again, and his eyes blurred.

"There's something there." The redheaded healer frowned.

"I know. It's shielded somehow."

"There are trees, pines of a sort, and they're tall."

Out of the corner his eyes, Nylan could sense Sylenia's puzzlement as she squinted out into the glare of the low sun, trying to make out whatever the two angels discussed.

"Just a hillside . . ."

"Why are we sitting here?" asked Fuera.

"The smith and healer see something," answered Sias.

"Don't see anything," added Buretek.

"They see a lot we don't. He sees inside metal. She sees inside people." The apprentice smith and armsman paused. "I'm not sure it be good to see everything they see."

"We'll see," said Buretek cheerfully. "They see something, or they don't."

Except it wasn't that simple, thought Nylan. Nothing that involved the order and chaos fields was—that he'd already discovered, unfortunately.

"There's nothing there," said Ayrlyn. "I mean, no animals, no big ones. There are the trees, and the stream."

"Let's see." Nylan turned his mount to the left and off the road, heading downhill.

". . . not even a road . . ."

". . . knows where he's going . . ."

". . . so does she . . ."

As they rode downhill toward the well-sensed but unseen valley, if a place that tried to fool human vision could be claimed to be unseen, Nylan noted a growing sense of calm, of balance before him, and a growing consternation in the saddles behind.

". . . something there . . . but my eyes . . ."

". . . told you . . ."

Finally, he turned. "It's just a grove of trees. There's some sort of magic shield around it to protect it from being logged or destroyed. That's all." *Not quite all, by a long shot, but nothing to harm them.* Whether it might harm Ayrlyn or him was another question. *And it isn't really a shield, either.* He took a deep breath.

"Not quite all," murmured Ayrlyn as she eased her mount closer.

"I know. I can feel it, but it's not harmful."

Abruptly, when the ground flattened near the base of the hill, they no longer had to use their order senses to force their eyes to see the grove.

"Oh . . ."

"Where . . . the trees come from?"

Even Weryl added an "oooo."

Less than a dozen huge and spreading pines formed a circle, shielding the needle-carpeted center area with a canopy of green. The area under and immediately around the trees was open, covered only with a deep carpet of pine needles.

A narrow and fast-moving brook bordered the grove, appearing out of the tangled thorn bushes and redberry bushes to the southeast. Was it from some sort of underground spring? There wasn't a stream south of the valley. Of that Nylan was certain.

Downstream, on the northwest side of the grove, the same

stream vanished into another tangle of bushes, except far enough away to leave a clearing in the open.

The cool and shadow of trees and the hills were more than welcome to the smith. He took a deep breath, a breath free from dust for what seemed the first time since they had left the Westhorns a long season earlier, a breath filled with the clean scent of pine.

The smith turned in the saddle. "We'll camp in the open space at the end. We can sleep on the needles around the trees, but keep the fire clear of them."

Sias glanced up at the towering evergreens, and then at Buretek. "Did you see these up on the hillside?"

Fuera reached out, leaning sideways in the saddle, and thumped the ridged and age-darkened bark. "Solid . . . most solid." He shook his head.

Nylan smiled slowly. Maybe there was something to the trees . . . and to the dreams . . . maybe. He hoped so.

"There is," Ayrlyn affirmed as she dismounted and led the chestnut to the downstream area just before the brook vanished into the thicket again. After a moment, as the mare drank, she added, "The redberries are ripe, and there are plenty here. But watch the thorns."

Watch the thorns—wasn't that the general prescription for life? What other surprises might there be?

After a moment, he dismounted and followed Ayrlyn, as did the others.

Overhead, the pine boughs whispered ever so faintly in the late afternoon breeze, a breeze that only the trees showed.

XCVI

No one steals the copper of Cyador. No one mocks the Mirror Lancers. Triendar . . . I want to teach those barbarians a lesson," snapped Lephi. "Turn the white fires on them, make them white dust—you know, unwrap the ancient chaos on them."

"I fear that I do know, Your Mightiness," replied the slight and balding figure, brushing short white hair off his left ear.

"You fear that I know what I want?" Lephi laughed, harshly.

"What you want will destroy you and Cyador. Not to mention me," replied Triendar dryly.

"Explain this," demanded the Lord of Cyador, Protector of the Steps to Paradise. Silence fell across the hall, and the polished white stone tiles appeared as cold as the ice of the Northern Ocean in midwinter.

"The ancient mirror towers were based on the powers of chaos. So are our powers. Chaos by its nature must be balanced by order. That is how the firewagons operate. The order of the boilers and chambers and the tubing contains the chaos of water heated into steam. The chaotic force of the moving wheels is balanced by the order of the stone paving blocks." Triendar paused.

"You have belabored those points before, Triendar. Why do they mean you cannot turn chaos upon the barbarians?"

"I did not say that, Your Mightiness. I said that turning chaos upon them would likely destroy Cyador and us. Such chaos would allow the Accursed Forest to surge beyond its boundaries—"

"One moment, ancient Triendar. You have always claimed that the forest held equal parts of order and chaos. How can your use of chaos allow it to expand?"

The white mage sighed. "It is not simple to explain, but I will try. If I marshal chaos against the barbarians, that concentrated chaos allows order to be concentrated elsewhere in Candar. The forest will use that order to expand, but once expanded, will balance order and chaos within its boundaries. For us to contain it will require more chaos, which will free order to strengthen it further."

"How is Themphi containing it?"

"Poorly—and with the less concentrated chaos of men with torches. Even so half your foot and lancers labor around Geliendra."

"That is why we must use your weapons against the barbarians," pointed out the Lord of Cyador.

"Then too, as I have explained before, there is the problem of the fireship, and all the chaos it must carry," Triendar continued, as if he had not heard Lephi.

"How does that affect the Accursed Forest? Even the shipworks are stoneworks built up from the water, and water contains order, much order, you have said." Lephi's voice sharpened. "You do not listen to me."

"I do listen, but chaos is never simple. A fireship, with the fire cannons you wish and the bombards and the chaos engines, it creates much chaos. Add that to all that has been stirred up this past year . . ." Triendar looked at the man in silver and white.

"You tell me that I cannot bring chaos against the barbarians and contain the Accursed Forest? That I must not complete the fireship."

"No. The fireship will not be ready. While it embodies much chaos, some is contained by the waters of the harbor and by the ordered iron that binds the engines and fireboxes. Most of the chaos it will create will be when the engine operates, and you cannot bring it to Lornth, can you?"

"I had thought, if the conflict drags on, to bring the ship around the point of Dellash and to fire that northern port—Rulyarth, I think."

Triendar shivered.

"Forget the fireship for now. As you say, it is not ready. But I will dare the fates. We must take the risk. To allow one small barbarian clan to seize our copper and destroy white lancers unpunished . . . what will stop the Jeranyi from surging west across the Grass Hills? Or those Kyphran traders . . ."

"Your Mightiness . . . Cyador, as you have pointed out, is scarcely powerless."

"Triendar . . . we have few firewagons, and they only operate on the stone roads. We have none of the ancient fireships, and but one under construction to replace them—"

"The ancient ships were destroyed because they were failing." Triendar nodded. "As this one will fail in a few years under the pressure of chaos."

"We will build others."

"And you will build chaos, and the Accursed Forest will use that to grow."

"We will face that when we must. For now, the barbarians must go, before they become a greater threat." The Protector of the Steps to Paradise stopped and surveyed the closed doors to the hall, the wisps of steam that drifted around the fittings. "We have instilled order and obedience into our people, and we cannot turn them into warriors overnight, and if we tried . . ." Lephi shook his head.

"They would strike first at the Mirror classes, you fear?"

"No. But the taxes and tariffs would rise, and then, so would disobedience, and that would make the Mirror Lancers and Foot more arrogant . . ."

Triendar laughed softly. "None would suspect a lord of Cyad to be so considerate and thoughtful of his people."

Lephi snorted. "We have no choice but to use chaos."

"As you wish, Sire. I have told you the risks."

"And I have told you those of not employing it. I have not mentioned the risks to you." Lephi gestured toward the wide window and the open waters of the Western Ocean. "Do you not understand? You worry about what *may* happen in the years ahead. If we do not stop the barbarians *now*, neither of us will need to worry about the future. Already, we have peasants who challenge the white throne. We have eastern traders who would charge our merchants double because they no longer fear Cyad. And now we have barbarians who would seize our copper mines. We have no fireships, no spare firewagons, no fire cannon of generations past. We have lancers and troops . . . and we have the power of chaos that you can muster. And you will muster it against the barbarians. The forest can wait; it must wait."

Triendar bowed. "As you wish."

XCVII

BURETEK, FUERA, AND SIAS sat around the low coals of the fire, a fire ringed with stones used by others, but not in years, if not in centuries, stones so old that the soot was burned deep into their pores and crevices. Sylenia sat slightly apart from the armsmen. Low murmurs drifted southward to where Ayrlyn and Nylan sat on the soft needles between two gnarled roots, their backs propped against the rough bark. Nylan listened for a moment.

". . . peaceful here . . ."

"They need it . . . probably we do, too."

"Spooky, though . . . ride by and never see it . . ."

"The angels, they saw it."

"They see too much, sometimes . . ."

With that, Nylan agreed. He looked to his left. There, on the other side of the root, lay Weryl on his blanket, eyes open, but heavy, half-looking into the dark canopy above that blocked the stars.

"This place is ancient," the smith murmured, his fingers touching the smooth crests of the deep-rutted black bark, his eyes going up toward the tip of the èvergreen—a tree that made even the groves of the Nomads of Sybra seem young by comparison.

"Older than any other trees we've seen," agreed the healer. Her hair, still damp from washing in the clean and clear brook, glittered with a light of its own in the dimness. "And it feels like the dreams."

"So what do we do?"

Ayrlyn took his hand. "Lean back and relax. Just open yourself up to your feelings. I know that's hard for you, but it'll be all right. I know it will."

With a deep breath, Nylan shifted his weight on the soft needles piled around the gnarled roots, in a space that seemed as comfortable as a pilot's seat, or more so. The scents of clean pine, the hint of moisture from the brook, the sweetness of crushed redberry—all created a sense of aliveness he had not felt in who knew how many eight-days.

Smiling, he closed his eyes, following Ayrlyn's example, ignoring the low murmurs from around the fire.

First came a sense of peace, of comfort, yet there was more.

Lines of fire flickered, white lines, force fluxes like a chaotic power net, firebolts white-infused and red-shaded like those thrown by the wizards who had tried to storm Westwind. . . .

. . . and the dark flows of blackness and the white chaos were mixed and twisted—and balanced. The trees grew and grew, and some died and fell, but always for all the changes, the white and darkness turned in and out, but balanced . . . until the heavens shivered, and the ground trembled.

Then, white lines of fire, fire that reflected light and darkness, burned through the forest, and the gray ashes fell like rain.

The rivers heaved themselves out of their banks, and the white mirror fires turned their waters into steam. Metal mountains grumbled across the water-polished stone hills and smoothed them, ground them, and suffocated them beneath strange new soil, and grasses that had never beén.

Green shoots struggled through the ashes, and were turned into more ashes, and the ground heaved and trembled.

Lines of white stone slammed down like walls, pinning the trees behind lines of force that burned . . . and burned, burned somehow because the force of the ordered chaos that prisoned the trees was backward, because chaos bound order. . . .

A sense of eternity followed, inaction behind walls, until the heavens shivered again, and the white walls cracked, and crumbled, and lines of white fire and darkness cascaded from ice-tipped peaks.

And the balanced flow of light and darkness resumed, with a sense of something like purpose and joy—except it was neither.

Nylan sat up abruptly, his hand reaching for Ayrlyn. Yet nothing had changed. The boughs still whispered in the wind; the insects chittered; the brook burbled in the darkness, and the four around the fire still talked in low voices.

"You know what it was?" asked Ayrlyn.

"The images reminded me of an early Rationalist colonizing force," Nylan said. "Bring the native ecology into line." He shook his head. "All that power—"

"The grove—the trees remember. That . . . that is hard to believe." Ayrlyn's voice was hushed. "And do you think this . . . Cyador . . . is what's left of the Rat expedition?"

"I think so, but how would you prove it? Would it matter?" Nylan shrugged. "I don't know. It's an empire, of sorts." He cleared his throat. "I just wonder if this grove is part of what was a larger, sentient forest—or a colonizing outpost . . . or—"

"As you said—does it matter? There's a larger forest to the south, one that's broken its bounds in a way that's connected to our arrival."

"Do you think the Cyadorans know that? Is that why they're expanding into Lornth?" asked Nylan.

"I don't think so. They couldn't know, or feel, what the trees . . . or the forest does. If they did, then, they couldn't have destroyed so much of it."

"The old problem—cultivation is always better." The smith shook his head. "Do you think our forests, places like Guljolm on Sybra—?"

"It could be," said Ayrlyn, "but since we're not likely to ever return—"

"Right." Nylan shifted his weight, turned his head, and looked through the darkness at Weryl.

"Da . . . reee . . ." In the darkness, less than two cubits away, Weryl sat on his blanket, a smile on his face, looking at a pine cone, turning it in his hands. Beyond him, on its hind legs, stood a brown tree rat. The tree rat chittered and was gone.

"He has the night vision," Ayrlyn said.

"Do you think he felt . . . ?"

She shrugged. "Probably, but feeling and knowing what it means are two different things. The sense of balance was stronger than anything, and that couldn't have hurt too much. He seems fine."

Nylan hoped so. His son was too young to be burdened with the meaning of those images. "What can we do?"

"I don't know that, either. Except that we're both getting the same message about balancing order and chaos."

"And no one else is? Why us?"

Ayrlyn moistened her lips, but did not speak for several moments. " 'Why us?' " she finally repeated. "I don't know. Why can we heal? Or have strange-colored hair?" She laughed, softly, ironically. "Maybe the whole twisting of underspace, the bringing of the *Winterlance* to this universe . . . maybe it was because we were needed to return balance—"

"An automatic stabilizing mechanism . . . strong enough to cross universes?"

"Maybe just chance, and now that we're here, this . . . balance . . . seeks us out. Does it matter?"

"I don't like being a player's piece . . . or the universe's." The whole idea bothered Nylan, especially when he saw how much he had changed . . . been changed. Poor Sillek, from everything that he kept learning, had seen and understood. The dead Lord of Lornth had been intelligent, perceptive, skilled, decisive, and a leader—and he'd been swept away by forces of ignorance, sexism, and barbarian tradition. Were he and Ayrlyn in the same position, condemned by some . . . force of balance . . . to try to right things . . . only to be drowned in the usual welter of blind human power lusts?

"That's pretty grim," she said.

"I feel pretty grim." Nylan rubbed his forehead, and found that he didn't have to, that the residual headache he had scarcely been conscious of had vanished. He found himself frowning.

"Order and chaos . . . balance . . ." he murmured.

"There's something there," Ayrlyn pointed out. "I think we need to stay here for a time. A little while, anyway. Just to see."

"Maybe you can sing again?"

"I wouldn't go that far . . . yet." Still, a ghost of a smile crept to the corners of her mouth and eyes.

"Is it safe?" His eyes went back to Weryl.

"Is anywhere safe on this world?" Ayrlyn's response wasn't an answer, but it was the best either of them could do.

XCVIII

NYLAN GLANCED BACK over his shoulder, and his eyes wanted to twist away from the grove in the valley. This time, knowing what he knew, he resisted the impulse, and took a long look at the grove and at the trees.

"It's gone . . ."

"It's still there," said Buretek. "We just can't see it. It's got a magic shield, like the angels said."

Sylenia, riding between and slightly behind the two angels, nodded. In his seat behind the nursemaid's saddle, Weryl waved a hand clutched around a small brown pine cone.

The smith glanced at the redheaded healer, whose preoccupied look indicated her thoughts were far from the dusty road leading southeast to Syskar, the Cyadorans, Fornal, and more battles. He took a deep breath.

After two days in and around the grove, while he and Ayrlyn were certainly more rested, neither had learned much more than they had discovered on the first night. The "dreams" or visions or images repeated themselves, with virtually no variation. The grove held the same balance of order and chaos, yet order—and peacefulness—seemed to predominate.

"That's the key, you know," Ayrlyn said.

"What?"

"Balance."

"It has been anywhere," Nylan half-agreed, "but the problem is that human beings don't accept balance. We may talk about it, but our actions are something else. Human desires for anything—love, power, coins—seem unbounded, and that doesn't fit with the idea of balance." He paused as a pain stab of discomfort flicked through his skull. Where was he deceiving himself? "I'm as bad as anyone," he added. "We needed to survive. We got that. Then we wanted some shelter and comfort. We got that. Then I didn't want to always worry about what Ryba had in mind . . ." He shrugged. "It just goes on and on. Sure . . . putting things in balance would help. But how do we get the Cyadorans to stop trying to take over the rest of Candar? We can't just tell them that they're un-balancing things."

Ayrlyn glanced at the dying scrub tree just off the shoul-der of the road. "I don't know. Not yet. But it's clear that everywhere, and here more than most places, in the end things do balance."

Nylan wondered. Did they? Or was the balance that of equalized power? Or did power triumph? Concentrations of power—like Cyador and Westwind—seemed to endure for a long, long time.

XCIX

IN THE DIMNESS of the hot twilight, with the orange glow at their back, the six—and Weryl—rode over the last hill. In the valley below, to the southeast, glimmered a few points of light—torches on the shed barn and the headquarters dwelling.

Against the purpling of the sky, against the openness and sweep of the dark brown hills, with its few lights the camp in the valley at Syskar appeared small, fragile . . . insignificant. Then again, was anything particularly significant except to human beings who persisted in the search for significance?

Nylan glanced upward, as the still-unfamiliar stars began to appear. How were he and Ayrlyn any different? Wasn't everything they were trying insignificant? What difference did it really make? Wasn't Fornal's belief in honor, even when the black-bearded regent had to know honor was futile, as sig-nificant—and perhaps more understandable—as the angels' efforts to move Lornth toward a less repressive and oppres-sive society? Especially since honor had a clear meaning?

"They're both insignificant," Ayrlyn pointed out quietly. "In the greater scheme of things, anyway. Being human is the struggle to bring meaning into a universe where order and chaos normally create meaningless patterns that resemble a balance."

"Cynical . . ." Nylan laughed.

"Of course."

"Wadah, Enyah? Wadah, pease?" begged Weryl plaintively.

Sylenia twisted in the saddle to give the boy a swallow from the water bottle.

They did not speak, nor did the three armsmen, on the rest of the ride back to Syskar. Even the sentries only nodded as the group rode slowly into the yard, and unsaddled and groomed their mounts.

Lewa stepped perhaps twenty paces from the barracks, surveyed them, and turned back into the dimness.

Nylan didn't like the silence, as ominous as the Cyadoran threat, in a different way, but he shouldered his saddlebags, picked up a sleepy Weryl, and started toward their quarters.

Nylan and Ayrlyn walked up onto the stoop—hotter than the open yard. Nylan carried Weryl, and Sylenia followed, several steps back. The strap hinges Nylan had replaced creaked as he pushed open the door.

Fornal sat on the sole stool before the rickety table—alone. On the table were a mug, a bottle, the candle with the glass mantle, and a scroll. "Welcome back, angels." Fornal glanced down at the half-empty bottle on the rickety table, then at his mug. "You would be pleased to know that my coregents appreciated the copper."

"We are glad to hear that."

"Ser?" murmured Sylenia.

Nylan turned and eased Weryl into the nursemaid's arms. With a quick inclination of her head to Fornal, she slipped around the angels and into their room; saddlebags slapped against the door frame before the door shut with a dull *clunk*.

The angels stepped toward the regent, then dropped onto the bench on the left side of the table.

A low murmuring came from behind the closed door, a lullaby. Nylan smiled faintly, momentarily.

The candle flickered behind its glass mantle with soot thick enough to block much of the dim light cast. The shadows on the blotched walls of the dwelling's main rooms wavered in the heat of the summer night.

Nylan wiped his forehead with the back of his forearm.

"Even I am hot, angel mage," admitted Fornal.

"You know how we feel about the heat." Nylan waited, then asked, "What has happened with the Cyadorans?"

"Nothing. They squat there," Fornal said. "They do not ride forth save in masses, in scores and scores, and their lances and their shields shimmer. Sometimes, they go far enough to raid. We do little. We have killed nearly half their force, and still they have five times the men I do."

"Cyador's bigger than Lornth," Nylan temporized, wondering, fearing, where Fornal's words were leading.

Ayrlyn watched, her eyes on the regent.

"What do you suggest I do? You are the dark mages. It nears summer-end, and we do not have the mines back. They have fired a dozen hamlets, and they will keep doing so. You counsel patience. My armsmen fight among themselves unless Lewa or Huruc or I watch them every moment."

Fornal lifted a scroll and handed it to Ayrlyn. "Read this. Even my patient sire and my practical sister share my worries. Even after the copper, even after we have reduced the forces of the white demons by half, the holders question the levies and the tariffs . . . because they see no results. We have not reclaimed the mines." Fornal snorted. "The holders ask if the angels are advising us to bleed Lornth dry in the Grass Hills . . . so that the dark angels may feast on the corpse of Lornth. Did I not warn you about our holders?"

"You did. Weren't they the ones who caused Sillek's death?" asked Nylan.

"And if they are not satisfied, they will cause ours," suggested the regent.

The redhead unrolled the scroll. As he watched her read, Nylan could see the darkness in her eyes, and the circles beneath them. She finished and handed the scroll to Nylan.

Nylan read the dispatch quickly, his mind catching the seemingly temperate phrases that hinted at more, far more.

> . . . holders have requested that the Regent Fornal seek a speedy return of the mines or another alternative that does not require levies needed for the forthcoming harvest . . .
>
> . . . the Lady Ellindyja and the Lady Erenthla have both reported that a number of young women have fled to the Westhorns . . . and their consorts and holders petition the regency council . . . feel that such problems cannot be ignored because of one set of mines in distant southern Lornth . . .
>
> . . . Suthyan traders, led by Lygon of Bleyans, are increasing the prices of iron stocks. . . .

Nylan rolled the scroll back up and handed it to the regent. Fornal had translated Zeldyan's—the hand was feminine— seemingly temperate phrases accurately enough, if with his own twists.

"So, angels? Has your magely journey revealed some answer that I may provide to my men? Or my coregents? Or the holders of Lornth?" Fornal finished the last of the bottle and stared at Nylan. "I know that you have done much, yet that is not enough. As harvest nears, the clamor for the return of the levies will grow, and so will the numbers of white lancers. The holders will claim that our fight has been worthless and without honor. Can you offer me any hope?"

"Perhaps," said Nylan. Did Fornal really think they could just come up with an easy magical solution? Or was he as frustrated as the two angels? "In the morning, we'll tell you how we'll destroy all the Cyadorans in Lornth."

Fornal rose with a sweeping bow. "I look forward to that. You do not know how I look forward to that." With the precise steps of a man who had drunk too much and knew it, he walked slowly, carefully, to his room, closing the door behind him.

"You were right," Ayrlyn said tiredly.

"I was?"

"About people not being interested in balance, or even their long-term self-interest."

"Fornal can't find an answer, and he knows it. So he's shifting all the responsibility to us."

"Isn't that human nature?" Ayrlyn looked at the candle and the sooty glass mantle. "I won't clean it."

"No one asked you to. I cleaned it the last time."

"Nylan, we aren't keeping score."

"Sorry." He wiped his forehead once more.

"You said we'd have a plan. What do we do? Burn up more Cyadoran mounts, and get everyone even angrier?"

Nylan shook his head. "We have to get something in the grenades that clings and will burn through timbers." He paused. "I don't know. More wax, animal fats? I'm an engineer, not a chemist."

"It would have to burn hotter," said Ayrlyn. "Much hotter."

"More experiments . . . and we'll need something that will act as an oxidizer." Nylan took a deep breath. "Just so the horse-lovers of Candar won't be too offended."

"That's not the only reason, and you know it."

"No," he admitted. "We need to upgrade what we've got distilled and improve it enough to make a larger mess out of the Cyadoran base, and the barracks and the soldiers. That way, it might just be enough to push them out of Lornth."

She winced.

"I know." And he did. They could burn the entire base, and it wouldn't solve the problem.

"For now. It might buy time. They *might* retreat back to Syadtar or wherever in Cyador," the redhead ventured, "but they'll be back with an army that will make what we faced on the Roof of the World look small."

"And they'll gather enough force to burn all of Lornth to a crisp?"

She nodded.

"Well . . . that would stop all the holders from complaining and believing that they can just negotiate some sort of agreement with Cyador and that life will go on and they can still abuse their women and have their limited honorable battles—"

"Nylan . . . in a way, they're right. At least about the honorable battles. So long as they just fought each other, it provided a rough balance . . ."

He saw where she was going, and nodded. "Except that Cyador has its own ideas about social balance, and so does Ryba."

"And Sillek and Zeldyan have been caught in the middle. And so are we," she added.

"Do we really want to make this worse? By blowing up or firing the Cyadoran base?" Nylan blew out the candle. The flickers and the shadows were harder on his eyes than the darkness. He wondered how much dissolving candle wax into the distillate would help . . . and what else was handy that they could add to that demon's mix.

"I'd rather run back to the grove and hide," Ayrlyn confessed. "But that won't work. Not for long."

Not for very long at all.

Whose thought was it? Did it matter?

They turned toward their room, steps slow and deliberate in the dark.

C

TRIENDAR CONCENTRATED ON the glass in the middle of the polished white stone table. As droplets of perspiration popped out on his forehead, the white mists swirled across the glass.

Finally, they wreathed an image, and the wizard swallowed. "This is for younger wizards . . . gets harder these days."

As the traders had said, a black stone tower reared against the mighty western peaks, and the plumes of smoke from the chimneys bore witness to its inhabitants. So did the stone roads that linked an outbuilding with smoke from its square chimney, and a stone bridge. A line of unfinished low walls on the west side of the black tower testified to the growth of the angel holding.

"It is small," said Lephi, almost dismissively.

"Small, yes," Triendar reflected, letting the image fade from the glass. "But it continues to grow. It did not exist three years ago. A year ago, they defeated two armies. And your lancer officers are suffering great losses to the barbarians who could not have touched them a year ago."

"Barbarian armies, of less than a corps of the Mirror Lancers," pointed out the Protector of the Steps to Paradise, Seer of the Rational Stars.

"Exactly," answered the slim, white-haired wizard. "Your lancers, you say, have counted no more than fivescore barbarians—if that. You have lost more than tenscore lancers, and more than that in fine mounts, supply trains, and an entire shipment of copper ingots. What has changed? Have the barbarians changed?"

"How could barbarians change? They never have." Lephi stood and turned toward the open archway that framed the west balcony. The shipworks lay beyond, out of sight.

"Then they should not be able to defeat the Mirror Lancers."

"You and Themphi, with your words and logic."

Triendar lifted his shoulders, then dropped them. "What would you have me say? That Majer Piataphi is handily defeating the Lornians? That the dark angels do not exist? That the Accursed Forest is not threatening to reclaim all of the east of Cyador?"

"Enough. What would you have me do? Throw my hands into the air and cower under the malachite throne and say I can do nothing? Am I to let all Candar pour into Cyad and destroy civilization? No, that will not be!"

Triendar rubbed his smooth-shaven chin.

"Well? You can tell your emperor what not to do. Tell me what actions will best preserve Cyador."

"Over time, Mightiness, nothing will preserve Cyador." Triendar smiled ironically. "For now . . . I would let the Accursed Forest grow as it will, and bring your might against the barbarians and their angel allies. From the days of the Rational Stars have the angels foreshadowed turmoil and trouble. Even the Accursed Forest can grow but a few kays a year, while a barbarian army can take far more than that."

"That is what I said. You rejected my words."

"That was as a mage. You asked what I would do were I you."

"Cyad will return to glory. It will. Have all your mages gather in Syadtar, and I will order all the lancers and the foot and all manner of weapons and supplies to be gathered there, and the barbarians will feel the might of Cyador."

CI

NYLAN SAT ON the end of the bench in the shade, finishing the last of the hard bread and cheese. Then he swallowed the last drops of water in his mug and looked toward the well. His forehead was already oozing sweat, although the sun had barely cleared the eastern hills.

He glanced at the smithy area, and at the rough shed farther away from both barracks and smithy, where were racked all too many of the makeshift grenades—with the emulsified mixture that seemed all too close to jellied naphtha—at least in effect. He frowned.

"You wince every time you look there," Ayrlyn said quietly.

"So do you. Our success . . . another triumph in bringing total warfare to Candor." He turned his eyes from the shed and its ceramic grenades to the well, where Sylenia and Weryl drew water. Beyond the two was the corral, with what appeared to be additional mounts milling in the group.

"Our choices are limited," she pointed out.

"Looks like Fornal got some reinforcements." His fingers

touched the hilt of the blade at his waist, not that he really wanted to use it if Fornal got nasty. But Fornal had been on edge ever since they had returned, ever since the scroll from Lornth, watching as Nylan and Ayrlyn had struggled with mixtures and compounds. That wouldn't have bothered Nylan, except that when Fornal was uneasy, he seemed to want to rely on personal combat to settle everything. Then, was Nylan overreacting?

Probably, but you've been feeling the need for the blade lately. Why?

"Not that many reinforcements." Sitting beside him on the bench, Ayrlyn sipped the bitter root tea that Nylan had given up on a good season earlier.

"And the holders are putting pressure on the regents for some sort of results. Win, lose, or surrender, but get our levies out and back in time for the harvest."

She glanced toward the half-ajar door into the main room of the quarters, then added in a lower voice, "That's why he's more receptive to our doing more of the dirty work."

The door opened, and the black-bearded regent stepped out onto the stoop and into the full sunlight. "Ah . . ."

Nylan watched impassively. How anyone needed that extra warmth when it was already sweltering . . . Except that it wasn't that hot for the Lornians.

"You have been saying you would tell me how you will destroy all the Cyadorans in Lornth." Fornal smiled pleasantly as he turned to the two angels.

"That means killing or removing them." Ayrlyn's voice was matter-of-fact, and she continued to cup the chipped brown earthenware mug in her hands. "You've seen us working on that."

Nylan sat up straighter on the bench and waited.

"You have not found that a problem before," the black-bearded regent said.

"You have had some . . . reservations," Nylan pointed out.

"I had hoped to make their defeat, and our victory, honorable." The younger man shrugged. "Now I am left in a difficult situation. I still have not the forces to defeat the white demons in a massed battle by means the holders would find honorable, nor the time to defeat them in a series of smaller engagements, even if they would oblige me." His face hardened. "I am no fool, angels, much as some may claim that I overvalue honor. Any loss the holders will find dishonorable, and any delay in returning their levies distasteful." Fornal offered a bitter smile.

"Even if we destroy all the Cyadoran forces at the mines, this war is not over," Nylan said slowly.

"No," admitted Fornal. "I know that if you defeat or destroy this force, all of Cyador will march into Lornth. If you do not, the lord of the white demons will reinforce those who remain, and march them northward, most dishonorably laying waste to all that oppose him."

"Do you want us to try to destroy the white forces at the mines?" asked Ayrlyn.

Fornal laughed, not quite harshly. "Have I any choice, angels? I do not find your way of warfare the most honorable, and I fear what you bring to Candar. Yet to reject your skills will mean the White Lord will dishonor Lornth." He shook his head. "Do what you must." The smile that followed encompassed only his eyes as he stepped off the stoop, pausing before he inclined his head. "I trust your own squads will suffice for whatever you plan?"

"One way or another," Nylan said.

"Good."

The stoop was silent for a moment, except for the crunch of the regent's boots on the sandy and dusty path leading to the corral. Fornal stepped around the nursemaid and Weryl without looking at either or back in the direction of the two angels.

Had Fornal been talking to his sire or sister? Nylan pursed his lips and turned to Ayrlyn. "That was pretty straightforward."

"Nothing of honor has been left to me; so you might as well do your worst to the Cyadorans?" Ayrlyn took another sip of the bitter tea. "He's a man in a difficult situation."

"He wants to be straightforward and honorable in battle,

but he knows that, first, it won't work, and second, what we do will change his entire world. But if we don't, he won't have a world."

"If we do, and we succeed, Nylan," added Ayrlyn softly, "he won't either."

"That still leaves us on the point," Nylan said, "not quite sacrificial goats, since we volunteered." He stood and surveyed the yard, watching as Weryl trudged behind Sylenia, his small sandaled feet raising puffs of yellow dust.

"After the time in the grove, do you think it's wrong?" asked the redhead. "It could be futile."

"It could be, but what are the alternatives? After what Ryba and we have done, we wouldn't last a moment anywhere else. We have to see this through, and I have the feeling that things will just keep getting harder." He forced a smile. "Why do I think that?"

"Because they always do."

He took a deep breath. "Time to check the makeshift distillery, and the makeshift forge, and the makeshift grenade fabrication facilities, and the makeshift whatever's next to be makeshifted . . ." Then he looked down at the blade. He really didn't need that—or did he?

"No! Leave me alone!"

Not two dozen cubits from where Nylan stood, a squat armsman had accosted Sylenia, grasping her free arm. He laughed, once, twice.

The nursemaid threw the bucket—water and all—at the armsman. Even before the bucket slammed into the man's face, Sylenia had scooped up Weryl and begun to run toward the dwelling.

Nylan jumped off the stoop and headed toward the armsman.

From the area by the shed barracks, another figure sprinted toward Sylenia, drawing a blade as he ran. A handful of levies turned, as if in slow motion.

With water and blood streaming across his tunic, Tregvo—it had to be Tregvo—pulled out his crowbar blade and lumbered after Sylenia—and Weryl.

Weryl! Almost without thinking, Nylan yanked his short-sword from the scabbard. As Sylenia darted toward him, he stepped to one side and threw the blade, automatically smoothing the flows around the dark iron.

The heavy blade slammed through Tregvo's chest and drove him over backwards, to the clay, pinning him there. The squat armsman's mouth opened, closed, then opened, and hung there, under sightless eyes.

". . . glare of the demons . . ."

". . . see why you don't threaten an angel . . ."

". . . glad he's on our side . . ."

Sylenia stood shivering on the stoop, shuddering despite the early morning heat. ". . . told me awful things . . . what he . . . would . . ."

"Enyah . . ." Weryl said plaintively. "Enyah."

Ayrlyn touched the black-haired woman's shoulder. "It's all right. It's over."

But it wasn't, Nylan knew as he walked toward the dead man, absently noting that puffs of dust rose with each step he took.

Tonsar reached the corpse first and tugged at the blade. Neither corpse nor blade moved. He yanked again, then pulled aside Tregvo's shirt. Metal glinted. The subofficer's mouth was the next one to open.

Nylan stopped beside the burly Tonsar, trying to conceal the headache that throbbed through his skull. The last thing he needed was to have to kill in camp. He bent and retrieved the blade, wiping it on the dead man's tunic, then sheathed it, squinting against both the glare of the low sun and his headache.

"I am glad you were near, ser angel," Tonsar said. "Though I would have liked to have struck him down."

"I wish you could have," Nylan said, meaning every word. His head kept throbbing, and his eyes watered from the pain behind them. For the hundredth time or so he wondered why. What was it? Why did it strike him and Ayrlyn? Did the sensitivity go with the ability to use the planet's order fields?

And why had he even been carrying a blade? He never did around the camp.

Had it been subconscious aggression against Fornal? Would Tregvo be dead if Nylan hadn't reacted to Fornal's baiting of the night before?

"I would have used mine on him, sooner or later," Ayrlyn said quietly, beside his shoulder, having arrived so silently he had not even noticed. "But I wonder about the mail vest."

So did Nylan. Another of Fornal's intrigues, designed to show the capriciousness of the angels, and how they interfered with the rights of "real" men? Or just coincidence? Or just an indication of the cultural conflict that he and Ayrlyn were generating, just by example?

Somehow, Nylan doubted that he'd ever find a clear answer. Nothing was ever clear. Of that he was certain, quite certain.

"Iyltar, Borsa—strip and bury this vermin," Tonsar ordered, sheathing his blade, his eyes turning to the quarters' stoop, where Sylenia sat on the bench, still holding Weryl, as though the child were a talisman.

CII

IN THE DARKNESS past midnight, the air was almost cool enough to be comfortable as Nylan stood and stretched, and stretched again.

"Ready?" asked Ayrlyn.

"Ready as I'm likely to ever be for this sort of thing." He turned and embraced the redhead, and they held each other for a long moment in the silence broken only by the faint chirping of some insect.

"Well . . ." she finally said.

Nylan let go. As she headed toward Borsa's inert form, he turned and walked over to the sleeping Tonsar, curled on his right side. "Time to rise and shine." The angel tapped the other's boot with his own, not quite certain how the burly armsman would react.

"What . . . ? . . . dark . . ." mumbled Tonsar.

"That's the idea, remember?" Nylan forced cheerfulness into his voice.

"Now?" Borsa asked. "It's still dark."

"Now," insisted Ayrlyn, moving toward Vula.

Slowly, the squad awakened, and began to check mounts and arms.

"No one will expect an attack at this demon-awful hour," grumbled Tonsar, adjusting his saddle, his fingers fumbling slightly in the darkness. "Truly, they are the dark angels. We stumble and trip, and they move as if it were daylight."

Nylan's night vision wasn't that good—the depth of night was more like twilight to him—but it probably seemed that way to the struggling armsmen.

The breeze was strong, almost a real wind, reflected Nylan, and he could understand why some animals in the Grass Hills might well prefer the night to the day. He would, if he weren't hardwired to be such a day person.

After checking his mare, he turned to Ayrlyn, who had stretched out on the ground again, presumably sending her perceptions out on the wind once more to check the Cyadoran camp. Nylan waited, while the rest of the squad packed bedrolls and formed up behind Tonsar.

"Anything?" he asked when Ayrlyn finally shifted her weight, indicating her perceptions had returned to her body.

"Nothing. I think half the sentries must be asleep."

Nylan could sense the sadness behind her words, and he half-nodded. He was beginning to understand Fornal's feelings. What they were doing was nothing short of despicable— but it was necessary to stop people who were despicable all the time, rather than just in war. The problem with honor was that history had demonstrated all too clearly on all too many planets that it wasn't terribly effective against an enemy unless you had superior forces, and that was what they didn't have. All they had was a better catapult that could heft larger incendiary grenades with a much nastier and longer-and-hotter-burning fluid and an even larger supply of the ceramic grenades. All in all, he hoped—mostly—that their "improvements" would penetrate the thick-walled barracks. He had no doubts about the deadlier impact on exposed men and horses.

Ayrlyn had insisted the changes would be enough to devastate the Cyadoran barracks. Nylan swallowed and forced himself to recall all the bloated bodies of innocent peasants in all the hamlets.

"There isn't much choice," Ayrlyn responded to his unspoken feelings. "We both know that Cyador is going to try to take over Lornth. They've got another army on the way, or they will. We have to reduce the odds while we can." She snorted. "Now, I'm the one who sounds like Ryba. Creating better weapons and promptly using them."

"The difference is that she liked it," Nylan said. His head twinged ever so slightly. Darkness! He couldn't even deceive himself about Ryba.

"I don't like her for a lot of reasons, but she doesn't enjoy killing either. She likes flaunting power, but not killing." Ayrlyn paused. "She uses people, and you've got reason to be bitter, but don't make her worse than she is." A soft laugh followed. "What she is . . . that's bad enough."

"Just as I thought you were getting soft on her."

"Not soft. Isn't it harder for you to distort things, even to yourself?"

He nodded, knowing she had felt his discomfort and his assent.

"Unless I've missed something, we're clear." She half-turned and motioned, adding, "Let's go."

The two mounted, the last to do so.

With the muffled impact of slow hoofs on grass and dirt, the squad eased their mounts and the pack animals through the lower swale between the two hills and out onto the flat below the mining camp walls, moving quietly and steadily toward the northwest corner. A single torch flickered from the northeast watchtower, but its light barely illuminated the walls within three cubits.

Ayrlyn swayed in the saddle, trying to split her senses, to judge where the best position for the catapult would be. Nylan tried to follow her perceptions with his, but, as had happened the last time, he was more aware of the strange wrongness of the ground beneath, far more aware, as though great violence had been done to the land, and then that violence had been sealed beneath the drying grass and soil. He tried not to shudder, even as the faint images of the grove and the distant forest slipped into his thoughts with the contrast between the balanced forces of the forest, always changing, but always balanced, and the great frozen imbalance beneath him, indeed beneath much of the southern part of the Grass Hills.

"This is fine. No sentries awake here." Ayrlyn reined up.

Nylan jerked slightly in his own saddle at the redhead's words, then eased back on the mare's reins and raised his hand to Tonsar.

"It's fine." Her voice was low. "Are you all right?"

"I'm fine. Just momentarily . . . disoriented." He shook himself. "We'd better get moving." He turned in the saddle. "We'll set up here," he whispered.

"I suggested that." There was a faint hint of gentle laughter in Ayrlyn's voice.

The smith followed her lead and dismounted.

Sias took the reins of Nylan's and Ayrlyn's mounts, leading them slowly back from the space where the redhead, Borsa, and Vula quickly assembled the catapult.

Nylan took a slow breath, aware that the insect chirps had died away with their presence. Would anyone in the camp notice? The night-shrouded walls remained silent; the only sounds those of the Lornians breathing, an occasional *whuff* from the mounts, those held, and those of the squad waiting, in readiness, if necessary, to defend the catapult team long enough for them to mount. He began to set out the thin clay-walled canisters on the flat beside the catapult, even before the other three had finished assembling the device.

Then he began slipping the fuses into the canisters, but had only reached the fourth canister when Ayrlyn straightened up.

"Let's wind up the catapult," she said.

A series of faint creaks followed her order as Borsa began to turn the wheel.

"Ser, ser."

Ayrlyn nodded in the darkness, but Nylan saw the gesture well enough, and eased the first fused canister tube into the catapult cradle. He took the striker. "You ready?"

"Yes, ser."

Whhsst-click. Whhsst-click. The fuse caught on the second attempt, and Nylan checked to make sure the flame was solid.

Ayrlyn adjusted the frame angle, then tripped the catch.

Thunk! The catapult's release sounded like thunder to Nylan in the stillness of the night, and the handful of scattered sparks that followed the canister seemed like warning flares.

The blackness that welled from Ayrlyn told the engineer that she was guiding, adjusting . . . something.

"It hit," she said flatly, even though Nylan could see nothing beyond the walls above and to the south of them.

"It's set," reminded Borsa.

Nylan belatedly slipped another fused canister into the cradle and squeezed the striker. Once was enough to light the fuse.

Snick! Ayrlyn released the catch, and another fire grenade arced into the darkness above the walls.

The engineer had the next canister ready when Vula—he and Borsa were taking turns—rewound the catapult. Ayrlyn readjusted the frame, and he squeezed the striker.

Thunk!

Borsa rewound the wheel even before the throwing arm stopped vibrating, and Nylan slipped another grenade into the cradle, trying to speed up the process, trying to ignore the headache that was so far just a twinge—but one that, were they successful, would be painful.

Thunk!

Another three grenades flew into the darkness before flickers of light—tongues of flames—darted above the walls, followed by calls of "Fire! Fire!"

Thunk!

With the growing light from the mining camp came the horn calls, haunting, demanding.

Thunk!

The four kept launching fire grenades into the dark sky, and still the walls remained black, except for the northeast watchtower.

Thunk!

Nylan sniffed. Smoke had begun to flow downhill from the Cyadoran walls. In spite of the growing pressure in his skull, he readied another canister and fuse. Beside him, Ayrlyn stumbled, and, after he placed the canister in the cradle, he slipped his arm around her. "Easy."

"So . . . hard," she murmured. "Already . . . some dying."

"I know." He put another grenade in the cradle and lit the fuse.

Thunk!

Along with the smoke came the white mist of death, and the small sharp knives that dug at their skulls. Then came a cooler wind from behind them, not quite enough to balance the heat that had begun to radiate from the mining camp— heat from their makeshift jellied demon fluids.

More intermittent trumpet blasts echoed into the night, as did the screams of horses, and the ever-louder crackling of burning timbers.

The smith dropped another canister into the catapult cradle, forcing back the bile in his throat, as he knew Ayrlyn did nearly simultaneously, bile created by the chaos of death and the rising odor of charred meat.

Ayrlyn's fingers trembled, but she flipped the catch on the catapult.

Thunk!

Vula bent over, double, while Borsa rewound the catapult.

"Best we leave," hissed Tonsar, touching Nylan's shoulder. "Someone's yelling to form up in there."

The smith nodded and dumped another canister and fuse in place, then squeezed the striker again.

Thunk!

How many grenades left? Surely, there couldn't be that many? Nylan half-sensed, half-groped along the lines he had laid out until he came up with another.

"Ser, we should mount up," Tonsar insisted.

Additional watch lanterns flared up, but not along the wall, and the four kept aiming, loading, and firing the clay fire-grenades over the wall a hundred cubits away.

Thunk!

Yellow-blue flames and greasy black smoke twisted into the night sky.

Thunk!

Thunk!

Nylan looked stupidly down. There weren't any more grenades.

"Need to get packed up." He wiped his forehead, damp from fear, tension, and the wall of flames they had created.

"That is what I have been saying, ser angel," said Tonsar. "I hear mounts and angry lancers."

Half-blind, using perceptions more than a night vision that strobed and burned, he tried to fold and fumble the empty quilted canister carrier back into a roll on the pack mare.

"I can do that, ser," offered Vula.

"Thanks." Was his unsteadiness so obvious even in the darkness? He tottered toward his own mare, stumbling.

No . . . so much death . . . so much heat and fire . . .

He struggled to turn toward Ayrlyn.

"Oooo . . ." With that soft sound, the redhead's knees buckled, and she crumpled to the ground.

Nylan, and Tonsar, lifted her onto Nylan's mare. The engineer hoped they didn't have to ride too far, but he led the redhead's mount toward the hills.

Behind him, Vula and Borsa hurriedly threw the catapult sections into their packs and scrambled after the squad.

"Let's go!" ordered Nylan, his voice raspy and unsteady.

"We go," echoed Tonsar.

As they trotted through the swale and the light of the burning camp vanished behind the hill, Nylan concentrated solely on holding on to Ayrlyn and staying in the saddle.

Anything more would have been too much.

CIII

THE LIGHT BREEZE from the north carried the faint odors of charcoal, smoke, dust, and burned meat to the two officers at the head of the column headed southward through the Grass Hills.

The two glanced back over the short line of riders straggling southward. The once-white uniforms were smudged with charcoal, some with blood. Nearly twoscore walking wounded limped before the three wagons that brought up the rear.

"His Mightiness will not be pleased," said Azarphi. A long fresh burn covered his left cheek, and his eyebrows had been burned to stubble. Like the others, he wore a uniform that appeared gray, spotted liberally with dark splotches of charcoal, dirt, and dark red-maroon streaks.

"No," answered the majer, his voice flat, as he glanced at the dusty road that led to Syadtar. "No doubt, I will face the Archers of the Rational Stars." He shrugged, and started to blot his forehead, then stopped as the back of his hand touched the burn at his temple. "There is no point in remaining. We do not receive supplies, and the locals have removed almost everything we could forage for. They will not stand and fight. We cannot tell how or when the barbarians will strike. The men cannot sleep for fear of being burned where they lie. Their new fireballs are far worse than the last. They burn through earthen walls and seek out the roof timbers, and the flame clings to everything."

"It is not the barbarians."

"It does not matter. We have no corrals left, and no wood to build more. If we stay, what is to prevent them from killing more mounts? Then we would have no way at all to leave. The Grass Hills are too dry, and Syadtar is too far, for lancers on foot, and we have but a handful of wagons left." Piataphi glanced back toward the trails of smoke that twisted into the morning sky.

"His Mightiness will send all the lancers, and the white mages to burn them to cinders. He must. For the sake of Cyad."

"He may. The thought does not particularly console me at the moment." Piataphi turned his eyes to the long dusty road southward, ignoring the smoke that still circled into the western sky behind them.

CIV

NYLAN ROLLED UP the bedroll in quick motions. Next came the few clothes that went into the saddlebags. He paused to wipe his forehead—the room that had been too small for the four of them was hot, but it had always been too hot. He lifted the shoulder harness from the pallet bed and strapped it on, though he increasingly hoped he did not have to use the heavy blade.

"Fornal's out scouting."

"Of course," snapped the smith. "He doesn't believe that the Cyadorans could have left."

"Would you?" asked Ayrlyn, tying up her own bedroll.

"They'll be back, and we'd better have found something with this enchanted forest, or—"

"Or what? We'll be fugitives again, which is better than staying here and being killed because we'll be too blind to lift a blade after either one of us kills one more Cyadoran. We just can't stay here and hope."

"So we're looking for a way out of this mess, another way to develop and use power. Through an enchanted forest?" The silver-haired smith shook his head. "Why does it always come back to power?"

"It always does," she answered. "Ryba was right."

No matter how often he was reminded by events, the idea

that the Marshal of Westwind was right about the use of power still bothered the smith.

. . . bothers me, too . . .

Nylan reached out and touched her cheek. "I love you."

"You don't say that often. Why now?" Her sunburned nose crinkled.

Because . . . just because . . . and because you understand . . . The engineer cleared his throat and looked down at the plank floor for a moment. "We'll have to sneak through the western part of Cyador, if the maps are right."

"Changing the subject, again."

Nylan grinned sheepishly.

"It's all right. I know it's hard for you." *And you're trying.*

"In more ways than one," he admitted.

After a long moment, Ayrlyn offered a gentle laugh. "Back to hard reality in southern Lornth. I can scout out things, enough to avoid any large Cyadoran patrols. It may be slow, but I can't imagine the Cyadorans being concerned about three riders and a child, especially if we avoid the main roads." Ayrlyn lifted her saddlebags and surveyed the room. "I don't see anything we've left."

"We've never had that much. Weryl has more than both of us," he pointed out, hoisting his own gear, and the larger bags that carried Weryl's things. "Do you think I'm right to bring him?"

"Who else would defend him? Tonsar would, but you can't count on his always being here. Besides, you'd worry so much you couldn't even think about why we're going."

"There is that." *And your promise to Istril to take care of him, and that didn't mean for someone else to.* After a quick look around the room, Nylan stepped out into the empty main room, almost as hot as their quarters, then crossed the dusty plank floors to the half-open front door where he stopped for a moment and watched.

Sylenia sat on the bench on the shaded side of the stoop, holding Weryl. "We will take a long, long ride, Weryl, longer than the ride here . . ."

". . . wide orsee, Enyah?"

"You have your seat . . ."

The smith stepped onto the stoop, with Ayrlyn squeezing out after him.

The nursemaid looked up. "We be ready. I have changed him, and given him a biscuit."

"You don't have to come, Sylenia. This could be a long ride." Nylan laughed gently and added, "As you told Weryl."

The black-haired woman glanced toward the near-empty barracks, then toward the still-blood-darkened dust beside the path to the well. "Better I go. Tonsar must not worry about my safety."

"Are you certain?" asked Nylan.

Sylenia nodded, shifting the squirming Weryl from one knee to the other. "I will be safer with you."

Nylan wasn't so sure about that. Safer crossing the Grass Hills and trying to sneak through some part of Cyador to something resembling an enchanted forest or the local equivalent? Based on a disruption in planetary order fields that only he and Ayrlyn and a handful of other interplanetary refugees or local mages could sense?

"Da?" pleaded Weryl.

Nylan bent over and kissed him on the cheek. "Hang on. We have to get the mounts and load them."

As he and Ayrlyn walked toward the corral, Nylan spoke softly. "She worries about him worrying about her. Does he worry about her worrying about him?"

"In this case . . . yes. Our boastful subofficer has a softer side."

"Unlike Fornal."

"He hasn't found the right woman."

"It takes that?"

"It helps to find the right woman. Or man," she added with a grin.

Nylan shook his head. "Fornal never will."

"You may be right."

After carting their saddles out to the corral, Nylan cornered the mounts, one by one, while Ayrlyn saddled them, almost as fast as Nylan could lead them to the shaded roof at the side of the corral.

As they finished strapping gear onto the pack mare, Tonsar crossed the dusty ground from the barracks area, his boots raising puffs of dust. "You are leaving?"

"For a time," temporized Ayrlyn.

"Tonsar . . . we need to take another magely journey," Nylan began. "I hope we'll be back before too long." He held up his hand. "You can lead the squads, if you have to. You know enough, and they'll trust you."

"It is not the same . . ." protested the burly armsman.

"It should be now." Ayrlyn's eyes fixed the brown-bearded and burly Tonsar.

"Remember," Nylan added, "there's no great honor in being killed if you have another choice that doesn't hurt others."

"Someday, mage . . . I will understand." Tonsar shrugged.

"We'll be back if we can make it." He paused. "It may not seem that way, but we wouldn't be much good in a battle the way we are now. We have to see what we can do about that, and there won't be any white demons around for a while. You can tell Fornal that. We left a note, too."

"I saw." Tonsar glanced back toward the barracks. "I saw again with Tregvo. You feel each death as though your blades struck you. Yet you would strike if it must be." He frowned. "To have the strength to suffer death and strike again . . . angels are terrible." A broad smile followed the frown. "Yet you love, and . . . you are good to Sylenia."

"We try."

"You will take Sylenia." Tonsar was not asking a question.

"She has asked to come, although she cares for you." Nylan frowned. "I don't know that it is fair, but that is her choice. She worries that worrying about her will distract you."

"She must go. You will protect her." Again, the armsman glanced toward the shed barracks, as if he feared one of the levies might hear his words.

"We will protect her as best we can," Ayrlyn affirmed.

A lanky figure stepped from the forge that had been a chicken coop, then dashed toward the group, stopping a pace back of Tonsar, waiting.

Tonsar turned, almost in surprise.

"You've got it, Sias. You are now armorer and general repairman." Nylan inclined his head toward the former apprentice. "And you fix anything that Tonsar needs fixed. Or ser Fornal," he added as an afterthought.

The lanky blond stepped forward. "You will be back, and I will show you."

"Good."

Sias flashed a shy smile. "I could be a smith. In a small hamlet, anyway. Except for the tools."

"Until we don't return, the tools are yours. I brought everything except the anvil—so . . . no matter what happens, you can keep the smaller hammer and the second tongs—they're yours. You earned them."

A broad smile crossed the young armsman/smith's face.

"Be careful with your blade. You want to live to start that smithy," Nylan advised.

Sias looked down sheepishly and scuffed a battered boot in the yellow dust.

"Best you go." Tonsar's eyes flicked toward the eastern hills.

After a moment of silence, Nylan nodded, then turned and walked his mount and the pack mare toward the stoop where Sylenia waited. Ayrlyn led her mount and Sylenia's after the pair Nylan guided.

The nursemaid walked forward and handed Weryl to Nylan. The smith eased his silver-haired son into the seat behind Sylenia's saddle, while she lugged her bags—and the two bags of hard biscuits and cheese and other assorted provisions Nylan had commandeered—toward the pack mare.

"Orse. Orse." Weryl jabbed his hand toward his father.

"Definitely a horse." Nylan fastened the straps in place, then stepped back and pulled the floppy hat from his belt. No sense in getting further blistered by the sun that remained far too hot for too much of the year.

"Ready?"

"I've been ready," answered Ayrlyn.

"I know. I've been talking too much." He swung up into

the saddle. After a last gesture like a salute to Tonsar and Sias, he turned the mare toward the lane and the road southward.

Tonsar raised his bare blade in return, holding it up for a time. Sias just stood silently by the subofficer as the four horses carried their riders out of the encampment and toward the brown slopes of the hills to the south.

"Wadah pease, Enyah?" asked Weryl.

"In a moment . . . a moment," choked the woman.

Nylan glanced back at the valley, more yellowed and dusty than ever under the pitiless sun and the green-blue sky, then toward the long and dusty road ahead.

CV

THEMPHI CHECKED THE saddlebags again, then mounted. The lancer officers behind followed his example. Belatedly, so did Fissar.

The white mage glanced back at the small house that had been his quarters for more than a season, frowning momentarily as he saw the green wall to the north.

"I don't understand, ser," said Fissar, easing his mount up beside Themphi's. "His Mightiness sent us here to hold back the forest, and now that you've pushed it back here on the south, we're supposed to leave it and go to Syadtar? And let it take over everything we've won back?"

"Yes," answered Themphi.

"One questions the lord of Cyad at great risk," offered Majer Jyncka, from where he rode on Themphi's left. "I know."

"You are pleased to leave?" asked Themphi, turning to Jyncka.

"It is a chance to redeem myself in battle."

"Battle?" asked Fissar. "The dispatch . . . it did not mention a battle," he finished lamely.

"I see you have mastered some of my lessons. The ones

about screeing what you could not see." Themphi laughed. "Would you were so assiduous with all of them."

Fissar kept his eyes on his mount's mane.

"Young magelet," offered the majer after they had covered another kay westward and toward the Grand Canal, "one must read not only what is written, but what is meant. Sometimes, the most important words are those which are not committed to parchment."

Fissar nodded solemnly, waiting, not glancing toward the white mage.

"Syadtar is the northernmost city in Cyador. If something is pressing enough that His Mightiness must recall your master and a disgraced lancer officer from battling the Accursed Forest, then either a great campaign is planned against the northern barbarians or they threaten us. Either way means a battle—or many battles."

"The news is not the best," added Themphi, "not for Cyador."

Fissar turned toward his master.

"For its size, Cyador has not that many lancers and foot soldiers and mages. Triendar knows that the Accursed Forest will swell in our absence, yet has chosen to summon us."

"No, that is not good news," Jyncka agreed. "Yet Cyador has always prevailed. How could it be otherwise?"

Themphi frowned, but said nothing as they rode westward.

CVI

AFTER ADJUSTING THE floppy hat and drying his forehead, Nylan stood in the stirrups to try to stretch his legs and thighs, and to unkink his knees. When he reseated himself, he glanced out across the rolling hills of sun-browned grass, hills that seemed to extend forever southward. "Two days and the hills still seem endless."

"Another day and they'll get flatter, more like steppes or high grasslands," predicted Ayrlyn. "Just think what it would be like on foot."

Nylan winced. His lips and mouth seemed dry all the time, and the water in their bottles was nearly gone. "We don't have that much water left."

After the first day, they had turned off the main road and followed a trail that led more to the southeast, back toward the still-distant Westhorns. Nylan thought he recalled that the mountains extended farther westward in the southern half of Candar, but that could have been wishful thinking. Then, anymore, what wasn't wishful thinking?

A thin stream from an underground spring that dried up as it flowed south had been the only water they had found. He licked his dry lips with a tongue almost as dry.

"If we keep on this trail, I think there's a small lake ahead."

"And probably a town, with a garrison of white lancers or the local equivalent."

"I didn't sense that. There might be some holdings."

"How far?"

"A good half day, maybe longer."

"We'll need water before that."

"We do need water," said Sylenia. "You are mages."

"Waada . . ." added Weryl from his seat behind the nursemaid's saddle.

"I'm not a mage," protested Nylan. Even as he spoke the words, his head throbbed. Was his internal lie detector insisting he was? "Anyway, just being a mage doesn't mean we can find water."

The sun continued to beat on their backs as they rode to the southeast, along the trail where the dust had gradually shifted from the yellow of Syskar to a grayed brown, mixed with sand.

Still, underneath the browned grass, Nylan could sense the boulders and stones that were too close to the surface, separated from the sun and light by that same thin line of chaotic order.

"It's still the same," Ayrlyn said. "They must have . . . I don't know what."

Neither did Nylan, but it felt wrong. He tried to lick his lips, but his tongue was dry, and there was no water left in the bottles on the mare. Had he drunk his too quickly?

By mid-afternoon they had crossed two or three more lines of hills and found no sign of streams, ponds, or springs—or of settlers, just more lines of hills covered with sun-browned grass.

They reined up at another hill crest, perhaps two more lines of hills later.

"There's something down there." Ayrlyn pointed almost due south, where a slightly higher hill cast a shadow over a flat, barely shining surface.

"I thought there weren't any lakes this close. That's not your lake, is it?"

"It doesn't feel like a lake," admitted the redhead.

"It be a lake," said Sylenia. "It needs be a lake."

With that Nylan could definitely agree.

As their mounts carried them downhill and closer, he could see that the flat surface was a small lake or a large pond, but it looked almost bright green, even in the late afternoon shadow. Even the shores of the lake were sere, without vegetation. There were no signs of houses.

Nylan continued to study the ground around the lake, finally noting several circular arrangements of stone in bare spots between the irregular clumps of brown grass on the higher ground to the south and east of the dried lake bed. "Someone's had a campsite here—not recently."

The mare's hoofs crackled as she left the sparse grassy flat around the lake bed and carried Nylan down the gentle barren slope toward the edge of the water. There, he dismounted slowly, and swallowed.

He bent and scooped up a handful of the water, smelling it, then licking his fingers. He winced. The water was saltier than merely brackish, and the white splotches that laced the barren ground were salt crystals.

"A salt lake?" asked Ayrlyn.

He nodded. "Maybe . . . maybe I can order-sort enough to keep us going."

Whuffff . . . The mare edged toward the water.

Nylan didn't know if she would attempt drinking it or not; so he handed the reins to Ayrlyn before he walked to the pack mare to unstrap the small bucket.

He half-filled the bucket with the salty water, and set it on the shore, trying to summon the dark order fields. His forehead began to perspire, though he couldn't imagine that he had enough water within for sweat, and his vision to blur.

The water in the bucket swirled, and white heaps appeared beside it. The smith took a deep breath, looked at the half bucket of water, then dipped his finger into it and licked. "It tastes all right to me."

"Waadah?" pleaded Weryl.

Nylan carefully poured some of the water into the bottle Sylenia proffered and handed it back to her.

Weryl slurped, but didn't seem to spill any.

In turn, the silver-haired angel refilled two more bottles, one for Ayrlyn and one for Sylenia, and drank the small amount in the bottom of the bucket.

The second bucketful was easier, and Nylan refilled the rest of the water bottles.

"What about our mounts?" asked Sylenia.

The smith turned and looked at the horses. With open mouths, all panted in the sun. Nylan wasn't totally certain, but he had the feeling that they wouldn't be panting unless they were in poor condition.

Nylan groaned under his breath. He hated to think about the effort involved in using order fields to get enough water for the mounts—yet if he didn't . . .

In fact, even if he did . . . He sent his perceptions out to his mare, then shook his head.

"What be the matter?" asked Sylenia.

"We'll be camping here tonight—one way or another."

"The mounts?" asked Ayrlyn.

He nodded.

Sylenia slipped out of her saddle, but left Weryl in his seat as Nylan refilled the bucket with brackish water for a third time, and began to marshal the order fields once more.

They really didn't have anything else to use but the bucket. So Nylan held it for the mare. Some water splattered over his forearms, but not too much. The smith took away the bucket after the mare had finished half a bucket and offered it to Ayrlyn's chestnut. His eyes blurred.

"I can do the next batch," Ayrlyn offered. "I'd better do it. You look like dead flame."

Nylan handed her the bucket. His legs were shaking so much that he had to sit down, right on the salt-crusted lake bed.

"You must eat." Sylenia pressed a biscuit upon Nylan, that and one of the water bottles he had filled.

He sat on the dry lake bed in the growing shadow of the hill to the northwest, and ate, slowly. On the grassy area by one of the old campfires, Ayrlyn had set up a tieline and tethered the horses.

After the shakiness passed, the smith stood and walked slowly up to join her. They both sat down, along with Sylenia, and Weryl, and ate.

Abruptly, Weryl stood and tottered toward a stone poking out of the gray-brown dirt, a stone that might have been calf-high on the boy. All three adults watched.

"I wish I had his recuperative powers," Nylan said.

"You do. You've just done more." Ayrlyn smiled and reached out and squeezed his hand.

More? Too much more? Nylan wondered, but he took another sip of water and watched his son explore the ancient rock.

CVII

NYLAN BOLTED UPRIGHT on the bedroll in the dim light of dawn. He was sweating, despite the light breeze. His mouth and lips were dry, and his heart raced. For a moment, he sat there, breathing deeply and looking down the gentle incline to the flat and dark green waters of the brine lake.

"Another dream?" On the bedroll beside his, Ayrlyn rolled onto her side facing him.

Nylan rubbed his temples with the fingers of his right hand, then squinted, finally nodding.

"About the forest?"

"You had it, too?" Nylan's mouth was dry and felt cracked, as if he had trudged through a stone desert. He glanced to his left, but Weryl still snored, his mouth partly open. Beyond Weryl, Sylenia lay motionless, her face toward the south and away from Nylan.

"I think so. It was about trees and earthquakes and white lightnings and dark clouds." Ayrlyn kept her voice low, barely above a whisper.

"Chasing me." He coughed, then glanced to the east, but the horses grazed quietly, still all on the tieline. "Symbolism."

"It's getting harder to tell the difference between reality and symbolism." Ayrlyn rolled into a sitting position, brushing her short red hair back off her ears.

"Isn't it? It's getting a lot clearer—no, it's not at all clear— but it's feeling more important that we reach this enchanted forest, except I don't think it's exactly enchanted."

Ayrlyn took a deep breath. "We're going to have the entire armed forces of Cyador pushing over the Grass Hills as soon as they can—or as soon as they find out about the mess at the mines."

"Do we know that for sure?"

"You're asking that now?" She shook her head. "Given the

ay rulers and empires work, and the fact that almost all peo-
le resort to force when they have it, a full-scale armed in-
asion's about as sure a thing as you could bet on without
ctually standing in front of a bunch of charging lancers.
ven Fornal thinks so."

"And we're riding through hills and dust to find a forest
e're not sure exists except in our dreams?"

"It exists."

Nylan tried to lick his lips again, and couldn't. He reached
or the water bottle he had left by his head, uncorked it slowly,
nd sipped. "I don't even know how or if it will help find a
ay to stop the Cyadorans." He took another sip. "But noth-
g else will." He shrugged.

Surprisingly, Ayrlyn grinned. "I'm game." She reached for
e water bottle.

Nylan handed it to her. "What?"

"For the first time in seasons, you're not the cold, logical
ngineer. You're not calculatedly whittling away at a superior
orce. You've said, 'This is what I feel.' It makes sense."

"It does?" Nylan wasn't all that sure it did. He tried to clear
is throat.

"Enough. We need to eat." Ayrlyn sat up straighter and
eached for her boots, shaking them out before pulling them
n. "I hate living in my clothes, and that's all we do."

"Ooooo . . ." Weryl rolled onto his side.

Nylan followed the redhead's example and pulled on his
wn boots, then turned toward his son. Nylan's smile faded
s his nose wrinkled. "You smell. I'll be glad, I think, at least
n certain ways, when you can take care of some things all by
ourself."

Weryl's smile vanished, and the boy turned toward Syle-
ia. "Enyah?"

"Your father be right, child." Sylenia shook her head as
ylan lifted Weryl and carted him down toward the lake.

By the time he had lugged the boy a good distance down
he shore and cleaned him off—first using the salty water, and
hen using some desalted water that left him with a

headache—and returned, Ayrlyn had biscuits and cheese lai
out for them.

The yellow brick cheese was hard enough that Nylan al
most had to use his belt dagger like a saw to hack off chunk
small enough to chew.

Weryl promptly spit out the fragment he had been offere(

"Manners, Weryl," said Nylan wearily, rubbing his fore
head.

"Wadah, pease."

Sylenia proffered a water bottle.

All four ate slowly, silently, as the white-orange sun peere
over the eastern hills.

"We ought to get moving pretty soon," Ayrlyn said. "Be
fore it gets too hot."

"I wish we knew more," Nylan said after swallowing th
last crumbs of a too-dry biscuit. "Like exactly where we'r
headed. A map would help."

"The Cyadorans don't leave those lying around," mumble(
Ayrlyn, trying to swallow her own dry biscuit crumbs.

"The white wizards use a glass to see," pointed out Syle
nia. "Could you not do that? I have a small flat glass."

Nylan shivered. The thought of using that twisted white en
ergy for anything—anything at all . . . he just couldn't do it

"That might be difficult," Ayrlyn said.

"Can you not do something?"

The engineer frowned. Lasers . . . lasers had a parallel i
the order forces, and he'd used that parallel in smithing. Th
glass was parallel to electronics. Nagging thoughts chase(
through his mind . . . piezoelectrics . . . glass, what was glass
Silicon, and what was silicon? Sand? Order out of chaos
Sand was chaotic enough, but you could make glass, mirrors
lasers, mirrors, mirror shields . . .

"Frig . . . I should have seen it!"

"What?" asked Ayrlyn.

"So obvious . . ."

"What?" Ayrlyn's voice carried an exasperated edge.

"The mirror shields. You don't keep traditions unles
they serve a purpose. I assumed—maybe you did, too—tha

those reflective shields were half practical, half traditional."

"Oh . . ." Ayrlyn nodded. "They're protection against lasers—and white wizards' firebolts. They don't have any lasers left, but—"

"Right. What else do they have?"

"There was a mention of fire cannon in the scrolls. Lasers?"

"Could be. Or it could be something like a flamethrower." Nylan frowned.

"Antique weapon. You shoot jets of flammable liquids at people and things and light it. If you keep the pressure up, it doesn't come back and burn you . . . something like that." Ayrlyn took a sip of water, then stood and stretched. "Sitting on the ground isn't my idea of comfort."

"Flamethrowers . . . we can deal with. White magic lasers would be another thing," Nylan said.

Weryl climbed up Sylenia's shoulder to a standing position, then tottered toward Ayrlyn, flinging his arms around her trousered leg. "Ahwen . . . ahwen."

"You are an imp." Ayrlyn smiled, but lifted the silver-haired child and hugged him.

Nylan corked the water bottle and stood. Despite the wind that blew out of the north, he could still smell the brackish salty water below. *Salt and sand and grass hills and enchanted forests and white empires . . .*

"What are you thinking about?"

"Maps, glasses, forests . . . you name it." The smith rubbed his temples. That was the problem with thinking. The more he thought, the more problems and ramifications he discovered—and each had more complexities than the last.

He pursed his lips. Could he create a map, an image? Well . . . if he tried and failed, it cost nothing, unlike tampering with white chaos energy. Sands, granules of sand—he walked slowly toward the burned-out fires of the salt-collectors.

"No . . . Weryl, let your father think for a moment."

Ayrlyn's words almost drifted around him as he reached the nearest of the old stone fire rings. He scuffed the ground with his boot. Was it sandy enough?

After a moment, he walked back down along the dried-out

section of the lakeshore. At the north end, where a stream had once flowed into the brine lake, or still did seasonally, perhaps, he found a depression less than three cubits across filled with sand.

A map, he thought, *a map.*

Nothing happened, except that he had the faintest twinge in his skull.

Piezoelectric crystals, order flows, how do you get a map from that? Flows . . . chaos flows, patterns?

The second time he abandoned the idea of maps, instead concentrating on the flows of order and chaos.

The sands swirled, darker grains appearing until a pattern appeared.

"Well . . . it's something . . ." The silver-haired angel squinted at the sandy pattern, then sat down abruptly beside it. His heart was racing again, and his knees were weak.

Ayrlyn and Weryl appeared behind him at the edge of the dry stream.

"Are you all right?"

"Takes . . . energy."

Her eyes went to the sands. "You did it!"

"Sort of. It doesn't look like much to me."

Ayrlyn pointed. "Could that be Westwind, and the river and Lornth here, and that border there, the reddish sands—isn't that the outline of Candar itself?"

"Maybe." There weren't any large-scale maps of Candar, not that the engineer had seen, and his view of the continent had been limited to the brief time when he'd been jockeying an unstable and overloaded lander through a turbulent atmosphere. There was a definite resemblance between his sand map and what he thought he'd seen—but did that really mean anything?

He hauled himself to his feet.

"And this dark splotch here—that has to be the forest, and we're here . . . it's not all that far."

Nylan hoped not, even as he followed Ayrlyn's explanation. Now they were reduced to real faith in the unprovable—

magic, sorcery, or whatever—following their instincts, the sun, and a map created by subconscious manipulation of sand. And he'd thought the U.F.F. High Command had been screwy!

CVIII

A SMALLER VERSION of the silver and malachite throne no more than four cubits high rested on the white marble dais. The white marble wall behind the throne rose to a balcony covered with open grillwork that concealed the Archers of the Rational Stars.

Lephi studied the throne, then turned to Triendar. "Be still, old friend, and just listen."

He gestured to the two tall Mirror Lancers who stood by the double doors, and they opened the doors. A tall man entered the hall, wearing the uniform of the Mirror Lancers, a uniform without the green sash and no longer white, but smeared with charcoal and blood, and with yellow and red dust ground into the fabric. The doors closed. The majer bowed. "Your Mightiness." His voice was even, resigned, calm.

"I have been told that you commanded the force that took the mines, and lost them, and that you returned with less than a third of your command." Lephi's voice was cold. "Is that accurate?"

"Yes, Your Mightiness."

"Is it also true that you failed to mine the copper and sent none back to Cyad?"

"We mined the copper, Your Mightiness, and sent the wagons to Syadtar. I do not know what happened after that. During the entire campaign, I received no dispatches and no supplies."

"I will not have it!" Lephi glanced around the room, less than a tenth the size of the receiving hall in Cyad.

Majer Piataphi stood below the dais, resigned, waiting.

"Why did you return? Why did you bother? The Archers of the Rational Stars have terminated many for far less. So have the white mages." Lephi's head inclined fractionally, in the direction of Triendar, who stood to his left, a pace back from the rearmost part of the throne.

"I saw no point in having the rest of the foot and lancers slaughtered." Piataphi shrugged. "We received no supplies. We lacked enough horse to attack, and there was no forage. The barbarians would not stand and fight, except when they could find smaller detachments and outnumbered them."

"You left with more than enough mounts."

"In the middle of the night, the barbarians cast fireballs over the walls and into the barracks and stables and corrals. They were not like the fireballs of the white mages, for they left no trails in the sky. We drove them off, but not before we lost nearly sevenscore mounts."

Triendar's hands, hidden in his flowing sleeves, tightened into near fists, but his face remained impassive.

"I need no more catalogues of failure." Lephi smiled. "You almost hope I will turn the Archers of the Rational Stars on you, Majer. I won't. You will lead the van against the grass-lands barbarians, and you will lead from the front of the very first squad."

"Yes, ser."

"Go!"

The majer turned, rather than backed away, and walked toward the double doors, which the lancers opened as he approached.

After the doors closed, Lephi walked to the window at the right end of the chamber and looked beyond the white stone walls toward the browned Grass Hills. "Fireballs, supplies and copper that never arrived—what do you make of it?" He did not turn toward the mage, but left his eyes on the Grass Hills.

"He tells the truth—"

"I know that!" Lephi turned but did not move from his position by the window. "The man is honest, and he saved troops that would have been slaughtered. But it should not have happened that way. The barbarians should attack valiantly and break against the lancers, as they have always done. There should be no fireballs in Lornth. You told me that the three white mages of the barbarians had been killed."

"There are the angels."

"Do we know there are angels in Lornth?"

"There is . . . something . . ." Triendar admitted. "I have seen a man and a woman and a child, but only those three."

"Only three?"

"Only three. There is the Accursed Forest—"

"Always the forest . . . will Cyad . . ." Lephi clamped his jaw shut. "Find out more about the three. And be prepared to bring all manner of fire upon the barbarians when we meet on the field."

"Yes, Sire." Triendar bowed, just deeply enough for the gesture not to be mocking.

CIX

THERE'S YOUR REAL lake." Nylan pointed toward the silver-tinged and elongated oval in the valley below as the mare carried him along the crest of the low ridge on a dusty road that was scarcely more than a trail. The stillness of the air made it seem far later in the day than mid-morning.

"I said there was one." Ayrlyn surveyed the valley. "Not much else here."

Nylan nodded. Ahead on the left was a holding of some sort, and a thin line of smoke rose into the green-blue sky from near the lake, kays yet ahead.

"With water so scarce, you'd think there'd be more people around a lake," Ayrlyn added.

"Maybe it's salty, too." Nylan glanced toward the holding as they rode nearer. Nothing moved.

"It didn't feel that way."

The angel smith reined up, and wiped his forehead. Like

everywhere in Candar outside the higher Westhorns, it was hot. And like all of southern Lornth—or northern Cyador—it seemed, there wasn't enough of a breeze to notice.

Sylenia slowed her mount gradually, clearly trying not to jolt the dozing Weryl, a slight frown wrinkling her forehead.

The lane on the left side of the road led arrowlike to three structures perhaps a hundred cubits to the west—a square house, what appeared to be a barn, and a large shed. A dark rectangular emptiness gaped where the barn door had been, and one side of the shed had caved in, imparting a rakish tilt to the sagging roof. The lane bore no tracks, but no weeds grew where ancient wagon wheels had packed the ground.

"No sign of fire," mused Nylan. "Just worn out." He flicked the reins and eased the mare back into a walk.

"Aren't we all?"

"I hope not." Nylan didn't have to force the grin too much.

"You're difficult, and when you're not difficult, you're impossible." Ayrlyn smiled.

"Good."

A half kay beyond the abandoned stead, the road turned south again and descended into the east end of the valley. The lake was at the west end.

"You can tell that the lake was bigger." Ayrlyn gestured. "The flat meadows there? That's old lake bottomland. And there are mud or sand flats around the eastern end."

A thin plume of smoke rose from the house on the low hill to the southwest of the marshy lake.

"Why would they build a house so far from the water?" asked Nylan.

"Wadah?" asked Weryl.

"In a moment, child," said Sylenia in a low voice.

Nylan grinned.

"I'd bet the water level's seasonal," Ayrlyn explained. "In the past, it might have filled the whole bottom of the valley. That abandoned holding was on the ridge too. Probably the well went when the water level dropped."

"Another part of the puzzle."

"It's no puzzle," the redhead said. "All of this part of Candar is slowly changing to a drier climate."

The road followed what might have been the former high-water level of the lake on the north side of the valley. The grasses they rode past were thicker, with traces of green, on the bottomland below the road.

On the right side of the road grazed a scattered flock of gray-white sheep, but there was no sign of a shepherd.

"Not many people," Ayrlyn said.

"I have the feeling that we're on the frontiers of Cyador."

"That's the real puzzle," she said. "Why would Cyador be so interested in taking over Lornth? This valley is a lot more hospitable than southern Lornth, and people have abandoned it."

"Maybe it's the copper, or coal, or extractive resources that they need."

"Maybe . . . but why?"

Nylan shrugged. He didn't know, and there was so much they didn't know.

"They do not like the old people of Candar," ventured Sylenia from where she rode slightly behind them. "Not those who live beyond their white walls."

The faint *baaaa*ing of the sheep drifted toward the riders, and Nylan glanced down at the animals. Still no herder or even herd dogs. A golden bird, heavy and plumpish, burst out of the knee-high grasses below the road and soared eastward toward the even higher grasses.

"That looked like some sort of pheasant."

"If it looked like a pheasant . . ."

". . . it probably was," Ayrlyn concluded.

"I'd bet they taste good." Nylan could feel himself salivating.

"They be most tasty," Sylenia affirmed. "In Lornth, only the lords may hunt them."

That somehow figured. Nylan studied the lake ahead. On the south side, across from where they approached, was a stand of reeds.

"You think this is safe? Or should we wait until it's dark?"

"If anyone's looking, they've already decided to do something . . . or not. If they have, we'll find out quickly. If not, why give them more time? Besides, we need the water now." Ayrlyn paused. "And I don't feel like there are many people around here."

"Probably not."

Golden sand stretched back from the water on the eastern end nearly a hundred cubits with the beach running twice that in width, almost like a resort bathing area on Svenn.

"The runoff carries the sand here. The reeds hold soil and organic matter. It's probably a very clean lake. I'd like a bath." Ayrlyn glanced toward the house on the hill at the west end of the small lake. "This is the first real water we've seen in . . . I'm not sure how long."

"Weryl, he could use bathing," suggested Sylenia.

Of that Nylan was also sure. "Let's water the mounts and fill water bottles first," he suggested. "Just in case."

"You're probably right, but it feels like that one house is the only one with people in it."

They reined up just at the edge of the sand. Nylan glanced across the lake, but no one appeared, and the thin line of smoke continued to rise into the hot midday sky.

"I'll water the mounts over there, and you and Sylenia fill the water bottles. If no one shows up, then you three bathe, and I'll watch."

"I'll bet you'll watch! But will you watch what you're supposed to be watching?"

"I'm trying to be practical," Nylan protested. "Even if someone does show up, it will take time."

Ayrlyn nodded. "I'm sorry. We'd have to hold them off while you scramble into your clothes? Or onto your horse?" She grinned. "I might just yell to see you do it, especially if your eyes stray too much when we're bathing."

"Thanks."

"You've been warned."

Once the water bottles were filled, Sylenia wasted no time in stripping off her riding clothes, and Weryl's as well, and wading into the lake, dipping Weryl's toes as she did. Although Nylan did his best to watch the house and the road in both directions, he could definitely understand Tonsar's attraction to the young woman—although he was glad Tonsar wasn't around to see Ayrlyn's charms.

"Watch the road," she called.

He flushed and ostentatiously turned his head.

"That's better."

Once the three left the water, he concentrated even more on studying the road and the hillside.

"All right," Ayrlyn called as she finished pulling on her boots. "You can stop being so obviously a prudish martyr. You saw more than enough, and don't tell me you didn't."

He couldn't help grinning at the humor in her voice.

"It's your turn."

He dismounted and handed all the reins to the redhead, then pulled off his boots, then his clothes. The water was barely cool, close to warmish, as Nylan waded in, very much conscious that both Sylenia and Ayrlyn watched. The slope of the sandy part was gradual, so gradual that he had to walk almost a hundred cubits before the water reached his thighs. By then the sand had given way to soft mud that squushed up between his toes.

Finally, he plunged in, enjoying the coolness on his skin. The golden sand helped scrub away the grime of what seemed more than a season, although he kept looking toward the house on the hillside as he washed.

As he walked back up the sandy slope to the beach, he turned and glanced toward the hillside house, but could see no change, no puffs of dust that might indicate riders, just the same thin line of smoke from the chimney. Was someone baking or cooking, and just not looking outside?

For a moment, he just stood in the sunlight, wiping off water with his hands before he tried to dry himself with the small square of cloth that doubled as a towel.

Ayrlyn's eyes flicked from the hillside toward the silver-haired angel. "Nice view."

"Thanks." Nylan couldn't help flushing, even as he saw that Sylenia busied herself with not looking in his direction and holding a water bottle for Weryl. "See anyone?"

"No one, and it's not as if there were any cover."

Nylan wasn't sure whether he had minded washing up in plain view, or if the tightness in his stomach came from wondering whether anyone happened to be coming. He pulled on his clothes.

Once he was dressed, he and Ayrlyn alternated washing out their spare sets of undergarments . . . and still no one appeared on the road.

"Maybe we should camp here?" suggested Sylenia.

Nylan and Ayrlyn exchanged glances.

Both shook their heads.

"Too open, and we need to get where we're going," Nylan finally said. Staying just didn't feel right, and he could sense that Ayrlyn felt exactly the same way.

He slipped into the saddle, looking back to see that the damp undergarments remained fastened to the outside of his saddlebags.

The road curved up the hillside and past the single dwelling where smoke still drifted from the chimney, but the doors were closed, and the shutters on the lower levels were fastened tight.

"They don't like strangers," Nylan said.

"I can't imagine raiders would come this far south. A xenophobic culture, you think?"

"This far away from any towns? I don't know."

Sylenia cast a longing look back at the blue of the lake as they rode over the hill crest.

CX

NESSLEK SAT ON the carpet by the armchair in which Zeldyan was seated with a stack of polished wooden blocks before him. The boy chewed on the corner of one, drool coming from the corners of his mouth.

His mother read a scroll silently, while Gethen sipped chilled greenjuice from a goblet.

Finally, Zeldyan looked up. "He writes that the angels brought down fire in the night on the mines, and destroyed many of the white demons. The remainder rode back toward Cyador, leaving a blackened ruin." She let the scroll roll into a loose cylinder and extended it toward her sire. "After vanquishing the white demons," she added, "the angels vanished, along with Sylenia and their child. None knew where they have gone. They left a scroll saying they would return."

"I will read what Fornal wrote later." The gray-haired regent shook his head. "So we have a burned-out mine and no white demons. And no angels. Did they ride the winds?" A harsh laugh followed. "The last time I looked, they rode horses."

"When mages do not wish to be seen, often they are not."

"That be true enough, daughter."

"I do not think they have abandoned us," mused Zeldyan. "Though I could not say why."

"They have abandoned Fornal."

"Have they? They drove off the white demons." Zeldyan offered a faint smile. "They did not even promise that."

"The lord of Cyador will send all his forces against us," pointed out the older regent, his right hand resting loosely around the crystal goblet. "You already prophesied that. More armsmen and lancers than we have ever seen."

"We agreed that we had no choice."

A wooden block thumped to the carpet, then clattered as it rolled off the fabric and across the stone tiles. Nesslek stood, holding the armchair and tugging at Zeldyan's leg.

Zeldyan laughed, but the sound was bitter.

"Maaaa," said Nesslek, pulling on his mother's dark green trousers. "Maaa."

"Oh, child." She swung him up into her lap and hugged him.

Gethen continued after a pause. "What does your heart tell you about the angels?"

Zeldyan frowned.

"Your heart," Gethen insisted.

"They are good," she admitted. "Did they not drive off the Cyadorans and send us one shipment of copper?"

"That is true, but . . . the horses . . . and the firebolts and sneaking through the night?"

"They have done what needed to be done."

"And, even should we prevail, Lornth will not be the same. That, more than defeat, is what our holders fear."

"One way or another, Lornth will change." The blonde regent disentangled Nesslek's fingers from her hair. "Still . . . my sire . . . you know I have not seen with the same eyes as Fornal . . . but he is worried, and he must face the white demons first."

"He has cause for worry. So do we, but—"

"We should feed the holders the fodder we have?"

"And tell them that we have done as they asked." Gethen snorted. "And send a dispatch to Lady Ellindyja pointing out that we have reclaimed the patrimony of her grandson."

"Best it be done quickly, before . . ."

Gethen nodded.

"Then we will send Fornal a scroll, telling him that we will raise what other forces we can," added Zeldyan.

"Few as they will be."

"Few as they will be," she confirmed.

CXI

NYLAN LOOKED AT the road ahead, almost flat as it curved westward around a low rise barely more than ten cubits high. Instead of the straggling, sun-browned stalks of the Grass Hills, the meadows flanking the road bore thicker grasses that, despite the approaching harvest time, were predominantly green. On the scattered hilltops not more than low rises, at infrequent intervals, were woodlots with borders sharp enough that they could have been trimmed flush with a laser.

Scattered holdings flanked the woodlots, joined to the main road by lanes. Unlike in the lake valley, a handful of farmers and herders were visible, separated widely. But none ventured near the road.

"Notice that?" asked Ayrlyn.

"Notice what?"

"In Lornth, the houses are close to the road. Here, they're not. And I don't think I've seen a single woman outside. Some small children, but no women. We've been riding two days straight since the lake—"

"We did sleep some."

"If you call hiding in a woodlot sleeping."

Nylan forced himself to take a long, slow breath. "I slept."

"You and Weryl did—that's true."

"It was hard to sleep," added Sylenia.

"About the women?" asked Nylan, trying to steer the subject away from his apparently ill-advised suggestion as to a place to rest.

"It's just a feeling—"

"It be no feeling, lady," said Sylenia. "Their women, they lock away. Even more now since the time in the years of my ancestors that the noble ladies fled to Lornth."

"Gethen or someone mentioned that." Ayrlyn stopped and looked toward the curve in the road.

A small wagon, pulled by a thin gray horse, rolled from behind the rise around the curve and toward the three riders, its yellow painted spoke wheels barely raising dust.

"First local we've seen on the road," Nylan observed.

The dark-haired and clean-shaven man on the wagon seat stared at the three riders, especially at Ayrlyn's flaming hair. His eyes widened as he glanced from Ayrlyn to Sylenia and back to Ayrlyn, with barely a notice of Nylan.

The angels and Sylenia drew their mounts onto the right shoulder of the road, and Nylan tugged the pack mare after them.

The wagon driver edged his horse and wagon toward the other shoulder, his eyes still fixed on the strangers.

Nylan smiled pleasantly, adding, "Good day," in Old Rationalist.

The driver's mouth opened, then closed in a convulsive swallow, and he looked away, flicking the reins abruptly as he passed.

Nylan glanced back. The pace of the wagon had definitely picked up. "I think we're going to be reported to the local authorities."

"That's not exactly surprising," said Ayrlyn. "He kept looking at us as if we were . . . harlots or worse. I'm getting a very bad feeling about the position of women in Cyador . . . a very bad feeling."

Nylan had to admit that she was probably right—very right. "The sooner we find this forest, preferably before we run into the local authorities, the better."

"Nylan . . ." said Ayrlyn in a low voice, drawing her mount closer to his.

"Yes?" His tone was wary.

"You were probably right about sleeping well out of sight. We're going to have to be careful."

"You think we should go cross-country?" He glanced over his shoulder again. There was no sign of the wagon.

"Not until we have to. The roads are always faster."

That was true, and the road ahead, past the curve, appeared clear, with only a handful of the same scattered holdings spread across the rolling plains. How long it would be clear was another question.

Nylan blotted his forehead and glanced back over his shoulder, but the road behind remained empty, except for the settling dust of the wagon.

CXII

THE LATE-AFTERNOON sun poured through the window, but the white marble appeared cold, as did the figure in white and silver robes upon the silver and malachite throne.

"Have you gathered all the supplies necessary, Queras?" Lephi leaned forward, his figure highlighted by the light reflected off the white marble dais and the white marble wall behind the throne. To the right of the throne and back stood a figure in the white robes of a mage.

The dark-eyed officer with the crossed green sashes bowed before the dais. "We continue to gather all that is necessary."

"An eight-day, and we still gather supplies? Surely, what I have seen cannot be all the Mirror Lancers and their equipment, can it?"

"Your pardon, Mightiness—"

"Yes?" Lephi's voice was chill. "Do explain, Marshal Queras. Please explain."

"Three more of the firewagons have failed . . . we have less than a score. We brought matched horse teams from Summerdock, but that has taken longer . . ." Queras's eyes darted to the balcony above and to the open grillwork that concealed the Archers of the Rational Stars.

"What else? Surely, the failure of three firewagons cannot account for such a delay. Cannot supplies come up the Grand Canal?"

Queras swallowed and looked down at the recently buffed and polished off-white stone tiles of the hall that separated him from the dais, then at the green carpet runner on which he stood.

"Yes?" Lephi's voice remained silky and cool.

"Three eight-days ago, another two firewagons failed . . . and you ordered that the ironmages supply the fireship first."

"I may have. Even the loss of five firewagons should not

create that much delay for a land such as Cyador." Lephi smiled.

"The Grand Canal . . . there have also been difficulties."

"What sort of difficulties?"

"Roots, Your Mightiness. They have choked the waterway . . . and there were several large stun lizards."

Behind Lephi's shoulder, the white-haired mage's ruddy complexion paled.

There was silence in the small hall.

Finally, Lephi nodded. "Go. Do not return until you are ready to march . . . or until I summon you."

"Yes, Your Mightiness."

The door closed, and Lephi turned to Triendar. "So I should leave the Accursed Forest alone, old friend?"

"No." Triendar stepped forward and inclined his head briefly. "I told you that attempting to expand Cyador's borders through the use of chaos could destroy us all. You said it must be done. We have done all we can, but like you, white mages cannot be in two different places at the same time." Triendar paused briefly, then added, "The iron mages are few and fewer with the talent are born each generation. There are not enough of them to create the fire cannon for the fireship and repair all the ailing firewagons."

"And no one else can do this?"

"No, Sire. As you commanded years ago, we have visited every hamlet, and every village. We have even made women ironmages, and you know what . . . difficulty . . . that created, but there are still few with the talent." He shifted his weight from one foot to the other.

"Is it so much to ask, Triendar? Is it so much to ask that you and the white mages merely maintain what has been?"

"According to the ancient records, Your Mightiness—"

"You have told me about the most honorable and ancient records—from the time I was much younger. You say the talent for managing chaos and order is appearing less, but why?"

"We do not know. We have bought captives from other lands, even, but none of them have the talent."

"And what of those three . . . angels?"

"They ride somewhere in the Grass Hills."

"Is that all you can tell me?"

"The glass shows them riding. It cannot tell me which hill they climb or descend. I will keep screeing until they are somewhere that can be recognized."

"Somewhere that can be recognized? What use are your talents?"

"I cannot change the way the world is, Sire, however much I would like."

"Is this entire cursed world out to bring down Cyador? Is it?" Lephi glared at the white mage. "You cannot tell about these angels that destroy my lancers. You tell me that I must either do nothing and watch as Cyador slowly crumbles—or that if I try to restore her power and glory, then I now risk destroying all my ancestors built?"

"I did not put it—"

"Your words were chosen more carefully, but they mean the same thing."

Triendar waited.

Finally, Lephi shook his head. "I will not accept it. Cyad will rise again—in my time, and under my name. It will. It must! Is that clear, Triendar?"

"Your words are clear, Your Majesty. Most clear."

"Then gather your mages! Go!"

CXIII

THE FARTHER SOUTH Nylan and Ayrlyn had ridden from the lake the more the hills had flattened, first into low hills, then rolling plains. Now they rode through what seemed almost flat and level farmland.

The fields to the left contained low plants, with faded yellow flowers rising above dark green leaves that had begun to curl at the tips. A hint of a fragrance like reisera, but not exactly the same, drifted on the faintest of breezes across the dusty road. That was like so much of Candar—familiar, but not exactly the same.

Gray clouds, the first Nylan had seen since they had entered Lornth more than a season earlier, covered the sky, and scattered raindrops fell, leaving an occasional dark spot on the road.

"I don't like this," murmured Ayrlyn.

"The rain? It's a relief from the sun."

"No, Cyador. The whole situation."

"Too exposed? You think we should abort?" Nylan glanced ahead, where he could see what seemed to be a gathering of dwellings. "There's a village ahead. Here comes another wagon."

"Let me check." Ayrlyn's eyes glazed, and she half-sagged in the saddle as the four horses walked slowly southward, and as the single-horse wagon rolled toward them.

Nylan glanced toward the wagon, but, like the ones they had seen before, it was small, with spoked wheels and an axle supporting springs—certainly more sophisticated than anything he'd seen in Lornth. The driver was a dark-haired man, who, upon seeing the riders, turned the wagon into a side lane and flicked the reins.

Nylan frowned. Had they seen anyone else on horseback? He didn't think so.

"There's a big river beyond the town," Ayrlyn announced, straightening in the saddle.

"How far be this forest?" asked Sylenia.

"It's beyond the town," Nylan said dryly.

Ayrlyn raised her eyebrows.

"Should we ride through or try to ride around?" he asked quickly.

"It's not a big town," Ayrlyn pointed out. "And we can either ride through some farmer's fields and ford the river—and get everyone asking who we are. Or we can ride through the town and use the bridge, and save a lot of time. There's no one that looks like an armsman or a soldier."

"Soldier?" The word was murmured by Sylenia, and Nylan

ealized that the term came from Sybran, that the only Old Rat
erms were either "armsman" or "mercenary."

"I guess we ride through, looking like we own the place,
eady to draw iron if we have to."

"If there aren't any armsmen," Ayrlyn said, "we won't be
drawing anything. The locals turn from a blade. Haven't you
seen that?"

Nylan nodded, then added, "Yes," after realizing that the
redhead's eyes were on the road ahead. "I don't think anyone
rides horseback unless they're military."

"That would figure."

Sylenia's eyes went from Nylan to Ayrlyn and back, a
slightly puzzled look on her face.

"Enyah! Piscut, pease?"

"I can hear someone's awake," Nylan noted.

"A moment, a moment." Sylenia twisted, struggling to
open the small sack fastened to one side of the back of her
saddle, just to allow her easy access to a few of their rapidly
diminishing provisions.

The longer the smith looked at the village ahead, the more
something bothered him. That was another problem—he
could feel energies, still looming beneath the ground, and
sense that Cyador was trouble, but so little of it had anything
concrete in the way of proof. Was he losing his mind? Or had
he lost it long before, and was he wandering through a mental labyrinth of insanity?

His eyes went to the woodlot behind the holding on the
right side of the road, a holding, like all the others, well back
from the road, and shielded by a screen of bushes. No trees,
just bushes.

He scanned the woodlot again. The trees—what was it
about them? Then he swallowed. So obvious—and yet not
obvious at all.

"Look at the trees," Nylan said.

"The trees? All right. They're trees, and they're in woodlots."

"See any anyplace else?"

After a time came a soft "oh."

"Do you recall seeing any trees that weren't?"

"No . . . now that you mention it. Do you think—"

"I don't know, but let's hope that means the forest isn't too far."

They neared a house—screened by bushes—that stood a mere forty cubits back from the road. A woman picked green berries from one of the bushes. At the sound of hoofs, she turned, revealing an advanced stage of pregnancy. Her eyes widened, even as she grabbed the berry basket and darted around the bushes. A door slammed.

"Here, it's the door they slam," Ayrlyn said.

"That's because the shutters are already closed."

Nylan surveyed the town as they passed several more dwellings, still set back somewhat from the road. The houses were built of yellow brick—large bricks, and each brick was more than two thirds of a cubit long. Some dwellings were covered with plaster or stucco, but all were brick. The yellowish tint pervaded all the structures, and green gratework and bars covered all the lower-level windows.

The silver-haired angel frowned.

A gray-haired man with a broom in his hand looked up, bowed quickly, and then scurried off the brick walk that bordered the road, and behind another screen of bushes before a house.

As though a wave had passed through the town, doors shut ahead of the riders, and the road emptied, nearly soundlessly.

"They do not like strangers." Sylenia's voice was matter-of-fact.

"How about people on horseback?" suggested Ayrlyn.

A light wagon raced down the street ahead of them, heading toward the bridge.

"We'd better step it up," Nylan suggested. "I'd rather be on the other side of the river before the local authorities arrive." He flicked the mare's reins.

Nearer the center of town was a two-story roofed building, with brick columns. The lower level seemed open, and Nylan could see people inside, gathered in small groups, groups that turned away from the riders as they passed.

"Covered marketplace," noted Ayrlyn.

On the left side of the road from the marketplace was an ornate fountain, sculpted to resemble a tree of some sort, unfamiliar to Nylan, with spreading branches, from which water flowed in smooth sheets, giving the impression of moss or shedding rain in a storm.

"That's beautiful," Ayrlyn said.

"It is." But the town continued to bother Nylan. "It doesn't smell," he said.

"What?"

"Most low-tech towns smell. This one doesn't. It's clean."

"The Old Rats were pretty organized."

They kept riding, now at a quick trot, as the people scurried inside and the doors closed.

On the southern side of the town was the river. The three-piered bridge was made of the same yellowish brick, with only the base of the piers that rose out of the sluggish gray water being stone. To the east, downstream, were several brick piers that jutted out slightly from the raised levies, embankments presumably designed to confine any seasonal floodwaters.

At one pier was tied a long and narrow barge of some sort, filled with woven baskets piled two deep. Three men relayed baskets from the pier to the barge, and none looked up as the four horses passed, even as their hoofs struck the brick-paved approach to the span.

The river itself was larger than Nylan had anticipated, nearly a hundred cubits across, and, while the dull gray water seemed slow-moving, he could sense that it was deep enough that fording it would have been difficult.

The roadway of the bridge was narrow, no more than seven or eight cubits wide. Sylenia let her mount fall back, riding across right behind the two angels and side-by-side with the pack mare, her legs no more than a cubit from the low brick railing.

Years of use had carved two wagon ruts in the brick paving. Nylan let his senses study the bridge, then range outward. "The river's new. At least the riverbed is."

"New? It looks like it's been here awhile," said Ayrlyn.

"A few hundred years," Nylan admitted, "but that's new for a river."

"More planoforming."

But why? Why move a river? Nylan jerked forward in the saddle as the mare started down the other side of the arched bridge way.

The fields resumed on the far side of the river, just beyond the base of the brick-faced levy, with no houses or dwellings in immediate sight.

"Floodplain," Ayrlyn said. "The levies are lower on this side. Very Rationalist planning."

"I'm impressed, but it bothers me, and I can't say why."

"There's another thing," Ayrlyn added. "There were no signs. Nothing written in any public space in that town."

"That's odd."

"Yes." Ayrlyn stopped, then said, "There's someone ahead, where the road forks. On horseback."

"Frig." Nylan's hand touched the blade in the shoulder harness, and the one at his waist, moving both to see that they would not bind if he needed them. "Should we cut across the fields?"

"There are only three. They know the roads, and their mounts are probably fresher."

"You really don't think we can talk our way out of this?"

"No. But it might work, and we'll create more of a surprise than if we start running right now."

That made sense, but Ayrlyn usually did, often more than he did, Nylan reflected. Still, there were three armsmen waiting. And only he and Ayrlyn were armed.

Three men in green, all holding white-bronze sabres and mounted on dark brown horses, waited at the crossroads.

"Sylenia, you stay back." Nylan reined up a good twenty cubits back from the local patrol, his hand ready to draw the Westwind shortsword.

"You must come with us," announced the center rider.

The tongue was unadulterated Old Rationalist, and it took a moment for Nylan to make the mental adjustment.

"Why?" asked Ayrlyn. "We have bothered no one."

"You are strangers. Strangers are not permitted. Cyad must ot be polluted." The almost leering look of the speaker conasted with the flat speech.

Nylan studied the area behind the armsmen, but could see r sense no one.

"Come!" snapped the Cyadoran leader, as though it were conceivable that he would be defied.

Thunk!

Nylan gaped as Ayrlyn's mount darted forward and her eavy blade slammed through the speaker's shoulder. Seemgly too slowly, he pulled his own blade from the waist scabard, and urged the mare forward.

The armsman to the right glanced from Nylan to the sagng leader and back to the angel before raising his sabre. ylan beat the white-bronze blade aside, and slashed through e other's shoulder, then knocked the blade from the armsan's hand on the recovery.

"Ser!"

At Sylenia's scream he turned in the saddle to see the third yadoran bearing down on Ayrlyn, who held her second blade eakly before her. Reacting rather than thinking, he threw his eavy blade, smoothing the order flows.

The backflash of chaos froze him in his saddle. His vision ared into the nova of a powerflux, and he shuddered, blind nd trying to grope for the blade in his shoulder harness.

"You don't have to, ser Nylan." Sylenia's voice wavered a and out of his hearing. "You don't have to. They're all ead."

He lowered his hand, his eyes still clinched shut— tilely—against the sparks of chaos that flared through them.

"What do we do?" asked the nursemaid.

"Just ride. Fast walk," gasped Nylan. "Need to get to a roodlot or somewhere . . . sheltered . . . but not close to here. ou lead."

"I . . . I could not."

"You're the only one who can see."

"Oh."

Nylan shivered in his saddle, letting Sylenia lead the way, letting the mare carry him forward. He knew Ayrlyn was in worse shape, barely able to ride. But she had been right to attack first. Had they any choice? Not in this situation. Not outnumbered and with Weryl and Sylenia vulnerable. Not against a culture to whom outsiders were worthless.

Again . . . and again . . . only force mattered. It was all that anyone respected. Not feelings, not reason, not balance—just force.

. . . *glare-damned . . . frigging force* . . .

He swallowed and tried to stay in the saddle, trusting the mare to follow Sylenia.

CXIV

A CRICKET . . . OR grasshopper . . . or something . . . chirped in the darkness from the grass beyond the trees of the woodlot. The faint reiseralike odor simmered in the late-evening stillness.

Nylan glanced briefly through the darkness toward where Sylenia and Weryl slept, then toward Ayrlyn. "Aren't you tired?" He closed his eyes as the intermittent light-knives stabbed through them.

"Yes, but I'm not sleepy. My head still aches . . ."

"I know." So did Nylan's, and every so often his vision blurred, and white flashes or sparks kept blinding him, sometimes so that all he had been able to do when riding away from the river was hang on and hope the mare didn't carry him into trouble, hope that Sylenia would just find somewhere halfway safe.

It seemed as though they had ridden through eternity, through a rainstorm that, paradoxically, had relieved the worst of the chaos backflash agony.

Where exactly they were, he wasn't sure, except that they

vere farther south and closer to the forest. He hoped so, any-
vay, but he was too tired to worry or ride anymore.

"A lot of this doesn't make sense, not to me," he confessed.

"That's because you're not a comm officer or a sociolo-
ist," she pointed out. "It didn't make sense to me at first, ei-
her. Look at it rationally, though, or Rationalistically, if you
vill."

He groaned at the pun, then rubbed his temples.

"This is a highly regimented and organized culture—and
ne in which women are held in very low esteem—as valued
roperty. There has to be something like an aristocracy with
ome pretty high-handed privileges. That whole town
creamed it."

"Huhh?" Nylan's head continued to throb. Then, he'd been
he one to kill two of the locals.

"All the houses are shuttered, despite the heat. The en-
rances are screened with bushes, or, in the towns, barred
vith grates. There are no signs indicating where anything is,
nd all the houses look pretty much alike. Have we seen a sin-
le girl? Just one pregnant woman. The only horsemen have
een armsmen in authority, and everyone runs from anyone
vho's mounted, even before seeing who it might be."

"Why do you think I attacked first? It's not because I liked
he idea, or that I'm bloodthirsty," she pointed out. "We were
nounted, strangers, and bearing arms. That meant we were
ot only fair game, but that they would have attacked as soon
s we refused to come with them. The good news is that no
ne is actually chasing us right now," Ayrlyn finished.

"We're strangers, and we knocked off three of the local po-
ce or the equivalent, and no one's chasing us? Are you sure
ou're all right?"

"I'd bet those three armsmen were the entire local con-
tabulary. They got killed. Now, that was outside of town.
irst, few if any of the locals are going to have the initiative
o go see what happened, and those that do aren't about to say
ecause it would implicate them. That means every local can
eny involvement, and most probably will. Plus, in this kind
f system, who is going to want to travel to the next town or

military district or whatever, to explain what happened—and risk rather direct interrogation? The reaction is bound to be slow."

"Systems like that don't work."

"Oh, yes, they do." She said grimly. "These . . . Cyadorans have a highly developed sense of passive resistance and absolute military or aristocratic authority over anyone who doesn't fit. It's pretty obvious that any woman out in public is free game, but safe behind her house walls. Local men are probably respected by the aristocrats so long as they scrape and bow in public, and the local men stay as far from the aristocrats as possible. Look at the houses. Unless you're a local, how would you even be sure who lives where? The nonaristocrats aren't allowed weapons, and I'd bet that even the aristocrats face stiff social restrictions on how and when they can use theirs.

"Except for stealing from the fields, we can't and won't get supplies, because they're locked up to ensure rigid accounting, and because every store will slam a very heavy door before you can get there. If we did get inside the walls, then the local rules would make us fair game, and these people have a lot of pent-up aggression, I'd bet.

"Every armed force has the right to kill or torture us," the redhead continued—"or rape Sylenia and me—or you, if that's how they're inclined. The borders are closed, and geographically isolated, which limits strangers, and singles them out." Ayrlyn yawned. "No, as long as they can keep out large numbers of strangers, the system will work fine. And in some ways, probably better than other societies in Candar."

Nylan swallowed in the darkness. What Ayrlyn said made sense, perfect sense—even the precisely edged woodlots. But he had trouble believing it.

"I know. So do I, but it all fits."

"I keep wondering if this is just a fool's quest."

"I have all along." She chuckled, except it was a low and bitter sound. "But what choice do we have? Could we hold up to another battle?"

"No." The brief encounter with the overmatched Cyado

n locals had proved that. As Ayrlyn had pointed out, they
ight not have been able to survive if they'd let the Cyado-
ans start the attack. The next time, even if they drew steel
nd struck first, he wasn't sure they'd be able to hold up as
ell as they had the last.

"Do you want to spend the rest of your life running and
weating your way through Candar, always looking to your
ack? Or do you want to crawl back to Ryba?"

Nylan winced.

"Well . . . any other ideas?"

He didn't have any—not that were any better. At least, if
ey could find . . . something . . . in the forest . . . some way
 stop the Cyadorans . . . then they might be able to retreat
 a hilltop in Lornth.

"We'll never be able to retreat anywhere, Nylan," Ayrlyn
roke in. "We might be lucky enough to have a permanent
ome from which we can sally forth."

The grasshopper or cricket chirped again, and the sound re-
erberated inside Nylan's ears and skull.

"Get some sleep. You're tired. I'll wake you if I get sleepy."

"You're sleepy, too," he protested.

"Not as sleepy as you are."

Nylan leaned against her thigh and closed his eyes. May-
e . . . maybe . . . he could sleep.

CXV

YLAN GLANCED FROM the back trail they took across the low
elds toward where the main road was, roughly paralleling their
ack, but both roads were empty, although even the smaller trail
ey followed had heavy recent tracks. He rubbed his forehead,
en blotted it. Now that the air was more humid, almost mist-
g, if only slightly cooler, he was sweating even more, and not
st from under his floppy hat.

From behind Sylenia's saddle came the plaintive plea, "Mah wadah, pease?"

An exasperated look crossed the nursemaid's face, and Nylan pursed his lips together as he turned in his own saddle. Weryl couldn't be that thirsty! Every kay the child asked for more water, and his own senses told him that his son was fine, and that meant he needed attention—or wanted it. Nylan knew he'd been neglecting Weryl some, but not totally, and certainly Sylenia paid more than enough attention.

"Stop feeling guilty," snapped Ayrlyn. "You exude guilt, and that's exactly what he wants. Young children have no sense of ethics or restraint when it comes to getting affection, and your son's no exception."

"Neither am I," said Nylan.

"You have some restraint. I restrain you."

The engineer grinned. "How far, do you think? I can sense something."

"Just something?"

"Trees are easier for you; the ground is easier for me, and the forces underneath are getting fainter."

"Somehow, that makes sense." Ayrlyn cocked her head to one side, as if listening. "A couple of kays, I'd guess, probably over that low rise ahead."

Although they'd been cautious and circled several towns, neither of them had sensed any pursuit. They'd been lucky enough to find a melon field, with a few nearly ripe fruits and a small orchard with something like apples.

Nylan had suffered a slight stomachache from too many of the apples, but they had almost been worth it after days of hard cheese and harder biscuits. He wished they'd had the presence of mind to search the saddlebags of the Cyadoran armsmen they'd killed, but neither he nor Ayrlyn had been in much shape to think of such.

He tried not to think of how they would eat on their return—or while they were investigating the forest.

A slight breeze cooled his face, and faint droplets of water began to fall, not quite rain, but more than mist. He shifted his weight in the saddle again, trying to relieve the soreness

bove the rise was a darkness in the distance, with a green-
h cast.

"Will it rain harder?" asked Sylenia.

"No," answered Ayrlyn. "It will probably stop in a while."

Nylan frowned, looking again at the greenish darkness in
ae distance, wondering if Ayrlyn was right about the rain.

The three followed the road up the rise, past the deserted
ean fields.

Ayrlyn reined up. So did Nylan.

Across the low depression from them, a depression filled
vith fields, perhaps two kays away, rose a wall of green,
arouded slightly by the misty rain.

Nylan shivered. Not clouds, but towering trees.

"The forest . . . never have I seen such," marveled Sylenia.

Nylan's eyes went to the low expanse before them, and he
udied the irregular lines of greenery that spilled across the
bandoned fields. Then he tried to extend his feelings, those
nadowy perceptions he used when smithing, toward the
cene below.

Like two hammer blows, a line of darkness and a line of
vhiteness, unseen, only felt, lashed at him, and he swayed in
ae saddle, grabbing on to the front rim to catch his balance.
lis eyes watered and flashed, and he gasped, trying to catch
is breath.

"What did you do?" asked Ayrlyn in a low voice.

Nylan rubbed his forehead. "Just tried . . . tried to feel what
appened down there." He swallowed, still trying to massage
way the throbbing in his skull.

"It's been abandoned."

"Not for long." He pointed. "See . . . those fields were
arned, probably last fall."

"But trees don't grow that fast. It would take several
ears . . ." Ayrlyn broke off.

"The enchanted forest," Nylan reminded her. "Over there,
looks as though someone tried to burn it back." He rubbed
is forehead. "There's almost a faint overlay of chaos around
aere."

Ayrlyn's eyes glazed momentarily. "That layer beneath th ground?"

"Not exactly." Nylan took a deep breath. "The chaos is o top. The stuff underground is almost gone." The smith close his eyes, and rubbed his temples. "I'm tired, and we need think. Let's stop there." He pointed toward a house on th upper part of the rise that was not quite a hill. Like all the oth ers, it was brick, with a tile roof. Even through the continu ing misting rain, he could sense that, behind the screen o bushes, the door hung open. There was a brick shed ju downhill of the house, also empty, with its door ajar. Th strain of trying to sense what he could not see intensified h headache, and he massaged his temples again.

"Are you all right?"

He nodded and flicked the mare's reins. Certainly, he wa all right. Stuck in the middle of an enemy's land, at the edg of an order-enchanted forest that didn't seem exactly friendl with almost no ability to defend himself, and little food, an a splitting headache and unreliable vision. Trying to prote his son and keep his word to Istril and keep faith with Ay lyn, not to mention trying to find a way to stop an invasio by the most powerful nation in Candar. Of course, he was fin Just fine.

CXVI

PLICK . . . PLICK . . . PLICK . . .

Nylan slowly opened his eyes, wondering what the strang sound might be for a moment before he recognized the im pact of rain dripping off the tile eaves of the house. Rain . how long had it been since he'd heard rain?

He sat up on the bedroll. Ayrlyn, Sylenia, and Weryl sti slept. They had decided to all sleep in the main room, at lea the first night.

Rather than wake them, he surveyed the house again, trying to learn more about Cyador from the house itself. Although it contained only three rooms, all the floors were glazed tile, with a design of interlocking triangles, and the interior walls were a clean and pale yellow plaster. All furnishings, and any furniture there might have been, were gone, which argued that the inhabitants had not fled willy-nilly, since the floors bore only a relatively thin layer of dust.

Set in the floor two cubits back from the door, and curving to shield all view of the interior of the house, was a floor-to-ceiling screen of fired ceramic lace, glazed green. A brick stove was built into the west wall of the main room, with not only an oven, but a copper cooking surface bordered by ceramic tile. The oven door was a burnished copper, decorated with intertwined roses hammered out in a raised design.

Wufff . . . uffff . . . Through the half-open shutters came the sound of the horses from the shed barely big enough for them. Nylan had been reluctant to leave them out, not knowing what might come prowling from the forest.

"How long have you been awake?" asked Ayrlyn sleepily, hushing her voice as she realized that Sylenia and Weryl still slept.

"Awhile," he whispered back, reaching over and hugging her.

"Oooo . . ." Weryl's chubby fists pumped the air.

Sylenia sat bolt upright, then looked around.

"It's all right," Nylan said.

Ayrlyn eased herself away from Nylan and looked around. "I never would have guessed. It's so plain outside."

"This is just a common house," Nylan said. "You can tell that by its size."

"But . . . stoves, and . . ." Ayrlyn frowned, then stretched.

The smith pulled on his boots and stood, slowly, stiffly. The roof had been welcome, but the floor had been hard, even with his bedroll.

Nylan did not attempt to explain again, though he suspected his explanation of the night before had not been exactly coherent. "It's in working order, but we'd need

something to cook—which we don't have at the moment—
and some wood."

"Wadah? Piscut?" Weryl marched almost stiff-legged to
ward his father.

"We still have a biscuit or two, young man, and water.
Nylan swept his son into his arms and hugged him.

"Wadah?"

"All right." Nylan set Weryl down.

The boy marched to Ayrlyn, offering a hug, and askin
"Wadah, pease?"

"I'm going." The smith unbarred the rear door, twice
thick as the front, and with double brackets for bars, althoug
Nylan had only used one on the rear door the night befor
since there had only been two bars left in the vaca
dwelling—one for each door.

The well had a long-handled pump. Although the hand
itself was a dark polished wood, the links and rods were
the white bronze that seemed the most predominant metal i
Cyador.

After filling the sole bucket, handleless and leaky, whic
might have been why it had been left, Nylan washed up
best he could, then refilled the bucket with clean water b
fore pumping more water and letting it flow into the troug
below the pump. Ayrlyn stumbled out into the cloudy mor
ing, opened the shed and led the horses out for water.

As he pumped, Nylan glanced to the wall of green to th
south and the abandoned fields. The green shoots that had i
vaded the fields seemed taller. His eyes dropped to the low
damp places in the hard ground of the yard where the wat
from the night's rain had collected. There were several spec
of green, and cracks in the brown clay—the kind of circul
cracks made just before growing plants broke the surface.

"Nylan?"

"Huhh?"

"You've pumped enough," Ayrlyn said, gesturing towa
the overflowing trough. "What were you thinking about?"

Whufff . . . The chestnut edged Nylan's mare before dro
ping her head to drink.

"The forest. I'd swear it's grown since last night—not the central part, but all the shoots in the fields."

"It probably has, but your son is still asking for water, and my stomach is growling." The redhead picked up the bucket and held it under the curved greenish bronze spout.

By the time they were back in the main room, Sylenia had opened the food pack and laid out half a dozen biscuits and the small slab of cheese remaining. Weryl was already half-chewing, half-gumming his biscuit.

"I could use tea, or something." Ayrlyn eased herself into a cross-legged position on the tile floor.

Nylan set down the bucket, then picked it up. "I'll have to fill water bottles. This leaks too much." Taking one bottle in his free hand, he walked back out to the pump. After setting the bucket on the trough, he filled the water bottle from the pump and walked back inside. He handed the water bottle to Ayrlyn, then sat down, hacked off a chunk of the ever-harder cheese with his knife, and extended it to Sylenia. He cut a smaller chunk for Weryl.

"Eése . . . eese!" The cheese went straight into the silver-haired boy's mouth.

"He knows what he wants. Like his father." Ayrlyn grinned momentarily.

"You know what you want, too, woman."

"Of course."

Nylan had to wipe off the bottle after Weryl slurped his fill, but then he was getting resigned to the fact that children equaled constant cleanup.

The biscuit and cheese took the edge off the gnawing in his stomach, but not much more.

"You must . . . explore this forest?" asked Sylenia.

"Some way or another," Nylan admitted.

"While you . . . I could find some food. There are bean plants and some yams, I think. We have a pot. But this . . . stove . . ."

Ayrlyn glanced at Nylan. "You're the engineer."

"I can show you how to use the stove. It's easier, much easier than a fire. Believe me. It's a lot harder to burn food. You can if you work at it, but . . ."

The redhead stepped toward the rear door. "I'll take care of the horses."

Ayrlyn had groomed and saddled the two mares by the time Nylan had explained everything he could about the stove, checked the chimney and the flue, and thoroughly reassured Sylenia. Belatedly, he remembered to hand her his striker.

After he mounted the mare, he glanced toward the rear door of the house, where Sylenia stood with Weryl.

"Best you be careful." The nursemaid's eyes dropped.

"We will." The silver-haired angel turned the mare, following Ayrlyn, and they rode slowly southward, across a neatly banked and empty irrigation ditch, and into the bean field.

Nylan glanced down at the bean plants, and the leaves that seemed to be wilting despite the night's rain, then started to extend his perceptions.

"Don't!" hissed Ayrlyn from her chestnut.

Even as she spoke, Nylan could sense that same coiling of dark order force and white chaos, as if poised to strike, and he pulled back into himself.

Whufff . . . Nylan's mare sidestepped.

"Even she can feel it."

Almost as if an echo, the chestnut shuffled her feet as well.

"I get the image," Nylan answered.

"They were pretty well organized." Ayrlyn's eyes traversed the fields and the well-maintained ditching.

"Probably still are, away from the forest." He had to wonder what they could find in an enchanted forest that would help them defeat or at least stop a land that could provide high-class ceramics, stoves, and large-scale irrigation works, not to mention firewagons, fireballs, and who knew what else.

Silently, Nylan rode through the green shoots that reached nearly to the mare's withers, trying to guide her through the more open areas. The flatness of the ground was deceiving, so deceiving that when he looked back toward the house, he realized that they had covered several kays, and still had not reached the taller growth, although the ground they crossed held black cinders, cinders and ashes.

"Someone tried to burn this back, with that chaos flame, I think," said Ayrlyn.

Once Ayrlyn had called it to his attention, he also could feel the faint residue of chaos laid across the balance that the shoots embodied.

"Didn't do them a lot of good."

"I wonder. There's more here that we don't know."

Despite his curiosity, Nylan did not try to extend his perceptions, but left them open to pick up images, hoping that would give him enough warning.

"Careful . . ."

"I'm just listening." Even without straining he could sense the order/chaos pulse of the forest, so strong that he felt like some sort of insect creeping around a giant.

"It makes you feel that way," Ayrlyn noted.

"You're doing it again."

"So? You could tell I feel that way, if you wanted. We've been through this before."

He did not answer, instead trying to sense not only the forest, but Ayrlyn.

Ayrlyn—flame, banked, who felt what? Awe, fear, and yet who *knew* that the forest held the key.

Nylan wished he had her faith.

The shoots got thicker and thicker, but not any closer together, and grew in a pattern of sorts that seemed more defined the closer they rode up toward the older growth that towered into the gray sky.

Abruptly, the mare sidestepped again, turning away from the dark line of the older trees. Nylan reined up.

"Mine won't either," announced Ayrlyn.

"Hmmmm . . ." Nylan dismounted, and handed the mare's reins up to Ayrlyn. "I don't see anything. There's not that much undergrowth here." He took several steps toward the older trees of the forest, then paused, looking back at Ayrlyn and the mounts.

The redhead shrugged.

He walked another ten cubits and paused, looking down at a knee-high growth of creepers that extended both east and west as far as he could make out. Between the leaves he could see scattered traces of white—some form of stone.

"There was a wall here," he called back softly.

"I can feel it."

Slowly, Nylan stepped over the low barrier, scanning the area around, listening with ears and senses. While the sense of looming dark order and pulsing white chaos was fractionally stronger, nothing changed. In a way, that bothered him as much as if something had changed.

Abruptly, he turned and walked back to Ayrlyn.

"Let's head back and think about this."

She nodded.

They both understood. Merely looking and physically searching wasn't going to yield what they sought.

CXVII

Two officers in white uniforms, with green sashes, stood in the small room that contained little more than a flat wooden table, five wooden chairs, and several easels with maps upon them.

"Angels . . . riding in the direction of the Accursed Forest." Majer Piataphi handed the scroll back to the marshal. "Ser . . . I cannot tell that to His Mightiness. I cannot tell him that three of them, just three, destroyed a local patrol and vanished."

"You are a lancer officer, under my command, Majer," Queras stated flatly.

"As such, ser, I must offer my best judgment. This is not a good idea. I am not in charge of the border patrols or the local patrols."

"You are under my command, Majer." Queras's voice turned chill. "All Mirror Lancer officers are. You will follow my commands."

"You can only execute me for failing to carry out an order—and then you will have to reveal what that order was." Piataphi smiled bitterly. "The way His Mightiness feels about me . . . I would be turned into flame before him. After he flamed me, or if he did not flame me, ser, how would he feel about your trying to divert responsibility? Remember what he did to the officers of the Eighth?" Piataphi's words were level, and he did not blink as he regarded the senior officer.

"Brave you may be, Majer," said Queras as he finally shook his head, "but wise you are not. You defy me, and you lost an entire command, and allowed the barbarians to drive you from our lands. Our lands. That shows little wisdom."

"Yes, ser. That is why I must be honest. I have little left but that. I know the white mage stands by Lord Lephi, and he would know if I deceived."

Queras's eyes raked over Piataphi.

"Follow the Emperor's commands," added the majer. "Do not tell him nor return until we are ready to march."

"And the angels, O wisest of unwise lancers? How, pray tell, would your unwisdom address them?"

"If we prevail against the barbarians, then there will be time to deal with them and the forest. Even the white mages have left the Accursed Forest to deal with the grassland hordes." Piataphi smiled again, tightly. "And if we fail . . . then we have no worries."

"I am certain we will have no worries. Very certain. You will lead every charge."

"Yes, ser." Piataphi nodded fatalistically.

CXVIII

THE TWO ANGELS sat on the grass before the bushes that screened the front door. The clouds had broken the day before, and the unfamiliar stars glittered brightly in the early night.

Weryl snored inside, and the faint odor of some form of

vegetable soup being undertaken by Sylenia seeped from the house, mixing with the damp and subtle fragrances drifting from the forest.

"Pleasant," Nylan said. "First time in I don't know how long that we haven't been running or fighting or—"

"Peaceful." Ayrlyn leaned her head against his, her hair still damp from washing.

"Almost like we're under the shelter of a huge unseen mountain."

"A growing mountain. There are shoots in the back now, all around the house and shed."

"It's been waiting a long time," he pointed out.

"Either that or sleeping."

Nylan yawned, as a dreaminess passed across him, and he could feel that Ayrlyn experienced it, too.

"Just feel it," she whispered.

He took a slow and deep breath, then another, and could feel . . . he would have been hard-pressed to describe the sensation, although the images carried by the flows of that unseen power were clear.

Vivid images . . . almost rising before them, yet ancient images, images of a distant past . . . that also was somehow obvious. A history?

A green spark, a living spark, with light and dark entwined, grew within a forest, and from that came other sparks, all linked, and the sparks spread, ever so slowly, until they carried flows, flows of light and darkness, order and chaos, that held the forest, that were the forest, as ever so slowly all the trees took on the sparks, the light and the darkness.

The rain fell, and under the green-blue sky, the trees grew, and died, and the deer roamed, and grew and died, and so did the tawny cats, and the tree rats, and the wide purple blossoms, and the ugly-snouted lizards.

The dark flows of blackness and the white chaos were mixed and twisted—and balanced. The trees grew and grew, and some died and fell, but always for all the changes, the white and darkness turned in and out, but balanced . . . until the heavens shivered, and the ground trembled.

Then . . . lines of fire flickered, white lines, force fluxes like a chaotic power net, firebolts white-infused and red-shaded like those thrown by the wizards who had tried to storm Westwind . . . and the white unbalanced forces lashed across the forest, across the grasslands to the north and west, across the stony hills beyond the grasslands.

White lines of fire, fire that reflected light and darkness, burned through the forest, and the gray ashes fell like rain.

The forest struggled, and sent forth new shoots, and the white fires slashed across the shoots, twisting the flows, sending shudders through the ground itself, creating heat and tangled fires deep beneath Candar.

The rivers heaved themselves out of their banks, and the white mirror fires turned their waters into steam. Metal mountains grumbled across the water-polished stone hills and smoothed them, ground them, and suffocated them beneath strange new soil, and grasses that had never been.

Green shoots struggled through the ashes, and were turned into more ashes, and the ground heaved and trembled.

Lines of white stone slammed down like walls, pinning the trees behind lines of force that burned . . . and burned, burned somehow because the force of the ordered chaos that prisoned the trees was backward, because chaos bound order.

A sense of timelessness followed, inaction behind white stone walls, until the heavens shivered again, and the white walls cracked, and crumbled, and lines of white fire and darkness cascaded from ice-tipped peaks.

And the balanced flow of light and darkness resumed, with a sense of something like purpose and joy—except it was neither—and the dark presence of the forest mountain loomed.

Nylan shivered and wiped his suddenly damp forehead. A tree . . . or a clone group of trees, like the ancient aspens of pre-Heaven . . . had that been the beginning of the forest? The forest did not know; it only felt and sensed. Yet it had a vague concept of self, a concept that . . .

"How would you translate that," he asked.

"I wouldn't. Just call it Nados or Naclos or Nasclos . . . something phonetic like that. It won't mind."

"Naclos," the engineer decided. "Not that it means much."

"It means 'Great Forest' or something like it."

"It is great."

"So much power," murmured Ayrlyn.

"It wasn't very effective against the Old Rats."

"It wasn't? How do we know? Also, it has a longer perspective. The old barriers, whatever they were, have failed, and the forest seems to be well on the way to regaining its former position."

"Unless those white wizards return with something stronger."

"Maybe they left to do something else?" she suggested.

"Like fight Lornth? Why would they do that?"

Ayrlyn shrugged. "We're missing a lot of pieces. That's just what I feel, but I couldn't tell you why."

Although the night was warm, Nylan felt cold, almost alone under the looming yet unseen shadow of the forest. "I'm too tired to think."

Ayrlyn slipped to her feet. "So am I. Maybe sleeping on it will help."

Nylan wasn't certain about that, either, but he rose, slowly, inhaling the half-familiar smell of the vegetable soup as they walked back to the small house under the glittering light-points of the still-strange stars.

CXIX

NYLAN BLOTTED HIS forehead one-handed as he rode through the young trees that nearly reached his chest. The air was moister, but even in full afternoon sun with the sun falling full on his back, not nearly so hot as it had been in southern Lornth. The forest's impact, he supposed.

As they neared the older growth, rising nearly a hundred cubits overhead, the mare sidestepped, then snorted, and tossed her head.

"She doesn't want to enter the old part of the forest." As he spoke Nylan realized how stupid the words sounded. He felt stupid.

They'd ridden up and down the borders of the forest, but everywhere was the same—spreading greenery, scattered and abandoned houses of a sophistication far above anything they had seen elsewhere in Candar . . . and the same unseen and looming sense of the forest, with its balanced flows of order and chaos.

It was like a riddle, a simple, but impossible riddle, and riddles had always made the smith feel stupid, because they were so obvious after the fact, and made him feel like he wanted to take something and bang his head or smash the riddler. But there was no way, and no point, to smash something like the forest. Still, he was beginning to understand why the Cyadorans had referred to it as accursed.

"It's not that bad," Ayrlyn suggested.

"I'm just frustrated. Every day we putter around here is another day that the Cyadorans could be attacking Lornth, another day wasted." The silver-haired angel dismounted and tied the mare's reins to one of the larger shoot-trunks. So did Ayrlyn.

"So you want to ride back to Syskar and get slaughtered after the first charge of the Cyadorans?"

Ayrlyn's commonsense retort just made him feel more imbecilic. Instead of answering, he began to walk through the growing forest back toward the older growth, the towering dark trunks that stretched toward the green-blue sky.

His boots crackled, and he looked down at the desiccated and browning bean leaves and stalks. "It doesn't care much for crops."

"Or monoculture," added the flame-haired angel.

Nylan stopped short of the creeper-covered wall, now only calf-high. "It's lower. It shouldn't be able to work this fast."

"There are a lot of things that shouldn't happen here."

Nylan half-snorted. About that, she was certainly right. But those impossible happenings occurred all the same. He took a deep breath, then another, and stepped over the disintegrating white gravel that had been polished stone not that long before.

"Careful . . ."

The angel smith glanced around. Where he stood was in full shade, but otherwise felt no different from the newer growth.

Whuffff . . . uffff . . .

"Easy . . . easy . . ." Ayrlyn's words carried, and both mares seemed to settle down.

Nylan continued to survey the deeper growth to the south, his hand on the hilt of the shortsword at his waist as he turned his head to see what might have spooked the mounts.

To the south the trunks were spaced more widely, and clear openings ran deeper into the woods, almost like pathways. There was a sense of . . . organization, but how could a forest without more than rudimentary self-consciousness be organized?

"Balance," suggested Ayrlyn as she stepped over the former wall and up beside him.

"Great. What do we do with balance?"

"Think about it."

All he'd been doing was thinking about it, thinking about it and walking around it, and studying it . . . and what had he learned? Not much.

"We've learned that it can flatten you from a distance," pointed out the redhead. "And that even the Old Rats couldn't destroy it, but only confine it."

"Or chose not to."

"If they could have destroyed it and didn't, given their inclinations, it meant there was a good reason why. One based in sheer power, I'd bet."

Nylan yanked out the shortsword and began to walk along the de facto pathway deeper into the forest.

With a look over her shoulder, Ayrlyn followed.

The deeper woods were quiet, shadowed, with the same sense of everything in its place. A mixture of odors, like a muted and unfamiliar floral perfume, permeated the cool shade.

Nylan edged around a smooth-barked tree a good four cubits in girth.

Grrrrr. . . .

Across an open space of less than ten cubits, at the base of a rough, gray-barked tree with fissured ridges and a trunk nearly as big around as the shed that stabled the horses, crouched a tawny cat. Bigger than any of the few Nylan had seen in the Westhorns, its body was more than five cubits long, and teeth like white daggers glistened in the shadows.

The smith's fingers tightened on the heavy blade he carried.

"Don't . . ." hissed Ayrlyn. "Just lower the blade and back away."

Nylan paused. He hated to be backing up if the cat tried to pounce.

"Nylan . . ."

He lowered the blade, and took one step backward, then another.

Grrrr . . .

As he backtracked, he lost sight of the great cat, but kept listening for movement, watching for the slightest sign. Ayrlyn retreated with him, except more silently, and she had left her blade sheathed.

Moving backwards, it felt to Nylan that it took most of the afternoon to reach the creeper-covered wall, but the sun still hung midway in the afternoon sky when he stepped out of the older growth. "Why did you tell me to lower the blade?"

"Balance. It felt right."

With a glance back toward the old growth, Nylan finally sheathed the blade, then wiped his forehead. He looked toward the towering trunks again.

"The cat won't follow us," she said.

"You sound so sure."

"I feel sure, and that's funny, because I don't know why." The redhead gave a nervous laugh.

"You were right. I wish you knew why," Nylan said.

"It has to do with balance." She spread her hands, almost helplessly. "I know it does. We're still missing pieces."

"We probably always will be, but we have to do something."

"Such as?"

"We need to provide it with some direction," suggested Nylan.

"How?"

Nylan sat up straighter. "I don't know. Even trying to use any control of order flows seems to set off a reaction."

"Balance . . . that's the message."

"But why? It doesn't really think, not the way we do."

"Does it have to?" asked the redhead dryly. "That's our job, and we aren't doing very well at it."

The silver-haired angel untied the mare. "We need to think some more. Or talk. Or something."

"You didn't want to think," she said with a faint smile.

"I have . . . we have . . . to think smarter . . . somehow. And I'm hungry." *And tired and worried and frustrated, and that's just for starters.*

"I know," Ayrlyn answered softly. *I know. . . .*

CXX

THE SILVER-HAIRED angel plopped on the ground in front of the bushes, setting Weryl down between his legs, and glancing out across the kays of lower lands filled with tree shoots that separated the house from the older growth of the forest.

He ran his hand across his chin, clean-shaven, and with a few cuts. His hand-forged equivalent of a straight razor wasn't especially forgiving, especially when there was no equivalent of soap around. Water oozed down his neck from his damp hair.

The grass that had covered the hillside was turning blotchy brown in some places, and not others, and he wondered what pattern the forest had in mind, if it had a mind, for where there would be grass and where there would not.

Weryl levered himself up by grabbing Nylan's right knee, then stiff-legged his way to the nearest bush, where his fingers closed on a branch, gently.

Ayrlyn sat down beside Nylan, her short hair damp from her efforts to wash it. "What are you thinking this cloudy morning?"

He glanced at the low gray clouds, then at her. "The forest is the key to it all." Nylan felt stupid—again—for stating the obvious, but the obvious was all he had.

"Do you know why?"

"No. Not exactly. The whole planet is like a ship's flux system—enormous power, constrained by order, with a continual swirl of lesser fluxes." Nylan swallowed, then rubbed an itching nose. "The white stuff—what we call chaos—that's where most of the power lies. Order—the dark flows—they're more like boundaries than real flows, and they maintain the system. You need both."

"You've made progress."

"It's all taxonomy, just reclassifying the stuff we've known already."

Weryl released the first branch, glanced back at his father, then walked perhaps ten cubits before sitting down with a *plop* to study a green shoot growing in a crack between two stones of the front walk. His fingers stroked the green, gently.

"If there's no chaos, there's no energy to run the system," observed Ayrlyn. "Without your order, then you'd have uncontrolled energy that would swirl out and dissipate in entropic heat?"

"I don't know. That's my guess. There's got to be a balance, and somehow the Old Rats maintained that balance. Something happened—"

"What are you going to do?"

"We're going to act as system engineers, I guess."

"I'm no engineer."

"This isn't a ship's system, either. It takes feel. That's where you come in."

"Oh?"

"I'm going to try to feel out the system."

"After what's already happened?"

"We'll try it just inside the old growth."

"We're going to walk into *that*?" Ayrlyn frowned.

"Why not? As we found out, it can hit hard even from a distance. What's the difference between being in the middle of a flux or standing at the edge if it goes chaos?"

Ayrlyn grinned wryly. "Only the size of the particles that you're reduced to, but I don't know that I'm in the mood to be reduced."

"Before you do battle with the forest," suggested Sylenia, standing by the edge of the bushes, "best you eat."

"She has a point." Nylan lurched to his feet and toward Weryl, scooping his son up and carting him back into the small house. The smith's shoulder brushed the green-glazed ceramic screen. Such artistry—all abandoned so quickly. Then he supposed he'd have abandoned it too, especially if there were a lot of those big cats prowling around. The locals, Ayrlyn had pointed out, didn't carry much in the way of weapons.

Several loaves of bread were spread on wide leaves, along with some nuts and what looked to be yellow apples.

"Those are pearapples," Sylenia explained. "Yusek brought me one, once. These are better. They are fresher."

Nylan sliced off a chunk of the loaf and chewed the moist and tangy bread. "What . . . is this . . . ?"

"It be squash loaf. I can bake. With but one pot . . ." The dark-haired woman shrugged. "Weryl, he is good at finding the healthy fruits and things. I follow him."

Ayrlyn looked at Weryl. So did Nylan. Was Weryl sensing the forest the way he did the notes from the lutar?

"Da! Ahwen!"

"Does this bread keep? For travel?" asked Ayrlyn. "We'll need something on the way back."

If we get that far.

Ayrlyn frowned. "Pessimist."

"I could wrap it in leaves." Sylenia shrugged. "Do you plan to leave soon?"

"Not that soon," Ayrlyn said after taking a swallow of water. "The nuts are good."

"They must be cooked, or they are bitter."

Nylan was glad Sylenia knew about the local vegetation. He probably would have starved. Then, those of them in Westwind nearly had in the first year, at least partly out of ignorance. He tried the nuts, and they were tasty. He kept eating until he realized that he was no longer hungry, but that he was almost stuffing food into his mouth.

"Nervous?"

Nylan nodded. "You?"

"Of course."

He wiped his mouth and took another low swallow of water, then stood.

"Da! Ahwen!"

Nylan bent and lifted Weryl, hugging him tightly for a moment. Weryl hugged him back, then turned his head.

"He wants to give you a hug." Nylan eased Weryl toward the redhead.

Ayrlyn embraced the silver-haired boy, and Nylan could sense her tears. "Be good, Weryl. Be good." She set him on the glazed tile floor, and Sylenia immediately took his hand.

Nylan swallowed. *Am I doing the right thing? Have I any choice?*

No, came the thought from Ayrlyn.

They walked quickly out the rear door to where the mounts they had saddled earlier waited.

"This is scary," he admitted after climbing into the saddle.

She nodded, pursing her lips.

They rode into the growing outer forest without speaking, letting the mares pick their way toward the unseen wall and the boundary between the ancient domain of the forest and its recent acquisition.

"We can do this. We just have to think about balance."

"Thinking about it is easy, but trying to make ourselves part of it isn't going to be easy."

"Nothing important ever is."

Nylan nodded. She was right about that.

After tying both mares to trunks that were noticeably thicker than the day before, the two walked slowly toward the creeper-covered wall that was measurably lower than the day before.

"For something that doesn't think, it's certainly removing its past boundaries quickly enough," Ayrlyn noted.

"Thought and intelligence are just illusions that primates glory in." Nylan's voice was dry. So was his mouth. The narrow gray-green leaves on the new trees seemed to rustle, though he could sense no breeze, and a mist drifted out from the older growth, carrying the unfamiliar mixed floral scent that was neither too cloying nor too astringent.

Nylan swallowed and stepped across the creepered and vanishing wall. He swallowed again, and tried to relax.

Ayrlyn touched his arm. "We're doing this together, remember."

What were they doing?

Nylan finally let his thoughts drift outward, as though he were still on the powernet of the *Winterlance*, letting his mind follow his senses through the mist, through the green shoots, through the intertwining of the hot reddish white of chaos, and the cool black bands of order. Beside him, he could sense the order-rooted solidity of Ayrlyn, and even the distant presence of Weryl, though his son seemed a more innocent balance between darkness and chaos.

Their progress seemed nearly effortless, as they stood there yet moved through the swirls of darkness, jets of chaos, and unseen and intertwined webs where the two forces merged. Yet there was no gray, only black and white, a blackness deeper than night, a whiteness tinged with sullen red, like the hot coals of a smithy.

Beneath the surface flows was a deeper, more intricate intertwining of order and chaos. Why was the pseudonet flux more simple in the open air? Was it the earth? Or was everything more complex the deeper one went?

Nylan took another breath, then tried to let his senses take the subtle mixtures of ordered red and white iron and white chaos that seemed pure fiery destruction. Mixtures of order and chaos, patterns intertwining, tugged at him, drawing him toward them.

There—amid a grove that seemed to grow as he watched—was an upwelling of pure black, somehow power-surged, white-red simultaneously, that wrapped itself around a fountain of white tinged with red. Beyond the fountain was a rhythmic pulsing of smaller order-beats against a squarer kind of chaos, like a powerboard balance.

Nylan cleared his throat, and Ayrlyn's hand touched his elbow, a tinge of dark and comforting order in the fluxes that swirled and rose around them. He relaxed, as he could, and tried to take in, without judgment, the intertwining of order and chaos, trying to let himself drift along the lines of order, along the forces that made the *Winterlance*'s powernet seem insignificant, toward a small fountain of blackness that somehow seemed to geyser deep out of the roots of the forest, deep out of the melting rocks far below Candar, far below Cyador.

Even as his senses neared the fountain, it shifted, toward chaos, and a torrent of white boiled around the blackness, and red chaos oozed, then spurted forth. A cool thread of black beckoned, and for an instant, Nylan felt as though he understood the interweavings of the patterns, like the webs of perfectly matched ships' nets holding and focusing against the Mirror Towers of the Rats.

A line of molten chaos, red with dull white, lashed from nowhere, and needles like precisely focused lasers burned through him. Another thicker band of white began to twine around the engineer's senses, wrapping itself around his knees and oozing ever upward, tightening around his waist.

Nylan started, realizing that he could not just stand and let himself be enfolded, and tried to wrench free—even as another thinner white line slashed at him again, moving impossibly quickly for something rooted in a slow-growing forest.

A band of black, ordered steel slammed at him, and his knees buckled, and another line of white, tinged with red, slashed, and he lifted his arms and turned, trying to protect Ayrlyn from the assault of chaos and who knew what else. His soul and face burned.

"I'm fine." Her words were more felt than heard.

Nylan held to himself, trying to stand above the fluxes, as must any engineer, struggling to pattern what could be patterned, letting flow free the chaos that must flow, and forcing himself, his senses, into a ball of ego.

Nylan! Nylan, the engineer, who holds the fluxes, rides the chaos—that is me. That is who I am! I am Nylan . . . NYLAN!!!!

The lashes of chaos and order continued, but Nylan permitted himself a grim smile as he felt the attacks pause. With another deep breath, with sweat oozing off his forehead, and stinging into his eyes, he could feel the powers of the forest weakening, or backing off, and he increased his efforts, trying to master both the flows and himself before chaotic fluxes rebounded—and he knew they would, for chaos always rebounded.

Ride the flows! Hold the patterns!

He sent that thought to Ayrlyn, pressing order upon her, and received a similar feeling in return, except Ayrlyn was not Ayrlyn, but an intertwined pillar of order and chaos, warm, yet cool.

An image formed—one that Nylan knew was not real—and yet it appeared alive and immediately before him.

A figure in the undress olive blacks of a U.F.A. marine stepped across the turned and settled soil between the lines of knee-high trees. She lifted a black blade shortsword, a blade of Westwind, a blade Nylan knew he had forged.

Nylan strained to see her face, but a shadow cast by no sun remained across the face of the marine who carried no shield, no sidearm, only the short blade. Then, out of the shadows, two dark eyes slashed the engineer.

I rode against the first chaos wizard you fought, face-to-face, and I died. I died, and you live. I understood that we must fight, and I died. You still fight against the need to fight, yet you live on. You are the great engineer, the one who rides the chaos fields, and you abandoned me to the depths of chaos. Great engineer, you sought order where there was none, and a mighty tower because of me, because of those like me are forgotten, and all will remember your name. You re a self-deceiving hypocrite. You claim you want peace, yet wherever you turn, death follows. You establish order, and chaos reigns.

Nylan could not move, and though he could feel Weryl squirm in the distance, he could not reassure the boy—or Ayryn. The words pounded through him: "self-deceiving hypocrite . . . self-deceiving hypocrite . . . self-deceiving . . ."

Then the figure of Cessya raised the shortsword, the blade he had forged, and turning it slightly, slammed it across the side of his face. His entire cheek burned, and he staggered, before catching himself, the words still ringing: "self-deceiving . . . self-deceiving . . ."

He swallowed as the chaos and order swirled around him again, as another figure shimmered into being on the mist-damp soil between the towering trees that seemed to ring him as he watched.

A woman in a brown tunic, dark-haired, barefooted, stood there, her head downcast. Then her face lifted, and she beckoned, as if for Nylan to listen. He looked and saw that her shoulder slumped, almost cut away from her body, and dark, dark red stained the tunic. Blood drooled from the corner of her mouth.

. . . oh, great mage, you saved me, and you saved my daughter, and then you cast me against your enemies so that you would not have to fight. I died, and my daughter wept, and you had no answers. I died, and you could not tell her why. I died, and you lived. How many others died so you might live, great mage?

"No!" insisted Nylan. "It wasn't that way." Except that the words remained in his mind, and his mouth did not move.

. . . but it was. Niera is alone, cold on the heights you have left, with no one to comfort her. You lived, and you built, and you promised. Then you left, and there is no one to explain, no one to comfort. . . .

"You left Gallos without my urging. I didn't even know you."

Nistayna lifted her face and spat, and a gobbet of blood left those dead lips and splattered across Nylan's neck, searing like acid on bare skin.

. . . I took the blade you forged, and I died, and my daugh ter is alone, without mother, without father . . . and you lef Westwind, left my poor Niera . . .

Even as Nylan pushed away the image of Nistayna, anothe swirled into place from the endless mists of the Accursec Forest—endless mists that oozed from the depth of ancien trees and greens. A redheaded marine officer in patchec leathers pulled over olive blacks urged her mount towarc Nylan, then reined up, her blue eyes leveled like lasers at the engineer. One of the twin shortswords jabbed at his chest.

. . . great engineer, great smith . . . the greatest in all Can dar . . .

Great smith? Nylan wanted to snort.

Who else forged the black blades of death that shea through the toughest plate armor? Who else forged the bow of night and the shafts that penetrate all? Who else built the tower that dared the Roof of the World? Who else? You have abandoned all you forged. Tell me I did not die for nothing Tell me that the cairns of Westwind will not wither into mean inglessness. Tell me . . .

Each question raised by Fierral ripped into Nylan. Eacl one. Had the marine officer died for nothing? Had Nistayna been right? No!

Nylan refused to accept that. Order did not require that a tower or a patch of ground be defended forever, to and be yond death. Neither did chaos. There was a time to defend and a time not to defend, a time to fight and a time to flee, a time to build and a time to tear down, a time to accept the past and a time to reject it.

He stood unmoving, thrusting away the image of the deac marine and guard. Yet, before she faded, the blade he hac forged spun toward the smith, turning end over end, so slowly The razor edge nicked his left shoulder, barely missing Ayr lyn, and a gout of flame puffed from the wound, his own blooc flaming as it oozed from his skin, burning, aching.

Come . . . great forger of destruction . . . welder o chaos . . . receive your just reward. . . .

Another figure rose from the swirling fog of order anc

chaos—a black-haired, black-bearded man cloaked in purple, who wore maroon leather trousers, and a tunic of purple that matched the cloak. In his shoulder harness was a two-hand broadsword. He smiled, and his entire body was consumed in flames, yet he was untouched.

Behind the black-bearded man, Nylan felt the rising hordes of the dead, felt the purple-clad soldiers that marched toward an unseen black tower, felt the shadowy presence of white-cloaked chaos wizards.

You mean well, great smith and destroyer . . . and so did . . . join me, for we are alike.

Nylan looked down, beyond Ayrlyn, almost unnaturally silent beside him, to the shoulder where blood, flame, and red-whitened ashes flowed, feeling more blood and ashes weeping from his injured face, wounds that ached with the pain beyond pain.

. . . join me . . . for did you not destroy thousands with the best of intentions . . . did you not forge death and more death to save but a handful of ungrateful women?

The smith forced his eyes back to the Lornian leader. What couldn't he see? Why had every figure he had dismissed brought up another with more disturbing questions?

. . . join us . . . join us, for you deceive yourself as you believe the world deceives itself. While you talk of balance, you believe in forging an order, your order. Like us, you are a believer in self-order, a believer in deception . . . deception . . .

The big sword swung toward Nylan, and he ducked, but his skull jolted, and fire seared across his eyes. Smoke rose, and he smelled burning hair. His own hair?

You cannot escape yourself. You would be a hero . . . and heroes never escape. They deceive themselves so they may always create more destruction to save yet another lost soul, another poor victim . . . until they lose themselves to their deceptions. You are the great smith, the great hero of Candar and the Westwind . . . and you will be lost to your heroism, great mage . . . join us . . . for you cannot escape . . . you cannot relinquish the need to save all who need saving.

. . . cannot relinquish . . . cannot relinquish—the thought

reverberated through Nylan. Why couldn't he relinquish the need to save? Why not?

As the burns seared his arms, and his skull hammered, he swallowed, and ignoring the burns, the smoke, the pain, lowered his head, accepting that he could not save the world. Accepting that he tried to save so many because of his own unworthiness, because he had to prove that he was . . . was always . . . had always been . . . worthy.

Above him, impossibly distant, the trees rustled, and the ground trembled, and a huge tawny cat padded toward Nylan, blue eyes burning.

Nylan waited.

Grrrurrrr . . . rrrrrrurrr . . .

Order and chaos swirled around and through him, and he understood, not just with his head, but with his heart, his feelings, that they were not separate, but two sides of the same coin, understood that one could fight neither chaos nor order, but only those who misused one side of that coin. He understood, too, that the evils fostered by Cyador and by Westwind would be countered by equal evils.

And the great smith's eyes burned, and, standing motionless before the great cat and the Great Forest, he shuddered.

Beside him, nearly simultaneously, Ayrlyn shuddered, and Nylan knew she had fought her own demons, and they shivered together, in a cold beyond cold, and a heat beyond heat.

So did the soil, and the trees, and even the grasses that surged along the new-forged lines of balance, seeking the old patterns sundered by the mighty planoforming engines of the Rationalists, engines that had ignored the balance that had been and would be.

The fluxfires of the Great Forest, of the depths, and of all that struggled slashed through Nylan, and through Ayrlyn, and their pain intertwined and redoubled, and they shuddered again, in the agony of discovering the balance of order and chaos within.

Nylan staggered, and glanced toward Ayrlyn, standing on the firm damp soil between mighty trees. Her fair face was crisscrossed with burns, and blisters sprouted on her forehead.

"Darkness . . ." he murmured.

"You, too," she choked back.

His head throbbed, as though it had been squeezed between his tongs or flattened by his own hammer and anvil. Small sharp lances stabbed through his eyelids. A heavy dark welt was turning into an ugly bruise on his left arm, as was another across his neck.

"You still think this . . . was a good idea?" Ayrlyn's words seemed to waver in and out of Nylan's ears.

"No, except I didn't have any better ideas." After several swallows, the smith finally was able to moisten his dry lips.

"Some day . . . some day . . . do you think we'll learn not to meddle?" she asked.

"I doubt it."

"Darkness help us." Ayrlyn staggered, then caught her balance.

RRRrrrrrrr . . .

They both suddenly looked at the big cat, sitting on its haunches no more than a dozen cubits away, blue eyes still fixed on them. Then, the cat yawned, showing long white teeth, long pointed teeth, and stretched. After another yawn, it padded back and was lost in the ancient trees.

"Whewww . . ." said Nylan.

"Frig . . ."

"That's another way of putting it." The smith swallowed, still trying to sort out what the whole experience had meant. He glanced toward the taller trees, realizing as he did that, even without trying, he saw, and almost understood, the ebb and flow of order and chaos, chaos and order. He sensed those flows, effortlessly, and he saw the wrongness that underlay it all.

He swallowed and looked back at Ayrlyn. "What did you see?"

"The worst of myself." Ayrlyn shuddered for a moment. "How all of Candar is slanted."

"Slanted?" As he asked the question, Nylan shuddered, involuntarily thinking about the worst of himself—the endless twists toward self-deception and trying to avoid facing what was.

"It feels . . . slanted . . . from way down."

The smith nodded. She was right. It did, and when he and she had rested some, then they'd look into it. But they needed rest.

He looked upward.

The featureless gray clouds were beginning to separate into still indistinct but separate, darker, and more ominous chunks of gray, and the mist had stopped falling. It appeared near midday.

Midday?

"It took awhile," Ayrlyn said. "That sort of self-examination usually does."

"And the cat was sitting there all the time?"

"Probably. We would have been dinner if we'd failed."

Nylan shuddered again, as he turned back toward the mares.

Overhead, the clouds roiled, and the deep roll of thunder rumbled across the forest.

CXXI

AYRLYN CAREFULLY BLOTTED away the flaking and blistered skin, trying not to wince as she did.

Nylan moved the pump lever with his left hand, bending down and letting the cool water flow over his face. A day later, he still felt blistered and burned, and the left side of his body—symbolism made real?—was bruised from his cheek to his waist, not to mention the slash on his arm.

He knew that the body could manufacture wounds—but the slashes and burns on his shirt and leathers were another question.

Slowly, he straightened, trying not to breathe too deeply to avoid the aches in his chest and ribs. The air was cool, still damp, from the thunderstorms that had raged much of the night.

"A pretty pair you be." Sylenia took the bucket, which she

ad made less leaky with wood slivers and some form of
aste glue she'd concocted, and began to fill it. "You walked
nto a forest, and you return as though you have fought the
re demons, and you ride back through a storm, and you
mile." She shook her head. "The storms rage, and you sleep
he sleep of the dead. This morning you look no better, and
worse than after many battles. Yet you smile."

"We weren't looking forward to meeting the forest," Nylan
dmitted.

"You did battle with it," snorted the dark-haired woman.
Battling the white demons, that I can understand, but a for-
st?"

Ayrlyn smiled, a bit sadly.

"The Cyadorans fought it. They tried to wall it away,"
Nylan pointed out.

"Much good it did them."

Although Sylenia had a point in one way, Nylan still won-
ered. Cyador had stood for far longer than Lornth.

"I do not understand," said Sylenia after a moment, slow-
ng her pumping. "They did not like the forest. They built
valls around it. There be much land, and yet some lived so
ery close to it."

"Good question," Nylan said. "And there's no one left
round here to answer it, but I have an idea."

"I'd like to hear it," suggested Ayrlyn in a tone that said she
new he wanted to explain, and would anyway, no matter
hat she said.

Nylan flushed, but continued. "The ancient Old Rational-
sts—the white demons—changed much of the land, and the
ower they used . . . it remains beneath the soil in many
laces. I can feel this, and so can Ayrlyn. It's . . . disturbing.
. . They squeezed the ancient forest back and back. But they
ither couldn't totally destroy it, or they worried that
hey shouldn't. Either way, that disturbance beneath the
round thins out the closer you get to the forest." The silver-
aired angel shrugged. "So the closer you get, the less dis-
urbance. That means that those people who might be
ensitive to the chaos beneath the ground, even if they didn't

know what it was, would feel more comfortable living closer."

"There couldn't have been that many," Ayrlyn pointed out. "We've only seen this small village."

"Probably not." Nylan took a swallow from the water bottle, then handed it to Ayrlyn, tightening his lips and trying to ignore the itching that was becoming more frequent from his various wounds. Were they beginning to heal that fast?

"This be too much for me. And young Weryl, he will have everything out of the packs. Again." Sylenia marched back into the house.

After a moment, the smith turned to the healing healer. "Fine. We've learned a little about balance. Now what do we do?"

"We walk back through the forest and learn more. It should be easier this time, now that we've begun to reconcile the balances within ourselves."

"How much easier?" asked Nylan warily.

"I'd still bring blades. We don't know much about the wildlife."

There was far too much they didn't know, and probably too little time. Nylan wanted to shake his head. Fine . . . they understood the balancing of the forest better, and its powers—but how could those be turned against the Cyadorans? Or could they, when the forest had failed before?

"The forest didn't have us," Ayrlyn said. "Let's get the horses saddled."

Nylan could sense the depth of her conviction, but it was conviction, not a plan, and he could also sense that they were running out of time.

The sun hung well above the forest before they reached the area outside the old growth. But even before he tied the mare to another one of the trees in what had been the edge of the Cyadoran field, Nylan could sense that the forest was different—or were they different?

"We're different. The forest grows, but it doesn't change."

"Everything changes but the forest?"

"That's not . . ." Ayrlyn paused. "It changes. Trees grow and die, and plants, but the overall balance doesn't."

"Isn't that life?" he asked, stepping toward where the older growth began.

"On a large enough scale, but humans distort things so much . . ."

Nylan understood the unspoken feelings. Humans pushed the natural balance so far that the reaction was equally violent. He stepped across the slightly raised creeper-covered line, looking down momentarily. "I don't think it cared much for the Old Rats' barriers."

"It instinctively opposes unnatural barriers."

"Whereas humans instinctively create them?"

Ayrlyn nodded.

Nylan slowly edged his way through the close-spaced trunks, his hand not on the shortsword blade, but close, and his ears listening for strange rustles or something like the tawny cats they had encountered earlier.

They continued to walk, Nylan glancing ahead as they followed one of the clear "paths" in and around the guardian trees. That was what they felt like. As they stepped between two of the gray-barked giants, Nylan stopped.

The whole forest before them had changed, become more like an amphitheater. Silently, the two surveyed the expanse before them. Towering brown-trunked trees loomed overhead, widely spaced, some perhaps two hundred cubits high, forming a canopy just thick enough to turn the sunlight green while admitting enough light for the lower-growing vegetation. Under the high canopy grew shorter trees and bushes, none touching the others.

"This is different. I hadn't expected—"

"The outer lines of the trees are almost like a wall," said Ayrlyn.

Nylan nodded and stepped toward a purple trumpet flower bearing a stamen that flowed like golden notes—like the ones Weryl had grasped from Ayrlyn's lutar—from the bell of the floral instrument. Around the trumpet flower was a cluster of lower plants bearing tiny white starflowers. Each plant had its own space, and Nylan could feel the intertwined balance.

"You could sing, now, couldn't you?"

"I don't know if I'm balanced enough. I've been afraid to touch the lutar."

Will I ever be balanced enough again . . . so many death . . . killings . . .

As he caught the fragments of her thoughts/feelings, he reached out and squeezed her hand. "You are, or you will be."

Treeeeaaalll . . . treallll . . . They both glanced up at the musical call.

The branches rustled in one of the lower gray-green-leaved trees to the right of the path, and Nylan half-saw, half-sensed something like a tree rat vanishing. The impression of balance seethed even more strongly around them, as did an ugly sense of imbalance that tilted or loomed beyond the forest.

"Almost an oasis of balance here," said the redhead as she bent to sniff a delicate four-pointed green and white flower. "Why . . ." *would the Old Rats have destroyed this?*

Nylan frowned at her unspoken question. "Power . . . that's what always drives people. I just don't quite understand the link."

"Let's keep walking. Don't think about it. Let your subconscious work on it."

His hand reached for the blade at his waist as he thought about the Cyadorans, and his stomach tightened. He still had no answers, and less time, but he took a deep breath and tried to relax. Some things couldn't be forced, no matter how pressured he felt.

CXXII

Is EVERYTHING READY, Queras?" asked Lephi, sitting back in the malachite throne.

"I had planned to begin by sending the van companies the day after tomorrow, Your Mightiness." The marshal stood on the green carpet and bowed.

"Why so late?"

"The Tenth Mirror Lancers arrived yesterday. The Grass Hills are hot, even at harvesttime. There is little water at this time of year. Their mounts need watering and rest to be most effective."

"I had heard that you added local district forces . . ." Lephi smiled.

"Yes, Sire."

"Does that not betray your lack of confidence in the finest of Cyador?" Lephi's white teeth flashed.

A thin sheen of perspiration coated Queras's forehead. "I do not believe so. The barbarians have proven surprising in the past, and I would prefer to be overprudent. If the additional armsmen are unnecessary, then they will have gained experience that will be useful in your future efforts."

"You are humble, Queras. It befits you. How will you proceed?"

"We will first go to the northwest, to the South Branch of the Jernya River."

"The mines are to the north. So are the barbarians."

"The water is to the northwest, and the grass is better. Also the other barbarians are there as well, and best we vanquish them so that none remain behind us."

"Hmmmm . . ."

Queras did not wipe his damp brow.

"You may go."

The marshal bowed.

"And I hope there are no more delays."

"No, Sire."

CXXIII

Nylan glanced at the two horses grazing in the morning light beyond the shed, cropping one of the few flourishing patches of grass. Not a hundred cubits to the west, the same grass had turned brown.

"Do you think it would be safe enough to take Weryl?" he asked.

"To the forest? If we're careful. You think it's important?"

Nylan offered a forced and wry smile. "Who's knows what's important? It feels right, but I couldn't say why. Again."

"Has unaided logic helped you reach an understanding of the forest?"

"I'm still not sure I understand it."

"Too logical." The redhead grinned at Nylan. "You have to trust your feelings more."

"That's hard when I've spent a lifetime repressing them."

"You're getting there." Her grin widened.

"Slowly. Too slowly, it seems."

"We do what we can do."

He couldn't exactly argue with either the words or the sentiment.

Rather than change the brackets from Sylenia's saddle to his, Nylan put the nursemaid's saddle on his mare and adjusted the seat for Weryl. For the relatively short ride to the forest, he could handle the smaller saddle.

"You would not take your son to a place like that?" Sylenia asked from the rear door of the dwelling. She lifted Weryl away from the mud puddle beside the rear stoop stone. "No one needs be cleaning you again, young fellow."

"It's safe enough, now. As safe as anywhere," Nylan added as a twinge of light across his eyes reminded him that overstatement was a form of imbalance. Half absently, he won-

lered if a human society would be possible under the balance
constraints of the forest, since most accepted forms of manners involved some degree of deception.

"You are not listening," Sylenia pointed out.

"Where are you?" asked Ayrlyn softly, and with a smile.

"Thinking about the future of manners if lying isn't possible." He bent to tighten the girths.

"That's getting a little ahead." Ayrlyn adjusted the chestnut's bridle, squinting as the mare dropped her head and the
morning sun struck the redhead's face.

"It is not wise to take the boy into that—"

"Probably not, but it's something I feel." Besides, as Nylan
reflected to himself, if the forest did destroy both him and Ayrlyn, it wasn't that likely that the Cyadorans would be terribly
charitable to Weryl and Sylenia, although, he was forced to
add, Sylenia was resourceful and might be able to escape. He
frowned. Self-deception continued to get harder.

"Much harder," observed Ayrlyn.

"You angels. You talk and yet there are no words."

Nylan took Weryl from Sylenia and hoisted the boy into his
seat.

"Oh orsee."

"Yes, you're going on the horse." The engineer fastened the
seat straps around Weryl, then checked the blades in the waist
scabbard and the shoulder harness. "Ready?"

"As ready as I'll be."

"You two." Sylenia half-lifted the makeshift broom. "You
will poke and prod where none should too many times, and
then—"

"Probably," admitted Nylan. "But do you want to live under
the Cyadorans?" He eased the mare around and flicked the
reins.

"They be even worse than Tregvo." Sylenia shivered. "Be
you wary in the forest."

"We will," answered Ayrlyn. "You can come next time."

"I should think no. Enchanted forests be for angels."

"You would do as well as any," Ayrlyn said softly.

Sylenia watched as they rode down the gentle incline and

toward the older section of the forest. The young shoots in the flat that had been fields were now closer to head high, and some of the trunks were as thick as the smith's wrists.

"The forest isn't wasting much time," he noted as he guided the mare around a more spreading bush and into what would be a forest lane before long.

"Either way, it wins."

Nylan understood. If the Cyadoran mages succeeded in subduing Lornth, by the time they returned the forest would have consolidated enough of its expansion that it could never be pushed back without the high technology that the Rat descendants no longer possessed. "Even here, they underestimate nature."

"That doesn't mean they won't defeat Fornal," Ayrlyn pointed out.

Nylan took a deep breath.

"You don't want to go back, do you?"

"No. But I don't see any choice. I don't want to live alone as a savage here in the new boundaries that the Rats will impose when they win. And—"

"We gave our word."

"Are we so different from Fornal?" he asked with a laugh.

"In some ways, no . . ." Ayrlyn reined up in the small clearing that remained near the former white stone wall.

The smith and engineer studied the area, then dismounted and unfastened Weryl, lifting him out of his seat. "I don't feel anything."

"It's quiet."

They slipped over the nearly flat green creepers that still worked to reduce the former wall and past the outer guardian trees. Nylan felt like he should be holding his breath. Even Weryl was silent.

"There's a big cat ahead."

In a way he could not describe, Nylan could feel Ayrlyn's perception of the big tawny cat, but the cat seemed almost disinterested in the humans, and was following a large-tailed rodent of some sort.

The angels slowed, letting the predator move away from them.

Nylan stood by the trumpet flowers, holding Weryl, trying to sense . . . something. The flows of dark order and white chaotic power swirled around them. The smith looked absently at his son as he did at the forest—and his mouth opened. For like the forest, Weryl was order and chaos, less balanced, with faster and stronger swirls of the competing forces. Nylan turned toward Ayrlyn.

She too held both forces, but with more deliberateness, more . . . majesty.

Balance—did it allow greater use of power? How could he find out? He moved forward, just trying to soak in the feel of the underlying energies.

Several hundred cubits beyond the cleared expanse where they had stopped on their last trip, past another line of guardian trees, was a pond, almost oval, more than two hundred cubits long.

Nylan shifted Weryl from his still-sore left shoulder to his right.

They stood above the eastern end of the pool, at the top of a short grassy slope that led down to the clear green water. A fish of some sort, with orange fins and a brownish and orange-spotted body, glided up to the top of the water and took an insect—a water spider perhaps—with only the slightest of ripples.

"Wadah!" Weryl smiled and jabbed his right hand toward the silver-shimmered and tree-shadowed green surface.

At the far end of the pond, beside a bush with narrow silver-green leaves, a gray loglike object, at least ten cubits long, slipped under the surface, and a line of ripples moved toward the three.

"We'd better—" began Ayrlyn.

"Yes." Nylan felt the menace of the big lizard. Although the balance constraints would certainly allow him to use the blades against the monster lizard, he had some doubts whether blades would be enough. At the moment, the lizard was merely investigating. That he could feel. With Weryl in his arms, prudence was definitely better. Nylan turned.

"Wadah . . ." Weryl lurched back toward the pond.

"Some other day. We'd rather not be lizard food."

"That's a big lizard, and it's got some sort of order-chaos storage, like a weapon." Ayrlyn began to walk quickly to catch up with the other two. "But it's balanced, like everything in the forest."

"Outside . . . all of Candar is unbalanced." With his senses, somehow extended but passive, on the lizard, Nylan walked quickly back the way they had come, Weryl on his shoulder. They passed another stand of the purple trumpet flowers, one that he did not recall. He could catch the hint of the reiseralike fragrance that drifted into the green canopied amphitheater from somewhere. "That's what the forest tries to right, except that it's blind."

"How will this help us—or Lornth—against Cyador?" Ayrlyn took a deep breath without slowing. "It smells good."

"Where's the lizard?"

"Oh . . . it stopped at the water's edge. There are two cats prowling around there. One might have been the one we saw earlier. They can feel the order changes, too, I think."

"Why aren't they following us?"

"Nylan . . . whether you recognize it or not, you've balanced a tremendous amount of order and chaos in yourself. It makes that lizard look puny. If I were a big cat, I'd be a lot more interested in the lizard."

"Great . . . I don't even know how to use it . . . not really." A thought struck him, and he turned and looked at Ayrlyn, seeing what she had described in him in her. He swallowed. "You . . ."

She shook her head.

He laughed. "You! You're just the same as me or that lizard."

"It's scary," Ayrlyn admitted, her eyes going back over her shoulder, even though nothing seemed to move in the greenlit forest. "I never thought of myself as powerful."

"The forest would."

"Wadah!" interrupted Weryl with a lurch.

Nylan reached up and steadied his son. "When we get to the horses." His eyes narrowed. "Look . . . at Weryl."

"He's got it, too, that balance."

"Do you think . . . ?"

"I don't know."

Neither did Nylan, but his scarcely more than infant son was somehow instinctively balancing order and chaos. Their ordeal? The forest? He didn't know.

They kept walking, the only audible sounds those of insects, the rustle of the high canopy, their own breathing, and scattered bird calls.

Once beyond the guardian trees of the old growth, Ayrlyn paused by the chestnut, reins in her hand. "Nylan . . . what did we learn today?"

"We learned something. It's like powerfluxes—the greater the potential difference and the better the balance . . . that's the key." He eased Weryl into the seat behind the saddle. "And that it's easier for children. Or Weryl."

"It's still unsettling. We walk in there, and we walk out, and each time we're a little different, and I can't quite remember how it happened, but I can sense that it did, and that we're different."

"Are we different in a bad way?" Nylan strapped Weryl in place.

"No . . . I don't think so. But how would we know, if that's what the forest wants?"

"That's why we have to leave."

"Oh . . . if we feel that way when we're beyond its power?"

He nodded. "And if it lets us go—"

"Then it leaves the choice to us."

"Exactly."

"Will it?"

"Somehow, I feel it will." Nylan mounted the mare. "The forest even gives the animals limited free will. The lizard didn't have to chase us. Nor the cats."

"It wants something." Ayrlyn swung into her saddle.

"Of course. Somehow . . . we're going to help the forest." A grim laugh followed his words. "And it will help us."

"That far from here?" she asked, drawing the chestnut beside his mare.

"The Old Rats took their planoforming equipment and used it to resculpt this part of western Candar, but they sort of overlaid the old topography, and some of it wasn't necessary. They probably didn't have enough power to do it right—and they sort of stretched out the marshes and the water and created grasslands over what was almost a desert, and moved streams. It wouldn't last forever, and maybe it shouldn't have lasted this long—but there's a lot of energy there." He shrugged. "Any time there's an imbalance . . ."

Ayrlyn nodded. "But some of this still doesn't make sense, ecologically. A larger forest would have maintained the grasslands because it would have cooled the whole region."

"I thought rain forests grew—"

"That's it! This isn't a rain forest."

Nylan waited.

"Rain forests usually develop in areas of thin soil and high moisture. The soil here is comparatively rich, and the normal rainfall would be more temperate."

"So, healer and ecologist, what's the jump point?"

She shrugged. "I don't know . . . exactly. The Rats didn't have to slash the forest back into a relatively small square. They could have adopted some form of large alternating bloc agriculture—there aren't that many towns here, and from what we've seen, they're not overcrowded. That would show that the population pressure was never that great."

Nylan rubbed his forehead. "You're assuming that the forest would let them. Look at how fast things are overgrowing the old boundaries."

"The Old Rationalists weren't stupid," Ayrlyn pointed out. "They planoformed scores of planets successfully. This place didn't even need planoforming, not if the forest were already here."

"This isn't just a different place," Nylan pointed out. "It's a different universe. Fusactors don't work here—"

"How did they get the power to transform the land, then?"

"I don't know," he admitted. "They use more of a laser-based technology . . . always have. Maybe some forms of laser fusion work—or they did."

"Wadah, pease," interrupted Weryl.

"I know. I promised." The smith eased out the water bottle and uncorked it, lurching in the saddle as the mare crossed one of the former irrigation ditches. He held the bottle as his son drank.

"Let's get back to your point," said Ayrlyn. "There's a basic instability surrounding the forest, but not in the forest itself. Why would the Old Rats do that? They knew better. They had to."

"Power, maybe. We've seen the power the forest has, and it's only a fraction of its former size." Nylan reclaimed the water bottle and recorked it.

"That means . . . do you think that the Old Rats actually set up a power imbalance as a power/energy source for the white mages?"

Nylan nodded. "It's the only thing that makes sense. They're experienced planoformers, but their conventional power sources failed—or were failing."

"Surely . . . they had to know it couldn't last forever."

"They probably did—but what's better? Something that works for centuries—or longer—with the hope that their descendants can work out something? Or condemning themselves and their immediate children to true barbarian or low-tech lives?" He gestured toward the south. "Cyador is the most advantaged and cultured civilization we've seen."

"Advantaged . . . that I'll accept. Given the way they treat women—"

"Wouldn't it have been worse if they'd lapsed into low-tech?"

"That's too theoretical, worse than engineering speculations." Ayrlyn cleared her throat. "You're going to use that force?"

"If I can."

"If *we* can," corrected Ayrlyn.

The smith laughed, less harshly. "I stand corrected . . . as always. If we can . . . and we can. I just don't know how yet."

. "Harnessing that power won't be as hard as surviving it," predicted Ayrlyn. "Especially in one piece."

Nylan feared her assessments were all too correct.

Ayrlyn reined up beside the shed and glanced toward the rear door of the house. As she looked, Sylenia appeared.

"You were not gone that long."

"You didn't want us to go at all," Nylan said.

"If one must do something . . ."

The smith glanced helplessly at Ayrlyn. While a glimmer of a smile flitted around her lips, she remained silent.

"We probably need to get moving tomorrow," Nylan said as he dismounted and turned to Weryl.

Ayrlyn pursed her lips.

"Will we learn any more by staying?"

"Probably." The redhead slipped lightly from the saddle.

"Will we learn it fast enough?"

The redhead frowned. "Probably not . . . but . . ."

"I know. It's risky . . . everything's risky." *But do we have a choice? And we did give our word, and . . .*

Ayrlyn nodded sadly. . . . *and there's a tie between keeping a promise and order . . .*

"Unfortunately."

Sylenia cleared her throat, loudly. Both angels turned to her.

"I have made all the bread we can carry, and dried beans, and even some wasol roots. They were in the garden." Sylenia beamed. "Much better than cheese and biscuits."

Nylan would have been surer about their travel fare before she mentioned wasol roots, whatever they were.

CXXIV

IN THE DARKNESS, Nylan slipped out past the bushes and downhill, stopping only after he crossed the first dry irrigation ditch.

What did he have in mind?

Did he really know, except that he somehow needed to

raise and channel the power of or in or from the forest? Ayr-yn's comments about not knowing enough had worried at him, and worried. Yet he *knew* that the Cyadoran hordes were about to descend on Lornth—if they hadn't already, and there was a time to act whether they had enough knowledge or not. Somehow, someway, they had to raise the power of the for-est, or a power like that of the forest, in Lornth, against the Cyadoran hordes. And he didn't have any ideas, except in a general sense. Too general.

He took a deep breath, drawing the mixed fragrances that held the hint of reisera and others he could not have named.

Slowly, slowly, he opened himself to the pulse of the for-est, of the order and chaos, of the flows, so similar to those between the poles of a fusactor, except the flows were a con-struct of the power differentials . . .

No! Get back to the basics.

Power . . . order to hold chaos.

Not to hold . . . to guide . . . always in balance . . .

The sweat popped out on his forehead, despite the cool breeze out of the east.

Guide . . . balance . . .

Rather than reach, he tried to open himself to that power, visualizing himself as a conduit, a circuit, insulated by order.

He staggered under the impact of the twin flows—dark-ness and the crushing might of chaos welling from the hot magma far beneath Candar, chaos hot enough to melt even ship alloys, with enough free electrons, unstable quarks, lep-tons . . . the terms swirled through his thoughts, but the en-ergy was real.

Around him light grew—from a glow to a glare, so much of a glare that he closed his eyes, and yet the not-quite-cold light turned the area around the house into nearly day.

. . . heat . . . but not too much . . .

Despite his efforts to hold off the heat, he could feel it building, feeling the surges of power.

. . . careful . . .

The ground beneath him trembled, ever so slightly, but in-sistently, as though the chaos beneath wished to obliterate that thin barrier laid between the surface and the depths so many generations earlier by the Old Rats.

. . . not now . . . later . . . when we get to Lornth . . .

Slowly, he eased the flows away, letting them subside.

His breath was ragged, and his heart pounded so hard that he felt the sleepers inside the house could have heard it.

For a time he stood, gasping, just trying to get his body back under control.

Then he turned toward the house.

"Very impressive." Ayrlyn sat on the patch of grass remaining in front of the bushes. "I'm glad I understand you. Someone else might not have taken it well. They might have thought you were out to get the power for yourself."

"I never—"

"I know. You were afraid it wouldn't work. Or that I'd get hurt. Like all good engineers, you wanted to test your idea with no one around in case it went wrong, and, as usual, you didn't want to worry me. So . . . all I knew is that you were worried, and I couldn't sleep anyway."

"I'm sorry."

"You are so dense . . . sometimes. Don't you understand?" *Nylan . . . don't shut me out . . . please . . .*

"I'm sorry. I didn't know, and I wasn't sure how it would work." He put his arms around her. *Didn't want you hurt . . . if it didn't . . .*

"It will work. You could have asked me."

"It's such a change. I forget, still." He shivered, feeling weak. He released Ayrlyn and sat on the grass.

"Try not to." *Or I'll do . . . something dreadful! Long before we ever get back to Lornth!* She sat beside him.

The engineer blushed at her unspoken comment.

"In fact . . ." *I'm going to do something dreadful right now.* Her lips were upon his before he could speak again, and she pushed him back on the grass. *While you're too weak to resist . . .* Her hands were at his waistband. *And if anyone hears . . . you get to explain. . . .*

CXXV

GETHEN DID NOT unroll the scroll he held as he sat in the green upholstered armchair across the ancient carpet from his daughter and coregent. "The traders—the ones who ported in Rulyarth. They bring disturbing news, daughter and regent."

"That the white demons ready an attack? We knew that. Do they say when?"

"They bring no news of what we face from the south." Gethen cleared his throat. "The lord of Cyador builds a fireship like one of the ancients that swept clean the Great Western Ocean. It nears completion."

"We need not worry of that." With a quick look at Nesslek, who banged two blocks at each other, not exactly in a coordinated fashion, Zeldyan raised her goblet of greenjuice, taking a small sip. "Not soon, in any instance."

"Perchance not. Has there been word from Fornal?"

"Except for another plea for coins and levies . . . no. We sent him all that the sale of the copper raised. It was not enough, he claims. Yet he did not seize the copper, not according to Diwer. The angels did, and Fornal called them highwaymen."

"Would we had more such highwaymen." Gethen snorted.

"They may yet suffice."

"You have faith in the angels, yet we have heard naught." Gethen stood and walked to the serving table where he filled a goblet, not with the greenjuice, but with a dark wine. "The demons must be nearing, and we hear little. I must leave for Rohrn before long."

"How soon, my sire?"

"No more than a few days."

"So soon?"

"So late."

"So late, yet I must have faith." She set the goblet on the

side table, leaned over, and disengaged Nesslek's busy fingers from where he picked at the ancient green silk border of the chair's upholstery. "What else is there? We have no coins left. No way to raise more levies beyond that poor handful you take. Our holders are openly grumbling, and the harvest has been poor."

"Not so poor as for the mutters we hear."

"The Lady Ellindyja?"

"Some still visit her," admitted Gethen. "We cannot remove her."

Zeldyan lifted Nesslek into her lap. "A poor patrimony for you, my son, and much because your grand-dame was overly concerned about that of your father."

"That is cruel, especially to tell your son," offered Gethen.

"It is true. Would you have me lie to him? Even as his grand-dame destroys his own patrimony out of spite and pettiness? Truth may yet be his only weapon."

"Truth be never enough. Cold iron—that be the only weapon that a lord can depend on. Wizards and mages and trade—they come and they go. Cold iron remains. To the cold iron we do not have." The gray-haired regent took a deep swallow.

Zeldyan hugged Nesslek until he squirmed, then set her son back on the carpet beside his wooden blocks. She looked at the goblet, but did not drink.

CXXVI

SYLENIA CARRIED OUT the provisions bag and set it on the rear stoop. She glanced at the mid-afternoon sun that seemed to duck in and out of the puffy gray and white clouds scudding from the northeast. "To begin travel so late in the day . . . ?"

"This time we'll travel more by night, until we get out of Cyador, anyway." Nylan checked the girths for Sylenia's saddle, then readjusted Weryl's seat, stopping to wipe his forehead. While the area in and around the forest was cooler than the Grass Hills, even with the cooling of the trees the harvest season was far hotter than mid-summer on the Roof of the World—or anywhere else in two universes that he could remember offhand, at least outside of Candar. "I'm still not up to any battles."

"You could handle them better." Ayrlyn did not look up from where she loaded the pack mare.

"Maybe." Of that, Nylan wasn't exactly certain. Theoretically, he supposed he could figure out some way to balance things, but the gap between theory and practice was awfully wide, wider in many ways than advanced power system operations and engineering theory had been.

"I don't want to leave." Ayrlyn held the saddlebag in her hands, almost as if she had been halted by an outside force.

Nylan understood. For the first time in years, if not ever, they weren't surrounded by all of the unseen imbalances that had rocked their lives from one side to the other. Already, they had begun to adjust themselves to the forest's requirement for balance, and when Nylan extended his senses to look at Ayrlyn, he could see the changes, almost, it seemed, on the cellular level. While some changes appeared in Sylenia, Ayrlyn and he—and Weryl—appeared vastly different. Was that because he had been a power engineer? Or Ayrlyn a comm officer? Because the forest had reached out to them? Or they to it? "It's not paradise."

"I still don't want to leave." *This feels . . . closer to home . . .*

They turned to each other and embraced.

"Stupid . . ." murmured Ayrlyn in his ear. "How . . . a forest . . . feels like home . . ."

"Does, doesn't it?" He squeezed her more tightly for a moment, then slowly released her.

"In some ways I feel as you, lady," added Sylenia. "But here is Tonsar—"

"And there's still the problem of the Cyadorans. Remember all those burned patches? Sooner or later they'll be back to deal with the forest." *Especially if we don't deal with them—if we can . . .*

"I know," sighed Ayrlyn, "and we made a promise." *A promise . . .*

It wasn't just the words, Nylan understood, all too well, but the chaos created within themselves by failing to keep their commitments. Anyone who had to deal with order fields, he was coming to understand—possibly too late and too slowly—had to live a life somehow in balance. And unkept promises were not good for balance.

At least, that was how it seemed to him.

"Me, too," said Ayrlyn. "We're in this together."

He smiled at her, taking in the warmth that radiated from her, the warmth he'd been blind to for too long on the Roof of the World. Then he walked over and lifted the provisions bag from the stoop.

Sylenia turned and reentered the Cyadoran dwelling, presumably to reclaim Weryl.

Nylan stood and surveyed the dwelling, the smooth pale walls, thinking about the ceramic stove, the tile floors, the apparent cleanliness—and the chaos behind its creation.

CXXVII

THE STARS WINKED on and off as the clouds slipped across the night sky, covering one unfamiliar point of light and uncovering another, all the time that Nylan and Ayrlyn made their way north along the empty highway. Only the muffled sound of the horses' hoofs echoed through the night as the four rode closer to the river and the brick bridge.

The smell of the fields, and the faintly acrid odor of something that had been cut drifted across the road on the light breeze.

"The beans, they have harvested," confirmed Sylenia.

"Wadah . . . eans?"

"You just had some." Sylenia turned in the saddle and, twisting her body, offered Weryl the water bottle. He pushed it away, and the nursemaid recorked it and replaced it in the holder without a word.

Nylan doubted he would have been that temperate, son or no son.

When they passed the crossroads where they had confronted the Cyadoran patrol, not even a lingering sign of chaos remained. The engineer glanced around, his ears alert for any noise, but the only sounds were insects, a soft bird call, and the breathing and hoofs of the horses.

As they neared the river, neither Nylan's eyes nor senses could distinguish any movements on or beyond the bridge, a dark outline above the darker water and against the starry sky.

"Quiet," murmured the redhead.

The mounts' hoofs *clacked,* if not loudly, not softly on the brick pavement of the arched three-piered structure that spanned the deep and smooth-flowing water that appeared black under the cold stars, a blackness darker than the unlit and silent town on the north side.

Infrequently scattered points of reflected starlight dotted the smooth dark surface of the river—wider than Nylan recalled. Even centuries after the Old Rationalist planoforming, the chaotic white-red hints of violence seethed beneath the ground and beneath deep and slow-flowing river waters, the unseen line between what had been and what now was as clear and implacable as ever.

And I . . . we're . . . going to harness that?

"Yes," answered Ayrlyn.

"I'd better start working out the practical details." *Especially since I haven't the faintest idea how.*

"I have every confidence in you."

"Thanks."

Riding two by two between the stone walls, they reached the top of the span, where the echo of hoofs seemed to reverberate into the night. Yet no lights appeared in any buildings on the north side of the bridge.

Downstream, the fractionally darker shadows that were piers loomed above the north side of the water, and a solitary dog barked . . . and barked. Nylan tried not to stiffen, wondering who would come to investigate, but no lights appeared near the piers and the dog and the *clack* of hoofs began to echo off the brick buildings once they entered the town proper.

"It's spooky." Ayrlyn's voice was low. "Like the world outside their walls doesn't exist at night."

"They have to shut it out," whispered Nylan, "but that makes it easier for us."

The open-columned marketplace was empty—yet unbarred and unguarded, and across the street, the water splashed quietly down the sculpted tree fountain, water holding the faintest glow. Some sort of chaos?

"The town still doesn't smell," Nylan said.

"You want it to?"

"No. The only thing I've been able to smell is harvested beans, and a dampness around the river. No flowers . . . no garbage . . . no . . . nothing . . ."

"It does seem odd."

"Better no smell than the smell of Lornth by the old wharfs," suggested Sylenia dryly.

Nylan wondered. Cyador was clean and ordered, but how high was the price for such cleanliness—and how much force had been required, and still was?

Too much . . .

But how many people preferred order at any cost?

CXXVIII

So NUMEROUS WERE the horses that the entire countryside rumbled like a massive drum. The white uniforms spread across the mottled brown and green of the grasslands so that the hills looked as though early winter had fallen upon them.

Behind the lancers and their horses came the foot, rows

upon rows, white and well dressed out even for all the kays they had marched. Behind them rolled the legions of wagons—supply wagons, armorers' wagons, and the glistening wagons of the marshal's equipage.

Behind the van rode Marshal Queras, Majer Piataphi, and the white mages. Triendar squinted from beneath a broad and floppy white hat. Themphi's face was red and blistered, while Fissar bounced in his saddle.

The van had slowed at the ridge line that overlooked a lower-lying and greener valley.

"There are the grasslands barbarians!" announced Queras.

On the far north side of the valley stood a settlement, flanking a large pond or small lake. To the west, above the grassy swale that connected the two ridges, waited a dark mass of riders under the fir tree banners of Jerans.

As the Cyadorans watched, the Jeranyi horse wheeled, formed a wedge, and then plunged down through the swale and up onto the west end of the ridge, toward the left flank of the advancing Cyadoran Mirror Lancers, the drum of hoofbeats echoing on the sunbaked grasslands.

"To the left!" ordered Piataphi, spurring his mount toward the van that had begun to turn.

The white-bronze trumpet sounded its triplets, and the shields lifted, flashing light spears into the Jeranyi ranks, and the white lances leveled as the massed Cyadoran force slowly swung around. Light spears winked from the polished shields, turning the front ranks of the Jeranyi into a blaze of reflections. Majer Piataphi reached the front rank of the lancers and lifted his sabre again.

The day filled with the clash of blades and lances, sabres and shortswords, and the dark knot of Jeranyi appeared ever smaller as the lines of white-clad armsmen swelled, as did the clangor.

Themphi stared as bodies fell from bloodstained saddles; Triendar shook his head ever so slightly, so slightly that the floppy hat barely moved. Fissar, pale white, looked at the small lake, well away from the blood, and swallowed convulsively.

CXXIX

FROM HER MOUNT beside Nylan's, Ayrlyn raised her eyebrows. "You all right?"

"Sorry." Nylan flushed at the growling from his stomach. "Sylenia's culinary inventions have definitely kept us from starving, but the side effects are . . ." Rather than finish the sentence he never should have begun, he glanced to the west at a hillside that had rapidly become all too typical, a patchwork of brown and black and gray.

So far, all the holdings that they had passed since entering southern Lornth were ashes, black lumps in the midst of blackened grass that stretched for kays around even the most humble of hovels. Four days of scattered ashes and cinders and more scattered ashes and cinders.

"We're eating, and we don't have to stop to forage," Ayrlyn pointed out.

Nylan wished he'd said nothing.

"Might have been better." Ayrlyn grinned.

"You would eat ashes were it not—" began the nursemaid.

"I'm sorry. I know." Nylan sniffed the air as the mare carried him up the long incline. "Something's burning."

"Grass."

"More than grass. More than just a holding." The engineer glanced at Ayrlyn.

The redhead's eyes glazed over, and she half-slumped in the saddle.

Nylan slowed his mare to match the slower pace of the half-attended chestnut that Ayrlyn rode.

"Gwasss . . . wadah, pease?" Weryl coughed after his request.

"You are not thirsty," Sylenia informed her charge.

Nylan suspected that Weryl just wanted to talk, but, precocious as his son appeared to be, his vocabulary was still rather limited. So he asked for water, and more water.

"There was a town ahead. Clynya, maybe, but it's hard to tell." Ayrlyn shivered and straightened in the saddle.

"Hard to tell?" Although he asked, Nylan had a feeling that he knew what she meant.

"Exactly. You know."

He did—the town had been burned the way the holdings they had ridden past had been.

They reined up at the top of the hills and looked northward. Nylan glanced across the blackened expanse, kays and kays, on each side of the river. Smoke still swirled up from blackened heaps. Was the smoldering mass on the right side of the river all that was left of the barracks where they had stayed?

Along with acridness of ashes and cinders came the odor of charred meat. Only the thin plumes of grayish smoke moved in the afternoon heat, rising in thin spirals—except for a single figure that might have been a dog darting along what had been the road through Clynya.

"Clynya? This be Clynya?" asked Sylenia in a choked voice.

"We think so." Nylan studied what had been the barracks and the stable, where even the collapsed sod roof seemed, if his eyes were reliable from the distance, to smolder.

"They are demons . . ."

Nylan nodded, absently wondering again how a people who could build such clean and advanced homes could so consciencelessly destroy whole towns and their inhabitants. Ayrlyn had once said that technology enabled mercy, but the Cyadorans seemed less merciful than their lower-tech neighbors, rather than more.

"Because they don't believe outsiders are real people." Ayrlyn cleared her throat.

"And because they understand that force is the only true arbiter?"

"Probably." Ayrlyn spoke dismissively, and Nylan felt her feelings, both her acceptance that people relied on force and her general but intense disgust that it had to be so.

"The Cyadorans and Fornal speak the same language in tha respect. Iron, cold iron, is the master of all." He flicked the mare's reins. Whatever they decided, sitting and watching the remnants of Clynya smolder wasn't going to further their efforts. "Now what? Keep riding?"

"Any better ideas?"

He shook his head. Even the dog—if it had been a dog— had vanished, and only the smoke swirled on the east side of the river. "How long ago, do you think?"

"A day, maybe two."

Why had everything taken so long? Why had he been so dense? And now, even if they caught up with the Cyadoran hordes . . . what could they do?

"We couldn't have gotten here much quicker. Try to remember that," Ayrlyn said.

"That's easy to say." *And I still don't know how to stop them . . .*

"Use the imbalance . . . like you said." Ayrlyn eased her chestnut closer to his mare as they continued down the road toward the ruins of Clynya.

"For destruction?" Nylan rubbed his neck, then eased his right hand behind the leather straps of the blade harness and tried to massage his stiff left shoulder.

"You're the one who keeps pointing out that people only respect force."

"I have trouble with that."

"You don't want to become like Ryba," Ayrlyn said.

"No."

"Using force doesn't mean you have to glory in it or flaunt it." Ayrlyn reached across the space between mounts, leaning sideways in the saddle for a moment so her fingers could squeeze the wrist of his rein hand. "Anyway, we have to figure out how to use that imbalance first."

Nylan nodded. If they didn't use what they knew to survive, morality would become quickly irrelevant. The problem was that, having opted for survival, most survivors in Candar never seemed to regain their morality.

"That bothers you."

"Absolutely. I know I'm no better than anyone else, maybe not so good. So how can I believe it when I promise myself I won't change the way Ryba did?"

"You're not the same."

Nylan would have liked to hope so, but self-justification was a specialty of human beings, and he was more than conscious of being all too human, of seeking self-justification all too easily.

CXXX

THE LOW CHIRP of crickets or grasshoppers or cicadas or the Candarian equivalent filled the evening. Nylan burped as he settled onto the grass uphill from their camp. He didn't know whether his indigestion came from the slimy wasol roots or the filling but heavy squash bread. All he knew was that his guts felt like they contained lead, and he hadn't eaten all that much. He had the feeling that the orange loaves were endless, that Sylenia had been so enchanted with the ceramic oven that she had baked enough for an entire squad for seasons.

"Only half a squad." Ayrlyn slipped through the dimness and sat down beside him by the small stand of scrub oak bushes that shielded the hollow in the ridge where Weryl snored softly and Sylenia lay.

The scrub oaks were all that passed for cover on the hills flanking the river plain. They'd taken the hill road because Ayrlyn's wind scouting had indicated the hill road was more direct and because that way they could slip past the slower-moving Cyadoran force that followed the river road. Tomorrow, she'd said.

"Tomorrow." Ayrlyn shifted her weight, trying to get comfortable on the hard ground.

"What are we going to do if they find us—or some of their scouts do?"

"I was going to ask you that. You are the engineer, and I do trust your feelings."

"I appreciate the trust, but I haven't been all that successful in applying engineering—"

"You managed to power and control the laser to build Tower Black, and I don't think that was just technology or luck." Ayrlyn patted his shoulder gently.

"This is different."

"How?"

"There's no technological basis at all."

"It still has to be a system. I'm quoting an engineer. A very good engineer."

"Thanks. He didn't know what he was talking about. He just thought he did." Nylan coughed gently and shifted his weight. The ground was hard.

"You mentioned the separation in the ground," she prompted.

"It's almost a power differential. And theoretically, if there's a power or an energy imbalance between two forces, there *has* to be a way to convert that imbalance into usable power." He shrugged. "I just haven't figured out the mechanism for doing it."

"You sound like an engineer, but maybe this is simpler."

"Maybe." Nylan wasn't convinced. Nothing was ever simpler than it seemed. Not in his experience, and when it was, there was usually an incredible price to pay. Add to that that they'd left the forest before he'd really had time to work things out because they both knew that time was short and hoped that they could puzzle it out while they traveled.

He snorted softly to himself, wondering if their "puzzling" would leave them even more open to white wizards. Then, he had to hope that the wizards were either farther away or concentrating on the battles. Just like him, they couldn't do everything at once. He hoped.

The insect chirping died away for a moment, and Nylan glanced around, extending his perceptions into the darkness. He smiled as he sensed a foxlike predator creeping after some sort of ground-dwelling rodent.

The rodent bolted for its hole, and the fox pawed at the round for a time, then slipped downhill and toward the alley.

"It wasn't a fox," Ayrlyn said. "It was something like a coyote, except it was fox-sized."

"Call it a foxote?"

"It probably has a local name that we don't know."

"Probably."

Nylan looked skyward, into the cloudless evening and the unknown stars that glittered as impersonally as ever.

"In the forest, does the order balance the chaos? Or is chaos balanced by order?" Ayrlyn asked into the silence.

"What's the diff—" He paused. "Oh . . ." He swallowed. "Well . . . order provides both a balance and . . . I'd guess you'd call it an insulator or separator."

"If that's so, then isn't chaos more powerful? Ideally, I mean?"

"I don't know." He shrugged, tugging on a long and dry stem of grass. "My guess is that in larger concentrations that would be so, but as you break down chaos into smaller and smaller fragments, order gets progressively more effective." The stem broke, and Nylan absently chewed the end, then put aside as his tongue tingled with a bitter taste.

"What if you tied up all the chaos?"

"You'd end up tying up all the order. But that's not our problem." He sighed. "Someday someone may have to deal with that, and I wish them well, but we're nowhere near that. I'm just trying to figure out—"

"How about experimenting? In little bits?"

Of course, that was what all his talk had been about—trying to avoid, subconsciously, actually plunging in. What all that white energy could do terrified him.

"It is a little awesome."

Nylan laughed softly. "A little awesome?" He turned and hugged her. "I love your understatements. A little awesome." He laughed again.

"I'm glad you find me amusing."

"A little awesome?"

"Nylan."

He closed his mouth. Did she know? Did she have any idea of the power that lay beneath Candar?

"I guess I didn't know. I'm sorry."

"It scares me." The smith shook his head. "It scares me a lot."

"You can do it." Ayrlyn reached out and squeezed his right hand. "We can do it." *We can.*

"I just don't know." Still, her warmth and her willingness to share the risk warmed him, and he squeezed her hand in return.

"What if you just used the order lines, like a pipe?"

Nylan frowned for a moment. While it might not work, that sort of experiment wouldn't be that hard, sort of like the way in which he'd held the laser together at the end.

"You can, you know," she said, quietly.

He wasn't sure, but the only way to find out was to try. He reached beneath the ground, his senses extending until they touched the chaos/order boundary.

"I can't follow you, not very far," said Ayrlyn.

"Can't follow you very far on the winds, either," he grunted. Already his forehead had begun to perspire. With as gentle a touch as possible, he urged, coaxed, encouraged the order lines to turn toward the surface, reforming them in one small area into a tube, except it was more like an open-ended cone.

He swallowed as the tip of the unseen cone touched the top of the ground. "Now what?"

"You have to break the circuit?"

That wasn't it, not exactly—more like creating a ground in the air, or something like it. He winced as the power sink, or whatever it was he had formed, seemed to glow. He could see his boots with his eyes, and not just his senses.

Whhhhhsssttt!! A jet of fire—was it fire?—exploded out of the ground, turning the night into dawn, and an unheard screaming slashed through Nylan's skull.

The engineer swallowed, his eyes closing involuntarily against the light, against the energy, against the heat. His mouth was instantly dry, his heart pounding. The line of fire rose higher until it had to have been nearly ten cubits high—a fountain of chaos-fire brighter than the sun.

"There!" Ayrlyn had closed her eyes against the burning light.

The engineer forced his senses back out, grasping for the order cone. He squeezed, prodded, and closed the tip of the cone, letting the boundary layer drop back into place, in effect damping the release of chaos.

"Whewww . . ." he sighed, his eyes still closed, sparks and flashes still sparking across them, though the darkness of night had fallen again. He rubbed his eyelids and then massaged his temples.

"You could say that," added Ayrlyn.

"Lightning! Was that lightning?" Sylenia demanded, sitting bolt upright on her bedroll. "How could there be lightning? There is no storm."

"Don't worry, Sylenia," Nylan lied hoarsely. "We're experimenting. Just experimenting." He swallowed.

"Experimenting? What is that? You are making lightnings from the ground? That is experimenting?"

In a way the nursemaid's statement wasn't a bad analogy, since most lightning did result from a power buildup and disparity between a cloud and the ground, but the engineer didn't want to get into that. "There won't be any more strange lights. Not tonight."

"You are sure?"

"I am sure." Nylan blotted a forehead that was both hot and cold. Suddenly, he felt like he reeked, reeked of sweat and of sheer terror.

"He won't do it again," Ayrlyn added.

"Thank you, healer." Sylenia lay back on her bedroll, murmuring just loud enough for the angels to hear, ". . . bad when they fling blades through armor. Now . . . now they bring fires from the ground . . . what would Tonsar say? Oh . . . he would say much . . ."

"He would, too," whispered Nylan.

"You," said Ayrlyn. "You have been known to say more than a few words when—"

"Enough." The smith touched her chin, then covered her lips with his, holding her tightly, letting her hold him, trying not to shiver too much.

What might happen on the morrow was left unsaid, unthought. So was the possibility that they had alerted every wizard in kays. But they were short of time, knowledge, and experience—and very alone and exposed.

CXXXI

TWO BLACK VULCROWS flapped up from the road ahead, black forms outlined momentarily against the green-blue sky. Nylan leaned forward slightly in the saddle and squinted to see what they had left behind.

For once, a breeze blew across the hills, out of the northeast, rustling the dry grass and the scattered trees and scrub oaks. The wind carried a residual coolness from the Westhorns where Ryba and the guards of Westwind, Nylan supposed, were doubtless forging another link in the chain of destiny that would change all Candar for all time.

The engineer snorted. So did his mare, stepping sideways momentarily on the dusty road to avoid the carcass of some sort of lizard, the form half-picked already, though the residual order and chaos seeping from it indicated that it had not even been dead when the vulcrows started.

Nylan's forehead felt hot, even though the light wind was enough to keep him from perspiring the way he usually did. He uncorked the water bottle and took a deep swallow, then splashed a little on his face.

"Your face is red, even redder than normal," Ayrlyn said.

"So is yours." Nylan glanced back at Sylenia, riding quietly behind the redhead, but the nursemaid's smooth skin seemed unchanged. "You think that last night . . . ?"

"Releasing chaos that way is dangerous, I think."

"I know. Any alternatives?"

"Not offhand." Ayrlyn followed Nylan's example and
ank from her own water bottle, but did not splash any on
r own reddened forehead and cheeks.

No alternatives—that had been the problem since they'd
nded on the Roof of the World nearly three years earlier. Had
been less than three years? Nylan took a deep breath. It felt
nger, much, much longer.

"Angels, there's someone behind us," Sylenia pointed out,
sturing with her left arm.

Nylan turned in the saddle. A wind-flattened line of dust
gged the hilltop beyond the one a kay behind them, dust
eated by fast-moving mounts ridden by figures in white, still
ore than three kays back.

Nylan had known it would be a risk . . . but all the choices
ey'd had were either bad or worse.

"Let me check." Ayrlyn's face blanked, and she half-
mped in the saddle.

The engineer looked around as he drew his mount next to
rs, in case she started to slip from the saddle. He couldn't
lp worrying when Ayrlyn half-left her body behind.

Beyond the grass-covered ridges to the west, on the low
ad that flanked the river, marched the main Cyadoran force,
th so many bodies that even Nylan could sense them from
ys away. According to Ayrlyn, the angels had slipped past
at force earlier in the morning, but they weren't that much
rther north than the Cyadorans, not yet.

Behind them was what seemed to be a squad or more of
ncers. To the east were the rougher hills and, another five
ys or more, a twisted and steep-sided gully carrying a thin
ckle of water that eventually joined the main river at Rohrn,
ll a good three to four days ride ahead.

"They ride quickly," observed Sylenia.

"Ooo . . . orses," added Weryl from his seat behind the
rsemaid's saddle. "Orses."

"Yes, horses. I wish they didn't have so many horses,"
ylan told his son. Alerted by a shift in Ayrlyn's posture, he
rned back toward the redhead.

"Little problem here." Ayrlyn coughed and tried to clear he throat.

Nylan flicked the reins to speed the mare into a quicke walk while he waited.

"We can't go east. We're not far enough in front of th Cyadoran van, and if we angle that way . . ." She coughe again.

"They'll catch up because we'll be going slower in tryin to cross rougher ground."

The flame-haired angel nodded. "They also have a prett big group ahead of us."

"Frig . . ." muttered Nylan. "We're surrounded, in effec and they've listened to whoever was at the mines. They'r scouting with forces large enough not to be picked off."

"They're not stupid," said Ayrlyn, "but we knew that."

"Can we go back and stand off the ones who are chasin us, and then sneak around—"

"I'd guess that there are nearly a score and a half behin us, and they've sent some off to the east along that trail w passed awhile back to cut us off from the little river. Up fron looks worse. Close to fourscore of those white lancers. The must have one of those wizards. I can feel that off-whitenes: I should have looked farther this morning . . . but it's tiring. Ayrlyn took a deep breath. "I'm sorry." *Sorry . . . sorry . . .*

"It's not your fault."

"It is, but I can't do much about it now," she admitted. "It' what happens when you try to keep stupid promises."

Except . . . they weren't stupid. The last thing we need Cyador taking over all of Candar. Then where do we go?

"About where we seem to be going now," suggeste Ayrlyn.

"Frig, frig . . . frig," muttered Nylan. "Why is it that an time that we make the slightest mistake, it comes back i fluxes . . . or anvils?"

"Balance," suggested Ayrlyn dryly.

"Is that because we're more susceptible or sensitive?"

She shrugged, glancing back to the south.

"I know. Now's not exactly the time for theoretical speculations."

"The white ones are closer," pointed out Sylenia.

"It has to be all or nothing," Nylan said. "I have this feeling that we won't be worth much once we disrupt the balance.
So we have to do something to take them all out."

"They're closing in from just about every direction."

"Put the chaos in a cakelike shape—one of the fancy
ones—with the holes in the middle—we're in the hole,
and—"

"I get the image." Ayrlyn coughed again. "Sorry . . . it's
dusty. We'll have to hurry. We need to get closer to the lancers
in front of us."

"How far are they?"

"Another three or four kays."

"Frig . . . we definitely need to speed it up." Nylan flicked
the reins and eased the mare into a faster gait—a slow canter? He'd never been much on riding terms. Then, he'd never
even seen a horse up close until finding himself plunked down
in a mountain valley in an improbable world and being called
upon to do the impossible—continually, it seemed.

Could he create a double order line and channel the forces
between the boundaries? He wouldn't know until he tried, and
he couldn't try yet. Their opponents were too spread out. He
tried not to grit his teeth and concentrated on riding, occasionally looking back over his shoulder or to the east, checking the dust plumes in both directions.

By the time they had ridden along another long ridge,
dropped through a swale and climbed another hilltop, his legs
and thighs ached, and his shoulder and neck had stiffened
again. His face burned worse than earlier in the day, and he
was sweating despite the light breeze, although the wind was
hotter and drier and irritated his face as much as cooled it.

The sun hung at midday, but slightly to the south, and their
pursuers were riding down the ridge into the swale, not less
than a kay behind them.

"We aren't going to reach that next hilltop before the ones
behind us catch us," Ayrlyn shouted.

"Stop here." Nylan reined up and staggered off the mare. His knees nearly buckled when his boots hit the dusty dirt of the road, and he grasped the saddle to keep his balance.

Sylenia had to turn her mount to avoid running Nylan down, and she glared at the angel.

Nylan ignored the look and handed the mare's reins to the still-mounted Sylenia. "Hold these."

"A stable boy I am not."

"Dead is what we'll all be if we don't figure out how to stop the Cyadorans. You can help most by making sure the mounts don't run off," snapped the engineer.

The nursemaid's head snapped back.

"If you would," added Ayrlyn, handing her chestnut's reins to Sylenia after dismounting. "Nylan is right, even if he's a bit sharp."

Sharp? Who wouldn't be with more than fivescore Cyadorans forming up for a charge to obliterate you? The engineer tried to concentrate on reaching the order-chaos boundary layer beneath the soil, noting as his perceptions extended themselves that the power differential was less than the night before. Did it drop off that rapidly north of the Grass Hills? Or had they depleted it the night before?

"It drops off, I'd bet," Ayrlyn answered the unspoken question.

"Great."

"Not that much. There has to be plenty of power there."

Nylan took a long and slow deep breath, trying to relax a little, trying to shut out the drumming of hoofbeats nearing from all directions. He didn't have time to relax. He pushed his senses downward, reaching for the chaos/order boundary.

Ayrlyn's thoughts touched his. . . . *can't go alone, but can follow* . . . And he was aware of her warmth beside him, both physically and perceptually.

His perspiring forehead was coated with rivulets of sweat, yet he forced himself to be as gentle as possible, coaxing nudging an inner order boundary around the small segmen of the hill where the four of them stood.

"They near, angels!"

Trying to ignore Sylenia's urgency, the engineer attempted to create an outer boundary, not caring if it felt wavery, tenuous. The inner barrier was the important one, and he and Ayrlyn eased dark order currents around them.

"Wadah, pease?" begged Weryl.

"Hush, child. Hush."

"Wadah."

Nylan forced himself to ignore Weryl as the sound of horses drummed louder. With a convulsive mental *snap*, he broke the "insulation" between the lines of order and chaos, holding on to the barrier around them as unseen white lines of fire, ugly red gouts of molten force and stone bubbled upward.

Dust puffed up in patches, and the ground heaved. Nylan went down on one knee, started to rise, then remained there as Ayrlyn knelt beside him and took his hand.

Whhhhssstttt!! EEEEEeeeee . . . Not only did fire flare from the ground, as a curtain of chaos flame rose around the four and their mounts, but a sulfurous mist/haze burned through his nostrils, and he almost gagged, dry mouth and all.

Whheee . . . eeeee . . . eeee . . . Horses screamed.

Nylan hoped Sylenia could control their mounts. He wished she'd dismounted, but forced his concentration back on the barriers that held back primal chaos from them, trying not to think about Weryl, continuing to focus on that insubstantial line of order between them and disaster.

Wheeeee . . . eeee . . . Another set of horse screams—more distant—rose above the rumbling and shrieking of released chaos.

A thin line of white force probed toward them, and Nylan could sense Ayrlyn bat it away as though it were an insect—once, and then a second time.

The ground lurched again . . . and again . . . and the fires that had exploded out of the ground screamed and slashed through Nylan's skull. He swallowed, his eyes tightly closed, his mouth and throat dry, his chest tight, and his heart racing.

The engineer, despite both knees on the ground, felt as though he rode both the powerfluxes of a translating subspace ship and a horse of chaos simultaneously—all while being skewered by a surgically thin, high-grade weapons laser that was trying to flay every nerve he had.

Blackness—and angry whitened red—swirled around the engineer and around the healer, jolting them, fusing them, then yanking them apart. Heat welled up and past the order barrier, and Nylan's face felt flayed by lines of fire, by dust that ground itself against his skin.

Whhheeeeee . . . eeee . . . The screaming of chaos rubbing against order barriers went on . . . and on . . . and on . . .

Almost instinctively, the two angels struggled to close off the rupture Nylan had created, pushing, pressing order lines back toward a smooth flow.

Balanced—they were balanced . . . all the way . . . Those were Nylan's last thoughts as one hand grasped Ayrlyn's and the other tried to keep himself from toppling forward onto ground heaving so much that dust rose everywhere.

Then he did pitch forward as the order/chaos rupture sealed, the barrier collapsed, and the backlash of both balanced forces swept over them.

CXXXII

THE MAGE UNDER the white awning staggered, then steadied himself on the portable white wood table.

"Something . . . terrible . . . terrible . . ." murmured Themphi, looking down at the shards of shattered glass on the white surface. Blood dripped from the gashes in his forehead, leaving watery reddish stains on some of the mirror shards and darker splotches on the chaos-bleached wood.

"What was it?" Fissar stood at his shoulder, proffering a dampened white towel. "The glass shattered. I could feel it."

"It felt like another, a powerful one, yet it had the feel of the Accursed Forest, and it was closer, far closer—no more than a half-day's ride to the east." The white mage blotted way the blood gently, then stopped and extracted another sliver of glass from his hair above his right ear. "Go tell Triendar . . ."

"Ah . . ." stammered Fissar as he glanced from Themphi to the wiry white-haired mage who stepped in from the sunlight and under the shade of the awning. "Ah . . . ser . . ."

"Tell me what, Themphi? Why is your tent set up? And with what new magery were you toying? I could sense the order-chaos pulses from the marshal's wagon."

"None. No new magery. I sensed something . . . strange, and I set up the tent, just the roof part, you see, so I could concentrate. I was screeing the flank guard. They had encircled someone—no more than four riders. There was a flare of chaos, and my glass exploded."

Fissar opened his mouth and then closed it.

The balding white-haired mage pursed his lips. "Perhaps Marshal Queras should know this. What happened to the flank guard?"

"I do not know." Themphi felt sweat mixing with blood, and he carefully resumed blotting away both. "Except I do not think they survived. Neither did the young mage with them."

Fissar's mouth opened again.

"With that much of a chaos-order mix, I would think not. Do you have any idea what caused it?" asked Triendar.

"It acted like a mage, but it felt like the Accursed Forest . . in a way." Themphi handed the bloodied towel to Fissar so that he could work a tiny sliver of glass from his left hand.

"You felt that the Accursed Forest has destroyed those lancers?" Triendar frowned. "Even in the ancient times, the forest used animals, not the white forces directly."

"It was a mage, but not exactly. It was *like* the forest, but it was not the forest." Themphi took the towel again, then paused once more to ease out another chunk of bloody glass.

"Are you certain?"

Themphi nodded.

"That could be most worrisome. Have you a spare glass?"

"Yes," answered the younger mage warily.

"Then try to seek out the cause of this . . . this problem.

Once you know, we will tell the marshal that we *think* there may be a problem." Triendar worried at his chin. "You had best hurry. The lancers have finished with the hamlet beyond the rise, and the marshal is having his tent struck." He paused. "Then, it may be best to wait until morning. We could do little anyway . . . but do your best to discover the source of this . . . problem." Triendar coughed, pursed his lips. "One of our mages?"

"Pirophi, I think."

"He was always a little oversure, but . . . still. Do what you can."

Themphi nodded, then turned to Fissar. The younger man had already opened the small chest beside the portable table.

CXXXIII

THE CANDELABRA HELD lit stubs, barely a finger in length. Wax drippings wound around the silver base and seeped across the purple cloth. Three empty bottles stood on the table. So did two goblets, one full, the other empty. Against the glass of the center bottle rested a half-curled scroll.

Zeldyan reached for the scroll again, then stopped, and looked across the table toward Gethen. "Reading it once more will change nothing. There is nothing left of Syskar, Kula, and dozens of smaller hamlets. Clynya is a charred ruin, and the field crops have all been fired, those that could not be harvested quickly before the white demons destroyed them." She glanced toward the half-ajar door to the adjoining room that served as Nesslek's bedchamber. "A poor beginning, my sleeping son."

"Poor indeed," rumbled Gethen. "I have found less than tenscore in armsmen to bring here to Rohrn for Fornal. Tenscore! Two small companies of the white demons' lancers would overwhelm them in a morning—or sooner. Tenscore.

nd the holders begrudge that, even while they demand we
old back the demons." His eyes fixed Zeldyan. "And you,
aughter, letting me go, and then bringing Nesslek to this run-
own place."

"You would have me wait helpless in Lornth? This way I
ould bring all the armsmen from the keep. You need every
lade that can be found." Zeldyan brushed back a strand of
lond hair, and her fingers dropped to the table, then curled
round the base of the crystal goblet that bore the etched seal
f Lornth, a goblet mostly full of the amber white of Carpa.

"I do not know that all the cold iron in Candar would stop
hem." Gethen touched his beard.

"Fornal would claim so."

"That we know."

"My brother claims much." Zeldyan glanced toward the
edchamber door yet again. "My brother . . ."

"You question . . . ?"

"I do not like the way in which he regards Nesslek," ad-
nitted Zeldyan. "Was it not Sylenia who brought them to heal
ny son? Was it not Fornal who insisted he was not ill? Yet I
eel much discomfort in saying such."

"You say it, my daughter."

"I feel it. As I felt it when Fornal suggested to Relyn that
e could claim the ironwoods."

"Fornal said that?"

Zeldyan nodded. "Did you not know?"

Gethen cleared his throat, lifted his goblet, sipped, set it
lown. Finally, he spoke. "Where are your angels now?"

"I do not know. I will not yet give up hope, not while
ornth stands." Zeldyan sipped from the goblet she had re-
illed but once.

"You have greater faith than I, my daughter."

"Faith? I know little of faith these days. I know people.
.ady Ellindyja will die prating of empty honor. Fornal will
se a blade at the slightest pretext. You will use arms, but only
f all else fails. And the angels, they will keep their word, or
lie. If they can, the angels will return." The candles flickered
n the momentary breeze that flitted through the open window,

bringing the sour smell of Rohrn, a town that had seen better days.

"If they can . . ." Gethen said.

"We have not lost that from which we would not recover."

"Not yet, but the white demons are like locusts, or like a grass fire, charring everything before them." The gray of Gethen's hair glinted in the dim and flickering light that shifted as the candle flames wavered in the gentle and cool breeze from the open window. "If your angels do not return . . . we will fight as we can . . . as we can . . ."

"They will return." Zeldyan's fingers tightened on the goblet, and her eyes went to the partly open door. "They will return. . . ."

CXXXIV

A COOL WIND brushed his face, and Nylan shivered. Shivered? In the middle of southern Lornth? He shivered again.

"You must drink. You are burning," said a voice.

Burning? Whose voice?

Images of chaos-fire, order bounds, and the screams of dying men and horses swirled through his skull. Force . . . force . . . always force.

". . . force . . ." he murmured. Was it Ayrlyn who talked to him through the darkness? Ayrlyn, who had always been there for him? No—she had been swept under the blackness with him. Ryba? The dark marshal?

"Drink."

A water bottle was pressed to his lips, and he drank, slowly, through cracked lips and a dry mouth, finally sensing that Sylenia held the bottle.

Nylan opened his eyes, then shut them quickly as lights strobed through the darkness. Propped up against something—packs or blankets—he continued to sip the water

Sylenia offered him. Even closed, his eyes twitched with the flickers of light, as though individual powerfluxes flashed through them. Unlike the mass of pain that had flowed through him after battles before, he felt more exhausted than threshed or beaten. An acridity came with the evening breeze, an acridity that carried the odor of burned grass and rock—and charred flesh. Nylan swallowed the bile at the back of his throat.

"Ayrlyn?" he finally asked.

"I'm awake," came a tired voice out of the light-strobed darkness. "Better than you, but not much. We may have overdone it."

Overdone it? Probably. Don't I overdo everything?

"Stop it," said Ayrlyn wearily. "We didn't have much choice, and we did it together."

"It is terrible," Sylenia said into the darkness. "All around, nothing lives. Nothing moves."

"Weryl?" Nylan croaked.

"He cried, but he sleeps. He is innocent, like my Acora was."

All children were innocent, supposedly. Weryl was, that Nylan knew, but the engineer had to wonder about people like Ryba and Gerlich and Fornal. He knew better, but he found it hard to believe they had ever been innocent. He could hear Sylenia moving, carrying the bottle toward the redhead.

"You, healer, must also drink again."

"Thank you," Ayrlyn said, after a time.

Sylenia returned the water bottle to Nylan. "Again."

The engineer drank, more easily the second time, even as questions flitted through his mind.

How much time did they have? Would the Cyadorans turn all their forces against Ayrlyn or him? Or did they think the two angels had perished? Either way, also, the Cyadorans would continue to march northward. Of that he was certain. He and Ayrlyn had to do something. But what?

Even as he attempted to consider the problem, he could feel his eyes getting heavier, closing, against his unspoken protests.

Finally, in the gray before dawn, Nylan pried his eyes open, relieved that he did not experience the shooting, flickering light-strobes of the night before. Carefully, deliberately, he sat up in the stillness, an unnatural stillness without even the chirp of insects or the rustle of grass. His mouth was dry again, and filled with the taste of ashes, a taste that matched the gray of the dawn. His head throbbed with a dull aching, and his shoulders and back were sore and stiff. The skin of his face simultaneously itched and hurt and felt crusty.

His hands trembled as he fumbled for his boots, boots that Sylenia had pulled off. He certainly hadn't been able to do that. Then he managed to reach the water bottle and take a long swallow.

Ayrlyn rolled over on her bedroll, and he waited, taking another sip of water, as she struggled to sit up.

"Good morning."

"Wiped out . . . and you're still cheerful," she grumbled, shifting her weight cautiously, clearly as stiff as he was.

He extended the water to her, watched as she put the bottle to her lips and drank.

"You two," said Sylenia, rolling over, sitting up, and pulling on her boots. "Stinks here. Will for a long time."

Nylan looked beyond Sylenia and Ayrlyn, toward the east and the orange glow that was the almost-rising sun. Thin trails of smoke rose from one part of the scorched hillside. The four mounts, on a tieline that Sylenia had set up, grazed almost disconsolately on the sparse clumps of brown and green grass near the charred border between their sanctuary and the ashes beyond.

"Will it be safe to leave?" asked Sylenia. "Once we eat?"

"Yes," Nylan answered. "If more armsmen don't come."

"Good."

Ayrlyn frowned.

"What?" he asked.

"You're older," Ayrlyn said. "It's not the hair, either."

He turned his head and looked at her, deliberately. Her hair was still flame-red, but there were lines around her eyes, and darkness within and beneath them. Her skin was blistered in places, ready to peel. "So are you."

She took another swallow from the water bottle. "We've got to figure out how to handle this better."

"Any ideas?" he asked.

"No, but after we eat and feel better, we're going to sit here and play with it, until you and I understand, because next time we try without understanding, we'll be old and gray or dead or both."

"Oooo." Weryl stretched on his small bedroll, thrusting out arms and legs.

"He feels better than we do, I'll bet," offered Nylan.

"That wouldn't be hard." Ayrlyn stretched and leaned toward her boots. "Ohhhh."

The engineer eased himself to his feet and lumbered the few cubits to the provisions packs that Sylenia had unloaded. There he bent laboriously, his knees and back creaking, extracted the heavy squash bread, and hacked off several slices.

One he proffered to Ayrlyn, once she had her boots on. She stared out at the gray desolation that was turning into a patchwork of brown and black and gray with the rising sun.

"Thanks. Need something . . . head aches." Ayrlyn took a slow mouthful and chewed mechanically.

In a way he couldn't fully describe, Nylan could sense both her headache and his own. He began to eat slowly.

"Wead . . ." offered Weryl.

Nylan bent and broke off a chunk of the orangish bread for his son, then reclaimed the water bottle silently from Ayrlyn.

"We do not leave? We must stay amidst this?" Sylenia made a sweeping gesture to encompass the entire hilltop.

"Not any longer than we have to," temporized the engineer, half-mumbling around the still moist and heavy bread.

"But . . . the white demons . . . they ride toward Lornth," protested Sylenia.

"Slowly," said Ayrlyn. "What good will it do for us to hurry up and get killed? That's what will happen if we don't work this out." She paused. "And Tonsar will probably get killed, too."

Sylenia frowned.

"Oooo!" Weryl sputtered forth orange crumbs, waving a chubby fist. "Wadah . . ."

Nylan uncorked the water bottle, took a quick sip, wiped the rim, and offered it to his son. After Weryl drank, he wiped the bottle again, gave it to Ayrlyn, and walked toward the circular rim of ashes around their impromptu camp, chewing another chunk of the bread.

The ground was burned in spots, turned in others, and merely cracked elsewhere, but some of the cracks were wide enough for a mount to be swallowed shoulder-deep. Everywhere reeked of chaos, ugly unseen white-red chaos, yet bands of dark order ran through the white.

Nylan shivered, but kept walking around the perimeter of the order-insulated island of unburned and unchanged grassland.

". . . terrible angels," murmured Sylenia to herself.

Nylan was inclined to agree. So far, he'd managed everything terribly, and it was a wonder they were still functioning, much less alive.

The mixture of ashes and cracked land extended more than a kay in every direction. The engineer shuddered again. Just what were they working with? Could the white mages call up similar energies?

He didn't feel that they could, though he couldn't—again—say why. But if they could . . .

Once again, balance was the key, somehow. Instinctively he understood that. He shivered as he thought of chaos, like a fever . . . like a fever . . . chaos as a fever, Nesslek . . . the chaos fever that had killed Ellysia. But he hadn't tried to drive out the chaos, just contain it . . . twist it within order.

Had they still kept order and chaos too separate the day before . . . kept them too isolated, too pure?

"Could be," offered Ayrlyn, as she stepped up beside him.

"How could we keep them less separate?"

"Use more order insulation? Smaller and separate chaos tubes?" She shrugged and took a sip of the water bottle she carried. "We could experiment with very small tubes and compare how they felt."

Nylan nodded. Empirical research—that might work.

"It will," offered Ayrlyn.

He glanced back to where Sylenia offered Weryl another chunk of the heavy bread, then nodded. "We'd better get started."

"Not until you eat and drink more."

"Yes, healer."

Ayrlyn smiled and handed him the nearly empty water bottle. "Don't forget it, master of the chaos balance."

He had to grin back at her.

CXXXV

A YOUNG MAGE killed? An entire company of lancers wiped out, and you would tell the marshal not to worry?" Piataphi raised both straggly eyebrows, but one hand remained on the hilt of his saber. His bloodshot eyes were hollowed with dark circles, and his white uniform hung loosely on his frame.

"What good will worry do?" asked Themphi, almost under his breath. "Queras must continue. He has no choice."

"Choice or no, I must inform him." Piataphi turned and walked toward the second tent less than thirty cubits away.

"As you see fit." Triendar nodded slightly at Themphi once the lancer majer had turned and walked across the hilltop toward the Marshal of Cyador, Fist of His Mightiness. "Remember. Do not mention the forest. Or the three angels and their visit there," he added in a low tone to Themphi. "We do not *know,* for certain, that they destroyed the lancers. Admitting that uncertainty would not be wise. Not in the present circumstances."

"No," admitted Themphi. "But how long can we keep it from His Mightiness?"

"Long enough for it not to matter one way or another."

Themphi smothered a frown.

In the early morning light, Queras stood by the chair under the awning, facing northward, his eyes on the autumn-browned grass and the scattered and abandoned holdings to the west of the river. Around him, men in white rolled up the side panels of the tent. His eyes went to the majer. "Yes? What other disturbing tidings do you bring?"

"The left-flank company has failed to return, and no trace can be found of the armsmen or their mounts. Or of the mage that accompanied them."

"Majer, have you not learned from your failures? Did your sojourn at the mines teach you nothing? How many were in the flank guard?"

"A full company—four and a half score."

"Replace them with two companies, and add another company to the right flank as well. You, above all . . . you certainly should know that we can never allow any group of armsmen to be outnumbered." Queras's eyes flashed.

"Yes, ser." Piataphi bowed.

"You worry, Majer, yet you refuse to learn from your experiences. But is it not the same as what we have already faced?" asked the marshal. "When our forces are small, they are vulnerable, as yours were when you held the mines. But the barbarians have not been able to stand against all forces, and we have reduced all before us." He gestured at the hills flanking the river. "And we will take everything from those hills to the Northern Ocean."

Piataphi and Themphi looked at the dusty brown grass that surrounded the green carpet on which rested the marshal's carved and green-lacquered chair.

Triendar stepped forward.

"No, sage one. I need no cautions. I know the enemy is treacherous, and we have prepared as best we can. Cautions are best when preparing for the campaign. Cautions only reduce the boldness we need. Now we must reduce the enemy and carry forth the will of His Mightiness."

All understood the unspoken sentiment—"lest we be reduced with the barbarians."

CXXXVI

A REDDISH GLOW covered the sky above the western hills as Nylan set Weryl on his small bedroll and then sank onto his own, sitting and catching his breath, barely able to move. His back and shoulders were stiff. His thighs and legs burned from the long days in the saddle racing to get ahead of the white horde. And his head ached.

Whuuuu . . . uuufff . . . Downhill from where the engineer sat, the chestnut lifted her head, then tossed it, before going back to grazing, trying to seek out the green clumps of grass buried among the brown. Nylan's mare grazed silently, if more intently.

After a moment, Nylan rose, wearily, and stepped toward the provisions bag he had set by the saddles and blankets. The four mounts grazed on the longer grass in the protected hollow below the scrub oaks, the tieline anchored to sturdy roots.

"Da!" called Weryl, lurching up from his own bedroll, trundling forward and throwing his arms around Nylan's left leg. "Da!"

His own aches forgotten, the engineer bent and lifted the boy, hugging him tightly for a moment, their heads close together. "Weryl. Sometimes . . . sometimes . . ." *Sometimes, it's so hard to appreciate that while you're little now, before I know it . . . you'll be grown . . . already changing so much . . .*

"Da . . . wadah?"

Nylan loosened his hug and grinned. "I'll get you water, you little imp."

"Wadah?"

"Yes, you can have some, even if you aren't thirsty."

"Da!"

"You understand more than you ever say, you sentimental man." Ayrlyn looked up from the provisions bag Nylan hadn't managed to reach.

"That's dangerous."

Not with me . . .

Nylan could sense both the thought and the warmth behind it. "Old habits die hard. I'm trying."

"I know." *I know . . .*

After a silence, he asked, "How are we doing? In getting ahead of the Cyadorans, I mean."

"Tomorrow we should see Rohrn," Sylenia interjected, stepping toward the angels. "If it has not been burned already."

"The Cyadorans are three days behind us, at the rate they're traveling," explained the redheaded angel.

"You angels . . . you know what you should not and cannot see. Me, I trust what you say, but I would see Rohrn first." Sylenia picked up the two water bottles. "There is a stream, and we need water." She swept her hair, just loosened from the bands that held it when she rode, over her shoulder and marched downhill through the swaying and dry knee-high grass.

"You think they're that far behind us?" Nylan shifted Weryl to his other arm. "They've only traveled one day in four?"

"They're really not traveling fast. They seem more interested in destroying everything than in making a quick assault." The corners of her mouth turned up sardonically. "What else would you expect of the descendants of the Rationalists? Nothing is human except them. No other ways or beliefs can be tolerated."

"With just a little force to ensure the true and rational way."

"Cynical, but accurate."

"Force again." Nylan sighed. "Will we ever escape it?"

"We can, but not by converting an existing system. We'll have to begin from scratch. You know that."

And he did. The forest of Naclos represented a different approach—the approach of balance, where the use of force became a last resort—only to balance order and chaos, rather than the first option or order of business. But even the forest had fallen before the Old Rats.

"There's one little problem," he pointed out. "We still have to make our strategy work."

"It's not little." Ayrlyn laughed harshly. "And you were calling me the mistress of understatement?"

"I'm following your example."

"My example? When it's a dubious virtue, it's my example?"

Nylan, still holding Weryl at his shoulder, looked down at the brown grass sheepishly, then back at Ayrlyn.

After a moment, she grinned.

So did he.

CXXXVII

RIDERS AHEAD." NYLAN noted the dust on the road south from the bridge that guarded the east entrance to Rohrn.

"A scouting patrol. It's not the Cyadorans, not under a purple banner." Ayrlyn's hand touched the hilt of the shortsword at her waist, then brushed back strands of hair off her still peeling forehead.

Nylan touched his own blade, but left it sheathed as the Lornians slowed their approach.

At the head of the column rode a redheaded subofficer, square-faced, impassive, backlighted by the low sun that hung barely above the bluffs on the far side of the river, the bluffs that held the roofs of Rohrn. The column halted. So did the angels.

"Greetings, Lewa," offered Nylan. "We have returned. As we said."

Lewa looked at both angels, then at Sylenia.

"It's the angels!" called a voice from the rear of the squad—Fuera, Nylan suspected.

"When will you leave again?" Lewa's voice was cold.

"Not until the Cyadorans are defeated," Nylan said tiredly.

Lewa paused, then nodded slowly. "Your word, you always keep. For good, or worse."

"We're sorry it took so long, but," Nylan admitted, "we needed to find a better way to fight the Cyadorans."

"They are like locusts, stripping the ground, and like fire, laying waste to all before and behind them."

Nylan almost swallowed, surprised at the unexpected verbosity.

"That is what ser Fornal says," added the subofficer.

"He's right about that," noted Ayrlyn.

"We must patrol," apologized Lewa, "else I would escort you. Fuera and Sias—they can be spared, and you should have some honor."

"Thank you."

"We did not see anyone within the last fifteen kays," Ayrlyn said quietly.

"That would be good." Lewa nodded politely, then called, "Fuera! Sias!"

At the subofficer's order, the two former levies turned their mounts out of the column and rode forward.

"I ask you to escort the angels, and their companions, to the barracks and their quarters."

"Ser." Fuera nodded, but with a glimmer of a smile.

Nylan and the others drew their mounts to the side of the road. With a vague salute, Lewa nodded, and the patrol rode south.

"You have fought much sun," offered Sias with a look at Nylan's peeling and blistering forehead.

"You might say that."

"We are glad you have returned," added the former apprentice as the smaller group rode toward the bridge. "Could I still keep the tools? Some of them?"

"The ones I said were yours?" answered Nylan with a laugh. "Yes. I may need the others, but we'll see."

The bridge was empty and dark, and the dull *clop* of hoofs echoed through the streets of a deserted Rohrn, a town with shutters fastened tight, streets empty, doors barred.

"When did everyone leave?" Nylan asked Fuera.

"They have been going for almost an eight-day. Even the great holders here have sent their families to Lornth, some to

Rulyarth." Fuera spat toward the open guttered sewer—a dry sewer, Nylan noted.

"They are cowards," added Sias. "Not like you."

Thanks for the setup, Sias, Nylan thought, sensing Ayrlyn's grin as they rode through the empty square and the closed chandlery. The white-plastered walls of the buildings looked gray and dingy in the fading light.

The burned-out inn remained burned out, but the charred sign had fallen from its brackets—or been knocked from them.

The far side of Rohrn was also shuttered and silent.

Several armsmen turned from a woodpile as the group rode past the perimeter guards and toward the barracks.

"The angels . . ."

"They have returned . . ."

The mutterings and the whispers seemed to go on and on, although Nylan and Ayrlyn had not even reached the stable when the dark-bearded Fornal appeared in the twilight, flanked by two armsmen with torches that flickered in the light breeze. In the wavering light, shadows chased each other across the regent's face.

"I am so glad you have returned." Fornal's voice was lazily cold. "The white legions are less than three days' march to the southwest, and they have seared the grasslands for kays around them. The holders ask what good was our victory at the mines, and you are not here to answer."

"We have returned, as we promised." Nylan's voice sounded ragged to himself, and he hated sounding weak, especially in front of Fornal.

"That you did."

The two armsmen glanced from the regent to the angels and back again.

In the whispering quiet, Gethen walked into the vague circle of torchlight, followed by Zeldyan, whose blond hair glinted in the dimness.

"You have returned." Gethen's voice was flat. "But you return alone."

"You suspect the worst, but we have returned before we

must fight," Ayrlyn said quietly, her hand on her blade's hilt. "And we are here to fight."

Gethen looked askance momentarily before turning his eyes back to Nylan and quickly smoothing his face.

"Fairly spoken," grudged Zeldyan, her eyes on Ayrlyn, ignoring Sylenia. "What aid or succor do you bring? Is there any hope?"

"Yes," answered Nylan. *For all the gratitude you have . . .*

Ayrlyn suppressed a wince at his thoughts, and the smith felt ashamed. The Lornians were desperate, deservedly so.

"Where did you go?" asked Gethen.

"To the magic forest . . . to the enemy of Cyador," replied Ayrlyn quickly.

Nylan added, "We went to the Accursed Forest. It is real, and it is accursed—at least for the Cyadorans. And it will help us defeat them."

"What is the price?" asked Zeldyan. "Our submission to some green goddess?"

"It is not a god or goddess." Nylan shook his head. "The forest—it thinks of itself as 'Naclos' or something like that—the one that is and always will be—only needs the lands that are now eastern Cyador. I doubt it will ever need or want more. That was its historic range, before the ancient whites destroyed and confined it."

"That is all?"

"Look at Nylan," Ayrlyn commanded. "Look closely."

Silence fell. Gethen motioned to one of the armsmen with a torch, who stepped warily toward the angels.

"He is aged."

"Ten years, maybe more."

"So have you, lady," Zeldyan acknowledged. "You did this for us?"

"No," answered Nylan with a faint smile. "We did it because it needs to be done. If it did not . . ." he shrugged, "we'd probably be dead."

"You seem to have risked much for a people to whom you owe little," said Gethen.

"We hope . . . we hope . . . to find a place where we are

welcome." Nylan took a deep breath. "We've been riding from dawn to beyond sunset for more than an eight-day, except once," he added. "We want to live in peace and in harmony." Realizing he was so tired that he was repeating himself, Nylan snorted. "And we'll spend the rest of our lives fighting to do so—that's what being human is all about, anyway." He paused, then added, "We would like some food and rest before the Cyadorans get here."

"As you wish, mighty angels." Fornal offered a deep bow. "As you wish." He turned and marched into the darkness.

"Have you heard what has occurred in your absence?" asked Gethen. "Ildyrom lies dead, and even his bitch consort fell. Their mounts are cinders or scattered hundreds of leagues across the grasslands. Clynya, on both sides of the river, is in ashes and ruins, and the white demons march toward Rohrn."

"We rode through Clynya. We know." Nylan dismounted slowly. "All except about Ildyrom. He was the lord of Jerans, wasn't he?"

Zeldyan nodded.

"They know of the demons and their fires. They have already destroyed fivescore of the white demons," added Sylenia. "Just to return to Rohrn."

"Is that true?" asked Zeldyan.

"Yes." Nylan coughed. His legs ached, as they did after every day's ride, and his neck and shoulders were stiff again. "We're still learning. It's costly." He led the mare toward the stable doors.

"That aged them," interjected Sylenia.

"You have a champion," said Gethen with a half-laugh.

"You have changed, Sylenia," said Zeldyan. "Best you remain with the angels."

"If I must." Sylenia nodded toward the regent. "If I must, lady."

"You are dangerous, angels," said Zeldyan. "You will change all of Lornth before you are done. In that, Fornal was correct."

"Hardly dangerous," suggested Ayrlyn as she dismounted. "Just tired and sore."

Zeldyan offered a faint smile. "I said you would return, and your quarters are ready." She inclined her head. "Nesslek is waiting for me."

"How is he?" asked Nylan.

"Well, and hungry." Another nod, and the blond was gone.

"I needs must attend to . . . certain matters." Gethen nodded and disappeared into the darkness.

"Once again, we've made ourselves so welcome." Nylan's laugh was low and bitter.

"You are too powerful for them," said Sylenia.

Was that true? They were tired and all too human. Nylan shook his head. Too powerful? When they were outcasts wherever they went? Powerful? Hardly. Just tired and grasping at less than straws in a world where the only constant was the need for force.

The engineer began to lead his mare toward her stall.

CXXXVIII

THEY HAVE RETURNED . . . as they promised," pointed out Gethen.

"Yes, my sire. They keep their word. Always do they keep their word, and each time, Lornth changes." Fornal's words were slow, measured. One hand dropped to his waist, where his fingers tightened around the hilt of the dagger at his belt. "What can I say? They have killed more of the white demons than any of us, yet still the white demons threaten to destroy all we hold dear. If whatever magic they have brought does destroy the Cyadorans, will it also not destroy Lornth?"

"Can we afford to lose their aid now?" asked Gethen, sitting upright in the old wooden chair, a chair pushed away from the table on which still rested a half a loaf of dark bread, a partly cut wedge of cheese, and an earthenware mug. The older regent's blade, still in its sheath, lay half across Gethen's knees. One hand was circled loosely around the hilt.

"Yet, in little ways, they will destroy Lornth. A nursemaid looks at me as though I were the serf. My armsmen question me silently. What will come next?" Fornal eased his fingers from the dagger's hilt.

"If we win, we can work out something. We still hold Rulyarth, and Ildyrom is dead."

"That may be true. Yet I say that should they bring down the Cyadorans, that success will bring down the Lornth I have known and given my life to serve. This I cannot prove, nor have they been other than honorable in their own way. But our Lornth will be no more."

"If they cannot defeat the white ones, our Lornth will cease tomorrow." Gethen touched his gray beard with his left hand.

Fornal shook his head. "For all that, *my* Lornth is perilously close to perishing."

"The Lornth we grew up cherishing, Fornal, perished the day the angels landed. Whatever may come, it is better than having all Lornth burned and dying under the white hordes."

"You will regret ever having listened to the silver tongues of these angels. For all their honor, they are as dark and evil as the white demons."

"Do we have a choice of demons?" Gethen rose from the chair, right hand holding the hilt of the blade fully as long and heavy as the one Fornal bore. His eyes did not leave his son's as he inclined his head but slightly. His lips crooked. "For that matter, in this life, have we ever had any choices, except to do what we have thought best?"

CXXXIX

THE MAJER STEPPED out of the direct sunlight and under the tent awning, past the two Mirror Foot guards. Neither guard moved as Piataphi approached the carved and lacquered green chair where the marshal waited, fanned by yet another guard.

The majer bowed.

"You have news, Majer?"

"The barbarians have stopped retreating, ser," announced Piataphi. "The van scouts report that they have gathered on the west bank of the river to defend the town called Rohrn."

"The name matters not." Queras raised his right hand, then dropped it. "Like all the others, it will stink. They all stink. Once it is razed, once we have the land in hand, then we will build a proper town, houses with tile floors, and baths, and covered sewers. A town worthy of Cyad and His Mightiness."

"When will the attack begin, Fist of His Mightiness?" asked Piataphi.

"Tomorrow."

"The only access from the east bank is a stone bridge, and they have removed the center span," said Piataphi carefully.

Queras frowned, then said coldly, "The engineers are constructing the bridges upstream of the town now. There should be no problems. The water is low. By tomorrow, all will be on the west bank."

Piataphi bowed. "You have foreseen all."

Queras offered a faint smile. "The river bluffs that protect them from any attack from the east will leave them nowhere to go. That will be more . . . expeditious than chasing the smelly wretches all over the plains." Queras smiled. "You see, Majer, there is no problem that cannot be solved with the application of adequate force."

"Yes, ser." Piataphi bowed once more, deeply, deeply enough that the marshal did not see his eyes.

CXL

IN THE DARKNESS that held but a glimmer of gray, the chime clanged, off-tone, off-key, once, then again.

Nylan looked across the darkness of the quarters with eyes that had been open for what seemed most of the night to the cots where Sylenia lay, and where Weryl snored softly. Despite the open shutters, the room was close, hot, and the sounds of men moving across the packed clay of the barracks yard grew louder. A horse whinnied, then another answered. A set of wagon harnesses jangled.

He turned to face Ayrlyn's also open eyes. "Not much for sleeping, was it?" he whispered.

She shook her head, then leaned forward and touched his cheek with her lips. "I'll be glad when it's over."

"I hope I'll be glad when it's over."

"Pessimist." Ayrlyn stretched, then rolled into a sitting position, her knees tucked up almost to her chin.

"Realist. We'll either be dead or the agents of a huge change, and no one likes agents of change, especially our friend Fornal." Nylan yawned and sat on the edge of the bed that was a cross between a cot and plank platform. His back was stiff, and he stood slowly, stretching. "Ohhhh . . ."

"It's not that bad," hissed Ayrlyn.

Outside, the off-key triangle chimes clanged again.

"Da? Ahwen?" Silver-haired Weryl sat up, his green eyes wide, arms extended.

"In a moment, son. Let your old dad get his boots on."

"Does no one here ever sleep?" grumbled Sylenia, throwing back her blanket with a disgusted gesture.

"Actually," Nylan said, "we were sleeping while you were out exchanging sweet words with a certain armsman."

"Sleeping you were not, not even when I returned."

Nylan flushed.

. . . *walked into that one* . . . Ayrlyn shook her head and headed for the provisions bag.

As Ayrlyn used her dagger on the remaining squash bread, Nylan hacked off several slices of the hard yellow cheese. Even more than an eight-day old, the orange bread was better than that turned out by the Lornian armsmen's cooks. On the other hand, the cheese, tough as it was, remained a definite improvement over wasol roots.

"The cheese, it is hard."

"It's what we have." Nylan refrained from comparing cheese and wasol roots. "The bread is still good."

Ayrlyn grinned, then erased the expression as she handed a slab of the orange stuff to Weryl, who sat on the end of his cot, eyes fixed on the food.

"Food."

"You can eat," Nylan told his son, and followed his own advice.

When they had finished their quick breakfast, the engineer looked to the redhead. "Can you find out where the Cyadorans are—without using too much effort?"

Ayrlyn's eyes glazed over, and Nylan waited . . . but only briefly.

"They're camped on the bluffs four or five kays south, and they're beginning to form up."

Nylan nodded. "The chimes were right, then?"

"Looks that way."

The two began to strap on their blades.

Then, Nylan picked up Weryl, holding him tightly. His eyes burned, and he swallowed. How long he held his son, he did not know.

"Nylan . . ." . . . *need to go* . . .

"I know." The engineer lifted his head and looked into the green eyes. "You be good for Sylenia, you understand?"

"Good, da?"

"He always be good," said the dark-haired nursemaid. "Greedy, mayhap, but good."

Nylan set the silver-haired child on his cot, but Weryl's arms stretched out again. "Da?"

"He has to go, child." Sylenia picked up the boy. "They both must go . . . and Tonsar."

Nylan and Ayrlyn eased out into the yard under a dark green-blue sky barely turning orange in the east beyond the roofs of Rohrn. The clank of harnesses, the *whuff*ing and *chuff*ing and neighing of mounts and the low murmurs of wary armsmen filled the space between the stables and the barracks.

As they crossed the yard toward the stable, the dark

aked figure of Fornal pointedly turned his back to the an-
ls, and began to talk to Lewa. Nylan frowned.

"He doesn't want to see us."

"I wonder why."

"Because he can't deal with us. He knows we're the only
pe, but we stand for change and for a lot of things he finds
rd to accept. And he's smart enough to know that there's
point in making a point until there's a reason to," suggested
rlyn.

"After the battle, if we have an 'after.' "

"Something like that, but there will be. And we'll have to
al with that, too."

"So . . . we're disposable if we win?"

"I don't know," Ayrlyn admitted. "Gethen's hard to read,
d there's Zeldyan. She's not happy with Fornal, either."

Huruc offered a half-gesture, half-salute as he rode past.
Both angels returned the gesture.

"Some people still think we exist," Nylan noted.

"The better ones."

Nylan tried not to breathe too deeply, not when the front
the stable smelled of manure, horse urine, damp straw, and
her even less appetizing items, but his nose twitched and his
outh curled.

"Pretty rank," Ayrlyn confirmed.

Like their choices—rank: Ryba's feminist dictatorship—
ean, ordered, and oppressive; Lornth's honor-bound, back-
ard, and filthy male autocracy; or Cyador's chaos-founded,
ean, male-dominated, and all-controlling empire.

"We have another choice," she pointed out. *The forest . . .
ore home than anything . . .*

"Not unless we defeat Cyador."

Still, his thoughts held the small and clean cottage that had
emed more homelike than most of Candar. Had it been
ore homelike than Sybra? He wasn't certain, and that com-
rison would have to wait.

Their mounts were near the front of the stable, for which
ylan was glad, having the feeling that matters got even
nker deeper in the recesses of the ancient structure.

They groomed and saddled the two mares quickly and silently, although Ayrlyn ended up helping the always-slower Nylan. By the time they led their mounts out to the comparatively less odorous yard before the stable, the sun peered over the roofs of Rohrn. Only a dotting of distant white clouds marred the green-blue sky—to the west.

"Angels!" boomed a burly mounted figure. "I have not my orders from you."

Nylan couldn't help but grin. "Tonsar."

"Lord Gethen, he told me to find you. And to do as you ordered." Tonsar's voice lowered slightly. "Sylenia—she told me the same, and she was not gentle in her words."

"She has gotten a little more forthright," Nylan observed cautiously.

"She speaks her mind, and you men . . ." Ayrlyn shook her head and mounted.

Nylan followed her example and climbed into his saddle. "Was I complaining? Did I say a negative word?"

"You didn't have to."

The chimes rang again, longer, more loudly.

"Ah . . . angels . . . my orders?" Behind Tonsar was at least a squad of armsmen, mounted. Nylan could see Sias's long face.

The engineer paused, fingering his chin. "Actually, it pretty simple. You'll need a squad or so just to keep anyone from bothering us while we work. It'll be easier if we can get out of Lornth, but we don't need to be on top of the enemy."

A figure in black galloped out of the barracks yard, holding a huge blade high. A good tenscore armsmen cantered after him.

"There goes the great armsman," muttered Nylan.

"Don't be bitter."

"We are ready," announced Tonsar. "We will shield you while you destroy the white demons."

"Let's go." Nylan turned the mare after the departing armsmen, but let her walk quickly. He doubted that a canter or gallop would make any difference, except to leave him sore.

The Lornian forces were drawing up to the southeast, less than a kay beyond the last houses that could have been deemed a part of the town. There was no wall, as was the case with any town the angels had seen in Lornth.

Gethen and Fornal had arrayed their armsmen in four squares, with Fornal positioned with a small mounted guard before the two squares to the right, and Gethen before those to the left. Nylan rode to a point even with the front rank of the squares and midway between the second and third squares.

Gethen glanced in their direction.

Nylan shifted his weight in the saddle, watching as the lines of white, the shimmering round shields reflecting the sunlight, formed a semicircle on the flat that had been fields and meadows, a semicircle of destruction that was more than two kays away from the outskirts of Rohrn, and more than a kay from the Lornian forces. The white troops and lancers stretched from the river bluff due south of the town all the way to the northwest road that led to Lornth itself—an arc of nearly a hundred and twenty degrees filled with armsmen and weapons, without a gap.

"Here?" asked Ayrlyn, reining up.

"As good a spot as any."

"Never have I seen so many armsmen . . ." whispered Tonsar.

Nylan hoped never to see so many ever again, either. "You better get your squad set up." He swung out of the saddle.

Ayrlyn followed his example.

"Someone will need to hold our mounts," he told Tonsar.

"Sias!"

"Yes, ser."

"Don't worry, Sias," Nylan told the young former apprentice as he handed over the mare's reins. "You won't miss a thing." *In fact, you just might see too much.*

The engineer let his senses range over the ground, just trying to get a feel, trying to extend his links to the distant forest, and to the order-chaos boundaries that felt all too far away.

"This is going to get nasty," he said in a low voice. "All that distance . . . hope we can do it."

"It already is nasty," Ayrlyn pointed out.

"So how do you plan to stop them, ser angel?" Gethen, flanked by a pair of hard-faced armsmen, and followed by the square-faced Huruc, reined up beside Tonsar. "You had told us to leave this spot for you. Will you rout them on foot?"

"Do you really want to know?" blurted Nylan. "I apologize, ser Gethen," he added quickly. "We hope to raise the forces of the forest to stop them before they attack. Or before most of their forces can reach us."

"Before?"

"Why not? There's not much doubt about what they intend, not after what they did to Jerans and southern Lornth." Nylan swallowed, his mouth dry.

"No." Gethen's words were cold, colder than his eyes.

A series of horn calls echoed from the south.

"Do what you must do," said Gethen gruffly. "The white demons are raising their banners. We will hold while we can." With a stiff nod, the older regent turned his mount toward the armsmen arrayed to the north of where Nylan and Ayrlyn stood. Stood alone amid the mounted host.

Nylan swallowed, or tried to. His throat felt dusty, dry.

Ayrlyn handed him a water bottle.

Another series of horn calls stabbed the day, and a faint rumbling, and trembling of the ground began.

Whhstt! A firebolt arced into the air and exploded.

"We'd better . . ."

"Just do it!"

Absently, Nylan corked the water bottle, bent and set it on the dusty ground that had been a meadow, and pushed his senses to the south, well behind and beyond the white and red blotches that represented the slow-advancing Cyadoran forces.

Reflected light flashed from the Cyadoran shields, and Nylan closed his eyes, concentrating, feeling, seeking.

The power he sought seemed so distant . . . so far south.

"We can do it." Ayrlyn's words and presence warmed him.

He tried to relax, to extend his tenuous probe, but much a

he pressed, that distant link eluded him, flitted from his mental grasp.

The ground vibrated with the impact of hoofs and feet, and the horns echoed toward Rohrn again.

Another blast of fire soared out of the south and splashed across the meadow before the Lornian forces. Little balls of fire rolled toward the mounted armsmen, each leaving a long charred line behind it before dying away. A gust of wind carried the odor of burned grass northward, and Nylan sniffed inadvertently.

The engineer tried to wrench his attention back to that distant and continual barrier struggle between order and chaos, even as yet another fireball *hissed* toward the Lornian armsmen.

For a moment, less than an instant, Nylan touched the dark bands of order, bands binding the very soil in place over the ancient rocks, slowly infusing those artificial planoformed established boundaries with the mixture of order and chaos that ran through the forest and through much of Cyador and southern Lornth.

Then . . . the link snapped, and he stepped sideways, off-balance.

"Again . . ." whispered Ayrlyn.

After another deep breath, the engineer tried once more, this time conceiving of the link as a network, an underspace connection. For a longer instant, his thoughts held the dark bands of order, but the chaos lines eluded him, snapping back so hard that he staggered where he stood, then sat down roughly.

"What the frig . . . the angel doing?" came a hissed whisper.

"Silence!" ordered Tonsar.

Nylan stood, helped up by Ayrlyn. Somehow he needed to and.

A huge white fireball arced toward the Lornian forces, shattering in midair and spraying liquid flames among the mounted armsmen of the first square, the one farthest left of the two angels.

"Aeeeeiiii . . . no . . . no . . ." The screams of dying men seemed like whispers against the growing thud of hoofs and the underlying shrieks of chaos lifted by the mages to the south.

Whheeeee. . . . eeeeee! The shrieks of suffering and dying horses climbed above those of the armsmen.

Another fireball flared, turning the grass before the Lornian forces into a wall of flame, flame so hot that it seared the skin and singed the hair of the men and horses in the front rank.

Sweat ran down Nylan's forehead, and into his eyes, burning them as the struggle to release the energy in the order-chaos boundaries throughout Candar burned through his skull and soul. His own hair crinkled in the heat.

Beside him, Ayrlyn tweaked the shallower lines of order, and a line of flames, dark flames, rose from the fields before the advancing Shining Foot, turning white uniforms black, charring the flesh under the blackened shells that had marched proudly instants before.

Nylan's stomach turned—or was he feeling her revulsion?

Somehow, someway, he had to tap some kind of order-chaos energy—before everyone was killed. But he couldn't reach it!

Whhhhsttt! Another white-red fireball flared across the morning sky, splattering death and flames through the armsmen to the angel's left.

More screams of mounts and men filled the morning, and the light wind carried cinders, ashes, and the odor of charred meat. Nylan's guts turned again.

The sun burned more brightly, or so it seemed, upon his back, and the oncoming Cyadorans appeared endless—endless ranks of white, of shimmering shields and clashing reflections.

His shirt was soaked, and his eyes burned from salty sweat from trying to reach and channel elusive chaos. But if he couldn't tap that distant force . . . how could the white mages? He didn't feel them doing anything like that—and they were certainly using order and chaos.

"If you can't reach the one you need," he murmured, "use the one you can reach."

Are you sure? asked a small voice.

He shook his head, but sent his perceptions down, straight down, to where rock met magma, to where a different sort of order and chaos met. There, there he seized the deeper boundary, the edge between rock and magma.

Do you want to do this? His jaw tightened. What choice did he have? He was too far from the forest and had too little time left. *There is always a choice.*

Do what we must . . . Ayrlyn's calm thought helped.

With a sound between sob and cry, he cleft order and chaos, struggling to hold layers and layers of order between him and the raw white energy, especially between Ayrlyn and that energy.

As they struggled, Ayrlyn adding her order, her force, yet another fireball sprayed the meadow, this time less than a hundred cubits before them. Nylan could feel his own hair crisping more, the heat of chaos fire washing over both him and Ayrlyn, their skin near burning from the chaos fire.

Concentrate on your work . . . Ayrlyn's calmness soothed the questions in his soul as he wedged chaos and order farther apart, building a channel up from the depths, a channel to the back side of the Cyadoran forces, even as he tried to create an order wall before their own armsmen.

Not much good if you turn us into cinders.

Ayrlyn coaxed and eased yet more of the black webs, the unseen black patterns, into that barrier.

Whhssttt! Whsstt! Two fireballs in quick succession splashed against the unseen barrier, with the gouts of chaos fire rebounding toward the advancing Shining Foot.

A half-score of white-coated foot flared like fatwood in a winter fire, and the line slowed, but only momentarily, before the Shining Foot surged forward once more, the second line of troops marching over the charred corpses of those who had led the charge.

Whhhstt!

The white mages continued to cast their fireballs, despite the barrier, despite the casualties to the advancing Shining Foot.

The trumpets sounded again, and the heavy drumming of hoofs rumbled the ground, nearer than ever before.

Not yet! Nylan thought desperately. *Not yet!* His eyes opened involuntarily. The Cyadoran forces were nearly upon the Lornians, and Gethen's blade was poised, raised.

Nylan closed his eyes, tried to speed the rising globs of chaos, to open order channels, hundreds of them, and his forehead spewed sweat. His eyes were blind, unseeing, as all his efforts went into pressing order against chaos, against the power from the depths.

But the Shining Foot surged northward, and the lancers pounded forward, toward the Lornians, toward them, toward Gethen, toward the chaos fields that had yet to rise where Nylan struggled to bring them into the open air.

The engineer's breath rasped from his laboring lungs and through his raw throat.

"Make ready," ordered Tonsar, his voice firm, far steadier than Nylan felt.

Nylan reached, straining, for the slow-rising deep chaos.

The Shining Foot to the left began to run, less than a dozen yards from Gethen's forces, building speed.

And still the demon-damned chaos seemed to float upward, ever so slowly, ignoring the straining, the order channels, and the need for its presence now.

Nylan groaned, knives flashing through his skull, pressing order against chaos, chivying the energies upward, ignoring the nearness of the chaos, ignoring the shivering of the ground, and the fireballs that continued to fall across the field.

Now . . . !

CXLI

THE MAJER SAW the white awning at the crest of the rise, barely a dozen cubits higher than the fields and meadows stretching east and north from where he sat astride the white stallion. With a glance at the still-forming lancers of the van, and the low and disorganized structures of the barbarians' town beyond, he chucked the reins, then turned his mount toward the mages' tent. Only one of the mages looked up as Piataphi reined in the stallion before the tent.

"Greetings," called Themphi.

"Why all these preparations?" asked the majer. "There are few indeed to guard their town. It is not worth guarding, or would not be were it ours." A grim smile creased his face. "Or are the barbarians more than you have admitted?"

"Often matters are not as they seem, you may recall." Triendar raised his head from the table and the screeing glass. "Did you ever find the fivescore Mirror Lancers who vanished?"

"No." The majer frowned, then glanced at the line of white mages that formed to the west of the small, open-sided tent. "You know that."

"We do," said the white-haired magician, an edge to his words. "That is why these mages gather here. Each is assigned to a unit and will use firebolts on your enemy."

"Just make sure that they don't flame ours."

"They won't." Triendar smiled coldly. "You command your men, and I will command mine."

Piataphi finally nodded his head brusquely when neither mage offered more. Then he raised his sabre in salute, and rode toward the left flank where the First Mirror Lancers waited for their commander.

After the majer departed, Triendar surveyed the line of white mages. "Once the horns for the advance are sounded, you will use your firebolts to destroy the barbarians directly before your assigned units. You will use your fire until the enemy is no more. You will not use fire if it will kill our armsmen. Is that clear?"

A series of nods punctuated the line of white-clad men.

"Go."

Triendar watched as the mages mounted and rode toward their separate units in the postdawn light.

"What do we do?" asked Themphi. Behind him, Fissar swallowed nervously.

"We watch for the mages who destroyed the lancers before.

We must destroy them." Triendar frowned and concentrated on the glass.

In the middle of the white mists appeared a man and a woman. The man had shimmering silver hair, the woman hair like flame.

"Angels. Just two, not three."

"But they fought Lornth," protested Themphi.

"They have always hated those of the Rational Stars," pointed out the older mage. "They are not rational."

"Obviously. They sought the Accursed Forest."

The two white mages watched the angels in the glass, the only two figures on the Lornian side who were dismounted though surrounded by a squad of armsmen who glanced nervously from side to side.

"Still, they do nothing," murmured Themphi.

"They do more than nothing. They are reaching beneath the ground. Perhaps they are earth mages, save I never heard of such."

The Cyadoran horn calls echoed across the flat, and the sound of marching foot followed.

A series of fireballs arced toward the north side of the Lornian forces and exploded. Triendar offered a quick smile that faded. A satisfactory series of screams ensued, and Themphi nodded.

In the glass, the male angel winced, staggered.

"Send a fireball toward the angels," ordered Triendar.

Themphi frowned, concentrated, and a whitish globe formed and accelerated northward, plowing into the ground and casting flame toward the angels.

Both angels stepped back. Triendar smiled, but the smile vanished as a wall of flame seared up in front of the advancing Mirror Foot.

"How?" The older mage snapped, "No matter. Another firebolt."

A huge firebolt arced deliberately toward the angels, and both stepped back. A barbarian armsman beside the angel beat out flames that had spread across his sleeve.

A series of smaller bolts cracked across the morning sky. More Lornian mounts and their riders flamed and fell.

"Another."

Themphi wiped his forehead and concentrated, then staggered as the ground shifted underfoot.

". . . they can't do that, can't keep doing it, anyway," muttered Triendar. "More fire."

The younger mage swallowed.

The horn calls redoubled, and the Mirror Lancers charged.

A firebolt exploded in midair, well short of the enemy.

Driblets of sweat beaded on Triendar's forehead. "They can't."

More firebolts splatted short of the enemy, some recoiling upon the Cyadoran forces.

Both mages exchanged glances, and the mirror blanked. The ground shivered, shuddered, and seemed to swell beneath their feet.

Themphi sensed the growing force, glanced at the glass on the table and threw himself prone, yelling, "Down!"

Triendar frowned and opened his mouth. The earth rolled, and the older mage grasped for the table to steady himself. The glass on the white-framed table exploded. Triendar shuddered, then collapsed across the table, blood welling across shattered glass and white splintered wood.

The ground heaved, and plumes of molten rock and sulfurous fumes rose, shrouding the sun, before the quick-forming clouds above cut off even more light. The screeing table collapsed under the dead weight of the white-haired mage.

Beyond the tent, the ground heaved, shivered, cracked, and then opened with a groan.

Themphi crawled to his knees, trying to stand, when another heaving of the ground cast him facedown into the dust.

"An earth mage. Who would have thought . . ." Themphi's last words were lost as the wave of rock and soil cascaded down across the tent.

CXLII

THE MAJER RODE from the mages' tent toward the van on the right. His eyes slowly scanned the vast semicircle of arrayed Cyadoran troops, from the Shining Foot to the Mirror Lancers between foot companies.

"Never so many," he murmured. "Never foot companies."

"Majer!"

Piataphi turned in the saddle.

Captain Azarphi raised an arm in salute.

The majer eased his mount toward Azarphi, who waited before a double squad of white lancers.

"You are still to lead the first charge?" asked the younger officer.

"His Mightiness's orders have not changed," answered Piataphi.

"They never do." Azarphi's voice was low. "They never will."

"No." Piataphi's response was as bleak as the grayness in his eyes.

"You think this is worse than the mines, don't you?" Azarphi shook his head. "There aren't that many of them, and we've crushed them every time."

Piataphi forced a smile. "We have. And the powers of Whiteness willing, we will again."

"I'll see you with the spoils of this barbarian land, even willing wench!" answered Azarphi with a wide grin.

Piataphi returned the smile. "I'd best be where I'm supposed to be." With a nod, he urged the white stallion northward and past the Shining Foot.

The serjeant raised his blade as the majer reined up. "Van squads ready, ser."

"Good." Piataphi turned his mount and studied the field once more. The seemingly small Lornian force was drawn up in four squares, with gaps between each, clearly stretching to avoid being immediately encircled.

"They'll have to draw together, won't they?" asked the serjeant behind and to Piataphi's left.

"I don't know what they'll do," answered the major. "They don't fight the way they used to."

"Pity. It was easier that way. It hasn't been that bad, though."

Piataphi nodded, then frowned. Between the second and third Lornian groups was a small squad. Two dark figures stood on the ground, and the mounted squad reformed before them.

"What's that?" questioned the serjeant.

"Mages. Black mages. We leave those for our mages."

"Fine with me, ser."

The horns rang out from the center of the arc, and the odd-numbered Shining Foot moved forward, heavy steps measured, in time, and the rhythm of their steps rose over the scattered murmurs of the Cyadorans. Light flashed from the polished shields, reflections cascading across the outnumbered Lornians.

A single fireball arched from somewhere behind Piataphi and crashed into the dusty ground well back from the Lornians. The defenders did not move, even as three more fireballs flared across the skies and burned their way nearly to the waiting barbarians.

The second set of horn signals bugled across the field.

The major surveyed his squad, then lifted his blade. "To the right center!"

"To the right!" echoed the serjeant.

Ahead of him, Piataphi could see another wave of fireballs, and these hissed down on the rightmost square of the defenders. Bodies flared like oil torches, their screams lost in the thunder of hoofs.

His eyes went to his left, toward the black mages. Had one fallen? No matter, one way or the other. His enemies lay before him.

The ground rumbled and swayed beneath the stallion's

hoofs, and the majer's knees pressed more tightly, holding his seat as he gestured with the blade. "Forward! Now!"

He urged the stallion into full canter, feeling the backwash of heat from the white fireballs.

"Fry us as well. . . ." came from behind him.

His squad was almost abreast the Shining Foot to his right, when the trumpets sounded once more, and the foot picked up the charge toward the waiting Lornians.

Piataphi smiled grimly.

Another set of fireballs arched overhead, so close that the majer could feel the heat picked up by his raised blade.

"No!"

The white fires *splattered* on an unseen shield, and flowed/splashed back toward the lancers and the nearer foot. Piataphi spurred the stallion into a leap over the low rolling clingfire, holding to his seat even with the jolting landing.

"Here! The lancers!" He turned the white back right, charging toward the outnumbered Lornians, blade again ready.

The ground lurched beneath him.

Fires, like red trees with flaming arms that grasped toward him, flared in a line between him and his lancers and the defenders. Heat, more intense than a furnace, hotter than the worse conflagration at the mines, welled around him.

Automatically, his blade went up in salute to the unknown mages, then vanished, as did the stallion and the bitter smile that was the majer's last expression.

CXLIII

. . . AND CHAOS BURST into the air, with dark dust, and the odor of brimstone, and the heat of furnaces stoked by the hearts of stars.

Nylan and Ayrlyn stood. Legs unsteady against the ground that surged beneath them, they stood.

The earth heaved like a chaos-fevered giant, and dust surged from every crevice. Gouts of fire flared irregularly from the hills and plains. Behind them, in Rohrn, even the lowest and rudest buildings swayed, and roofs sank and crumpled between splayed walls.

Farther north and east as well, as far east as Henspa, as far north as Carpa, houses, buildings, shuddered, and some fell. Others were etched with cracks across white plaster and stucco.

Soil flowed like water, in places swallowing grass, in places bursting forth like a muddy tide, slow-splashing across once-cultivated fields and once-grazed meadows.

The link with Cyador, prompted Ayrlyn. *Now! Do it deep.*

Deep? Of course. Nylan almost laughed as he reached deep, then sent his probes deep and south, as he could feel that intertwining of the forest reaching for what he fed, for what he channeled. And the forest swelled, and order-chaos tendrils swept and strengthened themselves beneath all Cyador, beneath the new rivers and the old, beneath the old hills and the new, beneath the towns of order built on chaos. And Cyador trembled . . . yet held against the forces Nylan and Ayrlyn raised.

Whhsttt! Whhstt! Whhstt!

Three fireballs slammed against the order barrier beyond the Lornian forces, rebounding into the charging white lancers. The tall force leader on the white stallion somehow dodged the firespray, still leading his force toward the outnumbered Lornians.

To the right of the struggling angels, a black-garbed figure raised a blade, and tenscore armsmen galloped toward the other company of oncoming Mirror Lancers. Lances of reflected light played across the Lornians, and some raised hands to be able to see against the glare.

"Frig . . ." muttered the engineer, trying to twist the rising gouts of order to separate the two forces, realizing he could not stop the fires that would strike Fornal and his men, not with the forces already unleashed and rising. "Frig . . ."

Chaos fire burst from the ground, not in a line, but like a

forest of fire trees. *Like a forest, like a forest.* The fire trees lifted the charging Lornians and the lancers on both sides of the black angels, strewing them like harvested grain, like stalks scythed, black-crisped instantly, and cast aside as fast-dispersing dust.

The tall Mirror Lancer officer raised his blade, even as he was no more, as man and horse crumbled into scattered and powdered charcoal.

Nylan sensed the death all around, closer, more immediate. Absently, the engineer winced, even as he knew the first two companies of white lancers had been turned into charcoal, and that Fornal was no more. The Lornian regent might have survived, had he waited.

The tripled notes of the Cyadoran battle orders echoed forth once more, and yet another line of Mirror Lancers heeded the horn calls. The ground vibrated again, as their mounts threw them toward the Lornian lines and the angels who struggled there. The horses charged toward the fire trees of order-bounded chaos. For a moment, but a moment, the white livery and shimmering shields threw back chaos, before the horses and Mirror Lancers flared into blackened figures that rose, and fell, crumbling like towers of finely powdered charcoal.

Another set of chaos fireballs splatted against the unseen order barrier.

The engineer's legs wobbled, and he sat down, still struggling to hold order and focus the deep chaos on the remainder of the Cyadoran forces, forces so numerous, numerous like the grasses of the plains.

But wildfire takes grasses.

With a groan, he/she visualized/coaxed/shaped the raging deep chaos into a wildfire, chevied by order winds, sweeping south and west from Lornth, incinerating all in its path, turning all above the ground into cinders and fine ash.

His/Ayrlyn's guts turned, and white agony stabbed through them both, and Ayrlyn staggered and dropped onto the dusty grass beside Nylan. He reached for her hand, unseeing, panting, still trying to hold open order channels, as hot chaos bub-

led upward all through what had been ancient Cyador, all
through what had been the domain of Naclos.

They could sense, could feel, the hills to the south shudder
as they shed their unnatural cover of soil. Could feel as the
marshes along the ancient riverbeds all the way south to the
great Canal of Cyador, all the way west to mighty Cyad itself, called themselves back into being, twisting neatly tilled
fields into sinkholes and pulling cultivated crops under oozing dark waters. As the great river that had been . . . twisted
and churned out of recent banks and into older ones. As lesser
rivers reappeared, and finely mortared canal walls dropped
beneath earth and mud and water. As the buried shoreline
boulders sprang forth again, shattering building foundations
and bringing down walls in cities as far distant as Syadtar and
Cyrad. As the Great Forest of Naclos rose from the ashes of
chaos to balance the steaming mass that had been Cyador.

Had that small cottage where they had learned so much . . .
had it survived? Nylan's single thought was twisted from its
question with an even more violent series of earth tremors.

With all the changes, the shudders deep within the earth,
the grinding of magma and congealed stone, the explosions
of superheated steam—with all the changes came the darkness that bound order and chaos, chaos and order, the darkness that held balance.

That darkness rose on the plains south of Rohrn, rose and
crashed over Nylan, over Ayrlyn, and night surged like a tide
across the grasslands, across western Candar, and even up the
ragged spires of the Westhorns.

The once blue skies darkened, and the storms rose, spreading southward and westward to touch the shores of the Great
Western Ocean with heavy drops of water darkened with soot
and dust, and northward to the Northern Ocean.

And Naclos . . . and all of Candar shuddered with the re-
birth . . . and the rerighting of the chaos balance. . . .

CXLIV

A DULL RUMBLING echoed from beneath the ground, and the man in silver-trimmed white robes stood and studied the receiving room. The floor quivered, and dust puffed from between the minuscule cracks in the stone tiles.

Lephi shifted his weight and glanced at the dust, a deep frown forming on his face. "Dust?"

He turned and walked from the smaller malachite and silver throne toward the window. He staggered as the floor stones moved again ever so slightly beneath his feet. When he reached the window, he grasped the white stone sill to steady himself as he surveyed the area to the south of Syadtar.

A hazelike darkness dimmed the sky, and the sun's light was cold on his face and hands.

As the floors of his command center trembled again, the white walls of Syadtar wavered as well, moving as ships upon a troubled sea. Beyond the white walls, the earth churned, as if by a muddy sea whipped by a massive storm out of the south. Slowly, as slowly as Lephi's mouth opened in protest, the brown waves rose and then crashed ponderously over those white walls, submerging first the walls, and then the houses that were already little more than heaps of shattered white stucco and stone and crushed roof tiles.

"Triendar . . . you did not say it would be like this." His eyes were fixed upon the relentless approach of the ever rising wave of earth and rock. "You did not say . . ."

Crackkk . . .

Lephi glanced from the advancing tsunami of earth back over his shoulder and up at the lacquer-screened balcony. The massive stone blocks of the building's walls teetered and began to bulge inward.

With a bitter smile upon his face stood His Mightines

Lephi the White, Lord of Cyador, ruler of all lands from the mountains of the skies to the oceans of the west, Protector of the Steps to Paradise, Son and Seer of the Rational Stars. Lephi waited in that moment of time suspended. Waited and watched as the very earth rose around him, as the long-delayed balance was righted, as the white stones of Syadtar fell around him, enfolded him, and then buried him beneath the churning earth.

CXLV

IN THE LATE afternoon on the Roof of the World, the guards stood silent on the practice ground, their eyes fixed on the blackness rising just above the western horizon as Istril stepped out of the main door of Tower Black and crossed the causeway.

Ryba, wooden wand touching the ground, gestured toward the silver-haired guard and healer.

Istril continued her measured pace toward the marshal. The other guards waited.

The silver-haired healer stopped three paces from Ryba and inclined her head. "Marshal."

"What do you think of that?" Ryba glanced at the pregnant and silver-haired guard, then gestured toward the west, beyond the ice needle that was Freyja. "That has to be the engineer."

Darkness swirled into the sky, slowly turning the entire western horizon into a curtain of blackness that slowly enfolded the sun, bringing an early twilight to the Roof of the World. For a moment, Freyja shimmered white, then faded into the maroon blackness that covered the high meadows and Tower Black.

"I could already feel the shivering between the black and white," Istril said slowly. "So did Siret."

"And you didn't tell me?" asked the marshal.

"What could we have done? Besides, it's more than him. More than the healer, too. Something bigger, a lot bigger."

Ryba shook her head before asking, "Do you still think it was right to send Weryl?"

"He's all right. I can feel that." Istril paused. "That means Nylan is, too . . . but there's a lot of pain there." Her eyes glistened even in the dimness.

"When the engineer gets into something . . . there usually is." Ryba's voice was dry.

"He doesn't do anything unless it's important." Istril continued to look past Ryba to the horizon.

"That just makes it worse, doesn't it?" Ryba's voice was rough.

"Yes, ser."

After another period of silence, Istril nodded, then turned and walked swiftly back across the practice ground and the causeway into the tower.

Behind her, Ryba continued to study the growing darkness of a too-early night as the faces of the guards shone bloodred in the fading light.

The faintest of shivers ran through the ground beneath the marshal's feet, and the meadow grasses swayed in the windless still of unnatural twilight.

Another ground shudder passed, and then another, as the gloom deepened. The marshal waited . . . watched.

CXLVI

. . . AND WHEN MIGHTY Cyad asked that her lands might remain hers, that her gifts to Lornth be remembered in honor and peace, Nylan spoke quietly, saying that the legions of Cyad would rain destruction upon Lornth, and that the white legions must needs be repulsed.

"Will you have Cyad take all that for which you and your

fathers and forefathers have worked and earned?" asked the dark Nylan. And all of Lornth said that Cyad must be destroyed. From the shimmering cities of order and their peoples to the polished stone roadways smoother than glass and the great firewagons that sped upon them more swiftly than the wind, Cyad should be no more.

None would stand and state that Cyad had been kind and just, and that her peoples lived in justice and peace. For such truth was struck down by the dark mage Nylan with his black hammer, and also by the dark Ayrlyn and her lute so that none would know the grace of Cyad.

The Mirror Lancers burnished their shields and lifted their lances, and the sound of the hoofs of their steeds echoed through rocks and stones of all Candar. The white mages, powerful in the paths of peace and wary of war, girded their robes and invoked the hopes of peace . . . but all were doomed.

For Nylan, the dark angel, again lifted his hands, and he unbound the Accursed Forest of Naclos, and the forest rewarded him, and rendered back unto him the fires of Heaven and the rains of death. And Nylan laughed and cast those fires and rain across the west of Candar. And Ayrlyn sang songs that wrenched soul from soul and heart from body.

The Mirror Lancers found their light lances turned upon them, and the very earth rose and smote them, and the righteousness of the white mages was for naught as their glasses exploded before them, and death rained upon all the armsmen of Cyad, until none stood.

The very ground heaved, and belched, and swallowed the great cities of Cyad and Fyrad, and the winds flattened distant Summerdock so that no stone remained upon another.

The Grass Hills were seared into the Stone Hills, so dry that nothing lives there to this day. And Lornth rejoiced . . . until its time had come. . . .

> *Colors of White*
> (Manual of the Guild at Fairhaven)
> Preface

CXLVII

NYLAN'S EYES OPENED slowly, but he saw nothing, and he closed them against the knives that stabbed through them. He lay silently for a time, smelling fire and smoke and death and destruction, odors that knifed through his nostrils.

"Where is she?" the engineer finally asked, except that he knew. Ayrlyn was standing outside the tent, looking southward at what had once been fields, except that she saw not with her eyes.

How did he know? He shivered.

The link, the link he had opened to the forest . . . and a sense of welcome, well-being, rushed through him, twining with the chaos of destruction, and the dull knives of death and devastation—life and death, order and chaos, except they were not parallel, not exactly, insisted some forgotten engineer's corner of his mind.

He sat up, ignoring the pain, the stiffness. After a moment he tottered upright, out of the tent into the sulfurous air that swirled and swept up the hillside. Although he could not see, what he could sense was more than enough. Churned and blistered earth and rock, the chaos of nearly endless death, and the smells. The screams of men and mages churned under a tidal wave of earth and rock and the shrieks of innocent mounts trapped and buried, never to tread the grasslands again.

What he could sense was indeed more than enough. His head and shoulders bent under that unseen weight, and he would have fallen without a strong arm, and the strong soul of the woman who helped him, and without the sense of balance provided by the distant forest—a Naclos that was already . . . different . . . more aware.

He swallowed and straightened slowly.

"You can't see, either, can you?" Ayrlyn asked.

"No. I can sense things. You?"

Yes. You . . . the forest . . .

"Agents of change."

Agents of balance . . . She nodded, and he could sense the nod he could not see.

Another figure joined them in the morning that still reeked of the slaughter two days earlier. "You two . . . you best not be . . ." Sylenia shook her head. "You raved about going to the forest again. You cannot see."

"We have to," explained Ayrlyn.

"Then we will go with you."

"We?" asked Nylan.

"Tonsar will come. We have talked. It is better. He could not follow any of the lords of Lornth now, except ser Gethen, and ser Gethen, he is old."

"Fornal?" asked Nylan, hoping in a way that what he recalled of Fornal's charge had not been so.

"He . . . he perished amid the fires and thunderbolts." Sylenia shrugged and glanced around. "That, too, is better. He would not accept what will be."

Nylan took a deep breath. "Weryl?"

"He slept between you. Otherwise he cried, and wisps of fire or light, they surrounded him. He sleeps now. He is an angel, like you, so young as he may be." Sylenia shook her head once more and turned back toward the tent, clearly erected over where they had fallen.

Are we so fearsome we couldn't be moved?

Apparently.

Nylan chuckled, but only momentarily. His body hurt too much to continue. "No laughing matter." He paused. "Weryl?"

"What else would you expect? He sensed the notes early; he felt the forest."

Nylan took a deep breath, then slowly walked back into the tent. Every muscle hurt. As Sylenia had said, their son—for he was Ayrlyn's as much as Istril's—slept. But Nylan could sense the intertwining of order and chaos, the inherent balance.

He turned to Ayrlyn.

"He needs the forest, and so do we."

Nylan nodded, then eased away from the sleeping figure and back out into the bitter open air.

"Nylan?" Ayrlyn paused. "Why was it so much greater than before? Just because you pulled a core tap?"

"Just because?" he asked wryly. "Anyway, it wasn't quite that deep. It just felt that deep. There used to be a natural balance between order and chaos—almost between the crustal layers and the magma beneath. Then the Rats came along and laid an artificial layer of order over another layer of chaos when they planoformed Candar—or the section where the forest was. I don't know if that was on purpose or just the result. Whatever the reason, the old white mages had used the artificial imbalance between those top two layers as a power source—like an electric current, if you will. That was on a comparatively low level in the past. I think," the engineer added hastily, looking around with sightless eyes, as he sensed someone else approaching, "when I used the weapons laser to destroy the Cyadoran forces and Gallosian forces, it was like a wake-up call—or the equivalent. Or maybe the forest— I'm still not sure if it's really conscious in the same way we are—blindly copied the impact.

"The barriers that held back the Accursed Forest in Cyador, except it's Naclos now—or again—were old, ancient technology. Probably they shouldn't have lasted as long as they did, but the way I twisted the weapons laser broke the field, and the forest began to try to regain its own territory."

"And the Cyadorans didn't have the technology anymore?"

"It's not just technology." Nylan coughed, nearly retching before he finally said, "I don't know. I don't think it was any one thing, but everything sort of reinforced everything else. And then when I went down to the crustal levels, that acted like a power reinforcement for the forest."

"It's more aware now," she pointed out. *Much more aware.*

"I know."

An entourage on horseback approached, and the two turned, still sightless. Nylan half-wondered if he would ever see again properly.

"You have delivered Lornth." Gethen's voice was flat. "Some would question the price."

"Do you, ser?" asked Nylan mildly.

"No." A sigh followed. "High as it was and will be."

"Cyador is no more, is it?" asked Zeldyan. Nesslek rode in the seat behind her, half-dozing.

"Some of it is still there," Nylan said. "The part that wasn't built on the Great Forest. Some of the western towns and cities are mostly there. Ruins probably. The destruction is . . . I think it's worse where there were cities and towns. . . ."

"None of the white armsmen, not a one, survived. Nor did the white mages." Zeldyan's words were low. "Were you sent to destroy all the white mages? No matter what the cost to Candar?"

"No. We were not sent to destroy anyone," Nylan answered.

"That does not matter," said Zeldyan. "In that, Fornal was right. You have changed Lornth, and all of Candar. You have won the battle, but my brother and regent was lost. You have saved my son's birthright, yet that right is not what it once was. You have raised dark forces, and shown in doing so that an outlander or even a peasant can bring down the mighty."

"You have brought down the mightiest empire in Candar," added Gethen, "and while none should fault you, I have lost both my sons." His head bowed.

Nylan understood where the regent's words had to lead, but he waited. Ayrlyn squeezed his hand.

"Lornth would not be grateful if we did not thank you for deliverance," said Zeldyan. "Yet no regent, nor my son, will rest easy should you stay in Lornth. Against your powers, I cannot prevail. Yet I must insist, though it mean my death, that when you are well . . . when you are well . . . you leave Lornth."

"We will supply all that you wish to ease that journey," added Gethen. "And some golds for your future needs. Though I wonder whether you should need such."

Another silence settled, and the south wind raised the odor of sulfur and death again.

"We will need some supplies, and a little time to recover."
For the land to recover enough to let us travel . . .

"It's better that way," added Ayrlyn. What she said was absolutely true, and misleading, but the balance was sufficient.

"You cannot see. Will you be able soon to manage?" asked Zeldyan, anger, confusion, and compassion mixed in her voice.

"We managed this." Nylan's arm gestured toward the smoke- and dust-filled skies, across the charred grasslands. "We'll manage. Naclos . . . the Great Forest will take us in. And there will be a place for those who prefer balance to force." *Like us.*

Ayrlyn's hand took his, and they stood, the unseen distant forest of Naclos behind them, with them, with the sense of balance that infused them—and Weryl—the balance that they needed, the balance that Sylenia and Tonsar, and others would come to accept and appreciate.

Sightless eyes turned south; the two angels stood, heads unbowed.

After a moment, both regents inclined their heads.

"Better you leave when you are ready," said Gethen. "Few will remember the good you did, and many the evil. Though the good be far greater, it has cost us dearly."

"It always does," said Nylan quietly.

Always, affirmed Ayrlyn.

"May you always be kind to Lornth," Zeldyan finally said

"So long as Lornth is kind to Naclos," Ayrlyn answered.

The regents rode silently from the tent and the angels.

"Where does it end?" Nylan finally asked.

"Never. The balance doesn't."

"You're awfully philosophical."

"No. Practical."

Arms linked, unseeing, but with sure steps, they went to greet the waking Weryl. Behind them, thin lines of white and black smoke swirled into plumes of gray. Before them—across the changed lands—waited the Great Forest . . . and the Balance.

And the Balance.